To:
Randy- Mi Amore.
Dorothy, my fellow sleuth.
J.A who started the whole thing
T.C. May this be your Hamlet
and to Steven…Just because.

Tender is the Night- Part 1

~The Don ~

...And in the hard light of an angry sun,
no one remembers what was said or done.
Tender are the words they choose-
You win, I win, we lose...
Tender is the night, in the benediction of the neon light.
Tender are the hunters, tender is the night...

"Tender is the Night" © Jackson Browne 1983. Electra/Asylum records.

Prologue

She was jogging briskly down the forest trail; this was something she often did. Hiking or jogging through the local forest preserve was her favorite way to exercise and also to meditate. It was not unusual for her to cover five to six miles in a single day, especially if something was troubling her. Today, she felt at rock bottom.

Sarah Duncan drew in a deep breath as she emerged from the pine forest into a prairie field, where the trail cut through. It was early spring and all around her the myriad of life in the forests and fields filled her with a sense of calm and enjoyment. Red-winged blackbirds with their lilting song and hidden katydids filled the background with the steady drone of springtime sounds, lulling her into a deeper state of meditation.

She pressed herself harder, running faster, allowing her mind to begin to give into the endorphins that now coursed through her. It was as if her heart and soul were running away from the reality of life around her, hoping and praying she could run to a comfortable numbness.

Finally, rounding the middle of the flowing prairie, she saw a large boulder and her body, near its limit of endurance, screamed at her to rest. Sarah pulled up, her breathing catching in ragged gasps as she unhooked her canteen and drank deeply, letting the water soothe down her throat. Sweat ran off her forehead in small rivulets, mixing with the unconscious tears that ran down her face and dripped steadily down her lean throat, her drenched clothing clinging uncomfortably to her skin. "Damn it," She cursed under her breath as she swiped at the sweat and tears.

Her mind flashed back to breakfast this morning with her fiancé Jim, and she felt the angry tears once again welling up again inside.

She and Jim had been seriously dating for nearly nine months. Both worked at the same retail store, he as the assistant manager and she as a department head. Both had grown up in the same small suburban Midwestern town in northern Illinois, both had bumped into each other on and off after High School graduation, and both had enjoyed each other's company. In Jim she found someone she thought she could really talk to, could laugh with and have great sex with. She had thought she had found a forever partner, and they had planned to be married, he had given her an engagement ring two months ago and they had set the date for three months from today, a July wedding. At age twenty-three she thought her life was perfect.

Sarah wiped her forearm across her mouth, wiping away the water on her lips and a few stray hot tears from her eyes; why had everything seemed to suddenly change when he had given her that damn ring?

3

Didn't he want to marry her? After all he had been the one to ask her, yet it seemed after he had proposed to her, after he had given her the engagement ring he had began to grow subtly distant. At first putting in for different shifts and longer hours, then spending less time with her and becoming more emotionally cold. She brushed away a few loose strands of long red hair from her eyes, and retightened her ponytail; a soft unconscious sigh escaped her lips.

Like many, she had been blind to that which was right in front of her, so trusting. She had been so damn naïve. It was not until she had walked in late last night at work and caught Jim with her own shift supervisor, Mandy, that the full awful truth came out and hit her like a runaway truck. Jim and Mandy were in the warehouse coupled, making out behind the new shipment of women's clothing. Sarah had ran out of there with no words to say, tears streaming down her face with Jim trying to run after her, pulling his pants on, trying to convince her it was "Just a one time thing, baby! Really!" but Sarah knew-

Just the way Mandy lay there, her brown eyes arrogantly looking at Sarah, the slight smirk at Sarah's naivety and foolishness, told her everything she needed to know: that the affair between Jim and Mandy had been going on for weeks, maybe months.

Sarah took another long drink from the canteen, and began recapping the lid. The last straw had come at breakfast this morning, after she had fought and argued with Jim- all last night. Even he didn't know what he wanted. He couldn't even give her a definite answer on their relationship; his final answer had been finally a half-hearted "Maybe we just need time apart to think." That told Sarah everything she needed to know. He didn't really love her anymore; maybe he never had. Maybe she had been the one all along who had been in love, and he had merely been in lust. Sarah had simply, silently, slid the engagement ring off her finger and dropped it on the table and gone to work.

Things were not about to get any better there. Mandy, had called her in and fired her. claiming was because of company lay off's district wide, but that same snotty arrogance burned in Mandy's eyes at Sarah, and Sarah was too numb to argue, too tired to fight, too empty to do or say anything at that point. In the space of thirty-six hours her entire world had simply collapsed like a small star shrinking into a black hole, and she had no way out and no clear thought, no coherent plan of anything. Right now she knew she was just a small atom in the universe, completely adrift in one hell of a vast vacuum of empty blackness. And right now the only thing she knew that she could even think to do, was to run, to where she had no idea, but she knew running always made her feel better, and it was a start.

Sarah stood up and stretched her slim, but muscular body, twisting around in an almost crazed contortion to unwind her spine. She

4

twisted her back the other way, loosening the muscles while glancing at a couple of blue jays scolding and arguing with each other.

As she looked up at the sky, she saw huge early spring storm clouds building to the west. She knew in an hour or two they would be here. Already the wind was picking up, shifting direction, and she knew she had better get running the five miles back to the parking lot where her old car was. She welcomed the numbing blissfulness of the endorphins coursing through her once again, the small temporary measure that would allow her to simply forget all this mess with Jim if, even briefly.

She felt a sudden prickle then, all along the length of her spine, almost like a soft charge of electricity, but only for a moment and there seemed almost like a whisper upon the wind and then it was gone. She squinted against the sky, glancing around, but saw nothing. It was an odd feeling gone as soon as it had come, like a hot dry wind before a dark storm. Whatever it was, her emotions clouded it. The hollowness in her heart and soul simply chalked it up to her own emptiness and the impending storm. Picking up her pace, she headed back to her car.

Louie "Kohana" Gambini sat in the low branches of the large oak tree, oblivious to the small mosquitoes that were flying around him and with itching annoyance piercing his skin. He leveled the scope on his modified high-powered rifle as his intense hazel eyes looked through the hairline sights at the trail rechecking in his mind the slight gust of wind, the distance of the shot, all of it. He knew she would have to come back through this way.

Quietly and methodically he chewed the tobacco plug in his mouth. Like a cat stalking a flighty bird, his steady but quiet chewing was the only sign that belied his intense concentration.

Slowly and silently he reached inside his camouflaged hunting vest and drew out a small case. He softly flipped the latch. Inside where six small darts: two inches in length with a small barbed needle and a yellow-fringed tip. Each dart was already preloaded with the correct amount of drugs designed to drop a 200 pound man in less than thirty seconds. Although, the formula wasn't exactly a tranquilizer, it was instead a ketamine mixture with a large hit of amphetamine. The formula actually caused the human body to go into a kind of neural overload and paralysis. The result was always rather amusing for the shooter to watch and rather uncomfortable for the victim, but damned effective.

"I'm fuckin' Marlin Perkins, darting giraffes in Africa," he thought with twisted amusement to himself, but it didn't matter. He got paid six to eight thousand for these little extra side jobs and he found them an amusing way to keep his skills honed for his real work, that's why he really liked it, the practice and the thrill of the hunt. For him it was always about the hunt, whether doing these side jobs or his real work as a hired gun.

5

He loaded two of the darts into the modified CO2 rifle; in fact this was the real deal. He smirked slightly. Stolen two years ago from the Lincoln Park Zoo in Chicago, "Hell it might have even darted that damn giraffe" he mused. With a quick but expert spit he shot a wad of dark sticky tobacco juice around fifteen feet to the ground below him.

A mosquito buzzed his ear with an angry high-pitched whine and settled on his cheek, deciding to drink there. He ignored it, slipping into his zone, his mind and soul becoming one with the land; he was very good at what he did.

Once the darts were reloaded and his gun ready, he gently re-sighted and settled into an unnatural stillness, becoming as immobile as the large, decades old oak branch he was hidden in. He attributed his talent to the Cheyenne blood, from his mother's side, that flowed through his veins.

He enjoyed hunting people, and to him they all were prey. He knew she would be coming back around the bend in a few minutes, he could feel it. He could always feel his prey, his instincts never failed him. The silent, but rapid chewing on the chewing tobacco continued. "Come on and visit Louie, li'l bird." his mind chanted the mantra to himself. There were now dozens mosquitoes happily enjoying the free meal on his body but still he did not move, was not even aware of them.

Sarah thought she heard the first far-off rumble from the large, billowing storm clouds. The muggy air hung heavily perfumed with the scent of pine, wildflowers and the distant rain. The thought of the impending storm only electrified her body more, giving her an extra strength in her step as she began her run back. Her ears listening for the familiar sound of the prairie birds and katydids as she rounded the bend, nearing the dark, thick pine forest, but all was unnaturally and frighteningly silent.

Before her brain could digest this fact further she suddenly felt a rude jab between her shoulder blades. The sharp pain was gone almost as quickly as it had come, instead replaced by a tingly numbness that began rapidly spreading down her back and up into her shoulders.

She had involuntarily jumped and half spun around in midair. She saw nothing; she only knew that all around it her it seemed deathly silent. Her first thought was that some angry horsefly or bumblebee had stung her. Unconsciously she fumbled blindly behind her back, her fingertips just brushing against the strange, foreign object embedded deeply through her shirt into her skin.

As the strange numbness spread rapidly into her system, panic gripped her nerves like steel wires, sending massive amounts of adrenaline racing through her veins. Her heart was beating far too loudly in her ears and her mouth felt as though there was a clump of cotton rammed down her throat. Panic ceded to a dreamlike feeling;

her vision began to tunnel as time slowed to an agonizing crawl, yet seemed to race along as well.

A strange taste and smell had permeated her nostrils from the inside out, a medicinal smell which reminded her of fingernail polish, metal and blood. Primitive instinct was now taking over, and blind terror filled her brain telling her to run. Just run, anywhere!

She thought her arms and legs were moving, she thought her brain was telling them to, but it was as if she had become displaced from own body. A grey fog was closing up around the tunnel vision; she felt a far away jolt and heard a sharp distant crack! She realized then she had fallen with a hard thud over onto her side on the hard packed earth of the trail.

All her muscles were paralyzed, unresponsive to even her simplest command. Even her eyelids were frozen open. The hot, white light of the sun seared painfully into her eyes and filled her vision. There was nothing she could do about it. Only her pounding heartbeat and ragged breathing seemed to be continuing on its own, the blood pounding loudly in her ears, competing with a high-pitched drone that seemed to come from deep inside her brain. Her breath came in rasping, moaning gasps like a dying animal.

What filled her the most with dread and panic, was the fact that despite her fogged vision and paralyzed limbs, she was coldly and acutely aware of everything, aware of the trickle of saliva that ran over her unmoving lips onto the dirt, aware of her paralyzed muscles painfully tense and unable to move. Aware of her ragged breathing sending up small billows of dust from beneath her mouth and nose, and worst of all she was cruelly aware of the relentless white light of the sun burning into her eyes that were painfully sore because they could not close, could not wet their tender surface.

Some dim shadow, a heavily blurred figure had entered her field of vision, but her sore, light-blinded eyes could not make out who or what it was. A jacket was dropped over her head giving her blessed relief from the painful light. She thought she could feel rough hands on her; a sharp jab in the bend of her arm and then finally, mercifully, nothing.

CHAPTER 1 - _April 10th 1987_

He owned New York City. If any man could make that bold claim, it was organized crime boss, Don Victor "The Arbitrator" Jerome. At least that is what the F.B.I and the news media enjoyed proclaiming. According to them his fingers lay on the pulse of the largest underground crime family on the East coast, The Jerome Family

Empire, the most powerful of the five famous ruling Mafia Families of New York and he was their decadent emperor, their Don Corleone.

Victor chuckled softly to himself as he stood in front of the huge picture window on the 16th floor of his office, VIJER Importing and Exporting. He knew the F.B.I was only partially right. He did know the city, he owned many businesses both legitimate and otherwise and he did know the darker side of people. He was a diplomat, a charismatic politician and shrewd businessman. He knew any organization was corruptible and any individual bribable, and if their staunch morals were that unswayable there were always less subtle methods. Darker and more permanent methods of getting what he and what his Family wanted.

He scanned the city below; it was nighttime now, New York City alive, glimmering with a pulse all its own, electric decadence and diversity at its finest.

He was in his late fifties, semi-retired. The only thing that kept him out of full retirement was his hated rival Tito D'Salvatore and his Outfit. The two Families had no love for each other, and war had brewed between them for over thirty years. Many lives had been lost, many dear friends taken in the war between them.

Victor turned from the large bulletproof window and sat back down in the leather office chair behind the huge mahogany desk. Maybe it was his "empire" but it had cost him dearly in so many immeasurable ways. He was exhausted and so wanted to retire, but he knew deep in his heart it could not yet be.

"Gio," Victor glanced up and spoke to the neatly dressed, well-muscled bodyguard in the corner of the office, "Tell Albert to fire up the helicopter, I'll be heading home shortly."

"No problem Mr. Jerome," the muscular man nodded and left the room. Outside this office's main front door stood another well-dressed man, a revolver concealed beneath his sport coat.

No, Victor Jerome thought, he wouldn't have changed any of it if he could, he did love this life. The power was addicting, more potent than any narcotic. He had made this decision willingly over fifty years ago. He knew the Family was a jealous mistress that demanded all from you. He knew all his power had come with a price, a steep price paid in blood by his own children, his wife and his dearest friends. The Family was a seductive lover, who soothed the pain of loss, with the caress of power, respect and a love that could be matched by no mortal lover. His men, his *Famiglia*, they were his life, his very essence. He knew they would live and die for him, and he for them. The Family demanded all, but gave back just as much. It took care of its own, who were protected under its dark wing. The Family was definitely not for the faint of heart.

Victor was the climax of the Felani-Jerome Empire, started by Victor's father, Louis Alberto Geromano back in 1915. Louis was a tall man, standing nearly 6'4". He and his wife had emigrated from Northern Italy, and Louis Jerome reflected his North Italian heritage with light, curly, straw-brown hair and deep –sapphire- blue eyes.

As many newly immigrated families in the old days did, Louis changed his last name from Geromano to Jerome, in order to fit in with his new country, America. Louis and his beloved wife Maria set down roots in the "Little Italy" section of New York City, and Louis got work at a corner market.

It was soon after that Louis fell in with his fellow co-worker, Mario 'The Mouse' Felani; a small, wiry Sicilian also newly immigrated.

Mario was everything Louis was not, and their opposite personalities drew them together in a deep friendship. Back in Sicily, Mario had come from a family lineage long associated with the Sicilian Mafia Families. So, once in the United States, he picked up with connections here. Already Mario was a valued street soldier who earned money with petty crimes, racketeering and loan sharking.

Louis was a quiet, hard working man, who was gifted with extremely high intelligence and book-smarts. He often spent long hours reading law books in the local library and doing accounting work and bookkeeping for many local merchants. In his old northern Italian homeland, the 'Mafia' was only spoken of in bad terms, but in his odd friendship with Mario he learned the Sicilian meaning of Mafia. Slowly through the Robin-Hood-like tales of Mafia exploits, he was unconsciously, seductively drawn in, until through his deep friendship with Mario he too became as deeply involved in various rackets as his friend.

Mario was a dreamer and was forever coming up with new schemes to earn money. Mario was also the "muscle" behind the dream and Louis was the brains. Louis was the technical man, finding loopholes in the law, or ways to skirt around tricky dealings and other gangs and crews. By 1918, both men had worked long and hard and decided to start their own crew, their own Family. By studying the other older crime bosses and families, they knew they could do better, move things into the new century.

Things moved slowly at first, many tributes had to be paid to those crime Families and Mustache-Petes' already in control, but soon they were noticed as big earners and taken seriously by the other crime Families. Their friendship held steadfast and soon they had a crew of nearly twenty other men working under them.

Then on January 16th 1920, the big break came that broke many older crime lords and catapulted others into a wealthy existence, Prohibition.

Through Louis's meticulous earlier planning, the Felani-Jerome Alliance supplied nearly forty percent of New York City with its bootleg liquor. Mario had also strengthened his other rackets in illegal gambling, prostitution and loan-sharking, so that when Prohibition was finally repealed in 1933, the Felani-Jerome Family still stood strong, while many others, not having seen the forthcoming repeal, were left high and dry and broke.

Felani-Jerome was more than happy to gobble up the out-of-work soldiers and capos of the other Families and welcome them into theirs. Through a series of alliances and takeovers, Felani-Jerome had now catapulted into one of largest organized crime Families in New York.

It was in 1934 that the great Felani-Jerome Family would be forever changed, shaken to its very core by the events that that would forever transform it and build the framework of hate that would forever haunt it.

Louis already had two sons, Massimilano (Max) and Eduardo (Eddie). His wife Maria had just given birth to their third son, Vittorio (Victor). Mario's wife Leona was pregnant with her second child, her first having died from measles when she was just four. While Mario still had solid connections back in Sicily, in 1933, the Felani branch of the Family back in Sicily decided to send a small delegation to work as crew and associates under the Felani-Jerome Family in New York.

They sent the ruthless and hotheaded Rudolfo D'Salvatore a capo from the Felani Family back in Sicily. For the first five years all went well. Rudolfo and his eight soldiers worked hard for Mario and Louis, but then Rudolfo's greed and treachery began to leech out. Rudolfo's crew started passing less and less tribute and money "up the ladder" to Mario and Louis and sending more to their old boss back in Sicily and keeping more for themselves.

Rudolfo and his men began recruiting more of their own crew and doing more jobs, while keeping information from Mario and Louis, but yet sending secrets and inside information on Felani-Jerome rackets back to Italy and setting up small rackets and trades for themselves. It was Rudolfo's hope that he would be rewarded by his master's in Sicily and given a contract to kill Mario Felani and Louis Jerome and take over the New York Felani-Jerome faction.

When Mario found out, he was furious. One dark and blustery autumn day Rudolfo and four of his crew were gunned down outside Giuseppe's Trattoria. Rudolfo managed to survive his wounds while the other four men didn't.

This of course caused the total divorce and split from the Felanis - D'Salvatores in Sicily. Rudolfo ran for his life and flew back home to Sicily. However he would return five years later with more crew and associates to build his own Family in New Jersey and to plan his revenge on Mario Felani and Louis Jerome.

For five years, Felani-Jerome continued to prosper, but always the cloud of the D'Salvatores' betrayal hung over them. Although there was no outright war, the constant back and forth of disruptions, harassments, assaults and the occasional loss amongst other New York Families took its tolls.

Mario sat down with Louis in the spring of 1938 outside Renaldi's Bistro, their favorite hangout, sipping espresso and talking business in their home tongue of Italian.

"I know you've always been kind of the silent partner, my friend," Mario Felani leaned over towards his tall partner as Louis lit his friend's cigar from his own expensive lighter. "You've never wanted more, always been my dearest friend and most trusted underboss and more importantly my right hand man. But things have changed; I don't have to tell you that..." Mario paused to watch an attractive young Italian woman walking on the other side of the street.

"I know that, Mouse." Louis' quiet baritone voice barely spoke. For large man, he was quiet and reserved. He looked and sounded as bookish as he was.

"We gotta cover our asses," Mario's, sharp dark eyes swung back at him. He leaned close speaking even quieter. "I have thought long and hard about this. The D'Salvatores will be back; they are our *nemico*, our enemy, now. They have more of a grudge with me, than with you, since they are a part of the Felani Family back home in Sicily." Mouse stirred his espresso with a small spoon and then sipped at the hot drink. It soothed his cold body that matched the cold feeling in his gut. He knew someday, that D'Salvatore would get their revenge, but he also knew the Family had to carry on here. What he and Louis built must carry on.

"We've done everything together, my *compari*," Mario continued. "But for now we are going to have to change the Family name. It is going to have to be the Jerome *Famiglia* crew, period. The Felani name is a curse to us, you know that Louis, but are too kind to say it. I know this life Lou; I have lived it all my life. Felani is a cursed name now after what we did to D'Salvatore."

"Changing our name won't keep the D'Salvatores away." Louis leveled his deep sapphire eyes at his most trusted friend.

"I know Lou, but it will give confidence to our crew, and associates and capos. It will allow us to continue and build and to totally divorce ourselves from the Felani and D'Salvatore name, period. The line must be drawn and it will be drawn now." Mario jabbed his finger at the table for emphasis.

This was not easy for Mario. So long had he worked in this illegal profession where a name was a sense of pride, a status symbol, one not easily given up on a whim. It was like losing an arm or leg.

A small, barely audible sigh escaped Louis Jerome. He knew this changed a lot more than just a "name". Sure, Mario might be doing more of the daily work as he always had. Sure, Louis would be more of a "figurehead" than anything else, but a figurehead whose ass would be hanging out there in the wind. He might be the great draw for new associates and other Family alliances, but he would also be a much more visible target for any future vendetta's and trouble, and that meant his children and wife as well.

"Look me in the eyes," Mario leaned even closer; his dark eyes boring into Louis' placid ones. "You know why else I really do this…" his hand reached up and grabbed Louis's shoulder. "You are –clean-, you keep out of trouble. You understand what I mean?"

Louis nodded; yes he had known this was part of it too. He handled more of the legitimate angles of the Family. He had been the one to start a legitimate import-export company, construction crews and a garbage landfill business that was doing quite well and bringing in a lot of money. He kept his nose clean, stayed out of the eyes of the law. In fact it was Louis Jerome who often supported a lot of politicians and other wealthy businessmen buying them into the Felani-Jerome Syndication.

"Times will be changing, the old days are over," Mario confided almost sadly. "The law, the government, they are going to be taking a lot of us down. This isn't Italy, this is America. We need our *Padrone*, the head of our Family, to be clean. Only by doing this, will our Family will grow and prosper while others fall."

Louis nodded, and lit his own cigar. He knew deep down Mario was right. Mouse was as a genius in street smarts and gifted with deep insight that had always served him well. "I know my friend, I know."

"Things will continue the same as before." Mario shrugged, "Nothing will change except appearances. I will be your underboss, but will handle all the same things. You do not have to worry about issuing orders; in fact the less you know the safer for you. Yes?" he re-stirred his espresso.

Louis knew that Mario would never betray him; the two trusted one another far too much, knew that each had to rely on the other too much. He just nodded grimly, "And I stand tall and give our Family the strong image of solidarity and look like a *stronzo* saint to the law." He said with a jab of sarcasm.

Mario smiled and nodded their eyes meeting in a deep understanding. Both knew the pros and cons of this bold move. Neither kidded the other, it was an aggressive and dangerous move but both knew they could make it work. "To *Famiglia* Jerome, *salute*!" Mario lifted his espresso cup, his face with his usual half-cocked grin.

"To *Famiglia* Jerome, *salute*." Louis lifted his own cup returning the toast and the oath to one another and to the Family.

Several moments later a young dark haired boy of five skidded up to the table. "Papa!" he smiled respectfully at Louis with intense black eyes. It was Louis' youngest son, Victor. The young boy hopped over to "Uncle" Mario Felani and pulled out a shiny quarter dollar. With grave sincerity he placed it in Mario's pocket. "I won it in marbles, here's your share." The lad spoke softly in Italian.

"Ah, my boy Victor," Mario kissed his forehead and smiled over at Louis, "Are you sure you are not a Felani?" he laughed, winking at Louis. "You're a good boy, eh?" He knew it would insult the boy to give the quarter back, even in a kind-hearted gesture. Of all Louis Jerome's sons, Victor, the youngest, even at age five was already obsessed with the comings and goings of the Men of Honor, and the Wise Guys.

Louis just shook his head with a dark glower. Unlike Mario, he was not pleased about his son wanting to follow in the footsteps of organized crime. "Why are you here, Vittorio Giadero Jerome?" he called Victor by his full name. Thankfully the two older sons seemed to not have any interest, but young Victor...

"Mama wanted me to pick up some sausage and cheese for dinner." He glanced at the butcher shop next door.

"Then get to it and stop gambling the money Mama gave you to shop with." Louis tried to sound stern.

"But I won four times as much!" The small boy protested quietly, sounding oddly like an old man in a child's body. Finally, with a glance of respect to his father and a small half-hidden smile to Mario Felani, the young boy ran across the street to get his mother's groceries.

"Why are you so hard on him," Mario laughed, "He has the knack, Louis, you watch. He is going to be something big someday. I know it. The Family is in his blood"

"Over my dead body," Louis gave his friend a dark look, letting him know he was treading on thin ice. Louis was determined that none of his sons would be in the Family business, at least not the illegal parts.

Things had progressed well with the name change, just as Mario said it would. New associates and new soldiers filled the ranks as other smaller Families who had made it during the Prohibition era now crumbled, dissolved or floundered around looking for strong leadership. It was the Golden Age of the Italian Mafia in the US and Louis and Mario commissioned a huge estate to be built about an hour out of the city in the countryside of New York, both as a show of wealth and power as well as a haven for his family. Victor, however, still managed to end up spending more time in the city, learning the ropes of being a small time crook, as well as studying under his mentor Uncle Mario.
While Louis lived and ran things from the estate, Mario lived and ran the day to day illegal operations downtown.

Often elaborate parties were held at the huge mansion in the countryside. Plans made, politicians bribed, and Family alliances forged. It was not unusual to see congressmen, union leaders, or neighboring crime bosses all at the same party-

Victor sighed almost inaudibly and wearily rubbed his temples; he was old, yes, but feeble, no. He was never that and never would be, although right now he was very tired. He picked up the tall glass of orange juice from his desk, just the slightest tremble to his aging hand. He hated these trips down memory lane. Not the early parts. Not the innocence and fun of childhood, his love of his wife Isabella and his children. No, those memories he cherished. Those weren't the memories he hated; it was the tragic times, the dark Sunday of 1957 that caused him to wince involuntarily. Always his memories wove and twisted to that dark, bloody day, no matter how benignly they started.

Victor would always remember that day; it was etched permanently into the core of his very being like some dark cancer. It was both a reminder of where he had come from and what still drove him now. How could he forget that day that forever changed everything? Just as Mario Felani had predicted. Victor remembered that sickening, warm, humid summer day. The smell of roses wilting in the hot August sun, the taste of tart lemonade and sweet red wine, the smell of roasting pig, pasta dishes and the smell of wet, human blood.

It was one of those elaborate parties that Mario Felani and Louis Jerome threw at the great Jerome estate. Louis Jerome had worked hard over the years to try and keep his three sons as far away from the illegal Family business as he could. Victor's oldest brother Max had just finished his bar exam and was ready to start a legitimate legal partnership in California. Max had married a gorgeous, but not too bright southern girl named Babette and they already had two children.

The middle brother, Eddie, was the dreamer, drifter and artist of the family. He had a talent for art and poetry and with Jerome and Felani money had already held several art shows in New York City. Eddie was 100 percent Bohemian all right. However he also had an affair with the "Black Orchid": heroin. And this made him untrustworthy as well as forever being in and out of jail for drug possession.

Both the older brothers were nearly their father's image. Blonde wavy hair, with eyes of steel blue and tall builds; handsome almost to a fault. Victor was the dark horse of the family, who looked more like his Sicilian mother. At twenty-three he stood almost 5' 7" with dark brown hair that was already getting a sprinkling of grey in it. He had penetrating, obsidian eyes. Eyes that burned with what Mario called in Italian "*Nero Fiamma*" or "Dark Fire"- eyes that reflected a shrewd restless soul and the mastermind of a genius; the intense eyes of a true warrior, a true leader and a true Mafioso.

No matter how hard he had tried, Louis had not been able to turn Victor away from the lure of the *Famiglia*. It was the one sore spot between Louis and Mario and a painful rift between father and son. Mario saw in Victor a greatness and intelligence that he knew would carry the Jerome Family into the next decades. Victor had an uncanny knack for making money, for influencing people and ruling with quiet calm and a shrewd, hard heart, all the aspects and requirements that made an excellent Mafia captain and leader. He knew all the comings and goings on the street, memorized Families, Bosses and players the way some kids memorized statistics on baseball cards. His own father had outright refused to teach him the ropes and sponsor him and so in secret it had been Mario, who had sponsored Victor.

It pained Victor deeply that the day he was given his induction ceremony and "made" by his mentor and underboss Mario that his own father had outright refused to attend. Victor had only love and respect for his father Louis, but Victor knew in his heart that he wanted to be a Man of Honor, part of the Family, more than anything else. He had met and married a beautiful woman named Isabella Disarro, the daughter of one of the Jerome crew capos. Although Louis Jerome had given his blessing on the marriage, Victor still could not penetrate his father's heart, nor earn his true respect and support for him to carry on the Jerome Family name someday.

Victor loved and idolized Mario Felani the way some men loved heroes. Mario had shown Victor the truth and meat of what it meant to be in the Family. Through Mario, Victor learned the roots and traditions of *La Cosa Nostra* or "Our Thing". However, Mario made Victor learn and rise through the ranks the same as any *cugine,* newcomer. Victor did jobs, rackets and collections directly for Mario. When Victor had turned nineteen Mario sponsored Victor himself, and at age twenty, Victor earned his bones was finally given his induction ceremony, becoming a true Man of Honor.

Of course such a thing could not be kept secret from Louis Jerome, and Victor could see the hidden disappointment each time he looked in his father's steely eyes. He could also see the cloud that had slipped between Mario and Louis. Faint, but it was there nonetheless.

It saddened Victor to see more pride and love for him in Mario's eyes than his own father's, but what was done was done. Already the Family had demanded a steep price from him -- a rift between him and his own father-- and he had paid it. Mario had long ago warned him the Family was a mistress who exacted harsh payment for her rewards.

Today Victor was happy though; it had been nearly six years since all three brothers were together. Today even Louis's eyes beamed in happiness at having all three of his sons here, along with his grandchildren, and Isabella pregnant with Victor's second child.

Mario and Louis were both now in their sixties and Victor knew today after the party that the Jerome Family would be naming a new crew of capos and the new underboss, Ruggerio "Reggie" Calucci. Victor had always liked Reggie. He looked like Dean Martin and had a penchant for smoking vile-smelling cigars, but he was competent and loyal to the Family. Reggie had been Mario's most favored Capo for years. Another soldier to be promoted to capo would be Patrizio Fantenelli, whom Victor had worked with for several years.

Today the Del Giorno and Roman crime Families were there, along with their wives and children. Mario and many of his crew, and of course his wife Leona and his two older daughters, their husbands and four grandkids. Several Teamster leaders and their wives and kids were here as well as Police Chief David O'Neal and his family as well as Congressman Joseph Wheeler and his wife.

Victor surmised there were probably close to 200 people all enjoying themselves on the sprawling hundred acres of the Jerome Estate; just another one of Louis and Mario's parties where they handed out bribes to public officials and seduced other crime Families to either merge with or pay tribute to the Jerome family.

Victor watched as dozens of children, dressed in their Sunday best, frolicked in the bright green grass. People clustered, talked laughed and gossiped. Older Italian men played bocce while others sat around drinking and talking. The women were all gathered around, cooking and serving food, laughing and gossiping about other women, or handing out sweets to the myriad of children who ran and played in the bright warm sunlight.

The bright sun made everything seem unnaturally white and alive; the humidity in the air settled on everything like a soft downy comforter, and in the southwest corner of the sky, Victor could see the huge billowing plumes of storm clouds looming larger and more ominous by the minute.

He finished his glass of beer and his conversation with his brother Eddie, who he knew was high as a kite on heroin again today and began to wander the quarter mile down the winding trails to his aviary. He knew he would have to secure it before the summer storm hit.

It was his one true hobby, a private place that was his and his alone to meditate in, to lose himself in. It was a thirty by twenty foot screened and walled building that housed hundreds of small finches. There were branches artfully set up in the common free-flighted area and dozens of covered nesting boxes. One could be in with the birds or sit in an inner space between the two screens to watch the myriad of small birds fly and play.

He had only gotten maybe a hundred feet away when he heard the soft footsteps of his wife behind him. He knew it was Isabella, and a smile played on his lips before he even turned around. She caught up to him and caught his hand in hers; together they wandered down past one of the dozens of well-groomed gardens. In this one, Victor watched four little emerald green hummingbirds hovering, dipping and gliding among the bright red trumpet flowers.

"Bored of the party already my love?" Isabella teased in a soft, melodious voice. "Or does something trouble you?" she knew about Victor and his sanctuary in the aviary.

"Both," Victor squeezed her hand. "I thought maybe my father would be more pleased to see me, the same old need for approval I guess." Victor eyed her playfully. It was taboo to discuss Family Business with women, non-made members or associates. Although Isabella might not know all the details, she had been born and raised in the Family Business, and she knew that the lack of closeness between Victor and his father Louis often troubled him.

"The same old problems with Eddie," Victor continued. "It tears me up to see him getting deeper and deeper into the damn *babania*. My God, he has so much artistic talent; he could go so far…" Victor trailed off. He pulled a handkerchief out of his sport coat pocket and dabbed at a few stray beads of sweat on his forehead. Damn, he couldn't remember the humidity being so oppressive before. It was almost smothering.

"So," Isabella continued, "Do not turn your heart against Eddie too, my love." She caressed her husband's face. "He idolizes you, you know." She glanced shyly at him. Even four years married to him, she loved him more and more each day. Victor still made her heart flutter like a teenager with a crush. Maybe it was because he looked far older than his twenty three years. The grey sprinkled handsomely in his dark hair and his neatly trimmed mustache, the light that radiated from his dark eyes. "Like royalty," she thought.

"Of course I'd never abandon him, Issy." Victor chided lightly back, calling her by his pet name for her. "I love him deeply." Of his brothers it was he and Eddie that were the closest. Besides Mario, Eddie was the only one Victor could confide his true feelings to.

Eddie had never judged Victor, never showed regret for Victor's choice in following Mario's footsteps. Even though Eddie was high most of the time and wanted no part of that life, he still supported Victor however he could. Eddie also knew how to keep his mouth shut; never did he betray any of his knowledge of Family business even though he wasn't involved. After all it was Victor who often bribed some judge for an early release or to drop charges against his brother Eddie.

"I just wish I could find a way to get him off that shit," Victor cursed briefly in Italian, then glanced at his wife's swollen belly that nurtured and grew his child; her soul which loved his heart and gave him unwavering devotion and loyalty. "I just wish he could have the happiness that I have." Victor looked deeply into Isabella's eyes and then gave her a quick, passionate kiss on her soft pouty, lips.

"Besides," he nodded his head to the right, "A storm is coming up quickly, I need to secure the aviary. Shouldn't you be up with the other ladies, enjoying pasta and gossip?" he winked at her. "Where is little Theodore?"

"Oh Victor," Isabella laughed, "There will be plenty of time for gossiping with the ladies as you put it. I so barely get you alone, that I steal every moment I can with you!" she laughed dancing out ahead of him. Her long dark hair flowing out behind her, and her soft brown eyes filled with laughter, playfulness and passion. "Theo is with the ladies in the kitchen helping with the cannoli," she called after him, speaking of their first-born son, Theodore Jerome, who was now three. "Besides, you know Emilia is guarding him like a mama bear." She laughed, encouraging him more.

Victor picked up his pace and playfully chased after her, until soon they came up on the large aviary half covered by huge oaks and maples. "I revel in this place." He spoke almost reverently. "There is something so special and calming in seeing these beautiful birds." He opened the first screen door, then the second one.

"I know," Isabella scooted under Victor's arm as he held the second inner door for her. Immediately dozens of the tiny finches took flight some of them alighting briefly on Victor and Isabella. "I find this place pretty relaxing and special myself." She moved closer to her beloved husband as she wrapped her arms around him and kissed him deeply, their tongues meeting as he reached up and cupped her breast. For at least half an hour, they lost themselves to the throes of passion, kissing and making love, oblivious to anything but their own bond and passion for one another.

A distant rumble of angry thunder caused nearly every bird in the whole aviary to jump up and fly in frenzied, crazed circles. "We need to hurry." Victor held Isabella at arms length. Something inside him felt as agitated as the finches did, but he knew it wasn't the thunderstorm. He only wished he knew what.

Victor motioned to Isabella, they hastily got redressed and together they began to secure the aviary for the incoming storm. A few minutes later there was another clap of thunder closer and more intense. It rumbled ominously, a low, vibrating sound that seemed to shake the earth itself. Victor would later call it the day the Devil took his revenge.

"We need to move faster Issy," Victor quickly began to secure the occupied nest boxes, which contained tiny baby barely fuzzed nestlings. In frantic chirping they peeped and cried relentlessly.

The adult finches were in a state of terror now, they cried in strange eerie wails and swooped together as one big swarm, flying faster and more erratically around the aviary. Several collided with the screens or branches, their tiny bodies plummeting to the ground, still and unmoving. "*Merde!*" Victor growled, more to relieve his own growing anxiety. His gut was churning now; never had he seen his birds this out of control, this terrified. Even worse he seemed to feel the same panic and confusion as them.

Isabella looked at him confused and frightened as she fumbled around trying to secure the remaining nest boxes and awnings, but her eyes caught the anger and agitation in her husband's eyes and maybe something else: fear? She had seen many emotions in Victor's eyes, but never this.

It was then Victor heard it, over another sudden explosion of thunder, as the skies darkened to an angry, violent black. The screams. As long as he lived on this earth, Victor would never forget those screams;

cries of terror and of death. His blood seemed to freeze in his veins, but already his body was on autopilot, propelling him through the inner door.

"Victor?" Isabella suddenly looked as lost and as terrified as the finches. "Little Theo?"

"Stay here!" he ordered harshly, "Stay here and don't move, promise me!" His body hit the outside door, nearly taking it off its hinges. Already on instinct his hand had pulled out his silver-and-pearl handled Magnum 38 that he kept concealed in his breast pocket. More unearthly flashes and cracks of thunder, taunting Victor like a laugh from hell itself.

"*Vaffanculo!*" he groaned running faster, willing himself to close the gap of nearly half a mile, to where the main party was. It was then that the heavens let loose and the rain fell in huge hard drops into the parched earth-- so fast, so thick that he couldn't see the ground in front of him. Through the onslaught of rain, he heard the staccato pops of gunfire, like thousands of cruel firecrackers.

Victor's foot slipped in the wet grass, and he stumbled and fell hard, the air driven from his lungs with a hard grunt of pain, the gun flying from his hand, his head ramming into the hard earth. "No! No!" he panted and willed himself back to his feet, limping he redoubled his efforts to get back to the main lawn.

As he rounded the last curve, he knew they were there. The lightening flashed and lit up the yard through the downpour like some bizarre strobe light. The thunder rattled his very bones like a huge bass drum.

He could barely see them, but he knew they were there. His family, his friends, the women and children he had seen earlier, lying dead on the ground. The smell of hot, wet, sticky blood and carnage permeated his nostrils and even the heavy rain could not conceal it from him.

"No!!!" he screamed above the thunder wind and rain. "No! Damn you!" Victor knew it was too late: several dark silhouettes of cars in the distance were already screeching off towards the front gate. Victor stumbled and lurched blindly down the slope towards the site of the slaughter. The first body he nearly stumbled over was Mario 'The Mouse' Felani, one side of his face completely shot away. Next to him was Victor's own brother Max, face down with a large gaping wound in the middle of his back and half his lung blown out next to his body. Near Max were Babette and their two children also unmoving under blankets of blood.

"Oh God, no…" Victor whimpered as he briefly touched his beloved uncle's face, then his older brothers. He staggered a few steps more, slipping around on the grass that was wet with rain, blood and carnage. Vainly he tried to wipe the rain from his eyes, hoping he'd find someone alive; anyone who'd survived this. Somewhere in all this he the heard moans, cries and wails of pain and fear of those still alive or wounded.

He stepped on the small hand of dead five-year-old Carlotta, Mario's first grandchild, who had looked like she'd simply lain down to take a nap on a large blanket of blood. "Oh shit..." Victor growled and staggered back the other way. Tears of rage and grief blinded his vision as much as the rain. He seemed oblivious to the lightning and thunder now, his mind in a total state of numbness and grief.

After a few more staggering steps he recognized the fallen body of his aged father, Louis Jerome. "*Figlio di puttana,*" he swore, "Oh, Papa..." he knelt down next to Louis's body. A huge bloody wound was in his chest and a chunk of Louis' throat had been blown away by gunfire. Victor knelt and stroked his fathers face, let his tears fall on his fathers ruined body, but Louis Jerome had no care as his dead, blank eyes stared up at the rumbling, roiling storm clouds. The rain that ran down the dead man's face seemed to cry the tears for all of the dead.

Mercifully, Victor's mind shut down after that, and the rest was a blur to him. He couldn't remember any more. But the sounds and smells of that awful day would live on deep in his psyche forever.

Surprisingly, most of the people had survived that massacre in that stormy Sunday in August. However, none of them were Felanis. Mario, his wife and his grandchildren were gone as were Victor's father and mother. His eldest brother Max and his family had been killed. Eddie had survived, but had been shot in the neck rendering him quadriplegic. The Del Giorno and the Roman Families had lost a couple of their capos. Thankfully Victor's eldest son Theodore had been inside the house and seemed not to remember the events of that day.

Senator Wheeler and his family and Police Chief O'Neal had been unharmed as well. Miraculously, the two top capos of the Jerome Family, Reggie Calucci and Sal Antonia survived as did most of the Jerome soldiers who had been there that day. So did young capo, Patrizio Fantenelli, who would always carry a bullet in his upper back as a remembrance of that day. Victor's wife Isabella, of course, had been unharmed, having stayed put in the aviary. However, her father, Frankie Disarro, the head of the Jerome bodyguards had been shot so full of bullets he had been nearly blown apart.

Rumors spread like wildfire, but it didn't take rumors to know that the massacre was revenge from the Felani-D'Salvatore clan back in Sicily. A vendetta finally sated against Mario and Louis. The New York and New Jersey Families were now thrown in turmoil; confidence was lost on all sides. The massacre had started to bring the government and federal agents down on them, watching all Mob activities vigilantly. All remaining crime Families would have to go into a quiet mode, curtailing their activities.

Victor immediately had a sit-down with the remaining Jerome capos and crew. He was fully prepared to step in and continue the Family as before. Mario had tutored him well, and Victor knew all the innermost workings and, even more importantly, had taken to heart all of Mario's comments on who was to be trusted and who was not, which rackets would pay well and which the Family should dump.

"The only problem," Victor talked with Calucci and Antonia, "Is that I am still young in most everyone's eyes. How can they take seriously a man as young as some of their sons?" He eyed each man in turn. "Mario trusted you, Louis, my father, trusted you, and I trust you. You have done well with the *Famiglia,* and it will prosper again! But for now, it must be you that the other Families see up front."

The others knew what Victor spoke was true and they also had the same trust in him as he had in them. They had watched for years as Mario tutored young Victor and like Mario, they saw in Victor that one bright spark of leadership, genius and luck that only comes along once in several decades. True royalty indeed.

For now, Reggie Calucci served as the figurehead leader of the Family and Sal Antonia as the underboss. Victor was the acting consigliere, but everyone within the Jerome Family knew that it was Victor Jerome who truly ran things, made the critical decisions. Six years later Reggie Calucci would voluntarily retire, the leadership would shift and Victor would be publicly announced as the head and Don of the Jerome Family. It was no shock or surprise to those capos, lieutenants, crew and associates of the Jeromes.

Victor had worked hard over the past six years to form strong alliances with the four other Families in New York: the Romans, the Del Giornos, the Giancomos and the Corellas. Victor knew well Rudolfo D'Salvatore was also building his own strong Family and alliances.

"The D'Salvatores are our mortal enemy," Victor would let his voice fill with hate. "Not because they even exist boldly in our territory, but I know I speak for everyone here, when I say our revenge, our vendetta will come because of that bloody Sunday in '57!"

It was now Victor who was the Boss and *Padrone* of the Jerome Family, A new underboss was named, Patrizio Fantenelli and Sal "Sonny" Antonia his consigliere.

His wife Isabella had given him two beautiful sons, Theodore in 1954 and Michael three years later, the love Victor felt for his wife and she for him only grew stronger each passing year. She knew who and what Victor was and never intruded on what he did, or questioned him. Not out of fear, but because she saw the same in his eyes as everyone else. A man gifted with a presence, leadership and charisma that never wavered: A man who could have ordered the sun to rise at midnight if he wanted to.

21

Victor ruled his crime Family with a quiet calm that would forever mark him. Rarely did he raise his voice, rarely did he lash out in anger and never did he make hasty decisions. In fact so calculating and gifted was he in business and insight that he was often asked to mediate disputes in other Families or Jerome allies. It was shortly after he became the Don of Jerome Family that he earned the nickname the "The Arbitrator", and it would be a short ten years later, that Victor's cunning instincts, alliances, profit earning and sheer power would get him a seat on the coveted Commission, making the Jeromes one of the Five ruling Families of New York, fulfilling the dream that Mario Felani and Louis Jerome had paid in blood for.

After the "Bloody Sunday Massacre," Victor had paid for the best doctors and care for his beloved brother, Eduardo "Eddie" Jerome. His own dearest childhood friend, Dr. John Thomas Weintraub had come to help him out and second-opinion the case personally.

Eddie never improved; he lived in a shell that few could penetrate. A total quadriplegic, his limbs forever frozen, nor could he properly talk. His once sonorous voice was now barely a ragged whisper, like a broken butterfly in a wintry wind. It tore at Victor's heart, even though he had paid for the most expensive nursing home. Worse, he knew it killed Eddie to live like that. The artist, poet, drifter and dreamer, now not able to properly voice his simplest needs, far less innermost feelings and visions.

Victor visited him several times weekly, but each time he went, he saw Eddie die piece by piece before him. Over the years, Victor and Eddie worked out a method of crude method of communication, between Eddie's ragged whisperings, his mouth movements, the Morse code blinks of his eyes and more importantly what lay beneath his eyes in his soul.

Each visit Eddie begged his younger brother to release him, to end his pain, to kill him. But Victor could not. It tore him apart inside to see his brother grounded like some wild, proud falcon whose wings and feet had been amputated, whose beak had been blunted. It tore Victor apart that each visit Eddie begged for death, and it tore at Victor's soul that he was forced into this situation of his brother asking such a thing of him. Victor had killed many in his illegal dealings over the years; he was neither proud of it nor did he feel any guilt, but what his brother asked him! This was so alien to Victor he couldn't fathom it.

It was a cold, blustery day in December 1966 when Victor showed up for his usual visit with Eddie. Outside, big, fat flakes of snow gently fell on everything, making a kind of unnatural quietness. Children played and sledded down the hills or made snow angels on the ground. Victor walked into Eddie's room and took off his hat, then leaned over and kissed his brother lovingly on the forehead.

"You look drained again, my brother," Victor said as he removed his coat and gloves and neatly folded them on a chair next to the bed.

Over in the corner, a game show host was extolling the virtues of some kind of laundry soap, "A housewives best friend."

Eddie's icy blue eyes stared at Victor, blinking rapidly in Morse code. "Window!" he mouthed, "Window!" He wanted to see outside.

"OK, OK, my brother." Victor soothed. He used the crank on the bed to raise it more upright then went and drew the curtains wide open so Eddie could see the gently falling snow.

"I want to... feel, Vic," Eddie mouthed. In code and crude face movements and twitches to his younger brother, he communicated. "Something, anything! Cold, hot, pain, comfort, the touch of a passionate woman, hell, getting my dick caught in my fly, anything!" he pleaded, tears trickling down his cheeks. It took him eons to get the sentence out, and he was exhausted afterwards, but Victor let Eddie rail against the world, against his predicament.

"I know, Eddie, I know." Victor adjusted the blanket around Eddie so he could see the snow outside, then held his brother's gaunt, pale hand. It was so lifeless, so dead.

"Victor," Eddie blinked in code at him again. It took long, drawn-out minutes to say even the simplest few words and only Victor had been insightful enough to bother learning Morse code by heart to communicate with his brother. With anyone else, an impenetrable wall separated Eddie and them. But today he whispered hoarsely with as much passion as he could muster; Victor could see the sweat, the trembling muscles, as though Eddie was giving every ounce of strength to say this. "Release me! I have begged you every time, every time you turn your face from me! Let go of your own cowardice and do for me what you know must be done." The tears were flowing faster down Eddie's face.

"You make it hard for me too!" Victor felt his own voice harden, his own eyes rimmed with tears, "You are all I have left! My only brother, you ask me to do a very difficult thing!" For it was not cowardice. Victor had killed several men in his time in the Family, but it was his own selfish love for Eddie he did not want to release. This was literally the last person left in his true bloodline.

"Then if you love me, brother, do, the right thing!" Eddie's eyes took on a depth of anger and emotion that Victor had never seen before. "Let my soul fly free from this useless body and go out there, in the snow, in the summer sun. Damn it Victor! Give me my freedom! If you love me, you will do this for me!" Eddie couldn't mouth or whisper anything else -- his body was beyond exhausted then. Sweat poured off him, his chest rose and fell in huge heaving gulps of air as though he had run a ten-mile marathon.

Victor wiped away his own tears. He knew Eddie was right; it was Victor's own selfish need of him that kept Eddie alive. Victor's own need to hold the last remnant of that Bloody Sunday was what made him deny his brother what he asked for week after week.

A deep sigh rattled inside Victor's heart and soul. He walked over to the window and redrew the curtains. "OK, Eddie." He barely said with a resigned sigh. He turned and faced his bedridden brother again, and for the first time since Eddie had been shot and paralyzed Victor saw actual peace in his brother's clouded blue eyes. Peace and anticipation, like a great eagle perched on the parapet of a huge canyon ready to take flight to freedom.

Victor walked over to Eddie's bedside and caressed his gaunt face, kissed again his brother's forehead. "OK, my brother." He felt so torn inside, but yet oddly at peace as well. Perhaps Eddie's need was finally reaching his heart; perhaps he had finally allowed the message to come through.

Victor paid no heed to the tears that ran down his own face, as he drew up the pillow from Eddie's head. Their eyes met one last time, and Victor saw his brother's eyes excited, already anticipating the flight of freedom, his release from this prison of his broken body.

"Go on!" he blinked in Morse code at Victor, "Go on do it. Please." He whispered.

Victor drew the pillow down over Eddies face, climbed on the bed over his brother's gaunt frame, and leaned his full weight and strength behind it. It seemed like hours that Victor leaned himself into that pillow. He was only aware of his brother's strong heartbeat growing more erratic, aware of Eddie's breathing becoming more labored, wilder. It seemed like eons before his brother's chest finally stopped trying to rise and fall, before the strong heartbeat finally faltered and stopped altogether.

Victor drew the pillow away from his brother's face. A look of peaceful death and release was etched on Eddie's face. Somehow Victor felt more at peace as well. He fluffed the pillow and gently replaced it back under his brother's head. He tucked Eddie back in and placed his hands gently on top of the blanket. It looked as though Eddie had just fallen into a content, peaceful sleep and died. Victor walked over to the window and redrew the curtains open and watched as the snow fell more heavily, the children outside delighting even more in this pre-Christmas snowfall.

Victor turned the volume down on the TV a bit but still left it running. "Isabella will be making her famous lasagna tonight." Victor spoke to his dead brother, as he dried his own tears and regained himself. "I know lasagna is your favorite. Issy cooks it almost as well as Mama used to make," Victor smiled.

He walked over to the chair and began putting on his coat and gloves. "I know how you always loved when I'd bring some of Issy's pasta to you." Victor walked wearily to the door, still not turning to look at his now dead brother. "Goodnight, Eddie. I hope you are enjoying that flight over the canyons. Someday I will fly with you, my big brother. " He then left the room quietly shutting the door behind him.

There was only one nurse at the front desk at the moment. "Good night, Mr. Jerome." She smiled kindly at him. Victor had nearly paid for this whole facility. Always he was polite and kindly to the staff and doctors.

"Good night, Margaret," he smoothed back the hair on his rapidly receding hairline and placed his hat on his head. "Hopefully things will be nice and quiet for you this evening."

Victor was well aware even before St. Rita's Home for the Assisted, called him to tell him Eddie had "passed away peacefully in his sleep". Victor had already phoned the funeral home and made arrangements--

"The helicopter is all powered up and ready to go, Boss." Gio Aprile's strong voice snapped Victor out of his dark trip down memory lane. Victor was glad he was facing the large picture window so Gio couldn't see the lone tear that trickled down his aged cheek. Eddie's death on that cold, snowy December day was something only Eddie and Victor knew about. It would be a secret he would take to the grave with him.

"All right, I'm ready." Victor absently waved one hand then heaved his weary body out of the chair. He very rarely carried a gun on him; he had scores of bodyguards like Gio for that. Sometimes Victor felt he was more protected than the President of the United States. No, his Family and loyal allies did not want what had happened to the Felani-Jeromes back in 1957 to happen to him. And Victor knew it wouldn't, not now at least. He knew the D'Salvatores were biding their time like the Jeromes. War was imminent, but not yet. Not yet.

Times change and the *Cosa Nostra* of today was very different from what it was sixty years ago, thirty years ago, or even ten years ago. Now it was more and more the government they had to watch for. Things like the RICO Acts, turncoats and weasels who ratted on the Family to keep themselves out of court, jail or worse. Rackets changed, technology changed, people changed. But the code of honor, the rules, they never changed, at least not with Victor. He was more than willing to bring the Jerome Family into the 21st century, but the whole glue and foundation of "The Business" was a code of honor and hierarchy that had to remain the same.

Victor still lived in the original massive Jerome Estates about fifty miles upstate in the country. He commuted by private helicopter whenever necessary to the giant VIJER Corporation, his legitimate business front, or his private penthouse apartment. Because of the government and FBI crackdowns, Victor now spent more time at the Jerome Estates than he did in the city, preferring to let his capos run the day-to-day operation and to work through his trusted underboss.

The huge downtown penthouse was nice; a trophy of his power, but Victor far preferred the estates away from downtown New York City. Even though it had been the scene of the Bloody Sunday Massacre, even though it held so many memories both good and bad, it was the very reason he felt compelled to stay there. It was as though the hundred plus-acre estate stored his memories for him, kept alive the most intimate and important part of his memories and drove him to run his Family as he did, so that never again would the Jerome Family be vulnerable.

The sights, sounds and smells of his entire life story were stored there in that fortified estate. It held many smiles, many tears and many ghosts of his past all of which were a part of him. It was where his top echelon of men did Family Business. Many of his soldiers or associates lived there or in the small town nearby. It was his center of power and his safe haven. It was what he had known all of his entire life.

He disembarked the elevator on the roof, flanked by two burly bodyguards, each man carrying a concealed handgun. Opening the helicopter door for him was Victor's most trusted soul in the world and his current underboss, Laurence Martel.

"Evenin' Boss." Martel nodded and helped Victor onboard. One of the armed soldiers also climbed in and then shut the door, as the pilot powered up, getting ready to depart.   Victor settled in as the helicopter smoothly lifted off the helipad from the roof of the VIJER Corporation building and began a circling ascent into the darkening sky.

Victor leaned against the window and watched the New York City skyline all lit up and coming alive. Night seemed to be a separate entity all its own, a different time, a different set of inhabitants. Victor's mind idly drifted as the helicopter flew out of the city on a straight northwest course out over the suburbs, for the thirty minute flight to the country estates.

Martel had already settled back and was flipping open today's edition of the *New York Times*. The other bodyguard, Tony Armanno, was putting his foam earplugs in and then digging around in a paper bag for a snack. Gio was using this time to peruse a magazine on guns. The steady beating of the helicopter's rotor blades made Victor drowsy as they always did, and he closed his eyes and settled in for his short nap.

This time he dreamt vividly. Perhaps it was the earlier unfinished trip down memory lane, or maybe it was the fact that he was feeling under the weather, more tired and weary than normal but his mind once again took him on a spiraling journey through time.

Victor remembered the day he met one of his closest friends, John Thomas Weintraub. It was 1948, and Louis had sent his three sons to a fancy private school in a nearby exclusive neighborhood, in a futile effort to keep them shielded from the Family business in the city. There were mostly Italian kids in the school, and the rest seemed to be

Irish kids. Even though Victor was a short boy, with a slim, wiry build, other kids just seemed to know instinctively not to mess with him. Not only had they heard the rumors about him, but many of the students were the children of men who worked with the Jerome Family.

It was also the penetrating dark-fire gaze his black eyes held. He always seemed far older than his young age. Even in the Upper New Darby Academy Victor ran his own rackets among his fellow students.

It was one day shortly after school had let out; Victor was fourteen and was waiting for a car sent by his father to pick up his older brother Eddie and him. He noticed a fight out behind the school dumpster. Normally he cared little about such things, unless he was directly involved, but he did notice this was not much of a fight.

Some student was getting pushed around and teased, but made no move to defend himself. "Come on, Jew Boy!" one of the larger students taunted, and roughly slapped the glasses off the victim's face. "Come on and at least fight, you big Mama's Sissy! Jew Boy!" the other kids laughed. Victor knew the tormentor, it was Christoforo Larusso, a large junior he often employed to collect debts on kids who didn't pay back loans to Victor. But this wasn't one of Victor's orders; this was nothing Victor was involved in. Larusso was always fighting other kids anyway; unless he was working his muscle for Victor, he didn't care what Larusso did. Larusso's father was another one of the many soldiers who worked at the Jerome Estate.

Finally, Larusso grew tired of taunting a victim who wasn't fighting back. With a series of a few well-placed jabs and a hard left hook, he knocked his victim senseless to the ground and walked off. All the other kids, seeing the show was over and maybe even feeling bad for the boy who had gotten on the wrong end of Larusso, quickly and quietly dispersed as well.

After a few moments Victor slid off the brick wall and walked over to where the victim was now on his hands and knees fumbling around in the dirt for his glasses. Tears stained the victim's dusty cheeks, and blood dripped from his nose. Victor squatted down, near him. "What's your name?" he asked levelly.

"Leave me alone." The embarrassed victim tried to put strength he didn't have into his words.

Victor saw the glasses just inches from his own feet. Gingerly he picked them up, noticing the frames badly bent and one of the lenses cracked and shattered. "Here." He gently handed the glasses to the teen who was blindly groping for them. "What's your name?" He asked again.

"John," the boy barely said, "John Thomas Weintraub." He winced slightly as though he expected Victor to hit him too. He still sat kneeling on the ground and fumbled with shaking hands, trying to get his bent-up glasses back on his face. "Oh shit!" John moaned as he put on his broken glasses and saw the ruined left lens. "I am going to get it from my Mom." He mumbled under his breath. He wiped his hand across his face and saw the drops of blood on his shirt, and his hand. "Fuck." He mumbled again, and his eyes seemed to water up. He glanced quickly at Victor and then shamefully looked away.

"Come on." Victor stood up, and offered his hand to John Thomas, still on his haunches. At first John just glared at him, untrustingly, half pulling back from him.

"Come on..." Victor nodded slightly exasperated and continued holding out his hand. "I can help get you cleaned up."

Grudgingly he grabbed Victor's hand and allowed the smaller boy to help him up. John and Victor were the same age, but the small, wiry framed Victor had strength in his hands like an ancient oak tree.

"Why do you let them push you around like that?" Victor asked John, genuinely curious. John half shrugged, head down, and gave the impression he didn't feel like answering.

Just then tall, handsome Eddie came sauntering up around the corner, looking like some wiseguy James Dean. "Would you come on, Vic. The damn car is waiting! I got a date in a few hours!" Eddie was in his senior year and old enough to drive, but lately, their father Louis had insisted that a car come pick them up and bring them home.

"Come on," Victor briefly touched John Thomas's arm, "I promised to help you out, follow me."

John Thomas knew who Victor Jerome was; or rather he had heard rumors like most kids, knew that even the toughest bullies deferred to Victor or worked for him. He had seen Victor a few times in the hall, and always he had seen Victor as a quiet kid with an inner fire and strength that made him stand out and be respected; a leader even among his peers. Even more important, like most kids, he heard the rumors of who Victor Jerome's father was and what he did. The words "mobster" and "gangster" were often spoken in whispers whenever Victor's name was mentioned, but never to Victor's face.

John knew his mom was going to kill him for ruining his glasses and getting beaten up yet again, but somehow he feared saying "no" to Victor more. So he hunched his shoulders, and like a beaten dog, warily followed Victor and his handsome older brother to the idling Buick.

"Who the hell is this *cafone*?" Eddie nodded his head towards the bloody, messed-up John Thomas. He threw the beat up kid a half sneer of disgust.

"Just stuff it, Eddie." Victor said as he and John Thomas slid into the back of the car, after Eddie. "Just worry about the *puttana* you're gonna get later? OK?" Then Victor grumbled something in Italian to his older brother.

This caused the lean, mustachioed driver in the front to chuckle and even made John Thomas hide a smirk on his face.

"Pete," Victor spoke to the casually dressed driver. He knew the man was one of Louis and Mario's bodyguards and knew that he carried at least a 45-caliber gun under the front seat. He continued to speak in Italian with the driver, so as not to be understood by the new boy, "Do me a favor and drop me off in town, eh?"

Pete glanced briefly in the rearview, and muttered, "Your father will be pissed if anything happens or you're late."

"Nothing will, and I will cover you, OK?" Victor spoke softly to the driver. Pete just nodded with a slight grunt.

Nothing else was said during the brief eight-minute drive. Eddie stared out the window and occasionally rolled down the window to whistle or gesture seductively to some attractive girl. John Thomas sat sullenly with his eyes straight ahead wishing he was anywhere else, and Victor leaned back and after bumming a cigarette from his older brother lit it up and just sat back, smoking it.

John Thomas eyed him nervously for a moment; Victor just smiled a cocky grin and lazily blew out the smoke. "You don't think I'd do this in front of my father do you? He'd kick my ass." It was the move that broke the ice and John Thomas finally risked giving his strange benefactor a quick, warm grin.

Pete dropped off Victor and John Thomas in the middle of the small town Victor had asked him to, and then took off.

"So what's up?" John asked, still wary, as he glanced around the small downtown area.

"Why you let people kick the shit out of you, John?" Victor answered John's question with a question. John just shook his head and looked away, still not feeling amenable to telling this new kid his innermost thoughts.

"Come on. Follow me." Victor led John at a jog across the street to Davidson's optometry and eyeglass shop. He opened the front door and went in after John when in.

"Hello Victor!" Patrick Davidson, an old man smiled warmly when Victor came in. Victor's father had done him several favors, and more importantly he was still indebted to the Felani-Jerome Family over rather heavy gambling debts at the track.

"I need a favor, Mr. Davidson." Victor said respectfully to the older man. "My friend damaged his glasses. Maybe you can help, yes?" he motioned for John Thomas to hand his glasses to Davidson.

Davidson picked up the ruined glasses and looked at them then quickly glanced at the embarrassed, bloody-nosed, gangly kid that had walked in with Victor. Davidson half shrugged, saying nothing.

"I know my father and I would be very grateful for any help you could offer," Victor said sincerely, quietly. For a brief moment the old man met the penetrating gaze of young Victor's eyes. Unspoken words seemed to flow between them. Patrick Davidson knew any favors he

29

did would lessen his debt to the Jerome Family and any disrespect could only earn him more problems.

"Very well," Mr. Davidson finally spoke, "I think I can help. I think I remember seeing this strength lens in the back, I bet I could get it to fit. Wait here." He took the bent and broken glasses and walked into the back room.

"I can't pay for this!" John Thomas half hissed at the smaller Victor.

"You want your Mama to kick your ass?" Victor half grinned at John.

"No," John finally acquiesced after a few moments.

"Take off your shirt; we'll try and get it cleaned up some." Victor motioned to the small bathroom in the corner. "Looks like your nose is broken, but at least we can clean you off before you get home."

"Why the hell are you doing this?" John Thomas grabbed at Victors shoulder. "Why are you helping me?"

Victor turned and looked into John Thomas's eyes, his hands on his hips, "Why are you always letting those kids kick the shit out of you?" he asked in a low tone that would not be denied.

It was John who now felt the dark charismatic pull of Victor's gaze and somehow he felt compelled, almost out of blind reaction to answer. "Because I'm Jewish," he seemed to wilt under Victor's gaze; it was a gesture that spoke years of being teased for his religion. There were only two Jewish families in this nearly all-Catholic town, and he was one of them. "Why bother to fight? I know who I am inside. Besides, stupid high school isn't forever." He glanced around, forcing himself to break from Victor's uncomfortable, scrutinizing gaze. "Screw what they think. I know what I am and what I want to do. I'm going to college in two years and then med school." It was the first time he had confided such an inner secret and deepest dream to a non-relative, let alone someone he had just formally met only about twenty minutes ago and who was the younger son of a reputed mobster.

"Because you want to or because your mama wants?" Victor followed him relentlessly pressing further.

"Because I want to." John Thomas actually stood a little taller, grew a bit bolder. "Because I want to!" he hissed more fervently.

A slight smile formed at Victor's lips and he crossed his arms over his chest. He blinked, and his eyes held a surprising warmth and understanding to them. "That's why I'm helping you." He simply said. "Because you believe in what you want. You are actually a lot stronger than you give yourself credit for, John Thomas Weintraub."

It was the first time John had heard his full name spoken by a kid his age, without malice or disgust. Even more eerie was the sage wisdom he heard in someone his own age. Victor Jerome was supposed to be a tough punk according to the rumors, but the kid spoke as eloquently and quietly as anyone John Thomas had ever heard.

"You know historically, Jews and Italians have been good friends, think of Meyer Lansky, Benjamin Siegel, Mickey Cohen and the Murder Incorporated gang," Victor teased John lightly. He extended his hand, and this time John took it without reservation.

John had no idea of what Victor spoke of or who such people as Meyer Lansky or Mickey Cohen were, but he knew that from this day forward for some odd and unexplained reason, a deep friendship had sparked between them.

Throughout their years in high school, they hung out together. In school, the teasing of John Thomas Weintraub abruptly stopped, even though he had never heard Victor speak to anyone. Somehow the other kids just knew John Thomas was now under Victor's unspoken protection.

Victor kept his crime Family side of business far away from John Thomas, and John Thomas wanted no part of that gangster side of Victor. He never questioned Victor, never wanted any answers, and Victor never offered any.

Occasionally Victor might have him hold a package for him in his locker, or help with science papers, but that was the extent of any favors Victor asked him to do. Theirs was indeed a friendship built on trust and enjoyment of one another's company, and not of need for favors or manipulations.

Victor enjoyed having someone who didn't feel they had to watch their every step in his shadow, or suck up to him and win him over. Someone who was proud of what they did and who they were and was in fact as removed from Family business, favors and debts as they could be.

The years passed, and after high school John Thomas did indeed follow his dream of going to college and then medical school. Victor had been there at John Thomas's side when his father had died and then a few years later his mother. John Thomas had often visited the large impressive mansion owned by the Jeromes and had been welcomed by Victor's parents and family, and while it would seem that the Jewish med student and the son of a Mafia boss would have nothing in common, the friendship grew and held over the years.

John Thomas had been there at Victor's wedding with Isabella in 1953 and a few years later for that dark day in 1957. John had taken a week off of med school, as soon as he had heard the news of the massacre and helped Victor through funeral arrangements for his slaughtered family members; he had held his friend together, physically and emotionally. John Thomas was one of the very few people in front of whom Victor had allowed himself to truly grieve for his lost family and associates. One of the few people who had witnessed Victor Jerome shed tears of grief and rage and mind-numbing pain. This was a weakness Victor couldn't show his mobster associates, but with John Thomas Weintraub, Victor could simply be human.

For many years after that, John and Victor got caught up in their own hectic lives. Victor, with his meteoric rise in the Family business, and John Thomas, with his studies in medical school in California and his own marriage. Medical school took over almost all his waking time and then the hard road of internship, residency and his actual practice. Of course, Victor and John corresponded, occasionally called one another. The wives sent holiday cards to one another's families for birthdays and other special events, but it never seemed to work out that the two men managed to get together in person. Things were even more difficult, since John was out on the west coast in California.

Victor had almost thought the friendship finally on the back burner until 1971 when out of the blue John Thomas Weintraub showed back up in New York City, and in Victor's life.

"My God, you've gotten so old!" John held Victor out at arm's length then hugged him tightly. "And so bald!"

"And you're just as ugly, my old friend." Victor teased him back and clapped his friend's shoulder.

John Thomas had grown taller, slightly heavier. Not fat, but definitely a bit out of shape. His face hung long like some dejected basset hound and his round wire glasses still perched as awkwardly on his face as when he was a gangly teen. His overall appearance gave him the look of a worried hound dog, or some sedate but absent- minded college professor.

The two were in the great penthouse apartment in the VIJER Corporate building. "Whew! Quite a view." John whistled as he took a peek out the window at the city below, hustling and bustling like some hive of ants. John tried his hardest to ignore the sharply dressed man in the corner who stood there motionless with his hands across his chest. Even though John Thomas had always seen these bodyguards around Victor and his family during their whole friendship, they still occasionally made him uneasy.

John turned and smiled at Victor as the smaller man began making drinks for them both. "He hasn't changed, except to glow even more like some cosmic supernova," John Thomas thought to himself. Victor was still a small, lean man;, his hair was thinner, greyer, his face angled and sharp, and his moustache added a more dignified look to his definite southern Italian features. But those dark, piercing eyes seemed even more intense, even more penetrating and even more intelligent. John had also noticed there was something else new since that tragic day in Victor's life back in 1957. There was a cold, calculating hardness to those eyes now. A strength and drive that did not exist before, perhaps even a barely contained darkness that John Thomas had never seen.

"I am glad to see you, my dear friend." Victor smiled, and the two began catching up, the talk light. Victor noticed that John Thomas often glanced nervously at the bodyguard in the corner, so after a few moments Victor spoke, "It's OK, Tony. You can stand outside. John and I will be all right here." Tony nodded silently and then stepped outside.

"I meant what I said earlier, John." Victor pinned his friend with his gaze. "It warms my heart more than you know to see you. In fact it may be destiny." He smiled, took a long drink and tried to read what was in John's heart. He could feel his old friend's frustration and pain and he was already formulating a plan, a brilliant plan that would help both of them. Mario had always jokingly called Victor "the mind reader" and indeed Victor had an uncanny knack in reading people, whether they were opponents or friends.

The friendship picked up with the same closeness and honesty as before. John held nothing back and for nearly an hour he explained how his marriage was rocky because he and his wife had not been able to have children, explained how even though he graduated top of his class and had great recommendations, he couldn't get into the top surgery positions on the West Coast because the wait was so long, and "…Damn it I want to practice medicine and not fight HMO's and insurance companies all day long."

Victor let John spill his soul to him, and listened patiently. After John was finished he looked at Victor, half warily, half with uncertainty. For a moment both were transported back to that day they first met in the schoolyard. "What do you really want? Deep in your heart and soul, John?" Victor asked him levelly, calmly.

"To do what I have always dreamed of doing. What I dreamt of as a naive kid; before I knew about HMO's and battling insurance companies, and every other type of red tape out there. To truly help people in need, not be told I can't, because some goddamn insurance won't cover this or that procedure or prescription. Damn it, to actually practice medicine!" John quickly downed his scotch on the rocks.

Their eyes locked on one another, and Victor saw that same fighting spirit he saw decades ago. He extended his hand and softly said, "I can help you out. I need you John. I truly do, I trust you more than you can know and I think we can help each other out, as friends." He walked over and placed a hand on John Thomas's shoulder and smiled warmly at him. "You have always been there for me and my family, always." He gave the shoulder a gentle squeeze, and years of friendship flowed between them. "You are perhaps the only sawbones I trust, eh?" Victor joked, and then turned serious, "You were there for my Eddie and you've always been there for all of us. Be with me now, John, be with me full-time. I will get you into a good hospital here, I will have you practicing more medicine than you know and I guarantee you no red tape, eh?" Victor's eyes smiled down at him. "I need you John Thomas, please..." Victor's eyes bored into his old friend.

And so on that day, John Thomas had become the personal mob physician and surgeon to the Jerome Family. He knew more about Victor than Victor's most trusted bodyguards knew. He treated Victor's wife and family. Treated his business and crime associates and never asked any questions or passed any judgments.

John Thomas still remained blissfully and purposefully ignorant of the actual crime operations of Victor's Family, he just simply didn't want to know. He knew of course deep in his heart of what Victor did and who he was. It was hard to not know when it occasionally popped up in the newspapers or on the evening news, but he accepted him for that. He had been Victor's close friend before while staying out of the business, and he would again.

Like a special gem, Victor worked hard to keep Dr. John Weintraub blissfully ignorant of the Family business. He made some calls and pulled some favors and got Dr. Weintraub a prestigious teaching and surgery position at Cornell Medical University and Presbyterian Hospital, as well as having a clinic built right there on the Jerome Estates, to treat any private, personal cases that could be questioned by authorities. Through John Thomas he could also get access to hard-to-get medical equipment or drugs, not for recreational use, but to treat his valued capos and soldiers.

Victor hardly asked for such favors, though. The most important favor was that Dr. John Thomas Weintraub be Victor's personal physician and to keep that information confidential. A rival crime Family like the D'Salvatores would love to corrupt a physician for knowledge of Jerome Family weakness' and health problems. Bribes could be given, offers made under the table. Victor needed the one person he knew would be incorruptible, the one person he could truly trust, to keep his two most deeply hidden secrets.

It was that day that Victor and John Thomas's friendship moved to an even deeper level of trust and closeness. It was also that day that John Thomas voluntarily stopped reading anything in the paper about "reputed crime boss Victor Jerome and his Mafia Family." He simply chose to be ignorant and allow Victor to keep him sheltered from any illegal operations. John Thomas would spend the next years of his life jumping between Cornell and the Jerome estates.

John Thomas' marriage had never fully recovered, especially since his marriage had been one of convenience. John's wife Melinda had come from old money, and she had promised to put him through medical school in order to use his wealth to add to her own assets. But he made enough money to keep his wife happy, and so she stayed with him. He proved to be sterile and could never have children of his own, so he put his full energy into his medical practice, his teaching position at the University and his caring for the members of the Jerome Family.

CHAPTER 2- *April 10ᵗʰ 1987*

Sarah felt herself in the throes of some bizarre dream, an almost psychedelic nightmare. She felt sick to her stomach and miserable. Was it that steak she had eaten last night that was making her ill? Or maybe that rotten smelling-egg salad she vaguely remembered eating at lunch. Nausea was rising in her throat, and she felt way too warm. She groggily and angrily thrashed and flipped onto her side; it seemed to take every ounce of effort and only made her head pound in pain. This didn't feel like her nice warm, bed. She struggled to wake up, to remember. She was confused and thrashed more, because she couldn't remember, because she was not where she thought she was.

She heard a far-off voice, real or imagined she couldn't tell. "Come on darlin' enjoy it! Don't fight it." It wasn't a pleasant or soothing voice but dark, cruel and vile.

Although her body seemed to have a mind of its own and seemed to be shaking and trembling in some kind of seizure or shakes, her mind began to jaggedly piece together events, trying to make logical sense out of them. She remembered the argument with Jim, his affair with Mandy, her being fired...

She remembered being upset and confused. Needing to jog by herself to think things through; she remembered the warm spring day, the bright trails and the scent of pine forest, then...

That was all she could remember. Memories and experiences floated on the edge of her memory, but like some taunting long-forgotten song eluded her. Somehow she knew she remembered, but just couldn't remember at this moment. Somewhere on the fringes of her hearing --or was it in her dream again? -- She thought she heard a woman's voice, screaming or crying? She couldn't be sure.

She had some sensation in her body, but seemed unable to fully coordinate her movements. She knew she was lying on her side on some hard cold surface, maybe concrete. She knew she was naked, as she could feel air washing over her body and didn't feel the weight of clothes or sheets.

Her hand tried to blindly grope for some blanket or something to cover her nakedness, and that is when she realized her hands were confined. Bound together in some metallic type bracelets or handcuffs, either way they were bound. That disconcerting feeling of being bound and held seemed to hit her like a rude slap and she forced her mind further up into layers of consciousness.

"Get up!" That same unpleasant male voice from before invaded her ears and mind more clearly, more loudly. No sooner had he said that, than she felt a sudden burning and tingling pain in her leg like liquid fire that traveled up her body and caused her muscles to painfully tighten uncontrollably.

Her world snapped awake, pushing through the drug-induced sleep that was ebbing from her brain.

"Up, up, let's go, time is money, bitch."

Her eyes abruptly snapped open then; and she saw a large, elegant black man, wearing a lot of thick gold jewelry and swinging some odd-looking stick at his side, which seemed to have some kind of electrical arc at the end. Sarah tried to get her knotted muscles to move. Panic burned deep inside her, and a moan escaped her lips. She tried to rise and ended up flopped over the other way like some unsteady drunk.

The man swung the stick again and she felt it touch her bare ass. It wasn't the stick that hurt; it was the electricity it spat out that coursed along her nerves and muscles, making her twitch and burn. This instantly bought her to her feet, on pure adrenaline.

"What the fuck is going on? Where am...." She never finished the sentence that she screamed with rage and panic. The man had backhanded her and bought the electric prod down on her ribs, enough to make her brain feel like it was going to explode out of her skull.

"Look, bitch..." he growled, in a low voice that reminded her of James Earl Jones, "I can go on shockin' your ass all day long. Now either walk out on your own or I'll beat the fuck out of you and have you thrown in the truck unconscious." He grabbed her handcuffed hands, hauling her to her feet. "Yo! T.J., the next is ready!" he called out to someone.

Sarah's mind seemed to numbly obey on its own, even though it screamed with blind terror and panic. But terror of that cattle prod seemed to override anything else at the moment, and she blindly cooperated. Around her, she saw two other naked, bound and semi-conscious women on the floor.

Just at that moment a tall, skinny man came in and took hold of her manacled hands. He had an ugly, scarred face and eyes like a shark. His lean face half-grimaced in a grotesque leer, "Let's go darlin'..." he said sarcastically and dragged her out behind him. Behind her, Sarah heard the other women being awakened rudely as well.

T.J. dragged her out to where two other nude, women stood weaving, panting in terror and coming out of their own drug-induced nightmares. Their hands were tied in cuffs as well and through their shackles ran a common chain that connected them, much like prisoners in a chain gang. T.J. efficiently hooked Sarah up to the other two women and then walked back to get the next girl.

Sarah stared around in the cool night air, her body shivering and swaying uncontrollably. It appeared like they were in some enclosed industrial compound. Metal buildings and semi trailers were everywhere.

She glanced at the woman next to her, a small blonde-haired woman with dried blood and dirt all over her face who trembled uncontrollably, cried silently and moved her lips in unspoken words. Sarah looked up at the twinkling stars above, and wondered just what the fuck was going on and when she would wake from this nightmare.

The last two women were finally hooked onto the chain-gang, and then all five of them were led down towards a large semi trailer and truck. There was a ramp leading up to the back and the two men, the elegant dressed black man and the grungy, scrawny man kept them steadily and swiftly shuffling up the ramp and into the trailer.

The trailer was fully enclosed, with no windows or slats, a true cargo container truck. On the floor was about a foot of hay or straw. On the sides of the metal trailer were several large "O" rings that were low and close to the floor. The two men began unhooking the naked women from the chain gang and then forcing them to their knees and hooking their manacled hands through a short length of chain and through the "O" rings.

"Move it," the black man barked at her, swinging his cattle prod back and forth. Sarah didn't need to be told twice; the other man grabbed her hands, forcing her to kneel as he fastened her up to the "O" ring, locking her down tightly and cruelly. The trailer was dimly lit by a few lights on the ceiling, and Sarah noticed as the other woman was viciously shackled in next to her, that she had many bruises, her eyes swollen shut and dried blood on her lips. Sarah closed her eyes and looked away.

The tall, skinny white man was doing something to each of the girls and moving down the line. As he came up behind Sarah she saw that he carried five individual syringes. He roughly grabbed her arm and injected the fluid directly into her vein. A cruel smirk crossed his face, and he leered indecently at her as he roughly pulled at her nipple. "Have fun darlin', dancing with the devil." he hissed at her then moved to the next girl.

The two men quickly exited the truck, slid in the ramp and dead-bolted the doors with a cruel finality. Sarah began to feel lightheaded, euphoric. A peaceful, happy high began skidding across her mind. She shivered violently and began drooling but was oblivious to it. She felt nothing at all except that wonderful high.

She distantly heard the slamming of the driver's and passengers' doors on the truck, and the large diesel motor turned over and kicked to life. It idled, letting air pressure build up in the brakes, and allowing the engine to warm up to operating capacity. The inside light was switched off in the back of the trailer where Sarah and the other four women were chained. Sarah thought she heard quiet sobbing in the darkness, but she didn't care. She was stoned and high as a kite. She settled into the straw and let her eyes close in drugged, blissful sleep.

As the truck began to move forward with a small lurch, Sarah's mind began dreaming of her grandmother's farm and of cattle being loaded up onto trailers and going to slaughter.

The helicopter's low descent woke Victor out of his vivid dreams. He wiped the sleep from his eyes and saw that they were coming in over his estates. It felt safe, comforting to be home.

"Is everything OK, Boss?" Martel asked quietly, folding the paper neatly on the seat next to him and loosening the holster that hung around his massive shoulder.

"Yes," Victor said, stretching. "Everything's fine for now, Laurence." He stretched his limbs sending blood flowing back into his cramped arms and legs, which had fallen asleep with him.

Once the helicopter landed, Laurence Martel gently helped the aging crime boss out then shut the door and followed him up the well-lit, elegant pathway leading to the huge mansion. Here and there were several other guards; many nodded a respectful greeting or softly said "Good evening Boss," or "Welcome back, Mr. J." The few men patrolling the grounds carried larger automatic weapons like M-16's, or Uzis.

The front door opened, and John Thomas stood there watching Victor come up the walk; he had gotten here earlier and had been waiting for him.

"Oh, you're an ugly sight to come home to." Victor chuckled low under his breath.

"You're getting to be a feisty old putz!" John Thomas shot back at him. A few of the men chuckled quietly; it was always enjoyable watching the Boss and the Doctor play "grumpy old codgers". The two older men's banter had become a reliable way to gauge the health and emotional state of the other. Their friendship was just as deep as ever.

As Victor entered the house, he knew even before John spoke the words, "I had Rosette whip up your favorite pasta and gravy. That long skinny kind with the meat." John never could get straight all the different kinds of pasta and Italian food.

"Manicotti?" Victor said, already knowing that is what his head chef and cleaning lady had whipped up for dinner that night, just by the enticing smell. "You're being far too nice to me, John and I don't trust you," he gave his physician an exaggerated look. "I'm dying aren't!" he hammed it up; "Why else would you have Rosette make manicotti?"

"Don't say that." John Thomas said with an almost intense edge to his voice. It wasn't the expected playful insult and bantering Victor had expected. "Don't talk like that." John said again with as much harshness as his hangdog face was able to muster.

Victor discreetly grabbed hold of John Thomas's arm with amazing strength and drew him close. "I read you far too well, old friend." His voice was low, quiet and dripped with controlled strength that froze the room, meant only for John's ears, "I never believed in bullshit and I never gave any to you." Victor glanced at Martel and the other soldier, dismissing them without saying a word to them. "I would think after almost forty years of friendship you could be honest with me too." He unhooked his hand from John's arm.

"Victor," John Thomas glanced quickly to make sure the guards had indeed moved off. "We need to talk." This time there was no anger, no bullshit and no insults.

After dinner Victor sat in his elegant personal study; bookcases lined the walls and stately leather furniture decorated artfully. In the corner was a fireplace that crackled softly with a fire log. A real wood one; Victor hated that fake gas shit. The room was paneled in expensive teak woods and mahoganies. He leaned back in his favorite high- backed recliner; it felt comfortable on his tired body. Victor glanced up briefly, studying the ceiling in an attempt to quiet his exasperation. "Don't mince words with me, John Thomas. So you're telling me what?"

Dr. John Thomas Weintraub had been pacing back and forth in the study, watching with a harsh eye as Victor sipped on some cognac. "For the third time, Victor," he gruffly barked and stopped pacing in front of Victor, leaning down close to him. "Your kidneys are failing; your blood work is all out of whack..." John Thomas had learned long ago that Victor cared little for medical terminology and easily got bored at medical talk, even his where it concerned own conditions. If John Thomas didn't talk bluntly and in lay terms, Victor was just as likely to turn on CNN news or read a book as listen to him. "They haven't stopped functioning yet, but you need to get more blood work done, we need to prepare for dialysis, until we get a kidney transplant." Victor glared over his glass at John, narrowing his eyes at him. "At least we need to consider our options, especially considering your condition!" John Thomas finished.

"You say I've gotten to be a pain in my old age? Christ, John, you're like some nagging wife." Victor leaned forward in the chair forcing Dr. Weintraub to back off several inches out of his space. "I've lived for nearly sixty years on this earth, forty-two of them with -my condition-." He added with an acid tone, "I know I have old kidneys and an old heart-- I'm old damn it!" he scoffed at the doctor and sipped again at his cognac. "For an old man who can still jog three miles a day, bench press almost two hundred pounds and who is a brown-belt in Judo I would say I'm not doing to bad." Victor snorted a bit like a grizzled lion at an annoying fly.

"You're missing the point!" John Thomas rolled his eyes, and resumed his pacing. "I don't dispute your physical prowess, Victor! Hell, you could probably kick my ass ten times over, but let's keep you in good physical condition. I'm a bit worried here, OK?" he matched

Victor's hard glare with his own unwavering stare. John Thomas could be just as much a hard ass as his best friend and patient. "Because of your medical condition, we have to work that much harder to make sure you continue to be the grumpy old feisty coot that you are," John relaxed his gaze, "Besides I made a promise to you over sixteen years ago, as your personal physician to nag you and pester you and look out for you, remember?"

"So you did, old friend." Victor's face briefly crinkled in a rare smile, then sobered up to his usual dark seriousness. "So go ahead and do your tests. I'm sure they will only confirm what we both know. My kidneys are failing, and a transplant will be a long shot because I am unfortunate enough to have one hell of a rare blood type." Victor's level gaze bored into John Thomas. "I don't want to be hooked to a dialysis machine if they go, John. I don't want to be like Eddie. I cannot, will not be that vulnerable!" He made a harsh sweeping gesture. "We've already discussed this, you and I."

John gazed just as fiercely back at his lifelong friend. What could he say? As a physician, he was trained to never give up. It was his life, his creed always to heal, to find a way to make it work. He didn't even want to listen to this talk of Victor's, but he also knew that failures did happen. Knew that Eddie's debilitating injury from that dark day in 1957 had rode Victor hard; that his beloved Isabella's cruel death to ovarian cancer had only hardened Victor more.

He pointed his finger haphazardly at Victor and shook his head, speechless for the moment. What could he say to Victor's statement? He couldn't devalue what his friend felt deep inside. It was Victor's prerogative to feel that way. "You make my job hard, you know that Vic? I'm going to put you on a list for a kidney transplant, old friend. We both know it's one hell of a long shot but…" he turned to leave, and walked to the door. He paused with his hand on the knob.

Without looking back, John spoke, "Never forget you're my closest friend also Victor, long before you were my patient. I'm allowed to care too, you damn old curmudgeon. As a doctor, as your friend, I have to do what I must, you understand?" It was said softly, wearily spoken but with heartfelt sincerity. He opened the door and quietly left without looking back.

"I know," Victor said softly after his friend had left. "I know. And I make my living at long shots." Victor picked up his nearby copy of *Lord of the Rings* and leaned back to continue on where he had left off. He enjoyed losing himself in Frodo's adventures. It made the reality of the here and now disappear. Victor always thought Frodo would have made a great capo, and Gandalf a great Don.

A half hour later, almost as Victor was nodding off, there was a brief knock at the study door. "Boss?" a handsome, dark-haired male stepped into the room. He stood close to five feet eleven and reflected his southern Italian heritage. Olive skin, with dark brown eyes, and dark brown hair he kept neatly brushed back and slicked down. "Not disturbing ya, am I?"

"Joshua," Victor stood up, and both men briefly embraced and patted one another's shoulders. "Sit, talk to me." He nodded to a chair next to his own. Victor watched Joshua ease himself gracefully into the chair. He reminded Victor of a large, hungry predator. Every step reflected pent-up power, grace and control.

Joshua Demonico was Victor's consigliere and had been for close to eight years now. The consigliere was Victor's personal counselor and secretary. He had the boss's ear, and listened to the capos and the underboss. He did a little of everything and acted to keep communication between the top administration and the other branches of the Family tightly knit together.

"I thought I'd brief you on some upcoming business," Joshua's thick Brooklyn accent said while clicking open and rummaging through his briefcase. He was an immaculately dressed man who took extreme pride in his appearance; he wore only the most expensive suits and shoes. Wore an elegant thick gold rope chain around his thickly haired wrist and several small discreet gold chains around his neck and tucked into his shirt. On his other wrist was a 24 karat watch in gold and diamonds. Even his gun was custom made, a titanium and pearl handled 38 that he kept in a deerskin holster inside his suit.

Like Victor and Laurence Martel, Joshua Demonico wore an ornate gold, diamond and onyx ring on the index finger of his left hand. Also like Martel, Victor and several other soldiers and crew, he was a master at martial arts. It was reflected in his graceful moves and well toned body that was muscular and hard without being muscle bound.

Joshua had finished digging out his papers from his expensive leather briefcase, and leaned back, flipping open his monogrammed notebook. "Let's see here," he mused for a brief moment. "Tomorrow at two you have a meeting with Silvio Torturro from New Jersey and his two skippers. They want into the alliance and will be offering some stuff, cuts from contractor business for you and I'm sure a capo as well." Joshua paused, "Martel is taking care of some collections tomorrow, so..."

Victor nodded; he knew it was his place to be there anyway. As the head of the Family, he had to welcome any alliances and he already knew from Joshua's earlier legwork that the Torturros would be a good ally indeed.

"Next is that whole Buscamani fiasco," Josh tapped his pencil on the notebook with agitation. "They want a sit-down with you; they are not content to work with Laurence Martel or myself."

Victor sighed and rubbed his forehead, feeling a dull headache coming on. Angelo Buscamani was a royal pain in the ass. His was yet another small Family that had joined in an association with the Jeromes. Buscamani was never satisfied with the rackets he had and always wanted more from the Jeromes. "He's a fucking pain and gives me agita, Joshua." Victor growled deeply.

"I know Boss, but you know he's our lynchpin. They have some valuable shit to offer, and more importantly they wanted to ally with us and not D'Salvatores." Joshua explained what Victor already knew.

"Let's not forget also that Buscamani has a corrupt cousin in the New York F.B.I. branch." Victor smiled at him. "I just wish he wouldn't act like such a fuckin' princess and *coglione*." Victor cursed. "He knows we need his alliance, but he borders on pushing my patience to its limits." Victor stopped rubbing his temples for a moment, as a plan was already forming. "That captain he has working for us, Larry Cordoza, right?" Victor snapped his fingers, his mind racing, plotting, setting the pieces in motion.

"Yeah…" Josh wasn't following him, but knew when Victor was on one of his brilliant schemes.

"This is strictly off the record. Have him clipped." Victor said levelly and succinctly, "Use Martel."

Joshua just stared at the Don opened-mouth for a second, but said nothing. What Victor was proposing was very rarely done and considered risky and in very bad taste.

"I trust Martel implicitly, you understand?" Victor switched to speaking in Italian and leaned forward, pinning Josh's confused eyes with his dark fire gaze. "Tell Martel to make it look, -accidental- maybe a car accident, a robbery gone wrong- whatever- Martel does. I trust Martel and I trust you, Joshua." Victor put his hand on Joshua's shoulder.

He could feel the power, the strength, and the unchallenged leadership in that most simple gesture from his *Padrone*.

"After you talk to Martel, it goes no further, no one else knows, understood? You don't even mumble in your sleep. This is completely off the record and unsanctioned."

Joshua just quietly nodded; he was now beginning to understand where Victor was going with this. Beginning to see and comprehend the moves that would complete the play of this mental game of chess with Buscamani.

"Have it done tonight. When I meet with Buscamani in a few days, I will give him all my sympathy; assure him I'll give vendetta on the fool who robbed him etcetera. I'll offer him a larger percentage on rackets. Rackets that I want him to have and re-invite him to send a new captain over." Victor sat back with a slight smile to his hard, lean face.

Joshua nodded to his Boss, "Consider it done," he simply said. He knew this was what made Victor was who he was. He was a great mediator, but he was one smart and ruthless bastard as well. Joshua had never known someone to take advantage of Victor no matter how cleverly they tried. He knew this move of Victor's would quiet

Buscamani, make them think and also give the Jeromes a better capo than the whining pain in the ass-- Cordoza they had now.

"Make sure the sit-down with Buscamani is in a nice place, spare no expense." Victor added, and fished around in his pocket for a roll of Lifesavers. "How are the Axel brothers after that mock execution?" Victor asked Josh.

The Axels were small time hoods, spies and wiseguy wannabes. They were good earners, and paid their tribute regularly, but they had smart mouths and smart-ass attitudes. Martel had personally gone himself and beat the crap out of both of them, broken some bones and scared the shit out of them. "Much better now, *Padrone*. A few days in the hospital, some broken bones and fear of being whacked will do that." Joshua smiled a half grin and took a proffered Lifesaver, from Victor.

"Good." Victor idly waved his hand, and popped a Lifesaver in his own mouth. "They may not be true Family but they are good spies. They hear a lot on the streets, especially down in the docks. They know a lot of what D'Salvatore soldiers are doing down there. They watch and keep their mouths shut and more importantly they tell their information to us. Give the Axel brothers a nice gift, a little raise from the Jeromes." This is how Victor was: he punished any transgressions swiftly and cruelly, and he didn't like cocky attitudes and loose mouths. Loyalty and good deeds for the Family were well rewarded.

"OK..." Joshua slightly shook his head, sometimes he didn't always follow Victor's line of thinking, but this was why Victor was the respected head of the Family. He had an instinct for these things; he knew how people worked. Whatever Victor's methods for running the Jerome Family, it was obvious that they were highly successful and made the Jerome Organization one of the most loyal and tightly knot ones on the East coast. "It's been a couple a weeks." Joshua flipped another sheet; "You wanna do public relations downtown this Wednesday?" he looked up at Victor.

Victor nodded and took another swallow of his cognac, finishing it off. "Yes," Victor nodded. Every few weeks Victor would be driven downtown New York City, in his large armor-plated limousine, with four to six of his best bodyguards. They would drive to the most run down sections, the ghettos and the poorest areas, where Victor and his men would personally pick up tributes and earnings from drug or prostitution rackets. There was a two-fold reason for this. One was to make sure that the enforcers, the pimps, and the drug dealers were doing their job and not shorting their associates or the capos who normally collected from them.

But more importantly this allowed the small men at the bottom: the soldiers, the crews, and the lowest worker in the Jerome Empire to personally see the CEO and Family head. Even the lowest worker wants to know that the Boss cares about him, that even the smallest man is an important cog in the wheel.

Victor was not a miser, in fact, far from it. It wasn't the money itself that was an issue it was the loyalty. That one word: *loyalty*, was given the highest esteem and importance by Victor, and men were oftentimes executed for lack of it or richly promoted and rewarded over for devotion to Victor and the Jerome Family.

If Victor had one main pet peeve, one that set his blood to boiling, his heart and soul to become a raging dark inferno, it was a traitor. Victor was an old man and was raised in the old ways. The new crime Families often operated with different methods or slacked off in the old ways and codes, but Victor believed in the old values and those included respect and loyalty. It was these beliefs, these core values in running his Family, that kept Victor Jerome at the top of the pile with the highest loyalty rating of any of the East coast Families. It's what made his the most powerful Family in the Commission.

Josh reached into his pocket and pulled out a square of nicotine gum. He had been trying to quit smoking the last few weeks and lately had been on a razor's edge. "I have one small surprise for you, *Padrone*," Joshua said softly and there was a slight gleam to his handsome, dark, panther-like face. He unwrapped the gum and popped it into his mouth, "It concerns Vito Roman and that business you so detest..." he let the sentence hang for a second, knowing it was a very sore and delicate subject with Victor.

Victor gave a heavy sigh, he leaned back in his chair and his eyes took on a dark look. Some of the best-paying rackets for the Jerome Family were illegal gambling, loan sharking, and worldwide smuggling of both legitimate goods and stolen goods through the VIJER Import-Export Company. Union corruption and drugs also paid well and were good secondary money earners. The Jerome Family had even dabbled over the years in prostitution and money laundering although they had turned over most of those rackets to alliances of the Family.

For many years, the Roman Family had not only been the number one ally with the Jerome Family, but they also sat on the Commission as well. In fact, the alliance with the Roman Family had gone back in as far back as the Felani-Jerome days. They were one of the Families who had loudly supported young Victor taking the helm and helped convince the other Families in the Commission that Jerome (along with the Del Giorno, Giancomo, and Corella Families) would be even better and stronger than before the Bloody Massacre of '57.

Victor acknowledged that it was the ancient Don Joseph Roman, one of the original Mustache Petes, who had also taught Victor a lot of what it was to run a large Family--

It had been nearly four years ago, back in 1983, that Joseph, then a venerable eighty-nine year-old man with terminal emphysema, called

Victor in for a private sit-down and proposed a new racket. Victor knew that Joseph was trying to keep his Family strong for when his son Vito took over as head of the Romans.

"There is a new thing…" the venerable Don Joseph Roman gestured as he fished a large cigar out from his double breasted suit pocket. "A new money maker." He rubbed his gnarled, arthritic fingers together. They were sitting in Victor's penthouse apartment, atop the VIJER Corporate building. "These wealthy Arabs, they pay well for pretty American women, you understand, eh?" Joseph spoke in thick Sicilian. His hand trembled violently as he lit up and puffed his large Cuban cigar.

"Prostitution?" Victor asked. Prostitution was a common moneymaker in most Families.

"No, no" Joseph waved his hand, "Not like that. These *moolies* they want pure women, clean, not working women. You understand?" His old, dark eyes peered at Victor through a deeply wrinkled face. Around the room four well-armed soldiers from both Families stood around to act as bodyguards.

"What, like mail-order brides?" Victor said, still not fully comprehending.

"Eh," Joseph waggled his hand, "Yes and no, but more. Girls that can't say no, you know what I mean? What they call, harem girls. *Schiavitù, tratta della bianche*. White slaves." He explained it bluntly now, "Specialized pornography, snuff films; all this shit is big now in the Middle East. They are picky; they want fresh women, eh. *Innocente* women and blonde-haired, blue-eyed all-American women." Joseph had a coughing fit and pulled forth a handkerchief and hacked heavily into it.

"No, Joseph." Victor shook his own head, not believing what he was hearing "What is that nonsense? There are plenty of prostitutes available, women willing to…"

"No!" Joseph raised his voice, cutting Victor off, "No! That is not what they want. These fuckin' towel-heads, overseas they pay big money for these women, Victor. Hundreds of thousands of dollars." He leaned forward looking directly at Victor, like a grizzled old bear. "Victor, this is huge money for the Alliance, for the Jeromes and for the Roman's. We already have this thing figured out. These women; we take them from places like mental hospitals, prisons, poor ones, nobodies. Pretty ones, you understand? Ones that no one will notice missing. You control a lot of unions, most of the ports, you have a lot of corrupted officials in your pocket, and you own this huge fucking import-export company…" he gestured around the room. "All you have to do is say "Yes", that's it, we even package them up, you just have to ship them. Bribe the customs officials to look the other way, you understand?" Joseph sat back after his speech, wheezing deeply.

Victor had heard the term "white slavery" before, *schiavitù,* true captives and slaves, and what Joseph was proposing was exactly that. True slavery in one way or the other. Not prostitutes willing to turn a trick, or even get slapped around some, but women kidnapped, sold overseas to be used for sex, work, even killed or abused by rich, perverted masters.

Not only did this disgust and not sit well with Victor, but he also knew how dangerous this venture was. If even a whiff of this leaked out, the F.B.I's RICO division would come down on them like a ton of bricks and not just with prison terms. If caught, death penalties would be imposed. Victor was no angel, he had roughed up people who owed money or slacked off on favors or earnings, but it was always business. Very rarely were total innocent civilians involved. Corrupted officials could only look away so much, but the general public didn't like innocents killed. And more importantly, Victor didn't like it either.

"No!" Victor reiterated, this time in a deeper, harsher tone. "No! What you ask is suicide, Joseph! We're not talking trafficking in stolen cars here, but humans. Not prostitution, but kidnapping, overseas transport, who knows what else, do you realize if any of us are caught, if anything goes wrong, then we all fall, and we all fall hard?"

"Look, Vittorio," Joseph called Victor by his boyhood name, a purposeful disrespect towards Victor. "I loved your father Louis and your godfather and founder of your *Famiglia* Mario Felani; I have spent most of my life happy in this alliance with the Jeromes. I fuckin' helped kill D'Salvatore men after they murdered your family!" Joseph's eyes grew dark, hard, his hands clenching the air as though wanting to strangle Victor.

"Our Families have always been close. Hell, I helped you get where you are today, Jerome! You know it was me who pushed the Commission to let you in!" Joseph coughed up a thick sticky wad of phlegm, panting to regain his breath and went on. "I am a dying old man, my son Vito is already groomed to take over as head of the Family. Let me give you a little free advice, *Don* Jerome." The name was spat almost contemptuously. "Grow, expand and reward my Family for all the help we have given you, or we are through. The Romans pull out and the Jeromes will fall and be a Family that ceases to exist! Our alliance has bought much money and strength to both our Families, but it is time we get more! Always have we been in the shadows. You give us this small thing we ask, you wet our beaks or we are through! Broken! Divorced!" Joseph slammed his gnarled fists on the elegant table with a growl, his whole body trembling with anger.

Several of the bodyguards on both sides shifted or coughed nervously at the deadly quiet that hung in between the two Families. A split between the Romans and the Jeromes would guarantee a huge edge to the D'Salvatores and would shake the very foundation of the Commission and all the Families involved.

For a few moments, Victor sat there stunned; never had his mind comprehended such a threat as Joseph had lain out at his feet. Then an anger rose in him; so dark, so furious that he knew that he had to clamp it down or he would reach across the table and break up the Families' alliance himself, by throttling Joseph Roman right then and there. Victor called on his deepest reserves of strength and wisdom; if ever he needed to draw on his arbitration skills now was it. He must not let his own anger show; he must not let Joseph know he was rattled.

Victor sat back in his chair and steeple his fingers. His eyes grew as dark as a moonless night and his voice was unnaturally calm. Only Victor's underboss, Laurence Martel, knew that these signs meant Victor was dangerously close to uncontrollable, murderous rage. "This thing of yours," Victor said with distaste, "Proceeds only with the following conditions--"

"Now wait, Jerome!" Joseph sputtered, thick drops of saliva clinging to his drooping lips.

"No!" Victor glared, and this time his voice did rise to a dangerous growl of barely controlled rage, "You wait, Joseph!" the bodyguards on both sides snapped to attention in case need arose to break the two bosses apart in a physical fight or worse.

With a quick, subtle wave of his hand, Victor put his men at ease. "No." Victor continued, in full control of his voice and anger, but inside the shark circled and the dark fire in his eyes simmered with cold calculating fury. "I may be young in your eyes, but I am head of this Family. Of *mi Famiglia*, Joseph!" Victor leaned back again, "Go on to D'Salvatores, take your fucking bocce balls and go home, your idle threats only piss me off. Do not dare to challenge me, old man." Victor's eyes bore into his opponent, Joseph Roman.

Victor knew he was taking a huge gamble here of losing one of the strongest arms of the Alliance. That if Don Roman did not fall for his bluff, Victor would be indeed setting the stage for the break-up of the most powerful Alliance on the East Coast, and indeed weakening his own Family dangerously. All that the Jeromes, Felanis and Romans had built up for over sixty years would be gone in but a brief wink of an eye and yet a new war started. One that the Jeromes could not possibly hope to fight while still fighting the D'Salvatores. The Jerome Family probably would indeed fall and cease to exist as Joseph had threatened earlier.

The bodyguards, Victor's underboss, and the consiglieres from both sides, they knew this as well, and the immense tension hung in the air with a deadly silence.

After what seemed like an eternity, a wheezing chuckle finally emanated from Joseph Roman's throat. "Fucking Victor," he laughed, "You are not at all like your father Louis. Maybe your mother cheated with Mario Felani, eh? Your personality more reflects his." Joseph

47

wiped beads of perspiration from his forehead. "I will listen to your conditions as long as the Jeromes give us additional action, some of the union rackets. You're the fuckin' Arbitrator so start arbitrating." Immediately, the tension that had hung like a dark curtain lifted. And the bodyguards resumed breathing again.

Victor discreetly took out and popped a couple peppermint Lifesavers in his mouth, letting his own tension drain; not daring to let Joseph know just how much the bluff had cost him in nerves. "First and foremost," Victor stated, leaning forward once again steepling his fingers. "I deal with your son Vito, and no one else. Second, I will support but want nothing to do with this...foolhardy venture of Shanghai slavery." Victor nearly spat out the word. "I will decide when and how support comes to you in that area. I will be very generous and give you a forty percent cut of shylock business and swag. This comes from me and from the Corella Family, you understand? No union or contractor business. That is Jerome territory alone!" Victor knew that his underboss Martel had just drawn in a deep breath of disbelief but knew better than to say a word.

Joseph Roman's thick, cough-laden laughter resounded throughout the room. "Agreed, so be it. You are sly as a damned fox, Victor, but agreed." The two bosses stood and embraced in a hug, clapping each other's shoulders.

"Good," Victor smiled a forced smile; the smile of a shark about to devour its prey. "Send Vito to see me in three days. I will go over the details and give him his first points, his first payments on the new businesses for the Romans."

"Yeah, three days." Joseph grabbed his hat, coat and his cane. He ground out his cigar in Victor's expensive crystal ashtray. Joseph's bodyguards immediately helped their aging boss on with his coat and then protectively circled their infirm Don and gently led him out towards the elevator. As Joseph walked off, another round of chest-rattling coughs shook his body. Feebly he tried to wave off the concerned gestures of his men.

After they left, Victor said nothing for a few moments. Martel, his underboss, Joshua his consigliere, and the two bodyguards just stood there eerily silent. They dared not speak either. Finally Victor turned and looked at each man in turn, his dark eyes seeming to pierce their souls. "Martel," he swung towards his underboss. "Put Mr. Roman to sleep." Victor made the gesture of a gun with his hand; "I want him permanently retired by midnight tonight. With honor-- understand?"

Martel nodded. Victor's men knew this was coming, probably so did Joseph Roman's men. *La Cosa Nostra* was run like a tightly knit wolf pack. There were silences, rules, codes and more etiquette and intrigues than the royal families of Europe. Joseph Roman had committed the highest offense; not that he had argued with Victor Jerome, but that he did so disrespectfully in front of his men. He had outright challenged and threatened the alpha-leader, the Don. One who wanted to live a long life did not ever publicly humiliate or challenge the Don of a Commission Family.

As Martel and the other two henchmen filed out of the room, Victor smoothed back the hair he had left, a distinguished salt and pepper laurel of hair that circled his nearly bald head. "He is getting old, and he is dying." Victor thought to himself. "And he wants to die as a warrior, executed quickly for the highest offense possible. He didn't want to let his illness kill him slowly and agonizingly over the weeks and months. He wanted me to destroy him and put him out of his misery. He didn't want the Romans to be weakened when power was transferred to his son Vito." Victor immediately thought of his late brother Eddie and instantly understood what Joseph Roman was up to.

Victor sighed softly, clasped his hands behind his back and walked over to the large picture window to look out over the huge bustling city of New York. It had been perhaps the one of the most important decisions in the Don's reign of the Jerome Family, but he had passed it with flying colors.

Three days after Joseph Roman's funeral, Victor Jerome and Vito Roman went over the final details of the decisions agreed upon by Joseph and Victor. Victor knew right away that Vito was a cocky and careless boss, nothing like his father. Not by anything he did, just in his attitude. Victor knew Vito would screw up sometime and when he did, Victor would be there to mow him down and either get the Romans to merge directly under his leadership, or else let them leave, but with far less than they had now.

"Joseph told me, these women would be gotten out of mental hospitals and prisons. Virtual nobodies, that can't be tracked down." Victor fished out his roll of wintergreen Lifesavers. "This –thing- of yours will go on with the following conditions," he put the candy in his mouth and slowly savored it. "I will inspect whatever shipments I choose to, whenever I choose to. I will also be assigning my capo Leonardo Tagretta to work with you all as my eyes and ears. All your shit better be in order and smelling like roses. Any violations and this venture is done with. *Finito!* Do you understand?"

"No problem, Victor." Vito leaned back and sipped on his glass of champagne Victor had poured him. "My father had promised you good income on this venture, high points, and that is what you will have. Forty percent," Vito pulled out an envelope as thick as a paperback book and placed it on the desk in front of Victor.

Victor picked it up and thumbed through it; it was close to $65,000. He pulled out $35,000 and tossed back the remaining money to Vito. "I'll take half of this, and then only ten percent tribute." Victor sighed tiredly.

"That's all you want?" Vito nearly spilled his champagne, "Just ten percent? I don't understand?" Vito asked totally dumbfounded.

"I consider it devil's money, Vito," Victor eyed the awestruck younger Don. "Let it be known that I don't like this venture in any way. But I made a promise to your father; the only reason I take any money at all is because the code of *Cosa Nostra* dictates it." Victor quickly got up from his desk and left the room, before his temper caused him to say something he'd regret later--

Joshua Demonico snapped his notebook shut and called out towards the door. "Send in Marchelli."

Victor immediately snapped out of his drift down memory lane. That whole exchange with Joseph and Vito had been four long years ago. Victor had personally inspected maybe one or two shipments over the years, but he found it so personally distasteful, he usually let his imported Sicilian capo, Leonardo 'Len' Tagretta, inspect any shipments on a random basis.

"Vito Roman is getting a shipment in this Thursday, and you may want to go inspect it personally--" Joshua stood up and faced the door as a small, timid man was escorted in by one of Victor's burly bodyguards. Joshua motioned the nervous man forward. "This is Christoforo Marchelli. Martel and I secretly planted him four years ago in the Roman Family, specifically as a low-level soldier involved in that whole nasty business you don't like, to spy on Vito--" Joshua nodded to the speck of a man, encouraging him to step forward and show his respects to Don Victor.

"M-M-Mr. Jerome." The man had an obvious stutter and spoke in a barely audible voice. Victor stood up, and the two men formally embraced.

Joshua smiled; this time it was he who held a surprise that Victor didn't know about. It was always nice giving the boss a special treat he didn't know was coming. "Mr. Marchelli came back to us a few days ago with some very interesting information for me and Martel." Joshua walked up closer so that the three men were in a small circle together. "Tell him, Chris."

"We both know that for many m-m-moons Vito Roman has not gotten all the women from where he said he was, b-b-but I had no proof. I finally was able to get some; papers, photos, sh-sh-shit like that." The small man nervously dug around in his pockets pulling out envelopes stuffed with paperwork and half-crinkled photos. Being in the presence of the Don of the Family only made the soldier even more nervous, his stuttering worse. With a trembling hand, he thrust the paperwork at both Victor and Joshua. "H-H-He's using hired hands and independents to kuh-kuh- kidnap some of them, mainly women off the streets. He's getting maybe only one-third of them from institutions and shit. M-M-Most he is picking up randomly. I got paperwork with proof of p-p-payments and other shit to outside hired guns and lists of drugs used to d-d-dart 'em like animals."

The fire instantly returned to Victor's eyes, and the heavy weariness that had hung over him for days and weeks seemed to suddenly lift. "Excellent, my friend." A smile crossed Victor's face, the light in his dark eyes sending soothing warmth and strength to Christoforo Marchelli. He placed one hand on the small man's shoulder and squeezed it gently, then glanced up quickly at Joshua, unspoken words of gratitude flowing to his consigliere.

Joshua reached into the breast pocket of his suit and pulled out a thick envelope and handed it to Chris. "This is for your hard work. The Family is grateful for what you have done." Joshua gave Marchelli a quick embrace, as did Victor. "I'll have one of the men drive you to wherever you need to go. Consider your assignment with the Romans finished." Joshua winked at him. "In two days see Patrizio, he will have some work you can do that will bring you good profits." The small man nodded gratefully at Joshua and left the room, flanked by the bodyguards.

After they had left, Victor turned to Joshua and hugged him close again. "You certainly surprised this old man; you did well, my trusted friend." He held Joshua out at arm's length for a moment and then motioned Josh to pour them both a drink.

Joshua poured some Crown Royal whiskey for both of them and handed Victor a glass. "I am glad I was able to make your day, *Padrone. Salute!*" he toasted Victor.

"*Salute,*" Victor returned the toast. They both drank deeply for a moment not having to say anything, both grinning like two kids who had just pulled off the grandest prank. "I am definitely going to be visiting Vito Roman on Thursday. But before then, I will want a sit-down with the other heads of the Commission."

"Martel and I thought you would." Joshua winked, "Things are already being set up as we speak. The sit-down is for tomorrow with the other Commission heads."

Victor shook his head in amazement. "What do you need me for, eh?" he lightly teased Joshua. "Sounds like I am one of the luckiest bastards around to have such two loyal friends. You and Martel only show me more each day, that all of my decisions regarding you two have been the best ones I have ever made. Shit, I may just go into permanent retirement." Victor winked and they both chuckled and took another long drink of the whiskey.

CHAPTER 3- *April 12th 1987*

Sarah remembered very little of the trailer ride. She had drifted in and out of a tortured, drug-induced sleep, her mind filled with bizarre images and half dreams. She remembered she had been sick to her stomach several times; in fact the nausea still gripped her gut in a vice-like grip. Whatever drug they had injected in her was wearing off, because she was much more aware of what was going on. Sarah desperately wished she was still high so she would not have to deal with this, could pretend that this nightmare was not happening.

Her muscles ached from being cramped, her nostrils filled with the rancid smell of vomit, sweat and human waste, her nauseous stomach churned even more, and her head began to pound in pain.

The truck was stopped now, and suddenly as the back door was opened, bright, blinding sunlight assaulted her sensitive eyes, causing her headache to rise to new levels of agony. The trailer she and the other women were cramped in was suddenly invaded by fresh, clean air, and she gulped it deeply in her lungs, savoring the clean air, letting it clear her head. She and the other four women also were in a state of severe shock and hangover and all Sarah wanted to do was to be left alone to curl up and go back to sleep; to have someone shut that damn trailer door so that the bright sunlight would stop pounding into her head like a sledgehammer.

However she saw this was not to be. The well-dressed black man and the tall, skinny man were heading into the trailer and unhooking the girls one by one from the "O" rings and dragging them down the ramp into what looked like, some kind of kennel facility. Her vision and mind were blurry, unreliable, but she was certain the kennels were *not* for dogs.

Sarah was the fourth one unloaded and led down the ramp; her muscles were stiff and uncooperative. She could see the other ladies weren't faring so well either. The women seemed to be a groggy, hung over, in pain and shocked bunch. Her head felt thick and clouded; her senses rebelled at the sunlight and at her body's movement, but the grimy, scrawny man, T.J., kept her steadily moving down the ramp, always swinging that stupid electric cattle prod.

Her left leg was asleep from the cramped position it had been in during the long journey, but it was now beginning to reawaken, a strong tingling and numbness running up and down the length of it. She stumbled, barely keeping her balance.

"Move it!" the scraggly man growled at her. Stupidly, Sarah turned to say something to him and that's when her left leg gave out completely, sending her sprawling awkwardly on the hard, hot asphalt. Her head rattled with a deafening thud as she crashed down.

"Stupid bitch!" Thankfully T.J. just kicked her with his sneaker and didn't use that cattle prod he carried in his hand.

Slowly and ungainly, she clambered to her hands and knees, trying to regain a solid foothold and keep the ground from tilting and spinning like some bizarre carnival ride.

Feeling she was moving far too slowly, one of T.J.'s long arms snaked out and roughly grabbed her long, red hair, twisting it around his hand. "I said, up!" he growled dangerously at her.

In a moment of pain and surprise, Sarah twisted reflexively and lashed out blindly, catching the thin man hard across his lean, scarred face.

He brought the cattle prod down hard on her twice, once on her stomach and once across her inner thigh. Her body burned with pain and shock, and in blind panic and primitive instinct her body twitched and reacted against its own will.

Involuntarily her muscles tightened in painful bands, causing her legs to kick out backwards, like some wild antelope trying to escape the clutches of a lion. In a stroke of twisted luck, her feet managed to connect solidly with the thin man's crotch.

T.J. grabbed his balls and sank to his knees with a tortured grimace and a moan of pain. Sarah collapsed solidly to the ground about three feet away from him, to his left. The cattle prod fell from his hand two feet to his right. She was sick to her stomach, heaving, retching and panting from the physical exertion, from the pain inflicted by the cattle prod.

"Y-y-you fucking cunt!" the man spit out between painful gasps as he started getting his senses around him and was able to begin to move again after the rack to his balls. "I'll fucking break your fucking neck!" He panted and groped around for the fallen cattle prod. He scooped it up and forced himself to his feet, blind rage and anger now replacing the pain.

Sarah never heard him coming, never stood a chance. She was too busy vomiting her already empty stomach onto the asphalt. Her body was still absorbed in its own painful, hung-over state while slowly trying to climb back to her hands and knees. She suddenly heard a loud, far off "*crack*" like a bolt of thunder, and her mouth instantly filled with a wet, salty metallic taste. Her vision became an orange-red cloud, and all that she knew or was aware of suddenly ceased to make any sense.

Darius, the well-dressed black man, was just returning to the truck after letting one of Vito Roman's men know the new shipment was being unloaded when he saw his partner T.J., swinging his cattle prod like a madman on a prone and unmoving female. "T.J., stop!" Darius called and began running to where T.J. and the girl were.

T.J. was now on top of the unconscious girl and wielding the electric prod like a quarterstaff, jamming it against her throat, trying to break her neck. Beneath him, her unconscious form twitched and jerked like some obscene puppet as the electricity coursed through her.

"Quit it, damn you!" Darius grabbed T.J. by his scrawny shoulders and began to haul him off the girl, "You fuckin' dawg, would you stop!" he continued dragging T.J. off her, while T.J. was still trying to break free of Darius' grasp and finish killing her. "Will you stop!" Darius now growled in a dangerous voice, kicking T.J. hard in the back and then expertly wresting the cattle prod out of his grasp, "What the hell is the matter with you? Vito Roman will have your shit-eating hide! Have you lost your fucking mind?" Darius had wrapped his muscular arm around T.J.'s neck, choking his air supply off, cooling his temper. As T.J. finally stopped fighting Darius slowly loosened his death lock on him and let him go.

"The damn bitch kicked me in the balls, man!" T.J. wailed defensively, rubbing his throat where Darius had choked him, "She fucking attacked me!"

Darius held up both his hands, silencing his whining partner and letting him know he was close to pushing Darius's anger over the edge. He looked around T.J. at the unmoving form of the woman. He saw her chest rise and fall raggedly. She was still alive, but barely. Her throat was severely burned, a disgusting stench of charred flesh hung in the air. Her face, shoulders and ribs were horribly bruised and bleeding; blood flowed heavily out of her nose, mouth and out of her right ear. "Oh fuck you, man." Darius glared at his partner and then paced a few steps shaking his head in disbelief, "Ol' Vito is gonna be one pissed off mutha fucker! And you're gonna be the one to explain it to him!"

It finally dawned on T.J. what his outburst had done; Vito Roman and his associates were always very specific about the girls being in good condition when they arrived at his place ready for final shipment. Vito usually took a big chunk of payment out of Darius and T.J.'s share if any of the merchandise was banged up. TJ began to panic. "Maybe we can say she had an accident! Or maybe we can say she got in a fight with one of the other women, or…"

T.J. wasn't known for his intelligence and Darius was at the end of his patience. He knew the shit was going to hit the fan. "Get the other two out and gimme your Goddamn electric stick!" He growled in a deadly and dangerous tone, "You done lost the privilege of carrying that, my man. Stuff this injured bitch in the middle of the shipment; and you…" he jammed his finger into TJ's lean chest, "…are going to explain this to the man personally. Got it?" Darius turned and stalked off. He pulled a cigarette out from a gold cigarette case and tapped it on the inside of his hand. Yep, he knew Vito was going to be one hot-off-the-grill- guinea over this mess. He had been doing these runs for Vito now for close to three years, never with an incident like this. If Vito didn't kick T.J.'s ass over this, Darius vowed he would personally teach T.J. a lesson.

Victor sat in the back of the long black limousine. Next to him was his imposing underboss Laurence Martel; in the front passenger seat sat the Sicilian, Leonardo Tagretta, who was the Jerome capo who usually dealt with the Romans, and two armed bodyguards and soldiers. Leonardo and Laurence were armed as well. Driving the limo was one of Victor's favorite capos and his personal chauffeur, Cesare "the Elf" Ciccerone, a huge obese man, who looked like a walrus sporting sunglasses and a dark suit.

Following Victor's limo were two other imposing cars in the procession, one that held the Corellas Top Administration and the last car that held the Top Administration from the Del Giorno Family. Next to the Romans; these two other Families were the biggest and oldest allies of the Jerome Family. Each of the other Families had their own bodyguards as well. The dark procession of New York's most powerful crime lords slowly rolled through the gates of Vito Romans' isolated farm and kennels, out in the middle of nowhere near the New York / New Jersey border.

Vito Roman was in a foul mood to begin with, and his mood went from bleak to worse when he found out that Victor Jerome was arriving personally for an unannounced visit. "Of all the damn shipments to inspect," Vito thought to himself, "This one beats all." Vito paced like a caged tiger, "Come on, hurry up!" he yelled to his soldiers and henchmen, "Clean up these bitches the best you can before Victor gets here," Vito sucked on a large foul-smelling cigar, "And get this damn waste out of here already, throw him in the incinerator!" he motioned to the dead body of T.J. whom Vito had personally shot through the head.

"What about the real messed-up broad, Boss?" one of Vito's men gestured to Sarah's unconscious half-dead form.

"We don't have time to deal with that now, stuff her in the back unused kennel and close the door. We'll pretend we just have four this shipment. Also dope up the others with some more heroin; Victor can't examine too closely what's unconscious, understand?" he jabbed the cigar at his goon.

Vito had been agitatedly pacing, still puffing on his cigar when Victor and company walked down the well-manicured garden path towards the kennels secluded in the back of the large house, along with a large office. He nearly choked as he saw the procession of other Commission members as well. The additional entourage of Commission heads was completely unexpected. He knew something was up; something very, very bad. He felt a tremor of fear run through him.

Vito and Victor quickly and formally embraced, but Vito could feel the hardness, anger and coldness in Victor through the simple formal gesture. The same with Nicholas Corella and Enrico Del Giorno; their embraces were quick, hard, and distant. The expressions of all the other bodyguards, consiglieres and underbosses were unreadable. Even when he met Leonardo's, eyes whom he had dealt with for years, he did not find a friendly face; just cold hard expressions on all of them.

Leonardo Tagretta simply nodded with his chin towards the small building that was Vito's office, and the entire entourage moved off in that direction.

"Victor," Vito had to go into a slow jog to keep up with the fast pace Victor was keeping. "I'm a bit surprised, you know? Inspecting the shipment on such short notice."

"Oh?" Victor abruptly stopped. "It was in the agreement; I know you are aware of that." Soon Victor would close in and destroy his prey in one swift motion.

"Well yeah, I mean of course it is." Vito scratched idly behind his ear, "It's just that usually we deal with Len, you know? I mean it's been what, a year or so since you personally dropped by?"

"Three years and two months." Victor looked up at him and then continued his quick pace along with the procession of other crime lords and their henchmen to the kennels.

"Oh, yeah, three years." Vito jogged a few steps and caught up with Victor, "Ok, I'll be blunt..."

"You, blunt?" Victor abruptly stopped again, this time so fast it caused Vito to nearly broadside him. "Why Vito, this is a whole new side of you, my friend."

Vito grinned lamely, assuming Victor was making a joke. "Ya see," he leaned in close, trying not to be overheard by the procession of Corellas' and Del Giornos'. "I'm just kind of surprised is all; at the distinguished guests and "friends of ours" you brought with ya."

"I always liked a good surprise, don't you agree, Vito?" Victor turned on his heel and again began walking on. Vito's stomach began churning into a tight knot, and his blood began to run cold.

Victor and his procession had been silently walking around the kennels, for nearly fifteen minutes. As Victor stood and examined the four unconscious women, his look had gone from a steely grimace to a look of sour disgust and finally to utter contempt. Casually, Victor walked around as though he were taking a Sunday stroll. Not a word did he utter, just an occasional glance at his own men or his fellow Dons. He walked over to Vito's desk and motioned for Vito to show him the paperwork. The off-the-record codes and ledgers that showed the Jeromes how Vito was utilizing the VIJER Import/Export Company, supposedly keeping all this very hidden and clean.

"Level with me, bastard!" Victor without warning suddenly threw down the papers, spun around and with amazing speed and strength grabbed Vito Roman by the collar.

Vito was not about to make a move; he'd have let Victor beat him silly and not lifted a finger against him. He knew he was at a disadvantage. That something was going horribly wrong and he knew better than to piss off Victor more than he was already pissed off. "Whoa! Hey!" he held up his hands in a supplicating gesture. "What's up, Victor? I know this bunch is a bit rough-looking and all, but everything's in order. I mean..."

"Is that your final answer Vito? You have nothing else to tell me?" Victor spat at him, and then flung him away.

Vito just stepped back and shrugged, looking helplessly at the other bosses for support or answers, but none came. The others just stood stolidly and silently like an unmoving jury behind Victor Jerome.

"These," Victor picked up the papers he had been looking at and suddenly threw them to the floor, "- are trash, shit, worthless! Only good for burning the place to the ground with." He motioned to Martel and several of the bodyguards, who began pulling out lighter fluid and kerosene containers from their briefcases or overcoats, while others began stacking up the fallen papers and other flammables in piles around the office. Then began pouring the fluid all over the office.

"H-Hey, Victor!" Vito was sweating profusely now, "I don't understand! Please, what did I do? I thought we had an agreement?" Vito was about to light a cigar, but with the heavy fumes of lighter fluid and kerosene that hung in the air, he decided against it.

Victor eyed him, an unnatural calm to his dark-fire eyes. "An agreement, ah yes." Victor spoke quietly. He fished in his breast pocket and pulled out all the incriminating papers and photos that Chris Marchelli had given to him. "But you broke that agreement, Vito. You lied to me," he glared at Vito, slapping the incriminating papers hard across the Don of the Roman Family's face. "Only some of these women are coming out of prisons or mental institutions, the others are being kidnapped off the streets! You risked bringing the entire wrath of the government agencies down on all of us with your stupid, fucking carelessness and more important..." Victor walked up to him nearly face to face. "You lied to me. You broke our agreement! Your loyalty, your word, now means nothing." he reiterated.

Victor nodded to the soldiers who began pulling out lighters and matches, getting ready to torch the place. Behind him, Nicholas Corella and Enrico Del Giorno still stood unmoving, silent, dark judges.

Vito suddenly realized that he was caught, and that his life might very well end here and now. Not only that, but Victor had the full support of at least two other Commission Dons. There would be no mercy for Vito Roman. He felt his balls retreat deep within his abdomen. "OK, OK..." Vito panted in fear. He literally dropped to his knees in front of Victor Jerome, glancing at him and at the other bosses. "...I fucked up, Victor, whaddya want me to say?"

Vito's own men all flinched at seeing their boss so utterly humiliated. They dared not intervene, not in Commission business like this. It wasn't their place.

"I'm sorry! I swear it, I fucked up, and I am sorry..." sweat poured off Vito, and his heart pounded in his ears like a drum of doom. "I said I'm fucking sorry!" he shouted nearly hysterically to all the men in the room.

"Yes you are a sorry man, Vito." Victor casually spat the insult down at him. "But alas, this old heart is unmoved and not in a very forgiving mood." Victor walked over and took a lighter out of the nearest bodyguard's hand. He flicked the wheel, and it sparked a few times then kicked to life with a bright lick of flame shooting out from the top. "Sorry doesn't cut it." Victor's cruel stare tore through Vito's soul.

Vito Roman could have sworn that Victor Jerome was Lucifer himself; so hard and frightening was the old man's stare that he crossed himself, "What do you want, Mr. Jerome?" he begged; there were actual tears in his eyes. Still he remained on his knees, terrified to move. Certain that the next order out of Victor's mouth would be for his execution, "Anything, please I beg of you. Beg of you all!" he glanced up at Enrico and Nicholas as well.

"Ah," Victor stepped back and let the flame on the lighter go out. "So now you wish to negotiate, eh?" He stepped closer to the cowering Vito Roman. Victor motioned for Vito to sit at the chair at his desk, and then stood boldly astraddle over Vito. "Condition number one," Victor's hands pinned Vito's shoulders to the chair, his face mere inches from Vito's, "this white- slavery shit will be dropped from the Alliance, forever. Period."

"But," Vito tried thinly to protest, "there was a…"

Victor made a quick swipe of his hand to his henchmen and they all began lighting the papers and furniture in the corners of the office. Flames sprang up and began engulfing the papers and running up the elegant wallpaper. Laurence Martel, who had sidled up behind the chair, placed the ice-cold barrel of his 357 Magnum against Vito's temple.

"Nooo!" Vito screeched, in mortal terror, "OK, OK! I'll do it!"

"Condition number two," Victor calmly spoke, still holding Vito fast to the chair, oblivious to the rising flames and Vito's terrified shaking. "This shipment you have now will be destroyed, the bodies disposed of and this subject will never, ever, come up again in my presence or in the presence of this Commission or any of its Alliances" he nodded briefly to the Corellas and Del Giornos.

"OK, all right!" Vito was now crying like a child, tears coursing down his face, as he watched his office going up in flames. Watched as his men looked away from his humiliation and weakness in defeat and disgust.

"Swear your life on it, Vito Gianni Roman. " Victor took his hand that bore the Jerome Family ring on it and held it up to Vito's face; the symbol of the Jerome Family and its immense power.

Trembling like a vanquished child, Vito realized he was being given the ultimate humiliation in front of all his peers and his own Family. Usually such power displays and ring-kissing was no longer done, not for decades. It was almost as humiliating as if Victor had unzipped his fly and pissed on him. Vito pressed the ring with his lips and kissed it. He bowed his head in utter defeat, not caring at this point if he burned up along with his office.

"You are most fortunate I am in a merciful mood," Victor spoke and finally stood away from Vito, releasing him and nodding to Martel to back off. "I could have had you whacked instead of just broken and thrown out of the Commission, for your breaking your promise. You do know that." It was a statement not a question.

Vito could only nod; he could not even look Victor or the others in the eyes now. The Romans were now low men on the totem pole; the Commission had turned on him and taken his rank and seat in the Commission from the Romans, he was no different now from the lowest crew. He could either accept it or be shot and wiped out right here and now. Organized crime had little mercy; it was all about business.

"Martel, take Leonardo and the others. I want you to put all four of those women to sleep. One quick, clean shot to the head. They're unconscious they'll never know what hit them. I want any remains disposed of and this complex and office burnt to the ground. The main house can stay."

"Yes, Mr. Jerome," Martel's deep resonant voice acknowledged, and he motioned to several other associates to follow him.

"Consider yourself fortunate, Mr. Roman." Victor stepped back with his peers, Nicholas Corella and Enrico Del Giorno, looking at the shocked and beaten Vito. "You still live."

Nicholas Corella motioned to a few of his men, "Take Mr. Roman outside, and let him get a good view of the bonfire," he said in a thick Brooklyn accent. Two of Corella's bodyguards took hold of Vito and dragged him outside. Corella's underboss motioned to Roman's bodyguards and associates, "You too, move it." He gestured to the door. Vito's men were more than happy to comply as the office was now getting thick with smoke, the fire grew.

"I'll be out shortly," Victor nodded to Corella and Del Giorno as he watched the other two crime lords and their processions leave the building. Victor and Cesare began to quickly explore the kennels to see that Martel and the others had done their work. Victor was a tough crime boss who had seen much and done much. But this reminded Victor of some perverse concentration camp; shackles, manacles, cattle prods and other instruments of abuse hung along the walls. "Make sure the whole damn thing burns down to the ground," he muttered under his breath to Cesare as he began looking into the various cells. Most were empty; a few had the women who were now dead, with a quick bullet to the temple. In the last cell he saw Martel pouring kerosene on the last body of the "shipment".

"There were only four," Martel said. "All have been taken care of. You'd better leave, Boss," he gently said, "This place will be an inferno shortly."

Victor nodded and he was about to leave when he spied a half-concealed door behind several boxes. He could have sworn he heard some noise from behind that concealed door. His curiosity raised, he began moving the boxes; Cesare and Leonardo immediately began helping him. Victor opened the door and walked in. At first it appeared to be some large closet or large storage area, but as he walked in he heard coughing; it sounded like a female. Victor groped along the wall until he found a light switch and flipped it on.

He had seen many victims of beatings in his time, but there was something brutal in the way this young woman looked. A civilian, an innocent; viciously beaten, she was conscious, barely, but seemed aware of the haze of smoke that hung dangerously in the air.

Despite her severe injuries she was trying to drag her naked form to her feet. She wasn't very successful and kept collapsing, looking like some flopping, dying fish out of water. She turned and for a moment her gaze locked on Victor's, a total lucidness within them, her eyes, like Eddie's so long ago spoke the unvoiced plea, "*Help me.*" By this time Martel walked in after his Boss; he too saw the young woman, and slowly drew his gun.

"No, wait." Victor said softly and put his hand on Martel's arm, halting him and hiding his aim from the girl. "She is not unconscious."

Victor gingerly walked up to and knelt down next to the semi-struggling woman. He looked her up and down and shook his head. "They did a number on you, child." He spoke softly.

She immediately stopped struggling, her eyes trying desperately to focus on this strange person in front of her. It was a losing battle: horrid fatigue and weakness were again threatening to drag her into unconsciousness but his voice had cut through her pain-induced haze and she lay there half raised up, alertly looking his direction. Somehow she sensed safety in that voice. One arm weakly reached out towards him.

Victor gently stroked her bloody, matted hair and she grew more still and relaxed under his simple touch. "I know you are in pain; we will take care of it, eh?" He took off his own overcoat and draped it around her nude form, offering her warmth and dignity.
"We will take you to a doctor and have him fix you up." Victor stood up and nodded to Cesare, "Bring her along," he simply ordered. He looked up at Martel, "go ahead and finish up here. We'll be outside."

Martel nodded as Victor turned and walked out, his men following him like kittens after their mother. Cesare grabbed a nearby blanket and wrapped it around the girl in a protective cocoon, covering even her face and eyes, then gently picked her up in his arms and easily carried her out behind Victor and the rest.

The grand procession stood around seventy yards from the great kennel complex, watching it go up in a huge bonfire. All except Cesare, who waited in the limo with the woman who had slipped mercifully back into unconsciousness.

"I am content now." Victor barely whispered. Watching the huge flames engulfing the horrific kennels, only Laurence Martel heard the comment as he stood next to his Boss.

"Enrico has generously offered to go thirty percent with you in the stolen car and chop shop racket, Vito," Victor said without looking at him, "And Nicholas is willing to share twenty percent of his narcotics territories until you get on your feet again. You will work directly with him; don't fuck up this time Vito. I will give you ten percent in shylocking and swag." Victor finally turned to Vito, a pack leader re-welcoming an ousted member. "You will be doing far better than you did with this..." Victor gestured towards the burning buildings.

Victor had gotten what he once predicted he would. To rid the Alliance of this white slavery nonsense, to have the Romans over a barrel and off the Commission and to relegate them to the rackets of his choosing. To once again strengthen the Jerome Family and reward his two most loyal allies; the Corellas and the Del Giornos, the Families he wanted to see rise and benefit.

"Thank you, Mr. Jerome," Vito barely whispered. Some of his honor had been restored. Victor was right: it was more than a generous offer. After all, he could have been dead in the building, burning up with the rest of it.

"I leave you now." Victor faced Vito and embraced him briefly. "Do not lie to me again. Next time, there will be no mercy."

Nicholas Corella and Enrico Del Giorno repeated Victor's gesture of affirming Vito's new, lower rank by also briefly embracing Vito. Then the impressive procession of crime bosses and their henchmen, soldiers and bodyguards all left the still-stunned Vito to stand there and try to figure out all that had happened to him on this day. The lesson to Vito had only served to strengthen the tight bond of the Alliances and to further confirm that, although an aging Don, Victor was no pushover and still ruled with an iron grip.

Once in the car, Victor ordered Martel to call up Dr. Weintraub on his car phone. "Tell him we'll take her to Presbyterian Hospital downtown, to meet us there, and to keep it very quiet. We don't know what we are dealing with yet."

CHAPTER 4 - *April 13th 1987*

Tito Luciano D'Salvatore, son of Rudolfo D'Salvatore, the current 56-year-old Boss of the D'Salvatore Family, sat glumly in his living room. He looked every inch the part of a mobster. He was a big, blocky man with a head of thick grey hair, sharp Italian features and an even sharper tongue. He dressed in the finest suits, the most expensive leather shoes, and probably wore close to sixty thousand dollars in gold and platinum jewelry on him at any given time.

"He's gone too far this time," Tito growled at his Administration; Johnny Baldovino, his consigliere, and Joey Calendri, his underboss. "Victor is too attached to the old ways, he is like an old Mustache Pete, and now this thing he did with the Romans..." Tito paced a few feet then stopped to watch the Chicago Cubs get a homerun on his TV set. "*Testa di cavolo!*" he muttered under his breath.

"So are you saying the other Families are ripe for swaying?" Johnny asked.

"I dunno. I wouldn't push it, let them come to us, it's gotta be their idea. But I have heard through the grapevine that some of the Families, like Frankie Abruzzi and Tony Spinoza's crews are not happy with the leftovers that the Jeromes have tossed them. Not happy that the Del Giorno's and Corella's are being given more than their fair share. Victor's on the Commission, hell, the goddamn news calls him the fuckin' Boss of Bosses. Can you believe that shit?" Tito snorted in disgust, "He's powerful now, but he isn't forever. My father took down the Felanis' once and we can certainly take down the Jeromes now."

Tito took a slug of his beer and continued looking at the baseball game on the TV. "Felani was wiped out by us in the '57; our Family took care of that personally. This is an old vendetta and one not nearly over, just another chapter in the war." He mumbled to no one in particular.

Although the then-26-year-old Tito hadn't been there in person that day for the 1957 Felani-Jerome Massacre, he had heard that victory relived a thousand times in his fathers telling. A part of him wished he could have been there, could have wiped out a few Felani-Jeromes of his own, but his father had wanted to protect the sole heir to the D'Salvatore throne. Sadly, Tito's father had died shortly after his masterminded vendetta on the Felani-Jerome's. Only one short year after the massacre, Rudolfo suffered a fatal stroke which killed him instantly.

"Victor had two brothers," Tito continued to his men, "One died in our vendetta against the Felanis and the other died a cripple in the hospital as a result of it. Victor, stud that he is, only had two sons. The oldest, Theodore went MIA in 'Nam back in the seventies and Michael, well..." Tito paused and pulled out the faded and worn photograph from his breast pocket. The one he kept on him like a lucky rabbit's foot, the one he often bragged about, the one he still sent copies of to Victor to every few years to rattle his cage and chip at his morale. It showed Michael Jerome, shot so full of bullet holes he was almost unrecognizable, "—Well, he died an untimely death as a result of our *mannagge*, our war, with the Jeromes." A thin smile played along Tito's lips. "Victor has no more direct descendants," he continued, "No royal heirs to the throne. Once the old goat kicks the bucket, that Jerome magic will be lost, and I just know the Alliances will break and reorganize."

Tito looked away from the TV and eyed Joey and Johnny. "The old alliances will be broken forever, and a new Family will arise as the number one power. It will be our time to join the Commission."

A dark silence began to descend on the room, because every man there knew what Tito was saying.

"It's going to start up in full again, isn't it Tito?" Joey Calendri looked up at his Boss.

"Yes," Tito slugged back the rest of his beer, glanced once more at the faded photo and then replaced it almost tenderly back in his pocket. "To the end this time. The war begins again and this time does not stop until only either Jerome or D'Salvatore is left standing, and that Family will be us." He growled softly.

The three men sat grim-faced and solemn. For once there was no clowning around amongst the men, no jokes, no friendly bantering. Although D'Salvatores men were loyal to him and knew the D'Salvatores were a powerful Family in their own right, none of them relished dying. They knew exactly just how powerful the Jeromes were.

"Joey," Tito walked over to his underboss, "I have gotten very credible word from our strongest allies, the Armandanas, that Victor Jerome has been building ties with the Bonnaro Family back home in Sicily. Keep our best spies on it. I want to know why and what ol' Victor is doing with the Bonnaro Clan."

Tito then turned to his consigliere, "Johnny, I have a special assignment for you." Tito reached into his other pocket, pulled out a small key then opened a drawer in his oak hutch with it. He took out a thick travel bag and tossed it casually to his consigliere.

"For you, I have the assignment of corruption. See if the Romans would like to stay in the white slave trade. Unlike Victor Jerome, I will be more than happy to support him and in fact give him investment," he nodded at the bag, "To start up again. I also have it on good authority from our capo Frankie Scalia that there is a possible Jerome turncoat whom we might be able to get information from."

The game was over on TV, the Chicago Cubs had won. "Fuck!" Tito again cursed loudly. He had bet a healthy amount against Chicago and had lost. "What are you up to, old *nemico*?" Tito thought to himself. "What dangerous games do you play, humiliating the Romans and strengthening alliances back in the homeland of Sicily?"

Something wasn't sitting right, but his obsession with the war burned bright and deep in Tito D'Salvatore. He had to strike now. He had to finish what his father had started back in '57, to destroy Victor Jerome and his Family, permanently. It was his turn to be on the Commission now; it was time for the D'Salvatores to rise.

Tito's son walked into the room, "Hey," the swaggering 25-year-old Torenzo "Torry" D'Salvatore hugged his father and then gave Baldovino and Calendri quick pats on the shoulder as well. "Am I missing out on the retelling of the massacre on the Jeromes again?" he drawled and flopped down on the couch.

"You never mind about that, you've got your own crews to run." Tito shot his son a dark look.

Torenzo D'Salvatore would have been a dead ringer for Tito at that age: dark curly hair, light olive complexion and large brown eyes. Unlike his father, Torenzo had far too much swagger and bravado. He had been a capo for nearly four years now under his father near the New Jersey ports, and it was irritating the hell out of him that his father was not grooming him for a higher position within the family. "Come on, Pop, when are you gonna let me in on some of this action huh?" He fumbled around for a cigarette and lit it up, letting one of his legs dangle over the arm of his father's expensive leather recliner. "No offense, but I'm waiting for some higher purpose here than watching over some simple enforcers on the docks. I wouldn't mind taking out some Jerome bastards myself."

"You are too much in a rush with things, Torry." Tito turned to his son with a sigh. He did love his boy so, wanted to school him right, but sadly, in his heart, he knew that his son was far too careless and cocky, wasn't ready for the more skillful work of true leadership. "Maybe I will let you go along to the Armandana sit-down in a few weeks, how is that?"

Torenzo just nodded. He knew better than to push at his father. Tito was tense these last couple of days, and Torry had his own methods of getting in his father's good graces.

The pain washed over her like waves crashing into a rocky shoreline. Waves of bright orange pain that slowly receded then came crashing full force into her. When there wasn't the pain, there was nothing, a blankness that permeated her whole being.

Occasionally there were dreams, sounds, smells and tastes that filled her mind. People and events that seemed so familiar, and yet she couldn't place any of it. It seemed a part of her, but yet totally alien, unrecognizable. The whole thing looped in constant déjà vu, and then the whole cycle would repeat endlessly like an ocean of pain and bizarre tides of fragmented pictures.

"This is hell, and I must be in it..." was the only conscious thought she had.

CHAPTER 5 – *April 16th 1987*

In his office at Presbyterian Hospital of New York, Dr. John Thomas Weintraub sat at his desk in a state of near total exhaustion. He lay his head down on his arms for just a brief moment to rest his weary eyes, when he was suddenly aware that someone loomed over him. Whoever it was had thrust a cup of coffee under his nose. The familiar and comforting smell cleared the cobwebs out of his head. He glanced up at the towering form of Laurence Martel, Victor's underboss.

"I figured this might help you out." Martel spoke in a quiet, deep, sonorous voice.

"Thanks, Laurence." John gratefully accepted the cup of steaming black coffee. He gingerly sipped the rich, dark liquid, letting it revive him further. He glanced at his watch, squinting for a moment. "It can't be one in the morning; it feels more like 5 a.m." he said incredulously, he was beyond exhausted. Dr. Weintraub had spent days on Victor's special patient. Her bones had been set, surgeries performed, and now she was finally resting.

"It isn't one in the morning," Martel raised an eyebrow then went over and drew open the blinds on John Thomas's window, sunlight streamed in with a harsh glare. "It's one in the afternoon." He smiled thinly.

"My God!" John Thomas moaned, "Then I really am this tired?" he looked up, his glasses askew.

"Yep, you really did pull another 24 hour shift," Martel smiled with a slight twinkle in his ice blue eyes. "I didn't think an old dog like you still had it in you." He quietly joked good-naturedly with the doctor.

"I've pulled longer, my tall friend!" John Thomas straightened out his glasses, and sipped again on the coffee.

"Your humor is good today. Does that mean I can tell Victor the outlook is favorable for our patient?" Martel lowered one hip and sat on the corner of John Thomas's desk.

"Yes and no," Weintraub gathered up a bunch of folders and X-rays. "I've done all I can; the rest is up to her. She's stable but still unconscious." He slapped some X-ray films onto the viewer and flipped on the light. "Her skull was broken here and here," he pointed to the X-rays, "We went in and did surgery, removed some bone fragments that were lying on the brain."

"Any brain damage?" Martel asked. He was quite familiar with the human body and various medical aspects, only he normally caused trauma and death, he didn't heal it.

"It's too early to really tell." John Thomas wrapped his arms around himself; he felt so cold and tired. All he wanted was to go lie down and catch up on at least twenty-four hours of nonstop sleep.

"Preliminary tests and an EEG scan show that there is definitely some damage, but we don't know yet how severe and how permanent the damage is." He tried unsuccessfully to stifle a yawn, "None of us can know that until she regains consciousness, until the swelling goes down, and even then, we may never fully know if any damage she has is temporary or permanent." John Thomas dug around through some of his thick folders, papers scattering here and there like some absent-minded professor. In his mind, though, he had precise knowledge of where everything lay in his personal chaos.

"The good news is that all those electrical burns will heal nicely." He continued, "Any scarring at all should be minimal. Her voice box is shot though, gone." John Thomas knew better than too get to medically technical with Martel. Like Victor and his associates, he appreciated medical statements that were concise and in layman's terms or he got bored or lost.

"Without getting to technical, all the muscles and cartilage at the front of her throat that control the voice box were just too severely burned from the electricity to save. She'll be mute the rest of her life; maybe she can get an electrolarynx, but it's too early to tell." Dr. Weintraub returned to his desk and expertly chased Martel off of it with a few waves of his hand. "She also had a few cracked ribs and a collapsed lung; minor shit like that. Tell Victor the fact that she is merely alive is a miracle in itself. That is also a good thing. She's a fighter, he'll like that."

"Well," Martel nodded, "No doubt a testament to your fine medical work, as well." He meant the comment sincerely. "Then I can tell Victor the good news; he said if the prognosis was good, that he wanted me to ensure that she can be transported upstate to the Jerome Estate to heal."

John Thomas sighed slightly; he knew it would be better if she could recuperate here at the hospital, where she could have twenty-four hour care by medical professionals, but he had also known Victor long enough, his friendship deep enough not to question anything Victor asked of him. "Yes, yes. I suppose. But not until tomorrow at the earliest." he reluctantly agreed. "Thanks again for the java, Laurence." he held up the cup of coffee.

"Anytime, Dr. Weintraub," Laurence said, "I will be around personally in twelve hours to make sure that her transport goes smoothly." He picked up his own briefcase and prepared to leave, "Also," he added nonchalantly, almost as an afterthought, "Things may be a bit tense for a while. Don't be surprised if you see more of Victor's-'friends'- keeping an eye out for you."

John Thomas opened his mouth to ask a question, but Martel held up his hand silencing him. "Just know that you and your wife will be taken care of, OK, John? Do not ask me more." He placed his hand gently on the doctor's shoulder, gave it a squeeze of reassurance and friendship then turned and left.

John Thomas shook his head then went and sat back down at his desk, gathering up his files and charts so he could go home and sleep. Victor had kept his word from the time he and John Thomas had known each other as kids. Victor kept John Thomas ignorant of Family Business, and John Thomas didn't want to know. He loved Victor like a brother; they had been through good times and bad. Such horrible bad times, John Thomas remembered.

The first time he had seen Victor so vulnerable, so hurt, was after the Bloody Sunday Massacre in 1957. The second blow came in 1978 at the passing of the one woman Victor had ever loved, his soulmate and beloved wife Isabella. She had died of a fast-spreading ovarian cancer. They tried the most aggressive cancer treatments, but it was no use. John Thomas had watched the hardened crime boss, care for his wife with the tenderness of a mother. Even as she died, she and Victor shared a love and understanding that seemed it would transcend even death. It tore Victor apart to watch his soulmate die, but he stood steadfast and strong until the end.

An involuntary shudder ran through John Thomas's body as he remembered the final and even crueler blow to Victor's heart only a brief three years after Isabella's death. Victor's second son, Michael, had been gunned down unmercifully in the street while getting some ice cream. He remembered Victor cradling his son's bullet-riddled corpse at the funeral home and his oath of dark revenge, muttered over and over again as the tears fell in front of the one person he ever let himself see him as human.

All those times John Thomas had been the one person that Victor trusted, allowed himself to show his true emotions and grief to. The one person he let his guard down with and allowed himself the heart wrenching sobs that wracked his body as John Thomas held him, allowed Victor to be just a human being. Victor had been there for John as well, but John did not suffer the horrendous bad luck and loss that Victor had over the years.

John Thomas put down the empty coffee cup and stretched his creaking back, yawned again and gathered the rest of his things to leave for home. He and his wife Melinda had been married for over twenty-eight years, but it was a marriage of conveniences, a marriage of appearance only.

They had married for money and for the alliance of two wealthy Jewish families, in the last step his own mother had forced on him, an arranged marriage between the prestigious Weintraub and Rosenberg families. And while he and Melinda had grown to tolerate and even respect each other, there was no deep love between them, certainly not like had been between Victor and his beloved Isabella. John Thomas never could give her children, as he was sterile, and Melinda had no desire of adopting a child. Instead John Thomas's wife devoted all her love to small toy poodles, showing at prestigious dog shows around the country and breeding them. "At least she has something," he thought. They at least were friends and could have some fun times on occasion when they both managed to catch up with each other.

He shut and locked his office door, carrying a bunch of files; Victor's "Jane Doe" was among them. John Thomas definitely had a lot of respect for his dear friend Victor. The man had lost nearly everything he ever held dear to him, and for what? To be the Don, the

Boss of the largest supposed crime Family in New York. John wondered if Victor felt it worth all the heartache, the lives of his family, and if he could do it all over again if he would do things differently?

John knew he would never know. Such subjects were taboo between them and Family business matters never discussed, especially such personal ones as those. John was totally loyal to the man only because he was Victor Jerome, his best friend since high school, not because he was Victor Jerome, alleged Don of a Mafia Family. "I'm going home for the day and getting some sleep, Carla." John nodded to the head nurse as he walked off the floor into the elevator that would take him to the hospital's massive underground parking garage.

As the elevator doors opened in the parking basement, he got a chilled feeling, but adjusted his files and glasses and moved on forward towards his BMW. Suddenly two men stepped out of the shadows and to his side. They were somebody's goons and both wore dark sunglasses and showed no emotion. John felt his blood run cold, his heart pounding with fear in his chest and ears.

"It's OK, Doc," one of them said in a low, rasping voice "We're here to escort you home."

"What!" John Thomas stopped in his tracks, trembling and frustrated, one of his patient files slipping from his haphazard bundle. "What do you want from me?"

One of the nameless henchmen gently retrieved the fallen file and placed it carefully back on the pile back in John Thomas' arms. "It's OK," he soothed in a deep, rough voice, "Martel sent us. Remember? He mentioned to you that you'd be protected more."

"God damn it." John muttered angrily under his breath. "He didn't mention escorts! I wish he would be clearer on these things!" The men gently touched his arm and propelled him towards his car; they knew the doctor was tired and stressed.

"...Next time make sure he is more specific on these things." John continued grumbling, more to relieve his own stress at the surprise guests than any true anger at Laurence Martel. The goons had simply startled the shit out of him. John was too tired, to exhausted and relieved to put up his usual grumpy tirade. Though he'd never admit it to Victor or Laurence Martel in a million years, deep down he was thankful for the bodyguards. Little did John realize that the increased security was due to the impending war between Jerome and D'Salvatore, and in this case, ignorance was indeed the best gift of all from Victor to John Thomas Weintraub.

Victor eyed his war council, his upper management and the most trusted of his men. Among them was Laurence Martel, his underboss, second in command and his right hand man. Martel was the "mouth" of Victor, speaking the boss's commands and instructions and seeing to it they were sent smoothly down the chain to the capos. It was Laurence who relayed all the information from the lower ranks up the echelon, and it was Laurence Martel that most people in the Jerome Family dealt with. Few were privileged enough to meet the Don himself.

Joshua Demonico was Victor's consigliere, or "counselor"; he advised and updated the Boss on all aspects of the Family Business. He also acted as Victor's personal secretary, helping keep track of things for both him and the underboss. He also gave advice or helped Martel and Victor to stay in touch when they were on separate business. These two younger men and Victor made up the upper level power structure in the Family.

Victor's trusted capos or captains were the secondary bosses who were out there on the streets who gave the orders out to the soldiers of the Jerome Family. They also relayed information or problems up to Martel. The capos and their crews had the day-to-day job of collecting tribute, from the soldiers and associates as well as handling any minor problems that came up. Most capos were like "mini-bosses" and had a crew of anywhere from four to twenty soldiers and associates under them. In the Jerome Family, the capos, soldiers and associates, numbered well over 300, making the Jerome's one of the largest and most powerful crime Families in New York.

As a result, Victor held a coveted position on the Commission along with the other four powerful Dons of New York: Nicholas Corella, Enrico Del Giorno, Bruno Giovanni and Anthony Calavicci, who had recently replaced the ousted Vito Roman. While Victor was unofficially called the Boss of Bosses (usually by the media and the F.B.I) Most importantly, his own peers recognized the Jerome Family as the most influential and powerful in the tri-state area..

Victor's most trusted capos were here as well: Rocco Benedarra, Patrizio "Karloff" Fantenelli and Leonardo "Len" Tagretta. During war times with other Families, it was not uncommon for a very large Family like the Jerome's to have a second underboss to further help speed orders up and down the ranks. This fell on Patrizio Fantenelli, one of Victor's oldest capos and friends. He had been with the Felani-Jeromes since before Victor had ascended to the top. As chaotic as it appeared from the outside, the entire Family ran like a well-oiled machine, and rarely were there any screw-ups.

"So," Victor leaned back and sipped his cup of espresso. He showed no signs of tenseness or agitation over the impending war with the D'Salvatores. Like his hated enemy, he has known this time was coming long before. It had been in the air for years.

"It's the same old business, eh?" Victor gently questioned the small group of men:

"So what are my eyes and ears picking up, same old rumors or new talk?"

Patrizio shook his head slowly, "They already know about that shipment down in Jamaica and plan to intervene." He glanced up beneath his thick eyebrows at his boss; Patrizio had earned his nickname because of his uncanny resemblance to Boris Karloff, the horror actor. "Are you still sure you want to go to there in person? Surely, myself or..."

"I know, old friend." Victor held up his hand. "I plan to go in person. No need to disappoint ol' Tito; if I don't go, then that will make him even more suspicious, eh? I'll take good care of myself," he winked at his friend, "Besides, *compari*, this is something I must do in person. It's pivotal to the Family." A thin smile played on his lips.

Patrizio nodded. He knew nothing he could say would change the Boss's mind. "Just letting you know that Tito is onto that venture of ours."

"And that is precisely what I had hoped," Victor nodded back. "I worked hard to make sure he wouldn't think that information was just a rumor. If, or rather when, this war goes down that road to its final conclusion, it is imperative that Tito move here and there," Victor motioned as though maneuvering an invisible chess piece. "To move precisely where I want him. Not in our weak areas, understand?" Patrizio just harrumphed and dipped his biscotti in his espresso. "It's all one fucking, giant chess game my friend." Victor assured him.

"In two months from now," Martel's baritone voice quietly interrupted, "Tito is sending his top three capos, along with Torenzo and a few soldiers, down to Atlantic City to a meeting with the Armandanas." Martel smiled grimly while he refilled Victor's coffee.

Victor sat back a moment letting this glorious bit of information wash over him like a warm wave of water. Victor knew exactly why Tito was sending Torenzo D'Salvatore, instead of his underboss Joey Calendri or consigliere, Johnny Baldovino. Torenzo was Tito's son, his heir to the throne and probably soon to be promoted to underboss.

"Quite excellent, Martel." Victor softly spoke. He glanced at Laurence and knew what this would mean to both of them. Their eyes locked in a closeness that he shared with none of his other men. "Our vendetta," he barely whispered and then said, "Laurence, why don't you take some of our best hunters and make sure the Jeromes crash that party." Victor briefly closed his eyes, reveling in the scene he knew would take place. The long-awaited revenge for Michael's murder at the D'Salvatores hands, an eye for an eye, a son for a son.

Victor knew how hard Martel must have worked to ferret out that precious information, even Joshua looked shocked at the formidable underboss, as a small, dark smile of revenge briefly played on Martel's lips.

The door opened and Cesare "The Elf" Ciccerone, Victor's huge, heavyset driver and capo came through the door panting and puffing. He carried four white grocery-sized bags of take-out food.

"So what took you so long, Elf?" Patrizio lightly chastised the rotund man.

"Aww, gimme some fuckin' slack guys, will ya?" He began unpacking styrofoam containers, "You know Mario's is crowded this time of day!" He gave Patrizio a half sneer, "Here Boss--" he handed Victor his food first.

"You did just fine Cesare." Victor grinned while biting into a thick, chewy slab of garlic bread. "But next time, eat your lunch after you bring back ours." He said with a twinkle in his eye.

"Damn, Boss!" Cesare grunted, "Busted! You know me too well, huh?"

"It was the tomato sauce on your tie," Rocco pointed out with a stifled laugh; soon the whole room was filled with hearty laughter.

"C'mon, stop busting my balls here. Give a guy a break will ya?" Cesare grumbled defensively, but taking the teasing good-naturedly.

"You know Cesare, if you didn't handle a gun so well, if your crew didn't pull in so many points--" Martel said in deadpan seriousness while raising an eyebrow.

"You too, Brutus?" Cesare shook his large head and his double chins waddled like some obscene turkey. He feigned hurt; "You have cut me to the bone. All of you!"

"Hey, whatta this?" Leonardo Tagretta asked in his soft Italian accent and broken English as held up an extra unaccounted for foil wrapped sandwich that was steadily bleeding tomato sauce, "Who order extra meatball sandwich?"

"Gimme that," Cesare's pudgy hand snatched it from Len's grasp. "That's mine!" he huffed, and again the room was filled with the loud echoes of laughter. "Hey, I got one for later! Shit!" He hastily departed the room before the guys could tear him apart further. Although it was good-natured ribbing, Cesare was loyal to the Jeromes and the Jeromes were loyal to him. That was how it was.

Victor watched Cesare depart the room and a smile touched his lips. The camaraderie among his men was something he treasured the most. Business was over for today. The rest of the afternoon was spent watching *Scar Face* with Al Pacino.

"So Victor," Joshua quietly asked later while drinking some red wine, "What's up with the guest in the west wing of the house?" he eyed the boss. "The girl Martel bought up yesterday?"

Victor's face took on a dark, no-nonsense look. He eyed Joshua and the others levelly for a moment and then briefly pointed to his eye, the unspoken signal of "watch what is said around her, censor your conversations".

"Until I interrogate her further and unless I tell you otherwise, she is just that, a guest." Victor glanced around, "And she will be treated with respect."

"Understood." Josh casually nodded, as did the other men.

Slowly her eyes opened, working hard to focus on her surroundings. Her vision was fuzzy and there was a grainy, sandy feeling to her eyelids. Her whole body felt stiff, and very weak, and worse, she had no idea where she was.

It was someone's room. Definitely, a female someone. She lay in a warm, comfortable, frilly canopy bed. The room and bed were done in pink and peach pastels, and it was large; in it were a white dresser, chest of drawers and a huge mahogany armoire, laden with perfume bottles, hygiene needs and grooming items. Somehow, while the room was cozy, attractive and expensive-feeling, she knew it was not hers. It felt oddly foreign.

She stirred tentatively, testing her body, trying to reawaken and move muscles that had been immobile for almost a week. She lifted one bruised arm, and looked at it; bandages were gently wrapped around it where IV's used to be. She was also dressed in some kind of comfy cotton pajamas. She slowly lowered her arm and glanced around some more. What distressed her the most was a descending and solid blankness that overrode everything else.

She closed her eyes, thought and thought hard. Only fragments came to her, visions that made no sense. Tiny memory fragments of walking in the woods, a building on fire, cattle being loaded into trucks bound for the slaughterhouse and a well-dressed older gentleman with the presence and charisma of some celebrity or president. None of it meant anything to her; all of it was confusing.

Where was this place? Why was she here and what had gone on? There were no other memories to draw on. Not even her most basic memories, like her name or memories of her family. None at all; at least not at this time. She shivered involuntarily and a cold chill ran down her spine. Part of her mind panicked, but scariest of all, she didn't know why she was panicking.

She decided she was going to get up, look around and find a bathroom, because she really had to take a piss, badly. She forced her body to sit up, and suddenly a wave of dizziness swept over her, forcing her to nearly flop back onto her side. She swallowed and was keenly aware her throat was dry, parched and very sore. She rubbed the front of her throat and felt sore skin bound beneath gauze bandages that encircled her neck. The more she woke up now, the more she was aware of various aches and pain in her body. Her face felt sore, and she reached up her fingers to her scalp and forehead and felt a large patch of shaved hair, stitches and a healing but sore scar. What exactly had happened to her? A sense of uneasiness draped over her like a heavy blanket.

She really needed to get up and find a bathroom now, so she used all her strength to force herself back up and to roll off the bed into a standing position. As she did her legs promptly gave out from under her and she fell heavily with a loud thump to her knees as another wave of dizziness, weakness and now nausea washed over her.

The door to the room suddenly opened, and some strange man in his mid twenties, walked in. He had short dark hair and hazel eyes, with a young face that looked hard and yet boyish. He was well-dressed in slacks and an unbuttoned sport coat. He had a half-shocked look, and she noticed he had a gun tucked in a holster that he wore around his shoulder.

They stared blankly at one another for a few seconds, and the man spoke while holding his hands out, almost pleadingly, "Wait here, Miss. I'll go let them know you're awake, OK? Just wait here." He abruptly left the room and soundly shut the door behind him; she could hear him shouting and his footsteps retreating away.

She dragged herself to her hands and knees, trying to dislodge the ringing in her ears and slam down the wave of nausea as she gripped the bed trying to pull herself up. As she was halfway up, her body still swaying and trembling, the door opened again, and this time she saw the older gentleman with the balding head of grey hair and the distinguished moustache, the one she had seen in a memory fragment a few minutes ago. Dressed in a dark blazer, grey silk shirt and tie and a pair of well-pressed dark slacks; he still had the presence of a President or some powerful CEO.

"Easy child, let me help." He quietly spoke and quickly walked over to her. With unusual strength and gentle agility he easily helped her to her feet and then helped her to sit on the edge of the bed.

She glanced up and now saw two men in the shadow of the doorway. One she recognized from a few minutes ago; the other man was taller with strikingly handsome, but dark, sharp features and dark hair kept tightly slicked back. Impeccably dressed, in a stark white suit with a black silk shirt and white tie, he had the almost stunning good looks of a male model. Yet his eyes were dark, angry and predatory; an involuntary shiver ran through her. He seemed to glare right at her.

"It's all right, Joshua, Tommy..." The older man instructed the men, "Leave us and go page Dr. Weintraub, and let him know our patient is awake." The men nodded and shut the door quietly behind them, leaving the old man and befuddled woman alone. "How are you feeling?" he asked.

She tried to talk, to answer him and ask him a myriad of questions, but all that came out of her throat was a hoarse rasp; inside her throat she felt a dull aching pain.

She grasped at her throat, a look of confusion and surprise in her eyes.

"Shhh," Victor gently covered her mouth with one of his finger to her lips. "Forgive me, I forgot. Dr. Weintraub said your voice box had been damaged in the accident. He said talking would be out of the question. Hmmm," glancing around and saw what he was looking for on the nightstand next to her bed. "Here…" he got up and took the pen and paper and handed it to her.

She took the writing material and with a slightly shaky hand began to quickly pen out her questions, "*Where am I? Who are you?* "

As she wrote, the old man took out a roll of peppermint Lifesavers and offered one to her and took one himself. "Here, I bet your throat is sore and dry, I'll get some water." He left her savoring the minty sweet taste of the candy. "He was right.*"* she thought, it did indeed help ease the dry pain in her throat as well as give a jolt of energy to her body.

The older man had stepped into the bathroom connected to the bedroom and had filled a glass with cool water and brought it back to her. They traded, she handing the notebook to him as he handed the water to her. He slipped on his reading glasses and then sat next to her again. "Let's see," he read her questions. "I'll answer the second one first," he said with a slight smile. "My name is Victor Jerome, and to answer your first question, you are in my home, in one of my guest rooms."

She reached over to the pad of paper he was looking at, "*What happened to me?*" she quickly scrawled with a shaking hand.

Victor looked up at her over his reading glasses, "You were in a…" he paused just briefly, "…little accident." His lips thinned a bit. "You had some minor surgery and were in the hospital for a while healing. Once Dr. Weintraub thought you stabilized and near the point of waking up, we transported you here to my country home. It will speed your recovery. I never did like hospitals," Victor leaned over, confiding in her. "They are for the dying. That's what I always thought."

She began to feel at a major disadvantage and embarrassed. Obviously, this Victor Jerome knew her and yet she didn't know him. Or rather she couldn't remember him or his house. Was Victor her father, grandfather or who? He had said she was in an accident, but she couldn't remember any of it, or anything before it. Nor did she even have any emotions or memories, either good or bad, regarding him, or this house. Her lack of memory was causing her more distress and anxiety by the moment. Involuntarily, her body trembled and she turned her head so that Victor wouldn't see the tears that began to run from her eyes.

"What is it, child?" Victor put his hand on her shoulder and gently turned her face around to look into his concerned eyes. "Are you in pain?"

She shook her head no, and tried talking again, then remembered she couldn't. She grabbed the notebook and scribbled out "*I'm Scared!!! I don't remember you, or this house, nothing! It's all a blank to me!!!*" she handed him back the notepad with shaky hands.

"I know; I can imagine how confusing it is for you," he soothed her after reading her note. "I have heard of people having amnesia after accidents, you know? I'm sure it is only temporary, hmmm? I'm not a doctor, but Dr. Weintraub will be here probably within a few hours and I know he can fill you in a lot better than I on the medical aspects of all this." He smiled, trying to calm her with his words.

She snatched the notepad out from his hands and began to write again, feverishly,
"*I can't even remember my damn name, Victor!!! What happened to me? What kind of accident was it? How do I know you?!? I can't remember ANYTHING about me, my past or you!! I CAN'T EVEN REMEMBER MY OWN NAME FOR GODS SAKE!!!...*" Her writing was crying out in agony of unanswered questions, her whole body shaking with the effort of her rapid writing.

Victor snatched the notebook away from her before she was finished, before she worked herself into total hysteria. He briefly read her words and then put the notebook and pen in his pocket, out of her reach. His eyes got a more stern, more commanding look to them. Not harsh, but the look of a man who was in total control, "Look, child," he said matter-of-fact, "We'll talk more later, I promise. Let Dr. Weintraub examine you first, all right? I'll answer your questions then. Until then, I suggest you drink some water and lie in bed and slowly let your body re-awaken. You have been unconscious and asleep for over a week." He was about to pull back the covers and place her in the bed when she quickly motioned to the bathroom and towards herself.

Victor didn't need a notebook to understand the universal look of "I've got to go NOW".

"I suppose after that long nap you would have to go pretty badly, eh?" His eyes softened a bit again, seeing her fear under control. "All right, come on, I'll help you."

She used him as a crutch to lean against, as he helped her walk stiffly to the bathroom. He waited patiently outside for her to finish; then half-supporting her over his small shoulder with amazing strength, escorted back to the bed and tucked her in.

"Now," he spoke his eyes looking deeply into hers offering comfort. "That first man you saw is Tommy DeLuca. He has some nursing skills, so I will probably have him helping you around the house here and also tending to your bandages and such. I will have Tommy bring you up a pitcher of ice water and some cool cloths. I suggest you just stay in bed and slowly stretch your arms and legs and allow your tendons and muscles to gain blood and strength in them slowly and naturally. Dr. Weintraub should be here shortly; if you're really bored you can always read a book..." Opening the nightstand Victor grabbed the first two books he saw. One was the Bible, and the other was some paperback romance novel. "Here." He placed them on the stand near her, then turned and walked out, closing the door quietly behind him.

Victor, Martel and Joshua Demonico sat in the den area, where the fireplace and expensive bookcases were. "So what are you telling us, John Thomas?" Victor spoke for all of his Administration, while Dr. Weintraub sat opposite the three of them.

"I'm telling you: I have no Goddamn idea Victor, on how long her amnesia will last, what the extent of it is or if there is any other brain damage!" John Thomas tossed the Jane Doe patient's file on the desk. "It's like I told Laurence the other day," he continued. "Who knows with these things. People get amnesia all the time from accidents; usually the amnesia is limited to the actual accident. But in this case, with electricity being involved, the bruising of her brain, and her other injuries the amnesia may be much more extensive. From what you tell me, it is. With all that bleeding and pressure in her skull, and her preliminary EEG results in, it looks like she suffered a mild to moderate stroke."

"That doesn't help a whole lot, Doc." Joshua stood up to do his usual pacing, fiddling with a fresh piece of nicotine gum. "I mean we could have come up with that ourselves!" he grunted a bit harshly.

"I told ya, there is no way to be certain! No test that can tell for sure! People have strokes all the time; some recover fully, some not at all, and most fall somewhere in between. We can only see as she heals. Brain injuries are tricky; only time will tell!" John Thomas growled at Joshua and raising his own voice he stood up in a challenging posture. "Once I run some CAT scans and other tests I might know more!"

"Easy, easy." Victor settled them both down with a quick glance. "John Thomas," he turned back to his trusted friend, "I know you have given us your honest medical opinion and done all you can. For that I am deeply grateful. You know that. She couldn't have a better doctor." He then faced his pacing consigliere, "Joshua, it sounds like we will have to play this by ear, or eye rather, eh?"

"Yeah, fine." Josh sat back down.

"I mean," John Thomas hedged gently as he looked at Victor, "I can certainly tell a lot more about the extent of the amnesia with tests in the clinic tomorrow, but give me time tonight to research some stuff on through the medical texts. Neurology isn't my main specialty, you know." He explained. "Or perhaps if you tell me what happened to her exactly…" he let the question hang. No one had ever fully explained to Dr. Weintraub what had happened to the poor woman other than she was in a brutal accident that caused a lot of trauma and also involved electricity.

"John, you know I cannot tell you anything other than what I have told you. Research what you must, as usual, whatever it costs. She is a guest." Victor said quietly ending the whole conversation with a gentle finality. "John if you want to grab your stuff there, I will meet you at her door in just a minute. She's in Isabella's old room." John scooped up his file and his doctor's bag and with a nod walked out.

"So for now?" Martel spoke when he knew the doctor was well out of hearing range. Both he and Joshua looked attentively at Victor.

Victor steepled his fingers and sat back for a moment, thinking, analyzing potential outcomes. "So for now…" he finally stated, "Unless she specifically asks us anything about the whole kidnapping or Vito Roman or what not, we play dumb. We say nothing of that; perhaps it's a blessing she has amnesia; perhaps it's a curse for us. I don't know yet. We continue to treat her as a guest. If she asks anything about her ordeal, or remembers what happened, then we re-evaluate the situation."

Victor closed his eyes for a moment and began to wonder if listening to his heart was such a good idea regarding the mysterious woman upstairs. What would he do, what would he say if she suddenly remembered all of it? It would mean a hornet's nest of problems. Things might have been a lot easier if he had let Martel carry out his final commands over the whole Roman's white slavery fiasco and put her out of her misery with the other women. But his heart and anger at Vito Roman at the time had outweighed his logic. He would confront that when and if it came up. He did not become the Boss of the Family through needless worrying over trivial things. This impending war with the D'Salvatore Family was far more urgent of his thinking and energy.

He opened his eyes, and the other two men nodded their understanding of his orders. "Excellent." Victor stood up; "I'll meet you out on the lawn shortly, then."
The three men left the office going their separate ways.

As Victor walked up the stairs and down the hall to meet up with John Thomas, he shook his head and wondered. "Am I getting soft in my old age?" he chided himself lightly, "Family bosses have been brought down by a lot less than someone who could finger out people and rat on rackets."

John Thomas looked concerned at his old friends approach, "Feeling OK Vic? You've been slowing down a bit lately. Maybe you need to drop into my clinic as well. After all, we haven't done a full-scale lab workup on you this month. I've only recently added you to that donor list. It's going to take time. Maybe we need to make adjustments in your..."

Victor abruptly cut him off with a wave of his hand; "You took enough blood on me last month, you old vampire." Victor grinned lightly up at his friend then sobered up. "It's just working all these late hours." Victor assured the doctor. "I am keeping a close watch on -my condition-, I promise you." He patted John's shoulder.

"Oh, by the way..." Victor added as an almost casual afterthought. He knew he would have to broach this in a roundabout way with his mob physician. After all, he had made it a point over the years to keep John Thomas blissfully unaware of any of the exact details of the patients' lives that saw him from the Jerome Family. John Thomas just treated their medical needs and nothing else. "I know this case with the girl, her amnesia and all, makes this fuzzy and muddled. I..." Victor emphasized the word, "I will answer any questions for her, regarding her past. If for some reason she starts remembering things or asks strange questions, just let me know and I'll take care of it. All right?"

"Of course, no problem." John Weintraub slowly agreed. But then Victor's requests regarding Jerome Family patients were often like that, strange requests with no information given to John Thomas. He just fulfilled his Hippocratic Oath to heal them all.

She had spent the last two hours in bed, bored. All the while her mind had been spinning, trying to piece together who she was, what her past was, what had happened to her, who Victor Jerome was and who all these men running around with guns in his house were. She had tried to read the romance novel but found it boring and instinctively knew she didn't like that kind of reading anyway. "How come I can remember what kind of books and movies I like, but not my friggin' name!" she thought angrily.

Just then the door opened and Victor walked in along with another man. The new person was around Victor's age, but taller, with a demeanor that was gruff, caring and absent-minded all at the same time. He had a face like an old hound dog with round, wire frame glasses perched slightly skewed on the end of his nose, a lean, clean shaven face, and a head of thick, unruly dark grey hair.

"I'm Dr. Weintraub," he greeted her, "I don't know if you remember me? You were unconscious last time we met." He warmly shook her hand. "Let's see how you are doing, shall we?" He looked at her over his glasses and then, after opening his doctor's bag on her bed began to get to work.

Victor pulled up a chair in the corner and sat quietly out of the way, just observing. Occasionally she glanced over at Victor, and their eyes would meet. He could see the questions in them, but he kept his own gaze casual, almost nonchalant.

After a half hour exam of the doctor asking her questions, poking, probing and asking her to do simply neurological tests, Dr. Weintraub closed his file and sat on the bed next to her. "Now," Weintraub said, "We did all the preliminary medical evaluations, but I want to hear how you are doing? How you are feeling? What is your pain like?" He handed her a notebook and pen of his own.

"OK. I'm tired and dizzy, sore in my throat. No bad pain. But I can't remember anything! Nothing! Not even my name! Why can't I talk? What is going on???" she shoved the notepad back at the doctor.

John Thomas looked over at her, his eyes taking on a sharp look that bore into her with frank honesty. "You want the truth or some bedside mumbo jumbo?" he questioned.

She glanced then at the quiet, stoic form of Victor; his unblinking dark fire eyes told her he seemed to already know the answers. _"The truth._" She reached over and penned, then looked up at Dr. Weintraub.

"You had a bad accident that caused a break in your skull and bruised your brain. Your EEG, that is, an electrical reading of your brain, showed some damaged areas. In fact more than likely you indeed had a series of small strokes," John Thomas began to put his medical instruments back in his doctor's bag and closed it. "In all honesty, I don't know. You may get your memory back tomorrow, next week or next year, or you may get only partial memories, much of your life blank spots. Your injuries are the same as any stroke patients; the brain is a very little understood organ. Not I or any doctor could honestly tell you with total certainty what the full extent of your amnesia and neural injuries are, or when exactly it will all heal. " He smiled slightly, trying to give her some encouragement, "Look, I know it's probably not the cut and dried answer you were hoping for, but I'll be doing more testing with you in the next couple days, and we'll both try and figure this out and see what we can." He offered encouragement.

"As for your throat, your voice box was also heavily damaged in the accident. Unfortunately, you have lost the ability to speak. Until everything is fully healed in there," he lightly checked the bandages on her throat, "We won't know for certain if you can use an electronic larynx to talk. It depends on how much nerve damage was done to your voice box." He glanced up at her and offered a warm, sympathetic smile, "I'm afraid for now you are going to have to be a budding author and write everything. I realize it's a pain in the arse, but that's all we can do. As far as the dizziness goes, this should clear up in a couple days. That and the weakness you feel is from your being unconscious for quite a while. The body does that when it doesn't move much." He winked, trying to put her at ease.

"Hey, we're all good guys here; you're going to get the best medical care in the world! I assure you." Dr. Weintraub smiled. He glanced at Victor and both men nodded silently to one another. "I'll see you tomorrow, kiddo, OK?" John Thomas gathered the bag and her file and departed the room.

She nodded as she watched him leave. She liked the doctor; he had an honest and warm manner. Victor smoothly rose to his feet and walked over to her. "There, you see?" he said with a soothing demeanor. "You're getting the best care around."

She picked up the notepad and pen the doctor had left and jotted, "*Well, are you going to fill me in or what?*" she held it out for him to read.

He read it and smiled that annoying smile at her again. The one that seemed to say, "I know the answers but am not going to tell you."

"Yes, about your past, ah, well at this time I can't." he simply said. She glared at him then, truly glared at him in total disbelief and even anger at the old man.

Victor quickly hardened his features and shot a dark look of his own back at her. "*Basta*," He growled in a low tone, "Let's not get testy here!" He folded his arms across his chest and looked at her. "Besides," he lied, "Its Dr. Weintraub's orders. He said if we were to tell you too much about your past, that it could make things worse, because your mind wouldn't be able to remember it, oh never mind the details of it all..." Victor sighed in exasperation at her continued stare of disbelief. "The doctor said that now is not the time to try and force you to remember things. Period." He said in his; "I'm done with this conversation tone".

She sighed deeply and seemed to accept that answer for now, or at least she was resigned to the fact that Victor Jerome wasn't going to discuss it with her anymore. "*Well can you at least tell me my name, so that if someone calls me by it, I'll at least know they are talking to me!*" She wrote out and handed it to Victor, sadness in her green eyes.

"You do have a point..." Victor conceded as he eased back into a softer, gentler mood and unfolded his arms. However, he had no idea what her name was, or who she was or anything else about her other than he had allowed his mind to listen to his heart, had allowed her fate to touch his soul and had spared her from death at Vito Roman's kennels. But Victor's great genius was in his speed at thinking on his feet; it always had been.

"Alyssa..." he said, barely skipping a beat, his eyes looking deep into hers, "Alyssa Disarro. You are my niece." Victor said and left it at that, hoping for now it would satisfy her, for he was giving her nothing else.

"Now she is my niece? *Vaffanculo!*" He cursed himself out in his mind, surprised how easily the lie had come to him.

She smiled warmly and was pleased she had gotten that much from him. Gotten something, some thread she could at least hold on to, something to start with.

"I suggest you get some rest now, Alyssa." Victor smiled and put her notepad and pen on the table next to her. "Dr. Weintraub will go over your therapy and such tomorrow as he promised." Victor adjusted the sheets around her, tucking her in.

He walked to the door, was about to open it then paused. "Mr. Tommy DeLuca is right outside the door; if you need anything, he'll get it for you. As I mentioned before, he's also your private nurse for now, so he'll bring your medications, meals and such up to you. Since you have no memory of this place, of my home, it is best for you to remain here and go about reacquainting yourself slowly." He spoke to her without looking back at her.

Victor did not want to look at those hollow, questioning eyes of hers, not anymore tonight. She would take his explanations and use those and those alone for now. Until he knew more of what he could expect as far as her own real memories returning. "Tommy will bring your dinner up to you shortly. Rest well, child." He left and quietly shut the door behind him.

She heard him speak in muffled tones with Tommy, the man with the gun, outside her door: "What nurse carries a gun inside a house?" she thought, and then heard Victor Jerome's footsteps softly receding down the hall. She sighed and felt so alone, lost and somewhat smothered, a feeling that seemed to send a slight shiver to the core of her soul. As Dr. Weintraub had promised most of the dizziness was already passing, so she flipped off the covers and carefully padded to the window at the left side of her bed. She pushed aside the peach-colored lacy curtain and looked outside.

She was on the second story of a very large house; a mansion, no doubt about that. Below her, stretching out almost as far as the eye could see was a huge, well-groomed front lawn. There was a long, extra-wide driveway that circled the front of the house then disappeared out of sight to the right into a forested area. Off to the horizon she could see mounds of more trees. There were no signs of any other buildings that didn't seem a part of this estate.

Suddenly, down below six men galloped into view on horseback, large, wooden mallets in their hands. "Polo!" she thought to herself, "They're playing polo on the front lawn!"

The circular part of the driveway was filled with several limos and other expensive, sporty cars. Beyond the line of cars perhaps fifty people all elegantly dressed up in their Sunday best, sat around watching the polo match. There was a large group of men to one side talking amongst themselves, and several small clusters of exquisitely dressed women off to the other side talking and drinking champagne.

Walking alertly on the fringe of this party were several men in dark suits carrying rifles. They were dark, imposing and stoic, like Secret Service men. These mysterious guards talked to no one; they stood apart from the crowd and seemed to be calmly alert to all that was going on around them.

She saw Victor reemerging outside. He acknowledged a few of the guards and walked over to his crowd of guests. She saw him talking privately to one man, also in a neatly pressed dark suit, who literally towered in height, head and shoulders over Victor and everyone else. At one point Victor pointed offhandedly up in her general direction, perhaps to her window. Victor finished his conversation with the tall man and walked back over to an empty chair, sat down and chatted with his guests.

She continued to watch for a few more seconds until the giant Victor had been speaking to slowly turned and glanced behind him, staring right up to the window where she was. She could have sworn he looked right at her, could *see* her from that distance.

Her blood froze in a wave of fear, and she quickly let the curtain fall back into place. She backed up to the bed and quickly crawled back under the covers. Something was not right here. She didn't know what, but her gut instinct told her that something was decidedly wrong.

Chapter 7- *April 19th 1987*

Alyssa hadn't slept well that first night at all. She had been tossing and turning, searching her mind desperately for any hints about her past. Some things she remembered clearly. She knew the name of the forest preserve she liked to walk in, and what state she had been born and raised in. She knew she had certain strong preferences in colors, reading material, music; things that made her base personality, but everything else, especially people, places and dates, were a blur. Occasionally she thought she was on the verge of remembering something, a parent's name or if she had any brothers or sisters, but like an elusive melody that rode on the fringes of her mind, the memories ethereally danced away.

This house and Victor Jerome didn't sit comfortably with her. Not that she was afraid; it was just that her gut told her that she had never known him or his house, and the people who surrounded him did not give her a sense of comfort or belonging. She didn't know exactly how she knew this; if someone had put her on the spot and asked her how she knew Victor wasn't her uncle, she wouldn't have been able to tell them. It was just a vague feeling, a pervading uneasiness that told her that this wasn't her place and these were not her family and friends.

It wasn't that she disliked Victor Jerome and all his people. Obviously the old gentleman had saved her life and seemed to care for her. He had taken her in, given her wonderful medical care and for that reason she felt grateful to him. He had charisma, he had presence, he was a leader and he even caused a slight uneasiness to trickle down her spine at times, but the man was a mystery and at this point in her life, Alyssa had more than enough mystery with her amnesia. Even the name "Alyssa" seemed out of place, as though it belonged to someone else, but for now it was all she had.

She had gotten up, washed and completed her grooming. Last night, Tommy DeLuca had pointed out a few drawers in the dresser that held some clothes in her size. "Everything in this one dresser is yours," he had shown her. "Victor got all this for you, and everything in the bathroom is new for you; the toothpaste and hairbrush all that necessary stuff for hygiene. If you need anything else specifically, just ask and I or someone else will be happy to get it for you." he had smiled.

Tommy treated her kindly and seemed pleasant enough. Soft-spoken and clean-shaven, he appeared around her age. Even his carrying a gun didn't seem to bother her; it wasn't like Tommy intimidated like some of the Secret Service types. He brought up her medications, always with a smile, and some small talk. When she ate her dinner, he had sat with her and chatted lightly; when he checked her bandages, it was always with a gentleness that was professional and caring. Always he was seeing to her needs: if she was in pain, or uncomfortable. Always he treated her with dignity.

However, like Victor, he was very skilled at not answering direct questions. If she tried to ask him anything too personal about her past, how she got here, what her accident was, Tommy would say, "You need to speak to Mr. Jerome about that." and would quickly change the subject and look uncomfortable, or worse, leave. Since she enjoyed his company, she tried to not ask questions she knew would make him uncomfortable and instead just talked about neutral topics.

The next morning, as she was finishing brushing out her long red hair, there was a knock on her door and then it opened a bit, Tommy sticking his head in. "Good morning Alyssa," he said. "Victor said you were to join him for breakfast if you feel up to it."

She smiled and nodded yes. Put her hair back in a ponytail and then slowly followed him out. She still was a bit stiff and weak but there was no more pain in her muscles, just a slight soreness. A cane had been bought to help her walk without stumbling, and like a gentleman, Tommy held out his arm for her to use to balance on as he escorted her through the long maze of hallways and spacious rooms.

"A person could easily get lost in this huge mansion," Alyssa thought to herself as the eased herself down the stairs, through the foyer then to the left into a dining area. Even though the dining area was casual she could tell it was huge in here. There were a few side tables that held all kinds of self-serve breakfast items, everything from Danishes to donuts, pancakes to scrambled eggs and bacon. A large dark wooden table sat in the middle of the room with eight chairs all around it.

To her dismay, she could already tell this was not going to be a cozy breakfast for two. Already seated at the table drinking coffee and reading over a newspaper was perhaps the tallest person she had ever seen. In fact, she recognized him as the giant man who had looked up at her yesterday from the front lawn. With short blonde hair neatly combed back and handsome but dark features. He was dressed in a black turtleneck shirt and black pants, only adding to his unsettling appearance.

She had thought Victor unnerved her at times; this man caused her twice as much uneasiness. His personality felt more like one of the darker types that hung around, unreadable, unemotional and cold. His body was lean and hard, and his face appeared to be carved out of granite, all planes and sharp angles. It was his eyes, that unnerved her she finally concluded; cold, ice-blue eyes that seemed to be half asleep, but like some hungry dragon, was very much alert to the slightest goings-on around him. His half-lidded, bored look was merely his way of disguising what he was concentrating on. He briefly glanced up from his paper, his eyes seeming to peer into her very soul.

When he spoke, his deep baritone voice seemed to shake her very bones even though it was no louder than anyone else's. "Good Morning, Ms. Alyssa." He acknowledged her then paid her no more notice than a fly on the wall, directing his attention back to his paper.

Tommy led her to the breakfast buffet. She plopped a donut and some fresh fruit on her plate, grabbed some orange juice and sat down. As Alyssa was picking at her food she glanced around, admiring all the various oil paintings of landscapes that hung on the walls.

Just then, another man entered the room; she remembered him from yesterday as well. It was the man she had seen only briefly, the one Victor had called "Joshua". Stunningly handsome, with dark and dangerous features, he reminded her of some great hungry panther; always tense, always dangerously volatile.

For some unexplained reason she had an instant dislike of him, and he seemed to share the same about her. They glanced at each other like two strange cats, meeting for the first time. A hesitant, untrusting look with hair raised, stiffened backs and claws ready. He said nothing to her; Joshua simply chose to ignore her and proceeded to toss a few English muffins on his plate and filled his cup with strong coffee.

Tommy had finished buttering his four pieces of toast and was putting so much creamer into his coffee that it resembled brown milk more than java. "Where's the boss?" he asked no one in particular.

"Maybe he's got constipation," Joshua snorted, sitting down near the blonde-haired giant and snatching up a newspaper section that the man had finished with, "What do I look like? His damn keeper?"

Obviously Joshua was not a morning person. He sat down and buried his face in the newspaper.

"*Madonn!*" Tommy muttered under his breath, "Shoot me for asking, why don't ya?" He made his way back to the table with his toast and coffee, sitting down near Alyssa.

"If you want any more cream in that coffee, Tom," the tall, darkly-dressed man spoke, "I can just bring the cow in here for you." This was said with a totally straight face and only a slightly raised eyebrow for expression.

"Man, that's fucking cold, Martel." Tommy shot back with a grimace.

"Hey!" Josh snapped suddenly looking up from his paper at Tommy, startling everyone at the table, "Watch your dirty trash mouth, DeLuca! Company is present!" He said in a thick, harsh Brooklyn accent, "If I wanted a bunch of comedy I'd go to the damn comedy club. Give a person a chance to wake up." He glowered angrily at both Tommy and Alyssa then burrowed back into the paper.

"Yeah, yeah, whatever." Tommy grumbled under his breath, then turned to Alyssa. "Sorry," he mumbled and then turned his full attention to his toast and milk-coffee. He could feel the change in the atmosphere today, no good-natured teasing; the silence was like a heavy, smothering blanket.

She half shrugged as if to say "I don't care" and wished they would leave her out of this completely. This coming down to breakfast was a mistake, she thought, as silence fell upon them all again. Maybe she could see what Victor meant by staying in her room; at least there it was private and safe, a little enclosed sanctuary. She didn't know any of these men and felt uncomfortable around them. She picked some more at her donut and juice, listening to the soft sounds of people eating or the crinkling of the paper as Joshua and Martel read.

A few other men came into the room to grab coffee or various breakfast items and then left. Some glanced briefly at her, some stared almost rudely and coldly at her, but most paid her no attention. A few stopped and whispered privately to the large giant's ears. Usually his only reaction to their questions was a silent nod yes or slight shake of his head no. To one of the overly muscular, imposing, Secret-Service-looking guards that entered the room, the large man quietly said, "Gio, tell Cesare to bring the car around front, then let the others know of the morning meeting."

Victor finally entered the dining room; he looked stiff and unusually tired, like he had a bad flu or something, Alyssa thought to herself. But she was happy to see him; at least he was someone besides Tommy she recognized and felt somewhat comfortable around. The three men greeted Victor warmly as he grabbed a cup of coffee and a banana nut muffin. Instantly the mood seemed to soften some and become more bearable.

"You don't look so good today, Victor," the giant dragon softly spoke, "You all right?"

Alyssa heard caring and concern in the deep voice for the first time. But only, it seemed, for Victor.

Victor smiled weakly, "I'm fine, Laurence." He patted the man's broad shoulder and assured his men, "More than likely I am coming down with one bastard of a cold." Victor turned his glance towards Alyssa and raised his cup of coffee to her. "Ah, good morning child, I am glad you decided to come down for breakfast. Moving around will do you good." He smiled, took a sip of coffee and then continued with her, "In case you haven't all formally met, this is Laurence Martel ..." he gestured to the giant, who was shoveling the last of a glazed donut in his mouth and nodded towards Alyssa, -the Dragon-. "And Joshua Demonico," Victor indicated to the well-dressed, handsome man with the dark hair, -the Panther-.

"We met." Joshua said levelly; even his Brooklyn accent sounded low and harsh, like a hunting cat's quiet growl. He and Alyssa's dislike for each other grew even more.

"Well, very good then." Victor continued, seemingly oblivious to any dislike between Joshua and Alyssa, "And of course you already know Tommy." Victor sounded weary and drawn, almost as if merely talking was wearing him out. "After breakfast Alyssa, you'll be taken to my private clinic here where Dr. Weintraub will do some more medical tests on you, see if we can't figure out some more on that amnesia, hmmm?"

She nodded and continued eating slowly. She was ravenously hungry, but her stomach had gone without solid food in it for nearly two weeks, so it occasionally rebelled and threatened to up heave her breakfast if she ate it too fast. There was very little conversation at the table; in fact, only Victor spoke and mainly to Alyssa, small pleasantries such as --I hope you are feeling well, settling in, meeting all my family and workers--.

Obviously Martel and Joshua didn't feel as friendly as Victor, for they remained totally silent at breakfast. Alyssa got the distinct impression they felt her as strange as she found them to be. She also got the feeling that everyone, especially Martel and Joshua, were censoring their conversation by their stony silence. Finally, when everyone seemed finished, Victor turned to Tommy. "Tommy, take our guest to the car, will you? Cesare will drive her to the clinic. Then come see me afterwards."

"No problem Mr. J." Tommy acknowledged.

"Martel, Joshua; come talk with me in the office please." Victor glanced at them and then everyone began to move all at once, going their own ways.

Alyssa eyed Tommy levelly as he drained the rest of his coffee and pulled the napkin off his lap, "I have an ulcer," he said quietly to Alyssa as he gently guided her by the arm towards the foyer they had come through earlier, "That's why I put so much cream in it." He explained himself. Alyssa just smiled and nodded in agreement. She knew he didn't need to defend himself to her, but it made her wonder why one so young, and apparently healthy already had an ulcer.

Victor walked after breakfast to "the Office", his private sanctuary where he conducted Family business. Martel personally checked daily for any eavesdropping devices like bugs, phone taps, and wire taps: Victor trusted no one else. There was much to go over with the men today; the pieces had to be set into motion for his final checkmate against the D'Salvatores. The decisions still swam in his head; he knew there would be lives lost on both sides. This would lead to the final showdown, one that had been nearly thirty years in the making. Patrizio, Rocco, Sal Antonia and Leonardo would be here soon. There were a few things he could go over with Martel and Joshua before they came; after all, his underboss and consigliere were his most trusted.

He felt awful today. A dull ache permeated through his whole body. "Getting old sucks," he thought to himself. He knew sheer drive often kept him going now. He had so much to do, so much to accomplish. His biggest scheme and plan, the whole point of all he had worked for, would be coming to fruition within the year. He could not, would not, fall ill now.

With another sigh, he absent-mindedly rubbed the horrible ache in his lower back. It felt as though someone had beaten him with a baseball bat, repeatedly. He would have to talk to John Thomas about some decent arthritis medicines. What he was taking now wasn't working worth shit. He truly hoped John Thomas would indeed find a transplant for him, anything but that stupid dialysis. He would be far too vulnerable if he had that, even Martel would have a hard time protecting him. There were far too many easily corruptible people, especially now. Although he never voiced his true concerns to his friend and physician, John Thomas, he absolutely had to remain alive for the next year; only sheer willpower was keeping him running at this point.

"Why did I?" he asked himself. "Why did I really save that girl from the Romans' kennels?" He wondered again if he was becoming soft in his old age. He knew his men had wondered the same thing. What benefit was there in it? What could her rescue have accomplished except to act as a salve to his guilty conscience? He had no earthly idea what he would do with her, none at all. And what if, after all the medical treatment, she regained her memories? Then what? She would be a liability to the whole Family, and he would then have to kill her anyway.

He cursed himself again. Perhaps he would need to remain, as he always was, impassionate, aloof and hard. *Cosa Nostra* had no place for philanthropy and guilt. "I'm most definitely, becoming soft in my old age," he sighed barely aloud. Softness had no place in his world, especially not now when he was so close to achieving his goals. One wrong cog could screw up the whole machine, decades of work, the lives of his men and himself.

His mind flashed briefly to Eddie again, but there was something deeper, something difficult to explain. It seemed in some odd way, as though the woman was meant to be here. Victor was far from one to believe in coincidences, fates, superstitions, destinies or other such esoteric foolishness, but in that instant, as he looked out the window and watched Tommy leading her towards the parked limo, he had a feeling so profound it shook him to the depths of his soul.

She glanced behind her at the window, and though Victor knew she could not see him through the reflective mirrored glass, he also knew they indeed seemed to see into one another's eyes and souls if even for the briefest of moments. "Why are you really here, Child?" he whispered softly to himself. Somehow, unspoken, she seemed to answer him but he could not hear it. She looked away and the spell was broken.

Tommy had led Alyssa out into the warm mid-spring morning. Already there was the hint of humidity in the still air, a warm glare that seemed to be awakening the landscape, causing her to briefly shield her eyes. To her it seemed eons since she had been in the fresh air. She saw a huge black limousine parked on the driveway; bearing a license plate that read JEROME-1; Tommy was gently leading her down the steps towards it.

She stopped and glanced back for a moment, her eyes taking in the huge view of the mansion. The windows seemed to be covered with some reflective, mirror-like film. How could Martel have seen her the other day, she wondered? Even she couldn't see inside at this close range. Her eyes drifted to a window briefly; she could see nothing inside, but she felt him for a moment, the enigmatic Victor Jerome. "Who are you, old man?" she wondered. She knew he was alien to her memories, and yet there was something about him, some strange, magnetic pull between them and some purpose she seemed to be here to fulfill. The strange thought fled, and she quickly turned back to the limo and Tommy's small talk.

"... and Cesare will bring you back when you're done." Tommy finished speaking.

Ahead of him, Alyssa saw a very heavyset man step out of the limo, which rose a few inches when he got out, dressed in a rumpled suit and tie. "Morning, Miss Alyssa," the driver nodded and held open the back door for her. Tommy helped her into the seat as Cesare closed the door. She glanced around briefly, noting more of the dark guards around the huge estate. They blended like shadows, here and there

88

throughout the landscape, imposing, dark-suited men with guns. She shivered a moment and wished she could get to the clinic so she could question Dr. Weintraub until she had writer's cramps in both hands.

She felt the car lurch down slightly as the heavy man settled into the driver's seat. He had the window down that separated the passenger from the driver, and on the elegant sound system Tony Bennett crooned softly but erotically. The large driver turned down the sound even more and turned and looked at her, "Hey ya," he wheezed a bit, "The name's Cesare, but they all call me 'Elf' around here, and anything you need, you just let ol' Elf know, OK?" he smiled sincerely. As much as Alyssa instantly disliked Joshua for no unexplainable reason, she also knew she instantly liked "Elf": he was safe, and for whatever reason she trusted him.

"Stay with her, Elf," Tommy instructed, "Bring her back here when the Doc is done with her." He was fumbling in his pocket for his pack of Marlboro cigarettes and a lighter.

"Yeah, yeah." Cesare rolled up the window in Tommy's face before the smoke could blow into the car. "Go away with that coffin nail, will ya?" With a slight smirk, he smoothly put the massive limo in gear and started off down the driveway. Not away from the house, but down further, around it, into that massive tangle of woods she had seen before. "I tell ya, some of those guys are awfully high-strung," Elf spoke to Alyssa while deftly unwrapping a Hershey bar. "My philosophy in life is to take it slow and easy, ya know?" he broke off a piece and handed it to her, all while expertly driving, "I saw this special on some documentary channel the other day, about these sloth creatures, ya know?" he spoke as easily and casually as if he had known Alyssa all his life, "See, these sloths have something on us humans. All they do is hang around, eat all day and take it easy. They don't know the meaning of high blood pressure or ulcers or anything..."

Alyssa listened to him drone on in a cheerful way, her eyes taking in the majesty of this estate. Here and there, she would see a guard walking around, or smoking a cigarette, all of them with semi-automatic guns cradled in their hands, or slung around their shoulders; a few walking with large German Shepherds or Dobermans at their sides.

"...They are so slow," Cesare's voice caught her attention again, "That like moss and shit grows on them! Man it was amazing." He noticed that she was more into looking around than listening to him. "You never really got the royal tour of the Estates did ya?" he asked. She shook her head, no.

He nodded gently and pointed out some points of interest to her. "Here is the Boss' aviary, I never get what he sees in all those little birds, but he likes 'em and he's the boss, right?" he smiled softly.

Cesare noticed her looking still nervously at the guards. "Oh, those guys are OK," he assured her sincerely, "They're here to protect us, ya know? They're the good guys." He chuckled warmly. "They protect the sloths." He nodded absent-mindedly and waved to a few of them as he passed, and they waved back. They came to a fork in the road and turned down another bend to the right in the blacktop driveway, beneath a natural archway of trees and immaculately kept grounds.

In the opposite direction, Alyssa caught site of a good-sized house, partially hidden in the trees, and then it was gone in a blink. She turned and looked out the window, after it.

"Ah, that's just Martel's place," he glanced at her in the rearview mirror. "He lives down there, says the main house is too stuffy for him. He's kinda an odd fish anyway, real private like ya know? So, probably just as well, but don't tell him I said that."

Elf liked her. There was something so compelling about the young woman. He could tell something bad had happened to her, the bruises and scars and bandages attested to that, but beneath the uncertainty and hint of fear in her eyes was a strong soul. He could definitely see that.

He had been told that Alyssa was to be treated as Victor's niece, so that is how he treated her. He liked her fighting spirit, no sloth her, he thought. "Further down past Martel's place is some kennels and even some stables. The horses are cool, the dogs are not," he chuckled at his own joke. "Maybe when you're feeling better, you can go riding or something, ya know?"

She turned, and as though sensing him watching her, offered a shy smile and settled back into the rich leather seat, listening to him. He brought the car to a halt in front of a small brick building with no letters or markings except for a small, silvery Aesculapius; the familiar doctor's' symbol of two entwining snakes entwining around a pole.

Already in the parking lot sat a shiny silver-grey BMW and a covered golf cart. She had seen a lot of those golf carts around. From what she could see, nothing on this estate was a short walk; it was vast indeed.

"Well here we are," Elf put the car into park and opened his door, as he heaved his large frame out. "Over a half a mile and we haven't even left the Estates. Next time, I'll take ya on a tour of the other ond." He opened her door for her and helped her out. "There are some real nice gardens and such down by the other end, and some fountains and fancy shit like that. My kids like to come down and play in 'em once in awhile. The wife says it's a nice place to picnic, ya know?"

With still weak and shaking muscles, she accepted his sturdy arm as he helped her to the doctor's office and into the waiting area. "I hope he don't give ya a shot." Cesare looked around. "That would be a double bummer." He gave her hand a warm squeeze. "I'll be waiting in the car right outside." he assured her, then left the office.

She honestly did like Cesare; so far he had been the only one to truly treat her as a friend and the only person who had talked to her like a normal human being.

90

She was alone for the moment. It was a small waiting room, with only a few chairs. An eclectic mix of magazines lay strewn about, everything from "*Guns and Ammo*", to the "*Medical Gazette*", the "*Wall Street Journal*" to "*Outdoor Life*" and a couple newspapers that were a few days old.

"I'll be with you in a moment," she recognized Dr. Weintraub's voice call out from deep within the small clinic. "Have a seat."

She slowly sat down. It suddenly occurred to her that all medical institutions smelled the same, a sickly antiseptic and medicine smell that seemed to cover up the hidden scent of blood, illness and death. As she sat there, a slow chill seemed to creep down along her spine, and she felt herself swaying dangerously close to a wave of dizziness, her mind spun and then the dizziness cleared almost as quickly as it came. The antiseptic smell reminded her of something recently, but she couldn't pinpoint exactly what. Her mind danced on the fringes of remembrance: a light, a strange feeling in her body, a medicine-like smell in her nostrils, the hum of insects, the sun burning cruelly into her eyes that could not close, and then the fog of forgetfulness and amnesia closed back in around her.

"Hi there," Dr. Weintraub suddenly poked his head around the corner. He was dressed in rumpled slacks, a cotton shirt, with a wrinkled, opened lab coat. He looked like he had been pulling long nights with little sleep. "Come on back, I got everything set up for you." He gestured with his hand.

She pulled herself up, and felt another wave of weakness course through her; Alyssa's world seemed to tilt for a second. "Whoa," he said, "I gotcha." Again, it seemed to pass as quick as it had come on. "Expect that for a while," Doctor Weintraub reassured her, "Pretty common after all the time on your back, recouping and all."

Somehow deep within she felt it something deeper than just the recovery from her accident, but she had no idea what it was. Her mind came into focus, and she again remembered she had a battery of questions to ask this man.

For the next two hours, Dr. Weintraub seemed to run her through the wringer with tests, tests and more tests. Everything from psychological tests, to neurological tests, and he even pulled several small vials of blood from her. "I'll send these into Presbyterian Hospital; hopefully we can get some new information on how you are healing up." They had moved back into the main exam room, and finally he seemed to let up with his constant poking and probing. She grabbed one of the pads of paper from his desk and began to scribble out questions as fast as she could think of them. The first being, '*Am I going to get my memory back? What happened to me?*'

Weintraub read it and shook his head, taking off his trademark glasses. "As I said the other day, I honestly don't know, as far as your memory goes. The brain is just too complex of an organ for doctors to be sure of an exact diagnosis when it's injured, understand? We can continue physical therapy for your body and work on some different cognitive therapies to help you see if you can regain memories, but in all honesty it's anyone's guess." He rubbed his temples, "And trust me, doctors hate to say that. Like you, we always hope to have precise answers."

She did feel for him, she knew the Doctor was trying. His basic answer seemed to only confirm what she already knew. That she remembered certain things and forgot a lot of other stuff. Mainly the important stuff; like her true name, where she lived, where she grew up, the accident and how, if at all, Victor and these guards were related to her.

"Hey," Doctor Weintraub said gently. "Stop trying so hard. You just woke up; it's going to take some time. Nothing in medicine happens overnight, except my bill." He tried a lame joke to break the tension.

Fighting back the tears of exasperation that threatened to rise, she quickly scrawled out some more questions.

1) *What happened to me to cause, this amnesia?*
2) *How do I fit into this family?*
3) *Tell me about Elf, Joshua, Martel and the rest. Where IS this place?*
4) *Who are all these Secret Service guards with the guns? Is Victor the president or some kind of Mafia godfather? <Ha-ha!>*

"Ah, the budding novelist," Weintraub joked wryly as he took the notebook she practically waved in his face. He read it and glanced over his glasses at her while he re-read. He remembered Victor's words to him, about if she started to ask exact questions such as these. He coughed nervously at the last question.

With a sigh and a light-hearted attempt he said. "One, I can't tell you - Two, ask Victor - Three, ask Josh, Martel and the others yourself - and finally, ask Victor." He threw the pad down, out of her reach. He wished he could answer some of her questions but some were things even he did not know. That which he did was not for him to answer.

She glared at him, her whole small body nearly trembling in anger. All this secrecy and run-around was getting old, unnerving and just plain aggravating. She had been here two days already and in some ways felt more alone, confused and frightened than the she had first woke up.

"Hey!" Weintraub gently smiled and spread his hands in a sign of peace, "It's not that I don't want to help you out in that department, but your questions would be better for Mr. Jerome, your uncle, to go over with you..." He hated lying. He had never had to lie to one of Victor's patients before, not like this. "Let's finish up so you can go home for the day, fair enough?" He got up quickly so as to prevent any more questions.

Alyssa turned slightly so he would not see the tears of frustration that she quickly swiped from her eyes. She figured she was going to have to be more subtle in her questioning. Ask the right people, but not now, not Dr. Weintraub and not Victor. He had already given her the run-around as well.

Just as they were both getting up, they heard the loud squeal of tires in the parking lot, and then a resounding crash as the door of the office nearly flew off its hinges. The panicked voices of several men filled her ears, even Weintraub jumped nearly out of his skin at the sudden explosion of activity and sounds.

"Doc!" Joshua's voice roared, seeming to shake the very walls of the small clinic. "Doc, come quick, it's Victor!"

The physician in Weintraub took over, and he raced past Alyssa. She too got up and leaned on the doorframe, supporting her weak muscles. She saw Joshua along with two older men and Laurence Martel bearing the unconscious form of Victor Jerome in his arms. The old man looked like a child in the arms of the blonde-haired giant. Everyone hustled into one of the exam rooms. At the moment, she was completely forgotten, so she cautiously crept closer, silently watching.

"Put him over here," the doctor ordered and obediently the men followed his command. "What happened?" he demanded.

"He just collapsed!" Joshua was near panic, angrily chewing his gum. "Is it is heart Doc?"

"Easy Josh," Martel ordered, "Let John Thomas look at him." Martel began helping Weintraub hook the old man up to a myriad of machines, while Weintraub began to examine Victor. Alyssa noted Martel handled the medical equipment surprisingly well.

Alyssa crept closer to the doorframe of the exam room, where Victor lay; she could just barely make him out over the huddle of men crowded around him. Poor Victor, she thought. He looked awful; his skin was a sickly yellow. He looked so lifeless. His hands made small little twitches as he lay there, so vulnerable. Time seemed to slow down to a crawl, especially for the frantically pacing Joshua. The two older men stood unmoving, like dour statues in the corner whispering in some other language amongst them selves.

"His kidneys have shut down, gone into total failure. His blood is overrun by his own toxins." Weintraub looked up sadly at Martel directly but his words spoke to all the men.

"*Figlio di puttana*! Shit!" Josh roared in blind rage and frustration at no one in particular.

"Joshua!" Weintraub's strong voice snapped into Joshua's skull for a moment, calming and centering him, "Go tell Albert to fire up the helicopter. Victor has got to get to Presbyterian Hospital, you understand? Make sure Tommy comes along as well, I'll need his help on the flight down."

"Yeah," he nodded. Was that fear Alyssa caught briefly in the Panther's eyes?

"Goddamn it!" Josh raged at no one and everyone as he sprinted down the hall to tell the pilot to fire up the helicopter. Alyssa jumped slightly as he roughly pushed by her. Joshua always seemed so angry.

The two older men stood motionless, unmoving. Alyssa had not met them yet, but in their old eyes and age-lined faces she saw deep worry. The two men looked solemnly at each other, then back at the doctor and Victor.

Weintraub walked up to Martel, gently placing his hand on Martel's large one which covered the form of Victor, whose raspy breathing filled the small room. He and Martel looked into each other's eyes. Weintraub's words seemed just for the Dragon only, but Alyssa stood transfixed. She couldn't move, nor had anyone even noticed her. "Don't ask for a diagnosis right now. It's not good. He knew of this possibility. His kidneys have quit completely, they'll have to go, and he will have to go on constant dialysis until we can find a donor."

"If we can find a donor," Martel sadly shook his head. The half-lidded blue eyes that had looked so stone-cold at breakfast now seemed to be filled with a hundred emotions at once. "It will kill him. He wouldn't want to live like that, not my..." Martel quickly glanced away, towards the man on the table. "Not Victor." He said pulling the coldness from his heart back into the forefront.

"What do you want me to do, Laurence?" Weintraub forced Martel to look at him, "What? I don't have a donor kidney lying around. Not an AB negative, you can't match him, you're AB positive. I need the rarest there is, and I just don't have one sitting around! If he was any other blood type..." Weintraub pulled himself away from Martel's line of sight and began to work feverishly again on stabilizing Victor for his air lift out.

Somewhere in the distance the sound of a helicopter powering up was heard.

Alyssa began to realize that her benefactor was going to die. Maybe he really was her uncle, maybe not, but damn it, she liked the old man. Somehow she knew he had saved her from something so dark and vile she could not even remember its cold, cruel nature.

On the table, Victor's eyes slowly opened, and he appeared to be trying to focus on Martel and Weintraub, but he was not doing a good job. He turned his head slightly, and his eyes caught Alyssa's alone for a moment. She saw the dark eyes, so intelligent, beginning to flicker. They fought to focus on her a second. "Child, come here," he seemed to be calling to her. Was she the only one who heard him call out to her? Why didn't anyone else hear him?

She felt herself unconsciously drawn into the room. She knew she had AB negative blood: she had just seen it today on her medical file in Weintraub's office. Her world seemed to tilt for a moment, and it was as though one small lock clicked in her memory, one note of the elusive melody of her life sounded in her head. She knew, remembered, that she had AB negative blood. She waved furiously, trying to get Weintraub's attention.

"Not now, Alyssa," he angrily brushed her off.

"Someone take her out of here!" Martel ordered darkly.

She felt one of the older men step forward and grab hold of her wrist, leading her almost roughly out of the room. Still, she seemed to hear Victor calling to her; did no one else hear him? With a sudden surge of adrenaline, she twisted up and out of the older man's grasp, ran and grabbed onto Weintraub, hard.

Guttural hisses and grunts came from her useless voice box as she tried to persuade these men to see that she had the damn AB negative blood! "Eee!" she kept squeaking and pointing at herself and Victor. She was near panic. The pain of trying to talk was screaming agony in her unhealed throat. Still gesturing between herself and Victor, she latched onto Weintraub with such force she was sure she was leaving marks on the poor man. Although her voice was just barely above a whisper, she felt as though she were yelling at the top of her lungs. Tears coursing down her cheeks, "Oh, why wasn't anyone understanding?" her mind raged.

With a dark glower of slow anger, Martel looked as though he was about to unlatch her himself and throw her out and not very nicely. "What is her problem?" Martel's dark voice caused her hair to stand on end, but still she would not quit.

"I know you have AB negative blood, Alyssa," Weintraub tried extracting himself from her grasp, "But I doubt you could even survive a transplant surgery! You're not even healed yet from your injuries! Now get out of here!" Even his voice was raised with exasperation and anger.

Martel had already deftly grabbed her up and pulled her off the doctor as though she was a mere small animal. "She has AB negative blood?" he slowly released her and looked between her and the doctor.

"Yes, but..." Weintraub looked up suddenly, painfully aware that he felt every eye in the room on him. He stammered, "She can't survive the surgery Laurence, she's too weak! I mean..."

Martel cut him off with a wave of his hand, totally ignoring the doctor now. As he stood there looking down at her, his ice-blue eyes seemed to cut into her soul, the way Victor's could. "You are willing to do this for Victor?" He asked her levelly. "This isn't a pint of blood but a kidney."

'Yes!' she nodded emphatically, over and over as she continued pointing between her and Victor. Joshua had come back by this time, "The helicopter's ready and..." he abruptly halted as he heard the conversation going on. He stopped and stood quietly.

"You heard her, Doctor Weintraub." Martel broke his gaze from Alyssa and looked down at him. "She's more than willing." There was no room for argument in Martel's calm but not-to-be-denied voice. Joshua and the other two older men seemed to all take a breath at once.

"Then let's go..." Weintraub angrily motioned. Now was not the time to go into ethics. A part of him felt horrible inside: he knew this surgery would more than likely kill her. She had only a slim chance of pulling through because of her weakened state and recent injuries. But John Thomas also knew that Martel would not hear him, because he did not care. And worse, he feared what Martel might do if John Thomas refused.

Once again, the doctor had to kill yet another part of his soul. Victor was his best friend; he had to concentrate on that. Not the fact that this woman he had worked so hard to save was probably now going to die in the attempt to give Victor a donated kidney. And if she did die, then what? Then Victor would have *two* donated kidneys. He felt his own world waver for a moment, but John Thomas Weintraub knew exactly what it was. It was his soul being forced deeper into the dark web of Victor's organized crime Family. John Thomas's only solution would be to do his best to save them both, Victor and the woman. He knew that any complaining or lack of cooperation on his part would only drive Martel or Joshua to kill the woman outright, instantaneously thus making the choice for him.

No matter how hard Victor had fought to keep him innocent, John Thomas's innocence died there that day, under the scrutinizing gaze of Martel and the other mobsters, as the underboss once again scooped up the unconscious Victor in his arms. He was simply going to have to fight like a tenacious terrier and save them both. And so with an easy switch, the doctor moved all ethical qualms to the background as he concentrated on the hard surgery he and several other surgeons were going to have to perform on both patients.

CHAPTER 8- *April 22nd 1987*

The six men sat in the closed-off, second study of the Jerome Estates. The Office, the one Laurence Martel checked meticulously every day for any hidden listening devices. They glanced at one another, Martel, Joshua, and their four most trusted capos: Leonardo Tagretta, Rocco Benedarra, Patrizio Fantenelli and Cesare Ciccerone.

Patrizio was inhaling deeply on an unfiltered Pall Mall, smoking almost one third of it in one long drag. "So the shit is hitting the fan here." He spoke with decades of experience, voicing the thought each of them already knew deep in their hearts. "What is going on with the Boss, what is the plan here?" he ground out the rest of his cigarette and fished around for another one. He had been with Victor since before Victor had first been crowned Don. Patrizio still carried the bullet in his upper back from that Bloody Sunday Massacre in '57.

Martel sat in the richly decorated leather chair that normally would have been Victor's chair. As underboss the command now fell onto him. "First and foremost," he thrust an empty ashtray towards Patrizio to use as his was now overflowing, "As we know, Victor and the girl's tissue are a match." A murmur of nods went through the men.

Martel lifted a hand. "Weintraub said Victor has to recover from the surgery yet, make sure that he doesn't reject the transplant or get an infection. So we're not entirely out of the woods yet."

"But?" Josh left the question open, glancing at the man whom he trusted as much as Victor.

"But, Doc Weintraub says it looks very favorable," Martel answered, daring to name aloud the good news.

"What about his niece?" Cesare was waving his hand in Patrizio's face, trying to dispel the cloud of smoke that hung around him; "Did she make it?" he asked with concern in his voice. "Karloff" just blew a steadier stream of smoke directly at the "Elf". Everyone's nerves were on end, and Cesare's hackles were rising to Patrizio's bait; he suddenly snatched the cigarette out of Patrizio's hand and smashed it out into the glass ashtray with a dark look at him daring him to complain.

"She lives," Martel said casually, almost as though it were nothing, making a mental note of Cesare's question. He quickly leaned forward, physically getting between Cesare and Patrizio as though keeping two small children from getting into it and giving both men a hard stare. "I'm not trying to be overly pessimistic here," he leaned back once again and steepled his long fingers as soon as he noted he had everyone's attention, "But it's going to be rough for a while especially now, with what is in the air with all this *mannagge,* this war. In the meantime, it's business as usual," he stressed, his cold eyes taking in and meeting each of theirs in turn. "Especially now, not a peep of this is to get out; we don't discuss it outside this safe office. Not even casually around the soldiers. If the other Families get wind of this, they will lose confidence in us. And, more importantly; if our enemies, the D'Salvatores get wind of this, they will choose this time to attack. We just say the boss went in for some minor surgery and that is all we say." Not a word was spoken; all faces were frozen at his words. "Clear?" Martel asked matter-of-factly.

The other four nodded solemnly. This was not the time for joking, good-natured teasing or even petty differences. The Family had to continue to run like a well-oiled machine. There could be no flaws in the gears, no show of weakness, not with the D'Salvatores waiting for this kind of turmoil. "Not when we are so close to achieving the final move on the chessboard that Victor wanted," Martel thought to himself. If he had to, he would make the final move himself, but this was not how it was supposed to be, not yet. Not yet! "Fight, Padrone," he willed his thoughts into a solid mantra, "Fight and come back here, where you belong. Now is not the time, our vendetta cannot be fought without you. Not like this…"

"Patrizio," Martel glanced over at Fantenelli who had fished out a new cigarette and was about to light up.

"Huh?" the old man grunted.

"What are our eyes and ears picking up regarding the other families in our alliance?"

"The same minor shit and complaints…" Fantenelli finished lighting up, bored of hassling Cesare and glanced at the underboss, "You know, some grumbling with having to share with the Romans after the restructuring. They'll endure it for now." Fantenelli assured. "Victor offers them plenty; they are just making idle noise."

"Good," Martel leaned back, "Idle noise is good. It makes D'Salvatore think, makes him hopeful for turncoats. Just in case, though, throw some more points their way for now."

Patrizio nodded and gestured towards Rocco Benedarra, "Rocco's got the hard job now: he's the one watching the fucking Romans. Obviously we can't use Tagretta anymore."

This caused a few chuckles and nods as the men remembered Victor's humiliation of Vito Roman and the destruction of his kennels and white slavery operations.

"Now for the Romans," Martel let a wan smile play on his lips, "Obviously, none of us trust them as far as we can throw them. Victor worked hard at that, in fact left the door open for them to be swayed by the D'Salvatores."

"You know Vito Roman's crew is going to try and play double loyalties by straddling the fence or worse, try to join with other alliances on the Commission." Tagretta snorted in disgust.

Len's statement brought a robust guffaw from Cesare, "Ha! Good luck and good riddance! I doubt anyone but the D'Salvatores would take them, if even them!"

"Perhaps," Martel spoke softly, his eyes lidded a moment as he slipped deep into thought. "Rocco my friend, I hate to do this to you; I know I was going to pull you and you were going to start working with our contacts in Buffalo, but I need you here now. I'm going to have to post you longer on this Vito Roman thing; you're the only one I trust, and I'm a bit tied up at the moment."

Rocco and Martel's eyes met and locked, loyalty and the code of the Family flowing between them. "Hey," returned Rocco, a well-built man with olive skin, dark, curly hair and an expensive suit, smiled. "Forget about that, eh? Consider it done, my friend. It's an honor, Laurence; you know you don't have to apologize for that." He assured his underboss.

"I gotta time; I take care of what Rocco was to do in Buffalo."
Tagretta spoke decisively in his broken English, stepping in for Rocco.

"Thank you, Len," Martel nodded at him, "Make sure to stop at Presbyterian first and check that all our guards are in place to keep watch over Victor."

The other men nodded in agreement; they all felt the same way, with or without their Don laid up sick. This was their life also, they all had stakes and investments in this and they all trusted Martel as much as Victor did.

Martel eyed them all, and picked up his wine glass. The others followed his lead.

"Our Padrone chose well, my friends," he simply nodded and toasted each with his glass, "It is why the Jerome's are still number one in this city, and why we will stay that way." He emphasized the last part. "*Salute!*" he toasted them all.

"*Salute!*" they toasted back and spoke almost in unison.

Martel stood up to his full imposing height and stretched his back; he couldn't even remember the last time he had more than three hours of sleep in a row. "Now we take care of business, and we pray for Victor's health and recovery." He nodded.

One by one, the other men stood up, approached Laurence and gave him a quick embrace, each whispering their own promise of extra work or loyalty in his ears. They all willingly accepted Martel's role, honored his position as temporary leader and Boss. With a nod here and there, they began leaving.

Just as Joshua was about to leave, Martel stopped him with a hand on his shoulder. "He will be all right Josh," he spoke for Joshua's ears only. "Mark my words. I know my..." he paused for a moment. "I know Victor."

"Thanks." Demonico nodded up at his underboss. Joshua saw in Martel not an underboss but a true brother and mentor, as strong as blood family. "I know," he sighed. His worry over Victor was eating him, and Martel could see that.

"Have you cleared up that problem with customs at the docks? That shipment from Sicily will be here in eight weeks. It cannot be delayed," Martel gently reminded. He knew Joshua would have to be kept busy; it was the only way to keep the high-energy and highly volatile consigliere from worrying so much.

Joshua nodded, "It's as good as done, Laurence." He lightly joked and squeezed Martel's hand in an almost brotherly handshake. "Now I'm gonna order some extra flowers for the boss, for whenever he gets released."

"You do that." Martel solemnly nodded and watched Joshua depart down the hall, the consigliere's step a bit lighter than he had seen it in days. Martel knew why Victor so loved this life that he would risk all for it. The power was exhilarating, yes, but it was far more than that. It was the loyalty and friendships. Martel had known these people most of his adult years, some like Patrizio Fantenelli even longer. Others like Joshua Demonico he had mentored and sponsored personally. Outside, a sudden spring thundershower had now opened up and began to beat the house with a steady rainfall, and he could hear some low rumbles of thunder. "I hope no one has to learn of our secret early, Victor," Martel thought to himself, as he watched the rain beating with a sudden ferocity on the expensive ironwork windows. "This Family is in enough turmoil."

John Thomas Weintraub also watched the angry raindrops splatter against the window of his office in the hospital; it had already been raining for nearly four hours solid now. He stood up, rubbing his aching joints and walked to the window to look down the ten stories below. His mind drifted, watching as the rain cleansed the streets, made the colors of the city seem to run into one long wet mess, as though water had spilled over some artist's painting. Below him, people scurried to cars and taxis with umbrellas fighting the wind, or newspapers held over their heads as makeshift cover from the sudden spring shower.

"Hey..." an Italian-accented voice confronted him.

The sudden voice nearly made him jump out of his skin. He would have thought that after all these years he would have been used to it. It was always like this with Victor's people. He recognized the soft, almost silky, accented voice of Leonardo Tagretta. He spun around, but he truly didn't hold any anger. Perhaps the only anger was at his own conscience.

Surprisingly, Leonardo came over and forcefully motioned him away from the window, glanced around outside and then lowered and closed the blinds. "Like Martel mentioned before, there going to be more people here to keep eye on Victor. Some will be dressed like police or detectives, OK?" he softly soothed the doctor. Before the doctor could even mutter a complaint Len continued smoothly. "Is for everyone's protection, even yours, *Dottore*." He nodded towards the window. "You might not want to do so much window gazing, yes?" Tagretta was an illegal immigrant directly from Sicily, a capo sent as a representative of the Bonnaro Family, and his accent and deceptively silken voice seemed to make even the harshest restrictions sound as though they were good things, gentle things.

"Now you're telling me what I can and can't do in my own hospital?" Weintraub growled in a low, angry voice.

"No, not at all." Len soothed the ruffled doctor, "Just for safety, for Victor. You understand?" Leonardo was in his late thirties with blue-grey eyes and dark brown, shoulder-length hair he kept tightly tied back in a neat ponytail.

"God, these kids seem so young nowadays," John Thomas thought to himself, "The 'new Mafia'." He barely shook his head. If John Thomas knew how many men Leonardo Tagretta had beaten and killed over the years, he may have not thought him so wet behind the ears; the Mafia in Southern Italy and Sicily was far more violent and cruel than here in the States.

Tagretta seemed determined to not let the doctor get a word in edgewise. He had his orders from Martel. He also knew of the doctor's harmless grumbling, it was merely the doctor's way to let off steam and stress. "Martel not be able to come here for a little while, maybe several days. He make it very clear that I was to make sure all was OK, here. You know, for Victor, yes?" Leonardo eyed the doctor levelly.

John Thomas had long ago given up on ordering the men to do anything, even here in his own hospital. It wasn't like they rode roughshod over him, but with quiet, unbending finality, wherever Victor was, whatever concerned Victor, there they were; Victor's silent, dark sentinels. And no one, not even a prestigious doctor and surgeon at the big hospital was going to tell them what to do concerning their Padrone, their Boss and leader.

Leonard Tagretta decided to ask the doctor something he did know about, something to take his mind off all these new men in the wards watching over Victor. "How's Victor doing, *Dottore* Weintraub, eh?" Len asked softly, guiding the conversation back to his boss.

Always so softly this Len Tagretta spoke, John Thomas noted with amusement. Tagretta probably sounded the same way when he was ordering someone's execution as well. "It's a fucking miracle..." John said as he sank wearily into the chair behind his desk and in his eyes, it truly was. Victor had seemed to make an immediate perk-up with the new kidney, and even the girl, whom John Thomas had been sure was going to perish in the surgery, stubbornly refused; absolutely refused to give up. Rarely did John resort to stronger epithets than "shit," but this truly was a fucking miracle.

"Angels were watching over him, my friend." John Thomas conceded, "He's a strong man, Victor is. We will have him out of here as soon as possible. He's my dear friend as well, Len."

"I know." The elegantly dressed man nodded, rebuttoning his expensive black leather jacket. "And we all deeply appreciate that *Dottore.* Truly we do." He slipped a small package out of his breast pocket and gently placed it on the doctor's desk. "The angels will take care of you too." Len spoke sincerely, hinting at the added protection for the doctor, and his earlier act of closing the blinds. Any sniper worth his salt could have taken out the good doctor, and these were dangerous times, especially now with the D'Salvatore war gearing up into high throttle.

"What's this?" John Thomas's eyes narrowed a bit suspiciously at the package. It had ROLEX printed neatly on the box, and somehow John Thomas knew it contained exactly what it said, perhaps a few of them. "You don't need to bribe..."

Len cut him off as though the words that the doctor spoke were blasphemous. Even though his voice was still soothing, low, Tagretta's eyes darkened momentarily. "Is not bribe." He closed his hand harshly around the doctor's' forcing him to hold the package, almost a little too roughly, as if controlling a sudden insult. "We all know you be very busy with Victor lately, and the girl. It not leave much room to see other patients, yes? You're a stand-up guy, someone who is a dear friend to Victor. He know this; I know this, all the men kicked in for this. Is our way of saying thank you. Understood?" Leonardo left no room for argument and slowly removed his hand from the doctor's.

"Martel, he will call you soon," Len finished, "In meantime stay away from windows." Len cut off any further rebuffs or questions from John Thomas. "All of us are a very grateful to you. All of us." He nodded at the package and then with no other words, turned and left.

After Len had quietly left the office, John carefully opened the box. He was right; it did contain two Rolex watches, the most expensive ones, along with several neatly folded hundred dollar bills. "Shit," John grumbled under his breath and put the package in his desk drawer then locked it. It was not the first time that Victor's associates had given him these tokens, and almost always with the same words.

Alyssa awoke groggy and disoriented. Slowly it came back to her: Victor, his sudden illness and her willingness to donate a kidney to him. That whole scene in Dr. Weintraub's office as the men had rushed in the half-conscious Victor. As she awakened a bit more, she noted her back and side ached and burned. A drugged grogginess seemed to settle on her. She was aware of all the IV tubes around her. In her hand was some kind of push-button control. She vaguely remembered some nurse or maybe it was Dr. Weintraub, telling her to push the button whenever the pain was biting at her. She pushed it and felt something sliding down the IV into her arm. Already it was beginning to smother her again in warm, comforting sleep.

"Victor!" her mind fought the welcoming sleep; she struggled to snap her attention to the old man, "what had happened?" She turned her head to the left and saw him. He was in a bed next to her, actually awake. In fact he was partially sitting up and watching TV, oblivious to all the tubes stuck into him as well.
"Oh, thank God!" her mind sighed. The surgery must have worked; the old man didn't look so yellow or gaunt any more. He appeared weary, but when his eyes turned and briefly regarded her, she saw the dark-fire, his lucidness, the deep passion in him still there.

As though sensing her looking at him, Victor turned and smiled lightly at the girl. "Sleep, my dear child," he soothed, as though reading her mind. "You have earned it. Everything is going to be all right now. I thank you for your gift; now sleep and heal." His voice was rough and hoarse, but strong life flowed within him.

Those eyes held her; even in his healing state they spoke volumes and showed his quiet command, the depths of his soul and his strength. Any hint of vulnerability she had seen was gone. She tried to numbly move her lips, until she remembered she couldn't talk; the medicine she had self-injected was now taking effect and putting her into a soft, safe, pain-free sleep.

The next several days were as foggy as the rest of her memories. A catheter had been removed from her, IV's had been changed out, her surgical wounds checked. She remembered voices coming and going, all of them talking to Victor. She remembered some of the voices; the angry Panther, Joshua, the large, Dragon, Martel, and Weintraub's voice.

Time in the hospital had little meaning to her. It was either wake to pain or fall asleep to morphine; bandages, IV's and surgery sites, rechecked by Weintraub, Tommy or some other nurse, and so it cycled.

At one point she vaguely remembered awakening and Martel looming over her, looking down directly at her. His eyes seeming to bore into her soul, she had involuntarily shuddered for a moment, but his large hand then rested gently on her shoulder. What she really remembered was those compelling, blue eyes of his. They seemed to see through her, deep inside. For once, he was talking to her alone. "Thank you, Alyssa," had been his simple comment. His hand had lingered on her shoulder and then briefly touched her cheek. For the barest of instances, the hardness in his eyes lifted and she thought saw deep compassion in them. The gratitude in his eyes spoke volumes above his spoken word. Once again the soothing, pain-free darkness engulfed and cradled her.

Tito D'Salvatore sat back in his living room as he lit a big cigar, the TV playing some wrestling program in the background. He was still old-school enough to have some kind of noise running in the background when he discussed business with his Top Administration. He knew the only out-of-prison Boss was one who kept his secrets and plans silent from the prying ears and tapes of the F.B.I.

"So?" he took a long drag off his freshly lit stogie as he glanced with narrow eyes at his underboss Joey and his consigliere Johnny. "Is that thing with the Armandanas planned and settled?"

"Yeah, it's taken care of." Baldovino got up and grabbed a fresh beer from the bar. "We got two of your most trusted men going down there, Tony Trevello and that new skipper, Richie."

Tito nodded a moment, "I want my son Torenzo going along this time." He glanced up, "He needs to be given more responsibility, needs to get more involved."

"On this thing, with the Armandanas?" the small underboss asked half-shocked.

"Yeah, on this thing," Tito narrowed his eyes dangerously at Calendri, "Tony has been with me since the beginning, since he and I were just soldiers. He will be heading the negotiations, but Torry needs to be schooled in this, understand?" he jabbed his cigar for emphasis.

"All right, all right." Calendri sat back in his seat; he wasn't going to dare argue with the Boss.

"This other thing, with our independent friend out in California, I want you to handle that personally, Joey." Tito continued. "You got plane tickets to leave soon. I want Gambini on this and no one else. I know for a fact that Jerome is going personally down there to fuckin' Jamaica, and I don't trust anyone from our own outfit to take him out." The insult was definitely implied in his statement.

"Frankie was successful so far in making contact with that Jerome capo," Johnny interrupted as he turned up the TV slightly, glancing at the wrestling program on the screen, then sitting back down with his beer, "Looks like Paulie will leak out information, he is greedy and that is good for us." He winked, and they all had a quick chuckle.

Tito stretched out on his favorite recliner as he drank from his own beer, "That's good news indeed." He said idly, "But I got some other plans on the back burner as well, some additional help of my own."

"Like what?" the consigliere shot him a quick look.

"Never you mind for now," Tito gave a rather brief but smug look, "It isn't time to reveal those plans yet. But I swear this now on my father's grave, God rest his soul," Tito briefly crossed himself, "The Jeromes are finished this time, period, no ifs ands or buts. And, I will have you know, that Calavicci is now on the Commission, they are very good friends of ours and have promised to support us in our upcoming move against the Jeromes."

"They damn well better," Joey nodded in agreement, "After all, it was a lot of our money and support to them and to Antonio Giancomo that got the Calavicci's into the Commission up there."

Tito just nodded with a noncommittal grunt, "The Calaviccis and Giancomos support us fully, believe me. And I will be honest; as much as Del Giornos and Corellas vocally support the Jeromes they are probably only doing so because they don't want the Jeromes to turn on them next. I still cannot believe Victor had the balls to do what he did to Vito Roman. He is going to alienate himself from the other Commission Families, and that will be his undoing. You think any other Commission Families want to be next to be fuckin' humiliated and tossed out on their ass?"

"*Madonn*! Did you see that?" Baldovino interrupted suddenly as he pointed to the wrestling match on TV, "That guy just beat the snot out of him with that metal chair!"

"It's all fake, you *idiota*!" Tito growled at his consigliere, "Don't you know that? All that shit is fake." He shook his head.

"I knew it was fake." Calendri piped up in an almost sycophantic way, "I can't believe you thought it was fucking real, Johnny."

Tito rolled his eyes in disgust; he was beginning to feel he had the most inept underboss and consigliere on the East Coast. He knew they weren't going to be discussing any more business today, and he vowed to keep his plans and machinations to himself. "*Stronzo bastardo's*" he mumbled under his breath.

CHAPTER 9- *April 25th 1987*

"Why are we out here and that, empty suit, in there with Martel, huh?" Tommy DeLuca glanced at the huge limo as he pulled his sport coat tighter around him. He dragged deeply on his cigarette and looked around the desolate, rural countryside.

"Maybe they want some privacy, eh?" The older man nudged him, lighting up his own cigarette. "Besides, you, wanna be in there with da man Martel?" Paulie looked at the younger man with a knowing nod and then making a gun with his index finger and thumb lightly touched his finger to the side of his head; it was the universal sign of a mob execution.

"Yeah, yeah." Tommy said lightly but inside he felt an involuntary shudder. Paulie was probably right.

Tommy was one of the youngest of the Jerome Family soldiers; in fact, the last one before the Family had "closed the books" and decided not to take in any more made men. Tommy remembered his own ceremony less than seven months ago, that ice- cold underboss Martel had been in there, along with his sponsor Paulie Verro, Joshua and the "zip" Leonardo.

There was something about that underboss Martel that always seemed to turn Tommy's blood cold. Perhaps it was the giant man's, mob nickname, "The Undertaker." It was rumored and joked about by the Jerome men that Martel had well over one hundred killings under his belt, but it was more than that. It was as if the rugged giant had no heart or soul, like he could turn it on or off, be as cold as ice. Tommy had never seen an ounce of feeling from the underboss; even when most of the other men joked around, Martel seemed to hold back somehow. He never really seemed to trust anyone, never let anyone in and yet seemed to be able to get inside anyone else, be able to read their soul. It was those eyes, those cold, piercing eyes. They were like the Boss's, Don Victor's. Paulie had once jokingly told him that both Victor and Martel had eyes that were more accurate than any lie detector, and Tommy fully believed it.

Tommy was lucky. Shortly after being made, he had been given a great honor and been asked to come work at the Jerome mansion, a very coveted position that even seasoned men like his skipper Paulie Verro had not been granted.

Tommy DeLuca had been in the Army for three brief years as an Army medic and knew some doctoring, having the equivalent of an R.N, and since he helped Doc Weintraub a lot on the Jerome Estates, he figured maybe that was why the big bosses had granted him this nice transfer. Although, like today, he was expected to do the same dirty work as any soldier. He took another drag off his cigarette and glanced around. He could barely hear the subdued voices of the two men inside the car. Mostly, it was Danny MacCloud's voice.

Danny was what mobsters called an "empty suit." Someone who had no chance of ever becoming a made man, but who so loved the lifestyle of the mobsters that he hung around all the wiseguys and made men, acted like one and tried to get into their good graces just so he could brag to his friends he knew connected people. Tommy had his own nickname for them; he called them "Mob Groupies."

Martel had told Paulie and Tommy to pick up Mr. MacCloud from his usual Saturday route in South Jersey. Unfortunately for Danny MacCloud, he normally hung around the D'Salvatore wiseguys. Near South Jersey was strictly D'Salvatore turf and Tommy felt nervous even being here, what with the war gearing up and all.

Unconsciously, his hand slid under his sport coat and touched his Glock 9 millimeter he kept in his concealed shoulder holster. He knew better than to even dare question the intimidating Martel. After all, Tommy was just a soldier and whether it was taking care of strange injured women who suddenly showed up at the Jerome Estates or picking up local empty suits for the bosses, his was not to question why, just to do. He glanced at his friend and sponsor Paulie again, both men grinned lightly for a second, Paulie settled his shoulders inside his expensive overcoat, and the two went back to scanning the empty countryside for any suspicious activities or witnesses.

Danny MacCloud was simply ecstatic to be here in the car with Laurence "The Undertaker" Martel. In his late forties, Danny was a tiny speck of a man who wore outrageously loud, expensive suits, tons of jewelry, most of it not the real stuff, and often spoke in an exaggerated, hyped-up, mobster speak. The man was a living parody, some awful imitation of something out of *The Godfather* or *Goodfella's*. And now, the number two man of the Jerome Family, the head *Brugad* of the Commission was talking to him. Maybe he would be made yet.

So far, Laurence had been stroking the man's ego, letting him say whatever he wanted, ask whatever he wanted. His tactic had worked, and soon Danny MacCloud was speaking with such a loose tongue it amazed the quiet underboss. It disturbed Martel deeply that even though the man was not made, he had heard an awful lot hanging around the fringes of the D'Salvatore Family, far too much. It reminded Laurence that he was going to have to order his own men to censor themselves more strictly when speaking in public, to enforce and find even more secret meeting places, lest the empty suits that hung around the Jerome Family territory learn as much as this loose cannon.

"Excellent, excellent, Mr. MacCloud," Laurence leaned back, his eyes half lidded. Martel had already given the man a large envelope of cash, which had fueled MacCloud to spill even more information. "You know, there may be a place for you yet in the Jerome Family. I mean, I might sponsor you myself." Laurence teased the mobster wannabe.

"Oh yeah?" the man growled in his exaggerated New Jersey accent. "I would be a good earner for you, ya know? I mean hey whaddever you guys tell me to do, hey, bada bing, bada boom. I'll do for ya."

"I'm sure you would," Laurence began slowly drawing in his noose now. "Tell me: has there been some talk in your neck of the woods, maybe something about someone from outside the D'Salvatores being brought in to do a job?" he finally asked what he wanted to know. Either the man would be of use to him, or else all this had been in vain.

"Yeah, yeah!" Danny sat up excitedly, his cheap jewelry clanking around. "I heard Tito's underboss, Calendri, saying something about looking to hire someone called..." he paused, searching his mind for the elusive name. It wasn't one used very often, especially since the name he heard was a man who was a freelancer, someone not connected with any particular Family. "Um, Louis, Louie, Garibaldi? Nah, dat wasn't it." he said, a bit pissed at himself for forgetting his stuff, especially in front of the Jerome underboss.

"Gambini?" Laurence asked levelly.

"Yeah! Yeah, dat was it, Louie Gambini!" Danny piped up enthusiastically.

Laurence Martel sat back and closed his eyes for the briefest of moments. Louie "Kohana" Gambini was Martel's counterpart, the only man that Martel thought of as his equal in the realm of hits, murder-for-hire contracts and a host of other solo jobs like arson, kidnapping and strong-arming. Martel had a lot of respect for Gambini; he was good at what he did, accurate and deadly. If any other man could legitimately claim a number of murders even near Martel's, it was Louie Gambini. Gambini had been sought after by the best of crime Families. Although he claimed the West Coast as his home, Louie had firmly resolved to be an independent, a gun for hire, and next to Martel, he was the best. Martel's heart both rose at the thought of taking out his greatest equal and nemesis and sank at the thought that D'Salvatore had brought in the best hitman to use against the Jeromes.

Martel's lips thinned a bit at the man's name, but he showed no emotion that Danny would have ever caught on the stone-cold underboss's face. "Very good, Danny," Laurence allowed a brief smile at MacCloud as he shifted around and fully faced the man. "You have proven your worth here today to me."

If Danny would have had even an ounce of intelligence or truly known the quiet, deadly underboss, he would have known Martel's smile to be not of friendliness but of the satisfied dragon closing in on its prey. Before Danny could even draw another breath, Martel exploded with such lightning-fast reflexes Danny never saw it coming.

One of the Martel's large hands clamped down over the small man's nose and mouth as Martel's other arm came out and grabbed Danny's shoulder in a vice-like grip. With a twist as easy as someone opening the top of a bottle of soda and with the same horrible crunching sound, Laurence Martel expertly snapped the hapless man's neck. Danny MacCloud was dead before he knew it. Danny's reward for his information had been a quick, painless, death.

Martel rapped on the window, causing Tommy and Paulie to hurriedly get back into the front seat. Neither looked into the backseat; they both knew what Martel had done, for both had heard the hideous snap of the man's neck even outside the car.

"First we put our friend deep into the woods, and then we head back home," were Martel's only instructions.

"No problem, Boss," Paulie said from the passenger seat. He gave Tommy a discreet poke in his ribs, encouraging him to start the car and follow Martel's orders, especially since Tommy had a sudden distinct green paleness to him. Paulie knew what lay ahead; Martel was going to have them dismantle the body. He hoped his newest soldier wouldn't lose it on his first gruesome assignment. Paulie had worked with Martel before, so he knew what to expect, and he also knew Martel had little patience for those who weren't up to the task of efficient killing and dismantling. Butchering the meat, Laurence "The Undertaker" Martel called it.

Tommy's color had quickly come back, and he rammed the car into gear to get out of there, his eyes too nervous to look into the rearview and meet Martel's.

Two days later, Paulie Verro settled himself at his club and strip joint, The Harem, on the outskirts of the New York-New Jersey border. Here is where he did most of his work, running his crew and earning his points. He knew the D'Salvatore territory pretty well; it was one of the reasons Martel had ordered him along with Tommy to pick up that little wannabe punk, MacCloud.

"Hey Paulie!" a heavyset man came in and sat down near the back with him. Paulie's men raised no eyebrows; they knew these two were friends and doing business for the last several months. What Paulie's men did not know was that the man was one of D'Salvatore's many capos.

"Hey Frankie," Paulie quickly embraced the man, then ordered one of the topless waitresses to bring the newcomer a drink. "I wasn't expecting you today."

"You're doing good things, Paulie," the man flashed a grin, and pulled out a thick envelope. With a practiced move, he slipped the envelope under the table to Paulie's hand before he could say a word.

"Hey, hey…" Paulie warned, "Yer takin' a risk, eh?" he warily raised an eyebrow.

"No place to talk business here; come on back to the office."

After the waitress delivered their drinks, the two men got up and walked to the office.

Paulie knew he was playing a most dangerous game, a very dangerous one indeed,

but he was fed up and tired. Years he had been loyal to the Jeromes, years he had busted his ass, earned points and supported the boss and his regime. But time after time, had they passed him over for promotion and earning opportunities. "Instead fat fucks like Cesare, and boy-wonder Tommy, are getting the promotions and I am stuck at the rat's ass end of town," he thought angrily to himself.

Nearly a year ago, he had been approached by a "friend of a friend", a capo in the D'Salvatore Family who had promised Paulie a far bigger take, promotion and prestige in the D'Salvatore Family.

So far, Paulie had done very well for himself; he had gotten some rich payoffs from his friend Frankie, and so far they had not asked him anything he felt uncomfortable about. He was getting the best of both worlds, and Paulie saw that as his ace in the hole, his fair due. After all, it had been Paulie who had known about the whereabouts of Danny MacCloud after a tip-off from Frankie. Did Paulie know he was playing a bit of a risk? Yeah, but life was a bit of a risk, and he saw this as being a good thing. After all, wasn't he helping out here? Hey, he had found MacCloud, he was doing his part and he was earning a little extra income for himself, what the fuck?

"Come in, come in." Paulie let Frankie into the office.

"Ah, Paulie, my friend," Frankie glanced around at the pictures of nude women that hung on the wall and the closed circuit security camera monitors, which allowed anyone in the office to see what was going on in the strip club area. He sat down and relaxed savoring the drink. "Shit's gonna get tough for awhile, you know that, right?" Frankie fished a cigarette out of his pocket.

"Yeah, I know." Paulie nodded, offering to light the other man's cigarette. "Look, shit is quiet now, though, right? You promised me you'd let me meet with the Boss, Tito soon."

"I know, my friend; he has been busy, though. " Frankie inhaled deeply, "In a month or two, D'Salvatore is gonna open his books, I promise; I have already been whispering in his ear about you. He wants to meet you too, eh? He's got a place for you, Paulie; I told him of the hard work you do. Tito thinks it's stupid, that the Jeromes waste you out here like this, hard earner that you are."

"I know," Paulie agreed sullenly, "But what to do? Martel's got me running around like his personal bitch with all these extra activities!"

"Patience, patience, my friend," Frankie soothed. "Soon you will be with us; you will be safe when the Jeromes fall, eh? I promise you. I've always promised you. Just keep doing what you have been, helping us with information."

Paulie just nodded as he leaned back, relaxing now. Frankie was his friend; Paulie was certain that he was going to jump a sinking ship and end up on the winning side. As the two drank and talked, Paulie griped and moaned about his bosses and his dilemma, and Frankie sympathetically listened to every word, storing the information as if his mind were a computer. For now at least, Paulie was content with extra money, lots of extra money, but it was an investment well spent for the D'Salvatores.

Later that night, Paulie and his manager, Ricardo, counted the part of the profits from his daily take that would be kicked up the chain to Martel, his tribute, the boss's cut. "Hey good take tonight, huh Ricardo?" Paulie grinned, "Here, you worked extra hard," he shoved a couple hundred to his soldier and club manager. "I gotta hot date with my *comare*, Rinella, so I'm outta here. Catch ya tomorrow."

No sooner than Paulie had left the club, Ricardo walked over to the pay phone and dialed the number he had called a few times in the last previous weeks.

"Hey," he whispered to the silent Jerome family underboss on the other end, once the phone was answered. "That visitor was here again. I am sure the tapes recorded everything in the office. You want me to ship the copy to DeLuca?"

Ricardo listened carefully to the underboss's terse answer at the other end; the cold, deep voice of "The Undertaker" made him so glad he was not going to be on the receiving end of what was in store for his traitorous capo, Paulie. Ricardo only prayed he would not be asked to be there when the sentence was finally passed down and executed. "Yeah, I got it." Ricardo confirmed at the few instructions from Martel and then hung up the phone.

The days drifted in and out for Alyssa, and it wasn't until around day five that she finally fully awoke and was able to stay awake and alert. Her eyes had fluttered open, but what had shocked her most was that she awoke to Victor Jerome sitting in a wheelchair, his old hand clasped strongly and reassuringly onto hers.

"Hello child," he smiled. "You were struggling a bit as you woke up. I figured I'd come over and sit with you a while." He gave her hand an extra squeeze and then released it. "Dr. Weintraub told me of the precious gift you gave, donating a kidney to me." He nodded at her; that slight smile playing on his wrinkled face, those piercing dark eyes seeming to search her soul. "I am grateful, very grateful. Why did you do it?" He used the electric button on her bed to raise it up and handed her a notebook and pen that rested next to her nightstand.

"*Because*," she wrote, with a shaky hand, still weak, "*You saved my life. Even though I still remember none of it, I know that you took me in and gave me a place to stay, it's only fair the favor be repaid.*" She handed him the notepad.

A strange kind of smile lingered on his face, "Perhaps. It was a noble gift you gave me, one you certainly didn't have to and one that means than more you can ever comprehend." He leaned over and kissed her once on each cheek. After settling back in his wheelchair, he looked at her with a conspiratorial grin, "I say we bust out of here, kiddo." The fire still burned deep in those dark eyes, "I hate hospitals; I say we get Weintraub and Martel to spring us out of here and take us home." He gently patted her hand again.

She nodded in agreement. Then fumbling for the pad, wrote, "*I'm dying of thirst, is there anything to drink?*"

Victor slowly eased himself out of the wheelchair and sat next to her on her bed. He poured a glass of ice water from the bedside pitcher and then gently cradled her head with one arm and helped her steady the glass in her shaking hands, quenching her parched throat and lips.

What really began to bother Alyssa at this point was that Victor seemed to be recovering so well and yet she still felt so weak and frail, almost helpless.

As though reading her mind Victor softly spoke, "Easy Alyssa, we'll build you back up in no time. You've barely recovered from your first accident before undergoing this surgery." He nodded sagely and replaced the cup on the bedside. "We'll build you up right as rain in no time, eh?" he assured her.

With much wheedling and finally downright cantankerous demanding, Victor had indeed gotten himself and Alyssa released from the hospital and to his private home back upstate two days later. And only then because Dr. Weintraub and Tommy and he would be watching both patients constantly for the next couple weeks at the private Jerome clinic.

Joey Calendri, underboss to the D'Salvatore Family was already tired from the red-eye flight from New York to Los Angeles. Now he was here sitting in the warm California sunshine at some outdoor Bistro, with the infamous Louie Gambini. Joey thought the man a complete fruitcake but he had his orders, and his boss had wanted Louie Gambini for this hit and no one else.

Gambini sat across from him, sipping an iced cappuccino. Golden-blonde haired, long legged and tanned, dressed like half the other wild surfer-Hollywood types in a loud Hawaiian shirt and raggedy chino shorts. Gambini's mother was full Cheyenne Indian and he often used his Indian nickname "Kohana" when doing any kind of mercenary business. At age 35, Louie looked nearly 10 years younger than his real age.

Weird or not, Joey couldn't help but feel a little unnerved knowing that this casual looking surfer-type had probably killed more than 150 people, as well as done thousands of other countless dirty work and brutal jobs for various Crime Families all over the US. Next to the infamous Laurence "The Undertaker" of the Jerome's, this was the only man who came close to that league of assassination success and he was about to be paid to assassinate the best. Don Victor Jerome himself.

"Here," Joey shoved the briefcase with his foot towards Gambini, "there is the first half of your payment as well as a roundtrip ticket in there for the specified dates in October." Joey fiddled with his sunglasses against the overly bright Los Angeles sunshine and yellow glare of the air around the city.

"Cool..." Gambini nodded and then stretched out on the chair like some half bored gangly kid. He squinted up through his round blue tinted sunglasses at the sun, "I gotta go catch some waves here soon dude, so is like our business concluded or what?" He seemed to arrogantly smirk at Calendri with his every word or gesture.

This casual disregard for him and half-assed seriousness grated on Joey's last nerve. He was used to the way things were done on the East Coast, this Hollywood surfer type paid him no more mind or respect than if Joey was some casual empty suit, instead of the underboss of the D'Salvatore Family who had just delivered a partial payment of 60 grand in that briefcase. "Look," Joey said darkly, "can you do this thing or are you just going to jerk my chain, my 'Dude' friend, cause if not..."

Louie's hand shot out like lightning and with a strength that was both surprising and painful, grabbed Joey's wrist. "Hey relax man..." Gambini said still in that same casual voice, but Joey felt a sudden chill creep over him. Especially when he felt the cold steel of a gun trained on his crotch under the table. "You paid for the best remember? How the fuck do you care how I operate as long as you get what you paid for... *capisce*?"

Joey's wrist hurt where the half Italian-half Cheyenne hitman was holding him in an iron grip his face still casual as though nothing was going on between them, Joey dare not make a scene. He needed to hire this idiot, this whole plan of Tito's had been hinged on hiring Gambini no one else could even come close to succeeding. "Yeah, fine. Let go you fuck." Joey hissed malevolently under his breath.

Gambini released him with a chortle and just as smoothly slipped his steel plated 9mm back in his waistband while Joey rubbed his wrist, it felt nearly broken where the bones had ground together.

"Gotta go, dude..." Louie purposefully used the term at Joey Calendri, "The surfs up. Tell your boss Tito, thanks for the lunch money." After downing the rest of his iced cappuccino he picked up the suitcase, felt the heft of it for a moment as though gauging its contents and then walked casually off with not even a glance back.

Joey sat there mumbling, hatred in his voice. His damn wrist was still sore and he was not going to get any sleep yet. He had 2 hours to catch the plane out of L.A.X, back to New York. At least he had done his part; it was up to Gambini to do the rest in a few months. And if he didn't, Joey had half a mind to hire someone himself to take out the punk, Gambini. Before he hit the LA Airport, Joey called home to Tito. "It's done. The guy is a prick, but it's done."

Tito seemed to sigh with relief on the other end. "Excellent my friend, our work with Jerome's wannabe turncoat is proving productive as well. See me after you get in, your going to like the news and reward I have for you." Tito hung up.

"Fuck..." Joey mumbled to himself. He was definitely not going to get any decent sleep anytime soon. He'd be lucky of he could get an hour or two on the flight. He never did like airplanes; they were always so chilly inside, like the middle of winter.

For two days Alyssa had been just resting and lazing around in her room at the Jerome Estates again. She was actually glad to see Tommy and he seemed genuinely glad to see her back as well. Even though they talked about nothing but neutral topics, he was a huge help to her and was always taking care of her bandages or even massaging cramped up muscles. Mainly he talked about how happy everyone was that Victor was back home and what a "good thing" she had done donating a kidney to him. She was spared having to go down to breakfast, as Tommy had brought breakfast up to her the last several days, including his own; coffee that was more cream than coffee, and his usual toast or Danish.

As they finished up, he walked over to the dresser and pulled out a brand new folded set of sweat pants and a work out shirt. "After breakfast I got something fun for you to do." He smiled warmly, "So eat up, you finally get to leave this room." He said.

After meeting a few of Victor's men like Martel and Joshua, she didn't know how excited she was about the prospect of leaving the sanctuary of this room. Tommy left a few minutes later and she puttered around for a while, combing out her hair and changing into the workout suit.

There was a knock on the door and expecting Tommy, she was surprised when Victor himself came in. He walked in, using a cane to steady himself and carrying another but he moved surprisingly well, his strength and recovery time had been amazingly fast. He smiled warmly at her and handed her one of the canes as he gave her a quick, light smile. "Ah, you're looking much better, child." He nodded.

Alyssa sighed and looked up at him. Her uncle must have the constitution of a freight train, she decided. She felt worn out already and all she had done was eaten breakfast and done her morning hygiene routine.

"Now, now." Victor chided gently but firmly, "Worrying and self pity won't heal you Alyssa. As I said, you have fought a double round. You were not even recovered from your accident when you gave me the precious gift of your kidney. As one who had none working, of course my recovery would be faster." He winked knowingly and nodded, "Now come, follow me".

She nodded at him then using her cane doggedly followed him through the twisting hallways and steps of his huge mansion. Although he was dressed casually today, a dark blue polo shirt and neatly pressed chino pants, he still projected an air of charismatic nobility around him. "Always so elegant, Victor is." she thought to herself.

Victor paused once or twice to let her catch up to him as he eyed her with a glint of amusement in his dark eyes. It was as though he knew she was running him through the computer of her mind; trying to study him and figure him out.

If someone were to ask her what she saw in Victor's personality that was so charismatic or what drew her utter attention to him, she couldn't tell you. But Victor with his sage leadership, presence and force of personality was like a blinding light. A bright, fiery, sun that seemed to overshadow and engulf everyone else and like a moth on a hot summer night she was instinctively drawn to that light of his personality, his natural command and his sheer presence.

It perhaps was the one intangible thing about him that drew the other 300 people in the vast Jerome Family to him as well; the thing that had allowed him to make the meteoric climb to Don of his own Family in such a short time. The man had charisma and presence that seemed to outshine everything around him. He was both ultimate civility and raw emotion in the same breath, logic and chaos; he was a leader, a mentor, a father, and a devil.

No, not Alyssa nor probably anyone else who knew Victor could put a finger on exactly what "it" was about the man. But he inspired loyalty and he commanded respect. He could stun his adversaries with the very depth of his anger at times but his drive and belief was so contagious that one felt they could do anything; anything at all, if Victor suggested it. And so Alyssa followed him down those hallways of his massive house, pushing herself not out of fear of him but intrigued and obsessed like the moth relentlessly trying to bask in the presence of that great light.

Victor finally stopped outside a set of large wooden double doors. "Now child, we will heal you and build you back up." He pushed open the doors and beyond him Alyssa was amazed to see a rather good-sized, complete gymnasium.

She followed him while looking around her mouth half agape. Surrounding her were various weight machines and other weight training equipment, including benches and free weights. Against two of the walls there were also several treadmills, a couple exercise bikes and even a rowing machine. Most of the weight machines and free weight areas at the other end currently had several men using them, some chatting together, some watching the TV that was tuned into CNN news. On the other side of the gym were mats, and various punching bags and such. A few other men were dressed in work out clothes or even martial arts gear and were practicing boxing or martial arts. She could just smell the reek of male testosterone in here. With a slight chill she noticed Laurence Martel dressed in black martial arts robes, instructing another man on perfecting some kind of martial arts moves in the corner.

Victor touched her arm and pointed to the large boxing ring in the center of the room they had been walking up to. "The martial arts are a very, common sport around here." He casually regarded Alyssa, "My men need something creative to relieve their pent up energy." He chuckled slightly at some private joke. He suddenly turned his attention to that sparring ring "Good work Joshua!" he called aloud, his full focus on the two men in the ring.

Alyssa noticed then that the 'Panther' Joshua Demonico was in that ring; he also wore dark martial arts robes and was in a martial arts stance against some other man she did not recognize. Both combatants bowed at the waist and begun another flurry of assaults on one another. Even though they had protective gear on, Alyssa could hear the force of the punches, blocks and kicks. This was not just "friendly sparring" these men were training with deadly accuracy.

So caught up in watching the two warriors going at one another, she had not noticed Martel silently sidle up to where she and Victor stood, until his deep baritone voice called out, "Remember your legs, Joshua!

Go to kill." A shudder went through her, and she noticed that now nearly all the men were watching their consigliere in the ring. Many shouted encouragements to one man or the other.

At Martel's words of advice and encouragement, Joshua waded in with even more cruel and deadly hits, the action so fast Alyssa could barely keep up. Demonico had his opponent on the defensive from the get go, indeed like a tiger closing in for the kill; he used his feet to sweep them under his opponent taking him down. The other man went down like a ton of bricks and Joshua still holding his opponents' leg spun around with lightning reflexes and bent it at an angle that made Alyssa wince inside. He dropped his knee hard on the fallen opponent's back and the man grunted something that sounded oriental, Alyssa guessed some type of "Stop!" or "I give", for immediately Joshua released him from the twisted hold. The beaten opponent dragged himself to his feet and both men bowed formally to each other.

Joshua then leaped agilely over the ropes and down near Victor, "*Padrone!*" he beamed and hugged Victor and began to chat with him briefly in Italian. The men wandered back to doing what they were before, working out at various stations, and Martel leaned in and also in Italian joined the conversation briefly. The opponent Joshua had beaten was still rubbing the bruises and soreness out of him.

After a few moments Martel left, completely ignoring Alyssa as though she hadn't even been there at Victor's side, back to working out with the two men he was instructing in martial arts.

"…But now I ask you a favor, my dear Joshua," Victor slipped back into English.

"Anything, Victor." Joshua was idly running his hands through his hair tousling it.

"She is weak from her surgery and the accident," Victor smiled benignly and put his hand on Alyssa's shoulder, "I put you in charge of a physical therapy program for her, eh?"

Joshua looked at her for the first time, eyeing her levelly for a moment. "Of course, Victor," He spoke directly back to Victor, "It is done." He assured him.

"I have business I need to discuss with you and Martel within the hour." Victor nodded to Joshua. "Alyssa," Victor turned back to her, "I leave you in Joshua's capable hands. I will see you later my dear, for now excuse me." He gave her shoulder a light squeeze of reassuring and again nodded to Joshua and then quietly left, nodding to a few men who waved or nodded in respect or happiness at the return of their *Padrone*.

She and Joshua stood there for several long seconds regarding one another in a most scrutinizing, critical way. The two cats were still very wary and untrusting of one another. "Carmine!" Joshua called without breaking his hard, cold glare on her. "Come here, I gotta job for you."

Only when the man trotted up along side Joshua did Alyssa and Josh break their staring match. "Carmine," Demonico glanced at him, it was the very opponent that Joshua had just soundly thrashed in the ring. "Victor wants his niece on a personal training plan." Joshua said arrogantly, "Since you're head of the gym, you got the job. Rebuild her up; get her on an exercise regime."

The man just nodded silently but he looked about as ticked off as Joshua was.

"And you," Joshua pointed at her, his finger mere inches from her face, "Carmine here runs our gym and for now is yer personal trainer." His Brooklyn accent barked, "You better do what he says or you deal with me and I'll end up being your personal trainer." He narrowed his gaze darkly at her, "And you won't like that, understand?" Like Carmine, Alyssa simply nodded silently, if not a bit sullenly. "Carmine also works as one of yer uncle's personal guards," Joshua half spat the word 'uncle'; "So don't go pissing him off." Without another word he turned on his heel and left the two alone.

Alyssa looked at the short, well-muscled man who resembled a pissed off pit bull and sighed deeply.

Carmine Marcallo was not in the best of moods today, especially after his martial arts instructor and the Family consigliere had given him a sound beating in front of the boss and the rest of the men. And now this job, in front of him stood the scrawniest, *mezza-morte*, weakened female he had ever seen. He had heard from Martel and the rest about 'Victor's niece'. Why oh why, did he get stuck with this stuff? Carmine sighed deeply also and began to rub his thick blocky jaw muttering every Sicilian oath and curse he knew. 'Oh well,' he decided, 'maybe the Boss would reward him for this.' He could only hope.

"Ok," Carmine said in a sharp Bronx accent. "Let's go." He proceeded to work out a plan with her and then after awhile directed her to one of the Nautilus machines. Alyssa climbed into a thing that resembled some kind of medieval torture device determined to follow his directions. The contraption even had a seatbelt that made her wonder.

Only Victor, Martel and Joshua were in the office. Joshua was livid, pacing back and forth like a caged animal, his hands unconsciously clenching and unclenching, as though he wanted to beat the hell out of someone.

With Ricardo's tip off and help, Martel had instructed a hidden video camera be placed in Paulie's office at The Harem. The three of them had just watched over 2 hours of conversations between Jerome capo, Paulie Verro and D'Salvatore capo, Frankie Scalia.

"Let me do it." Joshua glared pleadingly at Martel and Victor, "Please let me be the one to take him out. Goddamn, *cazzone stronzo* traitor!" Joshua hissed.

"Perhaps Joshua," Victor sat thoughtfully for a moment, sharing a deep look with Laurence, wanting to hear from his underboss.

"This can be a golden opportunity for us." Martel raised an eyebrow at Victor.

"Yes, yes it can, my friend." Victor ran all the moves and scenarios through his head. Paulie might be useful as a pawn in the chess game, one that could unknowingly garner them valuable information. Victor steepled his fingers under his chin, deep in thought for a moment. "Paulie's censored now of course. He's fed only what we want him to hear." He looked at Martel who nodded almost imperceptibly at Victor. Martel had hoped Victor would choose this move.

"But Victor, Laurence!!" Joshua nearly groaned with pent up rage, "He's a fucking *cafone*! Let me torture the stupid shithead and send him to the D'Salvatores with a gunshot through the mouth! He's embarrassed all of us!" Joshua was nearly yelling with anger.

"Easy Josh," Victor said in a low, warning voice. His no argument voice, "I feel your anger, we all do. You will have your chance I promise you, Paulie will be yours but not until we've had him feed the D'Salvatores what, we, want him to know." Victor sighed. His own rage was hot and intense in his heart, breeches of loyalty were his pet peeve but these things happened and now it was time to take something bad and use it for something beneficial. "We need to let the D'Salvatores get sloppy." He pinned his consigliere with his gaze, "We need to let the *nemico* think we are so busy we don't notice one *stupido cafone*."

Joshua stopped pacing and came over to Victor. He wanted to say something, but he dared not. He knew Victor was right, Joshua could only see with hatred and rage right now, not the moves on the giant chessboard of this whole war with the D'Salvatores.

"You will get your time, Josh," Victor put his hand on Joshua's shoulder. "This I promise you. Right now he is censored and it's imperative Josh that he doesn't suspect in any way you know, because you are the one he deals with. You and Martel will be slipping him the info we want him to tell to our enemies." He glanced briefly at Martel, "Make sure Ricardo is well rewarded. After all, some time soon, he will inherit that place. But make no mistake, let Ricardo know he needs to be as silent as a church mouse and be one hell of an actor also." Victor glanced at both men in turn, "If Paulie even thinks anyone knows he will bolt faster than a rat off a sinking ship."

"Understood," Martel nodded. "Another thing we need to watch," he addressed both Victor and Joshua, "are these empty suits that hang around our Family."

"You mean the Jerome Fan Club?" Joshua smirked, while hastily unwrapping a nicotine gum square.

"Yes, them." Martel looked at directly at Joshua with a frightening seriousness in his eyes, "After my interview with a certain Danny MacCloud who was a D'Salvatore fan club member, I was rather amazed by just how much these *cafones*, know. They can be every bit as damaging as a turncoat. We need to reinforce omerta and censorship among all our men. The Axel brothers have been behaving quite nicely after my little talk with them, but there are others, many others, not to mention the Feds and anyone else who has an interest in our activities."

"Very true, Martel." Victor nodded. "You, Rocco and Patrizio can run it down the line to everyone." He turned back to Demonico, "Now Joshua, my consigliere," Victor seemed to convey a hundred feelings at once with his eyes, "Yours is the most delicate job of all and one I trust you dearly with, as I would my own flesh and blood son."

Josh's rage melted away. When Victor put things like that, he would walk over hell and high water to do whatever Victor asked. The man was like his father and he loved him as one. "It is done, *Padrone*," he nodded.

Alyssa sat downstairs in the richly furnished living room/ family room. The house was overflowing with people, banners proclaiming "Welcome Home Victor" and other well wishes were hung everywhere. All around, people seemed dressed in their finest.
Although she wouldn't know them, the Top Administrations of the whole five Family Commission were here; Jerome's, Corella's, Del Giorno's, Giancomo's, the Calavicci's and a few others who had crews who worked for the above. It was a giant *Cosa Nostra* convention of the New York area underworld crime Families, an F.B.I department's wet dream of a gangland bust.

While there were many Crime Families, many bosses, capos and Administrations throughout the upper east coast, the New York area had it's own ruling Commission known as the "Five Families", it was this Commission that settled disputes, and kept some semblance of traditions, rules and order up and down the Eastern seaboard as well as indirectly influenced activities even as far away as Chicago and Miami.

These were the true 'Godfathers' of legend, the Families who had shaped the core of the Mafia in the United States. Their arbitration and word was final, their combined force or vengeance unstoppable as a whole. Many in the Mob itself considered the Five Family Commission to be the most powerful entity in the underworld. But like any other politics, some Families had more pull and influence than others and the Jerome's were at the top.

It was no secret that D'Salvatore not only wanted vengeance but wanted Victor's seat on the Commission, however that matter was only between the D'Salvatores and the Jerome's. Only the most powerful Families sat on the Commission. A Families success or overthrow on the Commission was not interfered with, as long at the dispute was with the seat member and the over-thrower only; and so long as the war did not break any rulings or passes by the Commission as a whole. Since some of the other families like the Calavicci's and the Giancomo's did indeed deal with the D'Salvatores on a friendly business basis, this *mannagge* had to be between Jerome's and D'Salvatores only, the Commission would not interfere in any way. This was an old war, The Jerome's' and D'Salvatores from far back in Commission history.

All of Victors' and all the other Commission members were here with their underbosses, consiglieres, capos, and lieutenants. This didn't even count Victor's armed guards and the several bodyguards the Commission members bought with them, as well as some of their wives or girlfriends. There were so many comings and goings of everyone it was impossible to keep a count or tell who was who.

Except for the few people Alyssa had met since she came here to Victor's house, none of these people triggered any memories or looked familiar to her; in fact the whole magnitude of the event just overwhelmed her. She was sore and tired from her earlier workout in the gym. Carmine had kept her down there for at least an hour and a half until finally Tommy had come and rescued her.

"There's going to be a big shindig tonight," Tommy had said, already he was dressed in a dark suit, more fancy than he usually was, "The boss, er, your Uncle," he corrected himself, "said you were to be there for awhile and enjoy the party. There is a dress in your room that he said you were to wear."

Alyssa had followed Tommy's instructions, showered and put on the light blue, frilly dress that had been carefully laid out by someone on the bed, along with an elegant diamond pendant that had been wrapped up as a present. "*From your Uncle Victor*" had said the small tag, no more, no less; and finally a small matching handbag, which she put in a roll of Lifesavers and her notebook and pen.

Tommy had come and led her down to the buffet area of the living room, and then at that point bowed out with the excuse, "Gotta pull duty tonight. Sorry." She had noticed him later patrolling around with the various other guards, which walked around the crowds making sure everyone was safe and happy.

So Alyssa had sat here brooding over her ever-present amnesia and her now aching and stiff muscles. She had yet to have seen Victor, she had briefly seen Joshua stalking around the crowd chatting here and there but she didn't want to give any recognition or hello to him and certainly didn't expect any in return. She was debating on slinking off back to her room in a few minutes if she didn't see Victor when she suddenly saw the huge, rotund form of Cesare "The Elf". They caught each other's eye, he smiled at her and she waved him over.

He nodded and obligingly waddled over to visit with her, panting and wheezing as he arrived. "Here, hold this sweetheart," he handed her his overflowing plate so he could pull a chair over next to her. "Okay, gimme back," he motioned back to his food once he was settled. She had to bite back a snicker; it wasn't easy for his bulk to fit in the small folding chair, with a napkin in his lap that kept threatening to fall off. She handed him his food back, and he looked at her. "Where's yours darlin'?" he asked, concern in his voice.

Alyssa kind of half shook her head indicating she wasn't hungry. She actually was, she just didn't relish being in that press of people none of whom she knew. She swore there must have easily been close to 150 people here mingling about and even spilling into the back yard.

"Not hungry?" Elf half burst out, "Look at you girl. There ain't any meat on them bones. Nonsense!" he insisted, "Yo Tony!!!" he called out to one of the guards, "Bring this girl a plate of food for me, will ya??"

Alyssa felt so embarrassed as a few of the guests turned and looked at them. This poor bodyguard was trying to shoulder his AK-47, while filling up food on a plate for her as well as a glass of red wine. After a few cringing moments, Tony came back and silently handed her a plate of food mostly filled with pasta and other Italian delicacies. She nodded a silent 'thanks' to the man, too embarrassed to meet the bodyguard's eyes as he melted back into the crowd.

"There, much better," Elf grinned while shoving some type of overstuffed lasagna into his well-exercised mouth. "You look good tonight, 'Lyss." he nodded at her in the blue frilly dress.

Alyssa looked down at the soft, blue Chantilly lace dress. It felt so stiff and formal and it was one of those deeper base instincts in her that told her usually she didn't wear such things. That she preferred far more casual attire. She nodded kindly at Cesare for the compliment, though.

"You know, Victor wanted me to get you a dress for the party so I picked up that dress for you last week while you were in the hospital. I wasn't sure what size you wore but it fits ya pretty well," Elf, casually said while mopping up red sauce with a slab of garlic bread, "of course you lost some more weight while you were in the hospital," he flashed her a quick kindly smile.

Cesare was dressed also in a sharp grey suit and tie, made of an expensive silk. "I'll certainly say this for you," he looked her up and down, "even skinny as you are, you sure look a lot better than that day I drove ya from the Roman's place."

Alyssa nearly choked on the small piece of pasta she was eating, her heart slamming up against her chest. 'At last!' She thought, 'someone who was willing to speak to her of her past!' She also was aware that if she asked too many questions or asked them the wrong way, people around here had a way of quickly clamming up. So she realized she was going to have to be very careful if she was going to get Cesare to talk to her, lest he give her the silent treatment and runaround too.

She smiled softly at Cesare and then rummaged in her small handbag and fished out her small notepad and pencil. Her hand nearly flew across the page as she scrawled, "_Yeah, I don't remember much of that day, but they said I looked pretty bad._"

"Umfmmm," Elf muttered with a full mouth, swiping at his chin with his napkin, "Yeah, you were smashed up real bad, darlin'," he continued speaking his mouth still half full. "Beat up, burnt throat and all. I was the one who carried ya back out to the car and held you while they were finishing up business," he nodded absent mindedly towards the whole general throng of the room. "It was pretty touching, even all hurt and what-not, you kinda burrowed in my arms, ya know. Like ya knew you was finally safe, so I let you know it was gonna be Ok and all. Once you was safe in the car, you just fell fast asleep. I certainly don't blame ya." She saw a hint of a dark look cross his face, briefly, and he muttered something barely audible about "the fuckin' Roman's."

Alyssa decided to lay a small risk and ask a more risky question. "_Victor sure has a lot of admirers who are happy to see him healthy and back._"

Cesare read briefly while shoveling more pasta in his mouth, "Of course!" he looked up, shocked for a moment, "Who wouldn't be happy to see the Boss back up and around, except for maybe the D'Salvatore's, the Roman's and a few others." he winked at her and chuckling at his own joke.

Alyssa's suspicions of, what, Victor Jerome did were beginning to confirm her gut instinct: That he was some kind of Crime Lord or Mafia Boss, now to ask the risky part. She decided to play her hand, either Elf would either answer her and be her ticket to figuring this all out, or he would end any further questioning right here and now. "_So,_" she scrawled on her pad, idly, "_Who is the highest ranking one here?_" She casually held up the pad to Cesare the Elf's nose and waited for what seemed an eternity.

His mouth continued slowly chewing like some contented bull. His eyes suddenly shifted over to her and fixed her under his squinting gaze. "That's it." Alyssa thought to herself with dread. "Victor must have already told him not to answer any of my questions and I crossed that fine border and pushed ol' Elf too far."

Elf studied her deeply for a moment only making her uneasiness grow by leaps and bounds until finally in a near whisper he barely spoke, "Why, Victor, of course!" in a tone that one would use with a dimwitted child who had just asked a really stupid question. He kind of shook his head and then resumed cramming more garlic bread and sauce into his mouth, "Actually," he added in his usual more jovial, conversational tone, "Even though they're all on the Commission and pretty equal, this is Victor's turf that they're all on now and our Family is the biggest. Besides, it's Victor's party." Elf chuckled again, smug in his well-versed knowledge and grinning widely at his own joke.

Usually Cesare didn't spend a lot of time at the Jerome Estates; it was only more recently that he had been closer to home. Many times he traveled with Victor's entourage whenever he was needed to drive the Boss around. Being that he was married and with a family, he lived about 18 miles west in the nearest town and only hung around the Jerome Estates when he was needed to drive or help guard or help get orders down the chain of command.

Alyssa couldn't believe her good fortune! Cesare was going to be her link to the past, her teacher to fill her in on the blank spots, at least if she could pull it off he would. Now she wouldn't have to drive Victor, John Thomas and the others nuts with her questions that were only answered with vague innuendo's and empty information, back.

She ate her food with a renewed gusto, her appetite suddenly returning. She honestly did like and trust Cesare; to her he seemed lot different than many of the other men here. More relaxed, casual and less threatening and he definitely didn't seem as intimidating as most of the men like Martel or Demonico. Even more importantly the man would talk to her and seemed to actually take a genuine interest and concern in her and she was indeed touched. Even though Cesare was obviously a part of them and occasionally wore a gun, he didn't spook her like the looming and menacing Martel, nor did she fill him with fear and anger like Joshua or Victor's other bodyguards and henchmen. Whenever Cesare saw her he was always waving or nodding hello or giving her some little compliment. If Victor was an "Uncle" then Cesare felt like a kindly big brother to her.

"That's it," The Elf watched her enjoying the food and smiled approvingly at her, "we'll get some meat on you yet, 'Lyss."

She asked no more questions of Cesare that night, she merely penned neutral conversation with him such as her exercise program with Carmine and how happy she was that Victor was healing so well and what the weather was like, since she had been indoors and in hospitals for the last 3 weeks or more. According to Cesare it was beginning to slip into a prematurely hot, New England, late spring.

She had not seen Victor for hours, occasionally he passed by always whispering and talking with the other well dressed men who embraced him and expressed happiness and well wishes on his recovery. But because they mainly spoke in Italian or a mix of English and Sicilian slang and in low voices, she couldn't understand any of what was being said.

At some unseen signal, nearly all the men began to slip into that room down the hall with "Office" written on it. Alyssa had passed it by earlier in the evening and there stood no less than 4 guards around it, now even more guards casually converged on the area while others went to patrol around the outside of the house.

Even Cesare heaved his bulk out of the chair as he gave Alyssa a friendly kiss on the top of her head, "It was nice chattin' with ya 'Lyss, but I gotta go. Hopefully Carmine won't be such a hard ass with his exercise program. If he is, you come tell me, Ok?" he chuckled softly at her, "I'll be around here more, so if your ever bored, come look me up." After re-buttoning his suit jacket and leaving his plate and napkin on his chair, he wandered off with the rest of the men towards the Office.

It was then Victor came up next to her, almost silently. "Ah Alyssa," he smiled warmly and then gripping her shoulders gave her a quick hug and kiss. "You look lovely tonight." He studied her, holding her out at arm's length. "Of all the gifts I have received, yours has been the most precious and a Man of Honor never forgets such a favor." He hugged her briefly again, then released her. "I have business to attend to my dear, so feel free to help yourself to whatever you like at the table. I am glad Cesare was able to keep you company awhile while I was busy. I am afraid the next several days are going to be hectic for me, but I will visit you again as soon as I can. Keep up with that schedule that Joshua and Carmine have for you and you will heal up rapidly, eh?" then he too turned and walked off after the large crowd of fellow bosses.

"Oh he is so refined and civilized Victor is," Alyssa thought to herself, "No wonder he is in the position he is." Once inside the door marked 'Office', Victor closed the door behind him with a smooth click and four more guards stood outside the door. "No one would be disturbing the meeting in there." Alyssa thought.

She had no desire to sit around and watch a bunch of guards and people she didn't know, so she began to head back upstairs. Tommy saw her and then silently fell into line behind her escorting her back to her room. She didn't bother acknowledging him, her mind was swimming with a hundred questions and thoughts, none of which made sense or sat well with her.

Later that night, while she slept in the frilly bed, under the expensive percale sheets in the richly furnished peach-pastel room, Alyssa dreamed fitful dreams: Nightmares of 1930's styled Gangsters chasing her around in their old fashioned huge Buick's and Cadillac's, fedora's perched on their heads, dressed in expensive zoot- suits and all carrying huge intimidating Thompson submachine guns. They were faceless at first but as they cornered her here on the Jerome estates and piled out of their cars, closing in on her to 'rub her out'; she recognized the faces of Martel, Joshua, Tommy, Cesare, Dr. Weintraub and others.

124

She noticed one gangster that she hadn't remembered seeing at the house but felt she should know: He was tall, unusually thin, scar faced, grimy and carried a cattle prod which he swung threateningly back and forth with a sadistic leer on his face.

Smack-dab in the middle of the bunch was Victor Jerome but he was much heavier and looked an awful lot like Marlon Brando from 'The Godfather', down to the blood red rose in his lapel. In a Brando-like voice, Victor growled, "A Man of Honor never forgets a favor, eh? But you know too much, so ...." He shrugged idly and casually motioned to his men. At his signal a thousand machine guns blazed and crackled, spitting bullets into her body which jerked around like some horrid puppet.

Alyssa awoke with a start, sitting bolt upright in bed. Her body was soaked in sweat and she hugged herself trembling and shivering, her breathing still coming in ragged gasps. She sat there in the darkness, trying to regain her composure and convince herself it was just a dream. She glanced at the clock, it was only 2:10 am, Alyssa pushed back the covers as she walked stiffly, limping to the adjoining bathroom to get a drink and wipe the sweat from her body. When she walked back to her safe and cozy bed, she stopped by the window and drew the curtain aside to briefly watch the nightly guards patrolling, many with guard dogs and large guns at their sides.

A chill ran involuntarily down her spine and she let the curtain fall back into place. She knew outside her door stood another guard, Tommy's nightshift replacement, instructed not to let her out unless Victor gave his Ok or she was accompanied at all times by one of them.

Wearily she crawled back into bed with a heaviness that rode her soul, 'It's not just a dream,' she told herself sadly, 'it's all too frighteningly real.' However she knew nothing else had no other memories or remembrances to draw on. Who knows, maybe she really was Victor's niece but somehow it didn't feel right to the deepest part of her soul. A single tear rolled down her cheek and fell onto the soft blankets around her, outside her door she heard the night guard give a cough and stretch out on his chair. 'It's not a dream.'

At 2:10am, only Victor Jerome and Laurence Martel sat in the downstairs office. It was a late night after the large party and Victor knew all of them would be only more tired in the next six days. For the last three hours these two men alone had talked about the present, plans for the future and reminiscing of the past. On the stereo classical music softly played.

"Tomorrow all of this starts up in full and we play our hand. If we are lucky, then we get the checkmate or at least a stalemate." Victor swirled the last of his sparkling red wine in his glass. "It begins what we knew would be put into motion nearly 15 years ago, my *angelo della morte.*" he put down the glass and stood up to stretch his weary legs, getting the kinks out of his aching back. He too was still recovering from the surgery and even though he felt better than he had in months, the surgery scar ached and itched incessantly.

"Joshua won't be thrilled with his part." Martel lay sprawled out on a huge recliner, one long leg over the armrest, his own wine glass almost empty as well. "He wanted to go on this run with me."

Victor sighed and then walked over to where Laurence was and stood over him. He took his old hand and cupped it behind the huge underboss's neck until both men were nearly touching forehead-to-forehead. "It's our vendetta, my son." He barely whispered. "This is for Michael and Isabella and that dark day in 1957. You are my underboss for a reason, one we have guarded dearly with blood..." he released Martel and resumed his pacing. "Soon now, after all is set in stone with our openly declaring our joining with the Bonnaro's from Sicily, we will throw down our trump card and get rid of D'Salvatores. Be well aware..." he fixed Martel with a steely stare, "Calavicci and Giancomo are secretly and strongly behind the D'Salvatores, but if we take the D'Salvatore's down, we not only keep our seat but become as untouchable as the fuckin' Holy Ghost. We reward our loyal allies Del Giorno and Corella. We took out the Romans', and we did it in a bloodless move. Calavicci and Giancomo will remain as far away from this as possible."

Martel just silently nodded. "Our revenge will be sweet *Padrone*, I only wish you could be there, with me in a few days..." he referred to the little ambush that he would be setting for Tito D'Salvatores son.

"I will be with you." Victor went back and put a tender hand on Martel's shoulder, "God only knows I will be there with you and the rest in spirit. I will feel Tito's anguish as surely as we felt our own loss for Michael." He finished the rest of his wine. "It's late now, first thing in the morning make sure to have John Thomas bought here, tell Cesare to remain here as our contact along with Rocco and while Joshua will not be thrilled about being kept out of the ambush, he will listen to you Martel. He can have Paulie in a month or more."

Martel slowly nodded; the final two moves against D'Salvatore were coming now, this first to stun and deceive and then the second several months later to finish it to the end.

The next morning at breakfast it was only Alyssa and her shadow Tommy, "The men are taking care of business," was his only flat explanation. "After breakfast report to Carmine for your continued physical therapy and what not. I may end up staying here or leaving too, I don't know yet. I know Cesare will be here, and the Doc is supposed to come here for a while, so you'll just have to play it by ear.

Your Uncle sends his regards and hopes to see you soon." It sounded suspiciously like a rehearsed speech.

She just nodded and wrote nothing. After all if Cesare were coming here, she would be able to try and talk to him as much as she could. She noticed Tommy seemed to put even more cream in his coffee and ended up not drinking half of it. What really caught her attention though, was the slight tremble in his hand. He seemed even more high-strung than usual.

Tommy had escorted her to the gym and told her Carmine would be escorting her back when she was done. Once inside the first thing she noticed was how empty, it seemed in here. Usually there were 5-12 men at any given time in here, chatting loudly, laughing, joking and being their usual testosterone hyped-up selves. But today there was an almost palpable pall around.

Carmine was already working out on a weight machine, and motioned her over. As she made her way towards him, she could see the solitary form of Laurence Martel in the far corner, back in his black martial arts gear working out solo with a martial arts training dummy and punching bag. Only one other person was here, one of the nameless guards that were off duty and running at a breakneck speed on the jogging treadmill. Sweat poured off the fellow and soaked his tank top and shorts but still he kept pushing himself as if running away or towards something very emotional.

She didn't have her notepad so she couldn't write Carmine to find out where everyone was, but then, the head of the gym was not exactly as friendly as Cesare either. The first time Alyssa had tried writing and conversing with Carmine he had half growled, "Yer here to work, girl, not blab. Just do your exercises and hush." She already knew what she was to do, and so climbed in the machine next to Carmine to do her 30 repetitions of lower backstretches on the Cybex machine. The only sound in the gym was the steady whine of the treadmill as the guard ran all out and the unusually loud, whap, whap! As Martel worked with deadly and full force kicks on the battered leather training dummy.

No sooner had she done just 5 repetitions, when the two double entrance doors slammed open with a hard thrust. She looked up and saw Joshua stalking angrily over towards where Martel was. She couldn't hear the words at first, but she could hear the tone in Joshua's voice, he seemed as pissed off and livid with rage as she had ever seen him.

By now the guard had ran himself into exhaustion and he was walking on the treadmill, cooling down. His breathing sounded ragged, sweat still dripping off him like he was in a rain shower.

She was watching Martel and Demonico intently across the room. Martel standing there with his long arms folded over his chest and Joshua with his angered voice carrying on, his hands gesturing wildly.

Martel just kept quietly shaking his head, 'no' and that just seemed to enrage Joshua even more.

Joshua was wearing designer black jeans and an expensive, white silk shirt, he suddenly began to strip off his shirt down to just his undershirt, and for a brief moment Alyssa thought he and Martel were going to fight right there and then in the corner. Martel seemed to give a resigned sigh, as he roughly threw a pair of protective martial arts shin guards, gloves and helmet over to Joshua, who seemed to be running his mouth nonstop.

Joshua was stripped to just his jeans and T-shirt and was putting on the protective gear as was Martel. "This is fucked up! You know that!" Joshua finally screamed loud enough for Alyssa and the other two men to overhear. "You know I wanted to go on that run, it is my vendetta too! Victor is like my father, I should be going on this fuckin' thing!"

Martel suddenly hissed something at Joshua far too low and quiet for Alyssa to hear. But she briefly caught Martel making some kind of gesture of pointing to his eye and growled something to Joshua in a very quiet, dangerous tone.

"Fine! Come on then!" Joshua leaped nimbly like the angered panther he was towards the roped off ring in the center of the gym, egging Martel on, not content to let whatever argument he had with Martel rest, "Come on damn it, it's not right to deny me this thing for our *Padrone!*"

Alyssa noticed that Joshua was like raw energy seeming to be all electrical and hot-blooded where as Martel was stalking over to the ring with slow deliberate steps. She could see an almost tired resolution in his stance but Martel showed no other emotion in those stone cold eyes. He even moved carefully, exacting just like a dark Dragon, she thought to herself.

"Oh, *Merde!*" Carmine grumbled beside her just barely loud enough for her to hear. "This outta be good."

No sooner than Martel had entered the ring than Joshua leapt nimbly to the center gave a quick courtesy bow and already had leapt back into a fighting martial arts stance while Martel was still completing his slow, deliberate bow. Before Martel could even assume a stance Joshua had charged him with a primal, inhuman growl of rage; his fists and feet flying with uncontrolled rage as he launch his attack at the giant.

One of Josh's legs caught Martel with a sickening '*THUD*' against his ribs but Martel seemed to ignore it and instead had easily swept one long arm up and out and blocked Josh's fist from connecting with his throat.

Josh leaped back, "Well, can I go?" he pressed.

"No!" Martel's deep voice bellowed in a warning tone.

Joshua came at him again, this time Martel met his attack and pressed forward.

The sounds of the two men's blows and kicks hitting each others bodies other were far louder than when Martel was working with the training dummy and far more vicious and deadly than when Alyssa had seen Joshua and Carmine in the ring yesterday.

The gym had come to a complete standstill. She and Carmine just sat there on their machines watching the two combatants going at each other with unrestrained blows and strikes. Even the exhausted guard just sat down on a metal folding chair watching the battle between the underboss and consigliere with his mouth hanging open. Alyssa was certain that had the two combatants not been wearing protective gear, bones would have already been broken.

The Dragon unleashed a flurry of blows that sent Joshua staggering backwards into the corner and onto his knees. Martel just stood back in a rigid, unmoving stance that reminded Alyssa of some cold-blooded cobra, waiting to strike again.

Joshua dragged himself up slowly, wavering and staggering to his feet and it was then that Alyssa saw the blood freely running all over his lips and nose, dripping darkly onto the floor of the ring. Joshua swiped at it and looked at the blood on his own fingers; with a half crazed grin he smiled dangerously at Martel. "Can I go now, *compari*? Have I earned the right now, underboss?" he asked, it sounded like a heart-felt agonizing plead, in a sad, hollow tone. As though he knew Martel could tear him apart and he didn't care.

"Do not ask me this thing, Joshua." Martel never moved an inch from his stance, his eyes still half lidded like a great serpent. "I cannot grant it to you, the answer is no." It was almost as though it pained the man to even say it, as though he could see how torn in heart and soul Joshua was, as though he knew Joshua would have resorted to this, and it hurt him to have to settle this with Joshua in this manner. Had it been anyone else daring to make this disrespectful scene or questioning his orders like this he would have probably taken them out back and killed them.

Joshua ignored the blood pouring out of his face and with renewed vigor sprang at Martel; again the two moved with such lightening speed, Alyssa could barely keep up with the action.

"He'll never win," Carmine shook his head, forgetting he was talking to Alyssa, a woman and an 'outsider' for a moment, "Fuckin' Martel is the best, he taught all of us. He's a 6th rank black belt and true Master of Jujitsu, Karate, Aikido, and Tae-Kwon-do, not to mention he knows about 4 other styles. Josh is good in Tae-kwon-do, got a black belt in that and a brown in Aikido but he doesn't know half the shit Martel does. Wonder what he is so worked up about?"

But Alyssa wasn't listening to Carmine's comments. She was too engrossed in the brutality of the Dragon vs. the Panther. Whatever it was between them, Alyssa could tell it was something very deep, very personal. Joshua was still giving every inch of his heart and soul and

Martel was easily countering it all and throwing in his own punishment. She could already see Joshua was sporting fresh bruises on his shoulders, forearms and that earlier crack to the face would probably hurt for a long while and end up needing stitches. Even Martel had angry red spots and bruises on his forearms where he had deflected the anger filled hits from Joshua.

Finally pushed too far, Martel waded in, grabbed Joshua up high over his head and then slammed him down so hard onto the canvas Alyssa felt the impact resonate inside her own bones. Martel grabbed one of Josh's legs and arm, then dropping his full weight, drove a knee deep into Joshua's lower back holding him all tied up like a pretzel. He must have had the arm holding Josh's arm down around his throat, because Alyssa could see Joshua's face turning from red, to a bluish color, as Martel cut off his air. "No, no, and NO!!!!" Martel growled and finally the anger in the dragon's heart came out with an all-engulfing black darkness and presence that seemed to overshadow everything. A deadly hush seemed to engulf everything for a moment, as though time briefly stood still. For the briefest of moments, Alyssa thought of Victor.

Martel quickly released Joshua and nimbly got to his own feet and bowed deeply. "I am sorry Joshua. I truly am..." He said back in his normal, low, non-emotional tone. His anger gone as fast as it had shown, "I cannot ask any more than your trust. It will someday soon be revealed why, I promise you. But I cannot say any more and do not dare ask me too!"

Joshua had already pulled himself to his feet. It was very obvious he had been on the losing end; he was weaving like a drunken sailor on his feet, pain sketched on his face. Joshua bowed formally, anger still in his eyes, blood dripping all over his shirt, his designer jeans and the ring but he would not push it. He had to follow the Family rules and codes and he could only trust that Victor had his reasons. It tore him in half that he could not be in on this assignment for Victor. Victor literally was like a father to him, having taken him in from the streets as a teen and given him a home here on the Jerome estates and yet he also had a lot of respect for Laurence Martel who sponsored him in personally, had always treated him like a brother.

He had so wanted to avenge Michael's death for Victor, but Martel was not giving an inch and he could only assume that Victor had laid out reasons for it. He forgave Martel of course, but it didn't lessen his temporary hurt and anger at being refused this mission. Without another word he turned and after violently throwing his protective gear across the gym towards the martial arts corner, grabbed his shirt, shoes and socks and stalked off without another word.

Martel watched Joshua exit from the ring, the whole time his own heart in turmoil. He knew how much Joshua wanted this, but now was not the time. No one could know the ultimate secret Victor and he held so dear, one day Joshua would understand but today was not the day. Martel realized he probably would have felt the same had he been in the consigliere's shoes. He felt bad coming to blows with Joshua, the man was truly like a brother to him, had been his student but he had been left no choice: Joshua was always a volatile individual and he had expected a reaction like this from the consigliere.

Laurence turned and looked at Alyssa, Carmine and the stunned guard who were still all staring at him with gaping mouths, he narrowed his eyes and shot them all a dark look, "Problem?" he quietly and darkly asked.

"Nope! No problem Boss." Carmine said and quickly came out of his shock as did Alyssa, as well as the other guard in the corner. All three breaking their gazes' from staring at the underboss and went back to working on their machines, their eyes looking at the ceiling, the floor anywhere but at Martel.

Martel knew he had given Josh 10 times worse than what Joshua had give him but already he could see angry bruises raising on his wrist and forearm. His ribs felt sore and he was sure one was bruised deeply. He shook his head and gave a deep, tired, sigh. Then after neatly picking up the protective gear Josh had thrown and his own and neatly stowing them away, turned to walk out the gym. He paused a moment then turned back, "Carmine." His deep voice echoed through the gym, making both Alyssa and Carmine involuntarily freeze up and cringe on their machines. "I would be grateful if you could wipe down the ring for me, I've got to be somewhere shortly."

"N-no problem, Boss." Carmine stuttered. Without even looking back, Martel walked stoically out the double doors. "Son-a' bitch." Carmine half gawked; he then turned to Alyssa and fixed her with his dark, fiery Italian eyes. "I got a chore for you when you're done, Missy."

Alyssa wasn't going to argue with anyone. There was a palatable strain around the house that seemed like an explosive powder keg about to blow, and after just watching the underboss and consigliere come to some serious blows, over who-knew-what, she wasn't about to get anyone pissed off. She could tell all the men were on edge, not just Tommy.

John Thomas Weintraub had only four more hours, and then he would be spending the day watching the Yankees against the Padres, in his first class Box seats. He had waited all year for this game. His wife was out of town at one of her many dog shows, and after the game he had a date with doctors, Paul Davies, Neurologist and Richard Steinbacker, Cardiologist to go out and do what men did best. Drink beer and watch a few strip shows at one of the upscale gentlemen's clubs that the Jerome's owned. He had just finished transcribing a few notes and was humming a rather happy tune to himself, when the door opened and in walked Laurence Martel.

"Hello Laurence, my fine friend. You picked a bad day to pester me, for I am finally taking a much-needed break after 6 months on solid. The wife's out of town you know, and I have box seat tickets!" he pulled them out of his lab coat and waved them happily around, "Thanks to Victor, as well as…"

Before he could finish, Laurence held up his hand silencing him. John Weintraub didn't even need to ask; he could see the rather non-amused and serious look in Victor's underboss.

"It isn't Victor or the girl is it?" John asked a bit nervously.

"No." Laurence assured him. "They are both fine. But I'm afraid your plans are off, old friend."

"Oh come on!" the doctor complained his own temper beginning to rise. "Don't mess with me you oversized goon, not today." But even with John Thomas' heartfelt tirade revving up he could see something in the depths of those icy blue eyes, of Martel's, that told him he was not going to win this argument. "What? What!!" he angrily demanded. "What, is, it with you people!" he spat out the last part. "Not today, Laurence. Tomorrow, after the game but not today, I've waited all year for this game…" he waved the tickets in Martel's face.

Laurence nimbly plucked the tickets out of John Thomas' hand, tore them up and dropped the pieces into the garbage can. "You're going to have to cancel your vacation and your appointments for the next week; you will have to stay at the Jerome estates…"

John Thomas actually reached up and slapped Martel across the face. "Goddamn you!" his brown eyes filled with anger. Of course he loved Victor, but even this gangland shit got old, and it was only a testament to his being kept protected and uninformed that he never even noticed anything.

Martel pretended the doctor had not even slapped him, no emotion on his face, as he calmly continued speaking. "I am here to take you to the helipad at the VIJER Corporation and fly you to the estates for the rest of the week. Where is your wife?" he asked with a cold level tone.

"Out of town in Boston for two days at a dog show…" John Thomas slowly answered a slight fear creeping into his voice and soul. He began to feel quite badly now for his outburst at Laurence. He could tell something very serious, very deadly was now happening, and he began to feel the hair prickle at the base of his skull. "…And then visiting her sister in Camden."

Martel walked idly around the room a moment, as though thinking. "She should be fine then. Cancel your appointments, doctor." Martel picked up the receiver on John Thomas' desk, and held it out to him. "I am, sorry about this, John Thomas." Martel looked deeply and sincerely into the doctor's eyes.

CHAPTER 11-

The next day, Alyssa awoke to find Tommy was still here, he seemed a bit relieved himself, and she noticed he didn't add as much creamer in his coffee that morning.

She also noticed Dr. Weintraub at breakfast with them. She came over and hugged him briefly.

"Hey kiddo," he smiled at her, "How are you feeling? Has Ol' Tommy here, been taking care of your surgical wound and all?"

She nodded and grinned at Tommy and back at John Thomas.

"Good, good." John Thomas smiled and continued piling his plate with all kinds of rich goodies, scrambled eggs, Canadian bacon, Italian hash browns. If he was going to be kept here, he intended to continue his vacation regardless and let his hair down.

"Well as long as we're in this together, you might as well drop by later and we can go to the clinic and go over more tests and exercises and see if we can't squeeze any old memories out or help your amnesia."

This news brightened her immensely and for the first time since being here, she had a very enjoyable breakfast with Tommy, Dr. Weintraub and a few of the guards. She had noticed that while there was less than the normal amount of guards, there were still plenty to do the job nonetheless, and if anything they seemed to be armed a bit more than usual. Her good mood picked up even more when she saw the heavyset form of Cesare walk into the room.

He smiled brightly at everyone, "Hey Doc, hey 'Lyss, mornin' Tommy." He was dressed in a casual shirt and slacks today, with a NY Yankees cap perched on his head.

John Thomas glanced at the Yankees cap and morosely shook his head. "Man, if you only knew the game I missed yesterday." He half sighed.

"Ah don't feel bad Doc, Padre's trounced them, it was sad indeed. I had to catch the game on TV anyway myself." Cesare nodded and sat down at the table with his plate loaded with food.

"You know, Cesare..." John Thomas was about to begin, his voice in that doctor-tone that everyone around here knew so well.

"Ah-ah," Cesare waggled a finger at him. "I'm on vacation myself, so let a guy in peace, huh Doc? I know I enjoy my food just a bit much, but hell, I'm Italian, and it's my only vice, so lay off the diet crap for now."

"I know, but it's just that I am seeing all this saturated fat in your arteries, my big friend." John Thomas couldn't help but get the barb in.

"Now see!" Cesare was just about to shovel a country biscuit smothered in sausage gravy in his mouth, when he dropped it with a loud plop, on his plate. "See what ya gone and done? Ruined my appetite!"

This bought laughter from everyone, even the guards. For the first time Alyssa smiled broadly and felt included. This felt more like a family.

"Where are Lisa and the kids?" Tommy asked Cesare, while finishing off his Danish.

"They're visiting her parents in Philly," Elf quickly got over his ruined appetite and was drowning his pancakes in syrup. "They should be back here in a week or so." He pointed to his eye in a way that Alyssa had seen others do, almost as a signal, as Cesare glanced at Tommy, "Besides, Victor said it would be a good time for them to go on vacation, know what I mean?"

"Yeah, I was hoping to get Angela to be able to stay here, but she didn't relish the thought." Tommy bemoaned. "So she split to the shore for awhile."

"What?" John Thomas looked up at Tommy, "Your girlfriend didn't think staying at the Elegant Jerome Mansion with complimentary armed guards and an electrified fence that could stop a Mack truck would be romantic?" John Thomas said sarcastically while he waved his hand around, "Geesh! Go figure!"

Elf snorted a chuckle and Alyssa couldn't help but laugh a silent laugh as well.

"You still have to work out with Carmine today," Tommy decided to suddenly remind Alyssa.

She quickly sobered up and gave him this astonished look, but then even John Thomas piped in, "Believe me Kiddo, you need it. Get yourself healthy, come see me later on, and we'll do some more tests and what not."

"Oh, that sounds like a load of fun," Cesare rolled his eyes. He leaned in towards Alyssa, "Here," he tossed a Hershey bar on the table by her, "Here's some real food, and if you get bored later, look me up, I'll be around."

And so for the next few days, Alyssa had basically the same routine daily. Carmine had a whole morning and afternoon schedule for her. An hour and a half of exercise in the morning that usually included weight training, working on the treadmill and then an hour in the evening that included more stamina and weight training as well as some basic fundamentals in Martial arts. Although, because she was still recovering, she just learned the relaxing slow moves of Tai Chi that was taught to her by Rocco Benedarra, who was the lead man in charge while everyone else was out.

Although no one spoke of where or what everyone was doing, she figured it was something important. She had seen no sign of Victor, Martel, Joshua, Patrizio, Leonardo or several others that normally hung around before. It was Rocco who now seemed in charge of the guards and the house, and Cesare who shared a lot of that responsibility as well. Often the two of them went in the office or sat talking deep in thought or making quick little strange calls in code that made no sense to her.

In between her workouts as long as she pestered no one, she was fairly free to roam around, as long as it wasn't to the 'Office' or other rooms that were off limits to her.

On her free time, and when Cesare was around, she spent nearly every spare moment with him. He had taken her on a tour of the whole estate showing her Victor's private aviary, although she wasn't allowed too close to that, because it was Victor's private place, like his office. Her favorite though were the spectacular gardens and fountains in the back. It became one of her favorite places to walk, as it was there that there were no constant guards around and for a brief time she could just let her mind be free and wander.

He even took her up to the old orchards near the far west of the property where there were plumb, cherry, apple and even a few old rickety peach trees. Up against the Orchard ran the western fence that was around 20' tall, made of brick, wrought iron, and barbed wire on the top. It was even lined with several shimmering wires that always crackled with the malevolent sound of 50,000 volts of electricity in it.

"Never touch these fences, 'Lyss." Cesare had told her in all dead seriousness, a strange far off sadness in his eyes. "My eldest girl Gina was 14 and was up here playing football with the younger kids," he paused for a moment as a great shudder seemed to run through him, "She ran too far backwards to catch the ball..." Cesare's eyes had gotten briefly teared up at that point, then he seemed to quickly shut that part of his soul away and a shadow fell across him, as though a piece of his heart and soul was put away in a dark closet and he refused to look at her or discuss it anymore. "...Just keep away from the fence, Ok? Promise me." He solemnly said.

A day later, Alyssa had come across the barely recognizable charred remains of some kind of large bird of prey (an owl or hawk?) A gruesome shiver ran down her spine and she had no intention of ever messing with any of the fences.

She had gotten to visit the stables that held elegant white Andalusian horses imported from Italy, and 6 imported Polo ponies from Brazil. She had wanted to go for a ride, but the rude stable master, Mr. DeLoccasio, glanced down at her from the end of his overly long roman-nose, "These are highly trained sporting steeds," he said in a thick but elegant northern Italian accent, "Not common livery animals! They are not for casual rides. Stronzata!" He huffed indignantly. There were several armed guards down here as well, since the dog kennels were right behind the stables. So she didn't think she would be sneaking any midnight rides on horseback.

The kennels was a place she avoided at all costs, since inside were mainly a bunch of very, ill-tempered German shepherds and Dobermans, none of which were friendly to anyone, even their handlers had their hands full.

"Stay away from them pups," Cesare had warned her as well. "They are trained to kill, not nice pooches at all."

She had wanted to see Martel's place that was half hidden in the western woods but Cesare shook his head. "Nope, no way. Martel doesn't like anyone on his property, whether he is there or not. You would have a better chance petting one of those mean ol' guard dogs than getting on Martel's bad side." Cesare had not been smiling or joking either when he uttered that statement.

Their friendship had grown, and over the following days she looked to him even more as one would a big brother or protective but jolly cousin. Cesare had told her about his wife; Lisa and his three kids and Alyssa figured he had probably said the same things to them on his tour of the Jerome Estates.

With pad in hand, the two conversed whenever they could, and she had grilled him far more thoroughly than any F.B.I agent could. Not intentionally, at first Alyssa had only wanted to learn more about her own fate, her past. But even Cesare didn't know much about that, he only told her she was found at the Romans, that Victor had rescued her, humiliated Vito Roman, and brought her here. More importantly she had wanted to know more about the people around her. And while Cesare did not specifically come out right and say things, Alyssa was able to put together, through snippets and between the lines, quite easily the whole picture.

She had worded all the questions innocently, neutrally. Like how long he had worked for the Jerome Family, who were the various 'players' (like the Del Giorno's, D'Salvatores, etc.) and through Cesare's tales he had taken her with his colorful tales into the fringes of the dark world known as 'La Cosa Nostra', or "This Thing of Ours".

Perhaps it was because Cesare didn't know he was not to be telling her these things, or perhaps he had assumed Victor had already been honest with her. A week from now, when asked "Why he talked" he would say simply and honestly, "I just assumed she knew, that Victor had been honest with her. She never acted like she didn't know. She acted like one of us, she is a really nice woman and I liked her a lot. She reminded me a lot of how my Gina was, I felt kinda bad for her and all."

Alyssa had nearly all of Cesare's entire memoirs of their conversations etched deeply in her mind and instead of being frightened and repulsed by his tales she felt herself drawn even more deeply into the mystery and intrigue of 'the Family'. Maybe it was because she had no memories of her own to call on, that she so desperately wanted to be a part of something; to feel truly a part of a family, to have a history, to be needed and treated like a human being, that she so clung to his words and to him as a human being. He was the first one who had truly treated her like an equal, like he really cared.

From his tales and stories he made the men appear so close like brothers, (*Compari* he had called them) when she was at her most depressed because of her amnesia he seemed to want to buoy her spirits the most, and his tales filled that most empty part of her soul. He fulfilled in her soul a desperate need to belong and to be needed.

Cesare Aniello Ciccerone had been born in New York's East side, but both his parents were from Naples. Cesare's father Pete was a made man for the Roman family back in the early days, Cesare had an older brother named Valerio "Val" Ciccerone, and it was their father's deepest desire that neither of his sons joined in his footsteps. Of course it was not to be, Val no matter how many times was told of the virtue of hard work and an education saw the quick money and protection that could be earned by joining one of the many gangs. He found a sponsor from the Del Giorno family and shortly after was made. He was a good earner and a loyal soldier for his Family, but he died early, gunned down in a territory dispute with another Family. He had served his Don and capo's well.

Cesare purposely went shopping, searching out for the best Family. Much like a young Victor, he seemed to know the 'who's-who' and stats of various crime Families and players, the way some kids knew sports players. Cesare knew the Jerome's were the best, and that Don Victor was a legend even amongst his peers. Cesare worked hard until he was finally able to be sponsored in by a Jerome captain named Charlie Legavoli. Charlie taught Cesare and schooled him well, and soon besides being the closest of friends; the two were nearly inseparable. Cesare was pulling in some big earnings running several high stake games for Charlie as well as helping out Patrizio on the side, fencing stolen goods as well.

But what Cesare did best though was running cars through chop shops. His own older brother Val had taught Cesare how to break in, steal a car and have it dismembered and on it's way out of state in less than an hour.

As a result Cesare had a special knack and passion for driving. He was always well liked by his compari's, because of his sense of humor and loyalty. His heart was as big as the rest of him, and courage and loyalty flowed like hot lead through his veins.
Even though Cesare was about as easy going as they came, he would do anything for his Bosses and murder or acting as muscle to exact payment from a deadbeat debtor was something he never shirked from. Within six years of being made into the Jerome Family, he had caught the eye of the underboss Laurence Martel, especially since

Charlie had vouched for him and never missed an opportunity to let everyone know how big an earner Cesare was for him.

Cesare vividly remembered the day that Laurence Martel had called him in to talk to Don Victor directly. Apparently Cesare's big heart and loyalty caught the Boss's eye as well, for Cesare was promoted to personal driver to the Don himself. He couldn't have been more honored or happy; he knew it was his quick eye or gut reaction that would keep the boss out of any potential trouble.

In the Family, the position of driver was more like a special bodyguard, and it was well known that a boss's chauffeur were oft times more privileged to information than even many of the capos. After all, if a boss couldn't trust the loyalty and silence of the man who drove his car and protected him, he was in a bad position indeed. In many cases, the position of the Boss's driver was a prelude to the next highest rank of capo. Before Cesare had been promoted, Joshua Demonico had held the position of Victor's personal driver. He had even heard through Joshua Demonico that Cesare was being groomed as a potential future consigliere on Victor's retirement.

With all good things though had come the tests. And while Cesare had no problems with whacking someone, or enforcement, there was only one hit, that ever gave Cesare remorse. Probably, because it came from the last place he ever expected.

Because Charlie Legavoli had been Cesare's sponsor, he knew the man while a great earner and his best friend, had a drinking problem. Charlie could go on drinking binges like no one could, and while this was not the problem, the problem arose that when Charlie got to drinking his tongue loosened and his temper flared. Usually far to loose and loud, often revealing sensitive Family information.

Cesare would try hard as he could to silence his friend and sponsor, either by gently removing him from the situation, or at the worst, tricking him by getting him drunker in the hopes he would pass out and Cesare could bring him home and put him to bed before he did too much damage.

The other capos and Family members finally realized the best thing to do was to censor any conversation around him, or else feed him false information. However, sadly even this only worked for awhile, and while Cesare never did find out the full story, apparently one day Charlie revealed something, so damaging that their enemies the D'Salvatores were able to use it to find out where a Jerome-Del Giorno meeting was going on and it had cost several Jerome and Del Giorno soldiers lives in a skirmish.

It was the last straw; Martel had drawn down the orders to Cesare directly. "Cesare," the underboss had spoken to him, "My orders come from Victor. Charlie needs to be clipped. His mouth is far too big, his balls are far too big and he endangers not only you and me, but all of us."

Cesare had nodded glumly, "I know Laurence, maybe ..."

But Martel had abruptly cut him off. "I know you are friends, even deeper, he sponsored you into the Family himself. But he was given more than ample opportunity, and now he has cost us lives, Cesare, lives of our own people. I don't need to tell you how honorable, how far back in tradition *our thing* goes. My orders come from Victor, and his come from dictates handed down back in old traditions. Loyalty and omerta above all else Cesare, you know this." His icy stoic eyes pierced Cesare's soul like razor sharp knives.

Cesare knew Martel was right of course, the Family was all, and once accepted in then that Family came before all else in your life, the Family was everything. Cesare had only wished someone else would have been put on it. This was his best friend, but he dared not say anything. He knew better.

"I'm putting you on it," Martel ordered quietly in his deep baritone, breaking Cesare out of his daydream. "You're the only one who can get close to him; he's too suspicious of anyone else right now. He's become a liability and he knows what his slip has cost in Jerome blood. You, he still trusts, you, he'll let into his close circle. You will make his death a message job."

And so it had come down straight from the underboss himself. Cesare knew it would be done, and he knew with cold shiver that he would do it, for if he didn't, Charlie would be killed anyway and then so would Cesare for failing to carry out the orders. The Family rode you like a cruel master, and once in, the only way out was usually death. So with a heavy heart, he resigned himself that he must do this, kill his closest friend, his teacher and his sponsor.

It was two days later on a brutally cold, grey January day that Cesare had caught up with Charlie Legavoli again. He knew his sponsor would be at the usual high stakes game; earning money, drinking hard, and flapping his gums. Cesare arrived an hour early as he usually did for these high stakes games, to help set up, which usually meant lots of expensive booze and cigars and snacks, maybe even some prostitutes later in the evening.

"Hey, Elf!" Legavoli clasped Cesare in a hard embrace as soon as he entered the hotel room. It was Charlie who had dubbed Cesare "the Elf" as a play on his massive size, but nimble ability at breaking into and stealing cars. "We're gonna get a full fuckin' house tonight, my friend! I even invited a few lawyers who wanted in the game. Can you believe one even works in the fuckin' mayors' office!" he laughed a deep rolling laugh.

Cesare could already tell that Charlie was three sheets to the wind. He noticed that two of the most expensive bottles of Champagne were already gone. "Damn Charlie, you already drank the good stuff," he wheezed, "Whaddya gonna offer the guests? You know they come here to get some good eats and drinks as well!" Cesare mopped at his forehead with a handkerchief. Charlie had the heat cranked way too high in here.

"Fuck 'em!" Charlie went over and dug around the bar, "We paid for this stuff, besides we're gonna get all their money anyway."

"Come on, Legs," Cesare called Charlie by his mob nickname; he gently took the bottle away from him and placed it down. "Tell ya what; why don't I run us over to the liquor store, and I'll buy ya some good stuff myself, huh?"

"Oh yeah, I forgot, the little Elf got promoted to the bosses whipping boy now, huh?" He glared harshly at Cesare. It had been a sore point between them when Cesare had been promoted. Cesare was Charlie's hardest worker and best earner, and so he felt betrayed when Cesare had went off and worked as Victor's driver. "I bet you got your nose so far up Victor's ass it ain't funny Elf."

"Aw come off it, Charlie." Cesare looked at him exasperated. "I'm here now, ain't I? Have I ever missed a fucking game Charlie, huh? You and me we're still pals, quit breakin' my balls here, huh?"

"Yeah," Charlie backed down, "You're my only real friend Elf, you know that, right? I don't trust the rest of 'em. You..." he patted the Cesare's chubby cheeks, "You, my big Elf, are the only one I trust."

"You got the heat cranked so fuckin' high in here, Charlie." Cesare went and tried lowering the thermostat in the hotel suite.

"So what," Charlie muttered again and began scrounging around in the bar again, this time hauling up a 25 year old bottle of scotch. "Oh, bravo! Check this out, yes!" he cracked the seal and drank straight from the bottle.

"Come on, Legs, let's go out and buy some more, Ok? I gotta talk a little with you anyways. Before the guards and guests arrive."

"What? What business?" Charlie shot back dangerously, "More bullshit from the dear *Padrino* or his hulking hitman, that no good Martel?"

"No," Cesare cringed inwardly, "No, not that. I gotta ask you some advice on some rackets I'm running on the west side. Are you my teacher or not? I need your advice here! C'mon stop busting on me here." Cesare looked at him earnestly.

"Yeah, fine, sure." Charlie mumbled. "Poor Elf, promoted to the Boss's driver and he still can't keep his vig percentages straight." Charlie broke out in laughter, while putting on his thick, grey overcoat.

They had stopped at the corner liquor store and Cesare had gotten Charlie a few more bottles of high-end scotch, but as they were heading back, Cesare suddenly pulled over. "Damn," he muttered, "this fuckin' cold always makes me need to piss, come on, step back here with me and you can finish telling me those vig percentages again."

"You are so fucking funny, Elf, I swear." Charlie muttered, as he stumbled out, weaving on his feet. He was far too drunk at this point to even pay attention to the strangeness of Cesare's request.

As he and Charlie ducked down the dark alleyway, Cesare noticed that the heavy, grey afternoon was growing even darker, more impatient, and more ominous. Cesare felt as though the darkening sky was like Victor's wrath, pressing down on him to follow the orders of Charlie's execution. Cesare glanced up briefly heavenward, not even knowing what he was looking for, but nothing was to be found, just the angry, snow laden storm clouds and the relentless icy wind that moaned in a rattling sigh down the frigid alleyway.

The two men stood shivering as they finished pissing among the knocked over trashcans. "So, on the vig percentages," Charlie had begun, he turned to Cesare and saw him standing there with a barrel of a 9mm, clasped in his gloved hand pointed at his face. "Oh fuck, Cesare," Charlie barely whispered. "Why couldn't it have been anyone but you?"

The gun bucked and spat in Cesare's grip. The first bullet tore into Charlie's face, an arc of red-hot blood hitting the opposite wall as half his forehead was blown away. Charlie slammed back into the wall. The gun spat forth again and this time half of Charlie's neck was torn away leaving a mangled gape of red chewed up flesh. Charlie Legavoli sank down the wall; his legs sprawled at unnatural angles, his eyes still holding a look of both surprise and utter sadness. Cesare squatted down and delivered the final bullet deep into the mangled remains of Charlie Legavoli's mouth, the unmistakable message to all of one who has a loose mouth, one who had betrayed omerta.

Steam rose off the bloody corpse and the rancid smell of booze; piss and blood filled the small alley. In the distance a myriad of dogs had begun barking. Even the rats had run out of boxes and fled, frightened by the loud shots of the gun.

Cesare threw the gun down the alley and then turned and walked away, his thick shoulders hunched against the bitter wind. His heart felt as cold and empty as the drawing evening. The wind had ceased its angry wail and fat snowflakes now began to fall gentle down onto the city. It was the Family sated, it was Victor's vendetta carried out as the Grim Reaper slunk back out of sight into the bowels of Hell with another soul.

Cesare knew he had done what he must, what had been expected of him, what the Family had demanded of him. There would be no condolences for him from other Family members. It was something that Cesare knew it was forbidden to talk about, even to other Jerome family members.

Three days later at Charlie Legavoli's funeral, as his wife and children wept, Cesare noted the cold unremorseful stares of Victor Jerome, Laurence Martel and Joshua Demonico. And so the wheels of New York City continued grinding away, the Family would keep prospering and one annoying rat had been wiped out. It was that day that a tiny piece of Cesare died too, and he knew then what his father had tried so hard to keep him and his brother out of.

"_Did you ever regret your decision to join?_" Alyssa had penned out her question to him as they sat on the front lawn eating a couple of huge ice cream sundaes together.

"No." Cesare said with certainty, "I decided long ago what I wanted to do. My loyalty is to the Family, to Victor. I knew that along with the benefits," he paused for a moment remembering in his mind that January day, ten long years ago, "that one reaps the sorrow too."

Alyssa had never seen the darker side of Cesare, not even a hint of it. He was always so happy, so gentle with her. He could be funny, he could be serious, and he could even be bit of a scoundrel at times. He was usually a prankster and quite a bit of a slob but with her he was nothing but a gentleman and a friend.

She knew he had a strong love for his wife Lisa and his children for he often talked about them and was always happy to show her pictures of them, she knew he had an even stronger love of his job here with the Jerome Family, because whenever he did speak of his Mafia Family, he spoke of loyalty in the same breath.

Cesare and Rocco were the only ones to be able to come and go from the estates, and nearly every day Cesare bought her some kind of candy bar or sweet treat, always with the words "You need to put some meat on those bones, darlin'." Cesare made Alyssa feel not afraid of her predicament but to try and accept it, to learn who and what the Jerome's where.

On a rare occasion she might ask a question too personal, too deep, Cesare's jolly look would quickly fade away and with a stern seriousness he would let her know she was treading on dangerous ground. "We can't discuss that, you don't ask about that stuff. It's not for you to know." This was for out-of-line questions such as "_what did he do to become a made man_" or direct questions about the _Cosa Nostra_ in general, or such things as "_where all the men were off to now_."

On those even more rare times she asked a question that Cesare felt could get Alyssa, seriously hurt, if someone found out she asked him, he would snap quickly and angrily, "Shut up about that, and don't ever, talk about such crap again!" this was for real breeches of mob etiquette like "_What rackets the Jerome's were into_" or personal business between other Family members, "_Do you know what that fight was about between Martel and Joshua last week_?"

But Alyssa was no fool, and she knew better than to tread on thin of ice with Cesare. So rarely did Cesare ever shut her up with a closed, terse answer. In fact he unknowingly had set her education on an even further trend, when one day he joking looked at her after she had asked her umpteen question of him, "Damn woman, don't you ever watch movies, or read or something? I thought everyone had like watched *The Godfather*, or *Goodfella's* or *Scarface* or something."

And so, when none of the guards were paying to much attention to her, she often snuck into Victor's vast open library and devoured such literary works as *The Godfather* and few other Mafia related fiction books.

Torenzo "Torry" D'Salvatore sat crammed into the large Cadillac with Tony Trevello one of the elder, D'Salvatore capos, a couple guards and their driver, Richie Aponsarte. They had been driving for a few hours to make a meeting with the top Administration of the New Jersey Armandana Family. They carried a few gifts to cement their new alliance, and the Armandanas would be supplying a few guns and soldiers to the D'Salvatores as well as a few other favors to help them in their war with the Jerome's.

They were traveling extra light, knowing had they gone by convoy or with a larger group they would have drawn notice by either the Jeromes or one of the Jerome allies.
All the men here knew that Torenzo was being groomed to become the new underboss of their Family; he was after all, the only heir of Tito.

"So how productive do you think this meeting is going to be anyway?" Torenzo impatiently asked Trevello. Tony had been one of Tito's most loyal capos for close to three decades.

"Oh, I think if we know how to stroke them well enough they will be very productive," the older man spoke sagely. "If they weren't do you think your father would have set this little meeting up?"

"I still think he's wasting time, why not just buy weapons directly from some of the damn Russian gangs out of Philly or New York. We could be done with this and not wasting a perfectly good Saturday." Torenzo griped, sometimes he just couldn't figure out why his father made the choices he did, often taking the more difficult route than something simple or direct.

A few, stifled chuckles resonated around the car. "Are you fuckin' kidding me?" Richie half spun around in the drivers' seat, "Del Giornos are on a first name basis with the Russian mobs, and where there are Del Giornos there are Jeromes."

Torenzo was a bit miffed at having this pointed out, the heir apparent was not exactly a graceful learner, and many of the men knew of his hot headedness and rash decisions. They figured that was why Trevello had been sent along, to keep the meeting under control and heading in the right direction.

In fact, Trevello's coming along had also been a sore point between Torenzo and his father. "When was his old man going to let him make

143

some of his own decisions with out his father's capos acting as fucking nursemaids?" He brooded to himself.

In order to keep things even more secret, they had decided to take the most back end roads they could find, as Richie had proclaimed loudly, "Didn't you ever see that scene in *The Godfather*, where Sonny was gunned down on the fuckin' turnpike? Shit, I don't want to be in no place I can be boxed in!"

As they finally pulled up to the small tavern, they saw just a few cars outside, all of them bearing New Jersey plates. Every one seemed to visibly relax. "All right, let's go." Trevello and the others began to pile out.

What they didn't know was that the imposing figure of Laurence Martel was watching nearly invisibly from one of the windows, pressed deep into the shadows by the door. He made a quick motion to six of his other assassins who were stationed either sitting at tables or behind the bar. The real Armandana delegation had already been shot and crammed down into the cellar. "Remember," Martel said softly, "Torenzo D'Salvatore is mine." The men nodded at their boss and said nothing else.

The five men from the D'Salvatore group entered the dim bar as Frank Sinatra crooned away in the background on the Jukebox, before their brains could even register the set-up Jerome guns were blazing. For nearly two minutes guns roared nonstop, glass shattering violently mingling with the moans of anguish and shouts of fear, rage and death that hung in the air and then silence. Total deafening silence.

All six Jerome men stalked through the shattered and bloody carnage, checking on the fallen D'Salvatore men. It was then they heard the desperate, pain-filled sob near the door. They turned and saw Torenzo D'Salvatore, with both his knees shot out and sitting in a trembling and wounded ball near the underboss's feet. Martel had grabbed him up personally, disarmed him, shot him into submission and held him there out of the way so he would not be killed outright in the ensuing gunfight.

"Any other D'Salvatore men alive? Are any of our men hurt?" Martel asked in a calm commanding tone. The other men shook their heads no to both questions. A few Jerome soldiers were scratched up from flying glass or a few burns from a bullet graze, but not one of them were seriously harmed. However, the D'Salvatore's group except for Tito's son Torenzo was as dead as rocks.

"Excellent," Martel tossed his Uzi to one of his soldiers, then while looking down at his trapped victim reached behind himself and unsheathed a long, oriental assassins knife that he had strapped to his back. A cruel and malevolent smile ran along the length of his lips, making his face seem even more dark and vicious. "Gio, bring that camera over here..."

The shrieks that came from that shot up tavern lasted for only about five long minutes. But they were so tortured, so inhuman, that many of Martel's own seasoned soldiers would have nightmares for years at the sadistic, torture their boss inflicted on D'Salvatore's son. In the end, Martel rammed his knife deep into the base of Torenzo's skull and then hoisted him up with one hand like some obscene dead fish and had Gio take several excellent pictures, as Torenzo twitched in his final death throes.

Martel made sure to smile nicely for the camera. "Make sure a set stays with me, and a set is sent with our compliments to Tito D'Salvatore." He instructed, "Then torch this place to the ground and head on back home." He had then used his knife to saw off Torenzo's head from his body, and after wrapping up the decapitated head, as though it were a prized roast in several layers of cloth and butchers paper, he turned and with no further comments, walked out into the parking lot and to his rental car along with his grizzly trophy.

Victor Jerome was tired, bone tired and weary. It had been nearly 25 years since he had literally "hit the mattresses", a term that meant going into hiding and hanging low, usually during a Mob war. Victor and seven others had stayed cramped up in this run down apartment, far on the northern fringes of the city, deep in the heart of Del Giorno and the Russian mobs turf. He could hear some woman and man yelling and having an argument in Russian somewhere else in the run down building. To his left, Martel lay like some huge war dog half on and half off the broken down, stained couch. The man was exhausted and was finally sleeping after being up nearly four days straight.

There was a sudden soft series of knocks at the door; a few men silently snapped to attention, their guns aimed at the door. "It's me," Joshua slipped in the door with a grocery bag of take out food, which he passed around to the six other men in the room. Everyone went back to relaxing.

"Joshua, aspirin?" Patrizio asked hopefully. Of everyone he looked the worse for wear, it was known he had bad arthritis and had forgotten to bring his more heavy-duty painkillers.

"Yeah, sure Pops," Joshua reached into his jacket pocket and tossed Patrizio the bottle of aspirin. Joshua, like many of the men had several days of stubble on his face, but all of them were a bit unkempt. They only moved around to do their separate missions or when they thought that their hideout might be compromised. There was rarely any time for the luxury of showers and fancy dinners when you were deep in the middle of a blood war.

Joshua sat down next to Victor on one of the many plain mattresses and sleeping bags around, he gently handed Victor his portion of take out food and a couple packs of lifesavers.

"I feel it now," Victor turned to him. Even though he was as tired and unkempt as the others, there still sparkled an energy and strength in his eyes that seemed to feed all their spirits. "Tito grows tired. He is so risky, so ambitious that he takes stupid risks and now he is just realizing what his rash decisions and brashness has cost him. His only son..." Victor sighed.

Normally a man of Victor's importance in the Commission didn't go into hiding, but this wasn't a normal war, this was a fight to the death. Two mortal enemies locked in the deadly dance of combat of long vendettas that needed to be settled once and for all.

Victor's chest felt a bit lighter, although his memories would never be truly sated over the loss of his beloved younger son Michael: His dear, sweet second child, who was just weeks away from entering into his 1st year of medical school to be a pediatrician. Michael's life had been abruptly and hideously ended by Tito D'Salvatores men, who had come across him and assassinated him in broad daylight. To make matters worse, one of the animals had a camera on him and had snapped a quick shot of the two gunmen grinning into the camera and "flipping off" Victor in that insulting hand sign of a raised middle finger. No, that vendetta would only be settled with Tito's death, but Victor had now inflicted that same pain on Tito. Had forced his archrival to embrace and dance with the same misery and pain that Victor had felt so many years ago.

Martel had told Victor in private in every vivid detail of what he had done to Torenzo D'Salvatore, had given Victor the pictures to see for himself. Just the two of them sat there, looking at the pictures, as together their hearts burned as one. "Our vendetta, Padrone," Martel had said with one of the few times Victor had ever seen tears in the large man's eyes. "I felt you with me. He suffered with every agony we did." Martel had then embraced Victor and it took several long minutes until Victor could compose himself as well. Then neither spoke of it anymore. Victor just looked at the pictures and could imagine Tito as a father, seeing his own flesh and blood so mutilated, so tortured, the dreams that had died with him.

"We hurt him..." Victor barely whispered to Joshua as he came out of his recent memories. Victor glanced at the sleeping form of Martel and then back at Josh, "We hurt him deeply and unexpectedly and now he will pull back and rethink a lot of things; many things. Tito will be much more cautious next time; he will not underestimate the Jerome's again." He sighed and began to unwrap his food. "The next time we and the D'Salvatores go at it; he will remember what I, what we, did to him.

"But this pause that we gave him now, is giving us plenty of time to set up our final move. By the time Tito realizes what we are doing it will be too late." Victor took a bite of his sandwich, "His anguish, his rage will keep him from doing anything when we don't need him too and then play into our trap when we want him to move. He will pull back now and take awhile to decide his next move. He is angry and frustrated because he got no Jerome blood in the last six days."

Joshua just looked at his boss and leader without words for a few minutes. It never ceased to amaze him how Victor could always seem to eerily and accurately gauge people's moves and reactions. It was something that Joshua did not notice in the peers around his own age. It was a new Mafia out there for sure, but if indeed the old Mafia held men like Victor's caliper of manipulators and movers and shakers, than change was not always a good thing.

"You will get your turn in a few weeks, Joshua." Victor nodded and made a quick sign of the gun with his hand. "I'm putting you on that matter that you, Martel and I discussed a week ago, about our turncoat."

"Thank you," Joshua barely mouthed the words with relief. He was still a bit miffed that he had not been there on the raid on Torenzo D'Salvatore, but he gotten over his hot rage and believed when Martel had said there was a reason for it. Joshua realized there was one person who seemed to share Victor's uncanny knack of always coming out on top of any situation and reading people, friend or foe accurately and that was Laurence Martel.

"I wonder how much longer, we lie in wait." Joshua made small talk as he dug out and unwrapped his own sandwich.

Victor smiled warmly at him. "Not long Josh, I bet within five hours we get a call from Rocco and then we go home and all sleep in our own beds tonight." He toasted Joshua with a can of diet coke and then leaned back, sated deep in his soul. Tito was making all the moves he had hoped he would, "You're becoming too predictable my *nemico*." Victor thought wryly.

CHAPTER 12-

The scream of rage and anguish that flew out of Tito D'Salvatores mouth chilled the blood of everyone in the room. "Why is my wife crying her eyes out? Why am I preparing to bury my only son tomorrow? Why have I lost my best friend, Tony?" He lurched forward and slapped Joey Calendri so hard, the man's head shot backwards with a sickening crunch. "Why!" he roared.

"Whoa, whoa, Tito." Johnny Baldovino, his consigliere and two other older capos' ran forward and grabbed their boss. "Easy, easy. Come on, we are all grieving here. It's no one's fault." They restrained him.

"Why?" the Don sobbed. "Did you see what the fucking, Jerome animals did to my boy? Did you?"

Joey Calendri stood up, warily rubbing his jaw, testing if it was broken. He could taste blood inside his mouth. "I had checked everything; it was all a green light! There should have been no way that the Jerome's could have known!" he stayed out of reach of his raging Boss.

Tito had shrugged free of the other men, regaining his composure. It was not good for the head of the Family to lose it like this in front of his men. Not now, not when they were so scared, shocked and defeated.

"I know Joey, forgive me." Tito walked up to the skittish underboss and they briefly embraced. "My heart is in pieces, my soul is in pieces, do you understand?" He released Joey and walked over to his desk and then with a sudden renewed vengeance flung everything off his desk, sending everything crashing to the floor. He gave another primal scream of rage.

"Trevello, Cantata, Tutterro, DeAngelo, Delacraccio..." Tito began to tick off the names of all of his men who had been killed for the last four days.

The underboss, consigliere, and two remaining top capo's hung their heads. These were their friends killed as well. Their own hearts ached.

"...And my son, my only child, Torenzo Rudolfo D'Salvatore." He remained at his desk for a moment his aged shoulders shaking with silent sobs, his frame slumped, as strong hands grasped the wood of the desk so hard that his knuckles were white.

Johnny Baldovino looked down by his foot and saw one of the crumpled Polaroid pictures of the enormous Jerome underboss, holding the mangled, tortured body of Tito's son up like a dead fish. Even though Martel's face wasn't in the picture there was no mistaking the huge imposing man who easily held up Torenzo's lifeless tortured body. Johnny felt his own bile rise in his throat, his own eyes hot with tears.

"For each man, that fuckin' Jerome devil has killed I will take two of his! I so swear this on Torenzo's grave!" Tito turned around his eyes red rimmed with fury.

"They are dug in deep now Boss," Stefano Gualtiero said with a reasoned voice. Next to the now dead Trevello, and consigliere Johnny Baldovino he was the oldest most experienced capo here. "Our time will come Boss, but we must pull back and think now. We have set up everything with Gambini in a few months but now we must not throw caution in the wind."

"You are right," Tito stood up and walked unheedingly over his strewn about items, his heavy footfall crushing glass picture frames and other items. He threw himself down in a leather armchair and immediately the other men went to sit down as well.

Joey got out a cigarette and after lighting it handed it to Tito.

"The Jerome's would like nothing better, than for us to run helter-skelter all over the city trying to take them out. They have too many eyes watching us now, too many favors called in from other Families." Baldovino spoke as he began pouring out glasses of straight whiskey from the bar for everyone. "We have our capo Frankie Scalia who told us what Paulie Verro said about the Jerome's hoping we would do something rash, like going after them."

"Then we are lucky Frankie got that and we are lucky that we have a reputable link to Jerome info." Tito mumbled accepting the glass of whiskey.

"Oh, Paulie wants in bad," Baldovino half sneered. "I guess not all of Victor's men are as loyal as he likes to fuckin' crow about." He raised his glass. "I submit we wait then, do exactly what the Jerome's don't want us to do. They are probably counting on us to run around looking for them."

"Fine, agreed." Tito said only half-hearted, "We wait. Besides..." he paused as he suppressed another shudder of anguish. "I have a son to bury, what's left of him." His voice nearly cracked in anguished pain, his hand trembled in rage. Had Tito D'Salvatores heart not been in so much pain and shock he might have paid more attention to that tiny little tingle of instinct that was trying to tell him, something just wasn't right. But the emotion in his brain was clouding out every logical thought at the moment.

Between Cesare's friendship and answering her questions and reading novels of Mafia gangsters, Alyssa was completely drawn in. Even more so, since she still had no memories of her own. No links to any past, no remembrances of any relatives, family, people or places that once made up the fabric of who she was. Her empty mind, had hung onto Cesare's every words and those of the Crime Lords and their crews in the books she had read.

She finally wanted to confront Victor and at least have him fill in the truth of what he knew of her, of what had happened "From the Roman's place". She was tired of all the run around and would rather she know the truth. Only then did she feel she could embrace all of them as true family and hope they embraced her, instead of treating her like some protected outsider. She figured if she let Victor know that she knew at least basic facts, he would be more forthcoming with information he knew.

She had tried talking to Dr. Weintraub about it, but John Thomas would avoid the subject like a plague and whenever she even dared bring up anything even close to what Cesare and she had spoken of, he would visibly blanch, saying things like "Listen Alyssa, you better not push into what you don't know. Talk to Victor of these things, not me, because I am the last person to know anything just like you. And trust me, it is far, far better that way."

Alyssa didn't want to be ignorant like John Thomas, who grew uncomfortable when someone even pointed out to him the obvious all around him; she wanted to be a part of all of it, accepted by it. The day before the men had returned after their seven-day absence, she had written a simple note. "*Victor, I know who you are, and what you do. Let's not lie to one another anymore. Embrace me as one of your own. Alyssa.*"

She had stuffed it in an envelope, addressed it to Victor and then when the guards were changing shifts, she snuck up to the small area where Victor's personal bedroom was and shoved the letter under the door, where she knew the letter wouldn't be intercepted by any well meaning bodyguards. Then silently and quickly leaving the area she hoped and prayed.

Exactly seven days after the Jerome's had all went into hiding they all came back home, everyone exhilarated that there had been no Jerome bloodshed. Final score of deaths to the D'Salvatores 15, to the Jerome's 0, it was the largest recent mass of gangland slayings in thirty years. The New York and New Jersey branches of the F.B.I were putting in dozens of hours of overtime and many law enforcement officials and judges were being given large bribes to leave the Jerome's alone.

Among the fellow players of the East Coast Syndicates, alliances were drawn tighter as Families grew quieter and more wary. They knew that the huge, long overdue war between the Jeromes and the D'Salvatores was starting and sometime within the year would come to its final bloody and climactic end.

Alyssa was happy to see the returning men come back, as were the men who had stayed behind running things here. She had actually been in the kitchen with Cesare digging up a snack when Victor and a few other men walked in.

After embracing Cesare and Rocco, Victor had given Alyssa a quick hug. "You are looking far better child, so much more healthier. I am pleased; see I told you we would get you on the road to better health. You've been keeping out of trouble, eh?" he said playfully.

She smiled back and gave him a hug and respectful kiss on the cheek. After Cesare's tales, as well as her own reading research, she had much more respect and fear of the man than before, because now she knew exactly who he was. Soon, Victor was going to find this out too.

Victor and Martel once again, sat alone in the Office; Alyssa's crumpled, handwritten letter on the desk between them Victor glanced at it and half sighed, "This is exactly what I do not need." He said exasperated.

Martel just sat drawn and silent across the desk from him, the long fingers steepled, the icy eyes half-lidded, with just the smallest of twitches to his strong jaw of any indication of the mixed emotions inside him.

Victor wondered if his kindness was now coming back to bite him. The bullshit with Paulie Verro, his own heightened wariness as the war against the D'Salvatores had started and churned up, the important and impending deals with the Bonnaro's. He knew he merely had to give the order to Martel and what should have been carried out nearly two months ago at the Roman's hell hole, would be finished. He raised an eyebrow at Martel; he needed to hear his underboss's words. After all, both men knew soon Martel would be playing the biggest part of all.

"We need to know more information." Martel calmly spoke with quiet confidence, "I have an idea, I will need to get with John Thomas for some equipment, then dig up a few interesting goodies of my own." A brief smile played along his lips, "As you know, I have some interesting ways of getting people to..." he paused, "Open up and reveal the truth."

Victor nodded; Martel had said what he hoped he would. It pleased him to see that Martel often thought along the same lines and strategies that he himself did, but then Victor was not at all too surprised.

"We don't say anything to Joshua until I have gotten everything set up," Martel continued "I think we both know what his answer to all this would be."

Victor again nodded. "Agreed. How long until you can be ready?" He rubbed at the bridge of his nose trying to fight an impending headache.

"Just about an hour." Martel assured him.

"Good, then we all meet back here in two hours." Victor stood up and popped a few lifesavers at once in his mouth.

"Are you OK, Padrone?" Martel softly asked.

"I'm fine, Martel. Just wondering if I am getting far too soft in my old age." Victor took the letter and put it in the desk drawer.

"No." Martel said suddenly.

"What?" Victor looked quizzically up at him. Martel stood up, came around the desk and respectfully, embraced his Don. "No, you are not getting soft in your old age." He spoke honestly with a twinkle in his eyes.

Victor watched Martel quietly leave the elegant Office. "Soon our time will come, my loyal underboss and when it does, I know you will be ready." He thought to himself.

Dinner that night was a festive occasion; the house that had been empty and unusually quiet for seven days now rang with the sounds of animated conversation and laughter. In both English and Italian, jokes were being told, tales recounted, praise and camaraderie flowing between the men of the Jerome Family. Newspapers that carried the headlines of the "Mob Slayings in New Jersey!" were being passed around and laughed at, toasts of victory were being made and toasts of promised future misery to enemies were also being made but the mood was joyous, celebrant.

Alyssa ended up at the far end of one of the tables, between Rocco Benedarra and her shadow Tommy DeLuca. She had wanted to sit with Cesare but he was at the far upper end with Victor, Martel, Joshua, Patrizio and the Sicilian, Leonardo Tagretta. She guessed that once everyone had come back, that Dr. Weintraub had split, because she didn't see him at all at the dinner.

Even though the mood in the great house was high and jubilant, Alyssa noticed that she was not included much and no one certainly passed her any headlines to cheer at. She wondered if Victor had found her letter, 'He must have,' she reasoned to herself, it had been over 6 hours ago and he had been upstairs several times, as well as in his office with the imposing Laurence Martel. But yet, Victor made no mention of it to her, nor indicated to her in any way that he had seen it.

In fact although he carried on most jovially with his men, he often interrupted them insisting. "Because company is present, we don't want to bore her with what we did for six days." and like Cesare a week ago, he made that same signal, with one finger pointing to his eye as he looked a few men in the eyes, an unspoken signal flashing amongst them.

'I guess he didn't see the letter.' Alyssa figured finally, 'For his attitude is still the same. Still treating me as an outsider.'

As dinner wound up, Tommy looked at her and said "Don't forget you gotta do your workout at the gym." He glanced at his watch and seemed almost nervous with her.

Alyssa threw him an icy look and scrawled on her notepad that she constantly carried with her, "_Look, everyone JUST came back! Give me the night off, will you!!_
Let me visit with Victor and the rest!!"

Tommy read her note and shook his head. He looked almost more insistent than usual and again shook his head, no. "Carmine told me he would be waiting in the gym for you at 7pm and that you weren't to be late. It's almost 7 now, so you better go change into your workout clothes and get going." His voice was something she had never heard before in Tommy, darkly insistent.

Bitterly angered, Alyssa spun on her heel leaving the table and went up to her room to change. As she finished up and was coming out of the room she was taken aback as she saw a different guard standing there. One of the more dangerous types she often nicknamed the 'secret service guys'. Unlike Tommy, these guys usually conversed with no one and had very little emotion. They also tended to carry heavier arsenal with them like Uzi's, AK-47's or M-16's. These were the darker, more formidable men, who usually reported directly to Martel or Victor and just like Martel; most of them never had any expressions on their stone cold professional faces. Just a hard, unbending resolve and a deadly quiet nature.

As she headed to the gym she noticed that the guard followed her but at a farther distance, almost as if he was making sure she was heading there but not actually escorting her. She glanced around at him once or twice but he showed no emotion and just kept casually walking along 10 to 15 feet behind her. A small little tingle of fear and warning briefly shot up her spine but she ignored it and then just headed into the gym.

Once inside, Alyssa noticed the gym was unnervingly empty and silent with just a few lights on here and there. There were many different soldiers, guards and people who pulled many different shifts, so it seemed there was always someone, in the gym working out on the free weights or on the stationary bikes, sparring in the ring or even just sitting around chewing the fat and bullshitting. But now, there was not a single living soul in here, even the TV was off. Never had she seen the gymnasium with no one in it, like this! Alyssa felt her skin prickle even more, she saw no sign of Carmine and just as she decided she was going to leave, the double doors opened and Victor Jerome himself casually walked in dressed in a dark blue satin work-out suit.

"Hello Alyssa," he smiled warmly, benignly. "I was so impressed at your recovering health that I decided to give Carmine the night off and coach you myself." He motioned her towards one of the Nautilus machines. "You don't mind, do you child?"

Alyssa shook her head no. Of course she was honored to be coached by the Don! Even impressed that a man his age, who had just nearly 4 weeks ago had major surgery was still so fit, in many ways it seemed more so than her.

For nearly 20 minutes they had worked on the Nautilus equipment, Alyssa was indeed impressed with the physical fitness of Victor, on machines she was using only 10 or 15 pounds of weight, he was using 30 or more. On some machines she couldn't even match the weights or resistances he was using.

The whole time they worked out, Victor chatted to her amiably about nothing. Such frivolities as the weather, her improving health, that he was thinking of fixing up the west wing of the house and such nonsense. The man talked about everything but what she hoped he would, her letter to him.

"Come Alyssa," Victor rubbed the stiffness out of his upper arms. "Let's do some free weights and then finish up in here." He motioned to her.

Alyssa walked over to the narrow padded weight bench and at Victor's direction lay down on her back, above her head loomed the rack that held the weight bar. Carmine had been slowly building her up and only very sparingly had used the free weights with her, she had only worked up to around 50 lbs in a bench press, as Carmine and Dr.

Weintraub had been afraid she would hurt her healing surgical scars on her lower back and flank.

Victor stood behind her, almost over her head and added weights to the bar. He helped spot her in a few easy repetitions of 20 and 30 lbs. "Very good, Child," Victor smiled. "You have been working hard haven't you? I am impressed. I see you have the tenacity to stick to a task, no matter what it is." While he had been talking to her, he had been flitting around the weight bench, adding weights onto the bar. "I know Carmine said he had worked you up to 50 lbs but lets see if you can do a one or two reps of 60, shall we?"

Had Alyssa been looking into those charismatic eyes of Victor's she would have felt a very real danger but from where she was she couldn't see them and she was more concerned about impressing the old man. She would have attempted to lift twice that, had he asked. She gripped the bar with both hands above her head, tightening her hands on the bar in preparation for the lift.

This time however, Victor was not standing behind her, spotting her. Instead he had straddled the bench standing over her stomach, and suddenly his hands closed around the bar over hers harshly and painfully pinioning her hands under his.

Victor's eyes had now taken on a chilling and deadly glare and without warning he bought the weight off the rack. He had not set it up with 60 lbs as he had said but nearly 110 lbs of weight. Unprepared for it, the weight came crashing down on Alyssa's lower collarbone. In her weakened condition there was no way she could pick up the weight or get it off her and worse, Victor was not offering any assistance. Instead he leaned his own weight into the barbell, crushing it down against her lower throat. Tears of pain and shock sprang to her eyes as she made silent gasps of alarm.

Victor's hands still held hers in a crushing grip beneath his own and still straddling the bench he suddenly sat down hard on her stomach, further pinning her fast to the bench. "Now we talk!" Gone was any kindly look from Victor's face. His eyes burned with flaming ice, his muscles tightened in barely controlled anger. "You made a bad mistake," he hissed at her. "I don't know what kind of games you play woman, what kind of stupid threats you send me, but we are going to find out!"

Panic raced through Alyssa's brain, what the hell was going on?!? What had gone wrong? Had Victor misinterpreted her letter to him? With a sudden sickening revelation she realized that her life may very well end right here and now. These weren't the Boy Scouts she was messing with, it was the real "Mafia", and she had just pissed off, angered and screwed with the head of the Family and perhaps the most powerful Crime Lord on the East Coast. Realization hit Alyssa like a dash of cold water in her face as she remembered the exact words she had written '*I know who you are and what you do*...' her letter had sounded like an out and out threat some cheap, bold attempt at intimidating the man! 'Oh God! How could I have been so stupid?' She suddenly felt as though she were going to throw up.

Victor glared down at her even harder and his gaze chilled her to her very essence. The light of his charisma had turned into a cruel all engulfing angry sun of darkness so hard and raging that it overshadowed all rational thought in her brain. She was witnessing the wrath that had caused so many men fear, nightmares, and even their very lives.

His rage burned her like fire and although Victor only weighed around 150 lbs, his anger and sheer willpower made him as immoveable as a mountain. "Now listen to me, and listen to me well." Victor instructed in a clear, calm voice which made him seem even more malevolent and frightening. "After I leave this room, you will shower, change and come to my personal office. Don't even think about not showing up or running, for if you are not in my office in exactly 30 minutes, I will have my men kill you, no questions asked." He sat back on her; drawing a bit of the weight off her bruised and tortured throat and collarbone. "Am I perfectly clear?"

Terrified, she nodded yes, beneath him. Every breath she drew was an agony of pain and crushing weight.

"Good," Victor smiled darkly, sarcastically. He suddenly lifted the weight off her collarbone and hoisted it up to his own chest; his muscles strained, trembled but held the weight, his anger easily bore it. However for poor Alyssa this now threw the entire balance of weight onto her unprotected stomach where Victor was still sitting. All 260 lbs of the combined weight of Victor and the dumbbell rammed into her soft internal organs, an involuntary groan of pain was driven out of her lungs.

"I suggest you are prompt. Your life is in my hands, period!" The Don hissed, he gathered his legs beneath him, stood up and slammed the weight back onto the rack of the weight bench. He then swung his leg over the bench allowing Alyssa to crumple onto a heap on the floor gasping and panting in pain and sheer terror. Tears blurred her vision and she curled into a protective ball on the floor silent sobs racking her sore and bruised body. Victor calmly walked away and out the double doors without even looking back. Victor Jerome was the Boss and he could be the coldest of them all.

Alyssa was too numb to think of anything but blindly following Victor's orders, as she finished her shower and changed into a pair of jean shorts and a red tank top. 'How could I have been so stupid, and what is now to come?' was the only thought that ran through her brain like some mindless mantra.

When she exited the room 20 minutes later she noticed there were now two of the darker type guards waiting. Always impeccably dressed in dark suits with ties, expensive shiny Italian loafers and usually a large assault rifle in their grasp; whenever they were outdoors they wore sunglasses, and even occasionally inside, but either way, these ominous soldiers, the special bodyguards all seemed to look the same. Built like well muscled tanks, threatening and deadly. One now walked in front of her and one followed behind. Not a word, gesture or even acknowledgment of her, between them. All she could do was stare in numb fascination at the gunmetal grey AK-47 that was carried in the lead guard's hands, envisioning what a bullet from that thing would feel like entering her body.

As she walked onwards, her mind seem to suddenly shift again and she had a bold shining image and remembrance of her and 4 other women on some kind of chain, all manacled together hand and foot in some kind of chain gang and shuffling off towards a dark, cavernous semi-truck. She seemed to remember in the vision she had the distinct feeling of being led off to her death or some terrible fate, and as the vision began to clear as rapidly as it had struck, she felt the same mind numbing fear and panic.

They stopped in front of the important door marked 'Office', the one that Victor and his men conducted all their business in, the one that always had guards around it. There were already two more of the dark blackguards outside waiting. The lead guard knocked once and then opened the door, using his gun to motion to her to go in.

Softly, with her heart beating a terrified tempo in her ears she walked into the room, her body trembling uncontrollably.

The large room was richly furnished and decorated in subdued and somber colors. The rug was a deep, blood red color, the paneling an exotic imported teakwood. Elegant landscape pictures and a variety of antique swords decorated the walls and elegant lamps extended from the walls. Around the room were several expensive leather armchairs a couple couches, a few mahogany tables and an elegant wet bar in the far corner. A massive oak desk dominated near the back of the room and sitting on top of the corner of this desk was Victor Jerome, still dressed in his work out suit.

Behind him, chewing vigorously on a piece of gum was the immaculately dressed Joshua Demonico who paced like a caged tiger and to Victor's right was the ever imposing Laurence Martel who was now dressed in a tight fitting black T-Shirt and loose black slacks.

Victor narrowed his eyes at her, hitting her with a hard angry glare. Only one guard had come into the room and he locked the door behind him and then stood as a silent sentinel in the far corner. Joshua also threw Alyssa a look of pure hatred that froze her blood. Martel was the only one who ignored her for the moment as he was fiddling with something that appeared to be a medical IV bag, a metal pole and a metal medical tray that to held a variety of things on it. Martel briefly glanced at Alyssa, with no readable expression on his stone cold face.

156

"Come over here," Victor ordered her closer to the desk. "Sit down there," he motioned her to an elegant, heavy, large-backed chair that sat facing the desk.

Alyssa numbly obeyed, scuttling immediately into the chair. The chair was covered in smooth, olive green leather with two strong wooden arms on the sides of it. No sooner had she sat, than Martel leaned over her. He grabbed two strong leather straps, from a pile of straps on the floor and began tying down her arms. He said nothing to her, nor was his demeanor rough. Alyssa dared not move a single muscle.

"Pay no attention to Martel; he will prep you while we have a little talk," Victor eyed her levelly.

She nodded, her mouth feeling as dry as cotton, her heart still hammering in her ears. She noticed the letter she had written to Victor laying on the desk; Joshua had stopped pacing and now leaned up against the desk, his dark eyes boring daggers into her as he continued to vigorously chewing his gum.

Alyssa couldn't help but notice, as Martel secured both her arms to the chair. He tied one strap around each of her wrists and another other around each of her mid forearms. He then took an extra wide leather strap and wrapped it around her chest, shoulders and around the chair, pinioning her quite firmly in place to this massive chair. All of this was done in a most efficient and business-like manner by Martel who gave her no more thought or emotion than if she were a piece of stone.

"I see you wrote me some mail," Victor broke Alyssa's thoughts. "We are going to conduct an interrogation here today the outcome of which will determine many things."

Gone was any grandfatherly look he ever had with her. He was the Boss and he showed his business side now, the determination and even cruelness that had made him and kept him the head of the most powerful crime Family in New York.

Martel was now securing her legs to the thick wooden chair legs with two short lengths of leather straps around her ankles. She was quite efficiently, securely and utterly restrained. Martel turned back to the medical tray and began once again fiddling with some of the objects on it.

"I'm sure you have heard of Sodium Pentothal?" Victor continued, "To some it is known as 'Truth Serum', because it strips away your brains cognitive and reasoning responses. Lowers the curtain between conscious and subconscious and we will know if you are indeed a threat to us." He nodded briefly to Martel who turned back to Alyssa and wrapped a short length of rubber tourniquet around her upper arm.

Martel watched as the veins in her arm bulged out slightly, taking his large finger he roughly tapped one, bringing it to the surface of her skin, so as to find a good vein to sink the IV needle into. He then rubbed the area with an icy cold alcohol pad. Alyssa gulped once and turned back towards the impassioned Victor.

"Since you can't speak, we'll do a sort of yes and no answer session based upon written answers that you are going to give me now; before we put the drugs into you. In this way we can compare answers..." Victor explained and then idly waved his hand, "Don't worry about the schematics of it, that's my job."

Alyssa felt a sudden sharp pinch into her forearm and a red stream of blood pulsed strongly down her arm. Martel had stuck the needle into a good vein and expertly secured the small IV catheter in her. He then hooked up the tubing part of the IV system and hung a clear bag of liquid onto an IV pole next to her.

"It's just a water and glucose solution," Victor explained to the terrified Alyssa, "trust me, you'll know when we inject the drugs." Victor pushed forward a thick pad of lined paper and a pen. "Now," he explained, "this will be just like back in school. A written test, you number your answers and give me neatly written complete answers. Don't disappoint me now, child." The muscles of his jaw twitched slightly and his cold, hard gaze bore into her. "You've already bought yourself a hornet's nest of trouble by trifling with the wrong people." He nodded a signal to Martel, who unstrapped Alyssa's right hand so she could write.

The IV kept steadily dripping away into the veins of her left arm, feeling chilly and cold but Alyssa didn't notice for she was chilled by fear to the very core of her soul.

"Shall we begin?" Victor slid off the desk and now it was his turn to pace, hands clasped behind his back, "Question number one..."

Alyssa wrote feverishly to Victor's questions, most were broad such as 'How did she know who the Jerome's were?', 'What DID she think Victor Jerome did? ', 'What did she remember of her past'? 'Who was she'? Then Victor asked her strange questions that totally threw her for a loop and made no sense to her like; 'Who did she work for?', 'Who sent her'? 'Was she ever in prison? How did she end up in Vito Roman's Kennels?'

To these strange questions that her blank mind had no memories of, she could only answer with "_Huh?_" Or "_I have NO idea what you're talking about_" Other questions were personal, some that even she herself had no true answers for, 'Why do you think are or are not my niece?', 'Why did you donate a kidney to me?' and finally came the worst question of all. "_Who told you about me? About us?_" Alyssa felt sad, betrayed. She didn't want to squeal on her friend Cesare, it was unfair, he had never meant for all this to happen. "_I won't betray my trust to that person, Mr. Jerome_" she wrote, suddenly very afraid for Cesare.

Victor was livid and slapped her hard across the face "You don't seem to realize woman," he spat angrily, "answer the questions or this interrogation is finished right here and now!!!" he motioned to Martel who picked up a huge syringe. It was the biggest hypodermic Alyssa had ever seen, she figured you could have probably gotten half a pint of liquid in there. Yet strangely it was empty, just filled with air. Martel brought it down near her vein, the needle just puckering the skin.

"Listen and listen well, woman." Victor leaned into her face and growled malevolently, "I will have Martel pump that entire air filled syringe into your veins and just in case you are too stupid to figure it out, that much air pumped directly into your vein will stop your heart cold and you will die!!!" Victor was just mere inches from her face, his anger burning her like a raging nova and giving her a very clear picture of her consequences. "Now let's try this again," Victor backed off, "and this is the last time, I will cut you any slack!" He walked around back behind his desk and sat down in his richly studded black leather chair. "Who," he paused briefly, "told you about us, about the information you now know?"

With tears running down her face for betraying her friend Elf and for her fear at this whole predicament she wrote, "*Cesare, but I pressed him! I questioned him, since no one would speak to me of my past or how I got here or who I was. He was the only one who was kind enough to even try and help me understand anything. I didn't want to bother anyone, all I wanted was to have a friend and to have someone try and help me understand. That's all, to help me fill the total void in my memories, in my life. I just wanted to be accepted...*" She finished writing, and then slumped back in the chair, small little tears running down her face, not even daring to meet anyone's eyes.

The first part of the interrogation was over. Victor had slipped on his reading glasses and sat back with Joshua on one side and Martel on the other as they all read what she had written. Occasionally the men spoke briefly to one another in Italian or pointed to something on her answers seeming to compare information and weigh decisions.

After over 5 minutes of intensive reading, Victor looked up over the pad of paper at Alyssa, his gaze still impassive, a blank wall, totally business like. "Now," he said with a gentle sigh, "comes the fun part. We find out if you're telling the truth."

Martel had walked back around to the medical tray and picked up the first of six different syringes. Four had a slight yellow colored liquid in them; one had a light peach colored liquid and one a clear liquid. He picked up one of the yellow fluid filled syringes and stuck the needle into an injection port on the IV. He did not inject it all at once; in fact it seemed he barely injected any at all, very slowly, only a few drops at a time into her IV port.

Initially Alyssa felt nothing unusual. Then she felt a slight burning pain at the area where the IV needle went into her vein. She then began to feel a more intense burning in her veins, she grew scared. In the back of her mind she began to hear a distant high pitched whine or buzz, and instantly she had flashes of lying on the ground with a bright light blinding her. A shadow entered her field of vision and dropped something over her head, her mind cleared and she again panicked. What had they injected her with, some kind of poison?

She felt her heart pounding in her ears and thrumming along the nerves of her body, in the distance she could swear she heard the hollow thud of a large semi truck door being slammed, her own heartbeat felt like a droning diesel engine. Her mouth felt too wet and moist like she had bit into some bitter fruit. Everything around her seemed far away and muted; dream-like as though she were in some bizarre tunnel.

The burning inside her had stopped, but now her chest felt too constricted, too tight, as though the leather strap Martel had put around her chest were being tightened and cutting her literally in two. For a brief moment she could have sworn that her bonds had become living snakes, trying to constrict her body in half, panic began to rise again...

"Ride with it," Martel's deep baritone voice cut through her panic and fear and instantly her hallucinations stopped, the snakes dissolving away. "Imagine you are on a boat and you are far out at sea, the waves lifting you and plunging you. Don't panic don't fight it. Join with the rhythm, flow with the waves..."

For a brief moment she envisioned-hallucinated exactly what he said, her and the huge Martel on a small raft out in the middle of some vast ocean. In her mind she grabbed his arm and hung onto him and to his voice, clinging to it like a drowning swimmer grabbing for a life ring.

"Why is she shaking like that?" Joshua asked.

Alyssa heard Josh's voice as a far off sound, a muffled noise that made no sense and yet at the same time was perfectly understandable.

"*What the hell is the matter with you TJ? Have you lost your fucking mind??*" Alyssa heard a different voice in the background din of her mind, above the droning truck engine, above the voice of Joshua Demonico. It was as though three different movies were playing simultaneously at once in her head, three different realities. Three alternate universes all running at the same time.

"A harmless side effect, some people experience." Martel calmly assured him.

"*No wait,*" Victor's voice talking to the large figure of Martel who had a gun pointed at her, blocking his aim, "*She is not unconscious.*"

Alyssa once again focused on that deep, rich voice of Martel's she knew it was the only thing that would keep her from literally dying of fright or insanity. 'The Dragon' may be a stone cold killer but right now, in this delusional state and at this moment, he was her savior.

160

"Ride with it. Join with the rhythm, flow with the waves..." Martel's voice.

"Have fun darlin' dancing with the Devil..." skinny, grimy man's voice.

She felt all numb and detached from her body, high like she was floating on a sea of uncontrollable drunken stupor, half awake, half dreaming. She had no idea what was reality what was not. Her mind was now filled with so many thoughts that she couldn't keep track of them all and she didn't try. She began letting her conscious drift; her and Martel on a raft heading for dangerous seas...

"Alyssa!" Victor's voice was invading on the fringes of her hallucinations, "Listen to me and to the sound of my voice. You are in full control of yourself and will answer all my questions truthfully and to the fullest of your ability. You will give me all your answers by either a nod of your head 'Yes' or a shake 'No'. Do you understand?"

It was like Victor had said; she felt like she was partially in control of herself while around her everything else was in total chaos or went unnoticed. Now it was just she and Victor on the raft. It was a unique experience indeed. She nodded '*Yes*'.

"Now, from the beginning," Victor stated, "Do you work for another Family?"

She shook her head 'No'.

"Do you work for the F.B.I or any other law enforcement?" he demanded.

She shook her head 'No.'

"Do you remember your past?"

There were only jumbled pictures, flashes, nothing solid she could draw on, she shook her head 'No'.

"I am just a legitimate businessman, am I not?" Victor questioned.

She shook her head 'No.'

And so the questioning continued, for how long Alyssa didn't know. Time had no meaning to her and Martel kept her on a steady dose of the Sodium Pentothal, Midazolam and other drugs. All were hallucinogenic's and anesthesia's.

Victor's questions invoked images of fear, of confusion and of chaos. She promptly forgot any question he asked her as soon as she answered him. But he was an expert at this and even through 'Yes' and 'No' interrogation he was able to cipher all the knowledge he needed to know, by artfully asking a question one way, then perhaps several questions later asking the same first question but wording it differently.

Before Victor had Martel injected her with the truth serum he had asked her what she meant by "Embrace me as one of your own" in her letter to him. She had written back, "*Because you are all Family, Cesare told me how there is camaraderie, closeness, he called it compari. I don't know who I am, or even my past. But I need a Family now. I only have the highest respect for you Mr. Jerome, and for the other people in your Family. Cesare told me you saved my life and for that I feel indebted and grateful. You had told me when I awakened that I was your niece and while it didn't feel right intuitively, I so wanted it to be true, because I just wanted someone to let me be a part of their lives. I don't have any family, no memories, only blankness. I would donate a kidney all over again, because I really like you Mr. Jerome, just like I really like Cesare. I considered you friends. Compari."*

And now it seemed that Victor's interrogation was over. His voice was a bit softer, and she was numbly aware of sobering up, the hallucinations and the chaos seemed to be fading to the background, the war in her own mind seemed to be ending.

She had heard the voices of Victor, Martel and Joshua conversing with one another again in Italian for several minutes.

"Alyssa," Victor was suddenly back by her chair again, his voice cutting through the curtain of her mental fog, "I have talked with Martel and Joshua, they too have heard your words in this interrogation. We; I, believe you speak the truth. Cesare fucked up, he didn't respect omerta and he became lax. Fortunately for both of you he didn't say anything incriminating or specific. You will live and you will stay here until I figure out what to do about this whole dilemma."

Victor paused and then suddenly without warning his hand shot out and grabbed her by the throat as he leaned in face to face with her, again black fire shown in his eyes and even in this drug induced state Alyssa felt the power of that gaze, it chilled her to her very core. "Heed the words I speak child!!" he hissed his words for her ears only, in a dangerous tone, "You don't ever need the kind of Family I have. You don't want it and you could never be accepted, ever! *Finito*!! Nor will you be a 'part' of my world. You will pay the same respects as any other mans wife, daughter or niece."

She could feel the darkness of his angry light burning her once again, the ultimate finality of his words and the unquestioning ultimatum.

"*Omerta*!!" he growled, "It means you will keep your silence and show respect to the Jerome Family and the Men of Honor! You keep your nose out of anything that doesn't concern you and you ask only me or Martel or Joshua questions! Respect and silence!"   Victor released his clutch on her throat, realizing that in his anger he had been tightening his grip, slowly choking her. "Now," he stood up to his full height again, absentmindedly smoothing back down his bristled moustache and continuing in a completely composed manner.

"You will be treated as before; as a 'guest', as I would treat my niece or daughter. I will say to you now, as a calm man in full control of my capacities and in front of these witnesses. Do not ever speak to me again about *La Cosa Nostra*, or what I do. It is none of your concern or business and never will be. The same goes for Martel, Joshua or anyone else whom you meet. If you follow and obey that one rule, your life will be protected and revered. But ever talk to me again about 'the business', or mention anything about: Crime Families, *La Cosa Nostra*, The Syndicate, the Mafia or whatever you want to call it, and our association between you and I will be over permanently. Respect me as you wrote; not for what I am, but who I am as a person and we will live in harmonious coexistence." Victor gently touched one of her tear-stained cheeks. "But I say it as plainly as this child; do not ever fuck with me again."

Victor nodded to Martel who then took the final two syringes and injected them into her IV port. "It is an antidote, a reversal drug and something to help you sleep and forget this whole experience." The Don spoke softly, almost kindly.

Alyssa began feeling very sleepy and bone tired. The high was quickly fading and she felt drained emotionally and physically. All she wanted to do was curl up and sleep for a week.

"I have business to attend to, and will be gone for a few days." Victor informed her, "But I blame much of this upon myself, I should have had a better instructor for you. Someone to integrate you into my home and how you say; 'answer your questions' correctly for you." He glanced casually down at her, "You will be living with Mr. Laurence Martel for awhile." A slight grim smile played on Victor's lips, "He will show you about omerta, respect and anything else you need to know about living under my roof as a guest. Unlike Cesare, Martel will instruct you in the correct way, I suggest you heed his words and forget whatever nonsense Cesare told you." Victor casually ended this meeting with a dismissive wave of his hand. He was done now, finished. He stopped over by Joshua and whispered angrily in his consigliere's ear…"I want to see Cesare within two hours. Bring him to me here, in this office!"

Alyssa was barely aware that Martel and the guard had rapidly untied her and disengaged the IV from her arm. As Victor had said, whatever they had injected into was beginning to cloud her mind and body in a fluffy grey cloud of dreamless sleep and blessed forgetfulness. Her last conscious thought was of the underboss scooping her up like a small child in is arms and getting ready to take her back upstairs to the frilly, peach-pink room upstairs. Just as he was leaving, Victor stepped up to Martel's side. "Come back here in two hours Laurence, We are taking Cesare for a little walk and talk."

Still in a completely business-like fashion Martel took her upstairs to her room, undressed her, put her unconscious body into her pajama's and then tucked her into the bed. He lit a small nightlight in the room and turned down the lights and closed the curtains. He knew she would be out for a good 7-9 hours, before waking back up. The last injection had contained Ketamine, a surgical drug that would act to remove a lot of her memories of the last few hours. Laurence Martel knew a lot more than Dr. John Thomas would ever realize about working with medical and chemical interrogation techniques. After securing her safely in the room, he put one of his own trusted lieutenants by the door. "Gio, if I am not back by the time she wakens, call me." He instructed the silent guard in the dark suit. "She is not to leave the room until I come back." The guard nodded at Martel's instructions. Martel turned and then began to head to the gym to limber up for a few minutes. Victor, himself and Joshua had some unpleasant business with Cesare 'the Elf' Ciccerone.

Tender is the Night - Part 2

~The Underboss~

...No one knows what it's like
to be hated, to be fated to telling only lies
No one bites back as hard on their anger,
none of my pain and woe, can show through

But my dreams, they aren't as empty
as my conscience seems to be,
I have hours, only lonely-
My love is vengeance, that's never free...

CHAPTER 13

Laurence 'The Undertaker' Martel stood in front of his mirror in his master-bathroom; at nearly 6'11 he had worked to move things to a more comfortable height for him in his home. He was now throwing some hydrogen peroxide on his scraped up knuckles. It had not been a pleasant meeting with Cesare; he really liked the man, the man had potential, he was a good capo but more important Cesare was lucky that he still lived.

Laurence ran his hand down across the hard, clean-shaven angles and planes of his face. Right now, only three people knew of his deepest secret of all, however in a few months everyone would know.

He slipped out of his black T-shirt and tossed it to the corner. He caught a glance of the brand/tattoo on his upper arm, it was a Cobra entwined with a Dragon and the oriental kanji symbols for '*Bringer of Death*'. His long fingers ran across the tattoos lightly as his own memory swam down its dark corridors.

Laurence Martel was born as Theodore Vittorio Jerome and he was Victor Jerome's eldest son. Born in 1954 he was only 3 when the great "Bloody Sunday" massacre had happened and while he truly never remembered anything specific about that day at all, there were times in his deepest sleep and dreams when he could swear he could hear the screams, cries and sounds of death intermingled in a dark thunderstorm and weeks of long funerals afterwards. What he did know was how that date had always affected his father. It was Victor's personal living hell that rode his memory night after night and day after day.

His little brother Michael was born on that November of '57 and it was the one light that his father Victor and his mother Isabella saw from that horrid year. Theodore was always a quiet one even in his youth, and growing up he and Michael were nearly inseparable, Theodore was always looking out for his younger brother, who was the extroverted one. The brothers were completely opposite in looks as well, Michael was dark haired, dark eyed like his father with the soft smile of his mother Isabella. Theodore had the Northern Italian looks of his grandfather Louis Jerome, light pale blonde hair and startling blue eyes.

Theodore knew nothing of anything "different" growing up. To him armed guards were normal, he rarely saw many kids his own age. But his whole world was to change on his 8th birthday. His father Victor insisted he be sent to a private boarding school overseas in Brighton, England. It would be where Theodore Vittorio Jerome would spend the next 10 years living, schooling and growing up in; away from the armed guards, away from the mobster lifestyle of his father. Always his father or his mother and Michael would come there, to Britain for the holidays; only once at age 12 was he able to return back to New York for a Christmas Holiday vacation. It seemed that once his quadriplegic Uncle Eddie died, his father was even more overly paranoid about losing the last two living relatives of the Jerome bloodline.

Not that any of this was ever discussed with him. Young Theodore Jerome remained oblivious to the ominous build up of the D'Salvatore-Jerome war back home.

His younger brother Michael was also supposed to join him at the St. John's of Beaumont Boarding school, but Isabella after "losing" one son, to her husbands over-protectiveness and not having both her children to raise and take care of, put her foot down at having Michael sent away overseas. Instead Michael went to a private catholic school there in upper New York where he could come home on weekends and spend more time with his parents, especially his mother.

Theodore had learned from a young age to fend for himself, thrust at age 8 into a foreign country, where he was often the target of much teasing he learned an inner patience and discipline that was to forever mark his soul. Never was he one to run to his connected father or the headmasters for any assistance, his own battles were settled in quiet ways, often days or months after the teasing. A naturally athletic sort, he was finally accepted by his peers around age 14, especially when he began to skyrocket in height. By age 16 he was nearly 6'3 and 160 lbs of lean sinew. He was a voracious player of soccer, Cricket and the team captain on their school fencing team. Theodore had only limited interest in academics and while his grades were average, he did take a particular delight in history especially European and Oriental. He could feel for the true noble warriors and samurai's of old, and these were the men he idolized. Men with codes and honor, prowess and deadly martial skills.

Without fail his father Victor and mother Isabella and sometimes Michael, would see him nearly every school vacation. In the summer Theodore would spend time with his whole family in the old homelands of Sicily at the estates of Vito and Lena Bonnaro and their children and Family, who were not only close friends of his father, but whose clans had long ties with Felani clans in the distant past.

As Theodore grew into his mid teens, he had no doubt what his father did, especially because he was raised during the summers in the old tradition, learning about the 'Mafia' from the true Sicilian homelands with the Bonnaro's. Theo had no doubt that this would be *his* life also. In fact Theodore and Vito Bonnaro's son, Gino who was a couple years younger than Theo, often discussed their plans for being made and becoming Men of Honor when they reached the appropriate age. To Theodore it was just natural and normal; something a man did, like breathing.

His father Victor, seemed to sense all along that Theodore was a natural to be an integral part of the Jerome family and so along with Vito Bonnaro's teachings also began to groom his own son in the correct ways of the 'This thing of ours'. Theodore saw it as not lessons but just a normal part of life that surrounded him at all times. It was comfort, a part of him and a part of his soul. Every time he saw his father, Victor, he could see the pride and love in his father's eyes. It was the greatest reward to him of all.

His life stayed in this routine until he graduated St. Johns of Beaumont, at age 17. Already he and his father Victor knew Theodore would be a part of the 'Family Business' but his father now confided in him more and would often tell him of the *mannagge* now going on back home in New York with the old enemies the D'Salvatores. After graduating he spent another 8 months in Sicily with the Bonnaro's until he turned 18. It would be then, that his whole life would change as he knew it.

"Michael could never be a part of this thing of ours," Victor told Theodore one warm breezy day as they sat in a small café outside the small town Giarre, Sicily which was the Bonnaro's home territory. Theodore knew this area almost well as the London underground, since he had not been back in the states for nearly 7 years now. His homes had either been Brighton-Warwick England or Giarre Sicily on Holidays.

"He has no interest," Victor continued "and that is fine. He needs to stay legitimate; he's a good boy, not cut out for this life. Not like us, my son." Victor's dark eyes looked with pride into Theodore's sapphire blue ones. Victor sipped his espresso and shook his head with a playful smile… "Do I tell you that you could be a near ghost of my father, Louis Jerome?"

"All the time, my father." Theodore smiled back at him. He loved his father dearly, the man was his idol. "The D'Salvatores will be waiting for me, as you said before. We are between a rock and a hard place. What can we do?" he questioned his father.

"I don't know for certain, Theo, but I have a plan I have been thinking of for a long time. In fact you gave me an idea once." Victor sat back letting the warm air caress him. It was the early spring of 1972. "Remember in school when you were younger, all those stories you would tell me, about the warriors in the orient? It got me to thinking."

Theodore just raised an eyebrow and said nothing to his father. The man seemed to glow with an inner strength and power that was rarely seen.

"The States are all embroiled in this Vietnam war going on now. I have even heard that some *brugads* have their hands in this war, making profits in various ways. You are 18 now, you must sign this draft shit paperwork. It pains me but perhaps we can turn this to our advantage."

"You want me to go to Vietnam and fight?" Theodore said, not following his father's logic.

"Patience, Theo." Victor smiled thinly, "Yes and no. Yes you will go. I can pull some strings, favors; get you in a good position. But I am thinking there is a far more important reason for you to go. You will die there."

Theodore just sat back, his large frame sagged for a moment and his eyes hardened on his father in disbelief. He really was not following his father's twisted logic now.

Victor couldn't help but chuckle at his son's stunned look. "Do you know what a 'long play' or 'distance to mate' is, Theo?" he asked casually. Theodore shook his head no.

"It is perhaps the greatest strategy of all; it is a move on a chessboard that is set up perhaps 50-100 moves ahead of the game, before the first pawn is ever moved..."

Theodore still wasn't following but he knew his father's passion and mastery for the game of chess and Victor rarely if ever lost. Just as he rarely if ever failed in his gambits regarding Family politics and strategies.

"You are going to be my 'long play' and gambit, my sacrifice. I am counting on the D'Salvatores leaving Michael alone, since he doesn't want into this thing of ours. But you, if you were to 'disappear' over there..." Victor trailed off briefly then resumed, "If we could set it up to make it look as if you were killed, or Missing in Action, then bring you back at a later date. You would be my long play, my avenger who would be in place to take the reins someday of what I am building now. With you alive Theo, they will be after you, our *nemico's*. Your head will have a higher price than most, because you are my firstborn son."

Victor's eyes suddenly hardened, his gaze torn between anger and hurt, "We must never forget that day in 1957, Theodore, never! We lost nearly everything. I have always said in my heart that you were spared for a reason. This gambit will be our reason!" he pounded his fist hard onto the table. Victor sat back and sipped his espresso again watching a few children run down the street playing. On the other side some old men in the corner playing Bocce, a form of Italian lawn bowling.

"What I ask you Theodore is not an easy thing. In fact it is the hardest thing a father would ask his son. It will be a long time before you could ever see your family again. If you say no to this, I would fully understand. I don't expect..."

"I will do it *Padrone*." Theodore gently interrupted his father.

Victor nodded but leaned forward, "Listen to me well, Theodore. This is not a casual thing we set up here. I don't expect you to fully understand how hard this will be..." Theodore looked like he might open his mouth again but Victor hushed him with a finger. "Shhh, listen to me. You will have to 'die' to all those who know you, once on this path, there are only a very few who can ever know the truth. It will be one of the hardest secrets you must ever keep in your life. Perhaps harder than any secret the Family or anyone will ever ask you to keep. Even once you come back; it will not be an easy thing. You will have to be different, our relationship different. No longer can you look at me in public as your father."

It was here that Victor's eyes bore into his sons, trying to convey the seriousness of this request. "A part of me, the part that is your father, did not even want to ask this…" Victor touched his heart and his eyes briefly grew moist but then burned bright with inner passion, a deep sharing between father and son, "But, I see in you, something that my own father absolutely refused to see in me. I see in you desire, a true desire to follow in my footsteps and I will not deny you this Theodore if you want it. However it will cost you everything you know." Victor sat back then and said nothing a moment, watching the children and watching the old men. Then with a barely audible whisper he looked at his son again, "*La famiglia*, she is a hard mistress, she demands all if you truly want her embrace." He eerily echoed his own mentor Mario Felani's words. In his heart and soul it tore Victor in two for him to even ask this.

Theodore reached across the table and his large hand gently covered his father's smaller hand, the sapphire eyes burned with as much conviction as Victor's, a solidness and power behind them almost as strong as Victor's own gaze. He leaned forward and his deep voice spoke to his father alone, "I will do this father, because I want to. Because it is what must be done, we both know this. I would do anything you asked, not only because you are my father but because I want this as well, more than anything."

Victor reached over and cupped his son's head and they drew their heads together, forehead-to-forehead. It had been their gesture of tenderness between them ever since Theo had been a little child. Tenderly he kissed his son's forehead, "I will arrange the paperwork. We will correspond when it is safe to do so. I will send word to you here in Giarre."

And with that simple conversation, Theodore Vittorio Jerome's life would be forever and indelibly changed.

It was as his father had said. Theodore had spent another two weeks in Giarre with Vito and Lena Bonnaro and their daughter Lucianna and son Gino. A letter came to him one day, a draft notice for him to fill out and send back, and then 3 weeks later he had official orders from the US Army to report for basic training and then for training in Mortuary Services where he would go to Vietnam and work sending home those killed in action.

His connection in Vietnam was Staff Sergeant Angelo DiGallo, who was connected with a Chicago Family. Once there Theodore learned soon enough that even the US Military was as corrupt as any crime family. In Mortuary Services where he worked he learned from Angelo and a few others how to hide drugs and other contraband in the bodies of the dead soldiers coming back home into the states. It was a lucrative business and he was able to save a good chunk of money aside. Most of the days of his brief 1-year tour blended from one to the other. Rarely did he ever have to leave the Mortuary services, as most bodies already came into them from the medical and M.A.S.H units. Only on rare times did they ever have to go out into field conditions to collect bodies after a particularly bad battle.

 For obvious reasons most of the other soldiers kept clear of the "Vultures" and "Undertakers" knowing whenever they showed up it was because U.S. casualties had been taken, so rarely were they a welcomed sight. To Theodore it mattered not, he was enjoying a fairly easy and cushy job, with people like Angelo a fellow *compari* who understood him and his upbringing and the money was easy. They did not worry much about being caught as even officers and army intelligence often had DiGallo's crew smuggled contraband back home in the body cavities of the deceased.

 Theodore enjoyed corresponding with his younger brother Michael and often told his mother that he was safe and away from the fighting, rarely did he ever get any mail from his father Victor, except the occasional 'we're proud of you', 'things are progressing as I hoped' short messages, with little information. Victor was careful to keep his letters of Jerome Family activity at home very censored…

 Laurence Martel exited the shower and his daydreams from his earlier years, as dried off and then slipped on his comfortable jujitsu martial arts uniform. Black drawstring pants with a black shirt and bare footed, he padded silently down the hall of his home here on the Jerome estates and walked over to the refurbished 3rd bedroom. He had turned it into a Buddhist shrine/shinto. Inside dozens of candles burned and all along the walls were various kanji and Spartan decorations.

 He bowed deeply and respectfully at the door and then gathered some incense to his right of the door. After lighting it and whispering the correct prayers he walked over to the altar, bowed again and placed the incense in the special holder. He bowed once more and walked over to the various prayer wheels and went through his litany of his routine prayer mantras. After that he settled himself in the middle of the room on the wooden floor, and crossed his legs in the Lotus position of meditation he had learned long ago. He stilled his heart and mind, controlled his breathing and began to allow his body to settle into a state of slowed metabolism. For a while he achieved that perfect state of both oneness and nothingness, but then thoughts of the present flooded over him.…

Alyssa, now she was his responsibility. He knew how his father felt about her; for some reason his father had allowed past guilt over something to cloud his conscious of the here and now. She had proved valuable though, she had matched Victor perfectly and been able to donate a kidney, he had not seen his father this healthy in awhile. It deeply warmed his heart. He knew his father still had much to do, so close were their plans now.

But what of his own feelings toward her? Laurence knew he was ambivalent. There was a part that didn't trust her at all, saw her as an outsider and a liability; a part of him that felt compassion for her and even a part that recognized the womanly attractiveness of her. A part that saw her fear of him, of her situation and yet a part of her aching to belong. Alyssa, whoever she was, would have a rough road, this he knew. He wasn't sure what his father expected him to do with her but Laurence would train her in the only way he knew how, the way his own training of so long ago had been. Direct, hard and humbling. He knew no other way; it was the way all his teachers had taught him.

Laurence did wonder just how much she remembered and what she didn't. He knew from the interrogation that at this moment in time, she remembered very little if not anything about her own previous life. He knew that what she knew of the Jerome Family, what Cesare had let slip; was no more than anyone who read the papers daily, watched the news or read a lot of mobster novels would know. But what of later? What if she had a life somewhere, a family, children, and people looking for her? What if she 'woke up' from her amnesia and remembered everything about being kidnapped, tortured at the Roman's kennels and what she had heard here and then somehow ran to the authorities?

With a grunt of anger at himself, Martel resettled his body and thoughts... He was allowing his mind to drift to "what if" and that was never a good thing. His own life, his own teachers and his own father had taught him deal with what comes into play as it comes into play. Prepare for anything, but never dwell too long on what could be, or you will miss what is right under your nose. He took a deep breath, and smelled the exotic incense as it filled his powerful lungs. The familiar aroma, his strict training and discipline was able to bring his mind and body under sharp control. In order to stop thinking of Alyssa, he allowed his mind to wander again down the winding shadows of his past, a road he had not traveled down in over 10 years.

(June 9th 1973)
... It was June of 1973 when Angelo approached him one day, "Come here, Jerome." He waved a thick envelope at him. Theodore followed him into the Sergeants office as
Angelo tossed the envelope at Theodore and then sat at his own desk lighting up a marijuana joint.

Theodore tore open the envelope, inside were several documents, but the one that caught his eye first was a simple folded letter in his father, Victor's, precise handwriting.

'My Theo-
Our time has come, what we have discussed and worked for. The pieces are now in motion my son and favors have been called in. Today is the day that you will disappear. Now comes the hardest and longest road you must follow, and what pains me the most is that there is very little I can do now. Angelo will hook you up with another 'friend of ours', but after that, you must, no matter what, must, stay away from the states for at least 5 years!!!!

This is where your own road and cunning must come into play. We must not contact one another period, at all for 4 years. After that, write to me at home, and things will begin anew for your return. You will be welcomed back into the family, but as any other capo, you understand? I will sponsor you myself, but these things are for the future. Inside are things that can help you now, but the rest, you must do. Only myself, Michael, your mother, and John Thomas will know of the truth. No one else must ever know.
Love,
Your father

Theodore noticed inside were a multitude of things from passports to other official paperwork, and even more disconcerting, an official US Death-MIA certificate with his name on it.

Name: THEODORE VITTORIO JEROME
Date of Birth: 1/12/1954
Date of Casualty: 6/7/1973
Home of Record: WARWICK, NEW YORK
Branch of Service: ARMY
Rank: E-3
Casualty Country: LAOS
Casualty Province: LZ
Status: MIA

And all the other pertinent information of a soldier's life and death that he had typed out so many times himself.

"Come here *paisan*." Angelo chuckled at the rather pale Theodore Jerome. He glanced over at the death certificate Theo was looking at.

"Poor Theodore, alas, I knew him well." Angelo snickered wickedly at his own joke. "Killed in the prime of life at 19, so much *puttana* he could'a had."

Theodore just remained standing there. All was finally coming into play.

"Teddy my friend," Angelo teased him, "We got work to do. Poor Theodore Jerome is MIA now...Probably in some Vietcong Prison camp eating worm infested rice and being tortured, poor guy." He snapped his fingers under Theo's nose, "Come on man, snap out of it." Angelo said tersely, "We got work to do here, a lot of it in a short time. Now move, *paisan!*" he ordered his assistant.

Theodore didn't need to be told twice, the moment of shock briefly past and he now slipped into quiet efficiency. They walked down the hall and Angelo took a key out from under a potted plant and the two of them went into the Captain's office.

Captain Potter was the main officer of Mortuary Affairs, but rarely was he ever at the office. Most of his days were out playing golf, drinking or getting laid from the local mamma-sans. His three best workers, DiGallo, Jerome and Lester ran the office with such good efficiency and kept themselves and his reputation clean, so he was able to go off and enjoy the war by partying.

"Fuckin' Captain Potter," Angelo chucked, "he treats us well, eh, Lurch?"

Theodore liked Angelo; seven years older than Theo, he was a small, overly muscled, quick-tempered man, who was already a made man, "My old man and me are with the Abruzzi Outfit in Chicago. Although, I'm thinking I might wanna try working for some of the boys in St. Louie or Kansas City, they say there's gonna be a lot of growth there. Lots of money to be made, ya know?"

Theodore had his height that enabled him to easily move the bodies around in his profession, and Angelo had his great strength, for nearly 13 months the men had been good friends, although Theodore didn't go into a lot of detail about who he was, or who his father and Family was, Angelo knew Theodore was connected to the big boys of the New York Mob and that was good enough for him. After all, in this business, friends were friends.

"Ok, *goombah*..." Angelo dug around the captains desk and pulled out some official rubber stamps and letter head and then motioned for Theo to hand him that large envelope again, that had held his fathers letter. Angelo dumped out the contents of the envelope, inside were a passport, and a bunch of other papers. "Now we make you a new life, and I gotta tell you *paisan*, some one really likes you some heavy favors were paid off."

Theodore chuckled softly under his breath. Angelo was always calling him, "Lurch, Paisan or Goombah" In this line of work, seeing death day in and day out, a sense of humor was always needed. Besides, Angelo was a true compari, and a Man of Honor, Angelo understood.

"What's your new name gonna be now, huh?" Angelo half debated on relighting his joint as he slid the passport into the typewriter, but then thought better of lighting up a marijuana joint in the captain's office.

Theodore shook his head... "I hadn't even thought about it, I..."

"Aw come on, you gotta have some good name, *paisan*!" Angelo teased, "How about Vincent 'the scar' Costello? Wait, I know, I know... Richard Cranium! Get it?" Angelo laughed.

"Funny, very funny, Ange." Theodore's sonorous voice, played along, laughing.

"Michael Hunt?" Angelo tried again, a devious gleam to his eyes. "Freddy Fellatio?"

Theodore shook his head and dug out a cigarette, he lit one up and offered one to Angelo who took it. The two smoked in silence for a moment.

"Seriously, Lurch, ya gotta think of something good, ya know? Maybe Charles Von Wert, or some regal shit like that." Angelo prodded.

"Damn." Theo mumbled and rubbed his forehead, he hadn't even thought about it. But he knew he better think of something, and something that he could live with, since it would be his moniker for a very long time. "Let me think a moment."

His sapphire blue eyes darted around the captain's office, nothing really jumped out at him. Deep down, he thought it would be better if he didn't have an Italian sounding name. Not while he was in hiding, and when he came out, he could explain he used an alias, a lot of people in the Business didn't always have Italian sounding names, in order to disguise them from the law. His eyes had dropped to a large container he knew well. It was the civilian company that sent the various embalming fluids and other funereal equipment needed to prep the bodies for transport back home to the states. 'LAWRENCE-LOCKHART INC. – Martel, Kansas - USA.'

"Laurence Martel..." he almost whispered it at first as his mind looked at and then locked onto the combination of words. " That's it," he looked up at Angelo, "Laurence, with a 'U', Martel."

"Middle name Mr. Laurence, with a U, Martel?" Angelo looked at him.

"None, no middle name just, Laurence Martel." Theodore said.

Angelo typed furiously for several minutes, and then using several of the captain's stamps on certain documents he looked gravely at Theodore. "Theodore Vittorio Jerome, I hereby pronounce you; Missing In Action. Yer out of the Army now pal, by the way, happy 21st Birthday, Laurence Martel. I made ya a couple of years older on paper, goombah, makes things easier, more legal and you being as tall as Lurch, well it works out, ya know?"

Theodore felt himself gulp unconsciously as he watched Angelo neatly fold his new papers, the ones that said 'Laurence Martel' on them, back into the envelope and hand them to him.

"Take only a few things that you really need. The rest will be shipped home, along with a last note to your father, understood?" Angelo looked at him somberly.   Theodore just grimly nodded.

"Do not go out tonight, let no one see you. Tomorrow I will personally drive you to a location where you will hook up with someone different, a guide. I have no idea who, I only know the location I'm supposed to drop you at. After that, no matter what, you pretend you never heard of me in your life, got it, paisan?"

He nodded again. The two men stood up briefly and embraced quickly, as two Men of Honor, as friends.

Theodore scratched out a quick letter to his father Victor. He knew his father had risked everything, had spent much in money, in favors and in his very soul for this. Nothing could be risked now, he wrote simply.

Dear Mr. Jerome.

I am sorry on the loss of your son Theodore; however, one day in the future, you will meet the acquaintance of a certain 'Laurence Martel'. I think you will find him more than adequate to do whatever jobs you need done. I recommend him personally.

Your friend- Vito Bonnaro

He knew his father would understand exactly what he meant and what the message implied. It was done now; there was no going back, not ever. That night he packed up his money, a few meager belongings. The rest had been turned over to Angelo, so the Mortuary Affairs personnel could deliver 'Theodore Jerome's' personal belongings to his grieving family.

The next morning Angelo had Theodore ride in the back of the ambulance with the rest of the cadavers, then once out of the compound allowed him to ride up front. Laurence Martel now just wore only a black T-Shirt and his army fatigue pants and a small rucksack of his personal belongings and nothing more.

"You nervous?" Angelo asked him, as he drove Laurence to the final destination.

"If I said no I would be lying, my friend." Laurence said softly, idly watching the jungle scenery pass.

"You'll be Ok, eh?" Angelo smiled as he lit up a cigarette, "You're a fellow *goombah*, you'll be fine."

Angelo turned the raggedy green Army ambulance off the main road down a rarely used dirt trail, which they rode down in silence for a while. The only sound was Angelo's occasional cussing as the cadaver wagon bounced roughly along the muddy ruts and grooves in the trail.

They finally pulled up to a small clearing. There stood a man around Angelo's height, but at once Laurence sensed something very different about him. The fellow had dark eyes, a grizzled roughly chiseled face along with dark long hair he kept neatly tied back in a single long braid. He wore an old army uniform with no insignia, a large knife strapped to his side and a Russian AK-47 across his back; a black T-shirt accentuated his well-muscled body, with not an ounce of fat on him. Something about the man looked primal, feral and almost lupine, like a wolf.

"Oh fuck." Angelo muttered with an almost awe sounding fear. "I know him, that's Cochran!"

Theodore-Laurence had no idea who or what a Cochran was, but Angelo certainly seemed overly impressed and unnerved by him.

"*Madonn*, you do have some good connections." Angelo whistled briefly at Martel.

Laurence was about to get out of the ambulance when Angelo suddenly thrust something at him. Theodore looked down; it was a wad of cash.

"Take it, goombah." Angelo said softly, "You're good folks, a real stand up guy. Be safe, you understand?"

"You too *paisan*, take care." Theodore and Angelo gave each other a quick handshake, but deep friendship flowed between them. For a brief moment it was the hardest thing in the world for Theodore Jerome to get out of that ambulance, but he did. Now it was truly final. Theodore Jerome was indeed missing and presumed dead now.

No sooner had he gotten out, than Angelo slammed the ambulance into gear and hurriedly backed out the way he came. Apparently he was impressed by Cochran but had no desire of meeting the man, in fact if anything, Cochran seemed to have a dark reputation that preceded him. Laurence didn't bother to look back.

"Cochran I presume?" Laurence said.

The man raised an eyebrow at him and cocked his head slightly at the tall man in front of him. "That's one of the names I'm known as, if you want to use it, that's fine. Right now, I just need an additional $500 US dollars and we'll begin our little trip."

Laurence looked at the fellow darkly for a moment; he knew the fellow was skimming additional payment off of him but what could he do. He quickly peeled off some of the cash Angelo had given him and handed it to the fellow.

"Good." Cochran simply said, "Follow me." and without a further word he turned and walked towards the jungle. They walked deep in the underbrush to within a few feet of a stream and began to follow down the length of it. "Here," Cochran unslung the AK-47 from his shoulder. "Carry it, it's your protection."

Martel didn't know what to think of the man. He was arrogant, he moved like a stealthy shadow amongst the forest and there was something so compelling about the man it drove him nuts. There was some kind of inner grace and strength that alluded Martel's mind about Cochran. And despite the fact that Cochran probably only stood around 5'8, his presence and enigmatic charisma seemed to make him almost as big as Martel himself.

"So where are we going, what's the schedule here?" Martel asked him after about half an hour of walking through thick jungle.

Cochran stopped and abruptly turned. "A few rules here, my tall shadow," He said. "First, after this no more talking. I am your guide and teacher, not your friend. I have been paid to take you through some hostile territory and into a safe haven. That is my job. Yours is to learn and to be quiet and to follow without question. Later we will talk more and I might answer some of your questions, in time. From what I understand you are supposed to be dead," A slight smile tugged at the corners of Cochran's mouth. "I know death intimately and it doesn't talk and ask a lot of questions. I am good at what I do and you will be taken care of, if, you follow my rules implicitly. Fail that and you may very well end up truly dead, kid. Are we clear on that?"

Martel took a deep breath, his knuckles where white with rage where his hands gripped the gun but he said nothing. Slowly he nodded slightly but said nothing else. The look of daggers in his alone eyes spoke volumes.

This only bought another slight amused smile on Cochran's rough face. "You'll need that anger in time my tall shadow, but not today. Now follow me and do so quietly. It is already obvious to me you have no field experience." The man seemed to miss nothing.

The rest of the day was spent following Cochran's grueling pace through the thickest nastiest jungle Martel could imagine. Mosquitoes ate at him, leeches sucked on him, and within a few hours he was soaked in sweat and near exhaustion. Cochran looked relatively comfortable, he was neither exhausted nor overheated. Very few mosquitoes gnawed at him and he had no leeches on him at all. Thankfully Martel's guide was fairly patient and stopped frequently for him to catch his breath and drink his water. He had already drunk three canteens full and now Cochran was squatted down at the side of a stream filling the two canteens again, as he dropped some small iodine tablets into them. The only sounds were the relentless buzzing and droning of flies and mosquitoes or the various calls of jungle bird.

Martel knew Cochran was right, he had no field experience. Ever since he came here, he had never had to leave Mortuary Affairs except to run the ambulance full of cadavers to the planes for their final journey home. All morning long Martel had heard a cacophony of various birds, strange animals and weird jungle noises, but recently there was a new sound adding to the background din of the jungle, one that sounded like a bird making a weird sounding call he had not heard before. For some reason it made the hair along the back of his neck prickle.

Instantly Cochran was on his feet, swift as deer and as silent as a stalking wolf. Wordlessly he easily rammed Martel back off the path and into the jungle. "Down!" he hissed softly into Martel's ear.

Martel dropped down onto all fours as quietly as possible into the foliage. This obviously was not good enough for his mysterious guide who suddenly and soundlessly in one smooth martial arts like motion, knocked Martel's arms and feet out from under him and effortlessly grabbed the AK-47 from around Martel's shoulder. Just as Martel was pondering the graceful moves that Cochran had used to knock him flat, the man suddenly kneeled astraddle Martel's back and began to fire the gun sweeping it to the back and side.

Laurence was so stunned he dared not move a muscle. He had no idea what was going on. All he was aware of was the staccato sound of gunfire and a few screams of pain and cursing in Vietnamese. It seemed to be coming from everywhere and was over nearly as soon as it started. Cochran got to his feet and silently motioned for Martel to walk with him as they began to walk to the area he had shot at.

All was silent, too silent, not an animal or sound stirred. As they came out of the back end of the trail, Martel saw the 5 dead bodies of Viet-Cong enemies and then near the stream, scrambling to get away was a lone Viet-Cong female.

Cochran had hit her with gunfire in both her legs and now was stalking her down, growling angrily at her in Vietnamese. She screamed back at him, angry defiant. Cochran saw what she was reaching for and shot her dead before she managed to pull the pin from the hand grenade.

"Let's go," Cochran harshly motioned to him without looking at the carnage or the stunned Martel. "Our position is compromised; now we travel a bit more uncomfortably," he grumbled.

As Cochran led him back through the bushes they had just been at, Laurence noticed several bullet holes that had been right where his head had been. Had Cochran not knocked him as flat when he had and covered him, Martel truly would have been dead. It was then, Theo vowed silently to himself; as arrogant and gruff as the man was he was trustworthy beyond question. The man had put his own life on the line to protect him and he would never doubt or falter on Cochran's orders again.

The rest of the day was spent drifting downstream in the water itself. That night Martel pulled off 50 leeches, even his guide Cochran had his share of leeches. As an exhausted Martel finally lay on the ground, under the makeshift shelter trying to drift off to sleep, he caught a glimpse of his strange traveling companion. Cochran was standing in just his pants with no shirt or shoes, outlined by the large rising moon and going through the most graceful set of martial arts moves, Martel had ever seen.

Martel lay there that night pondering all that had happened to him that day. The cold, calculating deadly accuracy Cochran had handled the enemy snipers, the no mercy he had shown the enemy and the way he was at one with the very essence of the jungle; even the way he had protected Martel. And now even though both of them were beyond exhausted, the strange and mysterious Cochran was going through these graceful moves of martial arts that were so compelling to watch they were nearly sheer poetry in motion, under a starry night sky.

For the next few days, little was spoken between the two men. Cochran occasionally gave him orders, or had him collect firewood at night, but in the silence Martel truly studied the man. Cochran lived on the land as easily if not more so than the very people here. He set snares, caught fish with his bare hands and finally after the second day, cooked up some type of foul smelling fat and plant concoction that he told Martel to smear over his body. After that the flies and mosquitoes stayed away for the most part. Every night Cochran went through his ritual of doing his martial arts practice: The slow graceful moves of Tai Chi or the slow exacting moves and repetitions of Karate, or the rapid angry and hard moves of Aikido.

It wasn't until day four that Cochran finally seemed to visibly relax. This time it was during the day that they stopped. Cochran had caught some fish for them and one of his earlier snares had caught a small monkey-like animal that he had quickly killed and was now roasting over the fire, along with the fish.

"Soon we will be at a halfway house," Cochran took something out of his own rucksack; it was a small pint of whiskey. He cracked it open and took a long draught and then passed it to Martel.

"Thanks," Martel nodded and took a long swallow. He needed it more than he knew.

"You'll spend a few days in the halfway house while I do some business, then I'll come back for you and take you up to the port."

"Who exactly are you?" Martel asked, not in an unfriendly way, but genuinely curious.

A low wolf like chuckle barely escaped Cochran's lips. His intense hazel eyes looked deep into Laurence's. "I'm a run-away, Shadow, same as you. I've lived in and around these jungles for the last eight years. Originally I came here with US Intel but business was far more lucrative running guns, dope, whatever. I do a lot of things," Cochran alluded with a rare smile. Martel just shook his head good-naturedly and took another drink of the whiskey.

"Why do I stay," Cochran glanced around out of habit, always on guard. "That's what you really want to know, isn't it, Shadow." It was a statement not a question.

Martel nodded, "Yeah, I guess it is." He agreed.

"Because it's in my blood now," Cochran eyed him levelly. "You probably don't understand..." he paused and for a moment seemed to see deep into Martel's soul.

"Or maybe you do. Maybe you will understand in time. Sometimes, there are more important things than money, Shadow."

"This is very true." Martel nodded, God, how he knew that. As he looked into Cochran's eyes for a moment he had the oddest feeling; almost as though he were looking into a mirror, seeing within his own eyes, into his own soul. It was the most disconcerting feeling in the world. He chalked it up to exhaustion and probably some sickness from being sucked dry by leeches and mosquitoes. "That Judo shit you do, every night. What is that?"

Cochran eyed him quite harshly, his wolf-like eyes narrowing for a moment, as though judging whether Martel was insulting him or genuinely interested. He seemed to make his decision, "It's called Qigong, one of the more meditative Martial Arts..." for the next 3 hours

Cochran relaxed and talked about different styles of Martial Arts and their heritage, their plusses and minus' in combat and for healing, and like a magnet, Martel listened enraptured.

Martel had a hundred other questions he wished he could ask the man, but his own etiquette of being raised as a *Mafioso* forbid him. One didn't pry into another man's business. Cochran was one of those people who seemed both aged and ageless; his voice always seemed low and soft but yet at the same time could hold a hint of darkness, arrogance, playfulness, or soft contemplation. In those hazel eyes of his were the eyes of someone who had killed so many he had stopped counting, a man who had done a hundred crimes, who had loved, who had lost, who had lived, and who had died.

"Will you teach me?" Laurence finally asked that night after saying very little during Cochran's long talk that night. After all, it was the first time in nearly a week his benefactor-guide had felt in a talkative mood.

Cochran again looked at him with those penetrating lupine like eyes. "Stand up." He ordered, lightly. Martel complied getting to his feet.

"I want you to hold onto me and not let me go, even if it means death. Whatever you do, don't let me escape, understand?" Cochran looked up at him a bit playfully.

Martel nodded warily, but sensing that his teacher was testing him, he was determined to do his best. He did have Jerome blood flowing in his veins and he would call on all that was in him, no matter what.

"Go ahead. Get a grip, and do not let go." Cochran quietly ordered.

Martel stood behind him grabbed him in a chokehold, noting that Cochran didn't flinch a muscle as young Martel wrapped his long arms around the man and held him fast against him. "Hold tight, Shadow." Cochran chuckled a bit darkly.

It was then Martel's world exploded in nothing but bright oranges, reds and pain like he had never felt before. He knew his body was being punished with blows and that holding Cochran was like trying to hold onto raw fire. The harder he held the more it burned him and burned him bad. It was not until Cochran had driven his heel into Laurence's testicles and the huge man collapsed in a crumpled heap that the punishment stopped.

Laurence lay there; puking his guts out, tears and snot running out his nose as he lay on his side gasping for breath. He noticed Cochran a few feet away, blood flowed down his chin, his throat was scratched and bruised. While Laurence had gotten the worst end of the deal, Cochran had not escaped unscathed.

Cochran walked over to the crumpled heap of Laurence and knelt down. "I will teach you, Shadow." He spoke raggedly and then he used his hands to press on one side of Laurence's neck, the other pressing on his abdomen. Nearly instantly the excruciating pain of his balls being racked began to lift. Martel didn't know what kind of healing power those hands had but he knew that whatever simple maneuver

Cochran did, by merely exerting a gentle force he was able to relieve the extreme pain of the punishment that had just been done to him. This also made a lasting impression on him.

"You look like shit, Shadow." Cochran finally stood away from Martel. "Go to sleep."

Martel was about to do just that, when he noticed even banged up, Cochran had the dedication and self-discipline to go through his nightly ritual of his Qigong.

Dragging his own exhausted and still sore body to his feet, Martel limped over to where Cochran was. "I would like to learn Qigong too." He simply said. Cochran gave a satisfied nod and Martel's lessons began that night, with his first teacher, Cochran, as the two bruised and battered men began the graceful moves of Qigong together...

CHAPTER 14- *June 16th 1987*

Victor sat in his study with Joshua, as both men sipped cups of coffee. "You look healthier every day, my *Padrone*." Joshua smiled at Victor.

"And you flatter an old man, my consigliere." Victor raised his cup at him, "But today I received good news from my dear friend Vito in Sicily. Everything is green light for our meeting in a few months." Victor took a drink of his coffee and then put down his cup, watching Joshua unwrapping one of his ever-present nicotine gum squares.

"They must work, eh?" Victor nodded toward the gum. "I haven't seen you have a cigarette in five months, now."

"I don't know Victor," Joshua sullenly said, "I think I'm addicted to the damn gum now. Maybe we ought to get into this business, eh? We'd make a lot of money with it." He dumped the empty wrapper in Victor's garbage can.

Victor smiled at him. "I'm glad your humor is good, Joshua. I made you a promise and I intend for you to follow it up in exactly two weeks."

Joshua looked alertly at his boss now. "That business with Paulie, we talked of." Victor merely said, and made the gesture of a gun with his hand. He could see the thousand thoughts running through his consiglieres mind. "Joshua..." Victor said levelly. "It's to be a cut and dry hit, you understand? Pull him in, whack him, hide him and that is it. And do it far away from his business, here at the house if you need to, or down by the docks or in the city. Take Leonardo with you on the job."

"I understand," the consigliere nodded, "your orders will be carried out."

"I know they will, Joshua." Victor said softly with conviction, "No showboating and no grand torture. Not now, things must still be very

182

low key. He must simply disappear and never be found again. Believe me; I'd like nothing better than to have you make his death one that lingers for days and sets an example... But we have the F.B.I running around sniffing up everybody's asses now after that business with the D'Salvatores. We have the D'Salvatores running around with vendetta in their veins and we have other Commission members who are watching us with eagle eyes, wary over this whole thing. Now is the time for precision, stealth and coldness, cold like ice."

Joshua nodded grimly. At least he had gotten some of his anger out earlier on that prattling driver Cesare Ciccerone.

"Is something troubling you, Josh?" Victor said gently, watching Joshua carefully over his coffee cup.

"Nothing, *Padrone*." Joshua paced a bit, looking at the old Geromano coat of arms on the wall and at some of Victor's antique oil paintings.

"You wonder why Cesare got off as lightly as he did." Victor voiced what he knew deep in his heart his consigliere must be thinking.

Josh almost spun around with a shocked expression. "Am I that easy to read Victor?" he said almost sadly. "I meant no offense, you know I would never disrespect..."

"*Che metta a tacere*, Joshua." Victor said gently and reassured him. "I speak it because the question is there and I care for you as a son, so I give you an answer."

Joshua said nothing but came and humbly sat back down at the desk across from his beloved mentor.

"He lives; because he cared, Joshua. He fortunately said nothing any more damning than what the local newspapers say. Do you remember what I said to the girl?" Victor asked him.

Joshua looked up, blankly. "To keep her mouth shut?"

A soft chuckle played on the old mans lips. "Well yes, that too, but I told her I blamed myself and I meant it Joshua. I should have had her instructed better."

"It's my fault too." Joshua defiantly said, defending his boss. "I should have worked her myself, not had Carmine work her. I'd have taught her a few lessons." His eyes darkened.

"Joshua," Victor looked at him exasperated, "Why do you fight me so much all the time?"

"*Padrone*?" Joshua looked up almost stricken.

"Ask your real question, eh?" Victor felt his own eyes darkening, "You want to know why she is here, why I spared her."

Joshua said nothing as he felt his mouth go dry despite the gum he was chewing. He could only blankly nod, the last thing he wanted to do was piss off the man who was more loved to him than any blood relative.

"It is none of your Goddamn business." Victor said darkly, frankly, his eyes boring into his consigliere's. "Why did I take you in? Why do I do anything? Joshua it is not for you to second-guess me but to trust me and more importantly follow my orders."

Joshua felt as shame faced and stunned as if Victor had reached out and slapped him.

"Right now everything and I mean everything, in this Family must run as well as the most precise machine. From the lowest associate to the highest capo, from John Thomas to the fucking empty suits that hang around our family like vultures. All must run as I see fit, or we will lose this *mannagge* with D'Salvatores." Victor sat back and eyed deeply his consigliere. "You have the gift Joshua," Victor continued "you will be rewarded for your hard work, but the one thing you must learn is patience; *pazienza*. Sometimes what you think you see, is not what you really see, is not what is below the surface." He took another sip of his coffee, "You may not understand everything I do, or Martel does or even Cesare does, but you must trust in those whom you have pledged your loyalty. Even those grey areas that make no sense to you." Victor's eyes softened a bit, and he leaned back.

"I understand, *Padrone*." Joshua said quietly. The man looked hurt, "Victor, forgive me, I..."

"There is nothing to forgive Joshua," Victor said lightly, cutting him off. "You are your own harshest critic." He leaned forward with a slight twinkle in his eye. "You fight yourself worst of all Joshua. Sometimes we have to just stand back and watch, even the best warrior watches and learns." Victor drained the last of his coffee. "Enough of the lecture shit, eh? You're too old, I'm too old and there are more important things to be done. Have some of the bodyguards move Alyssa's things into Martel's house, she'll be out of your hair for awhile." Victor teased. "Don't think I haven't notice the two of you seem to have your own personal grudge going on." He chuckled. "I may be old, but not blind." He enjoyed watching Josh squirm a bit.

"Understood, *Padrone*," Joshua smiled back at the old man. "And point taken."

"Oh, and Josh?" Victor called out innocently before Joshua left. Joshua paused by the door and then hesitantly turned.

"You know, Cesare will be out for about a week, recovering. Make sure you and Rocco take up his work for a few days, run his route for him and collect his vig and tributes. Make sure you leave at least a little something for him to wet his beak in. He will be coming back in a week or two." Victor popped a lifesaver in his mouth and gave Joshua a half dismissive wave.

Joshua didn't know whether to laugh, curse or look shocked. He figured his best defense was no reaction. With a nod of understanding he quietly left. 'Damn Padrone, you're going to drive me insane yet.' He grumbled to himself. He did love the man though, Victor was indeed his father, and he also knew Victor had a maddening way of driving home a point.

Alyssa's eyes slowly opened, there sitting in a chair across from her was the large form of Laurence Martel. He was dressed simply in dark pants, a dark shirt and an unbuttoned dark grey sport coat. She could barely see the shoulder holster that concealed his gun.

"Good morning, Alyssa," his deep voice quietly spoke. "I hope you slept well."

She tried to say something, but the awful croaking noises that emerged from her throat reminded her once again that she had lost the ability to speak. She tried to remember all that had transpired last night but it was jumbled, clouded and disjointed. She had very vague memories of Victor talking to her in some kind of elegant office, bizarre dreams, but little more than that.

Martel stood up and swiftly and buttoned his sport coat, "As was mentioned, you will be moving in with me today. I will give you a half hour to get dressed and what not. Some of your things have already been moved into my home, further down the estates. We'll eat breakfast here and then later your Uncle said I was to take you into New York City to do some shopping. The change of scenery may do you some good."

With no further instructions the Dragon quietly and gracefully strode across the floor and ducked down out the door, closing it behind him. She heard him chatting briefly to some guard outside the door. It didn't definitely didn't sound like Tommy's voice replying.

As she got dressed she desperately tried to piece together what had happened last night. But so much of it was a jumbled mess and worse she felt hung over. The more she woke up, the more some of the memories came flooding back. Victor's angry fight in the gym with her, and then...blankness. There were some blurry memories of talking to him in his private office and him telling her that she would be living with Martel for a while. She vaguely had the feeling that Cesare was in trouble, but she could not remember any specific conversations with Martel or Victor from last night.

What had happened?!? Was her amnesia now spreading to her waking moments too? It had never done that before. With a cold chill, she turned on the shower and waited for the water to warm up. She glanced at herself in the bathroom mirror; it was then she noticed the deep bruises along her collarbone and throat. Saw the slight bruise on her arm where it looked like she had gotten a shot or something but had no idea what it was or where it had came from. Her hand lightly touched them and she remembered the deep anger in Victor's eyes and voice. Remembered a brief image of Victor on top of her, jamming a heavy weight against her throat but what else had happened?

As she finished up her morning routine 20 minutes later; all she definitely knew was that somehow, Cesare and herself had gotten in trouble for talking about the subjects they had talked about, "Maybe I should have listened to John Thomas' advice," she glumly thought to herself. That she was now sentenced to live with the formidable underboss Laurence Martel, who was to teach her the correct way, "whatever that meant," and that she was never to talk to Victor about 'mobster' stuff again. "Well I certainly am not inclined to! Whatever happened I know it was scary, even if I can't remember all of it." She thought with clarity but the rest was just vague, dream-like images that made absolutely no sense to her.

She dressed and went out the door to see one of the darker elite bodyguards. He grunted a rough "Follow me." and led her downstairs. She wanted to ask where Tommy was but she noticed there was no pen or paper in her room anymore. In fact someone must have come while she was sleeping and emptied most of her stuff out of the room.

Downstairs it was just Martel at the table and no one else. Already a plate had been prepared for her and placed across from him. "Eat up, Alyssa." He motioned with a 'no questions' gesture.

She slid into the chair and began to eat. The man caused the willies in her; he always had since her very first meeting of him. His sheer size, coupled with his stone cold expressionless face and the fact that she knew what he was capable of. She vividly remembered that argument with him and Joshua in the ring that day and for once, she was almost wishing even Joshua was here; anyone, other than her and Martel alone.

Somehow Alyssa sensed she and Martel were –not- going to be having long friendly conversations like she and Cesare had done. She was beginning to see exactly what Victor had meant in the statement: "Martel will teach you the –right- ways of the Family." First; she saw what kind of trouble that had gotten her and Cesare into and two, she certainly didn't feel as amiable towards Mr. Dragon Martel as she did towards Cesare. With her, Cesare had been friendly, kind, jolly. Martel was simply intimidating, stoic and had a heart that was as cold as winter.

Martel glanced at her deeply for a moment with those icy eyes of his, then picked up the nearby paper and began to read. "Take your time and eat up," he said quietly in his deep, sepulchral voice. "We have a long day ahead of us, my Shadow…"

(July 1973)

…"Let's go, my Shadow," Cochran marched himself and Martel out the next day to the halfway house. It was little more than a poor Vietnamese farmers hut with a husband, wife, 5 kids, 2 oxen and a bunch of chickens running around.

For the last week, Cochran had said very little to Martel except on day 5, and then had taken him and shown him some of the martial arts moves. He never called him anything but "Shadow" and rarely if ever explained anything. He just gave orders and Martel implicitly followed. Throughout this ordeal Martel had said very little, and just blindly followed whatever Cochran had told him to do but being in the dark and not even having an inkling of what plans may be coming up were beginning to grate on him sorely. He was tired, bruised, sick, exhausted and his patience at near end.

"Look Cochran," Martel said as wearily dumped his load on the shabby wooden steps, interrupting the conversation that Cochran and the Vietnamese farmer were having.

"Just what exactly is the plan here? I can't understand these people. You had mentioned something about a port; don't you think it's at least time to let me know something of what is going on here?" Martel was beginning to get thoroughly frustrated.

Cochran finished his conversation with the farmer in flawless Vietnamese, bowed respectfully then turned to Martel. "Walk with me..." He said in English a bit tersely.

The two walked away from the house for a few dozen yards, scattering chickens out of the way. "...I was paid to not ask questions and to get you out of the country," Cochran began, "I was supposed to take you to the port where you were to hook up with some other connection in Korea. I know the fellow, have worked with him a few times, but honestly I don't think he is for you." Cochran slung his own backpack down and kneeled down fishing around in it.

As he began talking again, Martel had to kneel down also just to hear him.

"You asked me the other night to –teach- you," Cochran continued, "at first I had just assumed you meant the martial arts but I have traveled with you, made my own assessments of you..." Cochran looked levelly at the strong young man who kneeled across from him. "There is much, so much more I could teach you. But I will let you decide." He pulled out a few small packages and then began re-buttoning up his backpacks. "I can stick to the original plan and take you to the port in a few days, or you can stay on with me. And in case you think I take up with any old run-away, never have I offered a partnership and training to someone." He said bluntly looking up then at Martel.

For a second Martel had that disconcerting feeling again of looking at his own eyes and soul within Cochran's. There was something about the man, something that reminded him of his father Victor; no nonsense and yet gifted with knowledge and strength that was immeasurable.

Wherever Cochran went he was treated as some great warrior, advisor/protector and respected person of all; of the North Vietnamese, South Vietnamese and Americans alike. He lived on the land as easily as a wild creature, could kill with a few lethal moves of his bare hands and seemed to hold a storehouse of knowledge in his head that he was now willingly offering to Martel.

Martel sat down, rubbing the stubbly growth on his own chin. "Why?" he finally asked quietly after a few moments. It wasn't a rude question, but Cochran could see the honest curiousness in it.

"Because, my tall Shadow," he grinned lightly, "I look at you and see someone I saw nearly 12 years ago. Myself. I don't want to know your story, that is yours and I won't ask and I honestly don't want to know. It certainly won't help your learning with me any. But I see someone who seems to be on some kind of inner quest and not just the average deserter-runaway." Cochran glanced up briefly around his surroundings, always alert to the tiniest details, "I see someone with brains, natural talent and perhaps it could even be because I'm getting older, looking for a true partner to share information with, someone who could eventually do some work for me in Korea or Japan."

Cochran pulled out another small pint of whiskey from a side pocket on the backpack and once again after taking a long drink he shared it with his traveling companion. "I won't lie and say it will be easy." Cochran said under his breath. "The last few days are fairly typical, maybe even easy but you've impressed me with your tenacity, your own inner codes and your own strength of spirit. But I guarantee you one thing; if you stick with me we could be one hell of a team, Shadow. You can earn yourself some money, but more importantly, I think I can offer you exactly what it is you're looking for."

Martel looked around at the two large, smelly water buffalo that wallowed around by the small sewage pit near the hut and the squawking chickens. He had nothing to do for the next five years but learn. He had seen Cochran in action a few times and whatever the man had, he definitely had charisma, intelligence, a sense of deadly and accurate survival and even a run of damn good luck.

Martel knew he couldn't say no, he felt almost compelled by the strange Cochran who seemed a perfect blend of East meets West. He was a smuggler, a drug-runner, a martial arts expert, an assassin, survivalist and who knew what else. Martel was defiantly intrigued. After the time the man had saved him from the Vietcong ambush, he had no reservation of Cochran robbing him or leaving him for dead. The man could have done that 10 times over already, in fact if anything he seemed rather protective of his younger traveling companion. "I'm in." Martel said looking into Cochran's hardened gaze. "You got yourself a student."

For the first time, Martel saw a genuine smile, spread across Cochran's grizzled, wolf like face and he simply put a hand on Martel's strong shoulder. "Excellent. I'm glad." was his only simple reply.

That night the two stayed overnight at the farmer's house, getting a good meal and some decent sleep. Cochran explained to the farmer that there was to be a change and that Martel wouldn't be staying with the family, he paid them anyway though. Both the farmer and wife had helped refill Cochran's supplies of survival gear, some medicinal plants, powders and some wrapped packages for trade.

"Raw opium," Cochran explained to his new student as he and Martel began the trek back into the jungles. "I trade a lot of it up stream in the larger areas, and bring back money or more importantly, needed supplies back to the producers the farmers. Now," He stopped abruptly again, so suddenly, that Martel nearly ran into him. He turned and faced Martel. "I can't go on calling you Shadow and its best if you use an alias around here, so, I am giving you the name 'Kageryu'..." the way Cochran pronounced the strange Asian name sounded like "Kah-Jer- Ree- You"

"What does it mean?" Martel looked at him a bit suspiciously, hoping Cochran wasn't calling him something insulting or worse.

Cochran gave an honest chuckle. "Nothing bad, my overgrown friend, I assure you. In fact the day you truly figure it out will be the day your ready to move on from my tutelage."

"Hmmm." Martel said raising a suspicious eyebrow but said nothing more.

It was slipping into late July on the Delta Cong, and now Martel, known simply as "Kageryu" began his longest road with his new teacher, Cochran. Over the next three years he would learn Vietnamese, Korean and the Japanese language. He would learn several styles of Martial arts (Aikido, Jujitsu, Shotokan Karate and Tae-Kwon-Do) as well as 'street combat' skills. For someone with no field experience he would learn how to be able to dismantle and rebuild a gun in 20 seconds flat and take out any witnesses or enemies with it. The two would spend months out in the jungles collecting opium or other high value trade items; transfer them into various towns for more trade. There they would party for a few days, restock up and head back out.

Cochran was hired by individuals to assassinate enemies, he was hired by governments to find hidden Vietcong Prison camps and he was hired by the enemy to sneak them back over to communist territory. The only one Cochran was loyal to, was himself and to his student. With Martel helping him, the two soon had a very lucrative business going.

Martel never really was sure who or what Cochran truly was; if the man really was deep undercover for the US Government, a double-agent or indeed a 'turncoat'. Martel learned everything from psychological and medical interrogation techniques with IV drugs and hallucinogens to tracking down run-a-ways or enemy camps in the jungles. He learned Eastern/Oriental healing techniques with natural plants, poultices and teas as well as crack shot assassination techniques both with weapons and with bare hands. He also learned to use his martial arts skills to heal as well as harm, learning where pressure and median points were to alleviate pain, to relax nerves, to relax trauma to a human body. He learned the healing touch that was a combination of Reiki and Shiatsu, a form of massage practiced in ancient oriental cultures like Japan and Tibet for centuries.

Kageryu-Martel had in those three years gone from a tall, gangly young man, to at age 22 his full height of 6'11. He had filled out to a hard toned body of strong, solid muscle. His long blond hair he kept at nearly mid-back length and usually neatly braided up in a single braid or a simple ponytail the same as Cochran did. The icy blue eyes had grown harder and deeper, the voice more baritone and sonorous. His soul had grown colder, harder with each life he had taken, even in self-defense. But killing never did bother him. Not once. Martel saw it as just a necessity, and for him it was easy to separate job from personal feelings, never did the two meet. This was something Cochran never had to teach him, for Martel it just came naturally to him. It was an instinctive part of his Mafia soul.

The other thing that had fascinated Martel about Cochran was how deeply the man embraced all things Oriental. Cochran was even a devout Buddhist and taught his student Kageryu the simple meditations and prayers. He taught him the Oriental culture, the language, the very essence of all that was 'Eastern' in philosophy. All of it Martel absorbed like a sponge, to him it felt natural not awkward and he eagerly drank in the knowledge and Asian philosophies and culture.

Perhaps Cochran's words had been true and he had indeed seen deeper into young Theodore/Laurence/Kageryu's soul than even he himself knew. Like his teacher, Martel soon adopted many of these same philosophies and they seemed a natural part of him. They just fit his soul and were an extension of him, no one forced him, in fact if anything Cochran tried to dissuade him. But in the end, Martel chose his own path; his own destiny and once down that path, Cochran fully supported his student's choice.

Like his Master, Kageryu now willingly straddled two worlds and yet was his own unique being and also like his Sensei Cochran, he too had soon built up his own reputation and he could see the fear and respect in others eyes when they dealt with him the same as they did his teacher and master, Cochran.

CHAPTER 15

(September 1976)

Laurence had learned over two years ago, as he worked on becoming more and more proficient in his Oriental languages, that "Kageryu" was Japanese for, literally "Shadow Dragon". But just that simple translation did not seem to satisfy Cochran.

"Yes, but what does it mean? How does it translate to you?" Cochran questioned him one day during their daily martial arts sparring.

Martel pondered to think for a moment and that is when Cochran caught him in a wide roundhouse kick to the head that dropped the huge man easily. Martel sat there glaring at his teacher. "I don't know," his deep voice rumbled, "but I have learned never trust your Sensei not to knock your jaw off if you let your guard down." Martel teased him with a serious face, rubbing his sore jaw.

Cochran bowed deeply with a mischievous gleam to his wolfish eyes. "Now you're learning, Kage." He called his student by his nickname, which sounded like *Kah-Gee*. Cochran offered his hand to help Martel up but with lightening speed Martel grabbed the proffered hand, flipped Cochran over his huge shoulder, then flinging his own body into a nearly backbreaking backward bridge he pinned his teacher cruelly beneath his own hard shoulder.

"Now you're learning a little too well." Cochran grunted in pain beneath him and Martel let him up. Both men leaped to their feet and bowed deeply. The sparring and lesson was over.

"You will be ready soon." Cochran suddenly announced out of the blue. "In three weeks I am making preparations for you to catch a freighter to Japan, where you'll start earning business and connections for me."

"No, wait!" Martel nearly hauled Cochran off his feet, "I just started with you! I mean I am sure there is still much more I need to learn! I can't be ready yet?"

"Kage," Cochran talked honestly, to his friend and business partner, "You've been with me for over three years now. There is very little more I can teach you. I consider you an equal now, not a student. It is up to you to take what I have shown you, and build it into your own. You understand?"

Martel just grunted and began cleaning up their latest campsite. He didn't really understand. He wished he could just keep working with Cochran, he knew it was too early to go back stateside yet and never had he had a friendship with anyone as closely as he had with Cochran. The man was like a father and brother rolled into one.

"You missed your calling my man," Cochran appeared over Martel's shoulder, "Counter-Intelligence would have loved you. You'd have been a natural but the only thing holding you back from being your best is your own fears."

Martel glared at his teacher harder. "I am not afraid, Sensei." He said levelly. "What would I be afraid of?" he glared, a young man's testosterone filled pride. "You've taught me more ways to kill a man than I can count, how to survive in hostile territory, how to make a living."

"You fear what you don't know, and you fear yourself, Kage." Cochran grabbed up his own gear, not meeting Martel's gaze. He was in his teaching mode and he knew Martel's Italian temper could flare like a hot fire when he wanted. But as Martel had long ago learned, Cochran never gave an inch; he could be the most hard and stubborn teacher of all. "You fear your inner self most of all. You're right, I did teach you all those things and more..." Cochran looked up, his own long braid flipped back over his shoulder. "I taught you how to heal with a touch, how to do psychological and physical interrogations, how to track a man down, how to run dope, find a POW camp, you name it. There is no reason you can't go on your own. You need to learn the world doesn't revolve around what you desire and want but where you best fit into it and how you can best serve those you are loyal too." Cochran began casually walking off towards the brush, not looking back.

Those words hurt Martel deeper and more painfully than had his teacher given him a few more roundhouse kicks. He had never seen himself as selfish or disloyal but what was his fear then, if not that? A simple but human desire and loyalty to remain here with his teacher and friend. He quickly trotted up alongside Cochran.

"There is an criminal type group in Japan," Cochran continued in his easy banter the one he often used when giving Martel missions or instructions, "They are kind of like your own people, what do you call it? Mafia? They are called the 'Yakuza', kind of like a Japanese Mafia, similar to the Triads. I have connections there with a Tashima Katsuro and I promised to be sending them a crack assassin and strong-arm. That is you, Kageryu and you will be sending information and business back to me on the sly." Cochran explained in a no-nonsense tone. To Martel it sounded eerily like his father Victor and in that moment his heart truly did yearn to move on, closer to his final journey back into the Jerome Family.

"You will need all the training I have given you Kageryu, like your own groups, the Yakuza have a lot of rules, loyalties and long standing traditions. You will be the outsider and need to prove yourself to the Boss and prove yourself well. Any fear they detect they will feed upon like sharks in bloody water." Cochran told him bluntly. "In three weeks, you will go." He finished, and nothing else was spoken of it that night.

Martel's heart and soul was heavy for the next three weeks. Only four times in the last three years did Laurence dare to send a letter out to his father, back home in New York. Always it was brief and always he wrote as Vito Bonnaro, usually just wishing the family a Merry Christmas and mentioning that Laurence Martel was in good health. It had been very hard for him to not be able to write to his younger brother Michael or even his own mother, or to receive mail from his father letting him know what was going on.

He had seen early on exactly the kind of sacrifice that Victor had talked to him about so many years ago on that summer day in Giarre, Sicily. That night he scribbled out two quick letters as Laurence Martel, one to his father and one to Michael. He knew he probably wouldn't be able to write to them right away in Japan, not under the noses of the Yakuza, Cochran had pretty much warned him outright.

Laurence looked up at the stars that night as his companion Cochran sat in a twisted yoga position deep in meditation, a joint hanging out the corner of his mouth.

"Two more years, *Padrone* and I will be back." He thought to himself, almost willing that his father could hear his inner thoughts. "I only pray that the gambit has worked my beloved father." He knew and trusted Cochran implicitly to deliver the last two letters out for him...

June 17th 1987

Alyssa's mind told her she had never ridden in a helicopter before and so like a young kid she stared out the window the whole trip from the Jerome Estates to the giant VIJER Corporation headquarters building in downtown New York City.

Martel watched her out of the corner of his eye a few times during the flight into the city. Her fear was giving away to curiosity and that was a good sign. The Ketamine mixture seemed to have worked well in making her forget most of the interrogation, as he had thought it would, of last night. If she did remember, she wisely seemed to show no reaction.

One of Victor's last private requests of Martel had been a simple... "Laurence, if you can't teach her or you feel at any time she is a liability, then I trust you implicitly to do what was not done months ago. If it needs to be done; then do it fast and humanely, but I think she is smart, I think she has learned and will learn. Call it a gut feeling but I think that is one problem we won't have to worry about anymore."

Laurence truly hoped it didn't come down to that. He would execute her if he must, but like his own teacher long ago, he saw a spark in her that he had not encountered in a very long time.

Once they landed, Laurence took her arm in his large long one and elegantly led her briefly around the VIJER offices, giving her a tour of the giant Import-Export company.
"This is the business we run." He said quietly, "The Family Import-Export Company. It has been in the Jerome Family since 1949..." and so he continued for awhile, feeding her the information he wanted her to know, telling her about the Families legitimate businesses.

Here the armed guards were non-existent, two had come with her and Laurence from the Jerome Estates but they carried their guns concealed and Martel had left his entirely back home. Any guards with heavier weaponry only showed up when Victor showed up, and even then it was only in the upper offices or penthouse apartment, not down in this legitimate area. Martel gave her a quick view of the penthouse apartment and spoke briefly to a man he introduced as Mr. Danny Valsiglio. "He is also our corporate attorney," Martel smiled grimly at some private joke.

While the two men spoke briefly in Mr. Valsiglio's office, Alyssa went and took in the view of the city from the 14th floor. It was indeed breathtaking, only one of the two guards stayed with her but said nothing. A half hour later Martel returned and again, leading her like a gentleman, he took her arm and they went downstairs to where a waiting limousine was. She noted that this one bore the license plate JEROME 2 and seemed a bit larger and heavier than the one at the Estate. There was no Cesare driving but some other man she had never met.

While Martel had been talking to Valsiglio, she had finally been able to find a small pad of paper and pen and so began to write out some questions for Martel, such as where they were going and what the plans for today were.

"I told you," Martel regarded her briefly, "Today you get to relax and have fun. We'll do some shopping, some sightseeing have lunch out somewhere. Have you ever been to New York City?" he asked.

Her mind told her she had not, so she shook her head no.

"You'll like it, trust me." He settled back. "Enjoy today, tomorrow I am sure I will have a nice schedule of activities for you to help you integrate better into our Family." He paused looking out the window himself, watching the street life of the bustling city. He could feel empathy for her, he was sure he had been this helpless and defenseless when he had first hooked up with Cochran. Hell, he almost got his own head blown off the first day. But his teacher had been patient, firm and even compassionate, when Martel thought for sure he was trying to make his life hard. The last he had ever seen of Cochran was over 10 years ago and until Victor had given him this assignment with Alyssa, he had not even thought much about it. Not that he didn't want to remember but so many other things had went on in his life, but now, with this new person underfoot that he was totally responsible for, his own memories began to weave down dark pathways he had not thought about for so very long…

(October 1976)

…Cochran stopped the old beat up jeep along the docks, where great cargo ships and freighters were being loaded. "You know how to contact me once you make it over to Japan." He handed Martel a few

194

wrapped bundles that Martel put in his duffle bag. "You'll be met on the docks by someone named Akinari, he's Tashima Katsuro's counselor, you'll know him on sight, he's missing the pinky on his left hand. He will probably show you to the boss today or tomorrow, I've told you the correct respectful greetings for the boss and give him both of those packages I just gave you. That's your 'passport' into the Katsuro clan," Cochran continued. "Also, keep all your original paperwork from three years ago, hidden and hidden well. You've worked hard to erase yourself don't compromise that to anyone. In fact my humble advice is say nothing to anyone about yourself. The story is; you're just there as my representative, got it? Most important, as I have drilled into you for the last three years, always remember constant vigilance." Cochran merely pointed to his own two eyes in the Army sign of 'vigilance'.

Martel just nodded. He had taken to dressing pretty much like Cochran and usually wore old army fatigue pants and either a black T-Shirt or just a black T-Shirt with a torn, sleeveless army fatigue shirt.

Cochran looked him up and down as he chuckled. "Here Kage," He reached in the back seat and handed Martel a couple of wrapped packages. "It's my gift to you, a nice suit some shoes and a hat, the whole works. They dress nice, the Yakuza. Even though you're going there as an independent you'll be expected to follow the same rules as their boys, if you know what I mean."

"I understand, Sensei..." Martel began.

"No." Cochran interrupted quietly, "I am not your Sensei anymore. I have nothing left to teach you, you're my equal. Just call me Cochran, Ok?" he smiled almost sadly.

It was the first time that Martel truly noticed the grey beginning to mix in his long dark hair, the deep lines of his face, the various battle scars all over him and worse the inner scars. In the years he had followed him, Martel could see why people had thought the mysterious "smuggler/trader/runner" a deadly and mysterious enigma and he indeed was. But for the first time, Martel saw him as just a man. The wolf was becoming grizzled and old.

"I will miss you, Cochran," Martel said softly, not looking at him. "And I thank you for what you have taught me. I assure you I will never forget it."

"No, I suspect you won't. That then that is the greatest thanks of all, my friend." Cochran slipped his sunglasses over his eyes and turned his head away from Martel. "Now go on, get outta here and send some good info and trade items my way. If not, I'll personally hunt you down myself. I give you my word these last two letters of yours will be mailed out as soon as I leave here."

"You got it. And thank you again." Martel gathered his stuff and like leaving out of Angelo's ambulance three years earlier, he did not look back.

It would be the last Martel would ever speak to or even hear directly from the man again. Rumors came to him six months later in Okinawa, that the untouchable Cochran had finally been killed. Some say he was double crossed on a deal, some said he was captured and tortured for playing both sides, still other rumors even said he simply went back to the Government he still loyally served and was just a damn good double agent the whole time but whatever the truth was, after that day, Martel would never directly hear from his old teacher and friend again.

Cochran had indeed given Martel the greatest gift of all; the knowledge that he now carried in his head, that was more valuable than anything. As well as his first expensive dress suit, as a professional hitman for the Yakuza, the Japanese crime syndicate. In the same box was a small gold neck chain, with a small dragon pendant on it. It was the only tangible items left from his mysterious and shadowy teacher.

Martel had indeed met Akinari Saitama and the Boss, Tashima Katsuro outside of Tokyo. For the first several months, he consciously chose to remember very little. He was kept very busy usually with the most mundane of tasks, and thankfully dealt mainly with Akinari who was like a consigliere.

Laurence Martel's true reputation was made on his first true terror killing for the Yakuza. He had worked for Tashima Katsuro's men for close to two months and he was not at all surprised to find nearly all the men not only hated him but also distrusted the tall, blonde haired American foreigner. Cochran had warned him; he was not born of their ways, or of their codes. But yet unnervingly Martel seemed to know them instinctively. He spoke flawless Japanese, he was a master at several types of martial arts, a natural born killer and he acted like no American they had ever seen before. He seemed to truly live up to his odd name of "Kageryu- the Shadow Dragon".

He worked directly for one of the Tashima's most profitable officers and counselor, Akinari Saitama. Since he had been placed here in a trade between Cochran and Tashima as a hitman and enforcer, he was expected indeed to be just that.

Martel knew he would have to not only work harder than other members, since he was an outsider but as his teacher Cochran had warned him, it was best that he prove himself a fearful opponent and get his reputation out fast.

Killing was nothing new to Laurence Martel. Under Cochran's tutelage he had already racked up close to 40 hits, many were Vietcong attackers, but many had also been people who had double crossed Cochran or even those who hired out contracts on others. So killing, whether in self defense or as an assassin was something that Martel was already intimately familiar with, including gruesome interrogation techniques.

Tashima Katsuro was a cruel, sadistic crime boss who seemed to take great delight in working Martel far harder and more dangerously than any of his own men and worse, he seemed to try and find whatever ways he could to humiliate the man. So it came as no surprise to Martel when he and Akinari were summoned before the heavyset Yakuza Boss.

"Akinari," Tashima growled at his counselor. "I have a special assignment and I want Kageryu over here to do it..." A cruel grin flashed over the pig-like face, "...and I want him to do it alone. However I will have you and four others watch the execution to see if indeed this American," he half-spat the word, "can show us anything new, eh?" he roared with laughter. Around him his henchmen and soldiers also roared with sycophantic laughter.

Martel could feel their hostile stares at him, the humiliating laughter. He merely stood stock still at his full height, no emotion in his deep blue eyes. Never would he give them the satisfaction of letting them see any emotion on him.

Akinari had been the only one who had even been decent to Kageryu, after all he worked with him on a daily basis and saw the humiliation the foreigner stoically endured, the expert and professional way Kageryu carried out whatever orders were given him, the way he never responded or 'lost face' no matter how cruelly the Katsuro men taunted him on his looks, extreme height, having had Cochran as a teacher or his being a 'useless American'.

In Akinari's eyes, Kageryu had already proven himself many times over; he doubted most of his own men could have withstood the constant verbal taunting and humiliating abuse.

"So what is the assignment, *Oyabun*," Akinari referred to Tashima as 'Father' which is how the Yakuza called their main Boss, almost like the Italian version of *Padrone*.

"Simple, Akinari." Tashima spoke to Akinari but his piggish eyes stayed glued to Kageryu. "One of the shop owners we collect tribute from, has begun to complain and is trying to get other local shop owners to resist paying our tribute. I intend to make an example of him. I want him and his wife to both suffer horrible deaths and be left in their store to be found. It will be a message job to any others who want to renege on deals and tributes."

Akinari gave a low bow in acknowledgement of his Boss's orders; "*Hai*, It will be taken care of within three days, *Oyabun*."

"I will be sending Hiryuu along as my witness." Tashima grunted, "And I want some witnesses from your group as well."

A short lean man in a casual shirt with his arms full of tattoo's stepped forward, he was Tashima's underboss. He glared darkly at Kageryu, a slight smirk on his sullen face.

Laurence already knew on this hit he would have no help or assistance whatsoever, in fact if anything probably all the men but

Akinari would find ways to try and trip him up making him look bad or foolish. However a dark plan was already forming in the shadow dragons mind. He knew how he handled this assignment would determine what his stay with the Yakuza would be like, either it would be a living hell with constant humiliation and torment or they would leave him alone to just do his job. He was determine it be the latter.

Three days later they were driving down towards the assignment, all jammed up in one of the henchmen's car. Martel being an outsider was the only one who did not have many of the extensive and elaborate tattoos that most Yakuza members had, so instead while they wore clothing that would show off their elaborate and intricate tattoos on this job, he merely dressed in his usual black pants, a black turtleneck and a black sport jacket. He wore a dark overcoat and thin leather black gloves as well in the cool wintry Tokyo air.

"Hey, stupid American, Kageryu..." Hiryuu teased him as they all headed to the shop owners store. "Why you all bundled up like a turtle? You have no tattoos on that white skin to show off eh?" this bought a round of laughter from the other men. Only Akinari was reserved in his emotions, he had no beef with the enigmatic foreigner. In fact like Martel, he just wished Tashima would leave Kage alone to do the job he was meant to do.

He gave a quick glance at Kageryu; still the tall man's face was as unreadable as granite. He just blinked once at Hiryuu as though the underboss was an idiot and said nothing.

"Hey, are you insulting me?" Hiryuu narrowed his eyes at Kage and growled at him.

"Why? Do you think I am?" Kageryu answered in a completely low and level voice.

This actually got chuckles from the other henchmen and a hearty one from Akinari.

"Oh, shut up!" Hiryuu roared at everyone and angrily spun back around to light up a cigarette and stare out the window.

Martel always thought Japanese one of those languages that sounded like you were being shouted at or insulted. It was just the low guttural tone of the language and its nuance that made it seem that way. Most Asian languages sounded harsh and angry to the 'American ear'. Thanks to Cochran he was fluent in Japanese, Vietnamese and Korean.

Ten minutes later they pulled up to a small general store, and all of them piled out. It was nearly closing time, so they knew they would be uninterrupted.

"Remember," Hiryuu instructed all the men, "This job is for Kageryu alone. Unless of course he is too weak or cannot stomach it," he sneered, "then we will show him what the true Yakuza can do." the underboss chuckled darkly.

The other men just nodded and cast furtive looks at the foreigner who still wore no expression on his stone cold face. This began to make even them nervous; didn't the American ever show any expression?

As soon as they went inside the store, Tashima's men acted arrogant, bold and loud. One turned the 'OPEN/CLOSED' sign from open to closed and stood by the door so no one could enter or leave. Another man quickly scouted the tiny general store making sure no customers were inside while Kageryu and Hiryuu strode to the counter.

Behind the counter stood an older man, at least in his late 50's; he was a tiny speck of a man but he had a strong inner fire. "What are you thugs doing in my store? Get out!" He stood up bravely even though he knew he had no chance against them.

Hiryuu leaned on the counter heavily and arrogantly shouted at him. "Ah, Satoshi, old man, you had plenty of time to pay us; over and over you refuse to pay our tribute. Now we take it out on your hide you ignorant old fool."

Still fear did not cross the man's face; he stood there bravely, glaring at Hiryuu.

"Kill him Kageryu." The underboss ordered casually and stood back. "And remember, slow and memorable, or you join him."

Briefly Martel and the shop keeper eyes met. The old man's look seemed to touch Kageryu's soul, almost the way a zebra's spirit touches the spirit of the lion about to kill it; a look that spoke of quiet certainty, fate and dignity between them. Satoshi knew he was going to die painfully and cruelly at the hands of this tall foreigner and he knew that the strange man had no choice either, that he was just as caught up in this game and battle as he was with the Yakuza.

At that moment the shrieking anger of his wife came from behind the store. Satoshi's mate came running into the room, "*Nooo!* You awful snakes, all of you! Leave! Leave our store! Leave us alone!"

Hiryuu easily caught up the old woman and disarmed her of the knife she had. "Akinari, tie her up let her watch her husband die slowly." He chuckled.

Only then did Satoshi's expression look terrified and horrified for his wife. 'Why hadn't she run out of the store? I don't care about me, but I was hoping to buy time for her life'. He hung his head, now he knew it was truly over. As Martel walked over and grasped his arm Satoshi barely whispered in Korean, for Martel's ears only, "Do what you must with me, but let her die fast when it is her time. I beg you great Dragon."

Martel nodded with the slightest of gestures. A slow blink to his eyes that seemed to give Satoshi's soul peace to endure what was to come.

"What did he say? What did he say?" Hiryuu demanded angrily since he didn't speak any Korean dialects.

"He just begged for a quick painless death for himself." Martel looked over at Hiryuu. "He won't get one."

Akinari and Kageryu's eyes briefly met. Akinari spoke fluent Korean as well and he knew exactly what had been said, but he looked away and played 'dumb'. His level of respect for the tall foreigner had only climbed higher and an involuntary shiver crept over him. What did the shopkeeper sense that these other men did not and more importantly how did he even know that Kageryu spoke Korean?

It was then that Kageryu let his dark presence and fill the store; a blackness so dark, terrifying and predatory that a thick silence seemed to descend on everyone there. The arrogant and snide faces of Tashima's men began to fill with horror as over the next hour Kageryu extracted such horrific torture and vengeance on the man that they had never seen in their lives nor imagined possible.

Not one man in that store that day would ever be able to cleanse his memory of what had gone on there. The nightmares would haunt them for the rest of their lives as they watched the Shadow Dragon's full terrifying force come out.

In this Kageryu did not do it to humiliate the storeowner but Tashima Katsuro's own men. Several times many of them including Hiryuu the underboss had to run to the corner to vomit; some looked positively green at the horrible vengeance the foreigner extracted with both weapons and in bare handed martial arts.

By the time Satoshi's mutilated body was finally tossed to the middle of the floor, a lifeless heap of meat, the men seriously doubted they could withstand another 'show' like they just saw with Satoshi done on the man's wife. They were genuinely relieved, that the shopkeeper's wife died quickly. They had figured she was in shock like the rest of them, little did they truly realize she died fast because Kageryu granted her a quick and merciful death. He had kept the promise to her husband.

Only Akinari stood silently by in support of Kageryu, doing his duty to watch, to humiliate his own men by not flinching at the cruelty Kageryu unleashed. The enigmatic foreigner truly was a Dragon, some great beast that seemed capable of destroying so easily. It reminded him of watching a great tiger tear apart a small antelope, limb from bloody limb.

Kageryu had mutilated Satoshi's wife's body only after she was dead and then easily tossed it onto the pile of meat where her husband was.

"You can arrange them however you wish." Kageryu turned around, great sapphire blue predatory eyes focusing on Tashima's underboss Hiryuu.

Not a single snide comment was spoken; in fact a horrified awe had descended upon Tashima's men. "That is fine," Hiryuu barely whispered, his bile still rising at the carnage. "That is fine how they are Kageryu..." he barely whispered the foreigner's name.

"He has done as the *Oyabun* has asked." Akinari spoke loud and clearly as he looked around at his fellow soldiers and at the underboss. "It seems to me the only ones who could not handle it were you." He said sincerely, honestly.

The men just quickly filed out, not daring to make a comment, fear still trickling through their veins like ice water. From that moment on, Kageryu would indeed get his wish. The fellow Yakuza members would never again doubt him; in fact they seemed to steer as clear and far away of him as they could.

Nearly all insults to his face stopped once Tashima had gotten word of the brutal killing that Kageryu had done, so brutal and cruel in fact it was in the news for weeks; and made the Japanese law enforcement come down hard on all the local Yakuza groups.

Later that week, Akinari would take Martel to one of the best tattoo men in Tokyo and personally pay for Martel to be tattooed on his upper shoulder with an intricate set of Kanji's and tattoos that read "Bringer of Death" as an honor of respect to the strange tall man, for the enigmatic foreigner truly lived up to that name.

It was during those darkest of times, when he was accepted by no one other than Akinari or himself did he learn the true nature of the name given to him by his ex-teacher, Cochran. Kageryu, the 'Shadow Dragon'. Martel hardened his heart and interior even further, he became the master of noticing the tiniest details around him without giving away anything. He learned to never give loyalty nor trust that was not earned and in his heart there was only one who owned that loyalty now, his father Victor Jerome.

Begrudgingly the small clan of Yakuza he was with learned to treat the strange American with a certain respect and even fear. He understood their language, their customs, he was a dark silent sentinel always seeming to be one step ahead and he killed with a precision and understanding of martial arts that even they were impressed with.

Finally just nine months into his work with the Tashima Katsuro's clan he was pulled aside one day by the boss.

"I have watched you personally, over the last nine months. I admit like the others, I owed you jobs because of past favors for Cochran, but the words he spoke about you in the letter were true." Tashima spoke to him. "This life is not for you," The boss idly waved his hand around, his small dark, pig-like, eyes still on Martel. "You have more talent, more dedication, more honor than most of these men. I want you to meet someone tomorrow. His name is Sen Yamashita and he will be at the Pool hall down the road. I am releasing you from my service with honor, Kageryu-san."

Martel bowed deeply and following the customs dictated, bid his boss an honorable farewell. He could only hope that what the fat, pig-like Tashima had in store for him was not a set up. However his inner instincts told him it wasn't and that while Tashima was being honest,

201

he was indeed not telling him everything. Somehow he sensed there was a lot more to Tashima's releasing him from his oath-bond.

The next day he got there early, very early. But apparently, Sen was on the same wavelength. No sooner had Martel come in and gotten a booth near the back where he could watch the door, when a small, middle age man with short cropped dark hair came over to him.

"Kageryu-san?" he asked respectfully. Martel nodded yes.

"Good, I am Sen." The man spoke in broken English, "Come; I have much to talk with you about, but not here." The small man then turned and walked to the door.

For a moment, Martel nearly lost sight of him. If Cochran was noticeably impressive, the thing that struck Martel the most about Sen was how the man could seem to literally melt into the surroundings in any situation. Martel had to watch the mysterious Sen nearly the whole time, or he simply blended in and got lost in the crowd even while next to Martel's side.

Martel and Sen had gotten a taxi to one of the famous high speed train stations then taken the train up north, far out of the city and out to the deep northern rural areas. Once there Sen led them both to a beat up looking pick-up truck and drove them even deeper out in the rural area. During the whole ride, Sen chatted a little about nothing. Once they got there, Martel could tell it was a medium sized family farm with fields and orchards. He had seen plenty of these in both Vietnam and here in rural Japan.

What he didn't expect was the beautiful female his eyes locked onto as soon as he exited the beat up old truck. She was over by the porch scattering corn for the geese and chickens. And it was not just her appearance, for she was a dressed in dusty farm clothes, the wind playing in her long dark hair, but something within her soul that captured his eyes and heart in a vice-like grip. It was her heart and eyes that shined like the glorious full moon upon very his heart and soul.

"Kageryu-san," Sen snapped his fingers catching his attention. "Come. You meet my sister later, Ok?" Apparently Sen wanted to work on his English with Martel, because every time Martel spoke to him in flawless Japanese, Sen replied in broken, rather poor English. Feeling embarrassed and not wanting to offend his host, Martel quickly apologized for looking at Sen's sister the way he did.

Sen led him down past a few orchard trees to a small grassy area that looked like dogs or roosters had been in pit-fights there. The ground was scuffed, torn up, and there were stains that look suspiciously like dried blood. "We spar, I test." Sen said simply and then shrugged out of his oversized sweatshirt. In early middle age, his body was still in perfect condition, his lean muscles rippled. But what caught Martel's eye, were the Dragon and Cobra tattoo on Sen's upper chest, and all the other various tattoos on his back and chest. In fact his whole body seemed to be almost literally covered in tattoos, except for his neck, hands and face.

Martel and Sen both bowed respectfully and for a few minutes Sen seemed to put Martel through every move that Cochran had ever taught him. Within ten minutes, Martel was already working up a sweat and the small man was barely taking a deep breath.

"Kageryu is trained well, Tashima Katsuro not lie. Now, I want you fight me freestyle. You try block-fight back whatever I throw at you Ok, Kageryu-san?" the small man smiled with a strange glint in his eyes.

Martel was as humbled as he was that very first day with Cochran, the small man seemed to never be where Martel's kicks and blows aimed at and when the small Sen hit, it left devastating bruises and excruciating pain. In just a few moments Martel could already see his own blood was mixed with his sweat. Whatever the style the small man used it was deadly, accurate and brutal. With a single blow to the mid-chest Sen easily knocked Martel down, where he lay much like he did that day with Cochran, coughing up blood, dust and puke. His eyes watched the small man, who stood poised like some deadly cobra, his eyes were hard with a deadly intent, and Martel knew this man could finish him off as easily as swatting down a fly. Martel was truly hooked! The accuracy, deadliness and brutality of this new style was like nothing he had ever seen.

"The Dragon and the Cobra, Kageryu." Sen now spoke in perfect Japanese. "It is called *shinobi no jutsu* or ninjutsu; the art of death, life, of stealth, assassination and survival without ever being seen. But also much, much more: it is the art of being perfectly synchronized with your body, mind, soul and the very essence of the life force that surrounds everything."

Sen came out of the stance and bowed, but made no move to help Martel up, who clambered to his own feet and bowed deeply, "I am impressed with your effort and dedication Kageryu. I will teach if you are ready to take that step. But a very hard and different step, it is a very personal step. Not an easy path." The small man spoke frankly.

"Darkness and hardship is something I embrace easily, Sensei Sen." Martel acknowledged his new teacher. "And so far very little has been easy the last four years. I humbly submit to your teachings, Master."

"Very different code here, Kageryu." Sen grabbed his sweatshirt and shrugged back into it. "This art is also very deeply spiritual. What I have been told about you was right; you are different from the others. I can see it in your eyes," Sen was walking around Martel now, examining him as a farmer would a prize horse or oxen. "What is your heart, Kageryu, Eastern or Western?"

"Eastern," Martel dared not make a move, he knew that Sensei's-Teachers often had their own paths, their own styles of judging and in his heart he so wanted this. Tashima had been right, Martel wanted more of what Sen had given him a taste of, and not the rowdy, showboating style of the Yakuza. He would be with his own Jerome Family clan soon enough. If Cochran had ever had a teacher, it would have been someone like Sen.

"How do you make infection fighting poultice, Kageryu?" Sen asked.

Martel told him, often having to resort to the Vietnamese names of plants and so for the next half hour, with the small Sen circling him like a hawk, firing off questions like barbed darts, grilling him on his knowledge of herbal lore, living off the land, and even his very spirituality, he was judged.

Finally Sen faced him. "Ok, you kinda weird, Kageryu-san, but I will teach you." He tried to look stern, but there was a playful glint in the small man's eyes. "I am down one brother and sister. You stay in the shed over there, fix it up how you like. You work for board and instruction here on my family farm; you also help me learn English."

Martel bowed respectfully and went to get his small duffle bag, his whole last four years of life in one small compact space.

"Oh, and Kageryu ..." Sen called after him. Martel abruptly turned. "... My sister's name is, Miyoko." Sen chuckled as Martel ran the name silently over his lips. "But you worry more about my rice fields, orchards and the martial arts training I give you, Kageryu-san, understand?"

Martel nodded again, but Sen saw the first hint of a true human emotion on the large man's face all morning.

"Miyoko!" Sen called gruffly as he rounded the corner, knowing his sister had been watching Kageryu's testing in secret, "You stay away from Kageryu-san, he's here to work! He doesn't need to get his brains more addled then they already are!"

Miyoko giggled and disappeared back around the corner out of range of her brother's growling voice, she knew her brother's gruff tone was an act and he was approving of her to meet the new man. She would bring dinner out personally to the tall, foreign stranger tonight...

CHAPTER 16 -*June 17th 1987*

Inside the limousine Martel was keenly aware of Alyssa's emerald green eyes seeming to peer inside of him for a moment and he quickly shut that past door of his drifting thoughts. He tried glaring back at her in his intimidating way, but she actually smiled at him, then with a blush turned her attention back out the window.

With a soft 'harrumph' he ordered the driver to stop at the main shopping area on 5th Avenue. Again, Martel and the two guards escorted her through nearly the whole 5th avenue shopping district. Never was she told no, she couldn't buy something. In fact if she hesitated too much, Martel simply picked up the item and insisted she get it with the words, "Mr. Jerome said you were to get whatever you wanted, my dear. Do not worry about the cost, you're not paying for it, enjoy and indulge."

Although she stayed in the conservative price range, she was finally able to get some of the clothing styles that felt right for her. A few times Martel made a few purchases as well, but she didn't pay to much attention to what he was buying.

The only odd place they stopped at were a few shops in the Little Chinatown section of New York. Martel had her wait in the long limo with the two guards as he stopped in a few Asian markets and then finally they stopped at one place that was unmarked, except for some type of hand painted Asian writing on a small sign. All four of them got out there and entered the small dark shop. Once inside her head was filled with the exotic scent of incense and the dimly lit room held just about every Martial Arts weapon she could imagine. Even the guards were like kids at the candy store checking out throwing stars, butterfly knives or other exotic oriental weaponry.

She pretended to be looking over some swords as she heard Martel talking in a flawless Asian language to the small older clerk. He seemed to greet Martel as though he was a lifelong friend and the two exchanged several laughs and gossip. Of course, she didn't understand a word of their conversation, but after a few minutes the older man pulled forth from under the counter the most beautiful Japanese Katana she had ever seen. It was wrapped in black silk and Martel picked it up and handled it as though it were a delicate living creature.

"Sen, this is too special," Martel switched back into English. "I am deeply honored."

"Go on, try it out." The grey haired Asian man smiled with a dark playful glint in his ageless eyes.

Alyssa stood flabbergasted as she watched Martel go through several series of the most graceful sword moves she had ever seen. The skill and mastery he contained as he swung the weapon both single and double handed was so fast so full of deadly beauty she was barely able to see more than barely a glint of the blade in the dim light of the shop.

The small man had picked up a delicate, paper-Origami swan no bigger than a tennis ball that he held outstretched on his palm, as though willing it to take flight.
Martel's sword seemed to whisper on the wind and then come to a stop mere millimeters from the man's open palm. The paper swan lay neatly cleaved in half.

Alyssa found she had been holding her breath and suddenly let it out with a rush. Apparently the guards had been also; for they seemed to have been watching the sword mastery of their boss as well.

"Sen, this is a clan heirloom..." Martel began, gently rewrapping it.

"Now it's yours, should have been a long time ago. Took me awhile to get it back." He winked at Martel, "Now, you take it home where it belongs." The older man smiled with genuine affection.

Martel bowed "I am honored, Sen." They switched back into speaking in Japanese for a few more minutes and then Martel handed one of the small packages he had bought over to the clerk. One of the guards bought a few throwing stars and a butterfly knife from the clerk, as Martel finished gently re-tying up the sword. Martel also made a few more purchases that Alyssa didn't pay too much attention to, as she was still remembering the grace and deadly skill that the enigmatic underboss had swung that sword with. Like his argument with Joshua that day in the sparring ring, this also made a lasting impression on her. The incense in the shop was making her a bit heady and drowsy in a pleasant way.

It was when the three of them exited outside the shop that it happened for the first time. Yes, she gotten little glimpses and memory whispers during the last few months, small wisps of dreams or jumbled images but none as vivid or that hit as intensely as it did this day. It was almost as if a door was suddenly smashed opened in a far dark corner of her mind, revealing a clear and dark image that seared on her brain.

As the guards were loaded the packages into the already stuffed trunk of the limo, Alyssa noticed a small diesel semi-truck crammed into the small one-way street. An oriental woman and a black man were arguing loudly, but Alyssa's attention was suddenly drawn to the empty black yawning opening of the back of the idling truck. Her vision seemed to fade, and then tunnel.

...She saw two men, a tall, skinny grungy one, and an elegant black man, both wielding some kind of electric cattle prods. "*Move it bitches!*"

Alyssa had sudden flashes of being struck with those cruel electric sticks, being manacled with other beat up women, the fear and hopelessness in her heart. She remembered the smell of blood, vomit and feces, the smell of utter and palpable fear; "*Look, Ho... I can go on shockin' your ass all day long, either walk out on your own or I'll beat the fuck out of you and have you thrown in the rig, unconsciously.*"...

"Alyssa..." a deep, far away voice seemed to briefly penetrate her mind like a misty shadow.

For an instant she saw herself on a raft in the middle of an ocean with a hurricane raging all around her. Trembling on a raft, while snakes constricted her arms, legs and chest...

"Alyssa..." The voice was more insistent, more of a quiet command. Her vision began to fade from the hallucination, but she was scared and terrified. What if the men came back for her? In her heart she was certain they were looking for her!

Martel pulled her in his embrace close against him with one arm wrapped around her and with his other hand he discreetly pressed on the side of her temple, on the precise pressure points he knew were there that would help calm and center her. To anyone watching it would look as though he were just giving her a casual, lover's hug and a caress. He had no idea what had set her off, but he could smell the terror on her; see the total fear in her body. "Come on little one." He said quietly and led her into the limo.

Martel had touched and gently pressed on the side of her temple, jaw and neck, and whatever he did, it seemed to all but melt away the sudden terror that had been rapidly engulfing her. The feeling that she was going to pass out or throw up was diminishing rapidly once she was back in the safety of the limo, back inside the closed protective world that she had known for the last couple months. At that moment, she wanted nothing more than to be back in the Jerome Estates, safe, protected, hidden from whoever those two men were.

As soon as she got in she pulled out her pad, and wrote: "*I'm scared, I want to go back home to the Estates. It's safe there.*" She knew it sounded ridiculous, she didn't know why all of a sudden the thought of not being back home safe within the Jerome Estates panicked her but she knew in her heart something very bad had happened to her; and those two men, the elegant black man, and the tall, grungy scrawny man were responsible.

Martel read the note, and then simply nodded. "All right Alyssa, it's Ok. We'll go back if you want." His calm voice was low and soothing.

She nodded emphatically, not even noticing that unconsciously she had scooted over until she was nearly pressed up against the formidable underboss, who just a few hours ago had unnerved her. The two guards sat across and raised an eyebrow at their boss, who merely shook his head briefly at them.

"Take us back to the VIJER building, Frankie. Once there tell Albert to fire up the 'copter." Martel told the driver. He turned back to Alyssa; "We're heading back now. Is that better?" he asked softly.

She nodded yes, feeling a bit foolish but still she noticed her body trembled ever so softly. She didn't think she would feel truly safe until she was back through the gates on the Jerome Estates, as far away from the wide-open throngs of people as she could be.

Cesare's exact words from the other day flooded back to her... "Oh those guys are Ok," he had assured her, "they're here to protect us, ya know? They're the good guys." He chuckled in a warm way. "They protect us sloths."

Alyssa would never think of the guards as scary again. Not after today, not after whatever hidden demon had just scared her so badly. Unlike memory flashes of the past, where images faded after the memory, she still vividly remembered the faces of the two men. The elegant black man and the pock marked scarred grungy scrawny man. Remembered them clear as a bell.

She didn't remember why, she was being loaded in that awful truck or what had happened to her before or after, but she remembered them and the truck and those goddamn, horrific cattle prods. She also somehow knew deep in her heart the Jerome's had nothing to do with them.

Martel carefully watched her discreetly out the corner of his half lidded gaze. He had no idea what had just happened with her, he would have to talk to John Thomas. The doctor had mentioned that she may have some of these flashbacks, but Martel couldn't help but wonder if some of the drug interrogation used on her the other day didn't unlock other doors in her mind. She had specifically said she wanted to go back home to the Jerome Estates. This comforted him; she wasn't afraid of them, in fact if anything she quieted down exceedingly fast once they were in the limo and he assured her they would go back. But he remembered the way her eyes had looked when she had stared at that truck, and the two people arguing.

One of the things Cochran and Martel had done in his time with his strange teacher in Vietnam, was occasionally scout out locations of Vietcong American prisoner camps, so that U.S. armed forces could move in later to rescue the American POW captives. One time while was Martel there, hidden deep in the bush the Vietcong captors moved a few of their American prisoners from one makeshift camp to another. He had caught the eyesight of a few of them and some of those American prisoners had that same glazed, terrified look on their faces as Alyssa earlier had. As though their minds had been broken and were on the very verge of insanity. Martel met one man's gaze, whose hollow terrified eyes looked so far gone that it burned an image in Martel soul even to this day.

During Alyssa's flash-back her eyes had almost looked like that. A sad, terrified, almost catatonic look; she looked fine now, but how deep were her mental scars? No one but her knew all that had happened to her. Would she be strong enough to handle it if she did remember?

This one's life was going to be complicated; he could feel this. He was going to have his work cut out for him, but he had made a promise to his father and like his father, he remembered earlier when she had actually met his hard gaze and smiled back at him.

Deep within Alyssa there was a strong spirit but it was wounded, broken. He would not give up on her unless he absolutely had to.

(November 1977)

...Martel awoke stiffly to the sound of metal hitting metal. His body was aching badly from just the simple sparring he had done the day before with Sen, his new teacher. Sen had given him this shed area to

fix up as his living quarters and Miyoko had come last night with
blankets, food and some lanterns to help him set up.

Miyoko! Martel remembered their conversation that had lasted for
hours as she helped him set up. He had of course been the perfect
gentleman; to do anything less would have been a huge disrespect on
his host and Sensei, Sen Yamashita.

Miyoko was 2 years younger than Martel and had explained to him
how her two siblings had been killed in some conflict she did not go
into. She told him it was just her older brother Sen, herself and her two
elderly parents living in the house and running the family farm. That he
would be a huge help to them here, with his added muscle.

She seemed quite taken with the enigmatic, stranger and while she
acted the proper, graceful unmarried lady, Martel noticed she had an
inner fire and spirit that burned brightly. She commented on his good
forms of his martial arts moves and by the way she spoke, he could tell
she was accomplished in the martial arts as well.

Miyoko and Martel had worked to set up quite comfortable place for
him here, she had even given him her own quilt from her bed and
promised she would make him a new one and he could use hers until
she was done. Martel knew it was a very kind gesture and one that
also spoke of her interest in him as well. That night he had dreamed of
nothing else but her and now, Sen's shouting voice was yelling from
across the yard, waking him up.

"Kageryu!!!" he barked, "Rise and shine!! You sleep in far too much,
get up and help me!"

Martel was truly astonished that such a small man could have such a
loud voice that could carry probably about a mile, as well. Then again,
that metallic and deep, BANG! BANG! BANG! Laurence stretched,
threw on some clothing and padded out the door. He looked down and
saw Miyoko had left a bowl of covered porridge for him. He was
touched by her gesture and began to eat the now cold rice porridge as
he wandered off towards the barn where the banging was coming
from.

"Kageryu!!!" Sen's deep voice shouted at him again from somewhere
deep within the barn.

"I'm up! I'M UP!" Martel yelled back, his own loud resonant voice
causing the various farm dogs to start up a barking ruckus. His breath
was fogging in the icy cold morning air and even the grass was
covered in crystalline frost. The cold bit at his skin waking him up even
more.

"Ha, ha!" Sen laughed, "Very good Cowboy, come back here!"

Martel expected to see just some barnyard animals in the barn,
which he did, but what really drew him in, was the modified area in the
back of the barn. It was a great blacksmithing forge, a huge furnace
was going and all around in various states of creation were various
Oriental swords. The small, short form of Sen was dressed only in

long pants and a full leather apron covering him. His well-muscled form began to swing his hammer on another sword on the anvil, as he shaped it, using tongs to expertly flip it this way and that. Sweat now ran down his body, making his tattoo's seem to come alive in the hellish fires of the forge. He handled the metal as a true master, as an artistic genius handled paint.

Martel blinked in wonderment and then putting down the empty porridge bowl he reverently examined a few of the swords. Between Cochran's tutoring and what he learned from weapons being smuggled by the Yakuza, he was a fairly good judge of martial weapons craftsmanship, but these items, never had he seen such beautiful and deadly martial swords and daggers: *Katanas, Tantos, Daito's, Daishos* and others.

Sen thrust the blade of the Katana sword he was working in a bucket of cold water, steam rose with a loud hiss, as he tempered the steel. Apparently he approved of the way Martel looked at his craftsmanship. "What do you think, Kageryu?" he asked his voice still loud, like the fires of the forge. But he already knew the answer before Martel ever opened his mouth.

"Come, sit down here." Sen motioned to him, while the sword cooled off for a few minutes. The two men sat down on a couple of straw bales. "Our family, the Yamashita's have made swords for many, many generations." Sen told him, "It has cost our family and clan in blood and in many other ways, but still we craft things as they have always been done. This I will teach you also, now, you will work and learn Kageryu and when we are done, you will be as honed as one of my finest blades." Sen smiled a wide toothy smile at him a moment, then ran his hands over his closely cropped hair. "Now, you go man the bellows Kageryu and while I teach you, you are going to teach me that English, Ok?"

Martel nodded his understanding and taking his cue from Sen, took off his shirt and grabbed one of the small leather aprons. Even in deep fall, the temperature in the forge was as hot as the fires of Hades.

"So, what you think of Miyoko's cooking, eh?" The small man asked him, as they worked together at the forge.

"It was the best I have ever tasted," Martel said slowly, his mind still savoring his and Miyoko's conversation from last night; the smell of her, the sound of her voice.

"Oh, you are so weird and brain-addled, my overgrown friend!" Sen shook his head, barely concealing his laughter. This tall one just opened himself up for the insults but he was glad to see the man had a sense of humor and played along. "Hopeless, you are hopelessly caught by her aren't you? Not good, Kageryu." He teased.

Martel just flashed him a small smile and said nothing, he could already tell this new teacher was going to be as relentless as Cochran had been, but for some reason he already felt as though he had known

Sen for ages. Their personalities so clicked well together, that theirs was an instantaneous friendship.

"You just remember that I trained her too, so no funny stuff with her! Otherwise we both kick your ass." Sen said gruffly, however Martel could already see the spark of humor and approval in his Sensei's dark, coal black eyes. "And what's with that long hair?" Sen teased him as he grabbed up his sword again, "You some kind of hippie? You gonna get that burned off at the forge if you don't cut it" he threw a few more friendly insults at his new student, as he cackled gleefully...

CHAPTER 17 – *June 17ᵗʰ 1987*

They arrived back at the Jerome Estates late in the afternoon. Because all she had eaten was a light breakfast, Alyssa was starving but she was just so thankful to be back that she didn't say anything. This time when she saw the guards patrolling like they always did, she felt not fear but a deep satisfying safeness, just as Cesare had once told her. They arrived at the front door of the Jerome Estates and she was about to get out of the limo and walk in, when Martel neatly caught her lower arm, stopping her and guiding her towards him.

"Ah- ah, this way," he steered her to his large, black, Buick Oldsmobile. "You're with me, remember." It was an older model, but she could see why he liked it, it was fully loaded, and more importantly had a lot more headroom than the average car. The day had been hot, hazy and humid, and already to the west she could see huge dark storm clouds billowing up, on the horizon.

Martel drove her past the main house, down past the aviaries and into the road that lead to the dark forest where she had not been before, to his large four- bedroom ranch styled house. Laurence Martel's private home, the one she was warned about never going to. An involuntary prickle of coldness ran down her spine.

She was a bit nervous at first; Laurence took out some packages from the trunk of the car along with his elegant, silk wrapped sword and led her up the neatly manicured lawn and stone inlaid sidewalk. Martel lived alone and quite secluded from the main house but once he unlocked the front door, she was suddenly overwhelmed by curiosity. What better way to get an insight into who this enigmatic underboss was, than by seeing how he lived?

The first thing that nearly stopped her in her tracks was how the house was decorated. Nothing frilly or pastel here, Martel's house was done in a completely Asian style, with elegant black lacquered and mother of pearl inlaid furniture, Japanese style wall paneling and even the pictures and various statues were all in an Oriental style.

"Shoes off at the door, always." He told her matter- of- factly, then his own shoes removed he disappeared down the hall past her with his bundle of parcels.

She removed her shoes, still taking in the oddness of his house. She could have expected many things from the unnerving Martel, but not this. The house itself held the spicy Far East scent of incense, covering the floor was stark white, deep pile carpet, with some black throw rugs tossed here and there. The whole place was fastidiously neat as a pin, looking like something out of '*Oriental Home and Gardens*' There were several large comfy looking couches and chairs done also in black, and on the walls there was simple large Kanji calligraphy or oriental paintings of birds, bridges, cherry trees and Imperial pagodas.

In the front room near the front door were a couple of large oriental Foo Dog statues and a large dragon statue in the far corner, all elegantly carved in the fierce Asian style.
The ceilings were fairly high for a ranch style house and she noticed the doorways were all much higher than the average door. Alyssa figured he probably got tired of ducking or whacking his head on the doorframes.

Near one wall was a gorgeous Asian scroll style painting of a great dragon, curled inward upon itself, its great sapphire blue eyes seeming to watch over the house like a regal guardian. It seemed to pull at her very soul a moment and she walked over and examined it, painted on an ancient parchment style of canvas it had the name 'Miyoko' on it but the rest of the writing was all in oriental kanji's. Upon closer examination the dragon was actually rather shadowy and indistinct not really solid at all, as though he was ghostly. Clutched in one of the dragon's taloned claws was a cobra and around his neck was a beautiful sword, it dawned on Alyssa then, that the sword around the dragon's neck looked identical to the one Martel had just gotten today from the strange little oriental shop. The whole thing looked like a beautiful picture someone had drawn with much symbolism but also with much care. Alyssa found herself strangely and compellingly drawn to it, although she didn't know why. Somehow, she could have sworn she knew the dragon.

Finally pulling herself away from the shadowy dragon, she glanced around for Martel. Since he was not there, she padded softly, if not a bit nervously down the hall and then nearly collided with him as he came out of the hallway bathroom.

"Ok, I guess we'd better get the tour out of the way." He said slightly exasperated.

She could tell he did not seem the type to have visitors often, especially not live-in ones and he seemed a bit terse at having someone under foot.

"Follow me," he said softly in his deep voice and led her down the hall to the end. "My bedroom," he said simply and let her glance in.

It was the one room that was not as immaculate as the rest of the house, here there were actually some clothes lightly strewn about as though they missed the hamper, there were several elegant oriental katana swords displayed on the walls, several bookcases and some shelves with oriental figures or more weapons on them. A huge custom-made California king sized bed, dominated most of the room, done in the same black oriental lacquer style. There were also a large dresser inlaid with mother of pearl and an armoire also in the same black lacquer oriental style.

Near his nightstand lay his holster and Beretta 9mm, and also a smaller black Colt police special. Another doorway led off to the master bathroom. More dragon type figures, statues and paintings dominated the room, along with some exquisitely detailed oriental cork artwork, and some elegant carved mahogany figures in various martial arts poses.

"You already saw the guest bathroom, that one will be yours," he pointed to the bathroom he had just come out of: It too was decorated in the simple, Spartan oriental, black and white style. "Here is your room..." he opened the black walnut door directly across the hall from the guest bathroom.

It reminded her of a comfortable hotel room. A nice, neatly made queen sized bed, two dark mahogany dressers and a nightstand, desk with chair, a closet and little else. A few simple Oriental-styled landscapes dotted the walls and a large, live, potted Ficus tree stood sentinel by a small window, but this room was not as heavily influenced in oriental decoration as the rest of the house she had seen. There were no weapons on any walls in this bedroom; however she did notice that on the small desk were several packs of blank notepads and a package of fresh pens, as well as a few blank diaries for her. She was touched by the caring gesture.

Already on the bed, she saw that some of her personal hygiene items from the main house had been delivered and meticulously placed here, "Someone will be down shortly to drop off the clothes and items you bought today." Martel explained.

He gracefully turned and led her back down the hall and to another closed room; this one had some type of beautiful Oriental calligraphy/Kanji on the door and the symbol of Yin and Yang beneath it.

Martel's eyes had a bit of a gleam when he opened that door, "My sparring and training room. You'll get to know this one well..." He said in a dry voice. He led her inside; it was actually the biggest room of the house so far, around 30' by 40'. Most of the floor was padded with firm, padding. The large back wall was completely mirrored from top to bottom, in one corner hung a leather martial arts training dummy like she had seen at the huge gym in the main house and also a large, canvas punching bag. However these were set more for his height and seemed of better quality. On the opposite wall hung an assortment of various training weapons from canes to quarterstaffs, wooden swords, to nun-chucks, and a host of oriental weapons she couldn't even begin to guess at.

"You'll know the names of all of them soon enough," he said as though reading her mind. "Trust me," a slight smile tugged at the corners of his mouth.

She gulped unconsciously, the mere thought of sparring against the giant underboss sent a shiver down her spine; she knew full well what he was capable of. Somehow she didn't think he would be as lenient as Carmine had been with her.

Martel turned out the light and motioned her out, then closed the door. He walked to the final room and picked up the neatly wrapped sword he had gotten earlier that had been sitting on one of the elegant black lacquered tables. "This is my meditation room, and temple known as a Shinto." He simply said. This room had no real door at all, just a simple oriental style screen that folded in on itself. Martel bowed very deeply at the door and then carrying the sword he walked inside.

Alyssa warily peeked in, without entering. The room was dim, but yet lit by dozens of candles and other Japanese lanterns. There was a large dais on one end, where sat a shrine to Buddha and in front of that was an altar to burn incense and several prayer wheels and other Zen and meditative devices. The elegant, dark, hardwood floor had several large black pillows and prayer-meditation rugs. Near the door were two holders that held thick bundles of unburned incense and on the wall displayed tastefully and respectfully were various scrolls with all kinds of Kanji and oriental lettering that Alyssa had no knowledge of what they meant.

Laurence Martel grabbed a few sticks of incense and after igniting them in one of the oil lanterns he walked over to the alter and after bowing deeply he placed the glowing incense sticks in two braziers that held some type of black and white sand. On the wall behind the statue of Buddha was the white and black symbol of Yin and Yang. Martel then took the sword, reverently finished unwrapping it and placed it on a special location near the back of his meditation room/temple on a wall that held two other elaborate Oriental martial arts swords. This one looked so much plainer in contrast to the other two, but yet it seemed to be the finest of the blades displayed.

Alyssa stayed at the door not daring to go in, somehow she felt she didn't belong in this sacred place of Martel's, that it was his alone, almost as if it was a part of his very essence that he never let anyone casually see. It was his personal space and she was not about to intrude on something as reflective and personal as a man's philosophies and spirituality. She quietly went to sit on the couch and wait.

Martel's house was nothing like she envisioned in the strange, enigmatic man. In fact, it only deepened the puzzle of him in her mind, made him seem even more distant and unreadable. It was beginning to seem as though she had very little in common with him. She was surprised that her own mind had envisioned him as a dragon because in many ways, especially now after seeing his home and a peek at his inner soul, he truly was.

Large, strong, aloof, deadly and mysterious, he was the strangest mix of anyone she had ever met, even if she didn't have amnesia and he certainly didn't seem to fit any "mobster stereotype" that one would read in a novel. But yet even knowing these facts about him, there was a part of her who found something so magnetic about him; she couldn't put her finger on it. Like Victor, Martel seemed to possess his own type of charisma, much more veiled than Victor's but there none the less. If Victor could be subtle at times, Martel was three fold that. If Victor Jerome was a great sun that burned brightly, than the mysterious Laurence Martel was a vast and powerful black hole that sat in the shadows of the great sun, but controlled and influenced events in its own shadowy but distinct way.

She was shaken out of her daydreams of Martel as the large man swept surprisingly quietly past her into the kitchen. As he began to unwrap some of the fresh foods he got earlier from the Asian markets, he continued his talk with her.

"I suggest since we are going to be living quite closely together for awhile, we set a few simple rules," he paused and glanced at her through the room divider that separated the kitchen from the living room. "First, you're here as my pupil and student, so don't expect me to be your maid. You pull your own weight around here, got it?" he eyed her levelly. Alyssa simply nodded.

"Second; the basement door, to the right, over there..." he pointed with a wickedly long carving knife to a door next to the refrigerator, "...Is off limits to you at all times, period. It is my job to teach you how to function as a normal part of this Family, and to respect the rules as well as how to take care of yourself, understood?" She nodded again.

Just as it looked as if he was about to say something else, there was a knock at the door. He closed his mouth and strode over to answer it. It was Tommy DeLuca and another guard delivering all of the packages she had purchased earlier and some of Martel's.

"Take these ones to the third room to the right, I will take these ones." He told the guards and separated out his own packages.

Tommy walked in behind the other guard and Alyssa happily jumped to her feet to follow him.

"Hey Alyssa!" Tommy grinned at her as he saw her. "How ya been? You doing good?"

She nodded happily, smiling at him. How she had missed Tommy, even though it had only just been one day.

"Here, help me carry these," he let a few packages slip into her grasp. She showed the guards where her guest room was and they proceeded to drop the packages on the bed. "Jeeze," Tommy said under his breath to her after the packages had been placed on her bed, "not the kind of house I would expect Martel to live in, huh?" he grinned at her, the two sharing a private laugh for a moment, "But then again, with Martel..." he chuckled.

"Problem, Tommy?" Martel suddenly interrupted Tommy's sentence as he glowered down at him, leaning against the doorway. None of them had even heard him come up on them.

"Uh, no, Boss." Tommy straightened up visibly blanching. "No problems at all."

Martel definitely did not look happy at having his private sanctuary over run by all these people, not to mention their comments of his lifestyle. "Good. Thank you and good-bye then." He said rather dourly.

"Yeah, sure boss. G'night," Tommy and the other guard ducked out rather quickly.   Alyssa felt a twinge of sadness watching Martel lock the door after them.

"Now, maybe there will be no other interruptions." He said tersely to the closed door without looking at her. Slowly he turned back to Alyssa, "Why don't you go unpack your things, set up your room, and freshen up. Dinner will be ready shortly." His tense tone had dropped, now he just sounded tired.

She turned and walked back to her room to do just that. She noticed past the potted ficus and out the small window, the rapidly setting sun was now blotted out on western horizon, by the storm clouds that had blown up darker, more intense. Already lightening flashed far off in the distance. She saw the car where Tommy and the other guard were driving back up to the main house. From here, she could just barely see the large gable on the eastern wing, where the mansion's library would be. Outside everything seemed to be hot, oppressed and tense as though awaiting the impending storm. Even the patrolling guard dogs were panting heavily in the muggy air, plodding along disinterestedly with their hot, weary handlers.

Martel worked with a rough fury on the oriental vegetables cutting them up for a stir-fry he was making for their dinner. For nearly nine years he had lived alone here, worked hard to be the enigmatic, quiet and solo underboss. It was a part he had worked to portray ever since he arrived back in the states in 1978. Rarely if ever had anyone ever shared his personal space at his home. Sen had visited a few times, and he had occasionally drank and bullshitted with Joshua, Leonardo or Gio who had crashed on the guest room bed... But any female companionship he had was always kept downtown. This house here was his personal sanctuary and he allowed very few to ever tread on it.

Ever since Miyoko he had not allowed his heart to truly feel for another. Any female companionship was strictly for pleasure. He had

216

one woman, a *comare*, whom he met occasionally by the name of Diana. Martel knew she loved him and would do anything he asked to be a part of his life, even if it was to be his secret mistress forever, but he did not feel the same way towards her. There was no connection in his soul for Diana at all; she was merely a pleasant companion and plaything to sate his sexual desires. Not to mention that it was almost expected in his line of work, a made man in the mob who didn't have a *comare* was considered a little strange, all the wiseguys had a mistress or two.

But now, with a student underfoot in his house and a female one at that...

He sliced a whole half frozen chicken in a single, hard chop of his huge cutting knife. With his bare hands he began to easily rip the raw meat off the carcass in order to slice it for the stir-fry.

But now, he not only had a female student underfoot but worse, one who seemed to spark an interest in him, in areas of his heart and soul he thought long ago stone dead, and buried behind layers of walls. He threw the meat and veggies into a bowl and began to toss it with sesame oil and other spices and seasonings.

What exactly about her touched him? Was it her dependency on him? Was it the way she had unconsciously sought out solace, protection and even strength from him both in her interrogation the other day in Victor's office and when she had been frightened downtown? Was it that beneath all that she had been through, that there was a hint in those emerald green eyes that held a playful, curious, strength and a soul who longed to be free and strong. Perhaps in some ways Alyssa reminded him of Miyoko. Even Alyssa's exotic Celtic heritage with her flaming red hair, her soft white skin, and those green eyes, stirred an aroused attraction in him. Perhaps deep in his soul he wanted her to grow strong again; confident, sure and safe and he wanted to be the one to guide her and teach her.

He watched her walk softly back into the living room and sit on the large, luxurious couch. Dressed in simple buttery soft jeans, and a loose but flattering pale blue tunic top, she curled her legs under her, but her eyes and mind continued to flit around the room, taking everything in, processing it. Always she seemed to be alert and watching, like a small graceful hawk.

"You know, you're not expected to be a nun," he said. "There is a TV, stereo, VCR, remote over there. Have at it." He said with a slight smile of amusement on his face at the way she was always regarded him, both warily and also with curiosity. At only around 5'3 she was tiny compared to him and he remembered the way she had felt so small in his arms when he had carried her upstairs the other night. Yes, she was very different from anything he had encountered so far and the same way she was drawn with a fierce curiosity to his differences was the same way he was drawn to hers.

"*Kanashii-Taka*." he whispered in a barely audible voice. In Japanese it meant 'wounded or broken hawk' and that is how he saw her, a small graceful, fiery hawk with an arrow deep in its breast. Wounded and grounded. "I will help you." He thought to himself. "Here you will be safe."

(February 1978)

... For the next three months solid, Laurence Martel's days were filled with backbreaking physical labor. Either he was working the great bellows on Sen's forge, or working around the Yamashita farm and at night learning yet a whole new style of martial arts. He was sore from working the forge and hammers, sore from working the heavy plow and farm work and sore from the deadly new martial arts lessons his teacher had been showing him, but he wouldn't change any of it.

In Sen he had found someone both irrelevant and also very spiritual in his own right, with his crazy sense of humor and love of all things American. Even though Martel tried to convince Sen, that he didn't come from anywhere in the "wild west" Sen always called him "Cowboy" and was convinced that nearly everyone in the US lived like they did in the Old West. And it was also Sen who taught Martel that whether with a weapon or his bare hands, to make his martial arts a true part of him, and extension of his mind, body and spirit.

But the evenings were his free time and he was free to converse with Sen's lovely sister Miyoko. Often she would follow Laurence around the farm when she had time, and chat with him there, when she wasn't busy with her own chores or work. She was as strong in spirit as her brother and her smile would melt Laurence's heart.

However Miyoko was no soft or silent oriental woman. She also was quite proficient in the martial arts and occasionally helped her brother and Martel in the forge. At first Sen kept the two of them fairly chaperoned, but once he saw his student Laurence was indeed an honorable man and hard worker, he allowed Laurence and Miyoko more and more privacy.

Sen was not blind to the emotions and love that was beginning to engulf Martel and his sister. It had caused a few heated arguments between brother and sister, but finally when Sen realized if he pushed to hard, he would lose her too, he backed off.

Martel had learned that the older Asian families and small clans were not all that different from the ones that lived back in the hills and villages of Sicily, where he had spent a lot of time. Just like in Sicily, the elderly were usually revered and respected, and certain codes or etiquette and decorum dictated how different genders or age groups, or social standing behaved around one another. And while there was not a lot of planting and farm work to be done in the winter months, Martel worked hard fixing up the farm, the house and building his muscles on the great blacksmithing forge or learning the deadly art of

218

Ninjitsu from his mentor Sen, as well as other weapons based martial arts fighting styles.

It was on a cold blustery February day he would learn the dark secret of why he was here, at all.

Miyoko had just bought out a warm lunch for both Sen and Martel, along with some hot *sake*; a rice wine, to drink and even though she normally ate lunch with the two men, this time Sen chased her off. While she usually was not bluffed at all by her gruff but caring older brother, he seemed insistent. So with a rather dark toss of her hair and a slight but defiant bow of her head she finally recanted and left.

"We have known each other, for three months now, Cowboy, so we need to talk." Sen sipped his *sake*, without looking at Martel.

Martel had learned to read people like a book, courtesy of Cochran and he knew whenever Sen was troubled the first thing he did was have problems looking you in the eye.

"Weird as you may be, Kageryu, I have really gotten to like and trust you as a friend and it is obvious so has my addle-brained sister, Miyoko." Sen glanced out the corner of his eye, watching Martel still blush slightly at the name of his sister. "Over the last three months, you have more than proven yourself to me..." he switched suddenly to the Japanese language, to give the words the proper grace and fluidness of the full connotation of their meaning, "...Loyalty, honor, dedication to the craft and determination. Our hands are not clean in this either." he sighed a moment. Took another drink then looked over at Martel.

The foreigner just sat quietly, regarding the distant Mt. Iwate. His pale blonde hair had been cut extremely short, and in the grey, wintry cold, the sharp planes and angles of his face gave him the icy cold look of a block of ice, or a tombstone. But Sen knew Kage was listening intently, listening to his every word. He had learned much about his student over the last three months, studied him closely and he knew that the quieter and more still Kageryu got, the more he was listening and thinking. Just like his oriental namesake, the great Shadow Dragon.

"...About 10 years ago," Sen continued and refilled his glass with more *sake*, "Before my father became sick with the coughing illness, he made the mistake of selling a lot of his land to Tashima Katsuro. He had gotten in trouble for gambling debts, so had I. I was younger then, not at home as much. I was not the perfect son either; I make no excuses for myself. You understand?" Sen had switched back into English. He noticed that the name of the Yakuza Boss had gotten an unreadable flicker in the icy blue eyes of Kageryu.

"But my father, he was not, how you say.... *streetwise*." Sen sighed audibly. "Next thing you know, not only was more land than owed being taken by the Tashima and the Yakuza, but so was our weapons being promised to them, cherished heirlooms to be sold on the black-market. By then I had come back home, of course I had tried to reason with my father and in person with Tashima Katsuro…" Sen drank down the rest of the second cup of *sake* and then put the rest away.

Martel noticed the tremble to Sen's hand. Obviously, such humiliating things were not something easily spoken about, not for anyone. He was already beginning to see where this conversation was going before Sen was going to finish this tale, especially since on their first meeting Sen had told him 'I am down one brother and sister'.

"Tashima wouldn't take no, for an answer." Sen simply said after a few minutes. It was said in perhaps the most monotone voice Martel had ever heard a man use, as though every ounce of control was put into that voice to keep him from breaking down at that moment. "Unfortunately being young and proud and stupid, I lost my temper, said things I shouldn't have. My younger brother and eldest sister paid the ultimate price for my insolence."

There was another long silence as Sen looked at a few farm dogs snarling and fighting over a bone. "I blamed myself of course. But what was done was done…" A deep sigh escaped the small man's throat as he dug around and pulled out some of Miyoko's lunch items. Two bowls of covered *oodon* noodles with small pieces of chicken and vegetables in them. He silently handed one to Martel without looking at the man. "I put the word out through a few friends. Friends I knew were –not- friends of Tashima Katsuro. One name came back to me about 9 months ago. Haiiro Ookami, the 'Grey Wolf'." Sen opened the noodles and with his chopsticks began to halfheartedly pick a bit at his lunch.

Martel raised an eyebrow and glanced over at Sen but said nothing. 'No, surely it was too much of a coincidence to be the same 'grey wolf' he knew as well!' Haiiro Ookami had been an alias that Cochran had sometimes used. Martel just nodded for Sen to continue and began to nimbly shovel noodles into his mouth with his own chopsticks.

"I just received a simple answer one day in the mail…" Sen reached into his pocket and pulled out a letter and handed it to Martel. The note was fairly crumpled as though someone had reread it often, held onto it with hopes and dreams. Almost like the little pieces of paper that prayers are written on in the Buddhist religion and then placed in trees or temples hoped to be heard by forces that be. '…*Tashima Katsuro has a western foreigner currently working for him, a freelancer. He is an EXPERT in martial arts. I have convinced Tashima to give him to you as repayment for 'over stepping his bounds' with your family. He is not happy but Tashima considers all things 'equal' now. You must let this vendetta drop Sen. Train the foreigner, I guarantee you will not be disappointed with him. If vendetta is still in your heart, let the foreigner be your instrument, but that is for him to decide, not you. Treat him well, and he will protect you. His name is Kageryu.*'

Martel felt his heart drop down into his stomach and his throat painfully constrict. Had Cochran written this note? Was this Cochran's

220

last gift to him, to get him out of Tashima's service? Martel didn't know whether to laugh, be angry, insulted or elated. All he knew was that deep in his heart; day by day his own family, the Jerome's, were tugging at him now like a silent insistent siren call, an ocean and a world away. He wanted to be there at his father's side. If games were going to be played, he wanted to play them on his own turf with the rules and people he knew.

He chewed thoughtfully for a few moments and handed the letter back to Sen, with no emotion on his own face. "Interesting," he said simply, "Sen," he turned to his teacher. "You remember the promise I made you the day I came here, do you not?"

Sen nodded, his dark intense eyes looking at Martel.

"Well it still stands my friend. I still consider you my friend and teacher, you have lost no face in front of me and I still love your sister and always will. I will take good care of your family. But the letter is correct. I will not be a weapon for any vendetta that now stands settled. If the old treaty is broken then new rules come into play but as long as the old treaty stands as is, then it must stand." Martel slurped down his soup, then stood up and stretched.

"Ah Kage," Sen smiled almost sadly and patted him on his muscular arm, "I think you maybe not meant to be a Ninjitsu, eh, cowboy? Maybe you should have been a Samurai?"

"Trust me, no." Martel smiled with a slight dark gleam of hidden emotion in his eyes.

"Kage..." Sen stopped suddenly, his face rather pale. "I must know something. You worked for Tashima, so that means that you have done... You know, well..." Sen verbally danced without saying 'killed people', "...How long did you work for Tashima?"

Martel knew where this conversation was going too; and it was the first lesson he ever learned not from Cochran but from his earliest teachers, his father Victor, and also the Bonnaro's...*Omerta*. Never discuss 'crime business', even with others in the business. Not just because you may give away sensitive information, but for the simple reason that down deep, people really don't want to know. They say they do, but they don't. People will never look at you the same again if they know you have killed 20, 30, or 100 people or they have watched you beat up and tortured some poor slob, who reneged on his loan, stole from the Family or worse.

"Sen," Martel said softly but insistently. "I am your humble student. But do not ask me questions about that which I cannot tell you, do you understand?" It was not a harsh tone, it was not cruel, but it was said with a look that told Sen that the conversation was never to be bought up again, ever.

Sen bowed slightly and said nothing. There was a hint of sadness in his eyes. Part of him of course wanted to know but perhaps a part did not; he wasn't sure what, at this point. He was letting his own hurt and emotions cloud his judgment, he knew that of course there was nothing that could be done now, he was grateful that Haiiro Ookami, 'the Grey Wolf' was able to get his family farm out from under the thumb of Tashima Katsuro and the Yakuza, perhaps his own guilty conscious of not 'being there' when he should have been to prevent his father for making mistakes, to prevent the death of his younger brother and eldest sister.

The two men silently put away the empty lunch containers, and walked back to the barn, to work on some more swords and daggers. "Sen, I'm going to ask Miyoko to marry me in a week's time." Martel said abruptly.

Sen stopped and turned around, his dark eyes meeting the intense blue ones. "If she says yes, Kage?"

"Then she will come back to the states with me." Martel said softly.

"Kage, that leaves me with no one here who can work!" Sen rubbed his hand over his smooth jaw line. "My fields will die, my forge will die..."

Martel looked around for a moment, taking in the land, the forge. He crossed his arms over his strong chest deep in thought, "I will compensate you Sen. I will send you enough money to buy the labor of 6 strong men and 4 oxen for as long as you want, until you decide otherwise."

Sen looked a bit miffed and insulted at first. "I would rather have you, Kageryu!" He huffed, "they may work, but they are not friends and they are not students. Nor can they appreciate the forge or the workmanship of fine weapons."

"No Sen, they cannot," Martel agreed with a sigh. "Sen, you opened up to me and told me many things here today. I wish I could do the same but I simply can't. It has nothing to do with our friendship, and everything to do with silences and promises I made long ago. Oaths and codes I must keep. If you remain my friend and I am sure you will, as you will be my brother-in-law, then someday you will know the truth about me and you will know more of the story of Kageryu..." Here Martel actually gave a deep almost sarcastic chuckle. "Then I can share with you deeper. But not today, Sen. I can only ask you for your trust and I know that is a big step to ask for, sight unseen when you have been hurt once before by someone asking you to trust them. You know how I feel about your sister you know I have respect for you. For now I can only offer you compensation for my labor when Miyoko and I leave."

"If she says yes, when would you be going?" Sen asked.

"I am hoping to head back by April or May at the latest." Martel spoke solemnly and grabbed up one of the leather aprons. "Regardless if Miyoko accepts my marriage proposal or not." He quietly added.

"So soon..." Sen said, firing up the large forge. "So soon? Why couldn't you be a slower learner, eh, Cowboy?"

"I dunno." Martel said, "Why couldn't you be a worse teacher?" he teased back lightly.

That evening Martel and Miyoko sat in his shed near a small fire pit they had built up. She had bought the ingredients for a small stir-fry and he had shown her a recipe he had learned for a Vietnamese version of the dish.

"And you can cook too!" Miyoko laughed with the firelight dancing in her nearly coal black eyes. "I guess for sure that makes you a keeper, Kage. Or should I call you Martel?"

Martel had just gotten done telling her a bit of his travels around the Vietnam countryside, although leaving out most of the details of what he and Cochran did.

"Well back in the states, I will be known as Laurence Martel. No one there will know me as Kageryu anymore." He answered quietly.

"Well then, maybe I should just call you Martel from now on." She smiled. She had a hard time pronouncing the 'Laurence' part of his name, pronouncing it more like 'roar- ants'.

She had gotten up to stir the rice to keep it from burning over the fire and one of her long black stands of hair had swept over her ears and down her shoulders. Absentmindedly Laurence took his finger and gently swept it back, she turned and blushed at him.

"Sorry, I didn't want you to get it burned in the fire." He mumbled.

Miyoko had to smile to herself; here was this giant of a man, one of the best martial arts fighters she had ever seen, who seemed to stumble over his own two feet whenever she was around. She remembered the first time they had ever sparred together in the ring, he had made the mistake of thinking because she was a woman, she must be more delicate than most and she had caught him squarely with a high kick between the eyes. After that Martel never underestimated anyone ever again, be it male or female, old or young. But yet during times like this, a simple smile from her seemed to disarm him totally. It was fair enough though; she felt the same about him. The sound of his deep voice or a gentle touch from him, made her body tingle with want for him and love.

Miyoko was a master of fighting with weapons, whether it was quarterstaffs, swords, daggers, nun chucks, or other martial arts weapons. When Sen wasn't teaching him bare-handed techniques, Miyoko was refining him and honing him on weapons fighting. Soon he was as good as she was with the katana or the throwing stars.

Martel appreciated the agility of her, the beauty and spirit and gracefulness she possessed. While to many outsiders she may appear like a quiet oriental woman Martel knew of her fiery spirit inside, the sense of humor, the independent soul, the quick wit, the passion, the drive and the depths of her feelings that ran inside her. When she believed in something she could be as resolute and immoveable as Mt. Iwate in the distance that overlooked their farm.

Just as she was not intimidated by the gruff, loud personality of her older brother Sen, neither was she intimidated by the tall foreigner, Kageryu. She respected him and his abilities, yes, but never did he intimidate her. He made her laugh, he made her smile, but she did not fear him the way other men and women seem to.

Sometimes, she wondered what made them each other so crazy in love for one another. The way she figured it was because they complimented each other so well.

Many times during their martial arts sparring, they simply had to call it a draw/stalemate, both of them standing there mutually sweating and laughing... They knew each other too well, knew one another's moves even before they made them and knew what was in one another's hearts and souls before they thought it. And like now, when they cooked dinner together or simply relaxed and talk, there was a feeling she had always known him, that he had always been a part of her and complimented her life, and he hers.

Martel had spoken to her briefly of his clan back in America, the Jerome Family and said that it must come first in his life but that no other woman other than her would ever come first in his heart, and this she believed 100%. She knew this because she saw it in his heart and soul. Unlike her brother Sen, she didn't want to know all that Martel had done before now, or what he had to do in the future. She was sure in her heart that Martel had his own Karma to atone for; whatever Martel had done or had to do was his business (regarding his 'clan/Family'). She was only concerned about the future of her family, herself, Martel and any children they bought into the world. She knew Martel would make a good gentle father for many children. From what she had heard about this Victor Jerome, he sounded like an intelligent, fair, and honorable leader of his clan, unlike Tashima Katsuro who double-crossed on deals.

Miyoko knew with the same uncanny ability they knew each other's martial arts moves that Martel was going to be asking her to marry him. She didn't know when but she was fairly sure it would be soon and that he had probably asked Sen about it already. She knew Martel was fairly old fashioned and followed Asian protocol very carefully. He would ask Sen's permission before he even asked her about it but he had of course hinted to her about it, fished around and asked her feelings to see if she would even be interested in being with him. He could be so silly sometimes, her Martel!

She smiled at him and he just looked at her, a slow blush around his temples wondering what she was smiling at him for. He may be 'Laurence Martel' to everyone else, but he would always be Kageryu to her. Her 'Shadow Dragon'.

"I made this for you." She handed him the gift she had bought over that evening, before they had eaten Martel's Vietnamese dinner. It was something Miyoko had worked weeks on, another one of her talents, her artistic ability.

It was a long tube like gift, ornately wrapped in origami paper and decorated with several origami designs on top. Miyoko had learned the art of the delicate paper folding, origami from her elderly, now bedridden mother. Sen did it also, but he was not as good as Miyoko.

Carefully Martel undid the package with his long fingers, careful to not damage the delicate wrappings and origami; he could see Miyoko had moved closer, her face seemed a mixture of emotions. He could tell she was worried if he would like her gift. He knew already he would because she had put so much thought into it. But he did not expect this...

Slowly he unrolled the parchment. It was, simply breathtaking. Done in the local Japanese style of watercolor, he knew Miyoko had artistic talent, but this, this was beyond stunning. He felt a lump grow deep in his throat... "Oh Miyoko," he barely whispered, his voice low, soft, almost hesitant.

"You don't like it." She sighed, her face falling for a moment, her eyes, downcast. She had tried; she had thought her heart had spoken true in this gift, in the making of it. What had gone wrong?

"No! No, you misunderstand." Martel unwrapped the whole scroll, looking at it. It was a beautiful oriental-styled dragon, a 'Shadow Dragon', the Kanji for his name artfully done to the left of it, the icy blue eyes of the dragon so beautifully matched his own, it was as though the great dragon on the parchment reflected all that Martel had lived during the last several years, what he lived now. It reflected his very soul. "It is the most beautiful gift I have ever received Miyoko." He studied it closely, running his finger along the outline of each of the kanji, appreciating the lettering and the brush strokes. She had made this for him, seen in his heart and soul and captured it. He saw the Cobra clutched in the talons of the shadow dragon and the sword around the dragon's neck. "You honor me by giving me the Ninja symbolism." Martel turned to her with a laughing twinkle in his blue eyes. "Sen hasn't even given me the mark yet."

"He will." Miyoko scooted up next to Martel and examined the scroll with him. Her shoulder resting against his great rib cage, "I know he will. It is also symbolism for this year, year of the snake, a cousin to the great dragon, one who is more subtle and in shadow." She smiled.

"But I don't understand this symbolism?" Martel pointed to the sword that hung around the shadow dragon's neck, "I have seen this sword before. It is the sword that hangs in your family's home, your clan family sword?"

Her hand gently entwined around Martel's fingers where it touched the scroll. "I know you will ask me a question soon..." she hinted playfully, "And I will answer 'yes', Kageryu." She smiled up at him. "That makes you of our clan too. When it is your time to be head of this clan, whether here or in the states, then that sword belongs in your hands. Then it goes home to you. Yes?"

"Yes." Martel simply said; she would be his, she would accept his marriage proposal. He kissed the top of her head, breathing in the sweet fragrance of her, and then engulfed her gently in his arms. Gods' how he loved her!

The next morning he realized he had the day off. Sen was going to go into town to get supplies, but there was now something he wanted to get. An engagement ring for Miyoko, for the first time, Martel felt something in his heart beside a deep cold hardness. He heard the farm dogs barking and realized he'd better hurry; Sen was out there feeding them and probably getting ready to leave.

Laurence hurriedly got dressed. "Hey Sen...." He bellowed as he screeched out of the house.

"What, Cowboy! Don't you ever take the day off?" Sen looked at Martel who had his shirt buttoned wrong and stood there in the snow barefooted. "You still so addled-brained." He forced himself not to laugh at his over eager student. He could tell Kage was deeply in love.

"I gotta go into town with you." Martel implored. "I'm going to get, you know..." He wiggled his fingers.

"You gonna get pneumonia if you don't put some shoes on first." Sen bit his lip to keep from laughing at the love struck Martel; who hurriedly ran back inside and grabbed his shoes and a jacket and then both men headed to the beat up old truck for the several hour trip to the near by town of Morioka, for feed, supplies and an engagement ring for Miyoko...

Chapter 18- *June 17th 1987*

"Hey Victor," Patrizio sat on the comfortable leather couch in the office. He never smoked in the Victor's office anymore out of respect for his boss' health condition. They were both old now, some of the last of the 'Old School, Men of Honor.' Him, Victor, 'Sal' Antonia, and Dante 'Danny the Wizard' Valsiglio, they were the last who were with Victor from the very beginning, from the get go, from the time he took the reins of the Jerome Family over from the Massacre in '57. "You still set on doing this thing in November? In going down there to this sit down with the Bonnaro's?"

"Patrizio, my dear friend," Victor came over and poured him some wine, "how long have we known the Bonnaro's, eh?"

"No, no. I know that, Victor. Forever, I know." Fantenelli toasted Victor with the wine and took a sip. "I mean, surely Len, or Martel, myself, or..."

"My dear old friend, no." Victor toasted him back. "*Salute.* Your offer is appreciated and doesn't go by unnoticed. Trust me."

"But why Vic, I don't get it?" Patrizio fiddled with one of Joshua's nicotine gum squares that were on a glass-serving dish, trying to figure out how to open it. Man, he needed a cigarette.

"Because the D'Salvatores are expecting me, Patrice, because they are expecting me down there." Victor watched him idly for a moment and then refilled his wine glass. "Look, if I go down there and take care of business, then business is settled there. You understand? But if I don't go, then business comes up here to be settled. If business gets settled up here, then it is not good for us; not now, with all the F.B.I's RICO shit, and everything else going on, including the wariness of the other Commission *famiglia's*."

"RICO..." Patrizio disgustedly threw down the unopened square of gum frustrated, "God, Vic, remember when 'this thing of ours' used to be fair, in the 'Golden Age'? Now they have this RICO predicates this, RICO acts that, it's all shit. I hate RICO; it's a bunch of *stronzata*. I tell you, it's too much like Communism if you ask me."

Victor smiled at his friends comment. "I do have a favor you can do for me, Ok? You don't worry about me, I've got Martel watching my back, as well as Len and several good button men, it's not my time yet Patrice. But you bring up a good point with this RICO shit. Now is where I need your special touch. Yours and Danny's."

Patrizio sat up. "Whatever it is Vic, ask it. You know that."

Victor unlocked one of his desk drawers and took out a good-sized elegant leather satchel he carried it over to the table and dropped it lightly between them. "There is 100,000G's in laundered money in there, courtesy of VIJER Enterprises, as well as 50G in stocks. I want that defense lawyer that was used last year by that outfit in Chicago for that high profile case."

"Jerry MacDermott?" Patrizio asked, almost with awe. "*Madonn*! The man is nearly a fuckin' celebrity himself! He could get an acquittal for Satan or Judas and have the Jury feeling sorry for him."

"Yes." Victor nodded solemnly. "Patrice, I will be honest with you, we are on the scoreboard now. We have bit the D'Salvatores and bit them hard, we have spent a lot on bribes, but the *mannagge* is far from over." Victor sat next to his lifelong friend, the man who was once his mentor, once his underboss and now who was one of his most trusted *capo-regimes*. He looked deep into Patrizio's eyes. "You know this life longer than even I, Patrizio; do you really think that no Jerome blood will spill? We will taste sorrow, we will lose men, we will have our people get pinched and go to jail. Possibly important ones, if this happens we need to get out our top people as quickly as possible, especially if it's someone like Martel, Joshua, or some of the other top skippers."

"Victor," Patrizio looked at his dearest and oldest friend, "I gotta ask you something about Martel."

Victor walked over and sat on the corner of the table and opened one of the squares of nicotine gum for Patrizio. "You may ask, Patrice..." he left the sentence hanging, but didn't look at him.

"Martel, he is..." Patrizio shook his head for a moment, "*Familiare*, you know, like I know him from somewhere."

"You do, he's my underboss." Victor dropped the piece of nicotine gum onto the table in front of Patrizio 'Karloff' Fantenelli.

"Yer not going to tell me are you Vic?" Patrizio looked at the gum a moment and then just left it.

Victor had been facing away from his old friend, at this point running a million thoughts and moves through his head. He had known that there might be a time, a day this very question may come up, that someone might detect the secret Victor and Theodore had worked so hard to keep secret, but he really didn't think Patrizio –knew- for certain, just suspected something. And unless Patrizio came and asked outright, Victor would dare not breathe the secret he had worked so hard to keep. "No Patrice." He faced his friend. "It is enough to know, that our underboss is a man I would trust implicitly and so should you. Support him as dearly you would me. He is the last hope for this *Famiglia*, especially if anything happens to me." Victor came and sat down next to Patrizio.

The two men just sat silent for a moment. Patrizio's old hardened eyes looked into Victor's and for the first time, in perhaps thirty years, a single tear rolled down Patrizio's cheek. "I understand, Vic." He nodded. The two men embraced briefly, tightly, as dear old friends. "I really need that damn cig...Forgive me." Patrizio dug around, fished out one of his trademark Pall Malls and lit up. He quickly wiped away the single tear, his 'Karloff' like face already composed in its usual stony mobster-like, look. He puffed down the cigarette as he gathered up the leather satchel. "Everything will be ready for ya, Vic, I promise. Come September, you will have no worries." He finished off his glass of wine and then so as not to fill the office with smoke he hurried out past the guard and quickly left.

Victor saw a change in the man, a purpose in his stride that did not exist before, it reminded him of the old days, shortly after the massacre when things were in chaos. Victor had done what he had wanted to. To drive home the importance of this war to his capo's. He knew Patrizio would now organize the lower rung capos and button men like a precise, well-organized army and he needed that. He needed everything to work like clockwork, with finesse and without question. Martel and Joshua were taking care of the upper echelons and he was taking care of joining things with Don Vito Bonnaro from Sicily. While Victor was responsible for his whole Family he could not do everything on his own, and he had to instill the same sense of urgency in everyone else as he had. So far things were going right on track.

He felt contented, if he could get good legal counsel on board then he would not worry so much if a few of them were arrested, knowing that the right attorney was worth their weight in gold in getting sentences reduced or dropped entirely.

Victor had two more stops he had to make, one was to check on how things were going with his corrupt judges and cops and bribed friends in the F.B.I and the other was with John Thomas, to have his blood levels checked after the transplant. He stepped out of the office and instructed the guard, "Gio, go bring the car around front for me, would you?"

"No problem Boss." The large baldheaded gorilla looking guard nodded and left. As Victor was waiting he glanced towards the darkening sky… It was going to storm bad tonight, he could feel it within his aching bones and already lightning was rumbling across the distant western sky. Outside the guard dogs were panting miserably in the muggy air, the guards wiping them down with damp cloths. He would have Gio stop by the aviary so he could secure his birds, they never did like storms and he wasn't so fond of them either. His mind wandered briefly and he wondered how Alyssa was doing her first day with Martel. He hadn't received any phone calls from Laurence yet, so that was a good sign but then somehow he really didn't expect any trouble either.

He still did wonder just who she was, what had her life been like before she had been unknowingly thrust into this dance with him and more importantly, why he had been so swayed to step in on her behalf? Still something primal and deep tugged on his soul as though there was some kind of connection or unfinished business between them.

"Gio's got the car here Mr. J." One of the other guards broke his train of thoughts.

"Ah, thanks, Tony." Victor smiled lightly at the man, and then walked quietly towards the long 'Jerome-1' Limo.

He truly did miss Cesare and would be happy when he was back. Hopefully Cesare would make no more mistakes like he did. Victor took no pleasure in enforcing what he had to enforce, what the rules and traditions of *La Cosa Nostra* dictated he must enforce. They had taken Cesare out late at night to the far end of the Estate by the gardens where Joshua and Martel had worked him over for a good five minutes with bare knuckles but even then with both men's extensive knowledge of martial arts, even holding back and pulling their strikes, they had done devastating damage to the man.

When it was over, Cesare lay there panting and barely whimpering in a pool of his own sweat, blood, spit and teeth. Victor had knelt half on top of him. "Cesare, listen to me." He spoke neutrally, under the chilling light of the moon. "You fucked up, you broke the most basic codes of omerta, you know that."

Cesare just lay there nodding, involuntary tears running down his cheeks, his mind dancing on the fringes of unconsciousness. He fully expected to be executed right there, and 'butchered'. His head probably chopped off by the cruel underboss.

"Damn it Cesare," Victor said softly as he kneeled in closer, one of his strong hands gripping the larger mans offering strength and yet forgiveness. He whispered quietly just so Cesare could hear him and not anyone else. "Caring is not a crime, understand? But you need to watch what you say. Don't be like Charlie; don't make me have to kill you. This time you live. Consider it a lesson learned." Victor had then slipped a wad of money discreetly in Cesare's shirt pocket. Only Martel saw what Victor had done.

"Listen to me, Cesare." Victor stood up and again raised his voice, so all the men could hear, "You will take the next week and a half off; heal yourself up. Do not fuck up again. Next time you will die a traitor's death that will be far more hideous than you can imagine, trust me. Do not insult me or this *Famiglia* again." Victor spat on the ground near him, then with an unreadable look ordered his men. "Clean him up a bit first, and then take him home."

Martel who had seen his father put the extra money in Cesare's pocket, probably to pay for the extensive dental work and setting of broken bones he would need, suddenly spoke up in a dark tone. "I'll do it." His eyes briefly met his father's and unspoken words flowed between them. He knew if Joshua or the other guards found the money they would more than likely take it as additional punishment for Cesare's breaking omerta and what could Cesare do? Nothing, the man would have no grievance to file, not after having been just humiliated like this.

"Fine, let Martel do it. So much the better." Victor said neutrally as he turned and walked into the deep shadows towards the car.

CHAPTER 19

Dinner had been fairly quiet. Martel had chatted a bit with Alyssa, asking her if she needed any assistance in putting her stuff away, she didn't, she had wrote she would put most of it away before bed. Then Martel just chatted a bit about some of what her schedule would be like for the next couple days and some general rules about the Jerome Estates. The very things that Cesare had already told her about, like staying away from the powerful electric fence, or not interfering with the guards on duty, or bothering Mr. Jerome's Aviary.

She was truly surprised at how good Martel's cooking was and a part of her mind told her she really did like Chinese food. She never would have envisioned the underboss as being a "good cook" of Chinese food, but then a few hours ago she never pictured that Laurence Martel's house would look like the inside of some Japanese

Shoguns house either. He was simply one mystery after the other, layer upon layer.

"Come with me a moment, Alyssa." He said after dinner. Martel led her to the back of the kitchen and then near the other back door, which opened up to a small, enclosed backyard. It was surrounded by a large 8' tall bamboo privacy fence and inside it was a meticulously maintained Japanese garden complete with Bonsai trees, rock gardens, some Koi ponds, rock benches, wooden bridges and other simple surprises. He unlocked the door for her. "Go ahead look around and enjoy. There is a Zen garden over on the far left. I am going to change and will be out shortly." Without a sound he turned and walked back into the house leaving her alone to explore the hidden Japanese gardens and sanctuary in his backyard.

The sky was fairly dark now and there were soft lights coming off from the oriental lights in the garden and from underwater lights in the koi pond. In the far distance she could hear occasional rumbling of approaching thunderstorm and she could distinctly smell the heavy scent of rain in the air, as though the very earth was taking a deep breath before the onslaught of the summer storm. She didn't know why, but the thought began to alarm her. She unconsciously wrapped her arms around her hugging herself and walked along the immaculately maintained stone path. She definitely thought the gardens would be more enjoyable in the sunlight, at night and before the onslaught of the impending storm they seemed shadowy, indistinct as though something ominous and malevolent was watching over her with a predatory eye.

She looked at a few of the bonsai trees and noticed that occasionally here and there was either the Yin and Yang symbol or some type of oriental Kanji symbol that seemed repeated a lot. The Yin -Yang symbols at Martel's house looked different than others she had seen; they always had the white on top and the black on the bottom. Most she had seen before had them side by side, but not his. The other symbol she saw repeated a lot around his house was the dragon and cobra theme often the two intertwined.

Here and there small sparks of dancing fireflies would occasionally glow, leading her deeper into the garden and almost dream-like she followed them. Occasionally the flickering lightning of the approaching storm would briefly illuminate the strange gaping mouth of some imperial dragon or Foo Temple dog statue that seemed in the dark; sinister, frightening and almost alive to her. The wind was picking up and the pine trees began to squeak and sway wildly in the wind. Wind chimes began to ring ethereally from somewhere in the darkness and the feeling of unease began to grow inside her, almost like a terror.

"The storm will come up soon." Martel's deep voice was suddenly up along side her.

She nearly leaped out of her skin at the sound of his voice! She spun around facing him; where had he come from? She hadn't even seen or heard him come up to her.

"Easy, I didn't mean to startle you, Alyssa." He said in a surprisingly soothing voice. "Let's go back inside." He turned and she could have sworn he instantly blended back into the shadows of the night, until the lightning flickered overhead illuminating him for a moment as he opened the back door for her to scurry under his arm.

She welcomed the soft lighting of his house, and was happy to be back inside. There was some soft classical music going on the stereo and she noticed that he had now changed into a rather tight fitting black T-shirt and loose black slacks. While he was not overly muscle-bound, she noticed that his muscles were most definitely lean, hard and well defined. Alyssa also noticed he bore several scars on his arms, most of them small, but so far from just his lower forearms and elbows she could tell he was a man who had been through a lot of physical action. He wore only one ring on his right ring finger; it was almost identical to Victor's insignia ring but a bit smaller, more subdued.

"Tonight, I am going to teach you the civilized game of Chess, Alyssa." He motioned briefly to the elegant chess set that he must have set up while she was out. "You'll like this, trust me." He flashed a rare, warm smile. He casually tossed a couple large oversized pillows on the floor and then lowered himself down onto one and motioned her to get comfortable as well.

She sat down, and listened to this enigma of a man across from her. Here relaxed, there was no fear from him, in fact just the opposite. She felt herself drawn in; a peaceful feeling soothed her senses as she listening to his deep baritone voice talk about each piece and how it moved across the board what the rules where, what the strategies where. She did not know why she often felt her eyes drawn to wander over him and even worse to cause her to blush on occasion. Right now he seemed a totally different a man than when she had first met him at breakfast nearly two months ago.

They had played chess for awhile and when she had taken a bathroom break and come back, she found he had made them both some warm chamomile tea and a snack. He made her laugh silently when her knight clobbered his bishop and he performed a wonderful death scene for his queen when Alyssa's rook had captured it. She was smiling and silently laughing hysterically, until he checkmated her.

However like a gentleman he did not gloat over his win, his blue eyes had only twinkled, "Always watch your king, Alyssa." He chided her softly, in a lighthearted way. "Don't let other peoples distractions get to you," he winked. For a brief moment she had a sudden vision of Victor. The old man had that same way of driving home a point with that conspiratorial but gentle wink.

It was then that the heavens finally decided to open up no longer able to hold back the storm. What had been before gentle rumbles of thunder now changed into violent crashes of thunder as though Zeus himself were trying to wipe out the Jerome Estate. Alyssa glanced around nervously as the lights flickered a bit, winked as though struggling to remain lit and then finally seem stayed on, at least for the moment.

"I always like a good rain storm." Martel idly glanced around. "It cleanses and refreshes the land." He looked directly at her, again that rare but genuine smile. "It also makes for excellent sleeping weather. People don't bother you when it's storming. Not normally." His eyes seemed to twinkle with a private joke that only he got.

Martel got up, easily unfolding his long legs from his cross-legged sitting position and turned off his stereo and began to tidy up. "With this lightning, we're probably going to lose power soon down here. The main Estate is kept on generators but I keep my house disconnected from it. I see no need for it, none the less..." He expertly tossed the two pillows back in the corner. "It's probably best if we call it a night for now. Goodnight Alyssa, if you need anything I will be up for a little while in my room." He inclined his head, giving her a slight half-bow and then padded gracefully off towards his own bedroom. "I'll turn the main lights off later after you're in bed..." His deep voice reverberated from somewhere within the back of the house, "until you're more familiar with my home."

Hurriedly she grabbed the empty teacups and plates, took them to the sink and placed them in. She nearly jumped a bit nervously with each terrible crash of thunder as she half walked-half dashed back to her room. She cursed herself, that she hadn't put away more of her personal stuff or unpacked more when she had time before dinner.

The rain was so heavy outside now it sounded like just a steady rush of water. It ran like a waterfall pouring off the gutters and drain spouts. She truly felt sorry for any guards pulling outside duty tonight. She dug around and pulled out an oversized sleep shirt. "Fine, this would work," she thought to herself, everything else could get put away tomorrow, when the storm was over. Outside the thunder was viciously crashing around them almost continuously as the lightning was flashing and flickering like some mad scientists lab gone wrong.

Martel began to light the two oil filled hurricane lamps by his nightstand. His mind drifted with the sound of the pounding rain to his evening so far with Alyssa. What was it about her that so caught his curiosity? Not since Miyoko had his soul ever felt so drawn to another person. He had discreetly studied her several times that evening, her graceful but wary moves, the way the light caught in her burnished coppery hair and the almost playful and happy spirit he could barely glimpse behind her own walls. Was that what attracted him so much to her? That like him, she was forced through her amnesia to literally begin a new life, to be someone and to be thrust into a life that was totally alien to her?

He sighed slightly as he replaced the glass chimney on the hurricane lamp and slid the T-shirt off over his body. A part of him felt a deep guilt tearing at him for even being so drawn to Alyssa, as though he was dishonoring Miyoko's memory. A loud crash of thunder snapped him out of his self loathing and he glanced briefly towards the hall as he heard Alyssa run into the guest bathroom. He wondered if the storm was affecting her psyche and soul, he could tell she seemed a bit on edge all night, that for some reason the storm was unnerving her. He knew his father often reacted the same way during bad storms, a tension and inner torment that resurrected dark thoughts from his past about the 1957 massacre. Was the electrical storm causing the same torment over past and hidden memories in her?

Alyssa had quickly changed and had dumped the rest of the packages on the floor to be put away for tomorrow, she wanted to simply crawl into the bed into a tight ball and try to shut out the raging storm outside but she had to piss badly, the tea from earlier had gone right through her. With a half sigh of frustration she flung open her bedroom door and then ran into the bathroom. As she was hurrying to do her business, another crack of lightning and thunder came crashing all around her. So close she could have sworn she smelled the ozone, felt as though the electricity connected with the top of her head. She was plunged into sudden and terrifying total darkness as the lights were knocked out.

Her mind suddenly swam with dizzying images so real she felt as though it was happening this very moment. She heard the distant droning of a large truck motor, her world began to tilt and spiral... 'Oh God, no! Don't let them find me here! Not now, please not now! Don't let this happen to me now! STOP!!!!' her mind screamed in terror, trying to will her fear away.

"...Enjoy it darlin' don't fight it!" the smells and sounds of that tractor trailer assaulted her nostrils, the vomit, the sour stench of palatable fear, the cries of the women and the electrical zap of that fucking cattle prod.

She struggled, fought, 'I've got to get free! Must get out of here!' it was the only conscious thought that overrode her brain. She remembered the grip of the grimy skinny man as he injected something into her vein, the way his hand lewdly grabbed her breast before he moved down the line to inject the next girl.

"Alyssa"... a deep voice so distant it rode on the fringes of her mind.

Her mind shifted again, now she was being beaten by one of them, helpless to do anything to stop it, 'Pain, extreme unrelenting, fiery pain!' That damn stick, she had no control of her muscles; she just knew the scrawny man was going to kill her in his rage. Oh please let it end! Let me go, please!!

"ALYSSA!"…

"*Why* was that damn voice so insistent? Who was it?" her mind reeled.

"Enjoy dancing with the Devil darlin'…. The skinny mans voice, a drug induced high skidding over her body like the most glorious experience in her life, but it was like the gentle touch of death.

"No! No! Not them, Please not them again! Make it stop!" Her mind was in a total panic as the reality of the here and now slipped out of her grasp.

She suddenly felt powerful hands grab her; it was over now, she knew it was. She could feel how powerless she was in that strong grasp, certain they were going to simply and hideously kill her now. Her muscles strained with every last ounce of adrenaline they had, but she seemed to go nowhere, like being frozen in amber. Then there was that soft pressure against her face and neck, it seemed to make her heart and nerves thrum along with the very pulse and essence of her life force. It was a soothing feeling and it began to slow the madness in her mind. She became more and more aware of the large hand against her, soothing her.

"Alyssa, it's me, Martel." The deep voice cut through the fog in her mind. It repeated like some lighthouse on a rocky coastline and slowly, her mind focused on the mantra of that of that voice. Slowly the tractor-trailer and the men began to fade away, like the wisps of some long ago dream.

She blinked in the darkness and found herself sitting, trembling and quaking with terror in a corner of the hallway, the underboss literally wrapped around her, his long arms and legs pinioning her fast against his chest. His face along side hers, his lips whispering gently into her ear, his hand pressing against the side of her head, his voice low and soothing as though talking to a frightened animal.

"Shhh, It's Ok, Kanashii…" he spoke. Right now, all he wanted to do was get her mind on the here and now.

He had been getting ready for bed, when he had heard her crashing and thrashing around in the bathroom. When he had opened the door, she had charged blindly out at him and had that same terrified look as she had earlier today while downtown. Thankfully she had not hurt herself on anything. He had simply grabbed her up and wrapped himself around her to restrain her in a soft jujitsu hold until he could get her centered and focused. Somehow he had a feeling that all this ozone in the storm was going to be possible catalyst to setting her off, so he had been watching her closely, prepared.

Now she just lay back against him, limp in his arms, exhausted, numb and not fighting, tears silently running down her face, for she had no voice to give to them.

"Alyssa." Martel said and slowly, ever so slowly began to loosen his hold and unwind himself from her. He couldn't see her eyes in the darkened hallway, but he knew a hundred ways to judge the mood and intent of a person. He could tell she was still terrified, still worn out from her terror but she was rapidly calming. "Are you with me in the here and now?" he asked softly.

She nodded silently. Her muscles relaxed, there was no fight left in her. Not against Martel. "...They are the good guys, they protect us..." Cesare's words came back to her.

"Ok, good." Martel said and stood up, easily pulling her up with him. "Come with me, its ok, I will help." While the bulk of the crashing storm was over, it was still pouring heavily and thunder was still rumbling ominously. Martel knew that his house wouldn't have power until at least around 4 am. He led her to his bedroom and Alyssa just walked complacently in his grasp, her eyes still semi-glazed. Her body was as weary looking as if she had just run 5 miles, coated in a light sheen of sweat.

Martel's two hurricane lamps flickered softly with a warm light but even in this soft light she flinched a bit. "Easy, sit down." Martel quietly guided her to the bed, as he adjusted the flame in the light even lower.

He walked back around and looked down at Alyssa for several long seconds, his hand running along the sharp angles of his face, thinking... "Kanashii, do you trust me?"
He asked simply. The way he pronounced the strange name sounded like 'Con-Nah-She'

She looked up at him blankly for a moment one of her eyebrows raising slightly as she silently asked the question and mouthed the word "Kanashii?"

"Fair enough," Martel knelt down on one knee in front of her, so their eyes would be level with one another, sapphire blue eyes meeting emerald green eyes. "Kanashii is Japanese for 'wounded spirit.' I think you have probably figured out, that I have spent some time in the orient and follow a lot of their philosophies. Victor asked me as a favor to help you, and I want to do that. I truly am not here to be the bad guy, if I can help with whatever demons are inside, then I will offer that help as your teacher, however I can. But we must have trust in one another..."

He paused and stood back up and walked over to one of his beautiful black lacquered armoires, it was inlaid with mother of pearl and portrayed a scene of breathtaking beauty; elegantly swimming Koi fish, and lazy cherry blossoms, in the low firelight the scene seemed almost alive. "...I will share something of myself that very few people know." He said without looking at her. "In fact, it will be my test of this trust in you. There are only a few who know of this secret and most of them are dead." He turned back to her, a few small bottles in his hand. "When I was in the orient, I was known as Kageryu, 'The Shadow Dragon'. This name will mean nothing to you but there are some this name would mean much to. It is simply a matter of my trusting you, in telling you this, you understand?" His blue eyes bore into hers.

She understood then, the painting in his living room, the Shadow Dragon.

"It is not uncommon for a teacher to give their student a new name; at least it was that way in all my teachings. So I give you the name, Kanashii-Taka, 'Wounded Hawk'. Now, I ask you again. Do you trust me, Kanashii?"

She looked him squarely in the eye, no fear and no distrust and simply nodded yes. After all, right now at this moment she could use all the help she could get, whether it was with regaining old memories, her amnesia or just simply fitting into this place and with the Jerome's.

A small genuine smile played briefly on Martel's lips, "Good, very good. Then we can begin to make progress." He went about efficiently setting up a small brazier on one of his bathroom counters and lit a small charcoal disk in it. He then lit a stick of incense and also took a few of the small bottles and began to mix some of the drops together along with some type of light almond oil, looking like some tall wizard mixing a potion.

Alyssa watched him intently but didn't interrupt him in any way. She was far too exhausted and drained mentally and emotionally and far too curious as well. She so needed a friend right now, someone to guide her and help her heal and learn, and if Laurence was willing to do that, than she was more than willing to give her trust and loyalty to him.

"Now, remove your nightshirt, lie on your stomach and just relax." He said.

This caught her completely off guard for a moment and she felt herself blush deeply. She was beginning to wonder now just what this 'shadow dragon' had up his sleeve! But he was already headed back to the bathroom. He paused for a moment, as though reading her mind. "Please remove all your clothing. If you are self conscious, you may go underneath the covers. Just lie on your stomach and remember, trust. Ok, Kanashii?"

And so she had removed the long nightshirt and had burrowed under the covers of his huge bed. It was indeed soothing and comfortable, and she could smell the faintest scent of him on his sheets, the soothing masculinity of him and a faint trace of his after shave or cologne. The storm was retreating now, the rain just pouring heavily, not as intense as before, but more like a steady shower. The thunder was no longer crashing with the intensity of the gods fighting but with soft intermittent rumbles that rolled almost gently along the skies.

Alyssa had just about fallen into a soft light sleep when the bathroom door opened and the Laurence stepped out. He was wearing just his black martial arts pants, and no shirt. The first thing she noticed was that he had on one of his upper shoulders a series of intricate tattoos, again the cobra and dragon intertwined. On the other it looked almost like a series of kanji that had been elegantly branded in then filled in later with tattoo ink, almost like a badge of honor. He was carrying a small bowl in his hands, which he gracefully placed on the nightstand next to her.

"Now we begin to heal your body and mind, Kanashii," he said softly. And she lay there almost hypnotized; the way a bird feels when a great snake looms over it. He had dipped his hands in the bowl and rubbed the warm scented oil over them and for a few moments he barely spoke in some oriental language and seemed to center himself. Then he got more of the liquid on his hands as he slowly moved the cover away from her back and began to work on massaging her.

Time ceased to have meaning for her then. Whatever Kageryu was doing was pure blissful relief, the oil was fragrant and pleasing, it was warm and soothed her, where it touched her body it continued to warm. His hands seemed to touch not only her muscles but also her nerves, her sinew and then her very soul. She felt layer upon layer of her body and soul begin to relax under his touch.

Like someone delicately peeling an onion, he seemed to relax those areas of her that had been tense, sore and held in check with both fear and pain. She would not know whether his healing and massage had gone on for long minutes or hours, she did know that the oil seemed to burn quite low in the hurricane lamps and several times she drifted in and out of sleep. Occasionally he would speak in his Asian language and gracefully move this way and that over and about her, his touch always gentle, always deep and always it healed and relaxed.

But beyond that she had no idea of the mechanics of how it worked. Martel's healing touch was almost some kind of weird mysticism that he seemed to know and she simply wearily accepted and gave into it, needed it.

She vaguely remembered her teacher Mr. Kageryu Martel, blowing out the lanterns, and climbing into bed himself next to her. She wasn't too aware of anything at that point, nor did she even care that she was naked under the covers in bed with him, her body was so sleepy and her mind still floated on a state of bliss and relaxation. The rain sung its own lullaby now of soft, insistent slumber to her. And she snuggled down into a soft, small ball beneath the covers of his bed and for the very first time she could remember; since any of this, since her arrival at the Jerome Estate she felt truly and utterly safe and home.

Martel watched her for a moment, as she quickly fell into a sound and restful sleep. He turned back over onto his side, put the safety on his gun then slid it out the holster and quietly put it under his bed. "I'm truly losing my mind, just like the old man." He briefly thought. No, neither of them was. He knew better, he didn't believe that for a moment.

He had touched her body, mind and soul; felt her hungry need of his healing and her desire of simply being accepted and belonging. While he would never dare to profess any great knowledge of destinies or of karmic forces he too felt she was meant to here for some unknown reason. For exactly what, he had no idea. But for now, he would do precisely what his father had asked him too and that was to teach her how to fit into the Jerome family, for that was the only way she was going to be able to survive to fulfill whatever destiny she was meant to do.

He felt his own mind drift off into silent dreams and he dreamed then of such dark dreams that he had not dared revisit for nearly 9 years, dark remembrances that he had fought so hard to keep locked tightly behind the iron walls of his will. But that night the foundations in the underboss's great emotional walls cracked and the emotions and darkness he had worked so hard to hold in check came out with an awful clarity in his dreams as he relived them in a horrid and tormenting vividness.

(February 1978)

...Martel knew that grey February day as they came back from town that something was just not right, he had been feeling something gnawing at the back of his skull all morning long as he was helping Sen load feed and supplies onto the back of the beat up truck. The local townsfolk, normally fairly talkative towards Sen were unusually quiet today, not much gossip. This worried Martel, alerted him to something just not sitting right. But stupidly he kept pushing it to the back of his mind, as he kept making plans for him and Miyoko. After all, soon they would be back in the states at home with his father.

They had stopped at the only jewelers in town that carried halfway decent rings, and he had gotten her a lovely fiery ruby and diamond engagement ring. That purchase had gotten some gossip out of the local towns' people, as they had not seen a wad of cash dropped that large in years, especially not on a ring. Even Sen had smiled lightly and teased "You are so addle-brained in love, Kage. But you are good for Miyoko; I am honored to have you in our family, honored to be able to call you brother."

But now as they were driving back, the feeling of something not being right was gnawing even worse in him. Martel had offered to take the wheel and Sen was gripping the side of the truck, his teeth clenched in his jaw, glowering at Martel, "Will you slow it down Cowboy, before we lose half our supplies off the end of the truck!" he growled.

"Sorry." Martel mumbled and roughly downshifted the old truck, it groaned under his harsh treatment and then jerked into a pothole, but still Martel kept it going at a rather quick clip, following the contours of

Mt. Iwate towards the Yamashita farm, where Miyoko was. He just felt he had to get back to the farm, as fast as he could.

It was when he crested the final curve that they both first saw it, the smoke, even from far off. He knew it was far too much smoke to just be the usual smoke from the great blacksmithing forge. No, this was a greasy, vile engulfing smoke that rose like a malevolent, evil creature flying upwards to the sky.

"What the..." Sen leaned forward in his seat, fear in his eyes. "Go! Go!" he urged Martel.

But Martel needed no urging, he slammed the truck into its final upper gear and if he could have willed it to go faster would have. They bumped, sped and rammed down the road, oblivious at this point to whether anything fell off the back off the truck or not.

As they tore into the front yard, Martel already saw the house, barn and part of his shed in a fiery conflagration, great gouts of orange flames leaping towards the heavens devouring all. Around him were the loud sounds of hissing, crackling, and popping as the hungry flames ate and chewed and devoured everything they could, like living creatures.

He was barely aware of Sen screaming, running around, surveying. But Martel was doing his own surveying and searching. "Miyoko!!" He called out, he headed at first towards the house, but it was the most engulfed in flames. There was no going in or out of there. He nervously walked around towards the back; "Miyoko!!" he called again but his eyes now fell on the family's four farm dogs, with bullet holes in them. His heart sank like a lead weight and a horrid sense of despair began to overcome him. Miyoko was a skilled martial arts fighter, but the family did not own a gun and if there was more than one shooter... His heart began to beat a stronger tempo and his own blood began to pulse with adrenaline. He felt his throat grow dry as he trotted off towards the barn. He could hear Sen in there, screaming enraged and distraught with horror.

"No! No!" Sen was screaming, raging and cursing in Japanese. Sen was in the flame-covered barn, which looked half in danger of collapsing at any second. The smoke was thick in here, but Martel took off his shirt and wrapped it around his face, so as not to breathe in as much smoke, he crouched down warily, bringing his height even lower out of the choking smoke, every nerve alert and on guard. He saw the great forge and furnace had been knocked over, destroyed, used as a catalyst to start the fire in here. He saw the few livestock animals in here shot also.

It was then he saw some human remains, but just two. Martel recognized them, the elderly Yamashita's, Sen's parents. Not very much remained of them, most was charred beyond recognition. Nearly all of Sen's finished martial arts weapons were gone. Cleaned out, stolen or destroyed but there was no sign of Miyoko, somehow in Martel's heart and soul knew she was not here, not in this barn.

"Sen, let's go." He grabbed at his teacher. "There's nothing else you can do here."

"No!" Sen cried, as he sank to the ground, numb with grief, "No, it's my fault! I have brought this on my family! Let me die with them! I have nothing left!" he mourned incoherently.

Martel could hear the agony and pain in his friend's voice but he had no intention of letting his brother in law die. Instead grabbed the small man up, hoisted him onto his muscular shoulders and then carried him out of the inferno. "You can die with honor later Sen, if you want," he said hoping it would keep Sen from doing something stupid at the moment, "but I have to find Miyoko, understand?" He placed Sen on the ground by the truck where he would be safe out of harms way. "Please, just sit here Ok?" he briefly touched the median pressure points on Sen's head and neck that would relax him, soothe the traumatic shock and at least keep him from doing something dangerous or suicidal.

Laurence glanced at the shed; it was the only building that wasn't engulfed as completely with flames as the other buildings had; instead it just sort of smoked and smoldered, almost beckoning to him. A million thoughts and voices ran through his mind at once and somehow, some way he knew Miyoko was there. Knew she would go there no matter what, if it were within her power to do so. He glanced backwards at Sen to make sure he was indeed still sitting there, and he was. Then Martel stalked off to the shed that had been his home for the last four months.

He easily kicked down the door and then warily watched from afar for a moment. After all, since this building wasn't burning as much as the others and since Miyoko hadn't been found yet, it could be a trap. Cochran's lessons of constant vigilance were not wasted on him. Cautiously he crept in, it was smoky, but the thick smoke was actually good in this instance, it would show him any traps left behind, any tricks. There were none.

He slowly looked down and saw a dark stain on the floor then, like someone had spilled a can of paint. A feeling of dread settled on him then... With his heart slowing down, with all of time around him slowing down, he knew that red river intimately. He knew its smell, its viscosity and followed it to the small form of his beloved who lay unmoving like a small fighting animal in the corner. Even in death her face was defiant and determined, she held no fear of her attackers, only contempt. They had shot her 5 times at close range in her chest and abdomen.

"Oh Miyoko..." Martel dared to breathe her name, his heart still pounding out a funereal dread in him. He sank to his knees and cradled her body, kissed it gently and held it. As he gently moved her lifeless body away from the corner he saw what she had been so determinately guarding, it was the gift she had made for him, The Shadow Dragon scroll. "Miyoko, why did they do this to you? Why didn't you run away? Run away and wait for me somewhere?" He clenched her body tightly against him and let his warm tears flow down his cheeks and onto her lifeless body, where they ran with her blood to mix with the intimate red river that he knew so well. For a time he was oblivious to everything, to the smoke, to the soft crackling of flames overhead. Laurence was far to lost in his own tears, to his own gut wrenching sorrow that bit so hard into his soul that it literally tore him in two. His dreams of a marriage and family with Miyoko floated ethereally out of his grasp and life like the smoke of the burning Yamashita farm up to the heavens above.

Then slowly he picked her up and carried her by the door, it was there he suddenly saw the note pinned to the inside of his door. He gently laid her body down then snatched off the note and read it. "*Kageryu: Consider this repayment for a bad deal from your 'friend' Cochran. Since we cannot find him, we are taking it out of your hide. Since you seem to have such a good grasp of the Japanese culture and the Yakuza as you claim, I am sure you understand this, yes? Maybe you can explain all this to Yamashita Sen, especially since I did a favor for HIM on behalf of Cochran, by releasing you into his service and stopping collection on his debt owed. I considered that favor null and void too and took it out on his farm... But what I did with Miyoko, I did for you Kageryu. Go back home, you stupid American. Tashima~*"

Miyoko couldn't have run away, if she had wanted to. She had been used, beaten and violated as a personal vendetta to him, then shot. Her last defiant act had been to stand and face her death squad and defend the gift she had made for him.

Martel's first instinct was to allow himself to be filled with every vivid hue of hatred and anger that he could feel from every layer of his soul and body. The violence, vendetta and vengeance was there and it was deep: Such white-hot anger, hate and raging violence; that he had ever felt in his life, but not yet. Not yet...

"Kage??" he heard Sen's voice calling out to him from outside. "Kage?!?" Sen began to sound panic stricken now. "Are you Ok? What's going on in there? Is Miyoko...."?

Quickly Martel folded the note into his pants pocket and walked outside before Sen walked in to see his sister brutally murdered as well. Martel did not want to tell Sen about his sister being raped. That wasn't something you went around telling a man, not your best friend, it would do nothing to honor her death.

Sen didn't need to ask Martel what he had seen inside, the tall mans grim face and bloodstained clothes instantly told him everything. "They got Miyoko too then!! Oh why? Who did this?" more tears ran down Sen's bloody and smoke blackened face.

"Tashima." Martel said icily, looking off into the distance as though he could see his quarry out there somewhere, sensing and marking Tashima for his future vendetta.

At the name, Sen went in to a rage. "You see! You see what I told you! He double crosses, I will kill him!! He is a dead man! I am going tomorrow to Tokyo and kill him personally!!"

"With what?" Martel looked down at his friend, his own eyes filled with a hard look, "He took nearly all your damn swords Sen!"

"Look Kageryu, you gonna make fun of me or are you to much a coward to help!" He shouted angrily leaping to his feet, physically lashing out helplessly at Martel. "If so, you know what? Maybe you should just get back on that plane and go to New York and go home to your cowboy family. I thought you had the heart of a warrior but I was wrong. I must avenge my family for what they did to me, my honor dictates it." Sen stood there angrily, like a live wire ready to explode. Sen's heart ached, his soul ached and right now he was not thinking clearly, his mind was a mass of revenge. He wanted vengeance and he was filled with anger and hate.

This was understandable Martel felt it too. Kageryu looked at him sadly for a moment, his eyes filled with empathy. "Sen, I understand more than you could ever know." A took a deep breath, slowly letting it out, looking around as the great barn suddenly collapsed in a loud fiery heap. Neither man seemed to hear it. Their hearts were both too filled with hurt and anger right now, their souls with shock. Martel gently put one hand on Sen's small shoulder, a simple sharing of pain and hurt, "How many men have you killed Yamashita Sen?" Martel asked, not arrogantly but honestly, humbly.

"Well, none yet," Sen looked away, almost embarrassed, "But I will taste the revenge of Tashima for what he has done." The small man shook with anger and the shock of what had been done to his family.

"Tashima is a boss among bosses, Sen." Martel continued, "He is guarded closely night and day. To kill him you must kill many. To hurt him, you must not kill just him, but his whole family line; His wife and his children." All this was said in a cold, unemotional way, "Sen this vendetta is my vendetta as well; I wasn't going to show this to you, but..." Martel reached into his pocket and pulled out the piece of paper that he had found tacked up on the door and slowly handed it to him. "I found this inside the shed."

Sen read it with trembling hands then handed it back to Martel. He looked up at Martel with deep sadness and fear in his eyes.

"Do you remember what I told you a few days ago?" Martel looked down at his friend and teacher, "That I would do nothing unless the old treaties were broken? Well they are broken now. Now things can be changed." And at that point a chilling smile crept across the shadow dragon's face that made even Sen take a step back.

"We will go together then." Sen said softly. His face still wet with the tears that had run down his soot stained face, as he watched all that he owned, that his family had owned collapse and burn. All but the shed, that just smoldered a bit. "You and I will take out our revenge." But it was a voice filled with fear, hurt and uncertainty.

"Sen, come talk with me, my brother." Martel guided him to the side of the truck where they sat near the running board, that way their backs were protected from the conflagration of the house and barn, they could face the shed and they could talk together.

Sen just numbly followed. This whole thing was way out of his league now and he knew it but his soul and heart were in agony.

"Sen." Martel looked at his teacher and best friend with dignity, respect. "I feel your anger, I feel your heart. I know what Tashima has done to you, the insult. It is my insult as well." Martel had to stop and Sen could see the muscles in the tall man's neck cord up in white-hot anger as he stared at the shed, seeming to see through it to the lifeless body of his beloved fiancée inside. After a few moments, the icy veneer slipped into place and Martel looked back at Sen, "You are an honorable man Sen and you have the heart of a brave man, but you are no match for the Yakuza. You are a true warrior, but do not be a kamikaze, Sen. Do not let your death be in vain. Do not waltz into Tashima's territory with your heart so full of anger and allow him to shoot you down full of bullets, for that is exactly what he wants you to do, and then what? He will laugh at you and he will have crushed one small piss-ant under his shoe, do you understand?"

Sen just looked at him blankly. "Then what, Kageryu? What am I to do? What can one tiny piss-ant do against Tashima Katsuro? I must do something, I cannot just do nothing!"

"Even one tiny ant, can cause trouble amongst a large hive of bees, my friend." Martel smiled wanly at him. "You see the shed?" he nodded with his jaw towards it, "It stands because they wanted it to. It smolders but doesn't burn. It was meant to stand and be a message to me, along with the note. Thankfully I had enough good sense to keep my important papers buried and hidden somewhere else on your farm. I also hid some things under the floorboards in there, some of the earlier gifts you and Miyoko gave me, a few swords, daggers and other goodies that you gave me, including morning stars and some potions, poisons and powders. I think my old gun from a year ago may still be intact, it was dismantled and wrapped in oilcloth and buried out in the fields…"

"So many secrets you have, Kage." Sen said almost in awe, as though really looking at his pupil for the first time.

"And more yet, you will soon learn. Pray that all my foresight has paid off, Sen." Martel once again placed his hand on Sen's hardened shoulder and looked the man deeply in his eyes. "Now, is where you will come into play. I cannot do this alone, I may be the muscle and I

244

may be the stealth, but I need someone who can get me in and out when I am done, who can make arrangements. We will need to leave Japan when I am done and leave quickly."

Sen and Martel talked; putting together their plan as they began to first dig up the items Martel had hidden in the field. (They already knew calling any local constables or police would be useless, Tashima no doubt already paid them off). After that, they hurriedly went through the shed to gather Martel's humble belongings, which Sen neatly packed for him. Martel pried loose the floorboards and pulled out the two razor sharp daggers, the sets of throwing stars, and the two *wakizashi* short swords that he strapped onto himself.

Martel now sat crouched and quickly oiled up the Beretta 9mm and put it together. It had been one of his last gifts from Cochran; smuggled to him two months after he had arrived in Japan now it would be used to take his revenge upon Tashima Katsuro. He had 125 rounds of ammo in all, not a whole lot, he would have to use them wisely if he wanted to get in and out alive and his plan was to definitely get out alive. After all, he was not on a Kamikaze mission either.

Sen had been busily doing something else and Martel had not been paying much attention, Sen had also been busy trying to gather what he could from what little remained. He insisted he be the one to clean his sister up, even though he knew she had been brutally used and murdered and Martel knew that since he and Miyoko had not been formally married yet, it was better to let Sen tend to her, let him clean her and grieve over his family. Honor dictated it and he would need to do it for closure.

Martel had to let the anger of what Tashima did to Miyoko fuel his own heart right now, the vivid image of his precious love and that horrid river of red ran rampant in his heart and had to fuel the rage inside him, for it would be the catalyst that would carry him through this near impossible task.

"Kageryu," Sen's voice solemnly said and broke him out of his thoughts. Martel looked up at his teacher before him; the man seemed numb but also stood in front of him with a resolute determination as well. "Before you go, you need to be marked as a Ninja. You are ready, you have earned it and I hope it will strengthen you. Miyoko would have wanted it as well."

Martel just nodded and tucked the Beretta into his waistband and followed Sen.

Sen led him to the edge of where the collapsed barn was still burning and smoldering, still occasionally the tears would run freely now and again from Sen's eyes, when his body could make them. "My forge is broken, Kage..." he said rather apologetically. "I cannot brand the Symbol the correct way. But I think right now that it would not matter. I think it is almost better this way. This is the way it was done in the beginning, somehow it seems more your style anyway, Kageryu."

Martel noticed that Sen had thrust a few half finished daggers at some point into the broken part of the forge. Over on this side of the barn; the heat was so intense, that it was already making both men sweat intensely. Martel knew what was coming; he had seen the ancient brand-tattoo of the cobra and dragon intertwined, on both Sen and on Miyoko, the sign of the Ninja. Usually now a days it was tattooed on, some got it branded on rapidly and then filled in later but Sen was going to do it the old fashioned way, the way it had been done for untold centuries past, slow, stroke by stroke and then rubbed in with ashes on the fresh wound. Miyoko had hers tattooed on, but Martel knew Sen had gotten his own branded on in the old fashioned way as well.

"I can tie your arm to the tree to hold it still if you want, Kage." Sen offered.

"No." Martel looked at him quickly, darkly. He would not be restrained in any way with potential enemies like Tashima's goons on the loose. He simply sat down at that point, centered himself and let his mind play over and over and over the image of his beloved Miyoko and how her lifeless, violated body looked in his arms.

Not a sound came from the large, resolute man as Sen squatted down and worked slowly, carefully, to brand the symbol onto Martel's upper arm.

Slowly the work went a bit at a time; cutting, rubbing fresh ash into the wound and then branding with the searing red hot blade and repeating the whole thing over and over. Silent, involuntary tears flowed freely down Martel's face, mixed with his sweat.

The stench of his cooking flesh was in the air; the smell of pain but not a sound was uttered by either man. All that could be heard was the crackling of Sen Yamashita's burning farm and the occasional crashing boards as more of his barn or house collapsed. It was indeed a strange, surreal and nightmarish scene.

The white hot pain that coursed through Martel's body only reaffirmed the white hot pain of anger and hatred that filled his soul and each touch of the knife that Sen carved on him was another layer of him that died. It was as though Laurence Martel was watching this whole scene from outside himself as an onlooker as Sen branded him; watching each of his years of life from age 8 onward simply ceasing to exist. Age nine dead... ten, dead... eleven, dead... Dead, dead and dead, until such a wall was built around him of coldness and an unemotional void that he was indeed the Shadow Dragon and the Shadow Dragon was him.

Martel now realized that to care for something was to give it power and to give it power was to give himself a weakness and an Achilles heel. Finally there were no more physical tears to shed; he did not know when the pain stopped, for he was numb to it anymore, numb to anything.

He was only vaguely aware of Sen standing in front of him offering his hand,   "Kage?" Sen asked softly, hesitantly, "are you Ok?" his voice had changed; it was more concerned, softer and even…frightened sounding?

Martel fought to focus his eyes, clear his mind and stood up, his world wavered briefly for a moment and he thought he would pass out but it then came into a crystal clear focus. His arm ached relentlessly, was sore and stiff. He hoped and prayed it would not hinder him later when he needed it most. "I am fine," He said hoarsely, "fine Sen."

Both men had noticed the change. There was no need to formally verbalize it, like had been done with his last teacher, Cochran. There had just been a shift in the wind and now they both knew that no longer was Kageryu the student and Sen the teacher. Now they were equals. They were still dear friends and they were bound by a common hurt and vendetta. "What do you need me to do Kage?" Sen simply asked.

Martel reached into his pocket and pulled out the small box that held the magnificent engagement ring he was going to have given to Miyoko in two days. He opened it a moment and looked at it, but there was no reaction on his face this time. All the anger was internalized now, stored up to be released for Tashima. "Take this, Sen." He closed it gently and handed it to Sen. "It is worth enough to get us both tickets to Hawaii. I will give you some phone numbers to call and some messages to get through to people who will help us. I will be gone for two days and two nights. On the third day we will meet at the Kyoto Airport. Make sure your paperwork is ready to go as well. Hold onto my passports and paperwork for me. Do not open or mess with anything. I am holding you in my 'trust-oath' and honor." He said simply.

Sen bowed low, respectfully "It is done Kage-san, my brother. May the strength of Kwan-Ti be with you in avenging our retribution against Tashima Katsuro for what he has done to our family." More tears slipped from Sen's dark eyes.

Martel embraced Sen briefly filling him with strength. "There is no honor in this Sen." He said darkly, "for he and his family will suffer. It is the darkness of the Shadow Dragon Tashima will feel and I hold no mercy for him. Forgive me Sen for bringing this down upon your family."

"I hold no blame for you, Kageryu." Sen spoke honestly. "I blame myself for not being there when I should have all those years ago, I should have been at my fathers side. Now I am paying the price."

Martel said nothing and just looked around, would he have to pay a price for not being at his fathers' side? What would his own karmic atonement be for all his crimes and was it already now beginning with the death of Miyoko? Well, a penny for a pound then for he knew a lot more death was going to ensue in the next thirty six hours at his hands.

Perhaps because Martel had simply listened so intently during his 8 months in the service of Tashima Katsuro or maybe because the Yakuza simply did not expect two men, let alone one lone man to try anything, that Martel was able to penetrate and go to where he knew Tashima's family lived. To simply kill Tashima would be too easy. This was personal and to hurt the man, his whole family line must be taken out.

Martel knew intimately that during this time of year Tashima's family would be vacationing at the shoreline and so that first night, he was able to go there to the vacation house and sneak onto the grounds he was surprised that there were only twelve guards on duty. They were easily taken out with the Ninjitsu techniques he had learned from Sen and the deadly Aikido and jujitsu he had learned from Cochran. A few he used his blowgun on. Whenever he killed a guard he disabled their radio, and took any weapons they had. Martel saved the guns; they would be useful later. Since he had the key from one of the guard captains, he easily and simply shut down the alarm system to the vacation home. He remembered and knew the exact times between the guard shifts. He also knew Tashima was far too arrogant and predictable in changing any of the routines he engaged in year after year. He obviously thought he was safe and invincible, he was about to find out how very wrong he would be.

Once inside the elegant vacation home and starting with Tashima's children, the Shadow Dragon's vengeance was unleashed; one by one he killed them in their sleep. The young children he killed mercifully; a quick, painless beheading with the razor sharp short swords. Tashima's eldest teenaged son was not so fortunate, he was killed more slowly and the body horribly mutilated as a sign of disrespect. The same with Tashima's wife, Shaji Katsuro, Martel cut out her heart and placed it on the pillow where her husband would normally sleep, her body was then mutilated in a sign of disrespect. He then cut his sigil with her blood on the wall: 'Kageryu- the Shadow Dragon'.

He knew his time would be limited, the clock was ticking and he would only have around five hours to find the boss himself before they locked Tashima down tight. He had to get to the one place he knew Tashima would be and that would be across town, in the bed of his mistress for the last ten years, Haruko.

Martel grabbed one of the guard's cars and raced across town, praying for strength, praying to the fates to help guide him on his quest for vendetta against Miyoko's family and centering himself to call upon his deepest reserves. If Tashima was not there, then he would have to go underground for awhile and listen for news and see if he could flush him out within 24 hours. If not, then he had to get out and call it a draw.

He had killed the man's family, but it was still not as good as if he could kill the whole Katsuro line. Only then in Martel's heart would it be sated and finished for him, only then.

He was racing time and knew he had two hours to get to Haruko's house before the guards at Tashima's house switched shifts. He had cut the phone lines, to delay them some but it would only be a matter of time before word got out to the Boss about his family's massacre. Thankfully it was late at night and he knew where any 'speed traps' were. Here in the deeper city of Tokyo most police were busy elsewhere and not hanging around the territory of Tashima Katsuro. Any of Tashima's men who saw the car, would simply recognize it as one of their own and not be overly alarmed.

As if the fates heard his pleas the skies began to drop a heavy rain down upon the pavement. Martel said a prayer of thanks to Buddha, Kwan-Ti and to Miyoko. The rain would blind his enemies more than him. Martel parked the car about a block down from Haruko's house and then grabbing what he needed blended into the rainy night.

His arm was throbbing in agonizing pain where he had earlier been branded but his adrenaline was fired anew. His hatred and anger had honed his nerves to fine wires and every sense was alive, attuned like a million electrical wires plugged into the pulse of the night. Like a great predator he stalked silently every sense alert; smell, hearing, eyesight. Every lesson coming into play that Cochran or Sen had ever taught him, as well as every nuance and remembrance he had ever picked up about the Yakuza while working down here for them. He knew where the lookouts where posted, where the alarms where.

He screwed in a silencer on the rifle he had grabbed earlier from one of the house guards and expertly shot out one of the lookout guards on a low building. The man never knew what hit him. Martel then deftly cut two of the phone lines to this side of the neighborhood and walked on, staying deep in the shadows, keeping his great height low to the ground.

The walk to Haruko's house seemed to take forever and he easily and quietly took out two more guards who never saw him coming. The last man by the back door Martel had simply used the two martial arts swords to impale him and slice off the man's head. It was over and done with in literally less than 3 seconds.

Using an old trick Cochran showed him, he took two small metal nails and quietly jimmied the lock on the back door and popped it open. He knew there would be no guards inside the house. There may be one out by the front door but none inside here. No Boss wants his guards around while he is fucking his mistress.

Martel could hear some soft laughter and talking down near the back of the house. A man and womans' his heart rose in anticipation, they were still here and awake. Quickly and carefully he stalked down the hallway ready for anything. He could see the soft light on in their bedroom, the glint of a champagne bottle by their bed. As he nimbly kicked open the door, he saw Haruko's lithe naked body standing there pouring champagne for the pig faced Tashima who lay lounging on the bed under the covers. Her eyes suddenly grew large and her mouth froze in silent terror in the shape of an "o".

Tashima was much quicker and his flabby body moved surprisingly fast as he suddenly moved reaching for something under his pillow but Martel was already on him in a heartbeat.

To this day Martel did not know why he took the risk he did of a killing so personal, it was the first rule a hitman never broke. Never get "personal", kill from a distance. But to Martel this whole thing was very, very personal and at that moment some dam inside Martel just burst and he made the worst mistake of his life. He moved in close, leapt like a giant tiger on top of Tashima pinning him down and grabbed his pudgy hand that had been reaching for a gun. He expertly wrested it from his hand and tossed the gun out of Tashima's reach.

"You lose, stupid fuck!" Martel hissed at him in Japanese. "Thought I would pack up so easily after you threw your muscle around just a little too much? Your family is dead, Tashima! Your wife and daughters were good fucks and your eldest son, his head and his dreams are as dead as you will soon be!" The wrath of the shadow dragon filled the air and for a moment the arrogance left the fat piggish face of Tashima Katsuro and he paled visibly. Fear actually came off of him in delicious waves.

"You lie, Kageryu." He barely whispered in fear beneath the enraged man atop him. "Why go through all this? Eh? We can make a deal, Eh?" he tried to laugh. It was then that Martel saw Tashima's eyes briefly just barely noticeably cut to the right, for an instant.

Martel was just about to turn and kill her when he felt the pain and impact of something cold and steely ram deep inside his back. His base instinct and martial arts training had made him move at the last moment to avoid taking a lethal hit, it was the mistress Haruko; she had rammed a dagger up under Martel's shoulder blade.
He turned and with a cruel snarl pulled the trigger on his rifle with the silencer and filled her with 4 shots instantly killing her.

But that last action gave Tashima enough leverage to suddenly ram the heel of his hand up under the wounded Martel's chin, the other aiming for the tall man's eyes, trying to throw the giant off of him. It made little impact on Martel who had the superior position and utter hatred in his veins.

Martel took the butt of the rifle and brought it down squarely on Tashima's head. Once, twice, it smashed into him with a hideous crack causing Tashima Katsuro's blood to flow wildly down his face.

"You are a dumb fuck, Tashima!" Martel wanted to just hit him and keep hitting until his anger had run out and Tashima's brains were splattered everywhere. Part of him wanted to torture him all night but the voice of Cochran was in his mind telling him to be done and go into hiding, to think smart. He was badly hurt now and he needed to pull back and assess his injuries. He needed to get back to Victor and his own family.

"Ok, here is the deal." Martel tightened up his hold on Tashima, his legs and weight pinning him immobile again beneath him, "Your death is one of the very few that is going to be very slow and very personal Tashima." Martel suddenly grabbed the man's throat with his bare hands and clamped on. His thumbs pushing into Tashima's windpipe and carotid artery as he strangled the life out of him, "and as your dying I am going to sit here and tell you all about how I killed each of your children and your wife, deal? And then you can then go on to the afterlife knowing you were killed by Kageryu, the stupid American." A chilling smile played along the Shadow Dragons lips as he choked the life out of Yakuza crime lord Tashima Katsuro. "This is also on behalf of Miyoko Yamashita and her family as well as well, for I shall take from you what you took from me, my life." He whispered darkly.

For nearly 3 minutes he watched and felt the great crime lord thrash and die beneath him. Finally after he had stopped struggling, after he had felt the pig's heart stop beating under him he released his grasp on the man's throat. He broke Katsuro's neck for good measure; a double assurance of death.

There was a great commotion then at the front door, guards' voices calling out to Tashima. Laurence Martel knew that the bodyguards had either found Tashima's murdered family or else their fellow dead guards out back.

He cursed himself out silently, leapt off the dead man's body and then nimbly dove for the window. His back rebelled and he felt he would pass out. 'Stay focused!' he ordered himself, 'Stay focused!!' Blinding pain ran up and down the length of his side. He dared not look at the bed to see how much blood he had lost.

One of Martel's long arms reached up and nimbly unlocked the window sash and then closing his eyes and saying a silent mantra he flipped it open and dove through it in one smooth move, once again becoming one with the rainy night. Right now he centered every thought he had on Miyoko, all the pleasant things they had shared together, all the dreams they had dreamt. Whenever the pain in his back bit him cruelly, or he felt he might lose consciousness to that dizzying pain he focused on remembering his father, Victors face, or his mentor Cochran. Remembering every lesson in the bush Cochran had ever told him.

Even in a big city like this, he was now a wanted man, hunted by Katsuro's soldiers, he would have to lay low and survive the next 30 hours to rendezvous with Sen or he would not live to see his father Victor. A part of him wanted to scream with delight, he had done the impossible! He had killed Tashima Katsuro and his entire family line, a part of him wanted to slap himself silly for not watching Haruko more carefully. "Had Miyoko and Cochran taught you nothing, you giant oaf?" He chided himself. "Never underestimate a woman!"

There was only one man he could half way trust to go to but he had to get there now, before word of Tashima's death made all the headlines and news, otherwise the man would turn him in. He stealthily made his way back to where he had parked the stolen guards' car and slid in behind the wheel. By now he was bathed in hot sweat and blood, chilled with the wet rain and he felt on the verge of passing out but he forced strength into himself and willed himself to stay alert. He placed a few of the guns on the seat next to him and one of the daggers in his lap.

As he sped off into the early morning night, he saw a squadron of police cars heading towards the neighborhood he had just come from, he closed his eyes a moment and smiled, letting the warm feeling wash over him. He knew it would never, could never bring back his beloved Miyoko but for the briefest of instances, it had been so satisfying, taking his vengeance out on Tashima, watching the crime boss's terrified face as the man realized he was truly going to die. As Martel sat there atop him telling him in crystal clear detail as only one who intimately knew the bodies of his family, how he had killed one by one his family members. Seeing the tears of remorse, fear and utter sorrow finally come to Tashima's hardened face, as his final death throes came over him. That had been Kageryu's reward - that is what he had wanted to see.

A half hour later he had pulled into a dark and run down alleyway, on the far end of Tokyo. It was a very poor and run down section, very little stirred except rats, alley cats and some drunks or those addicted to opium and sleeping it off.

There was a healer here, one that some of the Yakuza used. Martel preferred the fellow, only because he was one who followed some of the old ways, the old traditions, he healed with plants and herbs when he was sober enough to do so. Martel hoped he was not too stoned out on opium tonight to help him.

Of course the shop would not be open until daylight but Martel simply used his little nail trick to pick the lock and stealthily made his way in. He already knew the healer carried a gun and he also knew where he kept it. So he carefully scouted out the closed business, found the gun and pocketed it, then silently walked upstairs. He saw the old man asleep on his bed, several empty bottles of *sake* scattered around his filthy bedroom and cockroaches running around the bed and the nightstand. Martel clamped one large hand down over the snoring mans nose and mouth.

"Shhh, Kisho-Sensei," Martel addressed him politely in formal Japanese. "I am not here to harm you, but I need your services. I am injured and require healing. Tend to me and ask no questions, pretend you never saw me and you will be well rewarded. But argue with me and you leave me no choice. Do we understand each other?" Martel slowly turned on one of the small nightlights and slowly released his hand from the healer's nose and mouth.

The healer slowly sat up and reached over for his glasses, cockroaches scattered in the light, there was no mistaking the huge foreigner standing over him. "Kageryu!" Kisho barely whispered in shock. "You're still around?"

Martel just inclined his head slightly and stepped back, allowing the healer to get out of bed.

"Hand me my robes, Kage-san." Kisho asked politely.

Martel was thankful and could tell that this night at least the healer had not been smoking the opium, just hitting the *sake*, he was hung over a bit, but didn't have the glazed, gaunt look of being stoned off his gourd.

Martel had been here before; this was one of the various back alley healers where most criminal types came to be 'fixed up', and while Dr. Kisho was not the most popular Martel liked him, because he could get the more natural medicines that Cochran had taught him about, the herbal remedies and poultices and sometimes the more harder to come by natural remedies. So he knew where the treatment room was.

"You've got my gun, Kageryu-san." The small doctor nervously said as Martel followed Kisho to the exam room.

"I will give it back Kisho-Sensei, when we are done. I just didn't want you shooting me when I woke you up." Martel gave him a grim half smile, while pointing the gun at him.

"Still so polite aren't you?" the healer snapped on the lights in the exam room, began gathering his supplies. Very few people ever called him by his formal title anymore of "Doctor" at least not the Yakuza thugs but Kageryu was different, always respectful and always polite. He never asked for the modern narcotics, he always wanted the natural drugs; he always wanted to remain clear headed.

As Kisho turned towards him, he couldn't help but give a little gasp, as Kage had slipped out of his coat and shirt. He saw the gaping wound under his shoulder blade; it was a bad injury, deep and ugly. He also saw the mark of the ninja upon him now; he had not seen that mark in decades. Much had happened in this ones life. He was surprised Kageryu had even walked to him under his own power. "Lay down. I will attend to you, Kageryu." Kisho said with a note respect.

Martel was grateful to finally be off his feet and still he had to fight to keep from sinking into oblivion. All Martel's body wanted to do was to drift off to blissful sleep and unconsciousness, but not here; he knew it was not safe. While he trusted the healer to fix him up for now, he did not trust Kisho to not turn him over to Tashima's underboss or some other Yakuza goons. "Before you begin work, give me some Mugwort root, Ginseng and Gotu kola." Martel quietly ordered.

"But that will wire you up, make your body wide awake and run you faster." Kisho looked at him slightly confused.

"I know." Martel looked him dead in the eye. "Believe me, I know."...

CHAPTER 20- *June 18th 1987*

When Alyssa first opened her eyes she was aware that she felt more physically rested and healed than she felt in a long time. Her body which normally ached, was not as stiff and sore today, for a brief instance she felt a bit disorientated. "This wasn't the peach frilly room?" light was filtering through a dark blue curtain and she could see the dark inlaid lacquered furniture, then she remembered. She was in Martel's house; she was living with him now.

She opened her eyes more and looked to see if her bedmate was still there but he was not, she heard the sound of an electric razor and then flipped over onto her other side and saw him standing in the bathroom, his back to her. She noticed that on his right shoulder blade was a long ugly scar, in fact like his arms he had many scars all over him, but that one stood out deeply; looking as though it had never healed quite right.

On his back and shoulder were also some more small Kanji tattoos; he was dressed still just in the loose fitting black martial arts pants. She watched him going through his mundane routine as she remembered last night, the chess game, the storm, the sharing of trust, his healing massage and his oriental name for her, what was it???

The razor abruptly clicked off, "Good morning, Kanashii." He turned towards her "I trust you slept well?"

Alyssa nodded at him still waking up.

"Excellent. I would say so," Martel grabbed a towel, which he draped over his shoulders and came back into the bedroom. "It's nearly 10 am." He smiled wanly, "Since it's your first day and your still healing I let you sleep in. But don't think your going to get a free ride every day."

Alyssa rolled her eyes and burrowed under the covers... She was not a morning person.

"Amusing, Kanashii." Martel said totally neutrally. He walked over and nudged her, flopping down on the bed half on top of her. "Listen to me," he spoke to the mound of covers, "I made breakfast and already ate mine, there is coffee or tea available in the kitchen if you want. Your breakfast is in the refrigerator, so eat up. I'm going to take a shower, when I get done we will go over a routine and schedule for you. We have lots to do today and a tight schedule to keep to and you've already slept away 4 hours of it." He chuckled lightly. He stood back up and whistling lightly walked into the bathroom and shut the door.

"I really don't like morning people." Alyssa thought grumpily. She hurriedly put back on her nightshirt and then padded off to her own guest bathroom to shower up and then eat.

"That was some storm last night, eh John Thomas?" Victor sipped his coffee as he spoke with his old friend. "I tell you, it knocked a lot of braches down here, even dropped some hail over on some of the gardens. I'm going to fix some minor damage at the aviaries later, thankfully nothing too serious".

"Well it's going to be another scorcher." The doctor gave Victor a quick concerned look, "Just don't go over exerting yourself, you feisty putz."

"I haven't felt so well in months." Victor smiled at him over his coffee cup. "You told me so yourself. What did that blood work say again?" Victor teased him back.

"Yeah, well." John Thomas Weintraub tried to be gruff but smiled back. "It looks damn great Vic, but let's keep it that way, Ok? Promise me."

"Of course I will my friend, why undo all that hard work you did, eh?" he winked at John Thomas.

"So what's this I hear that Alyssa is staying with Martel now?" John Thomas raised one eyebrow and pulled off his wire-rimmed glasses to clean them on his napkin.

"Eh…" Victor just idly let the comment drift. "Things came up here, Martel had extra time and I thought with some of her problems and such…" Victor let the statement drift around a moment more, avoiding any direct answers. "Well they just seem to click so well together." He looked almost innocently at the doctor and left the explanation at that.

Behind him, one of the guards nearly choked on his donut trying to keep from laughing, "S'cuse me!" He half choked out and stepped out of the room where he coughed, laughed and coughed some more at the same time. A few of the other guards just snickered softly or turned away to keep from laughing entirely at Victor's comment.

Victor just looked innocently at John Thomas with a slight shrug as though nothing was going on. Len Tagretta walked in at that moment and Victor couldn't have been happier. "Ah! Good morning, Leonardo! Come enjoy breakfast with us."

Len spoke first in his native Italian to his Boss, "Good morning Don Victor, you look well. Everything is fine here?" He briefly glanced at the snickering-choking bodyguards, but just ignored them. "Are you going into the city today?" He gave his boss the customary quick embrace.

"Actually yes to both of your questions Len, tell Alberto to fire up the 'Copter around 1pm. We will be going over to the VIJER building to do a little house cleaning eh? We want to make sure all our shit smells sweet as roses."

"Very good, *Padrone*." Len nodded and then switched back to English. "Good morning *dottore* Weintraub." He said in his Italian accented broken English. "I have little something for you, Martel wanted me to give to you this, yes?" he reached in his pocket and withdrew an envelope and placed it on the table in front of the doctor." Then proceeded to go and help himself to the breakfast buffet to grab some espresso and fresh fruit.

John Thomas picked up the envelope and looked over at Victor who just gave him a shrug of his shoulders, as if to say, "How do I know what Martel's business with you is?" but there was always that inner and slightly amused gleam in Victors eyes and John Thomas knew better, Victor knew what everybody in his Family did. The doctor opened it and glanced inside. It contained two exclusive box tickets to an upcoming NY Yankee's home game. 'Son of a bitch,' John Thomas though to himself with a warm smile, he shook his head and tucked the envelope in his jacket pocket and finished up his cup of coffee and the last of his Danish.

"Something good, I hope." Victor said nonchalantly but his eyes were smiling.

"It's not bad." John Thomas answered back in the same neutral tone but with the same playful glint in his eyes. He wouldn't say anything to Laurence; he knew it would only embarrass both of them. Ol' Laurence-Theodore was indeed a lot like his father.

"So did you only come to harass me today, you old goat?" Victor teased his friend, "Or are you here to see the girl too."

"Actually I came over to see Alyssa." John Thomas shoveled the last of his Danish in his mouth. "Her throat is healed enough now to know whether she will be able to use an electrolarynx."

"A what?" Victor looked up at the doctor.

John Thomas reached in his pocket and pulled out a small tube-like instrument, which he flicked on and placed against his throat. When he began to talk, the 'tube' actually did the talking and sounded very robotic and monotonously machine like. "An- Electrolarynx- is- a- machine- box- like- this." He switched it off, and used his normal voice. "You see? That's what an electrolarynx is, I'm gonna see if Alyssa can use one."

Victor shook his head with a bit of a grimace, "That," he paused, "that is awful sounding." Several of the guards had kind of flinched at the robotic voice too.

"It's better than nothing, Vic. It's better than her getting arthritis in her fingers and not being able to utter a peep at all." He glared at Victor.

"You're right." Victor gave a sigh, "but you would think they would make them more..." he paused.

"Like human sounding!" Len piped up adamantly. "Exactly," Victor agreed. "Human sounding, that thing sounded just hideous."

"Well that is up to her." John Thomas groused. "Besides, it takes a lot of work to even use one of these, weeks and months of therapy. It took me weeks of practice to be able to even be able to say that simple sentence with this thing." His mind drifted, "I still have to rerun that new EEG on her and see if those areas of her brain affecting speech patterns have even come back up to speed. It's not just her throat that was damaged remember." He glanced quietly at Victor. "I'm not even sure if she can use this, but I intend to give her every chance."

"Well good then." Victor straightened up and smiled warmly at him. "She needs some good champions on her side. Between you and Martel, you both will have her right as rain in no time, eh?"

"Well, I'm done here; I can go see her now." John Thomas drained the last of his coffee and stood up.

"Come *dottore* Weintraub. I drive you down there." Len motioned for doctor to follow him.

"Where is Cesare?" John Thomas asked looking quizzically at Victor.

Victor just raised an eyebrow refusing to look at Weintraub's eyes, "He's taking a little vacation for about a week, John Thomas." He said in his neutral 'no nonsense-don't ask-me-any-more-about-it', tone of voice.

John Thomas felt a sudden chill fall across the whole room, as though the air conditioner had suddenly dropped ten degrees colder. Several of the guards actually looked at him darkly for his breach of etiquette. "Whew," John Thomas whistled under his breath. "Geeze, take it easy fellas." He shook his head at them.

Alyssa had just finished eating the breakfast Martel had made earlier, it was some kind of rice pudding with cardamom, sliced nuts and milk in it and was quite delicious. It had an exotic taste that seemed to awaken and refresh her there was still some hot, strong Italian style coffee in the coffeemaker so she finished the last of it.

As she was washing and drying her dishes Martel walked into the kitchen. Dressed in his usual black suit with a dark navy tie, his hair neatly combed back and an aura of non-emotion and iciness about him, Martel was back to looking the part of the cold, imposing underboss.

He had bought in a stack of papers and books that he placed neatly on the kitchen table. She recognized a few of the blank journals from her room.

"Finished breakfast?" he slid gracefully into the seat opposite her as he watched her sipping the last of her coffee.

She nodded and grabbed one of the of the blank note pads. "*It was really good, thanks.*"

He inclined his head in acknowledgement, "Glad you like my cooking. Now let's go over some things." He said in his colder, more professional tone. Then began to rifle around in the stack he had brought out gathering things and pulling out a list and schedule.

She stared blankly at him for a moment and was genuinely confused. He seemed so different last night and now it was as though that impenetrable wall was around him again. What had happened to the teacher who had made her laugh when they were playing Chess? The man who had held her and rode out her terror with her? The teacher she had promised her trust to? The healer who had made her feel safe and secure for the first time she could remember?

Here once again was the cold, unreadable Laurence Martel in fact if anything he seemed as distant and reserved as the very first day she had met him. She didn't think he was purposely playing with her or jerking her around but she just didn't get it. What had changed in him between last night and now? Last night was a glimpse of someone she had never knew existed in him and she thought, that it was a glimpse of the real him, a genuine part of his real heart and soul. This morning that part of him was slammed deeply away and locked down more tightly than Fort Knox.

"Kanashii, Alyssa..." his deep voice snapped her out of her daydream. "Are you listening to a word I am saying?" He stared down at her. "Is something wrong?" he asked neutrally, folding his hands in front of him, waiting.

"*No, I... Go on. Sorry.*" She penned. She was going to have to pull back her own emotions now and reassess. Not jump to conclusions either way. Perhaps he was merely being kind and she had read far more into it than was really there.

"As I was saying," he continued, "In a few minutes you have an appointment with Dr. Weintraub to check you out. Routine physical and I think he wants to check your throat to see if you can be fitted for an electro-larynx. Now, normally your days will go like this..." and he droned on, going over how her schedule would be. It usually involved things like martial arts workouts with him, mandatory reading time, artwork or some sort of what he called 'creativity time', then working over at the Jerome Estates with either the cleaning ladies or the cooking ladies. Alyssa groaned inwardly to herself, now he was planning out her day minute by minute? What was this, military school?

"Humbleness, Kanashii," Martel chided lightly, "Humbleness and routine is often a good time for meditation. You need to re-learn some skills like cooking, sewing, things like that. I cannot be babysitting you 24/7, I do have a job to do you know." A small dark smile tugged at the corners of his mouth a moment. "Think of it as physical and occupational therapy, besides you need to keep your mind busy and structured. Need to study your surroundings to learn how you fit in here and to feel more comfortable."

Alyssa had no qualms about working in fact she was thankful for it she certainly didn't want to be spoiled like some 'Mafia princess' that was for sure. She figured whatever she could do to help repay her debt for all the care that had been given her, was fine with her. But it nearly sounded like Martel had her entire day planned out with a precision that made her almost feel like a small child instead of a 24 year old woman.

"Now, one thing that I do want you to do is this," He pushed two of the blank journals towards her. "One is yours and yours alone, it's for your eyes only. Write whatever you want in it, draw artwork write poetry, I don't care, just follow the rules of *omerta*, understand?" he looked at her his blue eyes penetrating her soul. "You can write what is in your heart, but 'Family business', doesn't get discussed..." he pushed that book further into her grasp.

"This one," he pushed the other one between them, "This one you write in and we share together. If something comes up, some question you have when I am not here or you remember something or you have another terror or anything," his piercing blue eyes seemed to see right through her. "Anything at all any question, you write it in here and we will talk about it and share it. Or again, it can be poetry, artwork, I don't care. But we share it as student and teacher." He paused a moment as if almost sensing her inner thoughts. "Kanashii," he spoke gently, "You promised me trust, remember? I promised to help you heal. I know this may seem overwhelming and even a bit over structured, but it will help you learn, to heal inside."

She nodded, scooping up the second book. That one had two dragons flying in the clouds over a great mountain near an ocean; it was one of the blank books he had bought at the Oriental store they had stopped at yesterday. It was actually a lovely book, well made a piece of artwork all on its own.

"And here is a gift from me to you." He reached inside the pocket of his sport jacket and pulled out a small leather case and handed it to her. There were two recently painted Kanji symbols on it, one she recognized from the picture in the living room where the 'shadow dragon' was and she had seen it again in his room last night too. The second Kanji she did not recognize.

She pointed at the one Kanji symbol she recognized and hesitantly pointed at him.

His eyes smiled briefly in that genuine smile she had glimpsed last night, the cold hardness dropping away for the briefest of instances, "Very good, Kanashii. Yes, you remember, that is the Kanji for *Kageryu* but we will keep that quiet, Hmm?" he gave her that little wink and slowly the wall around him slid back into place. "This Kanji," he pointed to the second "is yours, *Kanashii-Taka*."

She opened the case and inside was two beautiful pens golden hawks with fiery red tinged feathers encircling them, they seemed to fly wild and free against a black background. Each pen had a soft silken cord she could easily loop around her neck, wrist or jean belt loop to keep it handy at all time and never be without a writing instrument.

"*Thank you, Martel,*" she used the pen to write on her writing pad, it flowed wonderfully and fit her hand comfortably almost as if it were made just for her. "*It's a lovely gift!*" She smiled at him, trying to convey the honesty of the emotions she felt at the kindness of his gift, somehow she sensed he knew.

He briefly nodded his head at her again. "You're welcome." Was his simple reply, "Last is this," he took out a parchment of paper and unfolded it written on it was both English and some kind of oriental writing. "Much to Dr. Weintraub's' chagrin and grumbling, I got his Ok and I will be going out today while I'm in the city and get you some herbal supplements I want to begin to put you on. I assure you they are all natural. They will help you heal up faster and balance your mind, body and soul." He refolded that piece of paper and placed it back inside the breast pocket of his sport coat.

"I will be going into town with Mr. Jerome, so after your visit with Dr. Weintraub you will be staying at the Jerome Estates." Martel continued "For now, on days when I am not here to supervise you either Mr. Tommy DeLuca, or Mr. Gio Aprile will be your," he paused for a moment, "Supervisor. Mr. Aprile works directly for me, and you met him briefly once before. So treat him with the same respect you would give me, please."

Alyssa was fairly sure she knew who Mr. Aprile was, probably that bald large overly muscle-bound bodyguard who had been there that one night, when Victor had sent the guards to escort her to his Office. A gorilla looking type, who looked like he could punch a Cadillac into next week with his bare fist. He was one of the more 'elite' bodyguards, and barely said two words to anyone. He was almost as intimidating as Martel, probably because he was the main captain of the house guards. She just nodded and slowly gathered all the stuff Martel had given her still trying to absorb all he had told her into her mind, juggling books and schedules in her arms.

"Don't be so glum," Martel stood up and helped her carry stuff to her room, "it will be a good thing, trust me, you will get into a routine in no time, you will welcome it after awhile or you would go crazy with boredom here. You will still have plenty of free time," he reassured her, "One other thing," he gestured to a beautiful book he must have placed on her desk while she was eating breakfast, "Your first book assignment, since you seem to enjoy reading so much." He gave her an amused look, "Learn about us and our beginnings the correct way." He handed her the nonfiction hardback booked which was titled 'The Italian Immigrants Journey in American History.' She carefully placed it with her other items she carried. "Now, I think it's time to go see Dr. Weintraub."

Alyssa had spent the next several hours with Dr. Weintraub and they had went over and repeated nearly every test she had done when she first came here, to the Jerome Estates including some new EEG's and psychological tests where he had her looking at strange blobs on paper, which made no sense to her.

She had explained to him a little about getting some little 'Memory flashes' of partial remembrances back but didn't go into a lot of detail. Somehow she just didn't feel as comfortable discussing the actual details with him of what she saw (The tractor trailer, the tall skinny man and his cattle prod, the beating…) as she did when she had told Martel about it. This was just fine, since John Thomas didn't prod into what it was she had seen, either.

He had spent a lot of time examining her throat muscles and the nerves to her throat and looking at the EEG brain waves. He gave her the strange tube device but after a half an hour it only left her even more frustrated and riled, a few tears streaked her face at her failure and frustration of not being able to learn the machine.

"It's Ok, sweetheart." He soothed as she sat there shaking as she clutched the strange machine, utter frustration in her emerald eyes. He gently retrieved the electrolarynx from her grasp. He knew she had tried so very hard, had put her entire heart and soul into trying to make it work. "It may just take time." he put it down on his desk, and studied the EEG's again. He still didn't like the way they looked. The right sequences weren't firing in all the right order, he had hoped she may have been able to maybe make some progress but he could see now; they were both obviously trying to pin way too much hope on this. Her scans were beginning to look like she was going to have no hope of ever using an electrolarynx.

He took off his glasses and let them fall on his desk, absentmindedly rubbing the bridge of his nose. "Let's take a break, kiddo." He pushed some tissues and butterscotch disks towards her. Because of his friend Victor's need for lifesavers and other candies he always had some kind of hard candy around somewhere on him or in his office, the crap was everywhere around here.

Alyssa sniffed loudly into the tissue and rubbed at her eyes then grabbed a couple candy disks and stuffed them down into the pockets of her jeans for later. John Thomas smiled. "I don't blame you. I hear Martel has you on that Asian food and those natural supplements of his." He just lightly shook his head for a moment.

She actually threw him a rather dark look and this surprised him. "Hey, hey!" he playfully laughed, "I was just kidding." He replaced his glasses back on which perched in their normal half-askew position, ever since that kid had broken his nose that day he met Victor, his glasses had never fit quite right, "Since when has Martel ever needed a defender, eh?" the doctor lightly teased with a gentle smile. "I love Laurence like a son, trust me, he's fine. Look, the good news is your healing really well. Honest. I am really impressed how well things are starting to come together and heal after your injury and donor surgery." Dr. Weintraub offered her a kind hearted look.

Alyssa was composed again now as she popped one of the candies into her mouth and tossed the Kleenex into the waste can.

"Do you have any new memories at all of what caused your initial injuries?" John Thomas asked her hopefully.

"*Not really*," she wrote. "*We both know about the same. Electricity, someone whacked me around good with a cattle prod*." She thrust the pad of paper at him.

"Alyssa," John Thomas began in a very serious tone as started putting some of his medical equipment back in his cabinets but didn't look at her, "Are you comfortable living with Laurence Martel? I mean if you want me to talk to Mr. Jerome about you moving back into the Estates under Tommy DeLuca's care or perhaps even with my wife and I..." he continued, his face refusing to meet her eyes.

"Oh Jesus!" her mind raced horrified for an instant... "Did John Thomas think Victor's people did this to her?!?"

"*NO!!!! No!!!*" she scribbled rapidly on the paper. She reached up and grabbed him bodily by the arm and then forced him to watch as she wrote...."*John Thomas NO!!! Victor SAVED me... He saved me from the Romans!!! That's why I wanted to donate that kidney to him. Look, I don't remember much, not really ANYTHING that happened before. Someone took me, kidnapped me? From somewhere, I'm not sure where...*" Her writing came fast, screaming from her soul to be heard by him, "*I don't know why. I ended up at some place owned by Vito Roman but Victor saved me. All I want to do is get along in this Family, like you do.*" She knew this was a double edged test of her loyalty of what she had promised both Victor and Martel and also would determine if John Thomas would help her fit into the Family now, as he was, as a protected outsider and associate of the Family.

She saw John Thomas visible relax, as though he was almost holding his breath. "He did wonder!" she thought to herself. "He really honestly wondered."

"*I feel very safe with Martel, I just want to heal up and get along peacefully here and that's all.*" She finished scribbling with the pen that had the golden fire tinged hawk on it and in her heart she did. Martel had asked her to trust her and she had given that trust, what more could she do? She capped the pen and looked at him, her eyes pleading with him to understand.

"Of course Alyssa," He smiled. "I didn't mean to make you uncomfortable, I'm sorry, hun." He smiled and seemed much more relaxed himself, as though a deep dark question of his own had been answered. "I promise I'll do whatever I can to help you do that. Ok, Kiddo? I just wanted to make sure you were Ok."

Martel settled in the helicopter as the engine started up, the blades beginning their steady droning *chop, chop, chop*. His mind remembered last night with Alyssa, it had felt so right and natural to help her, she had unconsciously reached out to him and he had wanted to help her. But the awful dreams that came to him that night were now confusing him and rending painful cracks in his heart and soul he thought he had long ago been able to lock tightly away. This cruel and vivid remembering of his past was almost beginning to feel as fresh as if it had all happened the other day and for the first time the stoic underboss was forced to confront his own inner demons and confusions the same as Alyssa was doing.

He glanced over at Leonardo who nodded briefly at him a moment and then resumed looking with a bored expression out the window. He glanced at the seat across from him and saw his father, Victor, opening his briefcase and slip on his reading glasses preparing to go over some of the legitimate records of the VIJER Corporation. As the helicopter lifted off the helipad here at the Jerome estates, Martel settled back and closed his eyes hoping to catch a quick nap during the 45-minute commute to the downtown VIJER building. Only one other bodyguard rode with them, there would be already a few more downtown. It was just a quick meeting with Danny, so there was no reason to go down heavily armed. The droning of the helicopters rotors easily allowed him to fall asleep especially after his rather late night up with Alyssa and his dark dreams of last night. He groaned softly once in his sleep as his own haunted nightmares picked up right where they left off...

CHAPTER 21

... He vividly remembered his own return back to the states after his killing of Tashima Katsuro. While he had killed many men, before that, this had been his first true vendetta killing one that had raged through him like white-hot lava, because it had cost him so dearly. Cost him the one thing he loved, the one woman he was going to ask as his future wife, as well as his dear friend and future brother in law's family and farm. He had been stupid enough to let his own anger overcome him and that had almost cost him his life.

He had gotten himself stitched up by a back alley doctor named Kisho and while there grabbed some natural herbs, poultices and antibiotics; unfortunately, the back alley doctor had given him the wrong antibiotics and he had not properly cleared out the infection in the wound before stitching it closed. Martel dared not take anything stronger than aspirin and some natural remedies, he needed to be as clearheaded and alert as possible. He knew his head would have a high price now. The next 20 hours where the longest and most painful of his life, as he stayed hidden while infection, fever and pain wracked his body. He fought to stay conscious as he ticked down the hours, trusting in Sen to get everything ready and make the right calls to Victor and others here in the states to let them know he was coming home.

It was only when he was safely on the plane and finally airborne did he finally allow himself to fall asleep with instructions for Sen to watch over him. And in his heart he trusted and knew Sen would.

Sen kept him on a steady diet of the aspirins, antibiotics and other natural remedies, Martel's only words to him where the occasional "Thank you Sen. Thank you my friend." spoken in Japanese. Occasionally the fever would burn deeply in him and he would get a bit delirious as he would tell Sen "Cochran, I found another camp, over the rise. But we won't get there today, they moved the POW's again." But Sen would just hush him up with a cool cloth to his head and tell him "Sleep Martel, you're going home now, Ok? Sleep, it's all over now."

At one point, The Dragons' icy blue eyes opened up as clear and blue as the pacific ocean beneath them, he gazed straight at Sen and spoke to him in a low, deadly voice "He died as a coward Sen. He died with fear coming off him in such delicious waves that I wished I could share it with you." And then a chilling smile crossed Martel's face that made Sen's hair stand on edge and a chill run down his spine.

"Shhh, Kage." Sen whispered hoarsely, looking around to make sure no one on the plane had overheard. "Not talk of that anymore. Not ever again."

"I know." Martel said softly, the eyes growing dull as fever took him over again, "I just wanted you to know. You deserved to know…"

Sen never left Martel's side, he stayed with him as honor bound as any brother or best friend would. Even thought at times he nearly had to half carry the much larger man to the plane transfers or through customs. Often he would guide Martel's mind with meditative exercises to relax the pain or to center himself, or to sleep.

By the 3rd plane transfer over Chicago and onwards towards New York, Martel was at least able to stay awake much better but he was moving as stiffly as an old man and seemed in danger of collapsing at any moment. His back was one mass of fiery throbbing pain and he felt as weak as a puppet whose strings had been cut, but now at least he was able to make his own phone calls. He had set up a hotel in New Jersey and instructed Sen to get him there. "Listen to me Sen." He said, "We are going to have to split apart for awhile in the states at least for a few weeks minimum, possibly a couple months. Please don't be offended…"

"Say no more," Sen interrupted quietly. "I know." He smiled weakly. "You already told me this, as did a friend of yours."

"Who?" Martel looked quizzically at him.

"It doesn't matter." Sen said with a mischievous gleam in his eyes, "He asked to remain anonymous but he already gave me some American money to help me get set up in New York. He said you might be busy for a while but that if I needed anything in the mean time he gave me a number to call." Sen remembered in his own mind the private conversations he had had with the powerful and enigmatic Victor Jerome; the help the man had generously offered him.

"Sounds like a pretty wise fellow." Martel smiled.

"Oh he is." Sen smiled back, "He is. Important thing is this." Sen switched to Japanese. "Kage, no matter what happened I still consider you as my brother-in-law, whether you marry in the future or not. We have been through death and life and death together. You are Laurence Martel now but you are also my brother and my best friend. You understand, Kage?"

Martel nodded and no more words were necessary between the two friends.

It seemed like hours and it seemed like days until Martel finally got to that little run down roadside motel in New Jersey, across from the New York City border and waited. He got to the room and there was already a gun waiting for him under the bed. He smiled, it was loaded and everything. He had debated on lying down, his body desperately wanted to but he knew if he did, he may not be getting back up. He was so sore and weak that he knew he would not be able to properly defend himself if anything went wrong. So he instead he sat on the bed his infected, swollen back against the hard wall and he turned on the grainy TV to some obnoxious game show as chewed down some more aspirin and goldenseal root, dry. The bitter acrid taste nearly choked him but kept him alert.

After about an hour a car pulled up and he cautiously forced himself up to peek out the window, the gun clutched in his hand. However he already recognized two of the men getting out instantly. The first was his father, the leader and teacher he had held vividly in his mind for 5 long years. The second was his father's best friend and physician Dr. John Thomas Weintraub and the third man was a young, handsome man, with dark angry eyes who just stayed behind with the car. Martel figured there was probably another armed man inside the car and maybe a few armed guards in another car across the street. The Don of a Family as large as the Jerome's didn't just wander around unguarded, especially so close to D'Salvatore territory.

Martel unlocked the door, and opened it. "*Ciao, mio Padrone*, Don Victor," He spoke formally in Italian, as though he was truly meeting the great Don for the first time.

Victor walked in and the two men's eyes met. Father and son finally looked upon one another after over 5 years of not seeing one another, not talking to one another except for a few hurried letters and a few hurried recent phone calls.

Martel saw his fathers dark eyes fill with tears, he had aged visibly but his charisma and power were still all engulfing. He had changed but yet he was as strong and powerful as he always was, his father and idol.

Victor looked at his son with pride, concern and a love that only a father can look at his child. He grabbed Martel by the back of his neck and pulled his head down until father and son where forehead-to-forehead. "*Mio vindicare angelo della morte tornaro a mi.*" He whispered for only Martel's ears. "My vindicating Angel of Death has returned to me." They stood that way silent a long time, in that silent gesture that was alone theirs. Their two heads together no words needed to be spoken, gently they swayed as one as they reconnected their souls.

Then they spoke briefly a few moments in Italian, John Thomas was the only other one in the room and he didn't speak the language but he was looking with graver and graver concern at the slightly weaving form of Theodore Jerome.

"Victor," John Thomas broke in, "I hate to interrupt but I really need to look at the patient here..." He indicated to Martel.

Victor led his son to the bed. "Sit and let him look, we will talk."

Martel nearly collapsed with pain and exhaustion as he tried to slip out of his jacket, but John Thomas was already helping him out of it, Weintraub's voice grousing, grumbling and wondering how on earth 'Laurence Martel' made it this far.

Victor switched back to speaking in Italian, both men totally ignoring John Thomas. For them, the world around them had ceased to exist except for each other, the joy in being back together again. Victor let one tear slip out of his eye and wiped it quickly away, "I can only pray all this was worth it for us..." he ran one slightly trembling hand over his son's large, well muscled shoulders, looking at the strange oriental brandings. "You have changed much; I see the hardness in your eyes, in your heart..." Victor made the sign of the gun and raised an eyebrow at his son.

He watched as Theodore ticked off his fingers in groups of five until he counted sixty five times. Victor did not doubt him one bit, he could see the hardness in his son, a man did not get that cold, did not get a wall that large and strong unless he had killed many people, unless his life had been a hard road.

John Thomas was oblivious to all this silent 'code' talk between father and son, as he was far too busy and in shock at the damage inflicted on Theodore Jerome's back, which was now dangerously infected. If he didn't receive a transfusion and IV antibiotics soon, he wouldn't live long enough to worry about anything else. All John Thomas knew was that Victor had told him that from now on, he was to never refer to Theodore as Victor's son again, that he was to call him

Laurence Martel and pretend that he was meeting him for the very first time today.

It was one of the only times Victor had ever asked John Thomas Weintraub to really out and out lie about anything so drastic. John Thomas had no idea why all the hush-hush and why the Jerome's had faked Theodore Jerome's disappearance and now bought him back as Laurence Martel and frankly he didn't really care. At this moment all he knew was his patient here, 'Laurence Martel' or whomever, needed urgent medical care. Whoever had treated him, had stitched the infection right into him. "Ah, fella's?" he forcefully interrupted them again.

Victor looked around Martel's back over him and cringed as only a parent can, at the severe damage to his son's back.

"Exactly." John Thomas pointed out. "Can we move this conversation to the hospital with him?"

"Of course, John." Victor nodded. "Let's go, Theo..." he immediately stopped himself short, "Martel." He corrected himself. He was going to have to make sure neither of them had any slip ups like that ever again, especially him.

They talked a long time that first night just Victor and his son, as Martel lay in the private clinic, home and safe on the Jerome estates with an IV in him, with proper antibiotics and pain killers going into him and a drain in his wound.

Father and son talked and cemented their story of Martel's arrival. That the story would be that Martel was an independent that had come recommended from Don Vito Bonnaro and was now sponsored into the Jerome family. He would start as a capo, but would be quickly raised to underboss. "Right now Patrizio, you remember him, he is our acting underboss but he doesn't want it, he wants to retire. Patrizio may be the only other one who may figure out our secret but only because he remembers you from when you were knee high" Victor smiled, " but of course you've grown quite a bit, eh?" they both chuckled together.

"I have a few people I am thinking about for my new top administration" Victor continued as he sat next to his son, "There is a young soldier, I picked up off the streets, his name is Joshua Demonico, he has an interesting tale as well. You saw him briefly earlier he was the driver of my car. He has a lot of talent. I may have you sponsor him personally, teach him the ropes." Victor smiled.

"Consider it done, *Padrone*." Martel answered hoarsely. He was so weary and exhausted but he also was so happy to be here, finally safe at home and at his father's side where he truly belonged.

"Are you really that good a trigger man? "Victor leaned in towards his son, his dark eyes boring into him.

Martel felt his fathers own eyes searching into his own soul, "Unfortunately, yes." He barely sighed.

Victor relaxed a bit. "Ah, *mi angelo della morte*, this actually makes our story better for your meteoric rise to our future underboss." He refilled a cup of cool water for Martel, "However, it's going to mean a bit of extra work for you. For this I apologize deeply." He ran his hand along his son's forehead, kindly, soothingly. "I may use you as a 'loaner assassin' and allow you to do independent contracts on the side. This does a two-fold thing. One, it puts fear of you into others and gets your reputation out far and fast. Two, it shows that us Jerome's are not afraid to share in their specialties and their experience. It makes you look good and it makes us as a *Famiglia* look good. It also gives you a whole hell of a lot of experience and insight into the other *Famiglia's* out there, to get caught up in the politics of the other families as they are now."

"Fair enough, *Padrone*." Martel groaned softly. He could feel the painkillers wanting to knock him out now. He fought to stay awake; he still had not even seen his mother or his brother Michael yet! He wanted to stay awake, to talk with his beloved father for hours but it was beginning to be a loosing battle.

"Look, you are tired. I have not even told Isabella, or Mike, that you arrived yet, especially not with you being so injured. You need a good night to recuperate some, eh?" Victor seemed to read his mind. "Tomorrow you can see them; I know they are waiting to see you. Rest now," he leaned down and gently kissed his son on his cheek.

"*Padrone*, wait." Martel barely whispered. Victor paused.

Martel fought now with every last ounce to stay awake, "Please promise me to stop calling me, *angelo della morte*, your 'Angel of Death'. I don't want that as my mob nickname, eh?" he smiled weakly at his father and then the great blue eyes rolled back in his head and the large frame finally collapsed in total and utter exhaustion.

A small smile played on Victor's lips as he watched his sleeping son. "Welcome home, my dear Theo." Victor barely mouthed into his son's ear. Knowing no one could hear. "Welcome back home. Now you are back under my protection, Laurence Martel." He gave his unconscious son another light kiss on the forehead and then Victor left the small clinic.

Martel's time back had been a bittersweet blur of perfect harmony and yet as a stranger looking in from the outside. He worked at his father's side day and night and also worked as a 'headhunter', a specialist hitman loaned out here and there to other Families. But yet never could he acknowledge to anyone that he was really Victor Jerome's son, Michael Jerome's brother or Isabella's eldest child.

Since he had grown most of his immense height while he was away, since his soul had grown so cold and especially as 'Theodore Jerome' was MIA and presumed dead, the masquerade worked. No one questioned, no one asked. Indeed the secret would be revealed only if and when it had to, when the final checkmate would come.

And so Laurence Martel started as captain of the elite bodyguards guarding his father day and night, he sponsored in the young Joshua Demonico, he endured the smirks and stares from the other soldiers and capos of his odd mix of Italian and Asian ways and his martial arts. But it would be his own student Joshua who would unknowingly be the one who would break the ice for him.

Demonico was fascinated by the dark, quiet man who seemed to have come out of nowhere and win the heart of the Boss overnight. Like Martel had so long ago been enthralled by the mysterious Cochran, Joshua felt himself drawn to the imposing Laurence Martel and the two had struck up an unlikely friendship. Martel began teaching Joshua the deadly moves and soon Victor began insisting that he wanted all his elite bodyguards to be taught with some of the martial arts skills. Even Victor himself, began to learn some of the relaxing moves of Tai Chi and even worked his way up to a brown belt in Judo. Once Victor began to learn, it seemed that nearly all the guards began to become obsessed with learning the strange martial arts that this independent stranger had bought with him.

For that is all any of them ever knew about Martel, that was the only story they ever heard. That Laurence Martel had been trained in the old ways, in Sicily by Don Vito Bonnaro's family. That he had then spent many years in Europe and other places as an independent for hire and then was bought over here to the Jerome Family to begin cementing future plans with Don Vito Bonnaro. A few years later enforcer, Leonardo Tagretta would follow as well.

But for Martel the reality was much harder, much more heart-rending than he could have ever imagined. To see and be with his real family; Michael, his mother, his father, but not be able to not call them by their names. To not be able to celebrate openly his biological family's triumphs or sadness, birthdays or anniversaries or they to be able to celebrate his. When his younger brother graduated pre-med school he had to stand and watch as a bodyguard for his father, not as Michael's older brother. And when his mother lay dying of cancer, he could only comfort her on and off as an 'outsider' and tend to her when no was around. Then he would quietly sit by her side for hours.

If there was one pivotal moment in his career, in this whole charade from the beginning, that he bitterly regretted, it would have had to have been as he watched his father die twice.

The first was the prolonged illness of his beloved wife and Theodore's mother, Isabella. Within 3 years of him returning back to the states, Isabella contracted ovarian cancer. By the time it was diagnosed it was already in stage 3 and there was very little that could be done for her. But Victor wanted everything that could possibly be done attempted to save her. Victor was beside himself with anguish and misery.

Martel could see his father's grief and fear at losing his one and only true love and soulmate; even Isabella had spoke privately to Dr. Weintraub and her son, begging them not try anything heroic, to not allow her to suffer a lingering death. But Victor would not hear of it.

So Theodore was caught in an awkward middle. At nights, he would sneak down to the hospital, often bringing his essential massage oils and he would tenderly massage his mother's body with his large hands as it wasted away from the cancer ravaging her or simply sit with her and tenderly rub her head with damp cloths as she fought off the wracking dry heaves from the chemotherapy that would not save her.

Victor would come nightly and hold her closely, sleeping in the same hospital room with her almost as if he wanted to do private battle with the grim reaper himself, refusing to give Isabella up to him. But Martel knew death intimately, he knew this was one deal that even the great 'Arbitrator' was not going to be able to deal his way out of.

Finally, after one exhausting night, where Victor slept in the same hospital bed with his wife, refusing to leave her side, he came out and simply looked at Martel, the great dark eyes, finally defeated and downcast. "I am letting her go." His father barely whispered as a dry sob wracked his chest.

And right there, Theodore saw his father die one death in front of him. Just that fast, as fast as if Martel would have killed him with his own two hands. He wanted to reach out and embrace his father, hold him, hug him and grieve with him as a son would a father. But he could not, not here in public, for he was Laurence Martel now, a *caporegime* for the Elite Guard for the Jerome Family and it was not his place. Instead he saw his younger brother Michael coming off the elevators and he saw his father and Michael embrace each other, as Victor half collapsed in Michael's strong arms.

With a heavy heart, he went to bid a final goodbye to his mother. As he ducked into her hospital room he could tell she was already fairly out of it, massive quantities of morphine and pain killers being pumped into her and he wasn't even sure if his mother really knew him at that point or not. But she did open her eyes weakly and smile at him, lightly grabbing her nearly skeletal hand with his large one, Theo rubbed his thumb along the nerves that ran along the side of her neck that released pain and tension and told her that the doctors would be bringing her plenty of pain relief soon. At that point she had looked at him and in a whispered voice spoke in Sicilian, "But I don't feel any pain, my beloved Angel. Just the warm ocean breeze..." and then she slept permanently, never to regain consciousness again. She died later that night.

The second time a piece of his father died was even worse, for it was completely unexpected. It was barely two years after Isabella's death and Victor never fully recovered from his loss of his "Issy". Once Isabella was gone, the main house seemed a much quieter and dour place. There were not as many parties, not as many men bought their wives or families or children to play in the great gardens and fountains anymore.

Theodore's brother Michael though, he was always trying to liven things up. He had a love for horses, competing in elegant dressage or playing polo along with Leonardo Tagretta at breakneck speeds but he was never arrogant. Adventurous, brave, even a bit rebellious but always he was a humanitarian and a kindhearted man. Victor was right Michael had no heart for 'this thing of ours'. He accepted all the guards and never asked any questions about his fathers business but like John Thomas Weintraub he was happy to remain blissfully unaware, or rather he made a conscious decision to remain unaware. So much so, that he asked John Weintraub to help him find a residency to study pediatrics. Michael Jerome wanted to be a neonatal pediatrician working with newborn babies.

Victor was actually very supportive and proud of his younger son and instead of throwing his connections around to get things for him, let Michael do things the way he wanted to. Allowed his younger son to make his own choices how he wished to and since he wished to do everything on his own merit that is how Victor let him. In fact, if anything it only seemed to make Victor even more proud at Michael's strength and tenacity.

The one gift his father had gotten him was to imported some fine breeding stock of polo ponies from Brazil and elegant Andalusian Horses from Italy; today Michael, Leonardo, Enzo and five other men had just finished up an intensive Polo workout in the hot early May morning. Men and horses alike were dripping in froth and sweat.

Victor, Martel, Joshua, Patrizio, as well as several other guards had all been sitting around smoking cigarettes, snacking and watching the polo players cheering them on.

"*Bravo!*" Victor toasted his cup of wine towards his Michael as he came trotting up to the bleachers, "My boy, he can ride, eh!" Victor said with pride in his eyes.

"Maybe I need get me one of these *cavallo*," Leonardo said in his accented voice as he also rode up and dismounted, "Although I no hear any of the ladies complain about way I ride." he glanced around at his fellow compari's, with a mischievous wink.

This bought a round of raucous laughter and cheering from all the men.

"Yeah an' Martel probably gets his women by giving 'em the ol 'Kung Fu grip of death'!" Patrizio said which bought another round of laughter.

"Yeah, yeah, funny." Michael nimbly dismounted off his steed as one of the grooms came to lead the animals away to cool them down. "A regular bunch of clowns you are, everyone is a wiseguy," he teased lightly. They truly were but he loved them all and could 'break balls' as easily as the rest of them.

He reached out and grabbed the glass of water Martel was drinking, quenching his thirst, "You don't mind, do you Kung Fu Master of Death?" he winked privately at his older brother and gulped it down. He did love teasing Theo at times, knowing that there was nothing his older brother could do. Knowing that in public he was Laurence Martel. But yet let anyone else say anything bad about his beloved brother and Michael would have personally clocked them. The two brothers as opposite in appearance and personality as they were remained very close often spending time in the office to speak to one another quietly and honestly knowing they couldn't be eavesdropped on.

"Be my guest." Martel chuckled at Michael's gentle teasing as his younger brother took the glass.

"Hey," Michael handed the now empty glass back to Martel and spoke up to the whole group, "I have this huge craving for some Angelo's gelato. I think I will run down to the city and grab some. Come on! Who wants to come along? I can always bring back cannolis too." he smiled enticingly.

Talk suddenly erupted from the whole group as money and orders began to fly from people's wallets in a pandemonium of utter confusion. "Come with me." Michael quietly mouthed to his older brother, with a wink.

"I'll go with you." Martel nodded he had been hoping to get some time alone with his younger brother. Michael smiled as he finished collecting the monies from the various men for their orders.

"No, Martel." Victor turned abruptly and sternly said, "I need to talk to you about a matter regarding a problem with one of our captains, as well as other business."

For a brief moment Martel looked like he was going to open his mouth and say something, protest Victor's orders but he just closed it. "Of course Mr. Jerome." He spoke tight lipped. A part of him was angry at his father denying him this brief private time with Michael and would always be angry for the rest of his life.

"Bring Martel back some cannoli, Mike." Victor nodded then began motioning that the men should follow him to the house for business.

"Yeah sure, no problem Dad." Michael nodded and gathered up the money and stuff.

"Dante," Martel turned to one of his best bodyguards, "I want you to go with Michael downtown."

"Sure Boss," The guard smiled. A trip to Angelo's would be a nice change on a hot day like today.

Michael stopped by Martel as the group started dispersing, "Sorry you couldn't go with," he whispered into his older brother's ear "I tried..."

"I know, Mike." Laurence said.

"I want to talk with you when I get back though, ask you a favor." Michael said. Martel looked at him puzzled as he raised his eyebrow, questioningly.

Michael smiled, he loved making his older brother wonder, it was so rare he ever got the big man to show any emotion. "We'll talk later. It's a good thing. Sometimes a guy just needs his brother's opinion, you know?" Mike grinned and began heading with Dante off towards the helipad.

Martel could hear the helicopter firing up in the distance, their pilot Albericci, a new guy, warming it up. For some reason today, it eerily reminded Laurence of the helicopters they used to run in Vietnam. He felt a sudden terrifying cold shiver run down his spine. "Michael! Wait..." he called out.

"Laurence!" Victor called out to him almost angrily as he was walking towards the house with the other men in tow, "Let's go! Now!"

Michael turned, framed for a moment against the green of the trees looking at his older brother. His handsomely roguish face, the tilt of his head and the way his eyebrows drew together as he looked questioningly at Martel; he looked so much like Isabella. "What?" he shrugged.

Martel just made the army sign of 'Vigilance', he pointed his two fingers at his own eyes and then at Michael "*Be careful!*" he mouthed. For some reason when he turned away he felt almost an almost compelling sorrow, a desire to tackle Michael and prevent him from leaving but he forced himself to clear his mind and then turned and trotted off after Victor and his fellow compari.

The men all ate lunch together inside and Martel had actually begun relaxed a bit. Afterwards Victor moved himself, Joshua, Patrizio and Martel into the Office to discuss business. Mainly it was the same talk of restructuring within the Family, stuff that Laurence already knew was coming down the pipeline. Martel felt himself growing unconsciously restless again. He noticed almost subconsciously he felt an impending danger. Once again he slammed it down and centered himself, trying to concentrate on his father's voice as he spoke.

Patrizio would be getting ready to retire next month but could be called up as a wartime skipper if needed; Laurence would be promoted to full underboss. Joshua would be promoted to consigliere in training and there was the new one they were grooming now, the heavy-set driver that had recently been promoted, Cesare Ciccerone, whom they wanted to assign as a special bodyguard and driver.

"He'll be a good worker, I've watched him myself," Victor said, "however, there have been some problems with his sponsor, Charlie Legavoli but we can talk more about that later. Now," Victor looked directly at Laurence, "this next thing I want to discuss is..."

And that is when the phone in Victor's office began to suddenly ring nearly startling everyone. There were several phones in the Jerome estates, but there was one phone in Victor's Office that was on its own separate number and a lot of the men used to jokingly call it the "President's Phone" because that phone never rang unless it was a matter of life and death. It was meant to be used only in a dire Family emergency; In fact in all of Theodore's life he could only remember hearing it ring twice. And today was the first time.

Patrizio just blinked and looked up from his cigarette. Joshua, who had been in the middle of lighting one up sat there dumbfounded looking at the phone as though he had never seen it before and whispered to Patrizio "Shit! I didn't know there was a phone in here! I swear! I never heard it before!" as he nearly jumped out of his seat.

Martel felt as though someone had suddenly poured ice water down his spinal cord, as the muscles in his back became rigid.

For a moment no one moved; then Victor got up, his eyes narrowing as he went to the phone answering it on the third ring. It was as though all of time had suddenly stood still. Martel could have sworn even the smoke from Joshua and Patrizio's cigarettes had ceased moving.

Joshua just kept mumbling, "Did you know there was a phone in here, Patrice? Laurence? I didn't know there was a fuckin' phone in here."

Martel darkly cast his eyes towards Joshua for a moment, willing him to shut up and then turned back to his father. He could only see the side profile of his father but as he watched him he saw the life literally draining out of him. It was the second time he saw his father die before him, as though whatever was being said on the other end of that phone was literally sucking the life and soul out of Victor. Patrizio must have seen it as well, for the man was also on his feet just as swiftly as Martel.

Victor was growing paler by the second, his body beginning to literally shake as his wrath, sorrow and grief began to fill the room.

"Victor? What is it?" Patrizio said softly, almost in a frightened tone to his old friend and partner.

"*Padrone*?" Martel was now also at Victor's side. He knew, just instinctively knew whatever it was, whatever was being said on the other end of that phone was beyond terrible, that it would be like revisiting Miyoko's death all over again. Another horrific karmic retribution in his life.

Victor tried to numbly hang up the phone but the receiver just fell from his hand with a loud clatter to his desk.

"They shot my boy…" Victor barely whispered to no one and to all of them. "The *fottuto* D'Salvatore *stronzo bastardo's* murdered my innocent Michael…"

Martel went to hang up the receiver that had fallen from Victor's hand when Victor suddenly snatched up the phone receiver and all and with blind fury threw it across the room, where it slammed into the wall with a hideous crash, narrowly missing Joshua who ducked just in time.

"Damn." Joshua muttered. "Oh damn..." the handsome dark eyes filled with pain and sorrow.

Victor's wrath and anguish railed in waves and Martel could feel his own horrific blackness wanting to descend but yet there was nothing he could do. In here, in front of these people he was the capo soon to be underboss, not Theodore Jerome, son of Victor and brother of now murdered Michael Jerome.

Patrizio patted Victor's shoulder. "What happened, Victor?" Patrizio asked, "What went wrong?" There were tears in Patrizio's eyes as well.

Martel had forcibly guided Victor to the couch, his arms protectively and instinctively encircling his father as he supporting him, letting him lean on him. Already he could see the glazed look on his fathers tear stained face. On instinct Laurence quickly unwrapped two lifesavers and discreetly forced them into his father's mouth.

"They were coming out of Angelo's, apparently there was a few of D'Salvatores button men scouting around our territory. The fucking D'Salvatore soldiers decided to take the shot..." Victor barely choked out. He couldn't go on, he was too upset his sorrow was too fresh, the grief too deep. "...Michael didn't want into this thing of ours!!!" He hissed, "I worked so hard to keep him out, to keep him safe! He was going to be a doctor, like John Thomas...." Victor collapsed against Martel as his body sank into a deep and engulfing depression. "First Isabella and now Michael, too many innocents, too damn many."

"Patrizio," Martel nodded quietly to the older man, his voice in a business-like, unnatural calm, "Please do me a favor and set up a meeting with the top capo's including yourself, in one hour. We need to talk."

Patrizio nodded at Martel's instructions then briefly hugged Victor, as one father to another. He had children also. "I am so sorry, Vic... Buon' Anima." He whispered to him. Then Patrizio just numbly and quietly left the room.

Martel then looked over at his pupil and soon to be consigliere, "Joshua, I really need you now to work with me here." He spoke in that same calm but undeniable voice, "Get Dr. Weintraub down here as fast as you can, tell him it is an emergency, I don't care if you have to tie him up and drag him down here, capisce? Victor needs him now. Then be back in an hour and bring this new man, this Cesare Ciccerone, he's going to have to get broken in the hard way."

Joshua also nodded at Martel, drawing strength from his calm but strong leadership. He came over and gently put a hand on Victor, kissed him softly on the forehead. There were unheeded tears streaming down Joshua's eyes as well. Victor was more than just a boss or padrone to Joshua; he was his adopted father as well.

"Josh..." Victor looked up for a moment, "Joshua... I know Michael was like your brother too, wasn't he son?" Victor gave Joshua a quick squeeze on his shoulder and then just collapsed against the large frame of his new underboss.

When they were alone, Martel reached over and caressed the pressure points on his fathers temples, "Oh Papa, was it all worth it..." he spoke in Italian to him. "You should have let me go with him, today." If only he could have gone with his brother Michael, his mind tortured him, he might have been able to...

"And then what? And then I would have lost you to!!!" the old man suddenly exploded at his son with a ferocity that both startled and silenced Martel. "I would have lost both my sons, buried *two* of my boys today!!! Don't you understand?" he half- heartedly grabbed Martel in frustration and pain, almost as if some inner sense of Victor's had known he would have paid for his actions all along in not allowing Martel to go with Michael... "No! No! Don't ever bring it up again! No! We made our decision. Now we suffer the consequences, Mr. Laurence Martel. It was my gamble, damn it, mine to bear!"

Martel hugged tightly onto his father, "Shhh, Ok, ok. It will be our vendetta father." He whispered softly his eyes filled with tears that could not spill. "D'Salvatore blood will spill for this; it is my oath to you, to Michael to the Family."

Victor hugged tightly onto Martel, "Agreed. This is our vendetta my son. I will not go to my grave until I have personally terminated Tito D'Salvatore and ruined his family line."

It would be the last few minutes they would be able to speak as father and son before all the meetings, funeral arrangements and all the rest of it. These rare few times they could come in here, in 'The Office'. It was one of the reasons Martel checked it personally. He wanted to make sure that not only was there no law enforcement bugs, but no one from the Family itself who was nosing around who could find out their secret. And Cochran being ex-Intelligence had taught him many ways to check for ways of being watched. "I wonder if the pilot was killed..." Martel mused aloud, his icy blue eyes turning towards his father.

Victor glanced wearily at his son, "Albericci? No, he was the one who called."

"Then I think there is a turncoat or sellout in our midst." Martel said softly massaging his father's shoulder, "Our vendetta will start with him."...

..."Laurence?" Victor's voice cut through Martel's cruel dream. "I could just leave you in the 'Copter if you wish." he chided lightly. "We're landing old friend, wake up."

"Sorry boss." Martel stretched languidly and quickly woke up.

"Yes, wake up there Martel," Leonardo nudged him gently. "Some of us have to work, eh?"

"Not sleeping well?" Victor eyed him. "Don't tell me you had a bad first night with your new guest?" he asked seriously.

"With Red?" Martel said mischievously, "Nonsense, she's a sweetheart. What's not to like? What is the old saying about redheads?"

"That they curious, spitfires with the temperament of a tiger and *molto eccitante* in a the bed." Leonardo mused thoughtfully, "At least the red-headed ladies I know," he smiled and winked at Laurence.

"Well, I haven't seen that aspect yet," Martel glanced at Len, "but if it surfaces, I will be the first to let you know." Laurence said with a straight face as he adjusted his sunglasses and unbuckled himself.

"Hmmm." The old man said with a slight smirk. They all disembarked at the roof, and then took the private elevator down to the main penthouse suite. The whole time Victor seemed intent on pestering Martel about his new guest. "So what did she think of your decorating taste?"

"She liked it." He said nonchalantly. "And, I will have you know, she thinks my cooking is fantastic."

"Oh well, she really is brain-damaged then," Victor teased his underboss. "To choose that Asian stuff over some good old fashioned veal piccata, or lasagna I don't know..." This bought hearty chuckles from Len Tagretta and the accompanying bodyguard. "Well as long as your methods are working then my friend," Victor finally relented after harassing Laurence enough, "then everything will be fine for all of us."

"Agreed." Laurence smiled grimly as they hooked up with Dante "Danny the Wizard" Valsiglio, the head of the VIJER Corporation.

All of the men spent the day inside Victor's office going over paperwork, cleaning out files, making things look legal and getting things prepared for the merger of the legitimate businesses between the Bonnaro's and Jerome's.

"For years, as Leonardo can attest to," Victor began, "The Jerome's and Bonnaro's have worked together, one hand washing the other, one Family strengthening the other. Without each other the great VIJER Corporation Import/Export probably wouldn't be running as well as it has been. Believe me; this whole crap with the Romans was dropped just in time.

"My dear friend Patrizio is right when he says times have changed. Now they have these RICO laws and predicates, so now new rules have to come into play, things have to be done differently." Victor motioned to Danny, "So I have my man, aptly nicknamed 'the Wizard' here, who can fix about anything with numbers and clean almost anything. Money comes in dirty and abracadabra, The Wizard makes it come out clean for us." There were several low chuckles around the room at Victor's speech. Victor nodded and then continued. "The

Bonnaro's, they own a lot of banking interests in Italy and it comes around full circle my friends."

"This 'thing of ours', work much differently here in America for sure," Leonardo added. "I live here now for several years and it nothing like it was in Italy. No get me wrong, I am oath-sworn now to the Jerome's and wouldn't have it any other way. I have grown quite fond of America and all she has to offer..." He made a lewd gesture which bought more chuckles from all the men, "But Mr. Jerome is correct when he say that the game, here, is played much differently." Leonardo continued, alluding to illegal rackets and activities, "The *federale's* and government have much more power here than they do back home in Sicily."

"Very true," Victor nodded, "And Leonardo brings up a good point, especially more so for you Martel. But this 'business of ours' all of it, it will seriously change someday, I am an old man of the old ways and the old ways are dying. There are not many of us left. Even if there were, it cannot be run like it used to. There is not much left of the same honor, tradition; even *omerta* is not held in the same regard anymore." Victor sighed deeply for a moment and Martel perhaps most of all noticed the aging years in his fathers face, "But that is a subject for a different time. Eh?"

"So in October then," Danny Valsiglio was shuffling through paperwork and other items, "is when you want to have the items ready to bring down to Vito Bonnaro?"

"Yes," Victor nodded. "As you know, in early October, I will be meeting Vito in person down in the Jamaica and we will be settling our Family's formal declarations of merging and alliances. I will let you know right now, I am traveling light. Martel will be staying up here, as will Joshua and Leonardo. I'm bringing very little with me, as we are keeping this entire thing very low key. But by October, gentlemen, everything must be ready with our finances, and everything must be squeaky clean. Understood?"

All of them nodded.

"We also need to have extra available in the kitty for any legal aid, that may be needed, with this thing, that I am sure Patrizio explained to you Danny?" Victor asked.

"Yeah, yes, he did, Mr. Jerome, that is no problem." The smartly dressed Danny nodded vigorously. And so the rest of the day the men worked on getting their stuff straightened up for their final move in October.

Only Victor and Martel knew the full implications of all this really entailed, what this merger with the Bonnaro's in Sicily would bring to them. Victor would study his son from time to time as Martel seamlessly took over the meeting helping here and there, dividing duties and flawlessly running things.

He did not relish what he had done to his eldest son, there were many a night the Don lay awake and knew it would always be his biggest and most unforgivable sin. What would he be leaving for Theodore 'Laurence Martel' Jerome? A legacy that would have to become mostly legitimate eventually, for the old ways were dying as he had said. Yet his son, the future Don and *Padrone* of the Jerome Family, already had a heart and soul far harder and colder than Victors' own.

Whatever had happened in Martel's life before he had come back to him had killed that part of him that had been Theodore. Even his mother, Isabella had cried at his return and told her husband privately, "Victor, I don't even recognize my own son." That evening as they had lain in bed together, "What has happened to his soul? To his heart? It is dead, buried deep." Victor had held her close and said nothing but he had felt it too and it had hurt him deeply, for he knew he had been the instrument in it. Victor had not been far off when he had called Theodore '*angelo della morte*', Angel of Death that first night, on his return home.

Martel's soul truly did seem dead and deep inside Victor blamed himself and he would never truly forgive himself for it. If he could have turned back the clock to that day in 1972, he would have never asked Theodore to go to Vietnam, he would have scrapped the plan. The gambit would have not have been worth this but now it was committed, what was done was done. One did not cry over spilled milk, this business had no room for those whose conscious rode them night after night. And so while the decision did sit heavily on Victor, it was something that ate at him slowly and privately like a deeply hidden cancer.

This becoming legitimate was the other aspect that Victor and Martel had spoken of before. The VIJER Corporation and buying of other companies had been something Victor had been seen coming down the pipeline for a while. While some of the older men like Patrizio didn't understand; Victor knew and tried to implore his son to set aside "clean and legit" areas completely free of mob influence. Lately it was becoming almost a joke the way people were turning rat within their own Families and Martel was being kept busy being hired out by different Families for one hit after the other. Finally Victor had put an end to it and now it seemed even his own Family was becoming open to this traitorous trend with Paulie and who knew who else.

Martel stopped by Victor and refilled his cup of ice water for him and dropped a couple lifesavers discreetly on the table near him. Victor sighed softly and kept hidden the small smile that threatened his lips. Sometimes he wondered how his son did it. How did he keep going day after day? Holding up the charade, so efficient and smooth so patient and eerily calm and yet his heart as cold as ice.

He remembered all the times over the years that Martel had to be on the outside looking in. Isabella's death, Michael's graduation, and Michael's death; He wondered how the man always kept that unnaturally calm composure. Occasionally they had talked briefly as father and son, only when they knew it was absolutely safe. Victor had learned just the smallest sliver of what had gone on during the 5 years he had been apart from the Family.

He knew his son had been planning on asking a girl named Miyoko Yamashita to marry him and she had been killed by a crime family over there, named the Katsuro's and that Martel had taken his vendetta on them. He knew of Martel's friend and Miyoko's brother Sen, as Victor had personally helped set Sen up in New York City with some money. Occasionally Martel and Sen still hung around together but usually his son didn't go into a lot of detail about his time in the orient, most of that he kept inside, and Victor didn't pry. He knew some things a man kept with him until he went to his grave; that was just the way it was.

But still, Victor knew full well the darkness and occasional cold anger that lurked in that heart of Laurence Martel. He heard the tales of the hits, he had witnessed the pictures of the vendetta his own son had done upon Tito D'Salvatore's son, Torenzo in retaliation for Michael's death and he had been there personally that day when Laurence had interrogated that pilot, Albericci.

While Victor had seen many strong-arm tactics in his day, the wrath and anger that Martel let loose with was truly cruel and terrifying, even for a hardened man like Victor.

It had indeed been a set up: Albericci, their pilot was double-crossing them and selling out to the D'Salvatores, getting paid well on the side by them to sell information on the Jerome's to them. As soon as Albericci had gotten word that Michael was coming downtown he made a quick call while the helicopter was warming up and ordered a small, 3 man team to Angelo's. After all, he knew Michael would be traveling light, just Michael and one bodyguard. Albericci would claim to not feel well and stay at the VIJER Corporation, no one would be expecting any trouble and after all, why would the D'Salvatore's be so deep inside Jerome territory? Once landed, Albericci put in another coded call to the hit squad and that was it.

Michael and Dante never knew what hit them as they were coming out of Angelo's. A beat up Ford sedan came screeching around a corner but that was just a distraction.

While Dante was pulling his gun on that car, two masked men jumped out from the alleyway and shot at the two men first taking out bodyguard Dante DiSilvio and then Michael Jerome. One of the masked assassins paused long enough to have the other masked gunman snap a few photos of him holding Michael Jerome's bullet riddled corpse as he held up his middle finger in the age old insult. The photo that Tito D'Salvatore continued over the years to send copies of to Victor to anger the old man and try and provoke him into a stupid response.

Victor had watched Martel expertly use chemical interrogation, nearly the same he had used with Alyssa, to get the information from Albericci but afterwards there had been no reprieve and no quick death. It had been a hideous and horrible death one that Victor had allowed his eldest son to vent his feelings of helpless frustrations on. The headless and handless corpse had then been dumped back into D'Salvatore territory as a message. It had been one of the very few times; Victor had seen the normally levelheaded Martel, become so violent, cruel and unforgiving in his rage.

But it was understandable. It was his flesh and blood brother, Martel was avenging, that which he had a right to did he not? It was vendetta, Victor himself was no saint, these were codes handed down through countless generations of *Mafiosi* and this is what he had taught his son from the very beginning, he could not back down now. For this is the legacy he had created. And so the great Don had simply stoically watched his son and underboss sate his anger and vengeance, for all the times he could not be there and had been forced to be an outsider.

To apologize openly at this point to Martel would be to belittle everything they had ever worked for, to insult the five years the man had thrown away of his life, the pain he had wrestled with, the tragedy he had seen, the trials he had shouldered. No, Victor could only now pave the way for him, prepare the Family as was planned for Theodore to one day take the reins of the Jerome Legacy.

Victor knew when the secret of Laurence Martel's identity was finally announced there would be many of his peers who would look at him with such loathing and contempt and wonder, "What kind of man could do that to his own son? Could ruin his life, and set him up to take a dying Family?" And Victor knew it to, with all these changes now, with RICO and all these other government laws and turncoats within the Family. The Jerome Family would only be strong if they could have some solid legitimate ties that were strongly hidden away from their more illegal dealings. This would be his legacy to Theodore-Martel, this and his merging with Don Vito Bonnaro to strengthen things back in the old county.

It was the only way, that once the proverbial 'shit hit the fan' as Victor knew it would, at the end of the war between the Jerome's and the D'Salvatores that the Jerome's would be able to continue on.

He glanced idly outside the window at the city down below, knowing that somewhere out there, his *nemico*, Tito was regrouping as well. "Soon *bastardo*," Victor thought to himself, "soon, us old men will dance the dance of death together and we will finally be finished of this thing." He was growing tired as he listened to the voices of his men drone on, he wanted to go lie down and take an afternoon nap. He trusted his son and underboss implicitly and he was growing older day by day.

Alyssa spent that first day back in the Jerome Estates with the very muscular, darkly dressed and formidable Mr. Giovanni Aprile, or as he told her "Just call me, Gio, everyone else does." And while Gio was all professional and generally a man of very few words, he was actually quite nice to her. In most ways actually a heck of a lot nicer and lenient than Carmine, her sadistic physical therapy trainer had been.

"I assume you know what your schedule is supposed to be?" Gio asked her in a strong but surprisingly low and quiet voice.

She nodded, yes. Although somehow she was certain Martel had already briefed him.

"Ok, then." He said as he idly scratched his chin. "I guess I will let you have some peace and quiet then, Ms. Alyssa." He gave her a polite smile. "My main station is right over there," he pointed by the kitchen, "and I am also usually around by the gym or The Office," he pointed, "So if you need anything, just look me up and I'll help you with whatever you need. Since it's your first day, I'll stick nearby in case you need any assistance, all right?"

She nodded again. She couldn't believe her good fortune in that that Gio was just going to just turn her loose like this! She was about to turn away and nearly run off to the large private library that Victor kept, when Mr. Gio Aprile gave a slight cough.

"Ah, Ms. Alyssa?" He raised one eyebrow at her. "You do know what areas are off limits, right." He asked in that polite but totally professional tone.

She was beginning to see why these were the *elite* guards. They were very clever indeed; very professional, very polite but so very insistent. She blushed furiously for a moment and looked at the carpet. Well, she knew some of the places.

Gio sidled up to her and spoke quietly to her ears only, "No going upstairs, no going into 'The Office', no going into yer Uncle's private library…" and he proceeded to tick off a few more places, ending with the dreaded, "…And you're to stay inside the main house today, so says Mr. Martel."

Alyssa nodded again and slowly began to walk off towards the smaller open library that anyone was free to use.

"Oh and one other thing," Mr. Aprile watched with slight amusement as she spun on her heel at him, green eyes slightly blazing. Martel had been right; she could be a bit fiery. "Rosette and the other ladies are expecting you in the kitchen in an hour for your first cooking lessons." A small grin smirked up on one side of the captain of the guards face.

Alyssa made it a point to blatantly check the time on the elegant grandfather clock in the hallway as Gio idly watched her and then walked off to the library to read the book Martel had given her until it was time for her cooking lesson. With a small smile barely on his lips Gio watched her head to the library. She was a pretty good kid and she had spirit, he liked that. It reminded him of his sister.

Giovanni Aprile had been with Victor Jerome for nearly 7 years. He had been born down in Brooklyn the son of Salvatore Aprile who had served as a NY City Police officer and his wife Lucia Aprile. He had one sister, 5 years younger than him named Angela.

Most of Gio's early life was fairly unremarkable until he hit puberty, and then with his father always out working late shifts on the Police force, Gio was lured in to some of the various wiseguys and gangs running around the Bensonhurst area deep inside Jerome territory. As a child and young teen, Giovanni Aprile had always been rather thin and gangly due to many bouts of childhood pneumonia and as a result it was not uncommon for him to become the target of several bullies and larger kids. It was when he was around 15 though; his life would change dramatically as he met up with Vince Corrado at the local PAL-Police Athletic League in his neighborhood. It would be there that young Giovanni Aprile would find a love of boxing and weight training.

His father seemed pleased because Gio was now not running around the streets getting in trouble for petty crap, but what Salvatore Aprile did not know that Vince Corrado, a retired police officer himself, was also a corrupted man who was in the pocket of the local crime family, the Jerome's. It was Vince Corrado who first got Gio into using illegal steroids to bulk up his strength, muscle mass and temper.

Gio truly had a gift in boxing and a vengeance and strength that was devastating to his opponents. He earned the nickname "The Bull" and was poised to have a promising career as an amateur boxer when his life would be tossed upside down.

When he was 17, his younger sister had been out one night with a few other girlfriends when they had been accosted outside a movie theater by three black men. She had been taken, beaten and raped so badly she had ended up in the hospital for several months with internal injuries, her face broken in so many places she was in casts for months. However it was Angela's mind and spirit that truly never recovered, she was always terrified sinking into a deep depression. A year later she would attempt suicide, nearly be successful and then be committed for another six months to a psychiatric hospital. It tore Gio in half to see his sister who had once been so full of life and fiery, now a shell of a person deep inside her own prison of depression and mental illness.

All of Giovanni's promises to be legitimate went out the window, he had vendetta in his heart and soul, and he once again turned to those people on the street whom he knew were into criminal activity in order to find out information on these three men who had done this to her. He had tried getting information from people at the PAL league but Gio was beginning to find out very quickly that the American Legal system was a piece of shit and unfair. So at the nudging of his trainer Vince he turned to his own Italian wiseguys and thugs for justice. He fought a few more sanctioned boxing matches, but whenever he came up against black opponents he fought them so cruelly and with such vengeance that when the bell rang it took nearly seven people to haul him off his badly beaten opponent. He was dismissed from amateur boxing and began to hang exclusively around the wiseguys in his old neighborhood again. Gio and his father Sal had many fights and altercations over Gio hanging out on the streets, but at this time under the influence of illegal steroids and with vengeance in his heart Gio merely dropped out of High School with only three more months to go and left home one night after he had nearly beaten his father to a bloody pulp.

"You have no care what happens to your own daughter?" Gio had screamed in rage as he was atop his father beating him with fists that did devastating damage. Gio's mother had screamed and pleaded for her son to stop and then stood there sobbing, afraid to get between the two men, she seemed to know Giovanni was now lost to the street gangs and the old ways, his heart was *Mafioso* now and could never go back. She knew Gio would be the instrument of her daughters' revenge and her Sicilian part of course recognized it and even applauded it but this cruel and violent streak of Gio's frightened her beyond belief.

"Of course I care you fucking ungrateful prick!" Sal growled in anger beneath his son, "The police are doing everything we can to catch the son of a bitches! But this is how you treat your father?" but even he was a bit unnerved at the size his own son had grown to in musculature. He was sure Gio had gotten hold of illegal steroids to bulk up and keep his rage on edge, but even worse was the young man's violent temper and his taste for vengeance.

"Bullshit! Fucking, bullshit!" Gio had grabbed his father's throat now a part of him wanting to throttle the man to death. "You pretend everything is all right, Angela nearly killed herself the other day and what do you do? Trust the fucking cops?!" he ground more of his weight against his fathers neck, "And what do they do? Nothing! They are a joke! My way is better! Let me handle this, I'll have the fuckin' bastards dead in a month! This is your daughter we are taking about, my sister!"

"Don't go down that path Giovanni." His father had stopped fighting his son, trying one last time to sway him from the path of criminal activity. "It is a path you can't turn from once in, those worthless fucking wiseguys. The only way out is death. Trust me, please, Gio. Be a respectable Italian man, stay far away from those damn thugs and gangster groups."

Gio abruptly let go of his father and rolled off him with tears of both hurt and rage in his eyes, "Please, please, father just kill the fucking bastards, why do you let these pricks run free in the street while Angela is tormented in her heart and soul?" he begged with one last attempt at connecting with his father in heart and soul, both saddened and embarrassed at the anger he had unleashed at his own father.

However, no sooner than Salvatore Aprile was freed from his son's angry grasp than he launched to his feet and grabbing a heavy iron statue swung it hard into his sons head. The first blow merely stunned the large Gio and caught him off guard. His eyes looked at his father with such hurt and betrayal it broke his mother's heart. "Attack me you punk ass bastard?" Sal roared.

"Salvatore, Noooo!" Lucia wailed in agony, "Leave him be! I beg you. It's over now!"

The second blow from the iron statue sent Giovanni sprawled backwards with an arc of blood spraying forth from the back of his head, "You fuckin' dare to attack me?!?" Now Sal's own Italian temper was in full gear. "You dare to attack your own father? I will kill you, you fucking street punk! I bought you into this world and I can fuckin' take you out!" he kicked his downed son and continued to batter him with that wicked iron statue. Since Gio had been stunned on the first hit, not expecting it, there was little he could do as he was still trying to get his mind focused on the here and now.

At one point Lucia tried to intervene, half jumping onto her husbands back cursing at him in Sicilian, "Leave him be Salvatore! Let him go! Let it rest now!!"

With an angry grunt Salvatore Aprile flung his wife off his back and with a right hook nearly knocked her unconscious. But it was the slight respite Gio needed, seeing his mother thrown across the room, the rage of red burned in his heart and in front of his eyes. Unconsciously going to his boxing training he rammed one large fist dead center onto his father's face with a sickening crack. "You have already lost me father," he said with a deadly grin, his face streaked sickeningly with his own blood. Gio's other fist swung up from below catching his father in the gut with such force the man dropped like a ton of bricks, the air driven from his lungs with a tormented grunt.

Gio stood over him a moment, fists clenched as glared down at his father who writhed in pain trying to get his wind back. "I could kill you, I truly could. But you are not worth it. You are a fucking coward pure and simple." And with that Giovanni Aprile walked out of his parents' house and life never to return.

Not knowing where else to turn to, he hooked up with the one man he had ever trusted, Vince Corrado and was promptly put to work on small time heists and as enforcement duty, using his strength, skills and intimidating nature to beat those who were late in paying to bloody pulps. But still every day he worked hard to find out who the three men were who had raped his sister. By the time he turned 20 he got his answer one day and took the next few weeks to hunt them down. The first two men he caught and dragged to an empty chop shop and literally beat them to death with bare fists and iron pipes, breaking their bones hideously and slowly. One man died within an hour, the second man lasted for 5 hours under Gio's terrible onslaught. The last man he finally tracked down a month later and as Gio was beating him the man kept saying he worked for an a connected man for the Jerome Family, perhaps hoping this information would get him a reprieve from the vendetta ridden Gio.

"You can't do this man," the man pleaded as he spit out blood and teeth, "I fucking work for Charlie who is with the Jerome's. Let me go now and you can walk away from this man, but you don't wanna go down the wrong side of the Jerome's man..."

"I am already walking down the wrong road, you *cafone* punk." Gio took his time beating and torturing the man over the day, exacting his own vendetta on behalf of his sister. This third one, Leon, had a lot of stamina and lasted nearly 8 hours, or perhaps Gio's form of punishment and torture was far more exacting and controlled now. He knew how to break bones and prolong death until he was ready to deliver it.

After finding out some information on the Jerome's it was Gio who boldly went one day to meet up with one of the capos Charlie Legavoli along with his street mentor Vince Corrado. Gio was respectful and polite and explained the reason for his visit.

"I took the life of Leon, one of your dope dealers. He was one of 3 men who had raped my sister and I wanted my vendetta sated with him, however I know he earned vig and business for you. So..." Gio said in a totally straight voice as though he had been a skilled capo for years and not some wiseguy *cugine*, "I will pay you not only what Leon would have made for you, but pay you restitution as well. I do a lot of heists and jobs with the Bensonhurst gangs and Vince here, and you will get top choice of what I pick up."

Perhaps it was this polite boldness that impressed Charlie, or perhaps the simple fact the young tough guy did exactly what he said he would, giving Charlie and Vince repayment for his killing of Leon. Within a year Charlie Legavoli along with Vince began to school Gio Aprile in the ways of 'our thing' and began to use him as an enforcer and associate for Jerome deals or as a guard during his high roller poker games.

A year later the imposing and professional Gio Aprile would catch the eye of then capo Laurence Martel who would take Giovanni Aprile personally under his wing, training him to be an elite bodyguard. And while Gio never did pick up the elegant moves of the martial arts, he learned enough of them along with his fighting skill and sheer intimidating size to be a formidable and deadly man indeed. When

Martel made underboss, he got Victor's approval and Gio was given his button and became a made man in the Jerome Family. A short six months later, when the current head of the bodyguards was killed in a freak car accident, Gio already tutored, schooled and primed would be set in place to replace him. It was a move never regretted by any of those that Gio had ever worked for. He was quiet, professional and his strength and stamina was legendary. Although he had stopped using illegal steroids when he schooled under Laurence Martel, he still worked daily in the gym and was an imposing mob gorilla who could easily snap a man's spine with his bare hands.

Gio never did visit his parents again, but every mother's day he would send his mother a card or gift, and for every birthday Angela had he would send her a box of chocolates or flowers to the nunnery she was now in, St. Michaels.

CHAPTER 22- *June 19th 1987*

Alyssa was actually surprised and shocked that day when she went into the back kitchens. She never knew before just how many people worked behind the scenes here at the Jerome estates, for she had never seen them all. There were at least 15 various ladies in here, between the ages of 20 and 70 and nearly all of them speaking in Italian strong with Sicilian dialect.

She walked in hesitantly, head down, feeling very out of place and like an intruder. These people were a hive of activity working hard, cooking, cleaning and baking. So many delicious smells tempted her nostrils. Here and there a few off duty guards walked around, some speaking in Italian with the women, as other soldiers sat in a corner smoking, playing cards, openly cleaned their weapons or even counted their illegal gotten monies. A few other workers cleaned silverware or fixed minor household objects.

Suddenly it was almost as though a hush seemed to stop and spread around the room; Alyssa felt almost as though she did that day when she was asked by Victor to walk to his Office. A cold chill seemed to creep up her spine as all eyes seemed to suddenly turn on her and for the briefest of instances they were wary and hostile, like a pack of guard dogs wondering what 'stray' had come into their territory but then suddenly, their eyes all seemed to lighten and smiles came upon some of the faces. Several voices began to speak excitedly in rapid Italian at once and some pointed directly at Alyssa.

A very old woman hobbled up to her and gently cupped her face, speaking something to Alyssa that she didn't understand a word of but the older lady was crying and smiling and embracing Alyssa, seemingly very grateful and happy for something.

"That isa Emilia," a rather stern but matronly woman had walked over to Alyssa. She spoke with an accent that reminded Alyssa of Leonardo's but a bit more harsher and thicker, "She be here atta this house the longest, she isa our head cook, she says 'thank you for saving the *Padrone's* life', for giving Victor your *rene*."

"Kidney, Rosette, the word is Kidney." one of the guards translated with a light grin.

"Eh," Rosette shrugged, "Alyssa know what I mean, don't you girl?" she winked at the younger woman.

Alyssa just smiled and gingerly hugged the elderly Emilia back who was composing herself now but still going on and on in rapid Sicilian.

"I am Rosette," the matronly woman introduced herself formally to Alyssa and gave her a quick hug also. "Emilia," she spoke to the older woman briefly in Italian, then switched back to English, "I notta think Alyssa speaks Sicilian, Eh? But she thanks you for the compliment, I'll tell her." Rosette gently guided Alyssa to the side of the kitchen, "Emilia and a all of us, want you to know you are welcome ina here any time. You did a wonderful thing for Mr. Jerome, your Uncle. He is a good man, eh? We all love him very much." Alyssa noticed a few of the older ladies, like Emilia actually crossed themselves in the sign of the Cross whenever Victor Jerome's name was bought up.

Alyssa would be indebted to Laurence Martel for these cooking lessons and an opportunity for these Italian ladies to tutor her, far more than she could have ever imagined, because it was through here that she would learn the real meaning of *omerta*, and what the *La Cosa Nostra* was and what the real meaning of the word '*Mafia*' was.

The people who worked in Victor Jerome's' kitchen and house were people who often came over directly from Italy who needed to earn money and needed protection when they came into this country. They were the wives, sisters, mothers and cousins (or widows in some cases) of the soldiers and bodyguards who guarded the great Jerome Estate, or the Italian immigrants who lived in the nearby town and worked by day in the great Jerome Estate and then at night drove back to their houses and apartments that they owned about 10 miles away from here. All of these people were taken care of by Victor Jerome as well, so he truly was like a 'Father' to so many.

It was here she would learn what love, trust and *Famiglia* (Family) was and that 'Mafia' was not what was thought of by American standards, like an 'entity' or a "Gang of rogues" but a state of mind. "*Mafia*" meant in Sicilian, something virile, 'the best', it was a code of conduct, a standard, a way of living not in itself criminal in nature but by a code of honor and oath bound.

While she indeed learned to cook some of the Italian dishes and learned a smattering of the language, her real lessons she suspected came from as Martel said- to learn from the people and the traditions themselves- and that was the greatest gift of all. And so she happily sat in the corner and would polish the silver or work on stuffing the rigatoni or tortellini, as all around her the life blood of the *Famiglia* went on with its daily routine and mainly she would either listen like a hawk or smile. Even though many times she couldn't understand everything that was being said, they always they made her feel included and a part of them, an honorary Italian woman. She also began her road to learning to understand at least some basic Italian.

In the afternoon or early evening Martel would come back and collect her from the main house and the two of them would go back to his house. Where after one of his Asian or Italian dinners they would either play chess, or else he would go over a classic book with her. Often one he would read aloud to her, in his soothing baritone voice and they would discuss together.

The first time, he had taken her into that martial arts work out room of his, she had thought him mad and that he would for sure tear her apart. But he had been very gentle with her, teaching just the gentle meditative moves of Tai Chi. On day four, he added some moves of Kenpo karate starting with the most basic of moves and falls with her.

Never was he rough, always he was a patient and kind teacher. However she often noted when she went through her own Tai Chi warm ups the fury and strength the man used in his own work outs against the training dummy, either with his bare hands or with the dummy martial arts weapons.

During the evening they went over her journal together, the one she was obligated to write for the two of them to share. At first she had felt self conscious sharing things with the seemingly cold man and it still rather confused her how during the evening times, at his sanctuary at home he seemed almost like a different man; relaxed, warm and more at peace but come morning, it was almost as if some strange transformation had taken place. Once his business suit went on, once he was dressed for the Family, then the cold mask of "the Undertaker" was in place and he was no longer her teacher "Kageryu" but the stoic, cold and efficient underboss of the Jerome Family. And while she understood it logically in her mind, it still didn't make a whole lot of sense to her heart and soul.

It was the only thing that tempered an otherwise very satisfying journey. She still remembered that first night that she had slept in his bed with him and of course after that first night, she had moved back into her guest room where she properly belonged. While he still offered her the healing massages and they did indeed seem to help heal and meld her mind/body and soul together, there was never any invitation from the man to get as close in trust as there had that first night. If anything he had seemed to pull back a step or two emotionally.

At Martel's house Alyssa had offered to clean and cook for Martel as well but he was very adamant about not letting her, if anything he was very much the master of his own domain and preferred to tightly run his own sanctuary.

"Kanashii Taka," he had told her gently one day, when she had offered to help him out by doing his housework, cleaning, vacuuming, "It's not that I don't appreciate your humble offer, I do. It's just that..." He had paused as though trying to find the right words, "I'm not used to such attentive help."

The truth of the matter was he was not used to having someone underfoot, period. And while he did like his student and appreciated her curiosity and her eagerness to learn, he deeply guarded his heart and his secrets. Even worse was that day by day his own heart was wavering in deeper feelings for Alyssa as well as deeper guilt over his attraction to her. He saw her nod in understanding but her eyes were already filling with tears that he knew she would not shed.

"Wait..." he sighed. "I tell you what." He conceded. "I will let you tend to my Zen garden." He gave her a rather dour look, crossing his large arms over his chest but his student knew him well enough by now to know it was only his begrudging dour look he got when someone actually was able to out-maneuver him. "And, you can keep the living room dusted off, fair enough?"

Alyssa gave him a formal martial arts bow but was smiling brightly her green eyes alight and dancing with happiness. '*Thank you*' she silently mouthed.

"You are way too easy to please, Kanashii." Martel bowed back and unconsciously rubbed his thumb along her cheekbone, "Perhaps those gossiping ladies in the kitchens are teaching you a little too well, hmmm?" he chuckled lightly, playfully.

She had promised him her trust and to keep his secret about the Kageryu thing and while he called her Kanashii at his house, he called her Alyssa everywhere else. However, like Martel, day by day Alyssa was becoming more attracted and dependant on her teacher and mentor.

Paulie Verro was just finishing up for the night at his strip club, The Harem. He knew Ricardo would close up shop and he wasn't due to see his contact, Frankie for a few more days yet. Frankie had promised him next week he would get him in to see the underboss for Tito, a man named Joey Calendri. He would sneak out of town then to make the quick meeting, but for now, his mind was only thinking about the evening he had planned with his *comare*, Rinella. She was a hot little number he had hired a few months ago to dance at his club and this evening they had a hot date at her apartment for some fun and action.

Paulie cruised across town and spritzed on a bit too much aftershave and combed his hair back in the mirror as he pulled up in front of her brownstone apartment. He was about to get out of his Cadillac when he leaned over and grabbed a few condoms from the glove compartment. "You lucky dog," He chuckled as he read the condom package, "Ribbed for her pleasure. Yeah, fucking-A-right," he laughed.

He locked up his car and took the stairs two at a time as he bounded up the brownstone and hit the buzzer for her to let him in. "Hey babe, it's me." he gruffed into the speaker.

The main door opened with a buzz and a click letting him in. He walked up the steps to 2-D, gave a quick knock and waited for her to open the door. The door opened and he walked in noting the apartment was darker than usual. She must be lighting some candles for a romantic effect he thought, "Hey darlin' you miss your sweet stud?"

"Sweet stud are you now?" The voice was not Rinella's but the harsh rough Brooklyn accent of Joshua Demonico.

"Oh Fuck! Fuck You!" Paulie tried to back up, every hair on the back of his neck rising in utter terror.

The strong muscular form of Leonardo Tagretta had already been waiting behind the door and had closed and blocked it. As Paulie turned He nearly slammed into the silent, dark and unmerciful form of his fellow capo Leonardo.

Panicked, Paulie swung back around, nearly ramming into Joshua again as both men quickly and efficiently closed in on him springing their trap.

"Paulie, my fine friend, we have a problem here," the consigliere's gaze bore into the traitorous capo. "So we're all going to take a nice little ride back to the Jerome estates, *capisce*?"

But Paulie Verro already knew where this encounter was going, he knew he was busted and he was not going anywhere with these two. He knew they were here to execute him. "Oh shit, HELP!!!" Paulie screamed like a trapped animal and tried to bolt, he actually even took a halfway decent swing at Joshua Demonico.

However Leonardo was a master of the garrote, it was his specialty and before Paulie moved another inch the metal wire sung in Len's hands and expertly snapped around Paulie's neck immediately silencing anymore screams or struggles from him.

"Hold up his weight Len!" Joshua darkly ordered. With a swift martial arts move, he easily executed a side-kick and a hideous snap was heard as he snapped Paulie's leg at the knee. Not a sound could Paulie make as he was being throttled by the garrote in Leonardo's hands.

Only the glazing of the Paulie's eyes, the paleness of his skin color as his body began to go into shock was any indication of the brutality of what was being done to him.

"Give him some blood Len…" Joshua ordered, his eyes filled with utter rage. "Let him have a breath or two."

Leonardo loosened the garrote just enough to prolong Paulie's agony then hoisted him up again, bearing his full weight.

"Paulie, you traitorous pig! This is how you repay the Jerome's? Those you swore an oath to? You turn and want to join our enemies?" Joshua's anger was white-hot with another sudden angry kick, he broke Paulie's other leg.

Joshua wanted to do so much more, wished he could keep up the torture for several more hours but he had promised Victor, swore to him he wouldn't showboat would do the hit and do it correctly. "No, Fuck *YOU*, Paulie!" He hissed angrily at the man and spit on his face. "Finish him Len. This *babbo gavone*, disgusts me!"

Joshua watched with grim satisfaction as Leonardo kneeled down on top of Paulie's back as he expertly finished garroting him to death. Like Martel, Leonardo showed very little emotion during his hits he simply did what needed to be done, his face a mask of neutrality and total business. In some ways Joshua was envious of them, Joshua took all of his hits personally. He either enjoyed them or hated them all, for him the emotion was the catalyst that fueled his rage and hatred when he had to kill someone.

After Paulie was dead, both men quickly and silently wrapped him up in several large gunnysacks and then rolled him up in a carpet.

"Thankfully the girl had smarts enough to take our offer of going out to see a movie tonight and skip her date with Paulie, or we'd have two bodies to hide." Joshua snorted, as the two men hoisted up the concealed body of Paulie in the carpet.

"Maybe he notta be good fuck, eh?" Leonardo chuckled quietly in his soft voice. "Whatta we do with him now?"

"Now we take him over to our safe haven out by Wildwood, butcher the meat, and hide the car in Enzo's junkyard. As far as we know and off the record, Paulie is on vacation in Florida and that's all we know." Joshua sighed darkly, wishing he could have done a lot worse to the traitorous Paulie Verro he was not sated at all with the quick death of the rat.

"Florida sounds nice…" Leonardo trailed off as he and Joshua rammed the concealed body of Paulie into the back seat, then covered it with a blanket they had in preparation. "I wouldn't mind being there, on da beach you know?" Finished with that, Len slid in behind the wheel and started the car. "Shame to waste nice Cadillac like this." He said shaking his head as he retied his ponytail and ditched the garrote under the seat.

Joshua just glowered at him from the passenger seat and fished around in his pockets for a couple of his nicotine squares.

"Joshua," Leonardo chuckled softly at him, "Why you pissed off *mio amico*?"

"Because the fucker died too quickly. I wish I could have gouged his eyes out and broken all of his fuckin' bones," Joshua said in all seriousness.

"You are one angry man," Len shook his head at him, as he smoothly drove the car out onto the deserted road. "Save it for when we need it in a few months eh? You will have plenty to kill then, I assure you."

Joshua was going to say something smart-assed but looked warily at Len a moment and stopped. He adjusted the thick gold bracelet around his wrist and chewed vigorously on his gum. "I forgot you been through this *mannagge* shit before, huh?"

Leonardo laughed then again. Not a friendly laugh, but more a snort of disgust. His blue-grey eyes took on a look then, a cross between one filled with sorrow and with red-hot anger. "Oh yes, Joshua." He said levelly, his Sicilian accent hard. "I have been through this *mannagge* shit before. You notta understand. What happened a few weeks ago, that was not it." Leonardo glanced at him, as though looking through his heart and soul.

And for a moment Joshua felt the air chill in the car, unconsciously his hand went to the AC unit on the car to shut it off, but it was not turned on.

"You will getta you wish, Joshua." Len nodded as he stared straight ahead driving, "Save your anger for then; for the *nemico*, eh? Not one *cafone* rat. Back in my hometown, before I come here, when I worked for the Bonnaro's my clan was his clan our *Famiglia's* were tied by generations to theirs. Much more close than you alliances here with you Corella's and Del Giorno's and other Commission Families."

Len glanced over at the lane, smoothly turned left then continued on, only the occasional street light briefly illuminating the two men, as they drove on. "So anyway, Bonnaro's have been fighting the DiGiacomo's for many years back home, it was like you Jerome's and the D'Salvatore's. Hate, war, always war. My whole family had been killed by the war there, my brothers, my two sisters, four of my cousins, my father..."

Joshua just turned for a moment and watched as Leonardo ticked off all 15 of his blood relatives and family he had lost in the blood war between the Bonnaro's and the DiGiacomo's. He felt his throat go dry despite the gum. Here he had served with the quiet voiced Leonardo Tagretta for nearly nine years and yet had known so little about him, and tonight Len had shared more with him than he ever had.

"Oh yes, Joshua," Len said still in the same softly accented voice, neither with anger or pity. "They kill the women back home as well. Here in the states, '*Our thing*' is so different, so very different indeed. Back home, you can die simply by association. Women, children, none are safe. To make your bones you often expected to kill children, women it notta matter. *Mannagge* is *mannagge*, enemies are enemies.

You do what you Boss tells you, what the oath of the *Famiglia* demands of you. Victor understands he is of the old ways, Martel too..." Leonardo trailed off then, lost for a moment in his own thoughts as they drove deeper into the dark of night, off the interstate and onto the New Jersey freeway headed into the dark empty deserted forest areas.

Leonardo then turned his full attention on the road and the men didn't say a word to one another the rest of the night, but silently did their gruesome work. Joshua's level of respect for Leonardo definitely went up a hundred-fold that night.

CHAPTER 23- *July 2nd 1987*

For Alyssa, the same routine had gone on for nearly two weeks. Mornings and daytimes were spent at the Jerome estate with Rosette and the ladies and evenings at the home of her teacher, the enigmatic Laurence. Surprisingly during this time she had not seen anyone else she knew well at the Jerome estates, except for Joshua once briefly. He had come into the kitchen, to speak with Gio Aprile one day, glared at her as Joshua usually did and that was it.

She had not seen Victor Jerome at all and she had not seen Cesare, Patrizio or most of the other men she knew. She had asked Martel about Victor's absence one evening and he had simply said, "He's on a business trip for now, although I'm sure he'll be very happy to see how you have improved in health when he returns." He gave her a brief look though that said, -'and that is all I am going to say about it,'- and invited no more questions on the subject. Alyssa was beginning to learn quite quickly the nuances of *omerta* and what was permitted to ask or discuss and that which was taboo to bring up.

She did see her friend Tommy DeLuca a few times, he chatted with her and taught her how to play poker but he was back to putting a lot of creamer in his coffee and that spoke volumes to Alyssa. Whatever was going on, the Family was gearing up for something again.

"I dunno." Tommy complained one morning, "Things are tense." As he shuffled the deck of cards for another hand of poker between them, "My friend Paulie has dropped off the face of the earth, Joshua seems fit to be tied these last two days and for whatever reason, even the bosses are stretched thin and hard to be found." He riffled the deck and began to deal out the cards. "So honestly, you like living with ol' Lurch over there in the Imperial Peking Dynasty house?" he chuckled.

Alyssa felt her heart sink. There was a time she might have pried Tommy for information and told him all the details about the enigmatic Martel but now, how could she? She knew what kind of trouble that had gotten everyone into last time and worst of all, she really did like

Martel. For whatever reason, she felt there was something, under that stone cold exterior of his that very few were privileged to see, passion. She had seen it in the graceful way he swung the sword, or the way he had talked her out of her terror that night in the bathroom and felt it in the way he caringly gave her the nightly healing massages. To her, Martel had been nothing but nice and a complete gentleman so far and she had made a promise to trust in him.

She smiled lightly and just shook her head playfully at Tommy in a friendly way, as though he had asked a silly question. After all, Alyssa had learned often the best way to diffuse a situation around here was to just play it lightly, at least for her. With all these Italian male tempers, she had learned from Rosette and the other ladies if she took things lightly and easily, listened well and kept her mouth shut she was often allowed like a graceful cat, to saunter quietly past whatever dilemma was dropped at her feet. For the most part, the men just had a habit of venting out loud and it was the sign of a good wife, daughter, niece or any '*Mafioso*' woman, to simply listen, ignore (or smile and nod) and move on.

"Ah, yer probably right." Tommy finished dealing and threw some poker chips into the pot. "I'm sure everyone is just on edge is all." He smiled and changed subjects, "You are looking a lot healthier though Alyssa. Your wounds are healing up nice, you're not all skin and bones anymore and it's nice to actually see you smile." He nodded as he threw in a few chips into the pot, "Now if only this damn poker hand was as healthy." He grumbled.

But it would be later that day when the worst test of all would come to her. Martel had picked her up early from the main house at around 10:00 a.m. and they had worked on her journal and played chess in the beautiful Zen garden out in his backyard. Then they had gone inside to make a late lunch. Today Martel was showing her how to make a shrimp stir-fry with Oodon noodles.

Just as Martel and Alyssa were getting ready to start lunch inside, there was a knock on Martel's front door.

"Here," Martel instructed Alyssa, "keep stirring these noodles." He had thrown some noodles into a pot of boiling water then strode over to answer the door.

Alyssa heard his deep voice talking for a moment and then her blood seemed to run cold as she recognized the other voice; Victor! She had not seen the man since their last encounter when he had sentenced her to move in with Martel. Alyssa moved her head slightly to peek through the divider and she saw Martel's tall back bent down to speak quietly with his Boss and could only partially see Victor speaking with him.

She saw one of the bodyguards with them and it was then her eyes fell on the heavy form of Cesare. He looked awful. Even though he was dressed as usual in his suit, his face was horribly bruised and puffy on one side. He wore dark glasses and she was sure one of his eyes was swollen shut. He had a semi rigid cast on one elbow and he walked with a definite limp.

Martel had shifted from her line of sight for a second and she saw him give Cesare a quick warm embrace and whisper something to his ear.

That left Victor's line of sight towards Alyssa wide open and for a moment their eyes met, his dark eyes seeming to bore into hers. For a moment they were cold, hard, unyielding but then as easily as one turns on a light switch he smiled and his gaze became benign, gentle.

"Alyssa how good to see you again," Victor nodded. "Come, come here," he gestured to her.

Alyssa was suddenly aware that all eyes were upon her; she dare not meet Cesare's eyes, not yet, she just could not. Hesitantly she stepped forward, then finally walked confidently towards Victor and embraced him giving him a light hug and a respectful kiss on each cheek as she had seen others do.

She noticed Martel seem to give her an almost imperceptible nod, as though he had been judging her.

"Well, I see Martel hasn't been lying." Victor held her out at arms length in front of him, "He said you moving in with him has been working wonders and I see it has. You are looking much healthier and fit, Alyssa. This makes me happy," Victor smiled warmly and gave her another light hug, as an uncle would a niece. He smelled pleasantly of aftershave and peppermints, a soft comforting grandfatherly smell that seemed to reach into the deepest recesses of Alyssa mind. "I'm afraid I've been awfully busy lately my dear." Victor continued, "But that may change soon, so you and I can spend much more time together eh?" Victor's eyes seemed to take on a depth and intelligence that reached through her very essence. "After all, Martel here may be busy for awhile quite soon."

"Will you be staying for lunch?" Martel asked Victor. "I can throw on some more noodles for everyone."

Victor held up his hand. "No Laurence, that's Ok. We just need to briefly discuss some things then we'll be going." The Don made a nod with his head to indicate that the men should all move out to the Zen garden to talk.

Alyssa took the hint to move back into the kitchen and get out of their way and that is when she and Cesare nearly collided with one another, "Nice to see you again 'Lyss," He mumbled politely.

Alyssa looked up at the broken, bruised face and felt her world begin to tilt and spiral in a dizzying rush as her stomach threaten to heave up breakfast.

She must have gone pale and terrified because Cesare suddenly dropped his eyes and looked away, as though sparing her his condition.

Alyssa knew she was going to pass out, she just knew it. The voices of Victor, Martel, Cesare and the guard all just swam lazily around her head at once as she stumbled back to the kitchen. She had a vague memory of falling in slow motion and her head narrowly missing the boiling pot of noodles but cracking against the counter with an evil far-away sound as though it were all happening to someone else...

-CRACK-

"Have fun darlin' dancing with the Devil..." skinny, grimy man's voice. The scene shifted...

A vision of a woman and a man making out in a warehouse...She should know these people...Who are these people? She should know them for they evoked powerful emotions in her. The woman with hatred and anger, the man with sorrow and betrayal... The scene shifted...

"Ride with it. Join with the rhythm, flow with the waves..." Martel's soothing voice. An image of him swinging that oriental sword so beautifully and graceful, her heart filling with a sense of desire and arousal. The scene shifted...

The droning of a diesel engine and women in shackles being led towards a vehicle.

"That Goddamn tractor-trailer, not those two men again! TJ, I think one of them was named TJ, but which one?" Shift...

"I am just a legitimate businessman, am I not?" Victor's voice, his eyes intense like two black fire suns. "Oh no you're not, Victor, but I won't tell." Where have I heard that question before? Shift...

"YOU DON'T WANT THE KIND OF FAMILY I HAVE CHILD! YOU WILL NEVER BE A PART OF IT!" Victor's very angry voice, seeming to overwhelm all...

Why can't I just sleep without all these dreams? Somebody let me just sleep ...

She began awakening then, some far off intrusion on the fringes of her mind that was making her unwillingly come around, something offensive, rude.

Martel had grabbed Alyssa and carried her onto the couch in the living room. Victor had gotten one of the smelling salts capsules from Martel's first aid kit and the guard had snapped it open and waved it around under her nose.

Alyssa was coming out of it now, coughing and sputtering from the ammonia smelling salts. Martel was leaning over her, looking into her eyes intently and for the first time, Alyssa felt vulnerable, unprotected and naked beneath him. Almost how she felt when Victor looked at her. "Alyssa," Martel spoke softly. "Are you Ok? Are you with me in the now?" he asked gently.

She nodded yes. She felt weak but not like she was going to pass out anymore and not like she was going to throw up on Victor's expensive shoes.

"Here," Martel handed the smelling salts capsule to the bodyguard. "Throw this away in the toilet."

Alyssa was struggling to sit up she just wanted to go and melt away, to digest the memories and images she had seen in the dreams. This time the images stuck with her crystal clear like Polaroid photos in her mind.

"Easy, easy child," Victor half pushed her back down. "Cesare, call John Thomas up and tell him to come down and take a look at Alyssa."

Alyssa wanted to tell them all she was fine, just to let her be let her digest what she saw, just to step back and let her breathe. She suddenly for the first time in a long time felt overwhelmed by all of them, not safe like she usually did.

Martel sat down on the couch against her, his back to her holding her firmly against the couch, as he whispered privately to Victor for a moment in Italian.

Victor nodded then turned to the guard and Cesare. "Come, we will wait out in the garden, Martel will attend to Alyssa and will join us in just a moment."

Victor then turned and looked briefly at Alyssa, his eyes piercing but neutral. "You'll be fine child," he assured her, "We'll have Dr. Weintraub come take a look at you. I'm sure it was nothing." He gave her shoulder a light squeeze and she felt the strength of the Don in even that most simplest of gestures. Victor nodded to Martel for a moment and then walked out gracefully to the garden.

Martel watched Victor leave without turning towards Alyssa his great body still pressing against her holding her firmly in place; it was both reassuring and yet in a way frightening at the same time. She was going nowhere.

"Kanashii," He said finally after Victor and the others had gone outside and then turned to look down at her. His eyes held a look of puzzlement more than anything else. "It was different this time, wasn't it? We don't have time to discuss it now. But I am sure you can tell me later hmm?" His eyes were again piercing her, as though he somehow already knew.

Alyssa couldn't help the tear that slipped from her face. What was she going to tell her teacher? "I know what happened to Cesare and the realization of it so scared me and sickened me that I became cowardly and passed out? And how about now, Kageryu? Have I embarrassed you, Rosette and everyone else? Am I not 'Mafia' enough to be able to just pretend I did not see Cesare standing there all beaten up because he and I talked?" another tear slipped out past her eye, even though she fought it, because she knew in her heart of hearts, the whole reason Cesare had been so viciously beaten was

298

because Cesare had talked to her. Because she had questioned him and he had been nice enough to answer.

Martel shook his head gently and his thumb wiped away the two tears, "No one is angry Kanashii. There is no shame." Quickly he easily scooped her up, "This is what you fail to see." He carried her effortlessly to her room, the one with the potted Ficus tree that stood sentinel by the window. "Loyalty is prized above all else around here if you have not noticed." Martel laid her down and gently drew the drapes closed. He bought over her journals and a couple books. "Cesare has already been forgiven, but you have to forgive yourself. You know what we are and we make no excuses." Martel spoke plainly, but not harshly.

Martel was about to leave when he paused by the door and stopped. "Victor meant what he said," he spoke without turning to look at her. "He was indeed happy to see you again. I know him well. He was very happy to see you healthy and up and about and he was worried when you collapsed." Martel quietly closed the door behind him and left.

Alyssa curled into a ball as her heart and mind were thrown into a million different thoughts and directions.

Chapter 24

Tito D'Salvatore watched intently as the nurses tucked in his elderly wife and administered her medication. She muttered something in Italian about the saints and her son and then began to fall into a fitful sleep. One of his hands came up and lovingly touched her shoulder, "*Dormire sereno, mia moglie,*." Tito spoke softly to her in Italian. He knew his dear Concetta was ailing fast she had collapsed after hearing about their son's death at the hands of the Jerome animals and had literally suffered a stroke, thankfully it was minor but her depression hung around her like a black veil. His own mood and anger was not much better. It was all right, he tried to reason with himself, if his plan worked as he hoped, he would take her out of the country back to Sicily in five months or less. A muscle twitched along his jaw line and with a small grunt he turned and stalked off.

His underboss, Joey Calendri and his consigliere, Johnny Baldovino were waiting outside the door. "We need to talk," said Joey, "We haven't been able to contact Paulie Verro in a couple days. The manager who runs the place, Ricardo Orenda, said Paulie went on vacation to Florida."

Tito glared at him, Joey was always so high strung and he was growing weary with his underboss. Why was the man always so high strung? That and no matter what the weather the man seemed eternally cold, always he was dressing as if it was winter out.

"Joey, so the man can't take a fuckin' vacation?" Tito growled as the men walked stiffly down Tito's elegant mansion in New Jersey. "So what?"

"But Frankie said Paulie didn't say anything to him about a vacation! What if the Jerome's got onto him about what was up? Last thing Paulie was supposed to do was meet up with his *comare* whore for a date and he never showed up?" Joey skittered around to the front of Tito forcing him to stop and listen to him. "I say we gotta tread lightly here."

Tito finally stopped with a wheezing grunt and glared at Joey, "Joey, Paulie is a fucking *cafone*! All the Jerome's are fucking *cafones*! Whether they got Paulie or not, if he was that easy to turn there are others that easy to turn, don't you understand? Besides, it is a mere distraction for when our independent, Gambini comes and pays old Victor a visit in the islands in a couple of weeks, eh?" he winked at his consigliere and gave Joey a rather condescending pat on the cheek as one would a dimwitted child. Both Tito and the consigliere had a small chuckle.

"Joey may be a clown, but he has a few points, Tito," Johnny pushed gently. He always loved to dress the part, always the expensive suits, the most expensive clothing and jewelry he could find. He practically reeked of money. "I know for a fact, Jerome has pulled all his men close to home, locked down his own assets and people tight as newly harvested oysters. They've got even more *zips* coming in from Sicily setting up both in their estate and in the local town..."

"So what? We have our own connections, promising us extra muscle!" Tito growled. He was beginning to grow impatient with both of them, he physically pushed past his underboss and consigliere to his living room, "Look, I got a flight in three hours from now for a sit down with some 'friends of ours' down in Miami and so far things are looking very favorable as to them helping us get rid of this Jerome menace, you understand?" he began to spell it out for them.

Both the men looked in confusion at Tito they hadn't heard about this...

"Yeah, I don't tell you everything," he narrowed his eyes at them. "If this works out, we will have some added zips and muscle of our own in a few months, right here at home. Visitors helping out the home team and neither the Jerome's nor the Bonnaro's will be expecting that!" he grinned and walked over to his expensive humidor where he fished out a few cigars. "Renaldo!!!" he shouted at the top of his lungs to his top bodyguard-driver, "Is the Goddamn fuckin' car ready or not?"

A large thickset bodyguard walked over, "It's ready Tito; your bags are already packed inside."

"So are we coming with to this thing, or what?" Joey asked still a bit confused over this news Tito had just dropped on their laps out of nowhere.

"No," Tito said arrogantly. "Just me and a few bodyguards, I think I can trust you not to take the Family into ruin in just a few days, eh?" he flung the cold barb at his Administration. He still was hurting deeply over the loss of his son and seemed to blame his underboss personally for it.

"No of course not," Joey said with a snort. Tito had been acting so hostile and secretive lately, not keeping in touch with his men at all.

"Good." Tito eyed them both for a moment. "Then I will see you in 3 to 4 days. Here's how to get hold of me if you need to." he slapped down a piece of paper, some stationery from a ritzy 4-star hotel. "You can contact me here, through 'a friend of ours', Joe Cinno."

Joey raised his eyebrows and Johnny gave a low impressed whistle. They knew the name; Joseph "Joe Cinno" Cimino was indeed a big wheel in Miami, a capo in the DiMone Family.

Tito turned on his heel and left with a mumbling huff following Renaldo out the door to the awaiting Lincoln continental.

For a few moments neither man said anything and then Johnny motioned the underboss to the kitchen, he knew better to talk in one of the 'business offices' that would be the first place Tito would bug to listen in on his own people.

"So?" he fished around for some wine and cheese from one of the elderly ladies working there, "Whaddya think?"

"I think Tito's mind has taken a walk off the map ever since Tory was killed," Joey whispered and he crossed himself in the sign of the cross.

Johnny just nodded, stuffing some mozzarella into his mouth. "Agreed. I don't like this not talking to us. He doesn't talk to you, not to me. It doesn't bode well, ya know?"

"Wonder why he is suddenly all pals with ol' Joe Cinno down in Miami?" Joey mused as he took a piece of cheese Johnny handed him.

"Fuck if I know but it gives me *agita*. It's a bad move, I think. Tito is locking us out of his decisions and it makes me very nervous that there is something deeper going on there. He takes stuff way too casually and arrogantly. The 'Old Dinosaur' as he likes to refer to Victor as, is being very sly and Tito is not taking the Jerome's seriously enough. Tito should know better and this worries me." The consigliere gave Joey a deep look.

They both dropped the conversation. To discuss things further among so many people or potential ears would be a breech of sensitive information and omerta. They just glanced at one another and decided to move the conversation elsewhere.

Later that evening Joey Calendri sat by himself in the Boccari Trattoria, his favorite hang out and one of the D'Salvatore crews main downtown hangouts. Usually he would come in to bullshit and talk with his men, drinking and shooting pool or to play some cards, but tonight he sat by himself in the corner sipping some wine and thinking long and hard.

For the first time in his life, his mind began weaving down dark passages he never thought he would take. Tito called Victor a dinosaur? Victor was being the smart one, and now it was raising all kinds of alarms in Joey to see his own Family being led to ruin under the wavering and crushing hand of a leader who no longer seemed to be making smart decisions. He dared not breathe a word of this to anyone he almost dared not believe he was even thinking of such traitorous thoughts himself.

But who could he even go to if he defected? The Jerome's underboss, Martel would kill him before he got two feet into the Jerome territory. Maybe, just maybe... His mind agonized, he felt so cold, so numbingly cold all over. His own guilt and indecision chewed him up inside.

"Hey Joey, you all right?" One of the D'Salvatore capos and the owner of the place came over to refill his bottle, "everything Ok?"

Joey had nearly leaped out of his seat. "Yeah," he said, his body still trembling with cold or was it fear and indecision? "Yeah, I'm fine. Just leave the bottle. Thanks friend."

"Sure, no problem Joe," the man smiled lightly and moved on.

Joey sat quietly and continued running a million thoughts and decisions through his head. He had to be dead certain of what he was doing, because once on the chosen path there was no going back and he had to be sure he could even convince the Jerome's to even take him.

Weintraub had stopped over around dinner later and of course pronounced Alyssa just fine except for the small bruise on her head where she bumped the counter in her fall. Of course she kept writing him over and over she was "*just fine*".

Martel had been more subdued and quiet with her that evening, as though he was awaiting her to discuss it with him. What was she going to talk to him about? "I know what you all did to poor Cesare and it was horrible and I hope to God you never do that to me!" In some round about way it drove home with a certain finality that Martel, that all of them, were the Jerome 'Crime Family' first above all else, that there was absolutely no room for any breeches of etiquette.

She was forced to face with both her heart and ethics now, the blunt and cold rational of what was under her nose. These people who she was living with, who were taking care of her, were criminals they were not benign, law abiding folks. And while Laurence Martel may be able to make her laugh while playing chess and do wonderful things like relaxing her body with his oriental massage techniques he probably went out and killed people and who knows what else. He didn't get the nickname 'The Undertaker' because he did charitable grave digging work. She knew what he was capable of. She had read the books up in the library and heard the tales from Cesare, heard the conversations from the men when they didn't think she was listening.

However on the other hand, with her amnesia, she knew nothing else. She had no other memories to draw on but vague shadows and starkly terrifying scenes, like the two men and the cattle prod that would crop up from the darkest depths of her mind. A part of her was scared, yes. Knew it was 'wrong' on some level but yet this group of people, this man, Victor and his 'Crime Family' had taken her in and now housed her, fed her, clothed her and cared for her. They could have done a lot worse to her. They were obviously making some effort. Why? These were the questions that ran circles like crazed squirrels around her brain.

Some memories had definitely begun to come back to her... She knew she had been kidnapped, she thought by the grimy scarred faced man and the black man, for they were the only ones she really recollected. She only had the foggiest memories of being viciously thrown into in some darkened room and hidden or left to die, until she had found by Victor Jerome, who had offered her dignity and saved her life.

She was fairly certain she was not married nor did she have any children. Some deep gut instinct just told her she didn't but those past memories were still hazy as well. Nor could she remember if she had any other family such as brothers, sisters, parents, etc. Did she have a job? Was someone looking for her? Did anyone even care she was missing or was she just one of the nameless multitudes who disappear every year that no one ever misses that you see about on TV?

"Kanashii?" The familiar deep baritone voice gently broke through her thoughts.

She suddenly felt a finger gently touch her cheek for a moment, as softly as a butterfly alighting upon her skin. It came away damp with a tear. Kageryu was kneeling next to her his face still its usual stoic mask except for one raised eyebrow.

She had been sitting in the living room in front of the great dragon statute that guarded near the door there. She had not even been aware she had gone into a trance of thinking and meditation. She shook her head, embarrassed to have her own emotions so blatantly obvious, to have been caught by him as her own emotions so vividly betrayed her own turmoil inside her.

Neatly and nimbly Laurence Martel had sat down behind her, offering her dignity and privacy. "Ah, now I understand," he said with true understanding. His large hands came up and began to rub on the back of her neck and then down along the length of her spine. He was silent for several minutes as he continued his daily healing work on her body in fact his silence and his understanding only made the tears come harder for a moment. But then slowly, she was able to gain control of them.

Alyssa could feel the warm breath of Martel behind her, the power of him, the essence of him and the masculine scent of him. It began to relax her, as did the skilled touch of his hands as he rubbed and soothed the exact junctures of her nerves.

"I will be leaving for a couple weeks on some business," he said soothingly. "You will have to stay in your old room at the main house. You won't mind, will you? After all, you have made some new friends and your old friends will be there; Tommy, Cesare..." he paused for a moment at the name, "as well as my right hand man, Gio Aprile. He says the two of you have become pretty good friends; they will all take care of you. Of course Dr. Weintraub will be around whenever you need him. I've already ground up your herbs into the pills and bottled and labeled them so those are all ready for you to take." He leaned in even closer, his warm breath softly against the side of her neck and face, "And besides, you'll get a break from my Asian cooking." He chuckled softly, lightly, "The house will be locked up tight, so make sure to get out anything you need."

She nodded and unconsciously leaned back against him, leaning on his strength, needing his strength. Relaxing and enjoying his touch, his voice, the very essence of him.

Martel felt parts of his own body responding to her that he had thought long ago dead. Not just the parts that a man responds to an attractive woman but deeper parts, parts of his very heart and soul. For a crazy moment, a part of him wanted to simply enfold his arms around her and draw her into him to hold her, to caress her and to comfort her. He suddenly and abruptly slammed his emotional wall down with such ferocity, anger at himself and coldness that she must have felt it as well, for she suddenly felt an icy chill from the shadow dragon and nearly lurched forward.

"I've got to pack," he mumbled awkwardly and agilely climbed to his feet. "I know you've had a rough day, Kanashii, I'll let you just have the evening to yourself." He excused himself rather abruptly. Before packing he stopped in the martial arts room, where he vented his anger and frustration on the leather training dummy.

Martel felt for her, he honestly did. He knew she was gaining back some more of her memories, he could sense it in her but yet he knew that his student Kanashii was still the 'wounded hawk'. Grounded and lost, her soul adrift in confused memories and trying to desperately fit in, yet wrestling with her own ethics and heart over what she knew surrounded her on every level.

A part of him could only do what he had been doing, healing her with his touch, with the supplements he had been using, the exercises they had been doing and the gentle teachings of people like Rosette and the others helping her to try and fit it, to try and understand the Sicilian traditions but he had also felt her pain and confusion today as keenly as she did. A part of him wanted to sooth her, to hold her, to begin that journey once again that had been so cruelly interrupted long ago with Miyoko...But how could he? Alyssa wasn't ready; he wasn't ready, it wasn't fair to her. He shouldn't lead her on and he didn't want to give her the wrong idea. He knew his first duty must come to the *Famiglia* first, just as it always had. The war against the D'Salvatores was gearing up and getting ready for its final moves and he was Laurence Martel, underboss of the Jerome family first and foremost. Now was not the time in his life to be getting involved seriously with a woman. He was almost glad for the two week business trip, his own mind was in turmoil and he needed time away to think.

Victor and Laurence sat in Laurence's Zen garden later that night, long after Alyssa had went to sleep. "The girl is Ok?" Victor asked idly.

"She is fine," Martel said neutrally as he poured his father a glass of wine.

"Excellent." Victor took the glass, "Now, I hate to do this to you Laurence, especially when things are so hot, when the *mannagge* is heating up..." He paused and looked at his tall son half hidden in the shadows, "...And I had promised not to use you on these kinds of assignments anymore, however I think you will like this one." A slight trace of a smile crossed the old Don's face.

"It's as we discussed before," Laurence said smoothly, both men's voices soft whispers that were mere breezes in the night. Martel's Zen garden was quite safe from being eavesdropped. Another reason he enjoyed coming out here. "I take nothing for granted my *padrone*. All of it is important in the long run; all of it makes a difference."

"I know Laurence. But be aware that this is strictly unsanctioned work and must be off-record from the Commission and other Families; it must be off-record even within this Family. I cannot support this in any way," Victor explained.

Martel simply nodded and sat down next to his father. They had discussed the assignment before Laurence knew what was expected of him.

Victor handed him a list that had names on it. "These are the names to be taken out. The last four you will enjoy the most, Vito Roman and his Top Administration."

Martel raised an eyebrow and glanced almost in shock at Victor, "You're whacking Vito Roman, his underboss, consigliere and his two main war capo's?" the last four names were the only surprise, he had not expected those.

A deeper smile played along the old Don's lips. "Oh yes, my *Martello*. They not only fucked us over by defying us and switching sides with D'Salvatores while taking what money makers us and the Corellas and others gave to them." He growled with barely contained anger, "But they got back into that infernal racket of white slavery, I so detest. Make sure those four men disappear without a trace, leave nothing to be found! If you can, Make Vito's a lasting and painful reminder of why not to fuck with the Jerome's."

Martel just nodded and carefully folded the paper up, "I understand."

"Come back safe to me, Laurence." Victor whispered, "I need you back at my side. Things will begin going quickly then to our final gambit. All that we have worked for; all that we have worked so very hard for." Victor stood up and once again placed his hand behind Laurence's neck, holding his son's head forehead to forehead in that gesture that was father and son's alone. "I do trust and love you implicitly my son," he whispered to Laurence in Italian, "Be safe, come home to me *sano e salvo, mio angelo della morte.* Take this one vendetta for me this one last time."

"I will do it, father." Martel whispered back. He closed his eyes a moment, he would take the vendetta and do the assassinations for his father, but he knew such an action would not be kept silent from the Commission long. A family's whole top administration did not simply just disappear overnight without causing a panic among the other crime families. Martel only hoped that his father's rash decision would not cost the Jerome's when the final move against Tito D'Salvatore came down. If the Corella's and Del Giorno's stopped supporting the Jerome's in the final hour it would be disastrous. But he trusted in his father, he had to, and somehow in his heart and soul he felt it would work out in the end.

"*Mille grazie mio figlio.* Thank you," Victor said and sat back down next to the large figure of his son. Two men so very different but yet so much alike; one a great sun who's charisma overshadowed all, and one who sat like a great black moon in the shadow of the sun, a distinct and overshadowing presence all his own.

"While you excise and cut out this cancer of deceitfulness, the Roman's. I work more and more to dump more assets into legitimate enterprises for the Jerome's." Victor sighed as they finished off their glass of wine together. "Joshua has shown me yet more legitimate things that are becoming hot commodities now that are being run by our crews. And even some that have connections and can make profits the old fashioned way as well, you will survive, Laurence and so will the Jerome's."

Martel nodded again and collected the empty wine glasses. His body and mind felt almost as it had that night he had avenged himself on Tashima Katsuro, alive with tension and also icy cold clarity. "Good night," he embraced his father briefly. "Will you keep an eye on Alyssa for me while I'm gone? Make sure she's Ok?"

"What is it with you two?" Victor looked at him with a twinkle in his old dark eye. But he was beginning to know, even if his son didn't.

Martel grew rigid, slamming a wall over his emotions. "Nothing, nothing at all," his voice an almost unnatural calm, "I am merely doing what you asked, integrating her into the Family."

"Of course," Victor nodded solemnly. His heart told him otherwise.

The next day Tommy and Gio came down to get whatever belongings of Alyssa's she wanted back up at the main house for the two weeks, as Martel locked up his house and set the alarm system. The only one who had a key was Victor and he would personally be the one who would come feed Martel's prized Koi fish. This news had surprised Alyssa to no end, the Don feeding the underboss's fish!

While Giovanni Aprile was a formidable looking man and could even make Alyssa a bit nervous on occasion she really was beginning to like and trust him as a friend, in some ways even more so than Tommy. She knew Gio was Martel's most trusted ally and lieutenant. When Martel had been Captain of the elite bodyguards Gio had been the one man, Martel had personally handpicked and trained to be his top crack-shot replacement. Now it was Gio who was the Captain of the main Special Guards the ones who dressed darker, seemed more imposing and professional and were the full time guards here on the estate, as compared to the regular wiseguys and soldiers who just helped out now and then or visited on occasion.

Around 5'11 but massively built with a body builder's, overly muscled physique. Gio had a completely shaved head and dark brown eyes that only enhanced his rather intimidating presence. He was one of the few bodyguards who wasn't an avid martial arts nut and while he had taken a few of the street combat classes from Martel, his main specialty was guns and simply his sheer strength.

For a big man with a gorilla-like presence he was actually very quiet-spoken, with a calm demeanor and in many ways it was this quiet, professional voice of his, coupled with his well muscled size, that intimidated people the most or got them to quickly settle down and cooperate, he was always polite and never arrogant or rude. In many ways Gio Aprile reminded Alyssa between a cross of Martel and Leonardo but without the Italian accent.

Baby-faced Tommy DeLuca of course worked as just one of the regular soldiers, also known as a 'button man' he did whatever his bosses asked him to, whether it was filling in as an extra guard here at the estate, nursing Alyssa, earning money for his capo or whatever else was required. He like most of the Jerome soldiers, was a 'jack-of-all-trades' who did a little of everything.

Somehow she couldn't picture Tommy doing anything mean or cruel. But Alyssa knew that was just ignorance and naivety on her part. She couldn't picture Cesare doing anything mean before either, but now she knew better. She was much better educated into the workings of the Family than she had been a few weeks or months ago.

Martel's goodbye to her had been just a simple, "Remember your work we started together Alyssa and the assignments I gave you. Continue with the lessons we worked on and remember what we have gone over. I expect to have lots to read when I come back." He gave her a quirk of his eyebrow a quick grim smile and then just silently turned and left.

A part of her felt like chunking a stone after her teacher and whacking him on the back of the head with it but she had a dread feeling he would merely catch it out of mid-air and be amused by it all. Besides, she certainly didn't want to show bad manners in front of either Gio or Tommy, but she could already feel her eyes filling with tears. 'Did her teacher think so little of her? Was the time they were spending meaning so little to him, when it meant so much to her?' She felt her heart sink to her feet.

"Ready?" Gio asked as he touched her lightly on her arm breaking her thoughts.

She nodded and practically scurried to his car, she didn't want either man to see her sorrow at Martel leaving.

At first Tommy had wanted to grill Alyssa about Martel and his oriental-themed house and what it was like to live with the mysterious underboss; but finding that she wasn't going to give any answers, he finally left her alone.

Alyssa was just not in the mood to discuss Martel at all. Her own confusion was growing by leaps and bounds. Weren't these people criminals? She was not supposed to be falling in love with them and especially not the overgrown Laurence Martel. Why should she care if he was leaving for two weeks! Why should she care if he said a proper good bye to her or not?

Even though it was a hot humid summer day, she decided she needed to walk and wanted some time alone. So changing into a tank top, and cotton shorts, she went outside into the baking sun. As the glare from the sun hit her, her mind wavered and she seemed to remember, that once upon a time; she liked to run, wild and free… Almost like some wild animal or bird, flying across the landscape.

'Kanashii' the name Martel had given her came back to her, the way his deep baritone voice said it. She stretched and then began to walk swiftly; she would warm up and then try jogging. Maybe down by the fence line, where the glorious and vast gardens were, there was far more privacy there.

Gio had set one of the guards to just casually follow her at a far distance, just to make sure she was Ok, but not at her heels or guarding her. After all, she was considered safe now by the bosses and not a threat to anyone.

She had been jogging for nearly 15 minutes, sweat beginning to coat on her as she rounded the far corner, past Martel's house and coming up past the stables when she suddenly saw him; the heavyset form of Cesare Ciccerone. She was about to turn back but it was too late, he had already spotted her. In fact he eagerly waved her towards him.

"Come over here, 'Lyss!" he called out using the familiar nickname he always called her and began walking over to her.

She had no choice but to go over to him, to do otherwise would be rude and disrespectful. After all, she really did like the man; she was just so confused in her own heart and felt so bad about what had happened to him because of his kindness to her.

"Yer looking good 'Lyss" he said as he stopped walking, sweat rolling off him. He was dressed in a light satin work out suit and he carried a cane, sunglasses still on his face. "I figured since ol' Doc Weintraub's got me on this bitch of a physical therapy program anyway, why not lose a few pounds while I'm at it, ya know? Who knows, maybe we can be walking buddies or somethin'." He placed his hands on his meaty thighs leaning on his knees taking a breather. His breaths coming in wheezing, winded gasps. "Come here and gimme a hug, I missed ya kiddo."

She hugged him hard, and she suddenly could not control the tears that came this time, they rushed out her eyes and spilled down her face.

"Hey, hey," He looked at her with concern, "Hush," he soothed gently. "Easy, what's wrong darlin'?"

She fumbled for the pen around her neck, the one with the golden hawk on it. She pulled out the small pad of paper and quickly scrawled, "*Oh God Cesare, I am so sorry, so very sorry!!! I never meant to get you in any trouble, I swear! It's all my fault! I am so sorry, please forgive me, please...*" she was going to write more but Cesare could already read what she was writing.

He firmly but gently grabbed the notebook out of her hand, read it briefly, ripped the page out of it and abruptly crumpled it up, holding the book out of her reach for a moment. "No, Alyssa. Just stop a minute, damn it," he said a bit harshly, his 'no nonsense' tone he used for breeches of etiquette. He sadly shook his head, "It's over now, do you hear me?" he lowered his voice, gently, soothingly, a friend again. "You have nothing to apologize for. If anyone has anything to apologize for; I do," he gave her a brotherly kiss on the forehead, "Ok? And I'm sorry. I really am darlin'."

He closed the notebook and gently gave it back to her but kept the crumpled note. "Shit happened, we both assumed the wrong stuff and we both learned from it, Ok? Look at you; you're running around and looking healthy. It makes my heart happy to see you looking better." He smiled with honesty at her.

She could still see the stitches in his lip and it took everything in her not to wince at his healing injuries.

"That's my girl," he affectionately patted her shoulder. "Hey, I needed a little break anyway and like I said, maybe we can be walking buddies here in the future. Oh!" he dug around in his pocket, "I got something for ya…" he pulled out a fairly melted mush of a Hershey bar and looked at it rather apologetically and then back at her. "Yeah, well, sorry about that one kid. It's pretty hot out here, ya know? I hear you're staying at the main house for the next two weeks, so I'll make sure I bring ya in a fresh whole pack of the damn candy bars personally tomorrow. Unmelted even!" He grinned at her and then waved happily at one of the passing guards, just as he always did. The man waved back warmly at Cesare.

"Ah, it's good to be back," Cesare nodded as he wiped some more sweat off him and stretched his sore muscles. "You take care, Ok darlin'? Dry up them tears, nothing to cry at 'Lyss, Ok? Really, trust me. Victor, Martel, Josh and me, were like this!" he crossed his fingers and said it with such sincerity that Alyssa smiled at him, she knew it was true. Cesare loved his Family, this Family and the men in it.

Alyssa's step was lighter then as she finished her walk/jog around the stable and down the other side through the bowed ancient oaks and maples, the whispering poplars and the shadowy pines.

CHAPTER 25 July 5th 1987

Carefully and with the practiced aim of a sniper with years of experience Martel leveled the scope of the rifle with the silencer on it barely out the narrowest crack of the window of his parked rental car and watched the two men as they stood in the parking lot of the local strip mall making a drug deal.

He was around 600 feet out, it was a long hit but he had done longer and he had two of them to do within the next three days and then the final four assassinations that would be a bit more personal. Right now he just had to make sure no 'civilians' were hit.

He was about to squeeze off the shot, when a woman suddenly walked through his line of fire with a child in her arms and another in tow. He exhaled and re-focused his mind. With a small grunt he willed her with his mind to hurry up and move, if his target moved on now, things would get a lot messier fast and he would have to go onto plan B. He adjusted his large frame inside his parked car and again re-sighted hoping no one would notice him in the parking lot. However he doubted it, this was a run down but very busy section of Philadelphia.

There! Now he saw he would have a quick and brief shot, the two men were finishing their deal, he would have to plan his shot perfectly before a stray car pulled into the line of fire. Again Martel almost willed the forces around him and squeezed off the shot. He saw his victim's head seem to explode outward; the second shot was already off and aimed lower as he already was compensating for the victim's downward fall. Another arc of blood shot out the center of the victim's chest. The man was dead before he even hit the ground.

Quickly he pulled in the gun and dismantled it in less than 10 seconds, stowed it under the front seat and then calmly and smoothly had the car in motion and in the flow of traffic leaving the stores parking lot. Five men down and four more victims to go, these targets he was also enjoying immensely for they were associates of the Roman Family and since they had once again defied Jerome orders by accepting the bribes of their enemies the D'Salvatores and worse getting caught, they were now open game in this war. Martel would enjoy taking Vito Roman's life personally, but right now, they were being done off the record and anonymously.

"See what happens when you take a vacation Mr. D'Salvatore?" Martel thought to himself with grim satisfaction, "All hell breaks loose".

So far the first four days had dragged on slowly, since Alyssa had moved back in to the main estates. While she indeed had more freedom and everyone seemed more friendly, her mind and heart seemed somehow empty and hollow. Often Alyssa would find herself wandering near the locked up home of her teacher Mr. Martel. Or many times she would simply go walking or jogging down by the back fence where the gardens were, it seemed that was the only place where there was any real privacy from the main hubbub of the house.

Sitting on the elegant marble benches, surrounded by the old world Italian style fountains she found herself often vividly running through the times she had spent with the enigmatic Martel, their lessons together, his touch, and the sound of his voice. It was also in this place that she allowed her mind to dwell on the images her mind had dredged up and remembered from her visions and memories. Where she solidified them, catalogued them and tried to put them in some sense of order.

Some of these things she wrote in her journals and others she did not, others she kept deep in her own mind, the visions and images she knew she would never forget.

She knew now that she had indeed been kidnapped and she was sure it was this Darius and the TJ, the skinny, scarred up man. She also knew the vivid details up until the point that TJ had beaten her to a bloody pulp.

She knew before her kidnapping she had been named Sarah, that her boyfriend- fiancé had betrayed her, (But yet she couldn't remember his name) and he had been cheating with another woman. She also knew she had no feelings for this man anymore. Her heart was dead to him; she sensed that even before the kidnapping her heart was betrayed so badly by him that it was hurt beyond any feelings anymore between them. 'Is that why I am reaching out to Martel so badly?' she wondered, 'If so, what a strange choice to make. One doesn't go around on the rebound falling for the underboss of a Crime Family.'

She knew for certain that Victor Jerome was not in any way her blood relative or true uncle but for some reason known only to him, rescued her from Vito Roman's hellhole. She also knew that for some reason that even she could not fully explain there seemed to be some strange connection between her and Victor. As though for some inexplicable reason that she would never be able to understand or explain they needed one another. She also felt that there was still something more she had to do for Victor, but she had no idea what.

She knew that she and Cesare got in trouble for talking about too much stuff and that she had talked to Victor in his Office, but yet a lot of that was like her accident, blurry images and vague ghosts and shadows. She didn't remember all that was said in that Office that day, only that Victor said that she would be living with Mr. Martel and he would be teaching her the right lessons in *omerta* and getting along in the family. And that after that Cesare had obviously gotten the snot beat out of him, for filling her in.

Alyssa sighed and gathered her books and things, as she watched another summer storm rolling up in the southwestern sky. An unconscious tremor ran through her; for some reason storms always gave her chills and the electricity from them always seemed to make her nervous and on edge.

A small dark Honda Civic smoothly pulled up, it was Gio Aprile's. "There you are Ms. Alyssa," he said in his calm, professional voice. "Mr. Jerome wanted me to find you, said a storm was blowing in. Come on, I'll give you a ride back," he gave a quick nod with his chin.

She smiled politely back at Gio, then trotted over to his car as he reached over and unlocked the passenger door for her. The air conditioner was going full blast and on the radio was Pink Floyd's 'The Wall'. She looked over at him and smiled as she quirked an eyebrow in a good imitation of her teacher Laurence Martel. She never pictured Gio Aprile as a rock and roll kind of guy!

He just chuckled back at her as he drove her back to the main house, as his fingers absent-mindedly drummed out the rhythm of the song on his steering wheel. "Hey, Pink Floyd rocks!" he confided in her. Alyssa nodded in agreement with him.

As she usually did, she was just going to eat dinner with everyone else that night in the main area where the staff usually served a large, buffet style, dinner for all the guards and their families, including whoever was visiting. Especially since so many people had different schedules, but just as she was about to grab a plate Mr. Aprile gently pulled her aside with one well-muscled arm.

"Ah, Ms. Alyssa?" he asked gently, "Mr. Jerome would like to know if you would like to dine with him tonight. He has to make some phone calls first but he took the liberty of having a dinner for two set up in the study over on the west wing if you wish to join him?"

Alyssa nodded yes and put her plate back. She certainly wasn't going to say no to Don Victor! She almost wished she would have known ahead of time so she could have changed into something nicer. As they briefly passed the Office, that dark door where Victor did his business she could hear Victor's voice inside talking with a few others.

Outside stood another guard and Gio and the guard nodded briefly to one another as they passed. He led her down another hallway into a part of the house she had been forbidden before to go into, Victor's private library and study.

Rosette was just walking out, wheeling a cart ahead of her. "Ciao Alyssa," she smiled at her, "Giovanni, have you eaten yet?" she then asked Alyssa's shadow in a motherly manner.

"No not yet, later. In an hour my shift will be over and I'll get to eat." He smiled briefly at Rosette, "Besides, I'm taking Clarissa out tonight." Both Rosette and Gio smiled knowingly at each other and then Rosette continued down the hall wheeling her cart in front of her.

Gio opened the door to the private study-library for Alyssa and motioned her in. "I'll be right outside if you need me, Ms. Alyssa." He then quietly closed the door behind her.

Alyssa noticed Rosette had already set up a wonderful table for two in the middle of the room complete with glowing candles and covered dishes, already it smelled wonderful. A fire crackled low and inviting in the fireplace adding to the soothing ambiance. All around this huge study were large bookshelves filled with hundreds of elegant and rare books, the real kind; leather bound editions and classics. She walked around glancing at the titles, everything from Shakespeare's works to The Art of War by Sun Tzu. She followed Hemmingway and Twain down to Melville and even saw several rare 1st editions of Edgar Allen Poe; there was Dante's Inferno, Milton's Paradise Lost and Several of Mario Puzo's books on Mafia life, The Godfather as well as The Sicilian and several other 'mob-gangster type' titles. There were even Law Books dealing with the Federal RICO statute (Racketeer, Influenced and Corrupt Organization laws) and Legal books on the Organized Crime control Act, as well as other non-fiction work.

"Good evening child," Victor's warm voice suddenly filled the library as comfortable as the crackling fire and the burning candles.

She spun around, both nervous and happy to see him at the same time. She had not seen him since that day at Martel's when she had passed out.

"It's all right Alyssa, you can look at the books," he smiled lightly with that twinkle in his elderly but sharp eye. "Obviously I have a fondness for them myself, I see you do too."

She also noticed Victor had quite an impressive chess set in the corner. His was a massive set, much more elegant and intricate than

Martel's. The pieces depicted the ancient Romans vs. The Vandal barbarian horde. Each piece was nearly four inches high, made of solid Italian marble. They were stunningly carved down to the smallest detail like miniature statues of fine art, the playing board itself was made of onyx and marble, trimmed in solid 18k gold and inlaid with silver, a mahogany Chess clock sat near the board. As she was admiring his set, lost in the elegance and detail of it he had come right up along side her, it wasn't until she noticed his unique smell of peppermint and his aftershave that she turned and saw him there. Like Martel, the old man could move quite stealthy and quietly when he wanted to.

"Come, Alyssa," he said gently offering his hand to her. "I know that I promised to spend some time with you and here it has been already several days since I have had time. So, I thought tonight we would take the time to get reacquainted with one another, eh?" his smile was inviting, kind.

She accepted his old hand in her soft smooth one as he led her back to the table in the middle of the room. The storm had started outside it was not the violent storm like at Martel's that one night, just heavy rain and the occasional rumble of thunder.

"I always like a good storm, don't you?" Victor smiled.

Alyssa had a very weird sense of deja'vu then… in fact in many ways she almost felt as though she had done this before with someone else. 'Martel and Victor, they are so much alike' her mind thought.

"Now, let's see what Rosette cooked up for us tonight…" Victor opened up the covers on their dishes. It was one of Alyssa's Italian favorites, veal and eggplant piccata. Victor chatted lightly while they ate, mostly about the house, various books, and other light topics. This was fine with Alyssa as she was busy enjoying every scrumptious bite of her meal and the fine wine.

There was a shift inside Alyssa this time and she felt no more fear towards the old man. Yes she respected him, respected him immensely, she knew who and what he was and what he represented. She knew what he was capable of, she knew he was what the ladies in the kitchen called "Padrone" the father and leader of this Family and she knew he had a lot of responsibilities. She had seen him angry, she had seen him humbled and nearly dead (when she donated a kidney to him) and she sensed there was more to him than she would ever know. She would never see him as weak, in her eyes, never that.

"Come child," his voice broke through her thoughts as another soft rumble of thunder rolled across the sky. "Martel tells me he has been teaching you Chess, eh?" again that mischievous twinkle in the old man's eye. "I have quite a love for the game myself."

Alyssa's stomach was filled with good food and her body comfortably warm and sleepy from the glass of wine. But she felt that hollow feeling in her whenever Martel's name was bought up and she also felt naked at times in front of Victor. As though there was nothing that could be hidden from him. Again, it was like her teacher Martel, these two men seemed to be able to *see*, right through her!

"Do I sense you miss him, Alyssa?" Victor asked casually as he set up the pieces on the elegant chessboard.

She nodded yes and pulled up a chair, watching the rain gently cascade down the window on the now darkening evening.

"Ah," Victor nodded. "Understandable, considering the two of you have lived in close proximity for awhile." He glanced at her over his reading glasses, kindly not accusingly or strangely, as others might have. "It warms my heart to see you getting along with him then." He said honestly.

She was playing white so it was her move first, after some thinking she moved out her pawn and waited for Victor to move his.

He studied the board a few moments then looked back up at her. "I'll tell you what, Alyssa," he moved his pawn out strong and then sat back in his comfortable chair. "Tomorrow I will let you come with me as I feed Martel's fish I have something I want to show you. I think you might like it." A genuine smile played on the old man's lips that lit up his entire face. For that instant she truly did feel as though he was her Uncle.

She couldn't help but noticed as they played that Victor indeed played very similar to Laurence and while he didn't do any grand death scenes, he loved to chat lively with her. His mood was bright and cheery and he was quite complimentary with his praise, although Alyssa could tell right away she was playing against a true master of the game. He would play with her the way a cat would play with a mouse, to prolong the length of the game so they could talk and chat, but she knew Victor was in control of the chess board the whole time. Somehow she knew that old man was at least 40 steps ahead of her the whole time and she had no idea how he was doing it.

Each time he did win, he did it with grace and with a quiet dignity always making it seem close. Alyssa knew better in her heart, she knew Victor could have checkmated her a few times far more quickly. On a few of her moves, she caught her own errors immediately after she made them and knew he was just prolonging the game, keeping it going in order to keep the conversation and evening going. But she was truly enjoying Victor's company that evening, so she was in no hurry for it to end and he seemed to genuinely enjoy her company as well.

Finally around 9:00 pm she could hear the soft chiming of the great grandfather clock in the hallway. Both of them had been curled up on different couches reading, near the crackling fire. Victor had told her, "Go ahead, grab a book or two and we'll read." And so for the last hour they had simply enjoyed spending quiet time in each other's company reading.

315

A sudden insistent beeping of his watch startled her. "Ah," He rose almost apologetically. She noticed a slight tremble to his hand as he put down his book. "I'm afraid it's time for this old man to turn in. However, you are more than welcome to borrow a couple of my books from time to time if you like. I will let Mr. Aprile know you have my permission." He gently said.

She gathered up, Lord of the Rings, which she had been reading and also gently took down a book of poetry by Carl Sandburg.

"Wait," Victor grabbed a book and slipped it into the other two books.

She tilted her head to read the title 'The Seven Samurai'

"It deals with war, courage, honor, Family, duty. Kind of like 'The Godfather' but in the Orient, in ancient Feudal times over in Japan…" Victor let the sentence hang. His eyes bore into hers, in mutual understanding. He didn't need to say anymore. He was giving her a key; a key to begin to help her understand the enigmatic Martel.

She took a deep breath, holding back the tear of gratefulness that had threatened to spill down her cheek as she politely kissed his cheek and mouthed "*Thank you!*" her face splitting into a barely controlled smile that lit up the room.

"Good night child. I'm glad I made you happy." Victor patted her shoulder gently. "Now, I must really go to bed. I will see you at breakfast tomorrow."

Vito Bonnaro was a small man but his sheer presence made him seem much bigger than his 5'4" size. He dressed immaculately, had a neatly trimmed salt and pepper mustache and even though he was close to 70 he still had a full head of thick wavy grey hair. His eyes were as dark and sharp as black onyx, only the lines in his face and the age spots on his hands belied his age. He walked with a cane and a slight limp but his mind was also as sharp as a tack. For over 40 years he had been the head of his *Famiglia* here in Giarre, Sicily and one of the most respected Dons around. His elegant old world palazzo sat on the far eastern end of the Island near the shoreline, with a splendid view of Mt. Etna to the west, it was a testament to his Clan and *famiglia's* long-standing power.

"Don Bonnaro!" Antonio DiMone respectfully kissed embraced Vito Bonnaro and kissed his cheek. DiMone was the Boss of one of the Miami Crime Families. Antonio had grown up in here in Sicily not to far away as a young boy, but his family had moved to the U.S. when he was only 10. However his main missions here today was that he was the acting liaison right now between the Jerome's and the Bonnaro's and he was also setting up real estate and deals in Miami for the Bonnaro clan.

"Don DiMone, I welcome you to my home and back to your own motherland. I hope your trip in was good." Vito Bonnaro spoke in a quiet voice.

"It was thank you." Antonio glanced around briefly enjoying the view. The two sat on a wonderful patio in the backyard garden of Vito's Italian villa, framed by the shade of arched fig trees, under a large arbor that was entwined with grape leaves. On one side one in the far distance one could make out the slope of Sicily's volcano, Mt. Etna and one the other side the blue-green of the ocean. A warm breeze caressed both the men as they sat down, palm fronds swaying in the sunny air as small lizards scuttled around the stone fence. Neither man paid any attention to the several guards who sat around here and there with *luparas* the favored Sicilian weapons of the modified shotguns, while a few others carried rifles or machetes.

A heavyset woman, with a lovely face bought out a tray filled with wine and cheeses. Like her husband she was elderly but yet still retained a dignified youthfulness that seemed to defy age. A sageness and strength that was undeniable, just like her husband, together they seemed a team that fit as well as hand with a glove. Giving a small wink to her beloved Vito, she wordlessly served the wine to both of the Don's and placed the cheese and bread.

"Thank you, dear Lena." Vito Bonnaro said to his wife, as she quietly left the two Dons alone and went to see if the guards wanted some wine and cheese as well.

It was here in this rugged old world paradise that Theodore Jerome had grown up and learned values of the old ways of '*Cosa Nostra*' during his summer vacations. It was here that Leonardo Tagretta had loyally served as one of Don Vito Bonnaro most trusted enforcers and assassins, before being sent to work for the Jerome's and it was here that the final element of the destruction of the D'Salvatores was now being planned.

The two men enjoyed the serenity of the view for a few moments and then Don Bonnaro turned to Antonio DiMone. "I understand that you say Tito D'Salvatore is now down in Miami as we speak? Trying to forge a new alliance with you there as well?" both men spoke in Sicilian.

"Yes, he is trying to hook into a deal with my capo, Joseph Cimino. However, Cimino is totally oath sworn to us. We have paid Cimino well to play with D'Salvatore, string him along a bit, eh? Since we already have a lot of people coming in from the old country here anyway, it is a perfect cover. Tito will not know if we are truly helping him or not. The whole time, the immigrants are actually your people Vito; yours and mine, coming in to strengthen the Jerome's and your own Family and then just as Tito thinks he is calling the shots we give our final command and override them and it all goes to hell in a hand basket for him." DiMone smiled wanly.

317

"I like the way you think, my friend," Vito said. He watched as two lizards scuffled over the best sunning place on the stone wall, he trusted his gut instinct and it had never let him down in all his nearly 69 years. Right now it was as quiet as the mighty volcano in the distance. He felt Ok with this plan, trusted DiMone. Victor and he had been in constant communication but they had, had to censor a lot of their conversation because of all this 'RICO' nonsense. He still didn't understand all of what the RICO laws were, only that now the United States had been coming down hard on *La Cosa Nostra* over the last decade.

He couldn't wait to see his dear friend and fellow *Padrone*, Victor Jerome in a few months in person. He had hoped it would have been Theodore who would have come here today or maybe his old Capo Leonardo or even the 'new blood' he had heard so much about Joshua Demonico. But he trusted Victor and his decision to secretly ally with DiMone and send him down to meet Vito. He had to; Vito knew Victor wouldn't have sent him someone untrustworthy if he could have sent someone else. 'They must be being watched closely by both the enemy and the federal agents', was the only thing Vito could figure. Victor had to play it safe and quiet and keep his cards close to his heart.

"Ok then, my friend." Don Vito smiled. "I appreciate all your hard work in this." He reached in his pocket and produced a small bag; inside was close to 25k in loose diamonds. "A gift from the Bonnaro's to our new friends the DiMones. Keep up the good work and let D'Salvatore think he is indeed getting support from you, getting fresh soldiers in from Sicily. Let him think he is even getting a free ride back to the homeland when all is said and done. But in the end, when that order comes..." the Don's gentle voice was still calm but the onyx eyes held a hardness and control that would not be denied. "It better indeed go to hell in a hand basket for him, you understand?"

"Of course it will." Antonio smiled and bowed his head slightly, he swallowed deeply, feeling the power from Don Vito Bonnaro, "believe me; we want only the strongest alliance with you and the Jerome's."

"We will reward, all those who are loyal to us and to the Jerome's." Vito spoke honestly, neither harshly nor arrogantly. "And we will crush all those who oppose us or betray us. For we still have many friends hidden in many places. And we are watching the watchers. That is how it is done in this country, my friend." He toasted Antonio "*Salute.*"

"*Salute,*" Antonio DiMone drank with him. He could see just exactly why men feared, respected and clambered to follow Don Bonnaro, he and Victor Jerome were indeed a lot alike cut very much from the same cloth.

Later that night after Antonio had flown back to the states, Vito sat with his son Gino, now his consigliere. "What do you think Gino?" he asked him. He trusted Gino; his son read all of these new laws, especially all this "RICO" stuff pertaining to the U.S. and the Federal Laws, for an old man like Vito all these laws did was muddle his brain.

"If Victor had not contacted us personally, I would have been more worried but we got his last letter and the one from our friend Martel." Gino smiled. "I trust them both, so far all seems legit. Do I think DiMone is trying to skim a bit extra for himself?" he made the sign of skimming, "Of course, but right now that is the least of the worries, right now his loyalty to us and the Jerome's needs to be impeccable."

Gino came around and sat next to his father, Vito. "Look *Padrone*," he smiled at him. "Over there in the US, their police and agents know Jerome's and D'Salvatores are gearing up for *mannagge*, for war. They are all watching, even the other *brugads*. Victor has Martel running all over trying to get last minute business done and the D'Salvatores are trying to get last minute business done, right now it is the quiet before the storm. And then it will open up with the ferocity of the great volcano over there. Their *mannagge* will erupt like Etna. Now they have to pull back and prepare. Both of us know the feeling, eh? You will see Victor in Jamaica soon, in just a couple months. I will have everything ready for you here and everything ready to send to you in the United States."

Vito smiled at his son and consigliere. "I am lucky to have you at my side, eh" he gave him a light squeeze on his shoulder. "Make sure all is ready for my departure in when the time comes. Remember I am traveling very, very light. No bodyguards except for one or two good ones. It will be just Lena and I. That is part of the plan."

"But *Padrone*! Papa!!" Gino stood up then, alarm in his eyes. What his father was asking was so risky. A Don of his caliper out with just one or two guards was virtually naked, anyone could take him out.

"Gino..." Vito looked him deep in the eyes. "Trust this old man, please. The chickens are setting a trap for the fox, eh? If we don't..." he paused "If Victor and I don't do this, then it won't get settled in the 'old way'. We want the *nemico* to try and take Victor out down there."

"But what if they try and take you out down there as well?" Gino shook his head in disbelief.

"They can try, Gino but I have no intention of letting them." Vito smiled. "We do have a plan you know, us crazy old men." He smiled warmly. "Please trust us, eh?"

"I do, but I do worry about you." Gino sighed.

"I know. I'm sorry, it's a parents revenge, eh Gino?" he smiled briefly, playfully at his grown son, now a man. Father and son briefly embraced before moving on to discussion of other Family business.

Chapter 26- *July 6th 1987*

Laurence Martel had finished killing his sniper hits, he had already zigzagged over a 4 state area in 5 days and he now had to move onto hits that were going to require him to be a lot closer and more personal in his killing. These last 3 hits though were going to bring him some extreme personal pleasure, especially now.

While he had not allowed his heart to feel before on a hit, this time it was beginning to stir all on its own. The Roman's were a personal thorn to him, not only for their constant flip-flopping and disrespect to his father and the Commission, but their reneging on their deal to stay away from trafficking in white slavery. And while they were much more quiet and sneaky about it, funded under the table by D'Salvatore money, it would be one thorn Martel was going to utterly destroy once and for all. Martel was indeed very much a man like his father who followed strictly the same draconian laws of loyalty and respect.

As he drove back over the New Jersey border during the early morning hours he wondered briefly about Alyssa; if she was adjusting during his absence or if she had experienced any more of her terrors?

He hoped Joshua would not be there if she did, he knew Joshua had little tolerance or patience with her, he didn't know why the two so disliked each other. It was none of his business; in fact he mentally chastised himself for allowing his mind to wander down this pathway at all. He was supposed to stop and meet his mistress Diana tonight at 6:30, it had been nearly 3 months since he had seen her and he did have at least some reputation to uphold. His heart wasn't in it though and his mind kept repeatedly wandering to Kanashii.

As he turned onto the New Jersey turnpike, he briefly remembered that time he had killed Tashima Katsuro in revenge for Miyoko. It was one of the very few times a killing had almost cleansed his soul, even though it almost cost him his life. He knew killing the Roman's Top Administration would be like his killing of Tashima Katsuro, something that would almost cleanse him and in a karmic twist of fate, it would be his one unspoken 'gift' to Kanashii. For if the Roman's hadn't been in the white slave business, to begin with, she would have never been kidnapped.

He stopped at a gas station and checked to make sure all was in preparation. He was back on home turf and skirting both Roman and D'Salvatore territory so there was no way to really disguise who he was. He was only going to have the element of surprise, speed and stealth on his side. He had two of his martial arts throwing/stabbing knives in easy grasp along his beltline, and his gloves on for to assure no prints. He wore just his black pants, black T-shirt and black wrap around sunglasses. He had one 'quiet gun' (one with a silencer on) and one noisy, 'throw away' gun. (One with tape on the handle designed to make a lot of noise and attract attention but hold no prints). These he kept hidden under the seat.

He swung the car back into the lane and headed east, he would have time to get at least 2 of the killings done before seeing Diana tonight.

Alyssa had woken up a bit stiffly and after showering and dressing shuffled downstairs to breakfast. She had continued to take the 4 types of supplements Martel had prescribed for her but she sure did miss his massages. Even the Tai Chi and workouts he did with her always seemed to relax her. She occasionally worked out on the Nautilus equipment here at the gym but for some reason, she seemed to get extremely nervous of the gymnasium.

She was fairly sure it was more because of the one time her and Victor had their misunderstanding in here than anything else. Many of the men did the martial arts, but none seemed to have the same graceful moves as her teacher. Joshua had the ferocity but he didn't have the balance and overall grace that Martel did.

Joshua Demonico was just all raw emotion, The Panther. He grated on her nerves and made her wary and frazzled. She knew he felt the same way about her and yet she didn't know why there existed an animosity between them. None of the other men seemed to have that problem with Joshua when she watched them interacting with him, Joshua was all smiles; laughing and joking with his compari's, even with Cesare whom he had welcomed back just as Martel had said.

In fact since Alyssa had returned to the main House all of the men had treated Cesare as if nothing had ever happened between them. They ignored his injuries, made no mention of them and just welcomed him back and treated him as before.

"Hey Alyssa!" Cesare's voiced pulled her out of her thoughts as he poured her a glass of orange juice. He also was looking better, most of his bruises were fading now to a yellowish green, the cast had come off his arm and he wore a soft walking cast on his knee only and nearly all of the swelling on his face had gone down. "G'morning darlin', grab you some food and eat, before the morning rush comes through." His smile was a bit more crooked and he had a rather small angry scar that he would carry the rest of his life on his lip and nose.

She smiled back at him and grabbed some scrambled eggs, took the juice he had poured her and threw some pieces of bacon on there as well.

He was still lovable Cesare, but she had noticed the subtle change in him, the soft shadow that often seemed behind his eyes. He seemed a bit harder now, more serious. "How could he not?" She figured. "Aren't we both changed forever after that experience, Cesare?" She looked him in the eye a moment as they both seemed to smile grimly and nod at the unspoken thoughts.

A few more men came in and grabbed breakfast including Gio Aprile and Joshua Demonico. It gave Alyssa a deep sense of sadistic pleasure to know that whenever Gio was around Joshua seemed not to pester or bother her at all. Whether it was because Gio was Martel's right hand man and reported directly to him or whatever the deal was but it seemed whenever Gio was there, Joshua was actually civil and either ignored her completely or was nice. The only other time he acted like that was when Victor Jerome himself was there.

Gio Aprile slid in next to Alyssa, his plate loaded with food. "Good morning Ms. Alyssa." He smiled and spoke softly. He leaned in close to her, his voice for her ears only, "I have a message from a mutual tall friend of ours. He says to tell you 'hello', and he should be back in another week." Gio nodded and also casually slipped her over two cassette tapes of Pink Floyd and a wrapped present. "Thought you might like listening to them when you jog or whatnot." His plate held enough food for 3 people, "When you're done with those I have some AC-DC you can check out as well. The present is a walkman I picked up for ya, I see you jogging around here all the time so figured you'd like a little music with that." He grinned widely and then began drinking down some vile looking protein shake.

She bumped him lightly with her shoulder and gave him a brief but sincere hug of thanks. Her heart raced. He had spoken with Martel and Martel had actually sent her a message back! And she was touched at his gift of music to her, it seemed ever since she had moved back into the main house, that most of the people had worked hard to make her feel at home.

About that time Victor came down and joined the group as well. All conversation hummed along then in various English or Italian conversations. Occasionally some of the men made the signal of the finger to the eye or glanced at Alyssa, she already knew that signal. It was the 'censor the conversation' signal, but most of the men now knew to watch themselves around her anyway and just treated her like they would Weintraub or any of the other wives, mothers or Jerome Family women.

Once she remembered she would have felt an outsider at these conversations, even nervous and a bit anxious when the men began to raise their voices and argue, getting noisy, teasing one another in loud, raucous Italian. But now, after learning from Rosette and the others she welcomed the customary bantering between the men, it felt like "home". In all honesty it was the only home she knew, she didn't know any other. While she was getting some memories back, she wasn't getting any memories back on any level of any regarding anything that would have been a prior home life. What little she did remember had not been pleasant.

After they had eaten she and Victor walked down the winding drive together. It was going to be another very hot and humid July day, "They say some bad storms are heading this way…" Victor idly said as they meandered down the path. "Some kind of freak, summer tropical storm type thing but I don't think it will come this far inland. I don't feel it in my bones, the birds don't feel it." He looked around. "I think we will just get a lot of rain."

She had heard something on the TV lately about the weathermen watching a surprise tropical storm and about the remnants of it were supposedly blowing into the NY area.

"You know how those weathermen always want to blow things up to make a story bigger." Victor smiled wryly. "Pardon the pun." He chuckled.

Alyssa turned and noticed that the huge JEROME-1 Limo was trailing them with Cesare at the wheel just cruising idly about 10 yards behind them.

"I figured Cesare can give us a ride to Martel's house when we're done at the Aviary." Victor smiled. "But this part of the walk will do us good. Now..." Victor smiled broadly as they crested the small hill and she saw the building that had always been off limits to her, Don Jerome's aviary. "This is my aviary. My special place," Victor spoke almost reverently, "My thinking place and my meditation place. The one place where I come when I want to just be alone, to just come and relax..." gently he took her hand and led her down towards it.

As they walked up to the building that was around 100' x 60' Alyssa could see it was screened with a set of inner and outer doors. It had a well-constructed roof and additional awnings or sidings that could be pulled down to protect it. Already from here she could hear tiny peeping and chirping from the inhabitants inside.

Victor walked over to the first main door and carefully opened it. "It holds many memories for me, good and bad. Maybe it can be a place for you to try and find your memories?" he held the door open for her, his eyes warm and inviting. She ducked under his arm and he carefully closed the outer door.

They walked down the short foyer; in here were tubs that contained seed, medicines, cleaning equipment and a variety of implements to work in the main aviary as well as a few nets to catch any stray birds that escaped from the first inner door. There was a small portable radio here and one old rickety wooden chair. Victor walked over to the portable radio and turned it on, some static came on and then classical music came on over the radio from the local PBS station.

"Now Alyssa," Victor turned to her with a gleam in his eyes, "Come meet the kids." He motioned her to the second door.

Alyssa was truly impressed and awestruck. The main aviary held many branches and was free-flighted, inside there must have been close to 100 small colorful, tiny little finches darting this way and that as they cavorted, hopped from branch to branch or flew in nimble and agile formations. Victor made a soothing whistling noise and slowly opened the second door. The finches all collectively seemed to stop what they were doing for a moment, then in one collective swarm they took to the air and began to fly gracefully around the inside of the aviary, chirruping excitedly. "Go ahead." Victor smiled and motioned.

Alyssa again ducked under his arm and he slid in as well. It was like being in a maelstrom of birds! They flew gracefully all around them, a moving cloud of colorful tiny birds that swooped in spectacular circles as a collective whole and then alighted once again on branches, the walls, as well as on Alyssa and Victor. They chirruped, peeped and sang their little hearts out, hopping joyfully from branch to branch or from person to person.

She laughed a silent laugh of joy as she watched the birds playing around them. It was truly magical, never had she seen anything like it in her life! No, she was certain she had indeed never in any of her memories seen anything like this. It was like something out of a movie or book and she was like a child absorbing it all for the very first time and the utter and unadulterated pure joy lit up her face.

Gently she tried to pet one of the tiny, round whimsical birds and of course it flew off. She laughed and looked over at Victor.

Victor held out her hand in his and a bunch of little birds suddenly landed on her arm. She smiled and laughed again. Victor's face lit up as well in a warm sincere smile, as he watched Alyssa's reaction to his birds. "Isabella, my late wife loved the little birds and this place too." Victor smiled. "I see you do as well."

Alyssa nodded and then gently shook her hand so that the birds took flight again. She loved watching them fly together, how they seem to instinctively know to stick together in a collective formation and how they responded so deeply to Victor as well.

A few actually would dodge into Victor's pockets, "Hey," he chided playfully, "I have no treats in there, you little *bricconcello*." he winked and gently retrieved the bird from his shirt pocket. It quickly flew off from his hand.

At that moment there was no way that Alyssa could have even remembered Victor's anger from the other day, in here he was just Victor a kindly old gentleman, and not Don Jerome the most feared Mafia kingpin on the East coast. It was as though at this moment her mind could not even conceive of his other 'darker' side.

"I tell you what, child." Victor softly spoke to Alyssa, as he draped one arm over her shoulders, "This can be your place too if you wish." He turned and looked her in the eye. "I know sometimes with Martel out of town or what not, you may want a place to come and think, a place that is away from it all. I thought you might like it, so feel free to come here anytime, Ok? You have my permission."

She quietly reached over and gently hugged and kissed Victor on the cheek causing a few of the little fuzzlings that were perched on both of them to take off and fly around before alighting on them again. His strong arms encircled her body and squeezed her comfortingly as well.

"Good, I'm glad it makes you happy." He said honestly. "Now, come help me with these seed troughs and watering bins, I will show you what to do and when I am out of town, you can take care of my birds, do we have a deal?" he glanced at her. She nodded and then the two of them faced each other and seriously, formally, shook hands. She silently gave her heart and oath to Victor in this now, she would take the utmost care and responsibility for his birds when he was not here and was honored he trusted her with such a precious and wonderful task.

Together they fed and watered the birds and washed down the cement floor, all the while Victor chatted to her about the aviary and its inhabitants: How to tell the male finches from the females. Who were good breeders and who were not, how to slow breeding down or speed it up, how to check the nesting boxes and clean them out and other such important knowledge.

Alyssa enjoyed listening to his sage voice and gentle mentoring in the way of the birds and finally she began to feel relaxed and good again since Martel had left. She began to truly feel accepted by Victor Jerome himself and she began to feel a new and stronger bond beginning with the old man too. Through this gift of sharing his most special and private hobby with her he was not only opening a door to his own soul to her, but showing her that he truly was accepting her as his niece, giving her dignity and joy in a hobby they both loved.

Occasionally Victor would just look over at her and smile, as though those dark eyes of his were penetrating her very soul.

Alyssa would often wonder, "How does he sense my moods, read my thoughts? Is it by my body language? Or even more unnerving, as though with a single glance he seems to understand what is inside me. It must be because he is a warrior and diplomat." She figured. "He has to be able to read his opponents to see their weaknesses and strengths. To be a diplomat he must be able to know his allies and enemies most intimately."

She was partially right. Victor had that inborn ability which he had honed even further with Eddie when he had become quadriplegic. His son, Theodore was graced with that instinctual ability as well.

"Now," Victor broke her thoughts, "always remember to shut the double doors, so the birds don't fly the coop, eh?" he chuckled. He glanced around, "As I said, I don't think the storm is coming. If it was through, that is what the awnings are for. The coop can be secured from the outside or in."

Victor checked his pockets and with a soft chuckle fished out one tiny angry peeping finch who had found the perfect nesting spot in his shirt pocket. "Always you isn't it, naughty Peppi?" He chided sternly but playfully. The bird peeped and scolded right back at him. Victor showed her the tiny little band on its leg. "Number 416. I call this one Peppino, Peppi for short, 9 times out of 10 I have to check my pockets because Peppi will be in them." He slightly opened the inner door. "No jailbreak for you Peppi…" he gently tossed Peppino back in with the other finches.

Alyssa just laughed, but gently checked her long hair and clothes as well. She didn't have any little finches hiding on her, just some droppings from where they had landed on her.

Victor gave a little chuckle as they walked out. "I would advise wearing old clothes." She noticed he often kept an old sweater by the door here that he changed in and out of. "Now let's go over to Martel's and you can help feed the fish."

It was definitely hot and humid now and they both welcomed the relief of the AC in the long black limo that waited for them. It would have been a long walk to Martel's house otherwise.

Rain was pouring heavily down through the streets of New York City as the remnants of the storm blew into the city. All it was bringing with it was heavy rain and some rumbles of thunder along with some angry gusts of wind. He had indeed gotten two more killings done; once again the rain had worked in his favor not against him.

Martel paced around the 6th floor of the elegant penthouse apartment of his *comare*, Diana Dellano; he had paid for this apartment for her. Diana had cooked him some pasta with Alfredo sauce but his heart was not in it. Today she seemed to get on his nerves more than anything. He longed to be back in the sanctuary of his own home, in his space. He wanted to spend time meditating in his temple, to see the clan sword of Yamashita again, he wondered how Kanashii….

He wearily rubbed his temples. Kanashii, why was his mind drifting to her now? His mind began to wander down this whole mess with Diana, including the first time they had met. It had been a cool September night nearly six years ago…

Martel stood like a large silent sentinel at one of the high stakes Poker games that Leonardo and Patrizio ran downtown. Illegal poker games that bought some good profits for the Family, the players were usually associates and non-made members; everyone from doctors to lawyers to corrupt politicians.

Today one of the newspaper editors was there, Krelis van Courtlandt a rich man who loved to cheat on his wife and blow money at illegal poker games; along with a famous neurosurgeon, a lawyer and the Congressman from the 4th district in New Jersey.

Since there had been some shortages on tributes lately to the Boss, Martel was down today at the game to show face and make sure everything ran smoothly. With him were 6 bodyguards and of course the capos' and head of these high roller games, Leonardo and Patrizio.

It was the Family's job to make sure everything was supplied for these 'High Rollers' to keep them gambling longer and paying out more money. Expensive alcohol, women, good food, all of it was available to the men and doled out generously. After all it was not uncommon for some of these players to drop 100,000$ or more over a long night.

It was also not uncommon for some of the high rollers to bring in mistresses or women of their own. One of the players, the congressman from New Jersey routinely bought in a regular and long time mistress named Valerie, and the newspaper editor Krelis was known to bring in various mistresses or prostitutes on occasion. However today he had someone new and Martel could instinctively tell she wasn't a prostitute or mistress.

"Who is that woman?" he had casually and discreetly asked Leonardo during the game.

Leonardo almost looked shocked at his boss, "You not know?" he asked with genuine surprise, but his eyes held a sparkle of deep amusement and sarcasm. "That is the famous Diana Dellano she writes the weekly 'Crime Beat' column, for the big New York paper, eh?" he spoke in Italian.

"That is D. Dellano?" Martel asked his eyebrow quirking up in surprise. He had always thought 'D. Dellano' a male writer since they seemed to write so intimately about the Mafia life and the goings on of the various crime families on the NE Coast.

"You didn't know?" Len smirked gently, teasingly.

Martel just shook his head no in surprise. "I had no idea." He said calmly. It was a column that was read often by the various *brugads*, almost as a way to keep up what was going on in the different Families. Who had died, who had been arrested, who the FBI was bothering, etc. "Does she come here often? She doesn't look like a *comare*?"

"First time I see her here," Len said his arms folded across his chest.

"Then how did you know?" Martel asked the unspoken question 'who she was?'

"I see her picture before and see her on the TV, eh?" Len made a brief lewd Sicilian gesture, "One doesn't forget such a pretty face and sexy body eh?"

"No, I guess not." Martel glanced discreetly at the woman again. She was indeed a very attractive woman, with the good looks of some elegant model. Dark eyes and hair, and a light olive complexion, she had high cheekbones and the classic Mediterranean look about her that many Italian-American's in the U.S had.

Len chuckled then and nodded to Martel "Ah, I see she has caught your eye too." Leonardo was always known as the womanizer and sex god of the Jerome Family. It was rumored he had 8 *comare* and had an insatiable sexual appetite. His stunningly Adonis good looks and his silky Italian accent played a big part in that, Martel realized. Joshua who also was darkly handsome could be a rival Adonis, except he had one hell of a temper and usually not enough time to juggle so many comare, as Leonardo did.

"So, are you going to get lucky tonight my friend?" Martel teased softly to his capo.

"Eh, we see. She definitely not seems happy about being in Van Courtlandt's company does she?" Len winked and then moved on to watch the game, mingle and serve up more booze and food.

Martel scoped out the game and his guests making sure everything continued to run smoothly, but where as the other mistresses and comare were enjoying themselves, Diana Dellano seemed to grow more uncomfortable by the moment. Especially as her editor got drunker and kept occasionally trying to grab at her. Usually she nimbly stayed out of reach of his groping, but on as the night wore on, Mr. Van Courtlandt became more insistent about her being flirtatious and womanly with him. He finally caught her around the waist and hauled her over to him, "Hey there my favorite columnist, make sure you be nice to the hand that feeds you! After all I bought you that nice diamond tennis bracelet tonight."

Diana's eyes flared with anger. "You think I am some common whore?" She expertly twisted her hand out of Van Courtlandt's grasp. "That you can buy me off?" she hissed.

"Watch yourself my pretty..." Van Courtlandt's eyes got an angry look, "I can throw you off staff so fast it can make your sexy little head spin."

"You son-of-a-bitch!" Diana's temper was flaring. By now several people in the room had noticed the argument between the two people as it had grown in volume and intensity.

But this is what the large henchmen were here for, to make sure everyone behaved and didn't trash up the place. One of the large soldiers was going to walk over when Leonardo suddenly motioned to the guard to stand down and went over to the arguing couple himself.

"Ah, Mr. Van Courtlandt, Miss Dellano." He said with the skill and expertise of some foreign ambassador, "Why not take a break, drink some champagne or Crown Royal and have some snacks, eh?" Usually Len's silky smooth voice made nearly everyone comply with his wishes. His dark slate grey eyes could also flash with the unspoken intent of what would happen if his wishes were not followed.

Len put his hand firmly on Van Courtland's shoulder and while leading him a few steps from Diana nodded to one of the large henchmen as a signal to take the man to the bar and pour him a stiff drink. One of the goons obediently followed Len's instructions.

"Now," Len turned back to Diana Dellano, turning on his charm, "I think he will leave you alone for now, eh?" He nodded towards the direction where Van Courtland was being led off. "You know, I really enjoy you column." Leonardo said smoothly, "I read it every week myself." He went to grab her hand to link through his arm and put his own charm on her and that is when she tensed up again as darkly as she had with her editor and boss Van Courtland.

"I am not interested in being with some Mafia thug!" she hissed the insult low, under her breath at Leonardo. "So back off!"

Laurence Martel had caught the words though. Inside his mind he snickered, 'Len shot down by a woman! That was a first'. He was glad it was Leonardo though; at least Tagretta had the good graces to just give her a quick dark flash of his eyes and a slight gentlemanly tilt of his head and then move on. Had it been Joshua Demonico the man would have gone through the roof at the insult and probably done something not so nice.

The woman spun on her heel and went to head to the door Martel was standing by, probably to leave. But the rules of the house were no one left until the game was over.

"Not leaving are you?" Martel glanced down at her as she swept passed him, his hands simply clasped loosely in front of him.

"Actually, I'm leaving for the night. If you'll excuse me!" she meant to put anger in her words, but her eyes just kept sweeping up and up until they met the icy cold ones of the tall underboss.

"Sorry Ms. Dellano." Martel's hand then had flashed nearly quicker than the eye could see and he had her small wrist firmly grasped in his large hand. "No one is allowed to leave until it is 11pm, and it is only 10:15." He stated simply.

"Unhand me, you overgrown goon!" she tried to sound angry but her voice held more fear than anger.

Martel pulled her nearly right up against him, his muscles like iron bands against her. "I suggest that you settle down and just relax." He said in that deep baritone voice. "Go have a drink, go sit over by the bar or on the other side of the room if you want. But you are not leaving until 11pm."

She tried then a simple martial arts move against him, he recognized it as one of the most basic of the karate forms. Tried to twist out of his grasp and drive the heel of her stiletto high heeled shoe into his foot.

She suddenly found both her hands pinned neatly behind her by one of his large hands and his other hand pressed right against the side of her neck and shoulder. To anyone else it would look like they were talking, or giving a quick lover's hug, but she felt excruciating pain as he pressed on the median nerves that ran along the juncture and totally immobilized her in a high level Jujitsu move.

"Not very smart or very nice, for someone supposedly a reporter Ms. Dellano." And then his eyes did seem to bore through her like some dark angry entity.

For the first time all night she felt terrifying, primal fear course through her and knew that this huge man could and would easily end her life if he so desired. She knew it intimately then, this was not a man to yank his chain and she felt almost nauseous to her stomach. But there was also a different feeling growing in the pit of stomach, one that began to heat up her very soul...

"Now I suggest you calm down. Do we understand one another?" his voice was still calm and low but it resonated through her bones and sinew.

She tried then the only womanly charm she had, hoping to appeal to him. "Please," she barely whispered. "I'm sorry, Ok? Look, I just am trying to get away from my editor he is such an asshole, he made me come here tonight and I told me if I didn't do what he said he would make my life miserable." She even allowed her eyes to fill with tears.

"You're acting is very nice, Ms. Dellano." the underboss simply said and released the hold on her neck but still kept one of his large hands wrapped firmly around her wrist.
"If you sit over here, I will make sure he doesn't bother you, however you are still not leaving until 11pm."

Surprise, stunned anger, rage and then sadness seemed to fly through her eyes all at the same time. Never had a man read her so easily, seen through her as though she was so transparent! She nearly opened her mouth to say something, to allow her anger to speak again, but a single dark look from him was enough to make her clamp her jaws shut, as she felt the power of him cause her fear again. Finally she just gave up, dropped her eyes and the acting games.

"Ok," she said sincerely, "Look, I am sorry. I will cause no more problems." She had no more fight or argument with this tall man and worse she found herself awakening in the deepest parts of her sexual soul.

Martel nodded and let her loose and she indeed did keep her word and wander back into the party. But he could see her glancing at him every few minutes, a curious glance filled with both arousal and something else... He just deeply sighed and continued to watch the game. Martel was rarely interested in anything except 'one night stands' with women and especially not with anyone who wrote stuff about Crime Families.

Diana knew she had insulted Leonardo earlier and also had no desire to lead him on, so she instead walked over to one of the large henchmen and asked almost sexily, "Who is that tall man by the door?"

The man looked like he actually might not answered her, but she turned on the sex appeal and finally he leaned down and said softly, "Laurence Martel." then turned his attention back to watching the game.

Diana walked off some, her stomach in knots. 'Laurence Martel! That was the underboss for the Jerome Family!' she had heard of him, heard of his nickname 'The Undertaker' but yet had never seen him. Unlike a lot of the Jerome capos and soldiers he was rarely downtown in the city, at least not that she ever could spy out. Somehow for someone so big he seemed to nearly be unnoticeable. Her mind became only more and more obsessed and attracted to the one man who so easily was able to rebuff her, and yet arouse the deepest most secret parts of her.

Finally at a few minutes before 11pm Diana walked back over to Laurence Martel and spoke quietly to him. "I know it will be eleven soon, but I am afraid to leave, what if Mr. Van Courtlandt decides to do something to me for not giving him what he wanted?"

"Like what? Fire you?" Martel spoke with an almost dark amused tone.

How could this man be so cold, so harsh! It only aroused her more. "Please Mr. Martel. Maybe you could escort me home?" She spoke his name aloud then, daring to glance into those icy blue eyes.

One of his eyebrows quirked up slightly, "Ah yes, a reporter to the end, aren't you Ms Dellano." It was a statement not a question, "Don't you know you should not ask strange men to accompany you home?" he asked simply.

For a brief moment she felt something cold and dark slide down her spine but when she looked in his eyes he saw that they were not harsh but amused. "You I trust." She said it to him in a sexy way. "And I am only asking you escort me home, no more."

Martel was about to tell her he would have Leonardo or one of the soldiers escort her home, but he saw both Patrizio and Len glancing at him then Len flashed a quick discreet 'thumbs up' sign to him and Patrizio just watched in fascination.

No, he would have to do this, he had to uphold some kind of reputation or at least give his fellow *compari's* the impression he was sleeping with her or they would begin to wonder about him. The real truth was something he had dare not speak to anyone, and that was that his heart had been dead and as cold as ice ever since Miyoko had been killed. He blinked once lazily and then with an almost resolute sigh looked down at her. "Sure, I'll take you home." He said and forced a smile.

She blushed deeply and then murmured "I'll go get my coat and bag."

"You go big fella." Patrizio winked as he walked by him puffing on his Pall Mall cigarette as the lady walked off to get her things. "Have fun tonight."

Martel just nodded but said nothing. At one point he saw Van Courtlandt trying to insist that Diana leave with him, but Leonardo had walked over and spoken to the man for his ear only. A distinct paleness washed over Van Courtlandt at whatever Len was saying to him and he backed off with a huff, just grabbed his coat and left.

After all the players had left, Martel told Ms Dellano to sit quietly at the bar and wait for him, as he, Len and Patrizio counted the game's earnings out of view of the 'guest'. Laurence took his share and the *padrone's* cut. "Ok, I'm outta here." He said quietly.

"Have fun tonight, Boss." Len winked.

After stuffing close to $15,000 of the money in his breast pocket he walked back to where Ms Dellano was sitting, "Let's go." Martel said with no formalities and walked out ahead of her.

"Hey! Wait!" she practically scurried after him. She was not used to having a man be so unaffected by her womanly charms! In fact Martel's playing hard to get only aroused her more, made her aware of his commanding and no nonsense presence.

Martel knew precisely what it was she wanted from the moment she had been eyeing him after their encounter. He decided maybe if he played cold fish and act uninterested that would send her a message but instead it seemed to only arouse her more and egg her on.

Martel glanced at Diana then, a hard predatory glance. She was sending all the right signals. He knew implicitly then what she wanted; what attracted her to him was exactly his coldness, and cruelness. He would find out; a quick grin did thin his lips for a moment, but it was the grin of a hungry predator.

"Come in for a drink?" Diana asked him as they reached her apartment.

"Do you want me to?" Martel asked his eyes half lidded. If she wanted this she was going to have to ask for it. Let him know she truly wanted to give herself over to him. It was all one big mental control with him.

A shiver ran down her for a moment, "Yes." she almost whispered.

He just nodded and followed her in, ducking low through her narrow doorway.

"Let me go freshen up!" she said as she tossed down her bag and began to head for her bedroom.

"No." Martel's voice resounded through her small but attractive one bedroom apartment.

"What?" she stopped and asked, whirling on her heel.

"I know what you want," the big man was suddenly right up alongside her again, almost out of nowhere. "You want to ride the tiger but not get bitten. You want what you so often write about, but never can truly have; some '*Mafia thug*' to take you fully and utterly." He threw back the cruel insult she had said to Leonardo.

Her mouth just kind of hung open, in a most sexy and submissive way as she was truly flabbergasted by his cruel and utter honesty.

He grabbed her roughly then and his mouth closed on her lips, hard and insistent. His hands forced their way up the side of her shapely thigh and short dress to her underwear, forcing themselves between her legs.

She tried to struggle for a moment, to actually fight him; but he just applied more force and felt the dampness of her arousal between her legs that soaked her underwear. Martel pushed her from him away then. A cold chuckle resonated within him.

"Oh fuck you!" she yelled and leapt back from him. "Get out!" she growled and pulled one of her shoes off and threw it with total rage at him. He just easily deflected it with his large forearm.

His eyes narrowed in a deadly and frightening intensity and she turned and ran for her telephone in the bedroom, since he was blocking her off from her living room.

Martel was on her like a large predator. As she reached for the phone he yanked it out of the wall and with his other hand flung her to the bed. He then sprang upon her, pinning her down beneath him. Again his mouth came down hard on hers practically drawing the air out of her lungs. One of his hands easily captured her wrists and held them up over her head and his other hand reached down to her expensive dress and literally ripped it from her body.

"Do you know how much that dress costs!" she screamed enraged at him.

"I don't care," was his simple answer spoken in a low chilling tone. He still held her down beneath him watching her bare breasts heaving below him. "Do you remember what I said about inviting strange men home?" he asked. "Now what do you feel? Still trust me? Still feel safe."

Fear sprang into her eyes and she trembled briefly beneath him. But there was also a strange sort of arousal in her eyes. A look of hunger and a desire to be consumed by him; to reach forth and briefly touch the utter blackness, but only a tiny bit.

That night the two of them would make the most passionate love Diana Dellano had ever felt, as she gave herself fully to her 'Dark Laurence', her body and arousal at his total mercy. Never had she felt such intensity in sex with someone as she did this mysterious man. Such mind blowing sexual intensity and such tingles of fear that only aroused her more.

After dressing he leaned in over on the bed, close to her and with an easy flick of his hand opened his razor sharp butterfly knife, but this time it pressed at her throat and not very sensuously. This time she felt true terror in her heart, as his presence engulfed her. "Listen to me well, Diana." He instructed in a cold voice, the presence of the Dragon enshrouding her, "If you want to keep on learning to have a relationship with me, you will not speak or write one peep about the Jerome Family, or me. We are ghosts, all of us. As long as you respect that rule, fine. But if I read one word in any of your 'Mafia' columns," he spat the word with disgust, "About me or my Family then you will find me a very different man indeed, my touch much darker and our association will be over, permanently."

She could feel the knife nearly puncturing the skin near the front of her throat, this time however it felt icy cold like his demeanor. "I promise, not a word, my dark Laurence."

He abruptly stood up and replaced the knife in his pocket. He then reached into his breast pocket where the money was and pulled out close to 3000$ it was a part of his share of tonight's take from the game. With almost a cruel flaunt he tossed the wad of cash at her naked form. "Go buy yourself a new dress or some jewelry, or whatever…" he chuckled cruelly a moment, "after all, it's what comare's and whores crave."

He could see the look of shock and almost anger cross her face for a moment. But he held up one hand silencing it immediately, "Listen to me well, Ms Dellano." He ordered, "I don't give a fuck if you donate that money to charity. If you are wise you will appreciate whatever gifts I give you, but understand me well. There is nothing, between us, do you understand?" his blue eyes pierced her soul like his knife so earlier had, "Nor will there ever be! You are my toy, my plaything, my mistress and nothing else. If you push at me to be more, then I will be gone faster than you can blink. Do we thoroughly understand each other?"

She merely nodded her eyes unable to meet his. Slowly she gathered the wad of cash he had tossed at her. He insulted her, he humiliated her and he was as cruel as the devil himself but no man had ever taken her to such heights of sexual ecstasy, ever. She knew she was but his whore and would do whatever he asked, whatever he demanded. She wanted it too.

"Yes Laurence." She quietly answered him.

"Good." He merely said. "Good night Diana." He turned and then simply left. The underboss of the Jerome Family had taken a comare for now, and for nearly 6 years Diana had been indeed content to simply be the pampered mistress and comare of Laurence Martel. But lately, her heart had only grown more and more in love with him and desired him even more. She didn't just want to ride the tiger and not get bitten; she wanted to be glued to it…

He stood by the window wearing only his pants, naked from the waist up. "Laurence, are you all right darling?" Diana came up to him breaking his daydreams as she began to massage the hard muscles of his body; her long well manicured fingers running over the exotic tattoos and kanji that were etched into his skin.

"Yes." He turned to her. "I am fine, just tired." He looked her over. She was high maintenance. But most comare were. She was around 5'7, had the elegant looks of a model. Long classical lines, high cheekbones, and dark hair she kept swept up. She had intense brown eyes and a light olive complexion with full lips. She always wore a lot of expensive jewelry, usually whatever he bought for her. And she made it clear she usually preferred diamonds, platinum and emeralds.

"I've missed you, my dark Laurence." She always called him that. She encircled his waist. Holding him tightly, breathing deeply of him.

Martel unconsciously tensed. He knew Diana loved him far more than he ever loved her; to him she was just a simple mistress. He had never promised her anything more than that, never hinted there would be anything more than that, just the occasionally get together of passionate sex between them. She had often told him that would be fine, that she would be content to be his mistress forever and she would be happy with that, anything to please him. But today for whatever reasons his heart and inner self was in turmoil. "I bought you a gift," his deep voice murmured as he turned from the large window. He reached into his pants pocket and pulled out a small box, inside was a tennis bracelet with diamonds and emeralds on it. He watched her eyes light up. "Hold out your hand." He said quietly.

She did and he fastened it on her wrist. She admired it and then kissed him deeply. "Oh thank you, darling, my dark Laurence." she cooed at him, her hands running down the length of him.

He easily scooped her up, and began to carry her to her bed. "So you missed me, hmm?" He teased, his blue eyes, getting the sleepy, dragon eyed look he was famous for.

"More than anything, you know that, my Man of Honor." She whispered sensuously, her eyes looking deeply into his.

Laurence well knew she was more in love with the image of who he was and his profession of being a hitman and underboss. Martel knew had he been some poor blue-collar worker from the Bronx she probably wouldn't have given him a second look.

"Are you a jealous woman my love?" he teased lightly, laying her down on the bed and laying next to her, his hand running along her body. "What's the matter, you think I am out with some other woman?" he laughed lightly.

She moaned softly as his hands ignited sparks of pleasure and arousal in her body, where they ran across her flesh.

His mind drifted to Kanashii... The day he almost embraced her by the statue before he left... They were so much alike he and Kanashii, both forced to be people they were not, both fighting their own shadows, secret and hidden demons. Kanashii, now there was someone who while he could not logically understand it seemed to have wrapped herself around his heart and soul and even worse, he knew she felt the same love for him. Had seen it in her eyes, felt it in her soul.

Diana's eyes flickered darkly for a moment, her breathing coming in hot gasps of pleasure. She wanted him so badly, to feel him inside her, taking her roughly; the thought of him with another woman though showed through her with brief fire of anger and jealousy in her eyes. It did anger her to think of it! She so loved her dark Laurence, but she didn't dare voice the words she knew would drive him away. "Maybe" she teased lightly. But her heart her soul had already spoken for her. "But I would love you anyway."

"And if I were to ever leave you?" the blue eyes bore into her with electric like energy.

"Then I would not be able to stand it," she murmured, "It would kill me."

"I am sure it would." He rolled atop her, his weight pinning her heavily down; his face mere inches from hers. "Oh Kageryu have you lost your mind?" His mind screamed within his skull as his lips sought hers out. He closed his eyes. "Who's face do you see Kageryu? Who's?"

A small shocked grunt escaped Diana's lips as his hands expertly sought out her throat and tightened …

Sen Yamashita was sitting at home, watching another cheesy Godzilla movie when he heard the knocking on his door. It was nearly 11pm. "Go away, wrong apartment! I gotta gun!" he yelled.

"Sen…" the familiar voice was ragged, undeniable.

"Oh shit," He clambered to his feet and unlocking the doors he allowed his old friend in. "Martel?"

Martel stood there, drenched to the bone shivering and a dark look to his eyes. It bought back sudden bad memories of that night with Tashima Katsuro, so many years ago. Martel's eyes had that same haunted, haggard look.

"Come in, come in." Sen dragged his best friend in his apartment, "You're drenched," both men switched to speaking in Japanese. "Kage, what happened?" Sen used the old name and quickly locked the door behind him.

Sen helped Martel peeled off his overcoat; he wore no shirt on underneath. Sen just looked at him and shook his head, Martel had that same 'blank' look on his face he did that night he had killed a bunch of Tashima's family and men. Sen led him over to the recliner and pushed Martel down in it, then stood in front of him and placed both his hands on Martel's head at his temples and began to apply pressure to the median pressure points he knew were there. Using the ancient shiatsu techniques, he skillfully worked down ward towards his former student's neck and shoulders. Finally after he felt Martel's body relax, after the tormented look had left the man's face for now he stopped. "I'll get you some *sake*, and kava root." It was then as he walked away that he noticed the long handle of the razor-sharp, *tanto* blade at the waistband of Martel's pants. It didn't take Sen much to figure out that his friend had taken a life tonight that stirred up some very deep and powerful emotions within him.

After Martel had dried off, drank some *sake* and taken some of the Kava root, he finally sat back and relaxed, his body no longer one big rigid mass of muscle.

Sen had sat there patiently, not asking any questions, not demanding any answers. He knew when his best friend was ready he would talk and not before then.

"I need advice from a friend." Martel finally spoke after awhile.

"Anytime," Sen nodded cracking open another beer for himself. On screen both men briefly watched Godzilla demolish Tokyo.

"I think, after all these years. I mean...." Martel paused, took a deep breath and then just finally told Sen his feelings about Kanashii. He didn't go into the full detail of what had happened with Diana, only to say that he 'reacted badly' because he felt the need to protect someone he cared about and was confused about his feelings. "When I was with this other woman, all I could think of was Kanashii..."

"Kage," Sen gently interrupted him. "The only one you are punishing is yourself, you understand? It seems to me at least, you have very strong feelings for this girl Kanashii something about her obviously touches you, deeply. Makes you very addle brained." Sen smiled and for a moment it felt like old times. "No one says you must carry a torch for Miyoko or that you cannot find happiness again, only you put this restriction on yourself Kageryu. I told you once long ago, that you and I are already bound as family, no matter what. Miyoko would want you to go on as well. If you find happiness then you should find it, it is so rare that anyone out there even gets a second chance let alone a first one. I am still waiting for my first one. Victor Jerome he not find a second one, if you can find a second one, Kage then you are a lucky and fortunate man indeed. Seize it."

"I don't even know if she would be interested in me, or if it would even work out." The large man sighed and sank back, exhaustion catching up with him. He had been out in the driving rain hiding the pieces of Diana's body in one of the Families safe haven dumping grounds. He knew he had no one to blame for his tired state but himself.

"How will you know unless you try? You stubborn fool!" Sen took his leg and thumped Kageryu who glared back at him for a moment. "Oh go ahead and glare at me, you overgrown ox!" Sen glowered at him. "You run around with your insides twisted all up, your karma twisted all up, angst ridden and crammed with inner turmoil and then you come to me, an unmarried bachelor, wondering if you did the right thing? Kage, live life! Take down the damn wall and let the Shadow Dragon come out and fly a bit. 'Kanashii', it means wounded/sad spirit.... I think you have the names wrong." Sen growled at his best friend. "The only one I see harboring a broken spirit all these years is you!"

Martel sat up, fire in his blue eyes, his muscles tensed up; the muscles along his jaw rigid with anger.

"Yes! At least now I finally get a reaction from you, something. At least it's a start. Anger! Ok, now work on the others." Sen laughed heartily and sat back down and drank his beer.

"Sen you are a real...." Martel fished for the appropriate curse.

"Asshole?" Sen offered as he laughed.

"Shit-head." Martel chuckled, along with his friend.

"No, come on, you can do better than that!" Sen egged him on.

Martel let loose with a string of epitaphs and curses in both Japanese and Vietnamese that had Sen roaring with laughter, until soon both men were laughing so hard that the neighbor downstairs was pounding on the floor screaming in Korean at them to shut up in his own string of epitaphs.

The sun was beginning to break over a grey rainy day as Martel threw back on his damp overcoat. "I gotta go, Sen." He bowed formally again to his best friend and brother-in-law and still in many ways teacher.

Sen bowed back it was an equal bow they were both equals now and then they embraced. "Kage, whatever happened, think of it as your 'wall cracking', eh? It's a good thing, let the Dragon come out and be free. Don't fight him, you are Kageryu and he is you, remember your most basic lessons. You're Laurence Martel but you're also Kageryu, let the Dragon fly and don't tether him down. You will be a better man, all the way around in everything you do. I wish you luck in all you do and with this girl, Kanashii. If it is meant to be, it will fall into place. But do not fight it or force it. That is my only advice."

"Thanks Sen." Martel nodded and then slipped quietly out the door. He felt a lot more refreshed than he had in a long time, his head a lot more clear than he had been.

CHAPTER 27-

Alyssa sat in the aviary; yesterday it had been rainy and now after the remnants of last nights storm had passed it was the opposite. True to the crazy weather patterns of New York, it had went from oppressive and smothering humidity and heat the other day to barely 60 degrees out, the sky a clear cobalt blue.

She had finished feeding the little finches and cleaning the aviary and now she sat in here and worked on writing in her journals the classical music from the PBS radio station soothing her in the background. It seemed like time had sped along even faster once Victor had given her permission into his library and the aviary.

Since she was physically healing so well, she had seen very little of Dr. Weintraub anymore and she didn't really enjoy going to the gym, instead preferring to either walk or jog lightly around the many driveways and footpaths of the estate. She much preferred the quiet solitude of being able to keep her own schedule.

She did enjoy spending time in the kitchens with Rosette, Emilia and the others and while she was learning to understand Italian a bit better, the hard reality was, she was still as mute as a stone. This also frustrated her. It got to be a pain to always write everything; it seemed that very few had the gift like Victor or Martel to eerily and truly seem to understand her heart and soul. It made the ability Victor and Laurence had that much more precious, but even then, it wasn't true two-way communication. And writing with the pen, no matter how nice could be a long and arduous task. Not everyone had patience for her to scribble everything out and worse was times when she forgot her pad of paper.

The only thing she did learn from Doc Weintraub was that she wasn't ever going to be able to use one of those Electro-larynxes. According to him and the tests, whatever area of her brain, controlled speech was damaged beyond repair. That and coupled with her throat damage was not going to be able to allow her to use one.

Each day she worked on fitting in more and more here with her new home and also tried to figure out two important questions. First: What could she do for the Jerome's? So far, all she was doing was eating their food and hanging around. She wanted to do something, fit in somehow, and do something more to repay their kindness to her, but what? What did she know how to do? She wasn't sure herself just what she knew how to do. Obviously before her kidnapping she must have done something had some occupation or had a job.

While each day, more and more bits and pieces of memories came back to her, she still was not sure of everything that she did up until the point before the kidnapping.

Second, she was still sorting through her feelings for Laurence Martel. Victor had pointed her through a series of some books, many of them oriental in nature, which had given her some of insight into the nature and personality of what seemed to make Martel click, why was Victor doing this? Did he seem to sense her feelings towards Martel as well?

Alyssa wasn't sure how much to trust of Victor in this matter. What would she say to the head of the Family anyway? It sounded stupid, ridiculous, and childish. "I think I have a crush on your underboss, I'm not sure, but I think it's because he was there for me when I really needed him." She knew she trusted the side of him she had seen that night he had opened up to her, the real him, the part that was 'Kageryu', but then there was always Laurence Martel, underboss, the cold, unfeeling, imposing figure... It was almost like he was two personalities in one. Could she truly accept this fact about him?

These were the kinds of things she wrote in her personal journal, for her eyes only. In the one for Martel and her, it was almost strangely empty. She had not had a lot of time to write much, since she had been so busy with the aviary and bonding with Victor and now she began to feel guilt. "Is Martel going to be upset because I didn't complete the assignment?" she sighed.

"Ah there you are child." Victor's voice interrupted her cluttered train of thought. She glanced up at him.

The old man chuckled and lowered himself into a chair they had moved into the Aviary when she had started helping with the birds, so now there were two plastic chairs in here. His body leaned up against hers and she smelled his familiar and comforting scent of peppermint lifesavers and his old spice aftershave.

"It's almost dinnertime Alyssa, something troubling you?" he patted her leg. The birds all perked up, they recognized Victor's voice.

Alyssa pulled out her notebook and the beautiful pen with the fiery hawk on it she kept tied to her belt loop. "*I don't know Victor, I feel lost. Still not fully part of your family, and not fully knowing my situation. I want to do SOMETHING to help out here, but what? I don't even know what I can do? I don't even stuff a good tortellini! I do love you as an Uncle; these last two weeks have brought me a lot closer to you. I don't remember any Uncles in my past. But if I did, I would want them to be like you*.

Joshua still gets on my nerves, Ha, ha! *And Mr. Martel, well, I miss him a lot, and I appreciate all the books you lent me about understanding him more. I look forward to his return…*"

Victor noted she blushed as she wrote this part.

"*It's just sometimes I feel so overwhelmed by everything, I just want to I dunno, run away and hide out I guess.*" She handed the pad of paper to Victor a bit hesitantly. But she had given her oath to him now, they had made their peace and after all, the man had one of her kidneys in her, had saved her life from the Roman's. If he had wanted her dead, he could have done that many times over already.

Victor pulled out his reading glasses and read the note, then handed the pad back to her. "Alyssa," He placed a warm hand on her shoulder. "Listen to me. I know you are confused. Your situation here is very simple." They both watched the birds for a brief while. "Your place here in my home is as I told you before. One of understanding and kindness, the same as any man's wife, daughter, or niece. I want you to succeed in whatever you want to. Whether you want to be an artist, writer, brain surgeon or veterinarian, it matters not to me. While you live under my roof, you are surrounded by protection, love and care, eh?" he smiled and glanced at her. "I know you feel overwhelmed at times, you are still healing inside dear child, it is why I offered this aviary and my library to you to come to." Victor gestured around him. "Believe me, I understand."

Alyssa couldn't help but feel a tremor run through her, not of fear but like before, of one who truly understood her. She leaned gently against the old Don, not wanting him to see her eyes. "Oh god, how he could understand what was in her heart and soul? Just like Martel could."

Victor closed his own eyes briefly and thought of Eddie, his carefree older brother and briefly fought down his own inner demons. He quietly shook his head a moment and lightly touched her hand. "Alyssa, I know you and Mr. Demonico seem to have your differences. Why who knows? That is between you and him. Neither of you have ever done anything to one another but it creates friction..." Victor watched some more finches hopping around lining nest boxes. "I cannot 'order' anyone to like anyone else, but I certainly hope that all of my Family at least co-exists peacefully."

He stood up and tucked away his reading glasses, "Now, I am hungry, let's go eat. Mr. Martel will be home tomorrow afternoon and you will be able to see him then." Victor smiled. "Besides, I want to show you something, I had summer decorations bought in this year."

Sure enough as Alyssa walked down towards the main house with Victor she saw that they had tastefully decorate the large estate with beautiful potted plants, bright flowers and even some delicate Italian lights scattered here in there, for evening enjoyment. It seemed to brighten the moods of the guards and soldiers. During dinner Alyssa overheard a few guards mention they had not ever seen the elegant mansion decorated this way and only a few of the old timers mentioned they had not seen it decorated this way since the death of Michael and Isabella.

As they were eating supper that evening Victor stopped briefly by Alyssa's side, "See me after dinner, I need to talk to you." He spoke to her ear only. Then he, Joshua and Patrizio and a few men disappeared down the hallway into his Office.

'Dual natured just like Martel'. She thought, 'No, not dual-natured just, the Family comes first. The Family always comes first.'

Victor reread the letter for the 100th time. Joshua paced a bit and chewed his nicotine gum; he seemed torn between happiness and anxiousness.

Patrizio looked in misery, his advancing age was not doing well with his arthritis and he was hoping to be in sunny Florida in full retirement by now.

The letter was sent from a postmark in New Jersey, with of course no return address, it was addressed to Joshua Demonico at the Jerome Estates and it was from Joey Calendri, the underboss of Tito D'Salvatore. He was offering to "flip" to turn traitor on his own Family and to switch sides and come forward with information and turn on his own people. He was willing to follow whatever orders the Jerome's specified, meet them wherever they wanted.

"Son of a bitch," Patrizio muttered again for the 20th time. "Can you believe that? An underboss now, of all things jumping ship."

"Yeah but do we believe it, or do you think it's a trap?" Joshua leaned over Victor's desk to glance at the letter again, "I mean how do we know this guy isn't coming with a 'wire' and has already turned stoolpigeon for the F.B.I or worse coming in strapped with dynamite up his ass or something and then... BAM!"

Victor looked up at Joshua with weary eyes. Patrizio just snickered and guffawed despite his painfully aching arthritic knees.

"Because Josh," Victor tried to control himself, he was not going to guffaw in Joshua's face. "Despite that excellent plan, how would Mr. Calendri know he would be meeting with anyone important, eh? What if he would be meeting, say, just Patrizio?"

Patrizio's guffaws abruptly stopped. "Eh? What! Me? I'm supposed to be in Florida Vic!"

"Of course old friend," Victor said with a twinkle in his eye, "I am just making a point, here." he winked at him. "Seriously, Joshua; Joey would be picked up by our men, low associates, checked head to toe, striped down and ferried around for awhile to make sure he wasn't being followed, then bought somewhere. He wouldn't know, where, he was being taken too. So what is he going to hide, eh? His small *cazzo*? No I think Mr. Calendri is very legit in his offer gentlemen." Victor casually tossed the letter on the desk. "I think Tito's underboss is indeed looking to jumping ship and that alone speaks volumes in whether or not we agree to meet with him."

A sudden palatable silence fell in the room then. "You know what this means, *padrone*?" Joshua barely whispered.

"Oh yes." Victor smiled grimly, "It means Tito is beginning to lose the very foundation of his Family and either he doesn't see it, or worse, he does see it and doesn't care."

"I don't think he sees it," Patrizio leaned forward drinking some wine and downing a few of his more heavy duty pain pills. "I got word in last night, that our connections, Bonnaro and DiMone in Florida are still running all green lights. Tito went down there a couple of weeks ago schmoozing with Joe Cinno and hoping to buy a lot of newly immigrated Sicilian muscle cheap. Of course he got it, to bad he doesn't realize it's owned by Bonnaro and DiMone."

"And that at the right command from their *real* Don, they will simply turn on the person who hired them. Yes..." Victor paused savoring it already knowing the scenario.

"So let me get this straight," Joshua sat down next to Patrizio, "Tito hires a bunch of ' Sicilian immigrant rent-a-guns' who he *thinks* are working for him, but unbeknownst to him, they really belong to Bonnaro. Tito sends them up after us but during the thick of things, Vito Bonnaro gives his men some secret command and they all suddenly turn on Tito and his men?"

"You do have such an eloquent way of wrapping things up in a nutshell Josh." Victor teased him lightly.

"Holy shit! *Madonn*!" Joshua sat there actually in awe for a few moments. This was amazing even to him. He was beginning to see what Leonardo's earlier statement about what real *mannagge* was beginning to mean. He had a feeling this was going to be an ugly, ugly battle and an unconscious shiver ran through him.

"There will be a few minor exceptions of course." and Victor's eyes grew hard, full of unbridled hatred. Patrizio understood that look, but even Joshua glanced at the floor for a moment. He did not enjoy seeing the 'dark fire' of seething vengeance and hate come out of his *padrone* and Don. "Tito is mine. That is one vendetta to be personally settled." Victor rose smoothly out of his chair and his demeanor abruptly changed, quickly his anger was replaced by his neutral face again, his thinking face, the mask of the Arbitrator. "Martel will be back tomorrow afternoon. I want to see him first thing when he gets back to discuss this matter. I still have not decided exactly what to do with this..." he pointed at the letter from Joey, "I am curious why he contacted you though Joshua." Victor paused and glanced at Joshua.

Joshua just shrugged his shoulders helplessly, "I don't know Boss, honestly I don't."

"Maybe he likes your pretty boy looks." Patrizio teased Joshua.

"Funny, Pops, real fuckin' funny." Joshua accepted the teasing from the elder capo.

"Ok, Ok." Victor settled them down. "I don't know either, maybe he does like your looks Joshua, who knows." Victor threw the barb good-naturedly with a wink, "None-the-less, the point is we have the ball in our court now. We shouldn't make any hasty decisions. Of course, as usual, we keep as quiet as clams on a beach. Although he gave us a way to contact him, let him think and wait. I don't want to do anything until I've talked to Martel and slept on this more."

Both Joshua and Patrizio nodded. The three men finished off their glass of wine together and talked about some other business.

Vito Roman sat there his mind numb, shut down and stunned. He was bound and beaten; he was watching horrified as Laurence Martel was gruesomely dismantling his now dead underboss and consigliere and burying their pieces into the local landfill.

Handcuffed and with his vocal cords expertly cut, there was little Vito Roman could do but watch this nightmarish sight, he would drift in and out of consciousness, unless the cruel Martel would awaken him by throwing water or other liquid on his face.

"Wake up there, Vito. We wouldn't want you to miss the show; after all, you're going in there with them, soon." Then he would chuckle darkly and go back to his grim task.

Occasionally the big man would deign to talk to him. "I figured, at least these fellows were just following your orders, so they deserved to die before being dismantled and being buried. You on the other hand..." Martel glared cruelly down at the terrified Vito, "You were warned once, even given a second chance by Don Victor and the Commission and what do you do?" Laurence leaned on his shovel and looked down at the trembling form of Vito Roman. Laurence just shook his head in disgust, "Not one ounce of honor in you Vito, at least your old man, Joseph had honor and he died like a warrior. I know I killed him myself. You on the other hand, are just going to die like a traitor."

Vito Roman trembled all over, his eyes rolled back and he passed out again, Martel let him sleep for a while. After all he wanted his victim to have a lot of strength for his final dance of death; for the torture he was going to endure at the Undertaker's hands.

Martel's muscles were aching with pain, he was beyond exhausted himself, and all he wanted to do was sleep for three days straight. He couldn't remember the last time he had personally dismembered so many bodies and hidden so many corpses "I feel like a fuckin' dog, hiding bones everywhere." he thought, but he knew his tiredness was no excuse for any mistakes or mishaps. All his teachers had taught him that.

Tiredness breeds carelessness. He had been extra careful to make sure he had covered all his tracks, dismembered everything carefully; and hidden hands, skulls and feet separately from torsos. Constant vigilance, Cochran used to call it.

Thankfully Sen's tea and ministrations had given him a slight boost, but his own angst and blow up with Diana had thrown in its own set of problems and for that he had no one to blame but himself. But at least he was thinking clearer now.

"Good riddance" he said out loud, not sure whether he meant Diana or the current body he had finished burying.

He walked over to the unconscious form of Vito Roman and kneeled heavily astride him, while fishing out the razor sharp butterfly knife he carried. It was one of Sen's finest, able to slice through bone as easily as butter. "Wake up, Mr. Roman." Laurence Martel chuckled grimly while glaring down at him. "Sorry to keep you waiting, but I'm ready for you now." Martel gripped the knife in his teeth as he used a strong piece of thin rope as a tourniquet and wrapped it just above Vito Roman's wrist.

The man's eyes filled with utter and primal terror and he arched and writhed beneath his executioner, flopping like some terrified fish out of water. But he was going nowhere with Martel on top of him. His vocal cords had already been cut so all he could do was make small little wheezing noises of pain and fear. "Your punishment is getting dismemembered alive, Mr. Roman; it's going to take a very long time for you to die." Martel pronounced sentence with a neutral but dark tone. He had no glee, no remorse, no sadism in his voice; just a total unemotional business like tone. "You are now going to get to find out first hand why they call me the Undertaker."

Only then did the Shadow Dragon's eyes flicker briefly for just a moment with the slightest hint of amusement. But it was not for him, not in the least -never was it for him- as he did his grisly work, his mind thought of Alyssa, "What goes around comes around Mr. Roman." he thought. He would be so happy to get home, shower and go to sleep.

Alyssa and Victor stood on one of the various stone porches, on the second story near the west wing. It was a crystal clear summer evening and out here in the country the stars shown like diamonds in the night sky. Victor's telescope was set up and trained towards the Western sky. Around her were various lights on some of the pathways that lit up the great driveway. Martel's house was dark of course, a few small lights lit up the outside of the aviary and a few lights lit up the outside of the great mansion.

Below her, she could see a few guards talking quietly amongst themselves or patrolling silently. Occasionally she would see the glow of ones cigarette or the brief red light of one of their night-scopes or radios.

She was almost a tiny bit sad the two weeks was up. She and Victor had actually grown quite close during the last week and a half. He had seemed to taken her under his wing and shared some very personal things with her. Told her about his late wife Isabella and how she had been taken by cancer, told her about his son Michael who had been killed in a 'Robbery gone bad' in downtown NYC. (Alyssa had seen Victor's eyes grown very dark at that story and it chillingly reminded her a bit of that day when he had gotten angry with her, only what his eyes held during his story about Michael was far worse than what he showed even her, but he quickly slammed down a wall around that.) Victor briefly mentioned he had an older son, Theodore who was Missing-in-Action in Vietnam and never found, but the funny thing was something just didn't sit right with her about that. With Isabella and Michael's stories she saw so much emotion in the old man's eyes and with Theodore's tale there was no emotion, or if anything, it was veiled. Like when he played chess with her.

Victor also told her how he had actually adopted Joshua Demonico off the streets as an older teen and raised him here in the Jerome Estates. Again there was emotion in his eyes with this story, good emotions of reminiscing. It did make sense to Alyssa and explained why Joshua seemed to act like he owned the place, he obviously felt like the "prince regent". But Victor didn't go into the how and why of how Joshua ended up here. She had a sense that like her own tale, Victor was very good at keeping lots of people's secrets.

She and Victor both wore light sweaters against the slight chill that was in the air. For some reason tonight she felt especially chilled, as though something very dark and cruel was in the air, something she couldn't explain. Almost like some dark rage whispering in the night, a dark vendetta being unleashed. For the briefest instance she could have sworn it was like a dark shadow being pulled from her soul; some weird karmic fate done to someone who had done something horribly wrong to her.

"Are you Ok, Child?" Victor nudged her gently as he adjusted the telescope, and smiled.

She quickly recovered, smiled back at him and nodded 'Yes'.

"Here." He offered her a butterscotch disk. "Take a look in the telescope, I found Mars."

She looked down the telescopes eyepiece and looked at the bright angry red planet.

"The planet of War, named after the Roman god of War." Victor smiled. "As you know Martel is returning tomorrow, but I have a little proposition for you Alyssa…" Victor said as he casually rested his hand on the telescope. Even in the dim light she could feel his gaze seeming to bore into her, seeing into her very soul.

Alyssa turned and looked at him, all ears now, her hands thrust in the pockets of her sweater to keep warm.

"In a few months I am going on a very much needed vacation down in the warm tropical islands; white sands, beautiful beaches. I am meeting a dear old friend of mine there, Vito Bonnaro and his wife Lena. It will be just the two of us; no Joshua, no Martel, no plethora of bodyguards…" Victor paused. "I remember your note you shared with me, this vacation may do you some good Alyssa. Give you a chance to feel normal, you understand? Allow you to sort through some of your feelings and memories and to really think about things and get away from here. I will be with you. We'll have only two men with us, one of them will be Gio Aprile and I know you like and trust him."

Alyssa hugged herself tightly for a moment, she watched as a shooting star or satellite seemed to streak across the heavens brightly for a moment then disappeared. She did need to sort her feelings and memories out. Part of her wanted to so badly see Martel but she also knew he always seemed to keep her at arms length as well. One minute sharing a bit of himself and the next slamming that wall down between them.

She nodded her head, yes and smiled at him.

"Excellent, Alyssa," Victor gave her a soft pat on the shoulder. "I know you'll enjoy it. I know I will…" he chuckled softly, "more than you could ever know." He adjusted the telescope and looked for another planet.

The next day Alyssa excitedly waited to move back into Martel's house. It actually wasn't until the evening time, although she heard he had rolled in back into the estates around mid morning. He had come in, spent time talking with Victor in the Office for nearly an hour, then went to his house for another 6 hours and then finally sent for Gio to bring her and her belongings back down.

As she entered, she saw him cooking back in the kitchen, the familiar smell of incense going, and some soft music going on the stereo. She breathed deeply; she had so missed his Asian cooking!

"Everything's dropped off Boss." Gio said quietly, nodded at both Martel and Alyssa and then left.

She walked over to where Martel was and bowed formally to him, her eyes alight with happiness and mischief. She had missed everything about this house, but especially Martel himself.

"Well, well, Kanashii-Taka." He dried his hands on a towel and bowed back. "Did you behave yourself? Do your assignments?" he fought to keep to the smile off his own face but his eyes were alight with amusement. "Have you been working out on your martial arts training, while I've been gone?" he raised an eyebrow at her.

She did frown at him then. Standing there, looking at him almost with an expression like one of his dour Foo dog statues. She hadn't seen him in nearly two weeks and he wanted to talk martial arts training?

Now he did chuckle. "Kanashii," he smiled and turned down the heat off the steaming rice. "Martial arts training is good for you, builds great agility and confidence."

She stuck her tongue out at him then and tossed a cut carrot at him. Sure enough he just easily caught it out of mid-air.

"Tsk, tsk. Temper, Kanashii. Tell you what. The day you can defeat your teacher is the day your lessons with me are over, fair enough?" He faced her with his own playful look. "No? I thought not." he chuckled and turned back to preparing the meal. "Welcome back though." He was teasing her purposely, trying to get a reaction from her. Martel had his own rather dry wit.

She gave her head a playful defiant toss, as though to ignore him and turned to get a towel and dishes to help him cook dinner, then decided to be really wicked. She glanced over her shoulder to make sure he was not watching her.

His back, was, turned. Quickly she twirled the towel determined to get some reaction out of him. She turned to snap him but he was far faster and had already neatly grabbed it in an iron grasp. With a silent, soundless yelp, she let go and suddenly leaped out of his grasp and did the only logical thing she could against him. Run away like a coward! She wasn't going to let an expert like him get hold of her.

He went to cut her off, but she dodged out of the way and then ran exactly right where he wanted her too, the martial arts work out room. It was like he was a cowboy herding some wild filly into a corral; Martel simply casually walked right in behind her and shut the door an amused smile still on his face.

"So now you want to play Kanashii? Ok, your teacher will play." He chuckled in a deep voice; she had fallen right into his trap.

She knew she was trapped; this was not how this was supposed to go, she was not supposed to end up here. She did not dare grab any of the martial arts training weapons off the wall, she knew her teacher better than that. Whatever she grabbed is what he would fight her with, she figured she would just try to run and stay out of his grasp but damn if he wasn't truly enjoying this! In fact he was in the center of the room just casually following her every motion no matter which way she turned or spun, his blue eyes gleaming with playful laughter.

She made a feint to the right and then tried to dodge to the left but he simply exploded with blinding speed, grabbed her up in a classic and effortless judo throw and threw her up and over his shoulder.

Even though the room had a thick mat and was padded, since she had not been practicing any falls it was enough to momentarily stun her. Before she could recover or move a muscle he had easily sat astride her stomach in a schoolboy pin, his large legs on her shoulders.

"Ok, wiseguy." He smiled down at her in a rather kindly way. "Here's the deal. If you can throw me off, you don't have to take martial arts training. Deal?" his eyes took on a wicked, playful gleam.

Alyssa was already nearly suffocated under his 260-pound weight, but she valiantly tried anyway, in fact the more she tried the more impossible it seemed. If she used an arm, he merely caught it up and pinned it under his leg, if she tried to use a leg to ram into his back, he grabbed that and hooked it with his arm. This forced his weight even higher and deeper on her chest, making it increasingly harder and harder to breathe and within a few minutes she was coated in sweat, totally restrained and almost on the verge of passing out.

"Jujitsu, Kanashii." He gently explained, releasing her arms and legs, letting air back into her lungs. "*Osae Waza*, It specializes in pins and chokes and other such things." He still remained sitting on top of her though, his hand caressing her cheek. "Martial arts aren't so bad. Eh? We'll work on learning those falls together. The day you can throw me off, is the day your lessons end. Deal?" he said softly.

She nodded defeated and exhausted beneath him, but with a smile in her own eyes.

He gracefully leaped to his feet and offered his hand to help her up. She accepted and bowed low to him. He was still her Teacher.

He bowed back. "It's good to be home though. I really have missed your mischievous ways, Kanashii." He smiled sincerely.

She smiled back widely and then without even thinking about it threw her arms around his waist and gave him a tight, spontaneous bear hug. She noticed his hands hesitantly returned the gesture this time. Almost as if they were rusty to the simple gesture but his large hands did gently rest on her shoulders and then briefly encircled her and caressed. "Now, let's go eat some dinner, shall we?" he offered. "I have not had a decent meal in several days and I am truly starved."

They ate their meal together in a comfortable silence and after dinner he again began his ongoing healing work on her body with his hands; massaging those places on her that seemed to not only touch her muscles and bone, but the very depths of her soul.

Tonight when he massaged her, he bought her into the temple/shinto area; he had massaged her there before as well. The candles seemed to have both a soothing effect and also it seemed to open doors in her mind, causing her memories to jog down pathways. Somehow she sensed that's why he did it. It forced her to both confront her own dark ghosts and to deal with the unanswered questions in her own mind.

Never did he talk to her while he did his healing work on her body. He would light incense and candles. He would occasionally whisper or center himself in Japanese or Vietnamese but never did he talk to her directly.

He would manipulate bone and muscle, press on nerves and pressure junctures. He would use what he had once explained was a combination of massage and reiki, acupressure and shiatsu. Sometimes his touch was barely there, as light as a butterfly alighting upon her very essence and at other times he would gently lean his great muscular weight deep against her, not harshly but slowly, almost smotheringly. The way he did it was not uncomfortable but actually quite soothing, just when she thought she would not be able to bear the pressure of his weight anymore, he would release her, and the effect was as cleansing as surfacing from an icy mountain spring pool.

Whatever techniques he used, her sudden mind terrors had all but ceased. Occasionally she would have daydreams or ghosts in her night time dreams, or simply awakenings of images in her waking world, but no more of the sudden terrors like she did down in the city, or that day when she saw Cesare. It seemed now, whatever memories came back to her came back in fragments that she was able to digest in small little lumps, some that she could compartmentalize and other memories that she simply didn't know where they belonged.

She still had no idea of her full name before she was kidnapped. She had no idea of where she had worked at, she was sure it was some kind of retail store but she wasn't certain of the name or exactly what she did. She did know she was once engaged to a man to be married but yet could not remember his name. She knew that he had betrayed her with a woman named Mandy (it did amuse her in a sarcastic way that she could remember *that* name, but not the name of the man she was engaged to!) she knew that somehow she was fired by this Mandy so the woman must have been her boss. Her mind was still so 'Swiss-cheesed' and full of holes! But it was enough to convince her that her life was not that thrilling to go back to anyway.

Perhaps that is why she so felt drawn to Victor and his people. Somehow she still felt there was something more she was here to do for the old man, some favor she owed him... But what? What was it? Her mind and psyche gave her no clue.

A small grunt escaped her lungs as Martel adjusted her spine and then sat back on her hips relaxing his own muscles and taking a break.

"You are extra tense tonight, Kanashii." He finally spoke to her, his thumbs gently along her neck and shoulder blades. "But then it has been two weeks. However I sense a lot of thoughts in you tonight. This is a good thing, trust me." He rested a moment.

She turned her head as much as she could and tried to look at her teacher behind and over her. One emerald green eye shining in the candle lit room of the temple. She still always considered this place, his place. She always felt a bit out of place here. He seemed to somehow be a bit more different himself tonight, but nothing she could put a finger on. She didn't know how to read Martel - Kageryu he kept his feelings and emotions far too well hidden.

One large hand came down gently brushing away some long strands of her coppery hair which reflected in the candlelight with a fiery gleam and caressed her neck and cheek gently again. This she did notice. It was like his rusty embrace of her earlier, hesitant but heartfelt as though he were 'relearning' the moves of the graceful dance of intimacy all over again. "It has been a long two weeks Kanashii." He did indeed look tired. "So I'm afraid I'm going to have to turn in a bit early. Perhaps we can play chess another night, go over your journals tomorrow."

She nodded beneath him and he nimbly if not a bit wearily got to his feet and began to snuff out the candles and gather his braziers and oils.

It felt so wonderful to be back in her room in Martel's house, the one with the Ficus tree which she had dubbed with the name "Fred".

As she was getting ready for bed and putting her belongings back away she suddenly noticed he had gotten her a present, it was on the desk. She gently unwrapped it; a beautiful jade hawk that seemed to be soaring with a noble strength in its green eyes. She smiled and placed it on the nightstand by her bed. She was touched by his gesture, and it seemed to watch over her in the dim light as she drifted peacefully off to sleep.

Right now what Laurence needed most was an icy cold shower. He did not realize how truly deeply he had missed Kanashii and even worse was that the playful roughhouse between them and then the hugs and gentle caresses had ignited even deeper passions within him. "I am addle-brained," he mumbled to himself as he adjusted the temperature on the shower to as cold as it could go. "Sen is right, I've lost my mind."

He glanced once briefly in the bathroom mirror at the brand on his skin of the Dragon and Cobra, his mind bringing up images of Miyoko. Martel had honestly thought his heart would never, could never, have felt this kind of love for another woman again but damn, if Alyssa wasn't touching his heart and soul as deeply as Miyoko had. With a feeling of guilt his eyes hardened again and the muscles along his powerful shoulders and jaw tightened. He stepped into the icy cold shower.

Joshua Demonico shot his cuffs on his immaculate white suit and double checked his tie. He knocked on the Office door, Victor and Martel were already there and they were smiling as though they had just gotten done sharing some private joke.

"Sorry I'm late," he grunted as he slid into the office, his eyes already dark and moody. He was definitely not a morning person. While he had a part-time room here at the Estate he also had an elegant condo in the town around 20 miles up north, where he ran his crew from. He had spent the night with a few of the capo's partying and a few of his mistresses and now he was running a bit late for a meeting with his Don and underboss, not a good way to start the day at all.

"Josh, its ok," Victor assured him gently. "Martel and I were just discussing the note from your fan Mr. Calendri."

Martel chuckled dryly. "He must really like you, Joshua."

"Yeah, great" Joshua huffed, chewing his nicotine gum with a vengeance. "I have no damn idea why." His Brooklyn accent had a habit of getting thicker whenever he was riled.

"It matters not, why..." Victor turned to him, fire and wisdom in the old Don's eyes. "What matters is how it can be subverted by us, eh?"

"Exactly." Martel nodded. He poured coffee into both Victor and his own cup and poured a fresh one for Joshua.

"And, so, what did I miss?" Josh asked beginning to fear these two men had made plans already without him. Lately he felt it was not uncommon.

"We think you should accept his offer..." Victor sipped his coffee as he sat back, a dark twinkle in his eye. "We think you should indeed meet with Mr. Joey Calendri and even better do it while I'm on, ahem, vacation just so he doesn't think anything is up..." Victor left the sentence hanging.

Joshua just sat there looking from Martel to Victor for a moment as though both the Don and underboss had taken leave of their senses.

Even Martel had a slight gleam in his icy blue eyes, as sneaky as the old mans. "I agree, I think that is a very good idea."

Joshua just blinked once as though trying to digest this information. "Let me get 'dis straight, you *want* me to meet with Calendri?"

"Yes." Victor nodded.

"Sure, let him tell you his information." Martel sipped his own coffee, a grim smile on his face. "I'm sure he can have some great info to tell. If he's blowing steam out his ass, he will tell us nothing we don't already know. We'll see what kind of game he's playing."

Joshua was waking up now, and beginning to follow the plan. "Ah, Ok... I gotcha." His own dark smiled lit up his dark handsome face. "And then we whack him, right?"

"Sure," Martel said softly, almost teasingly, "If that's what you want and don't want your own personal fan club. Or if you don't think he might make a decent underboss or war capo."

Victor knew Martel was teasing. Neither Victor nor Martel would have any plans to let a traitor like Calendri live. Sooner or later, he would have been killed whether quickly or maybe he would be left alive for awhile to rub salt in the wounds of Tito for a bit or not. It all depended on how far Calendri would have been willing to turn and what he would have been willing to do for his 'new Family'.

"Ha, ha, funny. Fuck you, Martel." Joshua said a bit harshly, not jokingly. "I vote to whack him, after we get his information."

Only Victor caught the brief dark look on Martel's face, the quick darkening of the icy blue eyes and only Martel caught the darkening of the Don's gaze for a moment at Joshua. It was as though father and son had suddenly sent a few brief unspoken thoughts to one another.

"Very well Joshua Demonico." Victor's demeanor had changed imperceptibly.

Joshua felt the temperature seem to drop instantly in the room. He knew that tone in his Don, in the *padrone*. He had seriously overstepped boundaries.

"Martel, my underboss," Victor seemed to emphasize the word, "will talk with you more when it is time to solidify plans, on this."

"*Padrone*, Victor..." Joshua tried to begin, but he knew it was futile; he had made a bad error in judgment.

"Joshua," the stoic underboss turned to him, "I want to see you at my house in exactly 1 hour. Please be prompt."

Joshua knew better than to even flap his gums anymore at this point. He could just feel the iciness of two men glaring at him at this point.

"Yes, Mr. Martel." He addressed his sponsor formally, gave him a quick martial arts bow. "*Padrone*," He gave Victor a quick, respectful incline of his head and quickly stalked out of the room. Both men could feel the combination of anger and fear coming off him in waves.

Neither Victor nor Martel said anything for a moment after the consigliere had left. They just sipped their coffee. "This war has a lot of them on edge." Victor said, "All of us, in our own ways."

"I know." Martel gently put a hand on his fathers shoulder.

"He needs to get his emotions together or they will jeopardize a lot of things, a lot of plans." Victor sighed almost softly. "I don't know what has gotten into him lately. He didn't used to be like this."

"I don't know either but I intend to find out." Martel said as he began to clean up the coffee cups. "The Family does not need any turmoil right now."

"No, no it does not." Victor nodded and smiled at his son.

"I'll be sending Alyssa up here while I talk to Joshua." Martel said as he refilled his fathers' coffee.

"That is fine. I have her working in the aviary now, you know. She enjoys it." Victor said idly.

Martel turned and raised an eyebrow, "You... Let her in your aviary?" he said almost in surprise, he knew Victor didn't let anyone but almost blood family in his aviary.

The old man chuckled softly, "Don't look so surprised my son. She needed a place to think while she was staying here, besides she likes it and she does well with the birds."

"I see." Martel said neutrally. "I noticed you also decorated up the house this year, it looks," he paused, "nice."

"Well I thought the men and their families might like it, with the war looming on us and such." Victor neutrally said. He diverted his eyes while he said it and Martel didn't think it was the only reason. "Oh, by the way," Victor continued casually as if discussing the weather, "Alyssa is coming with me to Jamaica when I meet with Vito in a couple months."

Martel nearly dropped the cups he was straightening. "What?!" he turned, unable to keep the surprise out of his voice. Even though his voice was low, the deep tone of it was enough to reverberate through the bones of his father. Only Victor seemed immune to the intimidation of the Shadow Dragon.

"Well, I figured she might like a vacation to figure things out, get her mind together and what not. Her and I had much to talk about while you were gone," the old man chuckled again. "Oh quit running circles around me, Laurence! You don't think I sense confusion between the two of you?" Now it was Victor's turn to pin his son down with an amused but penetrating glare. "Look, my first duty is still to this Family and that includes you and everyone in it. Just because we interrogated her here in this office with your IV techniques doesn't mean she has a 100% green light.

"She's a nice kid, I do like her, but I must ensure this Family endures on and all of my members are safe. You, me, even hot head…" he gestured with his thumb towards the door Joshua exited out of earlier. "She wasn't born of our ways Martel, she's still an outsider. I don't deny your teachings of her, but she still has to pass my tests." Victor said this not cruelly, but almost wearily and yet with brutally honesty.

Martel said nothing. What could he say? His father was the Don. It angered him to hear this news out of the blue but he knew he had no choice in this decision. Victor would do what Victor would do. Martel's poker face was one of the best. "Of course father. I hope she has a relaxing time on the beach."

"Oh Theo," Victor's said softly and faced his son, his eyes gentle, "I am not out to hurt her. She is the perfect cover as my niece, since that is what we are claiming her as anyway. It would be stupid for me to go down there with some *comare*." Victor laughed with a twinkle in his eyes. "Besides, I'm checking in under the Disarro name anyway, so why not have Alyssa with me. You turned out just fine with Vito and Lena, do you not think they will welcome Alyssa as well?"

Martel relaxed then, of course they would. His real unspoken concern was if Gambini got lucky. He just knew he would have to be extra certain that his nemesis would not have to get lucky at all. Now he had four people he truly cared about to keep out of Gambini's clutches. "I really, really wish you would take more than just two guards father." He sighed.

"I'm taking Gio Aprile, as one of them; you did recommend him personally did you not?" Victor smiled warmly.

"Yes of course, but…" Martel began.

"Theodore we discussed this." Victor interrupted him by putting his hand on his son's arm. "Too many guards and it will scare this Gambini off. The hit won't happen and it will come up here. We want business taken care of down there, in Jamaica. Away from RICO, away from the Fed's, away from the prying eyes of our *nemico*. Unless this opening gambit kicks off just right, the war won't go down the way we hope and plan. Please, just trust in me."

Martel took a long ragged breath his eyes meeting his fathers. "I do trust you father. Please just take care of yourself."

"I will." Victor assured him, "and we will take care of Alyssa and the Bonnaro's as well." His eyes twinkled with inner amusement and assurance.

Joshua's mood had gone from sour to really bad now. He couldn't believe he had somehow pissed off both Don Victor and his sponsor, Laurence. It was the last thing he would have wanted to do.

He stopped in the gym; he had almost an hour to kill, yet he had a lot of aggression he wanted to get out of his system. No one had any desire to work out in the ring with him, in his current foul mood, so after changing into a sweat suit he went at the martial arts training dummy in the corner.

These people, these men, they were his Family and his life! He owed them everything, would do anything for them. Everything had been fine until, she, had come along!

He unleashed a flurry of blows at the training dummy, imagining it to be that stupid, woman, Alyssa. A dark part of him would love to either garrote her to death or break her neck! How he had hoped that day they had her in the Office, that Victor and Martel had simply finished her off then. He could see no viable reason the woman even lived, and worse the old man seemed to even like her! The *padrone* even let her take care of the stupid birds!!! He unleashed another round of blows on the poor training dummy. That used to be his job when Victor was out of town. Now some amnesiac, mute, *comare* had it?

Joshua took a break for a moment, his breathing coming in exhausted gasps, his knuckles angry masses of fresh, painful bruises. He had forgotten to put on his martial arts gloves or any hand protection. "Fuckin' shit!" he muttered under his breath.

…Joshua Demonico remembered when he had first came here to the Jerome Estates himself, he had been barely more than 17, he would have been the kind of person who would never even have had the chance to ever join a Mafia Family had it not been for Don Victor Jerome.

He had grown up a punk kid, in the bad section of town on the very outskirts of the city, where the drug pushers were. He worked for a non-connected pusher who worked for a made soldier named Nico "Two Bits" DeBasio but every one called him "Free-base" behind his back because he used his own stuff. Joshua never touched the stuff; he had seen daily what happened to those who used.

He enjoyed watching all the Men of Honor up on the west end all dressed up in their fancy suits and their fancy cars flashing their money. But because he was a dirty kid from the wrong end of town, like a stray dog, they kicked him away. His own mother was a heroin user who died of an overdose when he was around 15; even child services didn't seem to care about some "stinking guinea punk who fell through the cracks" as Joshua thought of himself.

His mother used to tell him that his father had been a made man in the mob. Or so she claimed, a result of a few one-night stands with some fellow named Tony Demonico, supposedly with the Cordoza crew, Joshua had never saw seen hide nor hair of him.

DeBasio would often have Joshua run his money and packages (usually wrapped up heroin or crack) over to various drop off points, assuming the man was sober enough to give him the right amount. Many times Joshua had to cover with his own earnings to avoid having his fingers or arms broken. It was beginning to grow in a tiring rut, and he had nowhere to turn, nothing he could do. He could graduate and move up to bigger crimes like grand theft and burglary, and he was seriously beginning to consider that, anything to get out from DeBasio's thumb.

Joshua had heard that once in awhile, Don Victor Jerome, of the Jerome Family would come and collect payment in person occasionally from some of his lower soldiers and capo's. Usually DeBasio was sober enough for these visits. However one day, DeBasio was far to stoned for the visit to the Don, after shooting up on some new heroin stock.

He had called Joshua over, and nervously gave him a leather satchel. "Listen to me kid... You give this to the man in the fancy car and you better show respect, 'cause that's Don Victor Jerome you're speaking to, *capisce*?" he slapped Joshua's face hard. "And no fuckin' me over! Lil' dago, *jamook*." he drifted back into his drug induced stupor.

Joshua barely had enough time to make it over to the meeting place where the huge Jerome limousine was waiting, let alone have anytime to decently clean up. He felt embarrassed, dirty, soiled. He wished he could melt into the shadows.

Here he saw other men, elegantly dressed, like lords greeting their noble king. They would gently embrace a small man who had the presence of a grand Emperor and whisper a few words into his ear. Packages or envelopes would be exchanged; it all seemed so noble and courtly to Joshua. The glares of disgust that the other soldiers gave Joshua made him even more self-conscious.

Suddenly a path was opened between Joshua and Victor Jerome. Even though Victor Jerome was no taller than Joshua he felt like a giant to Joshua. He wore an immaculate suit, with an expensive red silk tie. On his hand was an elegant ring, his shoes the most expensive Italian leather. The Don's eyes were like dark obsidian mirrors, alive with intelligence and charisma. He was the only one who did not look at Joshua with any hint of distaste.

Almost hesitantly Joshua slunk forth. "Hello, Mr. Jerome." He barely whispered.

A few of the men around began to chuckle and mutter curses or insults under their breaths. Don Victor Jerome held up his hand and silenced them with a gesture and a look.

"What is your name, son? You are new to me; I have not seen you before." His voice was as charismatic as his eyes and presence; it was warm but full of leadership. Instantly all joking from the other men stopped.

"Josh... I mean Joshua, Joshua Demonico." He felt faint. "DeBasio sent me. He wasn't feeling well today." Joshua said nervously.

More chuckles and a few cruel guffaws ran around the group from the other soldiers, "Stoned off his fuckin' gourd more like it." A few said.

Victor sat back in his limousine and motioned for Joshua to get inside. "Come in, son. I won't bite." he said.

Hesitantly but obediently Joshua slid in. He felt so ashamed to be sitting in this man's elegant car in his dirty jeans, ragged shirt. He noticed there were a few dark-suited large bodyguard type men. He knew they were carrying guns, protection for their Boss.

"Is that for me Mr. Demonico?" Victor asked gently nodding towards the raggedy leather satchel Joshua had been carrying.

Joshua felt so stupid. "Um, oh yeah, sorry Mr. Jerome." He quickly handed the leather satchel towards the Don but one of the oversized guards quickly intercepted it, emptied it and did the counting.

Obviously this guy was Victor's accountant. After a few moments the guard mumbled, "Its light," and roughly tossed the empty leather satchel roughly back at Joshua. "Yer short 5G's kid."

Joshua felt his heart drop in his throat. 'Oh fuck you DeBasio, no wonder you sent me! You set me up!' his mind reeled, 'I can't cover this; I don't even have it in reserve!' Joshua felt the hostility and tension rise ten-fold in the back of the limo and the other guard casually began to reach into his coat.

For a moment the Don's eyes seemed to search his and Joshua could have sworn Victor Jerome was seeing into his very soul. "Did you know about this Joshua?" Victor asked calmly, but yet with total bluntness his gaze boring into Joshua.

"No, Mr. Jerome, I swear it to you." Joshua said. It wasn't said in a cowardly way but honestly. At this point Joshua was at his rock bottom. Either they would believe him, or they wouldn't. If they didn't he figured at least he would be killed quickly by Men of *true* Honor. At this point in his life, maybe a bullet to his brain would be the best thing.

Victor lightly touched the arm of the guard who had been reaching in his pocket and shook his head 'No'. The guard withdrew his hand. "Joshua Demonico, I want you to take us to Mr. DeBasio's apartment." And it was then Joshua saw a dark look come into Victor Jerome eyes that chilled his very soul and made him truly afraid.

They had driven the short distance to DeBasio's and Victor, Joshua and three of the guards had climbed up the stairs to DeBasio's apartment. Joshua was amused to notice they didn't even knock. One of the gorilla-like bodyguards had simply kicked the door down, and everyone poured in.

DeBasio weakly blinked in the light but before he could move two of the guards were on him. For nearly ten agonizing minutes the beating had went on with brass knuckles, until Nico DeBasio was a barely conscious mass of humanity. Joshua noticed Victor just stood stoically there, neutral to the whole affair one way or the other as if he saw beatings happen every day of his life.

Finally it seemed to wind down, one of the guards still sat heavily on Nico's chest, forcing him to face the Don, as Victor finally walked over to him.

"Nico DeBasio, you disappoint me." The dark fire in Victor's eye burned bright. "You know the rules I have against using the stuff, the *babania,* we sell in the Family. You know the rules I have for setting up my monthly meetings. That's two strikes against you. Listen to me carefully..." Victor crouched getting eye to eye with the bloody and beat up Nico. "I think we both know what happens if you get that third strike, do I make myself clear? I'm going to assign another button man down here to keep a close eye on you and if he even suspects you're ingesting any product you are going to find a few pieces of lead inside your skull."

Victor nodded briefly and the guard still on top of DeBasio's chest gave him a few more bone crunching hits for good measure. It was already obvious DeBasio's face was a ragged piece of meat from the brass knuckles and his blood was spattered everywhere on the couch, the floor and on the two bodyguards.

"Now," Victor continued, "Since you short changed me, I'm taking repayment in the form of your runner Joshua Demonico, he'll be working with me now. Joshua seems to have balls, courage and at least a sense of honor and duty. Some people are born to be Men of Honor, DeBasio and some aren't." The Don's gaze hardened like cold iron and he spat in DeBasio's bloody, mangled face. "You aren't, Nico DeBasio. Break him and chase him." Victor ordered.

Joshua Demonico would never forget those screams as long as he lived. Not just because Victor's henchmen cruelly broke Nico DeBasio's legs and wrists, but because they 'broke him' out of the Family, kicked him out. He was lucky he still lived, but perhaps DeBasio would have wished they had killed him instead. His humiliation and fate was worse than death.

He was no longer a soldier of the Jerome Family. He was nobody, an associate and an empty suit: No longer a made man or a Man of Honor. Word of his humiliation and lack of trust would spread rapidly on the street and he would be hard pressed to find anyone who would trust him, definitely not any other Mafia crew. In fact he was open game now to be killed for any past transgressions against any one he had ever pissed off. He had lost his protection of being part of one the most powerful Crime Family in New York.

"Let's go." Victor put his hand on Joshua Demonico and steered him out of the dingy apartment of his ex-boss and ex-life.

Once Victor was back in the limo he was composed again, his dark fire extinguished. He was the courtly Don. But the lesson was well learned for Joshua; already he had learned several very valuable lessons in the ways of *La Cosa Nostra* and the Family that day.

"Do you speak any Italian Joshua?" Victor asked him.

"Very little, just street slang," Joshua said apologetically.

"Ah, not to worry," Victor smiled. "My son Michael speaks it, as do I and there are a lot of people at the Jerome Estates who do. You will learn it fast."

And so Joshua had been literally adopted by Victor Jerome as though he were one of Victor's own son's. The Don gave him a liberal allowance and treated Joshua as though Joshua was one of Victor's own son's. Joshua loved the man and he would do anything for Victor and the Jerome family. When he turned 18, his formal education in the ways of 'Our Thing' truly began, at first he was sponsored by some of the various older capos' and eventually when the enigmatic Laurence Martel joined the family Victor hooked the two of them up together.

Laurence would be the one who would sponsor Joshua and get him initiated and be there with him on the assignment when he earned his button and made his first official kill for the Family.

Never had Joshua formed a friendship as close with someone as he did with Laurence Martel. He was enthralled and fascinated with the way the huge man moved, and fought. The way the man had the boss's ear and by how much alike in many ways both he and Don Victor were. Both Victor and Laurence seemed to be able to read their opponents, to know the outcomes of moves way in advance and to mask their emotions, something Joshua never could be able to do. Laurence Martel was to him like a true brother he had never had, in many ways closer to him than Michael, since Michael Jerome stayed out of the Family Business...

Joshua's mind came back to the present. The Jerome Family and Victor, Laurence, all the capos from Patrizio to Cesare to the various guards were his life and his world. He truly cared for them all, enjoyed joking with them, being with them.

Why? Why, was he letting this outsider woman get under his skin? He pulled back again from the training dummy sighing deeply. He was a tired mass, he had nearly exhausted himself working out his frustrations and memories on the martial arts training dummy. Besides he had to clean up and get ready to see Martel. He did not want to be late and disappoint his sponsor and underboss; he already knew he was on thin ice with Victor and Laurence.

After taking a quick shower, and redressing, he exited the gym and went to the foyer to grab his coat and car keys.

The front door opened and Gio Aprile and Alyssa came in, Gio was talking to her; smiling and chuckling about something and Alyssa was smiling and nodding back at him.

Alyssa and Joshua's eyes briefly met. He almost couldn't control the anger within him but he quickly slammed it down. Instead he went to push by her and as he did he nearly knocked her off her feet.

"Hey! Whoa." He felt the impossibly strong grip of Gio Aprile on his arm. It was like being held in the grasp of a bull elephant. "Easy Mr. Demonico, what's yer problem?" The voice was low but firm. He'd only heard Gio use that tone of voice with outsiders.

Alyssa stood by the door; her shoulder had caught the wall and she stood rubbing her arm where it had hit the corner of the wall. Joshua had knocked into her fairly hard.

A part of Joshua felt glad he had hurt her but a part now felt even worse. How much worse was he going to make this day?

Gio kept looking at him expectantly. He knew he couldn't order the consigliere to do anything and as a well trained elite bodyguard he didn't want to cause any scenes. Would Joshua do the gentlemanly thing as a Man of Honor and apologize?

"Forgive me." Joshua muttered in his thick Brooklyn accent, briefly glancing at Alyssa. Then back at Gio. "I was in a hurry. Now if you'll excuse me, please."

The hulking Gio nodded, gently released the consigliere and went to tend to Alyssa.

After quietly exiting the door, Joshua stormed off, rage burning in his heart.

Alyssa had been told by Laurence she would be spending the day up in the manor and Gio had come over to pick her up. She was briefly surprised by the darkness that Joshua had shown her, however she was even more surprised by the strength and anger she had seen Gio show to the consigliere.

Gio had invited her today to train with him in the gym. To anyone else Alyssa would have firmly said no, the gym was just not her favorite place to hang out but she trusted Gio. He had set up a boom box and snapped in some Black Sabbath cassettes in it and went about helping her with the free weights. She found Gio to be a 100% better trainer than Carmine Marcallo ever was. Gio was patient, gentle with her and worked hard to figure out a program that would slowly strengthen the muscles where she had been operated on donating a kidney to Victor. After getting her started Gio did his own workout and Alyssa was beyond shocked at just how much weight the man could lift and work with. Of course, after seeing the build on him, perhaps it didn't surprise her at all. The man was built like Arnold Schwarzenegger.

After showering up, they met back in the kitchen where Emilia and Rosette whipped up some cappricola and provolone sandwiches for them. "Well ladies," Gio spoke to all of them, "I'm gonna ask Patrizio tonight." He grinned as he crammed half the sandwich in his mouth in one gulp.

Rosette smiled knowingly and after translating for Emilia the older matron got tears in her eyes and said something in Sicilian.

"What?" Cesare came in catching this last part and hoping Rosette would make him a few cappricola sandwiches, "You finally gonna make a married woman outta Clarissa?" he came over and patted Gio's shaved head.

"Yep, sure am." Gio nodded. It was common knowledge that Gio and Patrizio's daughter, Clarissa had been dating seriously for several months. Everybody began to congratulate Gio, including Alyssa who scrawled out "*CONGRATS!!!!*" in big bold letters, underlining it several times.

"We're all getting invites to the wedding now, right?" Cesare teased again as he joined them at the table with his own sandwich and a beer.

"Hell yeah!" Gio gave a thumbs up, "In fact, I'm gonna see if Victor will let me have the reception here at the Estate. That way everyone can be invited."

The kitchen ladies seemed to love this idea and already they began speaking in rapid Italian figuring out courses and dishes to whip up.

"Whoa, hey." Gio winked, "I haven't even talked to Patrice yet. He better hear the news from me, not through the grapevine, ya know what I mean?"

"Ah, don't worry about it." Cesare said with a jovial wheeze, "He'll be happy to have you as a son-in-law. I'm always hearing Patrizio saying good stuff about ya and you know how old fashioned he is. Of course you didn't hear this from me."

This bought a round of laughter from everyone, especially once Cesare spoke it in Italian for the benefit of those immigrants who didn't speak good English.

"So, who are you thinking for Best man?" Cesare leaned over to Gio, "Martel?"

"Actually," Gio leaned in close to Cesare and draped one muscular arm around him "I was thinking of you, man. Whaddya say Cesare? You willing to stand up there with me?" he then turned to Alyssa, "You think he should be my best man, 'Lyss?" Gio asked her with a wink Cesare didn't see.

Alyssa nodded an enthusiastic yes! She also noticed Cesare's eyes had taken on a very deep look, an almost honored look.

"Come on, see? Even Alyssa says yes!" Gio teased and put one hand on Cesare's shoulder.

"Yeah, of course!" Cesare found his voice, "Shit, I am honored your even asking me! Of course!" the two men stood up and embraced clapping each other roughly on the shoulders.

"Hey, you're my paisan! My good friend! Of course I'm gonna ask you Elf!" Gio grabbed Cesare's jowly cheeks and then gave him a playful punch in the arm. By that time everyone had surrounded Gio and was giving him congratulatory hugs, the kitchen ladies and Alyssa giving him kisses on the cheek as well.

Chapter 29-

Martel already knew who it was when he heard the knock on his front door. He had sent Alyssa up to the main house for a few hours, with Gio to visit the Aviary or something. He didn't want any disturbances when he talked to Joshua.

"Come in Joshua," He called out. Martel was dressed in his casual clothes, his dark martial arts workout clothes. Some people would be unnerved seeing him in that, but Joshua knew Martel often wore them because he felt them comfortable to wear around his house, his 'lounging around' attire.

Joshua took off his shoes and bowed as he always did when he came into the home of his ex-teacher and his sponsor "Sensei, Laurence." He nodded.

"I made some tea for us Josh, unless you want something stronger?" Laurence motioned.

"Tea is fine." Joshua sat in the living room.

Laurence bought out the tea; it was a green tea with some kind of herbal supplement in it served in the traditional Asian type of stone cups, he poured a cup for Joshua and handed it to him.

Demonico sniffed it; "Valerian, hops, chamomile, and..." Josh sniffed again, took a taste and then looked helplessly at Martel.

Martel smiled. "Kava root, but you're getting quite good." He was proud of his student's ability to sense and distinguish the different types of herbs.

"Man, you trying to put me to sleep or what?" Joshua teased him lightly.

"Perhaps just calm you down some my friend." Martel glanced pointedly at Joshua's hands.

"Oh," he glanced embarrassedly at his hands, "Stupid me forgot to wear my hand protection again." Joshua laughed softly, trying to lightly play it off but he knew very little ever escaped Martel's notice.

They drank the tea in silence for a few minutes, Joshua noticed Martel had incense going as well and he was indeed beginning to feel a bit sleepy and relaxed. 'Damn Martel' he thought, 'you're far too good at what you do my teacher'.

"Hey, how is that Koi I got you doing?" Joshua changed subjects to fight the sleepiness and heavy headedness that was invading his senses.

"Shikaru?" Martel laughed, "Come see." Both men walked out to the Zen garden where a huge Koi swarm around a well manicured elegant Japanese Koi pond. It was a beautifully silvery fish, with bright orange markings on it. Its whiskers broke the surface of the water a moment as it looked up hoping for some handouts. Two smaller ones broke the surface a few moments later.

"Ya should'a named it Godzilla!" Joshua laughed. "May I?" his eyes lit up as he motioned to the Koi food tubs.

"Go ahead, I haven't fed them yet." Martel nodded. This was the Joshua he knew and remembered; a more relaxed Joshua, one who wasn't fighting demons inside. 'But aren't you fighting your own demons inside Kageryu?' His own mind taunted him.

Joshua took the measured amount of Koi food and flicked it a few pellets at a time to the gaping maws of the fishes. His chuckles amused Martel. "Go, Go Godzilla, hey, leave some for the smaller fish! *Bastardo!*"

Martel remembered Joshua had gotten him that fish as a gift when he had finished formally training with Martel around five years ago, even though Joshua still came to him for lessons and continued working with him for different levels of martial arts. However Joshua would never have the patience to truly learn all the intricacies and be a full time student like Martel had been with Cochran or Sen.

"Joshua." Martel began after Joshua had finished feeding the fish. "Look, you and I have never beaten around the bush with one another so I will be blunt with you."

Joshua looked over with an almost frightened expression at his teacher and underboss.

"Is something bothering you? Some grudge between us?" Martel asked, "You're still not upset over that incidence about not going on that job against Tito's son Torenzo, are you?" Martel eyed him levelly, his eyes seeming to pierce Joshua's soul.

"What? That? Oh, no. No!" Joshua said firmly, sincerely. "No, that is forgiven my brother and teacher!" he shook his head. "I understand about that."

"Then what?" Martel walked closer to him, forcing Joshua to look up at his towering form. "Something is eating at you, at your soul."

"I dunno…" Joshua tried to look away from Martel but couldn't. Martel was his best friend and confidant, his teacher and boss. "I guess it's that new chick, ya know?"

"Alyssa?" Martel asked quietly a slight confusion to his tone. He made sure to keep his face a mask of non-emotion. He was no stranger to the tension between Joshua and Alyssa, and his father had bought it up as well. Like Victor, Martel could sense uneasiness in the Family and it bothered him. But he had to be careful here, his feelings were dual natured in this as well. "What about her?" he asked.

"I dunno," Joshua finally turned away, "see what I mean? Sounds stupid, huh?"

"Obviously not to you it doesn't." Martel followed him, unrelenting, "Joshua, whatever it is, I need to hear it. Right now with the Family gearing up for *mannagge* and Victor leaving for his trip in a few months, all of us need to be covering one another implicitly. There can be no room for error in this. The Family must run like clockwork, we cannot have friction. There is no room for hard feelings of anyone, not even..." Martel refused to use the word 'outsider', when talking about Kanashii; she had given him no reason to doubt her yet. "...Not even, Guests."

Joshua's eyes flared for a moment at his old teacher. "Has she gotten under your skin too, Martel?" And he walked a few steps away with a huff.

"Enough Joshua," Martel's voice was low, letting Joshua know he was close to pushing the wrong buttons. "What is with you lately Kageryu?" his own mind chastised him; "First you lose your temper with Diane and now with your old student and the Family consigliere too? Is Joshua's battle really almost the same as your internal battle? Perhaps because Joshua has been one to wear his emotions on his sleeve he can vocalize it more."

Joshua just shook his head. "Victor has given her my job in the aviary, my job, to a *comare* outsider! And that day in the Office, when we all interrogated her, we should have just whacked her right there and then instead of letting the worthless bitch live and..."

"ENOUGH, *BASTA!!!*" the Shadow Dragon roared in utter rage, "Drop the insults already with Alyssa!" Martel had unconsciously closed the gap between them, his hand suddenly catching Joshua under the chin around his throat in a deadly jujitsu chokehold. One slight move and he would snap the delicate hyoid bone that held Joshua's trachea and windpipe together. There would be no countermove or way out unless an emergency tracheotomy was done.

"Kageryu," his own mind screamed in desperation, "do not go down a path you cannot undo. Stop this now! This is JOSHUA you are contemplating killing, your *compari*, the Family consigliere! LOOK AT HIM! LOOK HIM IN THE FACE!"

Joshua had been totally unprepared for the sudden rage of Martel. And while he had sparred with his teacher, while he had even seen Martel do some hits he had never, ever seen this side of him. Not ever. Not the unbridled rage and darkness that now emanated from Laurence Martel and more important never directed at a Family member, not even when they had punished Cesare for his breaking of omerta. For the first time in his life he looked into the face of Death.

Joshua's terrified eyes looked into the eyes of his teacher, his underboss, his brother. "Laurence I'm sorry, what have I done? What?" he tried to mouth, it came out a tiny croak.

Martel abruptly released him and turned away, a million emotions going through the large mans mind at once. For the first time in his life he saw a slight tremble in his own hand and he clenched it in a fist so tight that his knuckles were white.

All he knew how to do was kill; he had spent so many years killing everything that was human in him, ensuring his emotions were dead that all he had become was a killing machine. Now he had to learn to feel again, and he was finding that it was as soul wrenching a journey as when he had to 'kill' himself piece by piece.

"Joshua, I am sorry. Forgive me." Martel turned around and faced a shaken and pale Joshua Demonico, his voice back to being in total control. "I have now disrespected you and for that there is no excuse." He placed one hand on Joshua's shoulder and squeezed lightly. Then with a heavy sigh he trudged back into the house.

Joshua felt emptier, more hollow and miserable than if Martel would have simply beaten him to a bloody pulp. Just what the hell was happening in the Jerome Family?

After a few minutes of letting his underboss cool down, Joshua also walked back into the house. "Sensei? Laurence?" Joshua asked softly, warily. He saw Laurence standing by the sink, pouring himself a huge glass of the valerian tea and drinking it down in one gulp, he noticed the underboss was also pouring himself a large whiskey chaser.

"Joshua," Martel poured Joshua a glass of whiskey as well and handed it to him. "Right now everything, and I do mean everything, must run smoothly. Regardless of your feelings about Alyssa or mine." Martel sighed a moment then continued, "Right now we are on the verge of a lot of delicate decisions and a lot of action between our family and the D'Salvatores. I certainly don't have to tell you that."

Joshua downed his shot of whiskey in one gulp and said nothing. He was going to listen now, some very powerful emotions had happened between him and Laurence and he was certainly not going to push the man the wrong way. At the same time he loved the man like a brother, had sworn an oath to him as an underboss and to this Family to serve it unto death. He needed to listen and be heard as well.

"Why did Victor save her?" Martel continued slowly, "I don't know Joshua, why did he save you? He just did. It was his decision; we all have to live with it. Victor asked me to take her in and teach her and that is what I am doing. Do I find her a good student? Yes. Do I find her to my liking?" the tall underboss faced Joshua for a moment, his blue eyes piercing his, "Yes." He answered bluntly, "Will I let my feelings towards her interfere in my duty to this *Famiglia* and what I need to do? No. Nor will I find anything interfering in my duties to you and my other *compari*. You are the consigliere Joshua, our counselor, act like one," Martel said not harshly, but almost sadly. "Now is when the *padrone* and all of us," Martel emphasized the words "Need you. Now is when we need your ear, your advice; like before." He refilled their whiskies. "*Salute*, Joshua."

Joshua didn't know what to say, what could he say? Martel had humbled him with a few words as easily as the *Padrone* normally did.

He was not used to Martel being such a wordsmith, such an arbitrator. "*Salute*," Joshua numbly returned the toast and both men silently drank for a moment.

Martel still felt bad for his outburst at Joshua but he was beginning to think he knew now exactly what was going on with Joshua. "No his battle is different. He thinks Victor and I don't need him anymore. Joshua's battle is one of jealousy." Martel was certain of it now.

"Joshua," Martel led him back into the living room and offered him some more soothing tea. "You know, now is when Victor will need you the most. I think lately, you must have felt as though you were left out of the decision making process…"

Martel could tell by the pained look on Joshua's face that he had hit the correct nerve. "Victor will be leaving in just under three months to meet with Vito Bonnaro, it is then when things will really begin to heat up. It is when our Boss will need his consigliere the most; need you to ensure that all is running smoothly up here for him. I will need you as well Joshua." Martel emphasized the importance of his words, "I will be down in the islands trying to head off Gambini to make sure he doesn't take out Victor or Don Bonnaro and I need you up here handling the Family with your expertise, in this I trust you fully my *compari*. Neither Victor nor I would not have groomed you all these years if we didn't entrust in you so dearly of this Family." He rested one hand on Joshua's shoulder.

Joshua felt such shame in him then, almost as he did that day so long ago the very first time he met Don Victor… "Oh fuck why have I acted such an asshole these last few weeks?" his mind moaned in humiliation, "No wonder Martel nearly lost it with me; I insulted and disrespected the woman he obviously cares about. I have been holding back the bosses plans, acting the *cafone* I never wanted to be like…"

Martel could see and feel the slump in his friends shoulder, saw Josh's dark eyes that struggled in vain not to look at him, eyes that held shame, embarrassment and great sadness. He had not wanted to make Joshua feel bad, he had certainly not almost wanted to kill him but he needed to have the Family consigliere fully in top form, free from his own inner demons and jealousies, he knew Victor had been worried about this friction with Joshua lately and it had to be settled.

It looked like it was finally getting settled. Martel as underboss didn't want any friction either, he didn't like it any more than Victor and he needed to trust all of his men, all of the Family. He couldn't be worrying about anyone in a couple months when he was concentrating on killing one man, and one man alone. Louie Gambini.

"Laurence, I…" Joshua stumbled over the words, "I'm…"

"Joshua, Shhh. Listen to me." Martel shushed him. He was not going to make the man embarrass or humiliate himself. He sat down next to Joshua, like the old times, their eyes alight with plotting and planning, their blood fueled with a few whiskeys. "You and I are going to have some fun, Ok? We're going to have some fun with Joey Calendri." A dark, cruel grin flashed across Martel's face. "He came to you because he trusts you, you are the Family consigliere. He didn't come to me because of my reputation. Now, we will plan this together and I want your input on this as well."

Martel saw Joshua's eyes light up again, the dignity and strength of the *Famiglia* return to him. He was like his old self, not the angry tormented self but his cunning dangerous self. The groomed and deadly consigliere, this warmed Martel's heart. This is the Joshua Demonico he needed right now, this is the Joshua Demonico the Family demanded right now.

Alyssa had returned late to Martel's house. Apparently he and Joshua had been talking and drinking for a while. By the time Gio dropped her off, Martel told her he would take her shopping in New York City again tomorrow, and to visit "A friend of mine".

The next day they took the same exact route she took the first time, enjoying the helicopter ride and then the limo ride into little Chinatown. She remembered the strange oriental store with all the weapons and the small old man inside that Martel had talked to before.

However this time, Martel brought her forward to formally meet him, "Kanashii, I would like you to meet a close friend of mine, this is Sen Yamashita."

The small man bowed slightly, even though he was an older man around Victor's age, his eyes seemed to light up with laughter and amusement. "So you are the Kanashii that Martel talks about. Nice to finally meet you; you keep this tall fellow on the right path ok? Keep him from getting too addle brained." And then Sen had laughed himself silly until he was wheezing and coughing so hard Alyssa was sure he would have a heart attack.

Martel just shook his head lightly in exasperation at Sen's teasing and the two men conversed in Japanese for a while. The two guards who had come today were Tommy and Gio and it made Alyssa happy to have a whole group of her favorite people. She enjoyed showing Gio some of the different weapons, now that Martel had taught her about some of the different ones. Although most she still had no idea what they were or what they were called.

"Here Gio," Martel's deep voice sidled up, "I'll help you find a good butterfly knife, or maybe a *tanto* knife, if you want?"

At that moment she saw the small Sen nearby her, "Come here," he motioned discreetly to her, "Come here Kanashii." Enthralled she followed him; she noticed he moved as gracefully and almost as unnoticed as Martel. One minute he was one place and the next seeming to be somewhere else, his eyes alight with an inner amusement. He took her around the counter and near the curtains to the back of the store.

"So you like that crazy ol' Shadow Dragon, eh? I can tell. Well good. He needs someone look out for him, eh? Here." Sen thrust something in her hands, a small black lacquer box.

She recognized one of the kanji right off; it was the *Kageryu* kanji, Martel's oriental name. She touched the Kanji and glanced up, as though looking for him.

"Oh ho!" the small man's eyes seemed to dance with inner amusement and laughter, "So he told you did he? Oh, he really addle-brained then." Sen chuckled lightly and wrapped her hands around the box with his, "You not open, you give this to him," he whispered close for her ear only, "You give this to *Kageryu*, later."

She nodded and obediently slipped the small box into her pocket.

"You are good medicine for him, Kanashii. Trust me," Sen said with a toothy smile, and nodded.

"What are you two up too?" Martel and the guards had come back around with their purchases to put them on the counter.

"Conspiring, as usual Martel, what else?" Sen cackled gleefully.

"I believe it, Sen." Martel harrumphed. He motioned to Alyssa who came back around over to Tommy and Gio to check out what they had picked out. She couldn't wait for tonight when she and her teacher had their time together to show him the box and give it to him. The rest of the day it seemed to burn a hole in her pocket.

Joey Calendri had expected more of a reaction from Tito D'Salvatore from the disappearance of the Roman's Administration than the halfhearted grunt as Tito read the New York Post. Even the Commission seemed more concerned at least.

"Look what the fuck do you want me to do? Send flowers? They didn't find anything to bury! All it says is that the Roman's administration is missing! Maybe they are all taking a vacation or left town!" Tito groused. "Besides that's less money we have to pay them and more for our new soldiers coming in. After all, we have our own Commission families who are backing us, the Calavicci's, the Giancomo's and more importantly promised help from our new ally's in Miami, the DiMones."

"Aw, come on Boss, we know it was the Jerome's." Johnny Baldovino said as he adjusted his expensive Movado watch, "It had to be, they might have not found Vito, or his underboss or consigliere, but several of the capo's were whacked as well as a bunch of men over in Cleveland, Chicago and St. Louis, people known to do business with the Roman's. And besides…"

"*Basta*!!" Tito roared suddenly as he viciously flung down his paper. "Do you *bastardo's* know what a *mannagge* even is?" Tito stared at them incredulously a moment. "It is a war, it means people die. Even those by association! *Mi fai impazzire!*" He cursed briefly for a moment weaving a tapestry of thick Italian curses. Unlike the Jerome's, very few of his administration even spoke fluent Italian. Somehow certain curse words just lost their power when translated into English, Tito thought.

Both Johnny and Joey felt the chill coming off their boss and they didn't like it, they were both beginning to become very certain he was deliberately cutting them out now of plans, making plans on his own without them.

"Boss, Tito," Johnny tried to calm Tito's apprehensions with a smile. "Come on here. We are behind you, remember? We are in this together. Don't close out your Administration, not now, not as we are gearing up for the most important move of the war. We need to avenge your son, Torenzo." He knew the right words to bring back the boss's wrath to the here and now.

Tito's eyes grew dark as night a moment, His fists clenching around the paper. "You are right, you are right. Fucking, *stronzo bastardo, Vittorio* will be mine; his heart will stop beating in my fist as I stab it out of his chest…"

Calendri shook his head and had wished Baldovino hadn't gotten Tito all riled up about his son, Tito was never cognizant about his son's death when he was riled up and prone to do stupid things and give stupid orders.

Joey Calendri lightly fingered the paper in his breast pocket. He had heard back this morning an answer to his request from Joshua Demonico. They would meet with him in 2 months! The note simply had a time and date and said, "*Offer accepted*" and a place where he would be picked up, alone. He hadn't expected any less. Now he could only hope and pray that the Jerome's would see him as sincere and accept him.

He had calculated the date; it would be the same day that Victor was leaving to go down to his meeting with Don Bonnaro so he already knew he would not be meeting with Don Victor Jerome in person. That meant and he hoped, he would probably be seeing, the consigliere, Joshua Demonico. He would have talked underboss to underboss with Laurence Martel, but frankly the man scared the shit out of him and had a very bad reputation and if he had went to a Jerome capo it would have looked cowardly and in poor taste.

Joey and Johnny listened to Tito rant on and off for a while about how he was going to decimate all the Jerome's with his newly imported Sicilian soldiers. Occasionally Joey would look over at Johnny and finally he was beginning to see realization dawn on the consigliere's face. That Tito was planning on leaving them high and dry to deal with whatever may fall up here, while he grouped everything he had in Miami and in downtown New York.

He was leaving these two in charge of the New Jersey area entirely. After they had lost so many good captains and old hands in the massacre a few months ago, they had very few seasoned professionals left. All new faces, all the people left were new kids new soldiers who had never even fought in a street dispute or turf war, let alone a huge *mannagge* like this, or these damn immigrant 'zips' from Sicily. Tito was leaving them a sinking Titanic.

Johnny pulled out an expensive cigar and chewed on the end like a dog worrying a bone, as Joey buttoned up his leather jacket against the cold air conditioner in Tito's house. He always felt cold; maybe the Jerome's kept their house warmer.

"Son of a bitch," Johnny glanced at his friend and consigliere and sadly shook his head.

As they returned to the Jerome estates by helicopter Alyssa glanced out the window of the helicopter, taking in the view of the countryside. From up here in the air it was a gorgeous site, so peaceful. She had enjoyed her day in the city with Martel, Gio and Tommy. They had eaten lunch at an expensive Italian place and had shopped at some more Asian stores, she noticed Martel always had to stock up on his herbs and supplies and also shopped at some other stores as well. They also bought some large supplies for the main Estate, huge jugs of imported Olive oil and some other specialty items that weren't readily available at the smaller local town nearby.

To her amusement, they even stopped at a large fancy hospital and paid a visit to Dr. Weintraub surprising him at the hospital she remembered being at when she donated a kidney to Victor. It had been a wonderful day and she had no scares and no bad memories, just good memories of her, Martel, Gio and Tommy. And even though Martel was always fighting to not smile in public, she even got him to chuckle and laugh a bit. Tommy got everyone to laugh; he seemed to always like to break the ice by getting people to laugh.

She and Martel returned to his house while Gio and Tommy went back off to estates. Today Gio had picked out and ordered both the engagement ring and wedding ring for Clarissa while they downtown in the city. With a smile he had told Martel, Tommy and Alyssa that Patrizio had given him his blessing to marry his daughter.

Alyssa and Martel shared a light meal of soup and stir-fry and then Martel teased her, "Ready to work on learning those falls?"

She gracefully nodded and after working on martial arts for an hour, they settled down and he brought out a book and read to her. This was often one of her favorite activities. Martel would often half sit, half lay on the couch and she could sit wherever she wanted to. She used to sit on a chair or pillow opposite him, but now often chose to curl up like a cat right up against his chest so she could feel the reverberations of his deep, calming voice, within him as he would read to her.

He was a master storyteller gifted with a beautiful, sonorous voice. Deep in thought, drifting, she could close her eyes and get caught up in the tale. Occasionally he even made up his own stories, tales of great samurai or ninja's.

Afterwards they would discuss her journal, the one he had designated to be shared by both of them and this was her chance to ask any questions she had or to discuss any feelings or remembrances. Lately however she really didn't talk too much about any.

She had been pretty straightforward with him; the only thing she wasn't honest about was her emotions towards him. The inner confusion of needing him and falling in love with him; and also the confusion of feeling that ever present wall of his between them.

After that would come the nightly ritual, which usually always included his healing massage work on her body. It had become a comfortable nightly routine between them, student and teacher.

That night he again invited her into his bedroom for her massage, like he had that very first night. It was the only other time she had ever been in her teacher's bedroom.

She must have hesitated unconsciously for his quiet voice spoke up.

"Kanashii," He broke her thoughts. "I won't bite. If I am being to forward or making you too uncomfortable, we can do your massage somewhere else. I just thought you might like a change. I notice sometimes the Shinto makes you uncomfortable as well."

She shook her head and climbed onto his bed. It wasn't that she was uncomfortable, it was that she so wanted to be with him in all ways, body and soul that it ached like a deep splinter in her soul.

"I just thought by working in this room, we could make sure there was no residue from that first night here when you had your terrors." He gently explained.

By now she was used to the routine of him lighting the braziers and incense, heating the oil and all the rest. She always enjoyed watching him work though, always liked watching his well toned body and the way he used his martial arts training to center himself.

As usual she lost herself to the massage and his work, allowed her mind to drift and swim down its passages, allowed his hands to do their work and heal and soothe her.

She turned her head the other way and saw his gun holster and his favorite Beretta 9mm hanging on the side of the bed. 'Underboss first and Kageryu second, aren't you my teacher?' Her mind drifted. She felt her mind coming out of the aimless memory drifts of the massage Martel was finishing up.

She remembered then, she had something to give him. The package Sen had given her to give him. As he was putting the oils and things away she wrapped the robe around her and padded out of the room and retrieved the black inlaid lacquer box and padded back in.

Martel came out of the master bathroom and saw her standing there, with something in her hands held out to him. At that moment Kanashii looked as beautiful as he had ever seen her at that moment. Her green eyes danced with the light of happiness and hidden surprise, the robe held around her demurely and she held something in her hands, proffered almost sensuously to him.

He was just wearing his dark martial arts pants and his own dark tattoos reflected in the candle light of the room as he stepped forward. "Kanashii?" he said softly, his head cocked slightly, "what have you got there?"

A smile crossed her face as she gently placed the box into his large hands, his fingers brushing against her small ones. He felt his soul and body stir.

However as his eyes glanced down at the box he felt a chill course down him...He recognized this box. His finger unconsciously traced the Kanji of his name, Kageryu, and of the one underneath, family Yamashita, 'Oh gods, this was to have been my gift from Sen when I would have married Miyoko!'

He felt strangely sad and happy all at the same time, a strange connection to the past-present. Slowly he turned away for a moment then carefully opened the box. Inside were two beautiful inscribed Kanji made of solid gold, one was his name, the Shadow Dragon, *Kageryu*.

The other Kanji didn't quite fit right in the original box and it was newer looking. It said *Kanashii*. A small folded note accompanied the two wedding Kanji's.

Martel opened it; his back was now to Kanashii. So intent was he on reading Sen's note, he had forgotten everything else for the moment. "Kage, forgive me, I know this may bring up painful memories, but is something I give to you as a friend as well as someone who cares. This was something I had made long ago when I knew you were in love with my sister and were going to marry her. I already knew that look in your eyes then, you addle-brained Dragon, and I saw it again when you came to me the other night and we talked. I had the Miyoko Kanji remade/reincarnated into one for Kanashii. You still are an addle-brained Dragon; you know that?

I meant what I said; let the Dragon come out and fly; tear down the wall Kage. I know you know how to kill, but do you know how to live? I have seen you die, Kage, but can you re-awaken? I know you know how to grieve, but can you love once again?

Your Brother in Law Sen."

Martel felt for a moment as if his own world were wavering, felt his heart catch and hitch in his chest, as though it wanted to stop beating right there and then. He could almost picture Miyoko's face for a moment as clearly as day, he could see Tashima's face as he squeezed the life out of him as well, but that was past. He could not bring Miyoko back no matter how much he wished, anymore than he could keep killing Tashima over and over for it. He felt something hit his arm, it was wet and he looked down. It was a tear, his own tear. How alien and odd it looked to him, to be his own. He quickly wiped it away there was no more.

'Oh Sen, do you know what dangerous memories you have stirred in me?' But was it Sen doing it? Or was it someone else? *Kanashii!* Quickly he turned around. She was gone.

After she had given him the box Alyssa had seen a several emotions cross her teachers face and a few of them didn't look so pleasant. She had hoped the box would please him -she had thought Sen said it would please him- but when he turned his back on her and she saw that scarred back of his tighten, she could feel waves of emotions coming off him. Sadness, regret, hate and something else... It nearly overwhelmed her. This was not the stoic teacher and underboss she was used to.

Quickly and quietly she had left his room, she certainly didn't want to be there if he was going to be in a bad or dangerous mood. She still well remembered that one day he and Joshua had come to blows in the martial arts ring and she knew what her teacher could do in a bad mood. Even more important she felt he deserved privacy and dignity. She knew how hard Martel seemed to keep things to himself and she had not wanted to intrude or be a voyeur on his inner emotions and thoughts, she knew well in her heart with her own fears and emotions at times over her amnesia that she felt uncomfortable if people 'caught her' crying or fighting with her inner feelings over the whole kidnapping and coming here with Victor and his *famiglia*. She had quietly gone back to her room, while leaving the door ajar as she began getting ready for bed.

There was a soft knock on the door. "Kanashii?" Martel's voice called gently to her, he opened the door. He had slipped on a robe himself.

She glanced up at him. He seemed fine now, no more uncertain emotions, whatever emotions the box had caused he seemed to be in control of now, calm in fact... Gentle.

"Kanashii, are you all right?" He came over and sat down on her bed. "Thank you for the gift. I assume Sen gave it to you to give to me?"

She sat down also and nodded at him. She grabbed one of her pens and a pad of paper. "*I thought you would like it?*" she looked up at him.

"I do, Kanashii," he smiled at her. "I really do. Trust me. It's just that it has been such a long time that I got anything so nice, it takes me awhile to get used to it."

To anyone else it may have sounded stupid, but she understood. "*Kinda like that sword he gave you? Like the one on the Shadow Dragon Picture that is special to you.*" she looked at him.

He nodded. "Yes, little one." His hand caressed her gently, she did understand. "Kind of like that." This time he did allow his arms to enfold her, to inhale the soft scent of her. A part of him wanted to join with her right there and then as a man joins with a woman, to take her and make love to her but he could sense she was still not ready for that move yet. There was still too much confusion in this one yet and worse he still had a test of his own he had to give her.

He briefly closed his eyes, 'Oh Kanashii, can you understand? Even begin to understand what must come first in my life? I had hoped Miyoko would have; now I have to see if you can understand. You have already been indoctrinated into it -this *Famiglia*- but now you must pass the ultimate test and I will not be here to walk you through it. A test of your own inner strength and omerta, and if you do pass, the next months will be a test in strength for all of us, will you be able to withstand the ultimate secret then, Kanashii? Will you forgive me?'

"Kanashii, Alyssa." Martel tilted her head up to look into his eyes. "If you want you are welcome to sleep in my bed tonight. Strictly platonic, but you are more than welcome to if you wish. The choice is yours." He gently kissed her forehead.

She looked at him, almost insulted, almost sad. Did he not think her attractive, or worse was she assuming that he even liked her? Maybe he had a girlfriend somewhere and Alyssa's attraction was only one way. Perhaps Martel did not feel towards her as she was feeling towards him.

"I meant no offense, Kanashii." Martel smiled. "Trust me; I would love nothing better than to be with you as a lover. But you are still healing in mind and body; I just don't feel it's fair yet..."

'Liar,' his own mind goaded him, 'you are the one who can't handle it yet, Kageryu! You're worried if she doesn't pass your test or whatever test your father has that you won't be able to...'

"...Anyway, so," Martel continued as he slammed down his own annoying voices. "Soon, we can be together in that way. But for now, you are still welcomed in my bed, if you wish." His mind seemed to go in a million directions at once. 'Then why tempt yourself you stupid, addlebrained fool! Maybe she won't accept!' Deep in his heart he did want her so, did want nothing more than to make love to her for hours on end, to explore her fully. Why was he even asking this then? Setting himself up for something he could not have, that he didn't feel right in having at this moment? He had meant what he had said; he did think she needed to heal more in mind and soul and so did he.

With a demure smile, Kanashii got off the bed and taking his hands in her small ones led him back down the hallway to his bedroom, her green eyes alight with emotions of love, trust and passion.

Thankfully, she didn't tempt him further and after giving him a soft kiss good night on his cheek she simply curled up in a small ball, her back to him, like she did that first night and was soon fast asleep. Martel watched her for a while, watched her small sleeping form, like a small graceful cat curled in on itself.

One of his large hands hesitantly and slowly reached out, barely touching her as he ran his fingers over the curve of her shoulder and the soft beauty of her red hair. She snuggled against the touch of his hand a moment then curled deeper into the covers, burrowing into a tighter mound, a slight unconscious smile on her face of peacefulness and contentment, as she dreamed of her and Martel sailing on a large sailboat free and unencumbered on turquoise blue oceans.

Chapter 30-

Alyssa woke up to the sound of Martel shaving again; much like the first time she has spent the night in his bed. She unburied herself from the covers and saw his lean muscular back in the washroom, the angry jagged scar that ran from his right shoulder blade to nearly his bottom ribcage. It looked as though it must have been a horribly painful ordeal at the time. She saw the strange kanji and tattoo's flex and tense as he ran the electric razor over the sharp angles of his face, the intense sapphire eyes of the shadow dragon catching her watching him in the mirror. A slight smile of amusement showed on his angular face, as he noticed her watching him intently however he said nothing until he was finished.

How she wished deep in her soul she could learn more about him. Who he was, what made him tick, what his past was like? How did had he gotten that horrible scar on his back? What did he do when he left the house in the mornings? What did all those mysterious kanji's mean on him. Those were the kinds of personal questions that haunted her mind about the enigmatic Martel. She had tried to ask him a few times in the past, but always he had nimbly deflected her questions of him and concentrated solely on working on her healing, as though he was guarding his heart very carefully.

"Good morning my dear Kanashii," He spoke once he had turned off the razor, finally facing her.

She smiled back at him. It felt good to sleep in his bed, safe, she felt no fear of him anymore. She noticed that this time, he had not put away his Beretta like he had the first night. It still hung on the holster on his side of the bed. She scrambled out of bed, she was wearing her oversized nightshirt that had a grumpy cat on it that said '*I am NOT a morning person!*' and indeed she wasn't. Like Joshua it took her at least a good half hour to wake up. She rubbed her eyes and went about straightening her teacher's bed.

"Enough of that," He chided lightly. "Why not expend some useful energy and make us some breakfast my student, Hmmm?"

She turned and with a grin gave a slight tilt of her head, it was hard to be grumpy with him. She had sensed a change in him as of late, since he had come back from his two week business trip, as though he was trying to bridge that gulf between them. She had wished she had known what was in that box Sen had given her to give to him but Martel had not uttered a peep about it. He had seemed to allow her closer into his life and domain but not made mention of the box. She did know whatever was in it, seemed to have stirred some very deep emotions within him.

"I'll be out shortly." Martel assured her and then turned and began casually disrobing out of his dark, loose satin work out pants he often wore to bed. Part of Alyssa wanted to look, she knew Martel could care less whether she saw him nude or not, in fact there was almost a hint of amusement in his eyes. He was just all rather blasé and matter of fact about it. A shower was a shower and one didn't take one with clothes on.

Alyssa on the other hand half hurried out, but caught a slight glimpse of him from the other mirror that was in the bedroom, that reflected into the bathroom. She just caught a brief side-glance but she was not disappointed one bit in what she saw. His lean muscular frame, the smooth curve of his lower spine and upper thighs equally as well muscled. Like the rest of him, he bore some scars on his thighs as well; before she could stare at him more he had disappeared into the shower stall.

It was her turn now, to notice that the sight of him naked had awakened parts of her she thought she would not ever feel awakened. Arousals in places she did not think she would feel and while she cooked their breakfast she imagined the large hands of Laurence upon her as the two of them joined as man and woman and made love. She was falling deeply head over heels in love with her teacher Martel - Kageryu.

Breakfast was actually shared in relative and comfortable silence, as both seemed to be in their own world. Today she noticed he was dressed rather formal. A dark blue, full suit and tie, she knew he had his 9mm and holster underneath his vest and jacket and probably a few butterfly knives, not that they were really needed. The man was literally a walking weapon.

"Today I am going to be downtown in the city with Mr. Jerome, Joshua and a few others." Martel explained as he finished the last of breakfast and coffee that Alyssa had cooked for them.

Martel had shown her how to cook the rice, almond and cardamom breakfast she loved, so she had made it, although it never came out as well as his. However he never complained eating it with gusto.

She fully expected him to say; Gio or Tommy would be coming to pick her up to take her up to the Jerome Estates but what he said next shocked even her.

"You will be staying here, at my house today, Alyssa." He did not meet her eyes when he said this, simply finished his coffee and adjusted his holster and gun, "You know what you're to do. Just stick to your schedule, work on your journals and enjoy the stereo, TV or what not. You know the rules. I should be home in time for dinner, I will go ahead and cook for us tonight, but there is left over ziti in the 'fridge for lunch and don't forget to take your supplements."

She gave him a half exasperated but playful look, like 'Do I ever?'

"No, I suppose your improved health is a testament to that, much to Dr. Weintraub's chagrin." Martel chuckled for a moment. "I want you to stay in the house, Kanashii." Martel said. "No running on the trails today, just stay in here. If you want to work out, you have the whole martial arts room to yourself." He nodded and gave a quick amused but grim smile.

Then at precisely 8:30 am he had put his dishes in the sink, rinsed them out and simply left while she had been in her bathroom cleaning up.

She was not too surprised his departure had been as cold and abrupt as it had. He was usually like this. There was Kageryu the teacher and healer, the one she knew and was falling in love with and then there was Martel the underboss, the cold one. The one who had that wall around him, it seemed with everyone. The one who was all business, the one who had earned the nickname 'The Undertaker', today it seemed the underboss was even colder than usual, his eyes often refusing to meet hers on several occasions, but she had not made much note of it at the time.

Everything had been going boringly well. She had stuck to her schedule, bemoaned the fact that she was missing Gio and Cesare's sense of humor not to mention the delicious smells of whatever Italian delicacies Rosette and crew could whip up. Next she worked overtime on her journals, including the one that she shared with him. "Kage wants something to read, I will give him something to read," she figured and threw a few of her emotions and honest thoughts into it, her own inner feelings of connecting with him and being attracted to him. "Let him digest that!" she mused with a devilish quirk of her soft lips.

She pulled out some tapes Gio had lent her and tried to listen to music or read some books, but it wasn't working, she found it hard to relax. She finally decided to clean up the kitchen and dust the living room and even some of the other rooms. She knew normally Martel cleaned his house, but she wanted to do something nice for him, to show her appreciation for his kindness for her.

It was when she entered finally the kitchen around 11:00 am that she noticed it... The door that went to the basement was just slightly ajar... She knew it had not been that way when she made breakfast this morning, so it must have been left that way when she had been in the bathroom after breakfast, when he rinsed his dishes and abruptly left.

She stood there dumbfounded for a moment, near the forbidden door, just staring at it. The door which was always kept tightly closed and locked was now opened a tantalizing crack. She had always remembered his words to her from that very first day. The way he had pointed that long Japanese cutting knife... "This door over here; is off limits to you at all times. Period."

She reached forward and gulped, her heart beginning to beat a staccato rhythm in her chest. "It's like Pandora's box," she thought, remembering the classical Greek story of the girl whose curiosity had driven her to look in the forbidden box.

Now her mind raced, she tried not to think about it, but the more she stood there, the only thing she, could, think about was that damn door. Slowly she walked away, "I am NOT even supposed to be going through the door, it is off limits, Martel said so!" But her mind kept drifting back over and over to that door that was ajar. "Surely I could just peek, just peek once and be done, before I close it!"

She paced the house, dusted the living room and then paced back and forth some more, but each time she somehow found herself in front of that door that was slightly ajar. She tried once to simply peek with her eye into the tiny little crack, but it was as black as the grave beyond. She opened it a little wider with her fingers and then paced some more before daring to go back and look, her heart thrumming with both fear and curiosity. "You are worse than a cat or a hobbit! You know they say curiosity kills both!" Her body almost trembled with fear. What was she expecting? Some guard to leap out and say "Caught ya peeking!"

From what little she could see it looked like six stairs going down, a washing machine and dryer near the bottom, and a light switch on the wall directly to the right. So far, it was all very boring. She almost sighed in relief. "This was it? This was the 'off limit area' her teacher didn't want her to see? It was just a couple of heavy-duty industrial washing machines and a dryer." It must have just been a test of trust she figured. She knew in her heart she should just close the door and leave it alone.

She flicked on the light and that is when she saw the stairs actually continued on, doglegging to the right, under the house. She instantly felt her palms begin to sweat. "Oh shit." Her breathing came heavier.

She would never know how and when her legs grew a mind of their own. It seemed as though suddenly her body had a will that was separate of her own common and good sense. "This is wrong!" her mind screamed. "We are NOT supposed to be going down here!" she noticed her body ignored her mind and seemed to be slowly walking down the stairs anyway, her eyes taking in everything, cautiously, curious about who and what her teacher was. What made Kageryu tick?

"Oh be careful what you wish for, you stupid body..." she cursed herself. It really wasn't a desire to break the trust she had promised him of not looking down here, but the simple curiosity of really and truly knowing who he was. He knew so much about her and yet she knew so very little about him, in fact virtually nothing.

At the laundry machines, there was another set of eight stairs that went down to another door. Again she felt her feet carrying her further down. This door was different; it was a heavy solid metal door, thick almost like a door one would find on an old bomb shelter.

She noticed that it had various keyholes in it and even deadbolts that could be locked as well. "Well see," her mind chided her, "end of the line. I bet this is locked solid, there will be no going in here."

Her hand came up and tried the handle to the door; with an ominous and heavy click it actually opened. "Damn!..." had she even been thinking straight or listening to her inner instincts she might have thought this all a bit strange, like Alice falling into Wonderland.

After all, why would the basement door even be open for her to get into if not some kind of test? But right now pure adrenaline was coursing through her veins: Fear, adrenaline and the insatiable rush of unbridled curiosity. A part of her so desperately wanted to run out of here, knew this was not right, had been told to stay out of this area by her teacher.

But another part was so falling in love with the mysterious giant that she was desperate to know anything, any hint about him and who he was. While he cared for her and shared his expertise with her, the one thing he did not share was himself. She knew virtually nothing, about Laurence Martel. Who was he? Where was he born? What did he like to do? What did he love? Hate? She just simply wanted to know more about him.

Slowly she opened the big metal door; it actually opened quite easily and silently. So nervous and single minded was she, that Alyssa did not have the stealth or common sense to look carefully around, but even if she had, she would not have noticed the tiny electronic laser alarms that were turned off or the tiny hidden security camera's that recorded her progress, for the master of the house to view later.

As the big door opened, it was as pitch black in here as the stairwell had been at first. Her eyes could see nothing. She opened the door a bit wider and barely saw some indistinct shapes in the room; tables, shelves and very little other than that. Quietly she entered the room, looking along the wall; she found a series of light switches and flipped them on.

Suddenly the room exploded in the overwhelming brightness of overhead fluorescent lighting. Alyssa's jaw dropped, she felt her stomach drop like a lead weight to her feet and her heart nearly stop beating within her chest. She thought for a moment she would surely pass out and at that moment she felt like a rabbit caught before the lair of a great huge predatory snake.

The large reinforced basement room must have been right under the great martial arts workout room above. It was around, 20' by 30' with two narrow hallways that led to other doors on each side. These other doors were securely shut and locked by various locked deadbolts and intact padlocks.

In the middle of this room were 3 long wooden tables around waist high, there was a metal drafting stool at the table. Scattered everywhere on the tables were various types of weapons, mainly guns and firearms, in various states of disassembly. She could see everything from shotguns to rifles, handguns to pistols. Old fashioned black powder guns to military AK-47's and automatic submachine guns.

Cleaning fluid and various accoutrements for gun cleaning, repair and modification were also scattered around on the tables. Here and there were bottles marked with acids and other fluids she had no idea what they were. Files, saws and vice grips were attached to the tables and in one of the vice grips she could see where a gun barrel was firmly clamped and obviously in the works of being modified. For what purpose, she had no idea. This was not her world, she had no clue what any of this meant, or what he was doing.

It was then her eyes were slowly drawn to the walls or rather to the shelves and cabinets that lined the walls. Along all four walls of this room were shelves that stacked from nearly floor to ceiling. They were modified to hold weapons of nearly every caliper and type, mostly firearm type weapons. Many were far out of her reach but obviously easily accessible to Martel's great height. She saw everything from double-barreled shotguns, to wicked looking sniper rifles. Collections of police caliper weapons, as well as heavy-duty riot weapons and armor piercing military weapons. Even simple 4-foot long blow dart guns that were powered by nothing more than a person's breath. From cheap looking rusty, beat up pistols, to expensive looking rare European guns.

Weapons of assassination, weapons of death and weapons of killing; perhaps close to 200 guns of every type in this room alone.

But what had truly caught her attention were not so much the weapons and the great number of them but something else far more compelling and sinister. Alyssa felt the sweat begin running down her back like an icy river, feel her very body begin to tremble in fear and even her eyes begin to tear up. Spaced here and there in between the guns, were skulls. Human skulls from real dead humans, many bore bullet holes in them showing how they died their grisly death, some right between the eye sockets. She knew in her heart, these were some of the victims of her Kageryu - Laurence Martel.

One skull sat alone, almost like a King on a black wooden stand. The initials, "T.D'S, *for my brother*", carved into the wooden stand; that skull bore no bullet hole. All the skulls sat there leering down at her, it was almost as if they were staring at her in silent judgment. Chastising her in a cruel and brutal reality as if saying;

"You wanted to know what he did! But did you not always know and suspect in your heart? Now you know!!! Now you face the cold hard fact girl.

Now what?

What are you going to do? What will you say?

Is he any different now that you have seen first hand what he is? You have always known.

Whom have you hid the fact from? ONLY YOURSELF!!!

You knew who and what Victor was, what this family was, is Martel any different? Either you accept him or you do not."

She dropped to her knees in the middle of the room, her body trembling uncontrollably, her arms wrapped around herself hugging herself unconsciously as her breathing came in ragged gasps. What did she feel at this moment? Was she afraid of him? Repulsed by him?

No... No, she was not. More embarrassed and angered at herself for coming down here, for breaking the rules. He had warned her! Had told her this area was off limits to her, *she* had been the one who had broken the rules and come down here, *she* had been the one to open Pandora's Box.

Slowly she gathered her thoughts and slammed down her emotions. She wanted out of here! Victor's words came rushing back to her... *"You do not want the kind of life and Family I have, you cannot ever be a part of it; do not WANT to be a part of it..."*

Only now did his words reveal a deeper connotation and sentiment. The Mafia was not glamorous, it was not romantic and no she did not want to be to be a part of it. Not like this!

She knew Laurence Martel was the underboss first and foremost and she would be most content to be his student, his friend/girlfriend and whatever else he opened up and allowed her to be.

She would be glad and honored to be Victor's niece and friend, grateful that he was kind enough and trusted her enough to feed his birds and invited her to a vacation with him. But he was oh so right; she had no want and desire to know anymore of what the men did behind their closed doors, that was their world and she knew she had no place in it.

With trembling muscles she shakily got to her feet, praying she would not pass out, praying she would not have a panic attack down here. "Please do not let Martel find me here!" she knew if he did, the results would not be good. Somehow she didn't think he would forgive her this trespass, she was certain of it. In fact she began to grow paranoid of leaving the place exactly as she found it.

She went to turn off the lights and that is when she noticed the carved notches in the wooden doorframe. They were slash marks in groups of five. She stood there transfixed, ticking them off in her mind. There was close to 210. "Oh holy shit..." her mind reeled numbly and began to shoot more adrenaline into her body again. Somehow she didn't feel it was a count of the number of push-ups the big man could do.

She felt her bile rise and carefully turned off the lights, retraced her steps out of there and then got the heck out of dodge. She made sure to leave everything exactly as she had found it, including leaving the basement door slightly ajar. She would never, ever speak of that day, or write anything about it in any of her journals, or treat him any differently. She was not stupid; her skull could just as easily be up there with the others.

That afternoon when he came home, she was reading a book in the living room. Her mind a mantra of *"act normal, act normal, act normal..."* he had disappeared in his bedroom for a while to change into his usual black martial arts clothes and then went directly into his shinto/temple area for a little while longer.

When he came out, at first his face was a mask of stoicism, like it had been at breakfast. "So how did your day go Alyssa?" he asked, sitting down next to her, nearly pressed up atop her on the couch. Even his voice sounded more 'The Undertaker' than Kageryu, the deep baritone reverberating throughout her mind and soul. "Get into any trouble while I was gone?" he asked and looked at her squarely in the eye.

For a brief instance she was 100% certain he knew everything, could see the deepest part of her soul... She knew her teacher well enough by now to know he could read her like a book, as the sapphire blue eyes peered deep inside her.

"It's a test." She told herself, "Play it cool, just play it cool." She put down her book and smiled at him, and shook her head 'no'. Then took out her pen and the pad of paper, "*No, just the usual. Followed the routine and read for a while. I'm glad you're back, my Teacher, I missed you.*" She spontaneously gave him a hug then and snuggled tightly against him, choosing to disarm him that way. After all, if he was going to kill her, than she was going to die remembering the pleasant things about him, not the hard-edged and cruel 'Undertaker Martel'.

Her tactic worked or she must have passed his test for she instantly felt the hard edge to him soften. His hands came up and caressed her neck and shoulder, soothing the pressure points that were there, relaxing her muscles. "I'm glad, Kanashii." His voice softened, "I missed you too." He released his breath he had been unconsciously holding. She had passed the first test with flying colors. "Now why don't you wash up and I'll make us dinner."

When she went to wash up for dinner, he quietly closed the door to the basement and relocked it.

As they ate dinner, he casually said "Tomorrow I'll show you where I keep the washing machines, so you can do your own laundry when you want." He had to truly fight to keep the amused grin off his face as he watched her struggle to keep her face a total mask of neutrality, but she did very well.

"_O.K. sounds great_." She penned.

He even pretended not to notice the slightest tremble to her hand. He did so enjoy Alyssa/Kanashii. She was healing well and she was a strong fighter, just like Miyoko had been. He knew he had not been wrong in his assessment of her.

TENDER IS THE NIGHT PART 3-

~THE WAR ~

*...I've seen your face before my friend but I don't know if you know
who I am.
Well I was there and I saw what you did, seen it with my own two eyes,
So you can wipe off that grin, I know where you've been,
It's all been a pack of lies...*

*And I can feel it coming in the air, tonight, Oh Lord...
Well I've been waiting for this moment all of my life, Oh lord.
I can feel it coming in the air tonight...*

"In the air tonight" by Phil Collins © 1981 Atlantic Records

Chapter 31- *October 12th 1987*

The months had flown by for Alyssa; they had been both the most wonderful of her life and also the most frustrating. During the time from August to October, she had learned to befriend and find her niche even more within the Jerome *Famiglia*, and those associates who dealt with them like John Thomas Weintraub.

She had fallen into a comfortable routine of staying at the main house during the days and spending nights with her enigmatic and compelling teacher Laurence, especially as it seemed lately he, Joshua and several others where spending a lot of time downtown in New York City. Victor stayed here at the house often spending some long hours himself working in his study-office or consulting with men like Patrizio or several others.

While Alyssa was more than happy to see less of Joshua, she was surprised to see more of Leonardo Tagretta, the connection from Sicily from the Bonnaro's. He often spent a lot of time with Laurence late at night, their voices speaking in low Italian out in the Zen garden or occasionally even downstairs in that secret room of Martel's. A few times they worked out alone in the martial arts room here, and she had heard Leonardo a few times refer privately to Martel as '*Maestro*' or Teacher-Master. It did make her wonder deeply, especially as Laurence would not discuss any of it with her and both Martel and Leonardo seemed to want to keep their association and training with each other a quiet thing.

The long hot and tired dog days of summer however found her spending time with her friends Cesare as they became walking buddies together, or with Gio swapping music and learning to appreciate some of the more 'heavy metal' music that he seemed to love. Alyssa had gotten to go to Clarissa Fantenelli's bridal shower in downtown NYC, which had made her a bit uncomfortable at first because she did not know any of the various women, wives and girlfriends of many of the men. But they seemed to welcome her none the less and just like the men had their own 'politics' of wanting to bend the boss's ear or get closer to Victor, it seemed many of the women worked hard to try and welcome in Alyssa and befriend her, especially once they had heard she was Victor Jerome's niece.

She had finally gotten to meet Cesare's family, Lisa and his children and found them as warm and kind as he was. It was obvious to Alyssa's eyes that Cesare and Lisa Ciccerone had a very deep love and affection for one another and it touched Alyssa deeply, made her long even more for her and Laurence to somehow move their relationship to something deeper, something closer.

It's not that her and Laurence had not been working as a synchronized team, not that she hadn't opened up more and shared with him, but he as always, seemed to keep her at arms length, to keep that wall up around his heart and soul as strongly as Ft. Knox. She had tried only twice more after that night of giving him the box from Sen, to initiate a more intimate relationship with him, but always he mumbled something about him not feeling she was ready for it and then simply deflecting those words and feelings into something else. What frustrated Alyssa the most is that somehow in her heart she knew he did care about her, his response to her was obvious, the tender way he caressed her or the occasional bulge of his sexual arousal she saw in his pants or the way his icy blue eyes would seem to soften as he saw into her very soul. The sexual tension between them seemed like a storm on a hot summer day, waiting to blow up with an incredible force of power.

However, Alyssa was no fool either and so after a few attempts at letting him know she desired more but finding no reciprocating actions in Laurence gathered her dignity and let him be. If he would have been interested in someone else she may have understood, but what frustrated her most was that she knew in her heart of hearts he wanted this as well but fought it as strongly as anything. Even worse, Alyssa seemed to sense that there were great cracks beginning to form in that tough exterior and wall of his and instead of being happy it began to fill her with a dread and ominous feeling she could not explain. As the days and months ticked closer to the fall, he seemed to be only more distant and stressed.

For now she would let him be, there was nothing else she could do. And so instead she buried herself in healing up, learning the martial arts with him and spending more time during the day with people like Gio Aprile and Cesare. Since Victor spent a lot of time at the main house, she learned the game of chess from him quite well or the two would discuss favorite books they had read from his library. He also mentored her fully in the way of taking care of his beloved finches and together during the summer months they welcomed a whole new brood of young fledglings and babies in the aviary.

Learning her own way within the Jerome *famiglia*, she never once bothered Victor with her inner feelings of frustration over Laurence's wall, did not ask any questions she knew she had no business asking (Such as Leonardo's increased time in working with Laurence). Thankfully Joshua seemed to spend a lot more time downtown as well and so Alyssa did not have to deal much with him, in fact after that time she and Joshua had literally slammed into one another he seemed to go to great lengths to stay out of her way.

By remaining silent and showing her ability to keep omerta, Alyssa had overheard a few conversations between the men talking about the continuing rising tensions between the Jerome's and the D'Salvatores. Many like Tommy and several others were now beginning to feel the distinct pause before the terrible storm in the air that would signal the final cruel move between Tito and Victor in the next several months, Tommy was back to putting huge amounts of creamer in his coffee. However, for now, it seemed as if all the Commission families were acting as quiet and low-key as possibly as the F.B.I poked around in earnest, especially looking for whatever happened with Vito Roman and his Top Administration.

During Labor day, Victor held a great picnic out among the gardens of the Estate for his men and their families and Alyssa often overheard discreetly from several of the guards they had not ever seen the house decorated up and once again so lively, it was only some of the 'old timers' like Patrizio and Sal and a few others that mentioned they had not seen such parties at the Estate in nearly a decade or more.

As the cooler weather of late September began to ride over the New England states, Alyssa watched with appreciation as the trees burst forth in glorious golds and reds, the sky often glowing with the clear cobalt blue hues that reminded her of autumn in the Midwest. Never once though did she have any urges or drives to ever dig into her former life. Her life was here now, with Victor and his family. Here is where she felt safe, cared for and for the first time that she could remember- with or without the holes in her mind that the amnesia caused- accepted and a part of people who seemed to truly care about her and for her.

Alyssa had not been the only one who had marked well the passing of the months; in fact Tito D'Salvatore had been working overtime, obsessed and determined to put into play his final plans to eliminate the Jerome menace that gnawed at him like a cruel hot iron. He would never, could never, forgive Victor his killing of his son Torenzo and it was this more than anything else that caused Tito to not only trust more and more in the DiMones in Miami but to leave his own top Administration more and more out of his decision making processes. Between Joe Cinno and the DiMones, Tito imported more and more hired Sicilian immigrants into his own *famiglia*, installing them as bodyguards and even capos, much to the tight lipped seething of his own men and administration. Had his heart not been so filled with rage, vendetta and hurt he might have noticed that some dark voice of danger whispered in the wind, but he was far to concerned about setting up his own final move with the hitman Louie Gambini and his new Sicilian muscle.

Each day both underboss Joey Calendri and consigliere Johnny Baldovino watched with silent but growing concern at Tito's illogical and rash decisions. Johnny kept trying to valiantly act as an intermediary between Tito and his men, imploring Tito to rely more on his own people than these unknown 'zips', however Joey Calendri was making his own silent plans and moves that he dared not breathe to anyone. Day by day like a silent calendar in his mind Joey was counting down the days until he would be meeting with Joshua Demonico of the Jerome's. He knew they could never accept him fully, but he would be more than happy to jump off the sinking and crazed ship that Tito was running. Even if the Jerome's would simply allow him to be a soldier in their organization, he would be happy. Anything to get out of the oppressive and irrational thumb of Tito D'Salvatore and as much as he trusted an respected Johnny Baldovino, as much history as the men shared together, Joey dared not breathe a word of this to anyone, for what he was planning on doing was nearly as unforgivable as a rat who flipped sides to the F.B.I...

Another sudden cold front had slammed into New York earlier than normal that year, bring lower than normal temperatures into the early October days. Autumn decorations had been bought in by Victor and set up; Indian corn, corn husks and various pumpkins and gourds had draped the Jerome manor in a festive fall mood, as though disguising the dark storm that would soon be blowing with an icy grip through all of them.

Martel stood with Victor and watched the brilliant oranges and yellows of the leaves outside the large windows of the estates, listening to the plaintive cries of Canadian geese as they flew overhead making their autumnal migration to the south. "So you leave in two days." He said without looking at his father his voice a mask of neutrality. Only Victor sensed the roiling inner turmoil in his underboss.

"Martel..." Victor turned and lightly touched the large man. "I am worried about nothing, don't you understand that?" the old man's eyes were filled with both an inner fire and yet almost a sense of peace. The pieces would be in motion now; this is what he had waited for, what he had planned for all these years.

"That is exactly what worries me." Martel said with a slight grimace and walked over to the elegant fireplace in the Office. He nimbly added another log and poked the hungry fire alive, awakened it into devouring the new log he had added.

Victor chuckled softly, "*Mio figlio; mi guardiano.* My son; my protector." He spoke in Italian, "You and Joshua are going to be seeing Mr. Calendri tomorrow, right? That will be one little flea of information..."

"And then," Martel interrupted his father politely, "I am hopping the red-eye flight to Jamaica that very night to come down and track Gambini." He eyed Victor levelly, as though daring his father to disagree with him.

"I know, Laurence." Victor sighed. "I had hoped you would wait a day until you came down, I didn't want Gambini tipped off at the last moment and canceling the hit but I know wild horses won't keep you away, nor would I even dare to try and stop you." He smiled warmly at his son.

Martel nodded grateful his father wasn't going to fight him on this. "Besides, Joshua seems much better now. He will run everything smoothly for us here. We have heard from Vito Bonnaro and DiMone got our message to him. Your ducks are all in a row, just as you predicted." Martel closed the screen now on the warm roaring fire and went to pour his father and him some coffee.

"But something still troubles you, Laurence..." Victor watched his son pouring the coffee with the grace and careful precision of a Japanese tea ceremony.

Martel closed his eyes a moment, how could he tell his father what was really in his heart? That he was still worried sick over this whole hunt of Gambini. That he had so many to protect that he cared for; Victor, Vito and wife Lena, Alyssa...

How could he tell his father that he had no idea what Gambini's plan was? That Martel had been running scenario after scenario in his own head trying to think as fellow assassin and hitman Louie Gambini would think, *where* and *how* he would attempt to make the hit. He and Gambini would literally be playing cat and mouse and at stake were the very people Laurence cared the most about. He was only staying for this whole Calendri thing in the off chance that Joey Calendri might know something of the hired killer's plans, or might have information of what he told Gambini.

This time, when Martel turned and faced his father, he was able to mask his emotions; they were hidden deep behind the wall of death that surrounded his heart. The blue eyes were cold, lidded, "Just the usual business that troubles us all, my *Padrone*." He handed him the coffee, "Nothing for you to worry about; nothing at all."

Victor felt a tremor of sadness run through him again, like he did before. So close was his son to taking up the mantle of running the Family, but at what cost had all these years of being on the outside cost his soul. Would he be able to make the shift from 'Laurence Martel' underboss and assassin back to 'Theodore Jerome' the future Don and head of the Family?

After their private conversation, Victor spent most of the day talking long distance in code to his friend, Vito Bonnaro in Sicily and then to some of his trusted capos' here.

Laurence Martel had his own business to attend to. He spoke extensively first to Gio Aprile and the other guard who would be going along, Tony Armanno, two of Martel's best crack shot special bodyguards.

After getting briefed by Martel, Gio pulled his boss and friend aside. "So what do you think Boss?" Gio opened the box and showed Martel the custom made large 2-carat diamond wedding ring. "Clara wants a February wedding and I said, eh, why not. Ya know? Hey what ever makes 'em happy." Gio winked good-naturedly at his boss.

Martel was pleased that Gio and Clarissa were engaged, both were good people and he knew it would be a happy marriage. Gio had asked her hand in marriage about 3 months ago and Patrizio had happily given his blessing, of course after busting Gio's balls relentlessly about everything from the elite guard's bald head to being built like the Incredible Hulk. "You better not break my daughter!" Patrizio used to tease him good naturedly, "Or I'll break your skull." this would always bring a lot of laughter from the men. Victor and the other Family members were as happy as well. A wedding would be coming soon, something to lighten the mood of the Family after all this *mannagge* with the D'Salvatores.

Martel felt both a strange deja'vu as well as sudden icy chill slide down his back where his scar was. "It looks real sharp Gio. I wish you and Clarissa all the happiness you both deserve." He put a hand on his second in commands shoulder. "We'll get you back up here as fast as we can. Take good care of Victor."

Gio looked up at Martel a moment. "Hold this for me, will you Boss?" he suddenly thrust the box at the underboss.

Martel looked confused a second. "What?" He asked slowly accepting it in his large hands. "Gio, why?"

"Just hold it for me. Please." Gio asked. His dark eyes piercing Martel's, "I don't want to fight it through customs or lose it or anything. I trust you Boss; you know what I mean?"

Martel exhaled and looked away for a moment. 'You want me to hold it for safekeeping my friend, in case you don't come back out. I understand.' Martel thought, as he slipped the box into his pocket. "Pack heavy and be wary Giovanni, promise me." He softly said. "This may seem an easy assignment but Louie Gambini is a force to be reckoned with."

"I will Boss." Gio rose to his feet and slid his sunglasses back onto his face. "I'll take care of all of them for you." He turned back to Martel and emphasized the words, "All, of them. I promise."

Martel nodded and went to go find Joshua. His mind was racing, his insides churning. Already this hunt was not feeling right to him, Gambini was no second hand hood and he knew that to kill him he would have to use every ounce of cunning or he would lose everything and everyone. 'Damn you father for taking this risk! Damn it!'

Joey Calendri, D'Salvatores underboss, sat with consigliere Johnny Baldovino and four other capos' at one of the strip clubs over on D'Salvatore territory called the "Champagne Lady". It was one of the places where the D'Salvatore Administration regularly hung out. Tito of course was not with them tonight; he rarely hung out with his upper Administration and crews anymore. Not since his son was killed by the Jerome's. Instead Tito had been acting like Captain Ahab from Moby Dick, locked away, paranoid, driven and obsessed with hunting down Victor Jerome and utterly destroying him.

The men where laughing way too loudly, drinking, whistling, bullshitting and occasionally thrusting $20 or $50 bills at the women who would dance seductively at the table or on their laps. All Joey could think of, was that tomorrow he would be meeting with the Jerome's. Someone from the Jerome's, supposedly and he hoped, Joshua Demonico their consigliere.

He was supposed to go to a little roadside diner called "Petey's" near the NY/ NJ border and supposedly he would be picked up there. He already knew he better come there clean, meaning no weapons or anything like that. He had no plans to dare try and sneak any weapons. He was sure they would probably search him, blindfold him and take him for a hell of a ride before he was taken somewhere to talk to whomever.

He felt so cold inside, that he could feel himself wanting to shiver uncontrollably. This change in weather had made him feel even more miserable. He could hear his men teasing him, laughing. He joked back, smiled wanly and laughed without even hearing what he was saying. It was like his body was there but his mind was drifting away from himself, watching everyone around him from the outside. He quickly downed another glass of wine and a shot of whiskey. It warmed him but only for a second.

A sensuous woman was dancing in his face, brushing her nude breasts suggestively against him, trying to seduce him from his money. He found her only irritating, however he laughed and threw a $50 bill at her, then tried to turn his attention to one of his capos. He threw a $100 bill to the stripper and told her to dance over by Johnny B, to give him a table dance.

Oh God, how he wished this would work out. Were his own men so blind to what was happening? How could they sit here watching women dance while Tito ran the Family into ruin? Maybe Tito was like Nero who watched Rome burn and fiddled away, and here they all sat, oblivious to it all.

Was Tito leaving them all to be picked off by the Jerome's? Not him, he hoped and prayed. "Oh please not me! Let the Jerome's accept me. I will turn, I will turn traitor on that son of a bitch Tito, that crazy, insane son of a bitch." His hand trembling a bit as he picked up a fresh glass of wine; he was so fucking cold.

That night a cold northern wind blew up, making the wind chimes in the Zen garden at the side of Martel's house ring softly and soothingly as Martel helped Alyssa pack a suitcase for her trip. Since she didn't have a suitcase, Martel had brought one of his own up from the basement to loan her. She watched as he showed her a strange way to fold clothes, it involved folding then rolling them into small little cylinders, but it sure made a lot more room in her suitcase.

"Hmmm," he teased lightly as he was helping to show her how to roll the clothes into the neat, tight cylinders, "How come you get to go to an island paradise? None of Victor's other associates get treated so well? I didn't get invited, either did Joshua or anyone else." He glanced at her with his serious but playful look, the one he used when he was trying to get a rise out of her, "Ah well, enjoy it Kanashii. I suppose you deserve the break and some rest and relaxation."

I plan to my teacher! BE COLD AND SUFFER! HA, HA!' she wrote back to him.

"Oh yeah?" he stood up at his full imposing height for a moment, glancing down at her, hands across his chest a rather formidable but playful smile on his face. "Maybe we should see if you've developed enough strength to throw off your teacher yet, hmm Kanashii?"

Alyssa shook her head 'No, no, you win!' she mouthed and quickly went back to packing. But they both had grins on their faces as they did so.

She noticed he was a bit more silent than usual at dinner that night. He seemed to be wound up inside himself about something. She also noticed he seemed to spend an extra long time working on her nightly healing massage, his hands running along her body, soothing, relaxing it, and working his magic on her body and soul.

"Kanashii..." He spoke up suddenly.

For a moment she had to work her mind through the haze of her own meditations and thoughts to realize he was even speaking to her. Usually he never spoke directly to her during their massage time. One of her eyes lazily fluttered open and gazed up at him, over her.

"Listen to me." His hands continued to soothe her body, relax the pressure points. But she noticed that they had taken on an almost more urgent and harder feel to them. "I want you to relax and enjoy yourself with Mr. Jerome, show the same respect to Mr. and Mrs. Bonnaro as you would to Mr. Jerome. The Bonnaro's are good people, I know them personally. But..." His hands had almost become painfully strong in their kneading now, almost harsh. Her body tensed and tightened beneath him, a small hiss of discomfort escaping her.

Immediately he eased off, angry with himself that he had allowed emotion to come into his thoughts. 'Center yourself Kageryu. If you do not, you will fall apart on this assignment, and Gambini will succeed. He will destroy everything that you care about, your father, the Bonnaro's, Kanashii'...

"But," Martel continued, his touch back to being gentle again, in control. "Be aware, Kanashii. You do not need to live in fear, but you know what life you live in. Always be aware of what is around you. Do not let your guard down, constant vigilance. Listen to what Gio and the other guards tell you at all times. Follow whatever Victor and the Bonnaro's tell you." He paused. "Promise me."

She half nodded with a small grunt and snuggled back into her arms.

"Promise me!" His voice did not rise in tone, but the deepness of it seemed to rattle her very bones for a moment and she could feel the overshadowing presence of the Dragon coming out, it was almost like that day he and Joshua had come to blows in the ring. She was wide awake now!

Her head snapped up, and she arched around as much as she could with him on her back, her fiery emerald eyes meeting his sapphire ones. There was no fear between them but there was total understanding, respect and heeding of his advice. She nodded clearly and mouthed '*I promise.*'

A deep sigh seemed to go through him and she felt him relax on top of her. "Good. Thank you, little one." He said softly. He finished up the massage and after gracefully rising to his feet offered his hand down to help her up as well.

He hugged her tightly for a moment. The gesture seemed to be becoming less rusty, for him. "Kanashii, I will be up very late, downstairs tonight. It will be better for you to turn in early tonight." He caressed her cheek. "I will see you for breakfast though before you go. I will have all your supplements packed up as well for you."

She nodded and bowed slightly and left back to her own room and then sat down at the desk. She knew exactly where downstairs he was; in that weapons room, the room of death. She could almost picture him down there amongst the skulls working on whatever guns and projects he was working on, the large frame of Martel bent over the tables and guns late into the night working at a feverish pace over whatever assignment that only he knew.

She pulled out one of the elegant stationary notepads he had given her recently as a gift. It had a beautiful scene of pagodas and koi fishes in the background. She uncapped her pen and carefully wrote out:

Dear Laurence:
You are my teacher, you are my friend but you are more. There is something about you I can't put my finger on, but it burns deep inside me like the fire hawks on the pens you gave me. When you are not here, all I can think about is you. When you are here, all I can think about is you. I love you, Laurence Martel/Kageryu. I know this now.
I'm sure you may ask how I can be so sure of my feelings, when I cannot even be sure of all of 'who' I am? Life comes with no

393

guarantees Laurence; I guess it never does. Sometimes I am not sure of anything, you know? But, I am sure of THIS, of my feelings for you. I have gotten nearly all of my memories back, at least the important ones. I have no one in the past I love, only those who have betrayed me. I would rather be here in this life with you, than anywhere else.

My biggest hurdle was accepting that there were two of you. Kageryu, the one whom I had promised my trust to that very first night; my teacher, guardian and caretaker. And then there is Laurence Martel, the underboss of this Family. For the longest time I tried to keep both separate, but that is a mistake isn't it? They are both you Laurence. I will always love you and always respect you Laurence/Kageryu.

I don't know if you believe in a soulmate Laurence. Someone who so just "clicks" with you that to not be around them is like a hollow emptiness. You are that person to me. I don't know what you will think of this note. But it's a risk I have to take telling you my feelings. Isn't that what you always tell me to write? To write down my feelings so we can discuss them in the journal together? Well consider this my assignment for when I am gone with Victor. Either way, I had to tell you what was in my heart; I owed it to you, and to myself.
Alyssa/Kanashii

She wouldn't place the sealed envelope with the note inside it on his pillow until the next morning, right after breakfast and right when Cesare pulled up with the sleek black limousine.

She ran back inside his house to pretend she had to go to the bathroom and that is when she quickly ducked in Martel's room and left the envelope on his pillow. She felt a small tear in her eye but quickly held it in.

As she raced back out the door, she saw her teacher was bent over talking privately to Victor. Martel was in his suit, so he was in his underboss mode now. She gave him a quick bow, but this time he surprised her by slipping something into her hand, a small box. He leaned down and whispered for her ears only. "Open it when you are on the airplane, Alyssa."

"Well we should be going." Victor nodded. "Niece?" he tapped Alyssa's shoulder in a kindly way, Cesare and Gio had finished adding Alyssa's suitcase into the trunk. Alyssa and Victor slid back into the back of the limo, she saw another guard already back there. Cesare got back behind the wheel and Gio rode up front with him.

"Now child," Victor leaned back and smiled. "We are going to have a good time." He patted her leg and adjusted the expensive stereo in the back as the sounds of Dean Martin and some other singer she didn't know crooned some Italian songs to them on the way to Kennedy Airport.

Joshua Demonico had spent all afternoon going over his plans with both Jerome capo Rocco Benedarra who owned the Blue Parrot nightclub in downtown New York City, as well as Martel. They had gone over every possible scenario regarding their visit and discussion with D'Salvatore's turncoat underboss Joey Calendri.

Joshua glanced over at Martel. There were only three men at the Blue Parrot right now, if anything did go badly wrong, they didn't want it becoming a major mess. The Blue Parrot was closed up for business, all the chairs were up on the tables, and the lights were dimmed low. Normally it was a nightclub and didn't open until much later in the evening, but it was also an important Jerome crew hangout.

One table was set up with a few chairs around it, Joshua sat eating some hot Focaccia bread while in the back Rocco and a guard was preparing everyone some fresh ravioli. "He should be getting a nice ride right about now..." Joshua said while dipping his bread in the hot garlic oil.

Martel checked his watch. "Sounds about right; Nunzio's driving, he's a bit of a speed demon, so they will be here probably within half an hour. We know our plan, I know my part." Now it was the usually quiet Martel who paced nervously near the shadows.

Joshua watched him for a few minutes, he was not used to seeing the Family's underboss unnerved and rattled. "Something wrong, Laurence?" he asked honestly, kindly.

"Nothing Joshua," Martel said levelly. "I am just anxious to get down there. I only hope this *cafone* traitor has something useful to tell us."

The two men nodded to each other, understanding between them. Joshua knew Martel wanted to be down in the Islands hunting Gambini and protecting Victor. He didn't blame him. The only reason Martel was staying behind was in case Calendri had any valuable information that might help him hunt down Gambini.

"Hey." Rocco came out with some fresh ravioli and more bread. "Joshua, here ya go. Martel? I got some for you too, eat up; it may be awhile before you get some hot food, eh Boss?"

Martel wasn't particularly hungry, but Rocco's words were accurate and he forced himself to choke down some of the food even though it was indeed very good. He just didn't have an appetite for it.

It was as though in his mind, his heart and soul beat a constant nervous rhythm out to him, like some cruel signal, mindless and instinctual pushing him to go find his prey, his nemesis, Louie Gambini.

However what ground on Martel's nerves was the simple fact that normally he usually was able to get inside his prey's head. To think like them, to second-guess them, stay a step ahead of them. It was the thing that made him so good at what he did. But for some reason Gambini was like a ghost to him, avoiding his radar and staying just out of his reach.

Joey Calendri had followed the instructions to the letter. As he thought and suspected he had been met at Petey's, by a couple of Jerome soldiers who pulled up in a rental car with tinted windows. They quickly and roughly searched every inch of him, and then blindfolded him. His hands had been roughly bound in front of him and he felt the cold steel of a knife on one side, and a gun on the other. He had not resisted at any point nor spoken. Neither had they asked him any questions.

The only words spoken to him were a muffled "Sit there, shut da fuck up and enjoy the ride, Calendri." He had felt the car swerve, jump a few lanes and double back several times. He was quite sure that no one would be following them.

He couldn't help but feel the cold ache in his bones; they had taken his overcoat and suit coat, leaving him only in a thin dress shirt and his slacks. He knew they were running the heat in the car, but even so, he couldn't help but feel his body shiver from time to time in cold as though the icy grip of death was closing in around him. He did not doubt his decision to defect and turn from his own Family, he was just so fucking cold.

At no time did his guards talk to him, occasionally they grunted amongst themselves or obviously communicate with some silent signals among themselves. Once in awhile he would hear one say "Yeah," or curse briefly, but that was it.

At one point he was roughly shoved down on the floor and he felt his coat dumped over him. He figured they must have been going through a tollbooth or some place they didn't want to have him be seen. But he dared not make a peep, nor utter one word or grunt of discomfort; for he knew his every move and response would be reported to Joshua Demonico when they got there. After all, his men would have done the same had the roles been reversed.

After a few moments he was roughly hauled back up onto the seat without a word or explanation. His blindfold rechecked and the wild ride continued. He could tell he was downtown in the city now, only because of the constant turning and the sound of the traffic all around him.

Now a slow fear began to settle in on him and he did something he hadn't done since he had been a small boy in Catholic school. He began to silently recite Hail Mary's in his mind, almost like a mantra. He knew if he didn't he would pass out from fear. "Hail Mary full of grace, The Lord is with you'"... Shit, he was so cold... "Holy Mary, mother of God, pray for us sinners now and at the hour of our death'"...

Joey Calendri was dragged out the back of the car unceremoniously. He felt several rough hands nearly dragging him through an alleyway, up some steps, through a metal door and then through another door.

"He's clean ..." Joey heard one of his captors talking to someone.

"Fine, thanks, cut his bonds. Leave us." The voice said.

All the hands suddenly let go of him and he stood there, daring not to move. He felt the cold metal of a knife blade slide through the ropes that bound his wrists cutting them free, and the same with the ropes that had been hobbled around his ankles. He heard the sound of several feet shuffling away then.

"Just stand there a moment, Mr. Calendri." That disinterested disembodied voice instructed him.

"Ok." He nodded.

It was silent, so silent. He felt so damn cold. Did he hear whispering? He didn't know, it sounded like some fierce brief whispering in English or Italian, then softly receding footsteps. "Pray for us sinners now and at the hour of our death…" his mind drifted.

More silence…

"You can remove your blindfold Mr. Calendri." The voice finally instructed.

Slowly he did. His eyes began to adjust to the dim light; he could see he was inside a closed club/restaurant. About 15 feet directly in front of him sitting at a table was a darkly handsome man happily eating from a plate of pasta and gravy and drinking a glass of wine, he openly wore a titanium and pearl handled Police 38. Joey recognized him as Joshua Demonico. Behind Joshua stood another man that Joey didn't recognize this man held an AK-47 in his hands, pointed at Joey, a hard look in his dark eyes.

"Pay no attention to Rocco while we eat," Joshua motioned offhandedly to the man with the AK-47. "This is his place and he likes to make sure people behave in his place. Come sit down." Joshua motioned to a chair that was at the table in front of him.

Joey quietly and respectfully approached the table and then slid into the chair that was opposite Joshua Demonico.

"Espresso? Wine?" Joshua nodded casually to the D'Salvatore underboss, as he continued to heartily eat slabs of warm bread and ravioli.

"No. No thank you, that's Ok." Joey mumbled slightly. He was sure there were other guards deep in the shadows watching him with guns pointed at him as well, but there was no way to see in the blackness beyond the table.

"Suit yourself." Joshua shoveled another forkful of ravioli into his mouth. "So we finally meet, eh, Calendri? You're the one who's been giving us Jerome's agita?" Joshua fixed him with a steely look for a second, his handsome face dark, but then a hint of amusement on it. "The great underboss for Tito D'Salvatore and crew."

"No. No, not anymore," Joey tried to put conviction into his words. He believed them in his heart, but the chill in his bones made him fearful and he knew he had to make a good impression.

These Jerome's, these *nemico*, they were so intimidating, how could Tito have been so blind? "My note said what was in my heart. I don't believe in the D'Salvatores anymore. They are dead to me, they make stupid decisions and Tito is leading the Family…" he paused. "His, Family into ruin."

"And so you are a coward and jump ship and come here, hoping we will welcome you with open arms?" Joshua paused a moment, pinning the nervous man with his dark gaze. "Joey," he reached over and drank deeply from a glass of red sparkling wine, "so many people on all sides playing jump ship and switch sides, has no one any honor any more?" Josh half snorted.

"No, that's not it." Joey tried to sit up, to sound brave. "I mean, I do have honor, I want to. That's why I come here to you. The Jerome's have honor. Your Don, he is in danger. I come here with good faith, I have everything to lose Mr. Demonico and you have nothing to lose."

So far this was not going how Joey envisioned. "We both know I am the one at the disadvantage here, I can only hope my information is worth enough, my integrity enough to earn a place in the Jerome's…" he felt his heart pounding loudly in his ears. The whole scene seemed surreal to him.

"We'll see, Calendri, we'll see." Joshua began to idly mop up marinara sauce with his garlic bread. "You said our boss was in danger. So speak, share this information with us and prove your worth." Josh looked at him again like a scientist watching a squirming ant.

"I was sent several months ago, to hire Louie Gambini, a loser fuck if I ever met one, but he is good, some say the best, next to your own man, Martel…" Joey gulped remembering what the big underboss did to D'Salvatores son, Torenzo and the group sent to meet the Armandana's.

"We already know –that- information, Calendri. Tell me something I don't know. We are not stupid." Joshua half huffed.

"This Gambini, he is already down there in the islands. Went down there a few days ago, he got another 1/3 of his money from me a few days ago and is supposed to collect the rest when he comes back up with proof of…" Joey let the sentence dangle.

This Joshua did not know. He kept his face a perfect mask of nothingness, he knew his friend and underboss Martel was in the shadows listening to this conversation as well, he could almost feel Martel's anxiousness in the air. Across from him Calendri seemed to shiver involuntarily. "What else." Joshua prodded, pretending that the info was no big deal, but he marked it well. "So far you do not impress me very much Mr. Calendri." He swallowed another drink of wine.

"Tito has set up with some new associate in Florida, Joe Cinno and the DiMone *Brugad*; supposedly he is getting a lot of hired muscle from the old country, *zips*, immigrant Sicilian soldiers. These are the men he is going to use for the war." Joey tried again, he was growing more cold and nervous, he better have something these Jerome men could use or what use would they have for him?

"Huh," Josh just made a halfhearted grunt. He didn't want to seem too interested or non-interested. Just to play the part he and Martel had worked so hard to set up. "More interesting, continue."

Fueled by the bone the Jerome consigliere threw him, Joey relaxed a bit and began talking much more freely now. Most Joshua and Martel already knew, but it was when Joey said "…The last little plan was that Tito had a final surprise planned for any one else near the VIJER corporation. A hit squad of button men, in case any returned from the islands or to take out any high level Administration still left behind here."

Now Joshua perked up. In the shadows he could feel Martel snap alert as well. Two tigers with their ears fully perked up. This was new info. "More of these hired Sicilian muscle?" Joshua casually questioned.

"No," Calendri shook his head, "it was the last assignment Tito gave Baldovino and me to send down the line two nights ago. It's to be our own men, D'Salvatore button men, along with some Armandana trigger men."

Demonico felt a small trickle of chill now travel down his own spine. There would be no turning these men. This would be a true hit squad sent out by the D'Salvatore's.

"When and where?" He fought to keep his temper under control to play the part.

"I don't know, I swear to you, Mr. Demonico. They won't get their final orders from their capos until probably a few days from now." Joey looked almost apologetic.

Joshua would have been surprised and suspect had Calendri told him anything different, the Jerome's would have played their assassin squads the same way. Keep information close to the heart until the actual time of the hit. A part of him still wanted to reach across the table and throttle the guy though.

Joshua casually pushed the finished meal aside and he reached into his pocket and pulled out a square of his nicotine gum, which he expertly opened and popped into his mouth. "Anything else, Mr. Calendri?" he leaned forward, his eyes seeming to bore into Joey's. "Any other help you can give to us, or to influence our decision before we make up our mind on whether we accept you into the Jerome Family?"

Joey Calendri looked down at his hands for a moment they were shaking. He felt so mind numbingly chilled, so icy cold. "No, only what I have told you. I have risked everything coming here. I am dead in my Family's eyes now, a traitor. I put everything on the line to come here. I only hope…" he paused a moment and looked almost pleadingly into

Joshua Demonico's handsome face. "…That you could find something for me to do; some way for me to help out the Jerome's. I would work as the lowest soldier, anything, just a chance to be on the winning side…"

"Or to save your own skin," Joshua sat back casually, glancing at his own well-manicured hand. "I appreciate the information, Mr. Calendri, I really do. Especially if it saves our Boss, Mr. Jerome…"

Joey never saw the huge form of Laurence Martel seem to materialize and step out of the very shadows of the darkened nightclub. Silent and deadly like the shadow dragon he was, closing quietly in on his victim. He was dressed all in black, with ultra thin black leather gloves on, his assassination gear. He wanted no blood in this hit, no evidence.

Joey never knew what hit him, he was suddenly wrenched like a rag doll from his chair by hands that clasped around his neck from behind and hauled literally upwards and lifted easily as though he were in the grasp of some huge beast.

Martel's expert hands finding the exact junctures on the carotid arteries that ran along the front of the neck and the nerves at the side. With the slightest pressure he merely squeezed, easily shutting off the vital blood supply to Joey Calendri's brain.

"But you see, Joey…" Joshua said still calmly as he casually watched Martel executing the D'Salvatores ex-underboss. "We don't take traitors in the Jerome Family. I am sure we are being much more merciful with you than your own Family would be, if they got hold of you, eh?" he gave a dry chuckle.

It was quickly ending for Joey Calendri, he felt his eardrums burst inside his skull, and for the only time in his life that he could remember, he was no longer cold. In fact he felt darkness and warmth descend on him like a warm, fluffy comforter.

Martel snapped the neck for good measure as he always did, as Cochran had always taught him and then dropped the stilled body lifeless and limp on the floor. He casually stepped over it and sat in the chair Joey Calendri had just been in.

Briefly underboss and consigliere regarded one another. "Well?" Joshua asked his friend and mentor quietly as he poured Martel a cup of espresso.

"The only thing that was new to me was that: One, Gambini was already down there and two, that there will be a couple D'Salvatore hit squads up here, running around gunning for us but with no information on where or when."

Joshua nodded as he motioned for Rocco to dispose of Joey Calendri's corpse.

"Oh and Rocco," Joshua nodded to the well-dressed capo, "hide the evidence. No sense in letting the D'Salvatores know we are onto their information, even as scant as it is. Let them think Calendri took an unexpected leave of absence or something."

Rocco acknowledged his boss' orders and then went to go get the other guards to help him clean up the deceased Calendri and go hide the body in one of the Jerome safe havens.

"You're leaving then tonight aren't you?" Joshua asked but he could already see the answer in Martel's eyes. Saw the restlessness in the underboss's heart and soul.

Martel just nodded silently and drained his cup of espresso. 'Center yourself', he kept repeating in his mind to still his own anxious feelings. Still he could not lock onto Louie Gambini and this troubled him immensely.

"Take care of everything Joshua," Martel said softly, almost wearily, "especially yourself. Be wary now my friend. I will be back up here with Victor and the others as soon as I can."

"I know." Joshua said, "I know, *paisan*. Everything will be locked down tight. At least we have some warning, eh?" Josh smiled weakly trying to lighten the mood slightly.

"Thanks, Joshua." Martel rose to his feet, the two men briefly embraced and he then left through the front door. He would stop at his house, pack light and leave.

Outside the icy autumn winds blew like ghostly fingers through the city streets and the grey clouds were rolling in, they obscured everything just like the tendrils of his mind. 'Center yourself'…

He buttoned his dark overcoat against the chill, hoping that Cochran, the spirit of Miyoko, the forces of karma or whatever fates existed would be in his favor and not against him. For the first time in his life, he could envision this whole plan of his fathers going terribly wrong and him arriving only to see the dead bodies of Victor, the Bonnaro's, and Alyssa, all of them… He shook the image from his mind… "Center yourself Kage," he could hear Cochran's voice in his mind, "or you will fuck this up and make your vision a reality".

Chapter 32- *October 13th 1987*

Alyssa had been impressed but not surprised to find that the old man owned a Private, corporate jet, or rather VIJER Enterprises did, Victor told her. It was elegant and roomy inside with fold out couches, office areas and even a bed in another section. But on this trip, except for the two pilots, there was just her, Victor, Gio Aprile and Tony Armanno.

She remembered Tony as well; he had been the one guard who had been there that night she had been escorted to Victor's office during the misunderstanding with Victor. He was the one who had carried the large AK-47 in his hand. He was one of the guards imported recently from Sicily, so like Leonardo Tagretta his voice was one that was heavily accented, and his English was not the best.

But now that she was fully accepted into the Family as Don Victor's niece, the guards were nothing but nice and pleasant to her. She could tell Tony did not like flying and he seemed to spend a lot of time nervously playing solitaire and doing everything to not look out the windows. Victor spoke to him soothingly in Italian a few times, and even offered the man a strong drink of whiskey, but ever the professional he just shook his head no and continued playing solitaire and occasionally stroking a cross he wore around his neck.

Gio put on some headphones, lined up his cassette tapes of Pink Floyd, Metallica and some other rock and roll and heavy metal bands and kicked back and relaxed for the trip. She noticed every once and awhile, one of his dark eyes would open like an alert cat to glance around and make sure everything was Ok, and then doze back off.

Victor smiled at her and chatted a bit, and then told her he was going to catch up on some written work he had to do. He told her there was some books onboard, tapes, whatever she wanted to do to relax, as well as a wet bar with soda's, wine, beer whatever she desired.

Actually Alyssa was glad to be left alone; she was dying to see what her teacher had given her and couldn't wait to go look at it in private. Since she saw this was to be a small, intimate flight and the pilots said it would run about 5 hours, she penned to Victor. "*I will go relax and read and maybe write some in my Journals. In a few hours I will make some lunch for everyone*."

"Ah, thank you child," he smiled sincerely, "how kind of you. I know it will be appreciated, especially by Tony and Gio, eh? They are always hungry." He pulled out his glasses and slipped them on pulling out some of his paperwork, "When you make my sandwich, I just take a plain turkey and tomato with no sauces." He smiled for a moment gave her a light fatherly kiss on the cheek and left her to her own time.

He glanced at her a moment and then with a soft sigh bent over his paperwork. 'Ah my dear, you are a sweet child and I can tell you have been working hard. Will you be able to pass this final test, my test?' He glanced briefly at Tony and Gio who were relaxed and at ease on the flight finally. If Alyssa didn't pass this last test Victor threw at her, then he wouldn't make his son make the ultimate hard decision. He knew Tony and Gio would do whatever their Don told or commanded of them.

Immediately she went to the small nook where there were some books and magazines and reached into her jacket pocket to pull out the box and also rummaged around into her flight bag to pull out her diaries so it would look like she was writing in them.

The box was just a plain black small jeweler's box, tied with an elegant gold ribbon. With trembling fingers she opened it. At first she just saw a folded piece of paper; she gingerly opened it and saw Martel's neat elegant writing.

"*Alyssa/Kanashii:*

I hope your trip is a pleasant one, I hope you are able to find some answers in your soul while you are there. I could sense lately that there were a lot of things on your mind, some that I know you did not share with me, and of course I respect that. I have been so very impressed and proud lately of your progress with me while you have been staying here with me and I personally have enjoyed having you around.

When you are down there, with Victor, please, please; Listen to any instructions he or Mr. Aprile or Mr. Armanno tells you, no matter how 'odd' or strange they seem. Just do them without question. Trust in them as you would me..."

Alyssa felt a slight shiver then run through her, she glanced around briefly but everyone was still busy doing what they were doing. She began to seriously doubt at that moment, then, that this was just a 'simple' vacation. She looked back at the letter,

"*You will meet Mr. Vito and his wife Lena Bonnaro, they are very lovely people. Trust them as well. They are dear friends to the Jerome's. I don't know how long you will be down there, enjoy yourself, but remember the relaxation techniques we practiced. If you feel any fears coming on, go to Victor or even Mr. Aprile if you are able, both can be trusted as much as I can, hopefully you know this by now. But honestly, I think that you and I have worked through a lot of those. I have not sensed anymore of those terrors in you, they seem to have subsided? Either way, it makes my heart happy.*

I am enclosing something for you Kanashii-Taka, my dear student..."

She looked inside the box and saw a beautiful sterling silver Japanese Kanji symbol, strung on a black silken cord. The simple elegance of it was both stunning and yet so comforting. It was a single Kanji, one she did not recognize; complex in its design but beautiful. She glanced at the note, again, almost envisioning him sitting next to her, his deep voice speaking the words in the letter.

"*...It is the Kanji symbol for 'Strength' Kanashii; the literal translation is 'strength of courage'. You have proven yourself and this attribute to me, and I want you to wear this while you are on vacation down in the islands. Let it protect and remind you, let it be a reminder of me your teacher, and also of your own inner strength.*"

Alyssa slipped the silken cord around her neck and felt the cool silver Kanji settle against her skin. For a moment it was cold, almost like him, 'The Undertaker', but then quickly warmed, like the heat of the Dragon. Unconsciously her hand went to her chest where she felt the gift nestled against her flesh.

She glanced at the note one last time, reading his final words.

"PS: Remember to do your Tai Chi it will keep you flexible and also to take your supplements. I do want you good and healthy when you come back."

She had to chuckle at this! Only her teacher would ruin the fun of a vacation by reminding her to do martial arts Tai Chi forms. She closed her eyes a moment picturing him, enjoying the gift, the feel of it. She wondered if he had found her letter yet, and if so, what his reaction would be.

Alyssa had dozed a bit as well, written in her journals after that, and then made a huge lunch for everyone. She made Victors turkey sandwich to order, and was fascinated to find that there was an interior section of the refrigerator that was locked, and needed a key. She couldn't see what was in it, for it was a metal door. But it definitely piqued her curiosity. What would be kept locked in secret in a refrigerator? She knew better than to be nosey and ask, so she just kept quiet about the locked section of the refrigerator. Maybe they kept the really expensive caviar or something in there she figured.

Alyssa knew Victor had spoken the truth about enjoying the vacation the minute the jet touched down and they stepped off the plane. She breathed deeply the sweet, warm, salty air, she could hear the ocean roaring nearby and palm trees swayed lazily under cobalt blue skies. The sun was bright and shiny illuminating everything; indeed it was a tropical paradise.

There was a white stretch limo already waiting for them driven by a dark skinned island man in a white suit, as the guards and the pilots quickly unloaded the luggage from the private jet into the awaiting limo. One of the pilots handed Victor a set of keys and a two leather satchels. Gio then grabbed one satchel as Tony grabbed the other.

"Excellent flight, Mr. Robison," Victor handed the man some folded bills. "You and Mr. Ardennes, relax and enjoy your stay, we'll let you know when we're ready to head back."

The pilots nodded and they left in a waiting rental vehicle. Victor took Alyssa's hand in his own and like a gentleman led her to the limo. "I have checked us into a fairly nice hotel, the Sheridan Sands" he looked at her kindly, "I hope you like it. We can sight see after we unpack child." Victor said kindly but firmly pulling Alyssa's gaze away from the azure ocean in the distance.

A 'fairly nice' hotel was an understatement. The Sheridan Sands was quite an elegant 5-star hotel and Alyssa noticed that all the hotel personnel greeted and fawned over Victor, as though he had been there before. "Welcome, Welcome Mr. Disarro!" they greeted him. "Everything has been set up as you specified."

"I've bought my niece down, and we intend to have a nice relaxing vacation." Victor said as he finished signing in as Albert Disarro.

"He's going under an alias," Alyssa thought to herself, "Obviously he doesn't want anyone to know Victor Jerome is here." And it only confirmed her feelings earlier about this being some kind of 'business trip' for him and not a vacation. However she just played along smiling benignly and playing the part of the happy niece. She noticed Gio and Tony stood near the bags the bellboys were loading up, although the two guards seemed relaxed and at ease, Alyssa knew them well enough that she could tell both were as alert as two guard dogs on high security. Only someone who knew them well would know the intense look in their eyes, or the way they casually seemed to be scanning the surroundings constantly for any trouble.

"Excellent, Mr. Disarro," The hotel concierge was finishing up and handing Victor two sets of keys. "Your rooms are all prepared and if there is anything you need, don't hesitate. I am always at your service."

Victor slipped him a tip and then he and Alyssa followed the bellboy and flanked by the two bodyguards went up the elevator to the fourth floor to two very elegant adjoining rooms.

The Bellboy put the guards luggage in 407 the less elegant of the rooms, the one with two queen beds, and put Victor and Alyssa's luggage in the more formal and elegant suite, 406. This room was closer to the stairwell and elevator.

As soon as Victor tipped the young man and he had left, the two bodyguards and Victor immediately began switching the luggage around.

"I signed us into room 406 my dear..." Victor was saying as he grabbed one of Alyssa's bags.

Quickly she began to grab some bags to help him but was not following his path of logic.

"...But in reality we will be staying in 407." Victor continued as he placed her bag on the queen-sized bed near the window. It did have a gorgeous view of the ocean. "Mr. Aprile and Mr. Armanno will be staying in 406." Victor said simply. He faced her, his dark eyes looking into Alyssa's. "It's just one of those things my dear. Trust and indulge this old man, eh?"

She smiled, nodded and gave him a hug and a kiss on the cheek. Of course she would, he was the *padrone* and she would do whatever he asked. It was as Martel had asked her; all she could do was trust in the Family.

It actually didn't matter to her one way or the other. Even this room was simply spectacular. It was a suite practically unto itself. Two large queen sized beds separated by two elegant night stands, a small area with a desk/office, a small kitchenette with a refrigerator, microwave and even a small stove.

There was a TV of course and in the room were two baskets of complimentary fruit filled with bottled water and an assortment of tropical fruits, fresh exotic tropical flowers sat inside elegant vases on the nightstands, in each room filling the air with their sweet island scent.

"So do you like the room, child?" Victor asked kindly.

405

She smiled at him and nodded yes, as she began to unpack.

"Good. I think we will have a good time here together, you and I. Later we can sight see as I promised and tomorrow we will be visiting some friends of mine the Bonnaro's." Victor continued amiably.

Alyssa noticed then he had taken one of the leather satchels and keys and unlocking it went over to the refrigerator. Her curiosity was in high gear; she had a feeling she was about to find out something quite secret. Something about the secret compartment in the refrigerator she saw on the plane. She didn't dare move from her place at the bed, as she discreetly watched Victor deftly unlock the satchel and disappear for a moment in the kitchenette.

"You might as well know…" he sighed and motioned to her. "Come here."

Slowly almost hesitantly she walked into the kitchen. There she saw on the counter multiple vials of something and loads of syringes.

"Insulin," He turned to her. "I am an insulin dependant diabetic, have been for nearly 40 years. Twice a day this old man gets his fix." He turned back with a small ironic grin and began to put the bottles into a special metal lockbox in the refrigerator and then lock it. "My condition is something I like to keep rather private. It's a little quirk of mine." He glanced over at her his dark eyes both seeming to see right through her and also with an intense honesty.

Now it all fell into place for Alyssa, the lifesavers, his habit of always having some sugary candy around, the eating turkey sandwiches with no sugary sauces his constant need for watching the time and balancing his sugar. For him the lifesavers were literally a way to save his life, and she could see darn well why he would want to keep his diabetes private. It would be far too easy for an enemy to get hold and taint his needed insulin supply somehow, an easy assassination of a powerful crime boss.

"It's one of the reasons my kidneys failed and why yours saved my life." he turned back to her. "Only a few people know of this Alyssa." His eyes looked at her with utter frankness, "Dr. Weintraub, Laurence Martel, Joshua Demonico, Gio Aprile and now you…" he suddenly took an extra key off a key ring and handed it to her, his eyes boring into her with seriousness she had never seen in him before. Not intimidating, not threatening, not even vulnerable; just a total and brutal honesty. "Even most people in the Family don't know about this Alyssa. But you now do as well. If something were to happen to me, if I am knocked unconscious…"

Alyssa felt her heart begin to thrum deep in her chest, 'Oh God, don't talk like this Victor! Don't say these words! Don't put this responsibility on me!'

"Don't look so afraid child." He smiled lightly for a moment, his hand resting warmly and with strength on her shoulder. "I will explain things to you; it is nothing to be frightened of. I promise."

'Strength and courage Kanashii' she remembered the note, could almost hear Martel's deep voice, his soothing presence and for a moment the Kanji felt warm against her skin.

She smiled and nodded, trying to put strength into her heart and soul. What could she do? The man had saved her life, she owed him, she had promised him, and now he was trusting her with this most intimate and vulnerable secret of his. She slipped the key he had just given her onto the necklace around her neck, next to the Kanji. Victor eyed the Kanji and the key and she could have sworn she saw a gleam of laughter in the old man's eyes.

Victor finished putting the insulin in the refrigerator and locking it up with his key, he then picked up a couple of oranges and two syringes. "Come here, Alyssa." He said soothingly. "I guarantee you in an hour you will have no worries at all, eh?" He rolled an orange to her, "Besides, all you have to really do is just make sure this old man has his lifesaver fix and I'm usually happy as a clam." He winked at her and bought over a cup of water. "But if you ever do have to give me one of the insulin shots, it's no big deal, I promise…" together they sat at the bar as she listened to his voice instruct and guide and together they practiced injecting water into the oranges.

Louie 'Kohana' Gambini was right at home on the island with his tousled blonde hair, his tanned surfer body and his loud tropical shirt, which was unbuttoned and opened revealing his well toned torso. He lay back on the sand watching some of the scantily clad bikini women walk by. He occasionally grinned roguishly at a few of them, and occasionally some grinned back at him. He had been out earlier in the morning catching some waves but these were not the powerful waves of the Pacific, so he really had no interest in these waters. Besides, he was here hunting.

He glanced casually to his right at the large Sheridan Sands hotel. He knew that was where the great Don Victor Jerome was to be staying; his target. If everything was on schedule the old man should be arriving right about now. He was in no hurry though he was following his instincts. He always found he did his best jobs if he just listened to his instincts.

He lazily rolled over onto his stomach as though he were tanning his back and then pulled out a small but ultra powerful pair of binoculars that he kept occasionally scanning the Sheridan with.

'There they were!' He saw the white hotel limo pull up and saw the Don himself get out, with just two guards. 'Just two?' Louie thought to himself. They really were traveling light, Calendri hadn't been lying. He grunted a bit with pleasure.

No Vito Bonnaro yet, they were probably coming later. Nonetheless, his contract was not for Bonnaro, only for Victor Jerome. It was then his eyes saw a woman exit out of the limo with Don Jerome. She was wary but yet almost childlike in her joy of the surrounding beauty as well as exotically attractive. She seemed captivated by the sights. The Don lightly touched her arm and moved her along, whispered something to her ear; she smiled warmly at him and followed him.

Something prickled then in the back of Gambini's neck… 'I know you.' He thought, 'But from where?' He didn't like when he got bad vibes on a hit and suddenly he had some, in fact a whole stomach full and he didn't know why. Where the hell did he know that woman from?

Martel sat restlessly in the small commuter plane. It was one that was often rented as a secondary plane by the VIJER Corporation, a bit larger than the other private jet they owned outright. This one they often flew overseas to Italy or South America, as it had larger tanks, more storage space and more clearances. More importantly it had better hiding places for weapons or illegal contraband, so that he could get the necessary tools of his trade safely with him where he needed to go. Stowed safely, hidden deep in the recesses of various hidden compartments were several of his best guns, knives and martial arts assassination equipment.

He was the only one on the plane. The two pilots were flying them straight down to the islands since they had already cleared everything necessary at LaGuardia. Martel was full of pent up energy, his nerves and blood thrummed like electricity along the very fibers of his body.

He glanced again briefly out the window but there was nothing to see, just the white fluffy clouds over the vast expanse of the blue unbroken Atlantic ocean. 'Center yourself'…

He had hoped to be able to stop and see Sen before leaving, but now after what Calendri had told him and listening to his own instincts, he knew he had no time. Time was working against him and his heart and soul told him he needed to be in the Islands now, hunting his quarry and his *nemico*, Louie Gambini.

He reached into the breast pocket of his black sports jacket and pulled out the letter written by Kanashii. He scanned it again; he had found it when he had returned back to his house to hastily pack. He closed his eyes a moment, feeling the chaos all around him in his heart both about the letter from Kanashii and about Gambini.

Why did she have to write this now to him? Her timing had been awful, now with his mind already fogged and clouded, with his heart as tight as an over strung wire and his nerves on fire over his quarry, her letter only fueled the chaos and fire even more; distracted him. 'Center yourself or you will lose them all!'

It was times like this when he hated and dreaded the secrets and games and the persona he had worked so hard to build up. He was not infallible and while he had worked to instill fear and terror with his very name; while he knew even some of his own men feared him and others expected miracles, he began to doubt himself. Did his own father belief the same hype? The same miracles?

'*Vindicare angelo della morte,* the vindicating Angel of Death. Oh father, do you have so much faith in me, when even I begin to doubt myself on this assignment?'

"CENTER YOURSELF!"

Martel grunted with an almost angry growl and after carefully folding Kanashii's letter back into his pocket he closed the window to the view outside and forced his mind to begin back at the beginning. The very beginning, letting his mind wander down the rote corridors of the very first lessons Cochran had taught him for stilling his mind, his heart, his soul. Going through the most basic and dull of the mental forms of meditation and centering rituals, as though hearing the words his teachers in his very essence, first Cochran, then Sen, then his own voice.

"Breathe in deeply and cleanse your mind. You are stone, your heart is stone; you feel nothing, breathe out..."

He fought in his mind to do what he had always done, put up the wall around him, the wall of death and non-feeling, and the wall of separation.

"Let the dragon fly, Kageryu." He heard Sen's voice pestering him within in his mind, remembering Sen's letter and his talk, "For he is you, and you are him; Kageryu means Shadow Dragon, embrace the shadow and do not fight it."

He wasn't sure if he dreamt then or merely was in a deep meditation. But he saw the clouds again, over the vast blue Atlantic. However this time he was zooming over them at an impossible speed, as though he was free and unfettered like a bird, or a shadow. Below he saw an island, and it rushed up to meet him. Scenes shifted, colors merged time had no meaning, exactly like a dream. He saw him then, Louie Gambini. His equal, his nemesis and the man who would take from Martel all he would want, all he loved. He could see Gambini, on a sand dune near a deserted stretch of ocean, laying on his stomach and a high-powered military sniper rifle in his hands.

Martel wanted to react, to do anything! But he could only watch in this vision, he had no control over it. It was as though he was there, but not. So instead he concentrated on memorizing, even the tiniest details around him.

He saw what Gambini was wearing, the way he seemed to be aiming at some small tiny one room shack in the distance around 1000 yards away. The ocean was near the shack, almost right at the doorstep of it, and the roar of it covered the muffled distant bark of the snipers rifle. Glass exploded, blood flew, and he saw his father and Vito hit the floor, blood running down his father's hands, so much blood, far too much blood...

409

Martel's eyes suddenly snapped wide-awake. He checked his watch; he had been dreaming-meditating for nearly two hours. He knew he had another hour before the plane would touch down. He forced his hand to stop trembling as he stood up, stretched and buttoned his sport coat. He was both unnerved even more but yet elated. He could feel him now, he could feel Louie 'Kohana' Gambini, the man was on his radar now. But he also knew he would have to work hard and swift to find this place he had seen in his mediation.

"How long until we land?" He asked the two pilots.

"About another 45 minutes, Mr. Martel, we got lucky and picked us up a good tail wind up here." One nodded at him.

Martel nodded his thanks and went back to his seat. Would things begin to come together again like it had so long ago when he had hunted Tashima Katsuro? This time he knew there would be no stupid mistakes, no fatal errors. He was more experienced, more mature. His vengeance could be tempered now; it had to be.

"Center yourself…"

The voice was quiet and peaceful and he found he was able to slip very quickly and comfortably back into his meditative trance.

Later that afternoon Alyssa and Victor sat on the beach together, he wearing tan slacks and a rather sporty yellow Polo shirt along with a straw fedora to keep the sun off him. She was impressed that even when the elegant Don was relaxing he always seemed to wear nice clothing. She herself had dressed in a one-piece swimsuit along with a large tunic cover up. She was still a bit self-conscious about her surgery scars on her side.

Both she and Victor wore sandals and she couldn't help but to note even at his age of late 50's early 60's he was still in excellent physical shape, with a healthy and fit tone to him. He was a bit thin from his recuperation of his prolonged illness and his transplant from her, but other than that, his recovery as she had seen with her own two eyes had been remarkably well. Much better than her own, which had taken months.

Alyssa saw both Gio and Tony were also dressed more casually, in Bermuda shorts and light T-shirts, sitting about 15 feet nearby them. They both wore sunglasses and baseball caps and appeared to be dozing or watching the beachgoers but she knew they were discreetly keeping an eye on their boss and *padrone*. Alyssa noted many of the women on the beach seemed to glance appreciatively at the well muscled Giovanni Aprile and the roguish Sicilian, Tony Armanno.

Victor had gotten Alyssa one of those tropical drinks in the pineapple with the colorful paper umbrella in it. She enjoyed the flavor, but whatever was in it sure packed a punch! Already she was feeling the effects of it in a pleasant way. Victor was just drinking a diet soda with a twist of lime.

Together they sat on comfortable beach loungers next to one another and watched people swimming in the sea, or windsurfing out on the crystal clear turquoise blue waters. Somewhere off in the distance she could hear reggae music.

"So, are you enjoying yourself so far Alyssa?" Victor asked kindly, smiling at her then regarding the windsurfers out on the breakers. 'So now we will talk my dear, and see if you pass my final test.' The old man thought to himself. A part of him didn't want to do this but yet as leader of the Family he knew he must.

Alyssa nodded enthusiastically and slurped some more at her Pina Colada.

"Excellent," Victor continued, "Tonight as I mentioned we will have together, and I will take you to a nice place, it's kind of fancy. I thought you might like it and I hear they serve wonderful seafood and such…" Victor smiled at her again briefly that unnerving smile and then suddenly out of the blue without a break in stride said, "So when did you get nearly all your memories back child?"

Alyssa nearly choked on the tropical drink she was drinking on. She felt as cold suddenly as though winter had blasted though, despite the comforting warmth of the tropical isles.

How had he known? How long had he known? Lamely and without even really thinking she just wrote out on her pad of paper "*How did you know?*"

Victor just half snorted, not an angry snort but almost half amused. "I make it my business to read people, remember child? I could see it in your face, in your actions. The way you responded to…" he paused a moment, "the people of my Family." This time the smile was genuine. "Now, I thought we had an understanding you and I?" he faced her again and this time the smile was gone. He was just the business-like Victor, to the point and the true *Padrone* of his Family. "Why didn't you tell me such happy news? I thought you and I were perhaps friends, eh? Surely such news as that you would tell a friend."

Alyssa could only sit there staring at the man. A part of her felt rooted to the spot. A part felt like she wished she could fly away like one of his birds, be anywhere but having this conversation. What was she going to say? "I didn't tell you because I hadn't come to grips with it myself? I hadn't come to grips with my feelings with Martel and a few others. I still have huge blank spots in my mind, and areas even I don't know about and don't know what I want to do with my life or myself but I know I want to be with you all. Part of me loves and trusts you all, but part of me does indeed fear you all…"

Her mind still remembered Cesare and the trouble they had both gotten into for talking too much. Her mind also briefly remembered Martel's weapon room in the basement of his house, "…And I am still coming to grips with that dark side of the Family as well, coming to grips with what this *famiglia* really is, an illegal Mafia Family… But

411

dealing with it because I want to, and I must in my heart and soul, but I never would betray you. I am just still so confused!"

She wanted to look away from him, to pull her gaze from the distinguished crime boss, but she could not. Instead she felt one lone tear trickle down her cheek.

"Listen, *whatever-your-real-name-is.* Don't you think ever since I rescued you that day from Vito Roman's I did not anticipate this very day?" Victor's voice was low, for her ears only but right now it seemed to drown out all other sound around her. He pinned her down with his eyes; his full business-was-in-session gaze, "How was I to even know you would be amnesiac? Think about it child!" he growled softly as he reached in his pocket for his roll of lifesavers and popped one in his mouth. "I never had to do what I did, never had to save your life or heal you back to health." He checked his temper and broke his gaze from her turning to glance back out at the ocean a moment.

"*Why did you?*" Alyssa wrote out with a trembling hand on the pad, holding tightly the elegant pen from Martel in her grasp, feeling the weight of the Kanji from her teacher around her neck and the key Victor had given her. He had given it to her, trusted her with the secret of his condition even after he already knew she had her memories back. She knew finally her and Victor were going to settle this one way or the other, permanently. She could feel it deep in her bones. She held out the pad to Victor with a small trembling hand.

Victor casually looked at it, then facing her again his eyes boring into hers as he spoke, "Because contrary to what a lot of people think or want to believe or what you want to think or believe, I am not a monster. I do have a heart and soul as well my dear; I can feel the same as any human being. What Vito Roman did angered the hell out of me, it burned deep in my heart and soul." His eyes took on some of his dark fire, "And I wanted it to stop any way I could. I worked hard to make it stop, the day I was there. And there you were, with your spirit, determination. Even grievously wounded you fought to live. How could I let that perish? You were a *persona innocente*, a victim of Vito Roman ..." Victor savored the peppermint candy in his mouth a moment letting his temper get under control, calming himself before he continued.

"...I saw in you helplessness, a desperate last attempt to reach out and live. How could I refuse that? When I talked to you that day, while you may not remember or maybe you do, there seemed to be a connection between us. Or so I thought." He paused for a moment. "And then, when you risked your life for me, to give me a gift of your kidney, I saw a loyalty repaid and I was honored and touched. I truly thought you understood. Your kidney makes me healthy, gives me time to do what I must in this lifetime. We've had our ups and downs in our relationship child, but I had always thought it balanced out in the end." Victor watched the windsurfers again for a moment.

For a while he was so quiet, Alyssa thought he was going to say no more. Then he spoke softly. "Even Martel's spoken and unspoken praise and report on you, told me volumes in the level of trust of how you were fitting in. I watched you myself; saw how you interacted with everyone from Rosette to Mr. Aprile to Mr. DeLuca even Cesare. Even I was impressed with you, trusted you, felt you had earned a place as we had spoken before, loved and cared for as a niece, a daughter."

Victor turned and faced her again, his full attention on her. "But I tell you this child. I have no room in my life for anyone who cannot give 100% loyalty to me or my Family. If you want to leave, go now. I will buy you a first class ticket to wherever you want to go, and Mr. Aprile will take you to the airport and drop you off, and I will never want to see or hear from you again. Our association will be over forever, *finito*." this was said in such a calm, soft, tone of voice that it chilled Alyssa's blood more than if he would have yelled it at the top of his lungs in rage.

"But remember one thing, child." He added, still in that unnerving calm. "If, I had merely wanted you dead; that could have and would have been done a long time ago, and I certainly would not have wasted my emotions, time and money on you."

For the second time in her relationship with Victor Jerome, realization hit Alyssa like a blast of icy water, rushing over her body. Her breath felt as if it was constricted in her throat and with a trembling hand she quickly wrote as fast as she humanly could, despite the painful cramping of her fingers, *"Victor, I don't want to go away! I want to stay with you and Martel and others, I want this life, your life, not what I had before, there was nothing for me before. I apologize, oh, Victor I am so sorry, I was so blind, forgive me! I don't know why I didn't tell you about my memories. I truly don't. Stupid fears on my behalf I guess. You are right, you have been nothing but kind to me, everything you said is true and I am honestly grateful and thankful for all that you have done for me. I swear to you, I won't conceal any more feelings or memories or anything else.*

"Victor I truly do love you as an Uncle, please don't make me leave. I want to earn your trust again, I promise not to let you down, I..."

She probably would have kept writing until the sun went down, her soul aching with desperation to make him believe her, but Victor had reached over and gently taken the notebook out of her hands. He sat there reading her scrawled writing that screamed with her anguished emotions.

She could only sit there and watch him as she held tightly onto her pen, silent tears still quietly running down her face. Either he would believe and accept her or reject her and turn her out and for some reason that fate seemed worst of all.

He reread the notebook then placed it face down in his lap. He sat placid, quiet in thought a few moments and then with a soft sigh turned back towards her. His hand reached out to her and with trembling hands she grasped it, feeling the strength and warmth in his older hand.

"Very well child." He said warmly, serenely. "You are one of my own then. My niece until death, I will adopt you. You are now forever a part of the Jerome *Famiglia*. Remember, you will show the same respects as any mans' wife or daughter. Respect and omerta." Victor spoke something to her in Italian that she had no idea what he said, but he gently patted her cheek when he said it, and it seemed a very important thing to him.

She just nodded solemnly.

"So what is your name anyway?" Victor looked at her with slight amusement. "I just made Alyssa up that night you asked, although I do have a familial line that is named Disarro, it was Isabella's maiden name." He handed her notebook back to her.

"*Once I was known as Sarah, I don't remember my last name. Many of my memories I still have a lot of holes in. But I prefer Alyssa, it means more to both of us anyway.*"

"I suppose it does." Victor read the note and laughed gently. "We'll keep it Alyssa Disarro then, it would just confuse everyone to change it anyway." He chuckled again and patted her hand.

He offered her one of the peppermint lifesavers, but Alyssa declined, noting he only had four of them left. 'Now I'm going to be worrying how many lifesavers my Uncle has when he goes out?' she gave a soft sigh to herself and vowed from that day forward to always carry an extra roll on her, just for him.

"So tonight is for us then," Victor reiterated again, "and tomorrow we will be meeting the Bonnaro's around lunch time. You will like them, their English isn't so hot, but not to worry." He gave her shoulder a light squeeze. "You'll get along just fine with them. Trust me."

And this time she did. She trusted her Uncle implicitly. She had given her solemn and soul sworn oath to him and the Jerome Family now.

Louie Gambini had been on the beach, only around 50 feet away from them, the Don the girl and the two goons. He chuckled to himself, "I could have walked right past on my way to go to the bar and just blown the old fart away" he thought. Of course he knew the two goons would have been on him in a heartbeat and he would have been dead and a good hit was only one in which you collected your payment. As a gun-for-hire he had no stake in this whole D'Salvatore/Jerome fiasco he only wanted his money.

Normally he would have spied only briefly on his target, not hung around so long, after all, he also was a semi-famous face in the underworld, despite the sunglasses and raggedy goatee he had been growing. However there were plenty like the two goons or the old Don who may possibly recognize him. He was half surprised that his counterpart, the enormous and rugged underboss Martel, wasn't lurking around here with his Don, but he had checked all the flight logs, scoped out the airport personally and no one fitting his description had come in last night or with Victor Jerome. He would have checked today's planes, but this woman had him intrigued now and he didn't like when he got bad vibes on a run.

"Lil' bird, lil' bird, where does ol' Louie know you from?" he grumbled to himself. It tasked him and irritated him and was beginning to piss him off. So he had sat on the beach, drinking a few Pina Coladas of his own and trying to figure out just where he knew this woman from. A few times he thought he may have had the answer, but like some shadow it danced away at the last moment from the fringes of his mind.

His bad vibes of wanting to figure out who this woman was, instead of checking the airports as he had originally planned that day would cost him dearly.

Martel finally landed, gathered his working items and guns in a plain duffle bag and then disappeared into the crowd, blending in seamlessly with the people around him. He paid cash up front and stayed at a rather inconspicuous, low budget out of the way place. He changed into some clothes that matched the colors of the surrounding islands, tans and whites and off beiges.

The whole art of ninjitsu assassination was stealth, as he had long ago learned from Sen. It was the ability to be able to literally disappear into a crowd of people in the middle of daylight if you needed to. Even with his great height, he was able to make himself able to disappear quite well when he had to.

While he was in the hotel he worked hard at covering the guns with a desert/sand type camouflage type coating and cloth to reduce their glare and to prevent them from standing out. He also made sure to wear his concealed throwing darts and stars as well as a few small knives and weapons. After all, he never knew when he might get lucky and just happen to bump into his quarry by accident and on this assignment his only goal was to kill Gambini as fast and quickly as he could, preferably before Gambini got to his father or Vito or anyone else.

Martel had an itinerary in his mind of his fathers first 2 days, and that was all. Victor wouldn't tell anyone where the final meeting place with Vito Bonnaro would be, it would be only him, Bonnaro and the guards. He figured even Vito and Victor might not decide until the last moment but Martel had an image in his mind, now if he could only find the place that resembled what he had seen in his dreams/meditations.

Martel was sure Gambini wouldn't try hitting Victor in a public place but if he were a good hitman he would at least be tailing him. After all, it's what he himself would do. Otherwise how would he know where Victor's final meeting place with Bonnaro would be?

Laurence could feel Louie Gambini out there, like a dull beacon his prey called to him, taunted him, but he knew he had to be patient. To run around too fast or to force things too quickly would be a mistake for all involved. He sensed something; some karmic force was working in his favor, just like the night of his vendetta against Tashima Katsuro.

"I feel you my old enemy, it will be good to dance the final dance of death with you, it will feel good to end your life." Martel closed his eyes briefly and gave a soft sigh. So many things in his life now were speeding down the track at a rapid pace like a train on a rail at breakneck speed on a collision course. Three years ago things seemed so simple and now. Now, so many secrets were ready to emerge from dark places, so many skeletons ready to exit from closets.

His mind drifted to Alyssa/Kanashii again. What was it that so attracted him to her? Perhaps it was because that like him, she was on a similar journey. Forced through her own amnesia and the predicament she was now in, to be someone different; to live in a new life, to start anew. Martel lived his own secrets, kept his own dark skeletons in his closets and played his own emotions and dark intrigues close to his heart. Alyssa, even though it was no fault of her own, was also thrust into a world where she now had a mask to wear and a part to play.

In her letter to him, she had written she had gotten nearly all of her memories back and yet she still chose him, had given her heart and soul to him. He hoped and prayed she would be able to withstand the tests his father would place on her shoulders.

With a loud click he assembled the final bolt and snapped the gun together, sighted down the scope to make sure of its alignment.

A small grim smile briefly played on his face; Martel knew Gambini would not withstand the final test from him.

This he had to keep telling himself and believing. Center yourself…

"I am, centered!!!" His mind shattered his self doubt like a crystal barrier and he knew it to be utterly true. The shadow dragon would go hunting and trailing tonight.

Joshua Demonico, Patrizio Fantenelli, Rocco Benedarra, Leonardo Tagretta and two other Jerome capos', Sal Antonia and Jerry Bartellino all sat around at Rocco's Blue Parrot Nightclub one of the Jerome crew hang outs downtown.

Joshua found he often liked taking care of business here in the heart of the city, where he could be in touch with the men, the streets and the essence of the Family instead of up at the secluded estate further upstate. After all, this is where he was from and where the soldiers and crews of the Family lived their daily lives.

"So what's the word, eh?" Patrizio was also able to enjoy his smokes in here. They had finished talking monetary business and now the real questions came out, about their boss.

Joshua knew he had to balance very delicately what he sent down the line with what he knew in his heart. He couldn't risk any screw-ups with Victor down in Jamaica so lightly guarded, Martel not here and Vito Bonnaro trying to make a formal alliance with them.

"Everything is going good for now," Joshua chewed on his own nicotine gum square, his dark eyes searching his men. "Be alert in your areas, know who your people are, listen to the fuckin' empty suits hanging around your areas. We have some pretty good information that there may be some D'Salvatore button men scouting around some of our areas."

Grumbling and cussing and talk rose up at once from all of them.

"Bold now, are they?" Len asked warily, he snorted in disgust, "bastardo's come around in my area and they will get their noses wiped off their faces."

"But I thought?" Patrizio looked at Joshua, leaving the question unfinished. 'Weren't the button men supposed to really be Bonnaro Sicilian muscle that would turn at the last moment?'

Demonico just eyed him a second and barely shook his head. "Just be wary Pops, Ok?" He conveyed unspoken messages to his friend and mentor. "Not everything is as it seems. Just keep yer eyes open."

"Yeah, yeah." Patrizio nodded and drew long and hard on his smoke.

"Also be wary of new associates you haven't seen around your territories before. No reason to get alarmed and do anything rash, like start icing people or doing whatever you want, but just be alert." The consigliere continued.

"Fucking D'Salvatores," Sal Antonia growled, "the fuckers are going down hard, I tell you that much, constant agita is all they ever give us."

Joshua and Leonardo glanced at one another briefly, then Len steepled his fingers looking at each man in turn. "We soon get some help of our own, but for now, Joshua is right, we need to be wary as hawks." His quiet voice made him sound even more dangerous.

An uneasy shift seemed to circle the men a moment.

"Yeah, sure, no problem," Jerry Bartellino, a large heavyset man nodded. He almost looked like some mobbed up, large war dog, "watch our areas- watch our asses." His thick Brooklyn accent barked. "Like Sal said, all the fuckers do is give us agita but we'll be watching for them. I know my crew will be." He laughed loudly, "I hope the fucking pussies do show up, I got a few button men of my own who'd like some action."

This got some chuckling and camaraderie from the other men.

417

"I know you would, Jerry," Joshua nodded with a grin finishing his glass of wine, "but hear me out. We need to keep in contact with one another, no solo shit, no showboating. Earn your business, do what you must to keep your area's clean and under surveillance, especially for people who have no business there."

"And keep and eye out for the damn Fed's." Rocco downed his own drink, "I've seen more fucking Fed's and F.B.I running around with hard-on's the last couple weeks than my whole life. They know this shit is in the air too."

"God damn I hate fucking RICO..." Patrizio eyes grew dark as he was getting geared up for his tirade. The F.B.I and R.I.C.O; the governments 'Racketeer Influenced and Corrupt Organizations' law, was Patrizio's special pet peeve and he never lost an opportunity to go on a rant against them. "You know this 'thing of ours' used to mean something, now with all this goddamn RICO shit..."

"Pops, I know." Joshua touched him lightly on the arm; he didn't need Patrizio going off on a tangent now, he needed to get orders out to his main capos and crews. "I hate 'em too, eh?" Joshua just smiled thinly, "So let's not give 'em any fucking excuse to get involved, understand?"

All the men nodded darkly in agreement.

"So then what..." Sal asked, he was almost as old as Victor and Patrizio, but had a lean hard edge to him. "We all just sit here until the fucking *bastardo* D'Salvatores' decide to come take a whack at us? Is that what you're telling us?"

"All I'm saying is keep your eyes open." Joshua wasn't made consigliere for nothing; he could be just as influential as the imposing Martel or the regal family Boss, Victor. His dark gaze bore into each man, his own dark charisma coming forth. "We need eyes, you are our eyes. This thing, this *mannagge* with the D'Salvatores, it will come. No one will abandon you or leave your ass hanging in the wind. Defend what is rightfully yours, but do not bring down any heat from any law enforcement or any problems from other *Brugads* and Families!" His hand hit the table for emphasis, "Remember, they are staying out of this shit between the D'Salvatores and us. This shit, this war, is only for Jerome and D'Salvatores. We can't count on any help from the Corella's or Del Giorno's or anyone else."

The men leaned back and grumbled quietly or nodded in agreement or just silently drank their wine.

Joshua, Leonardo and Rocco glanced at one another briefly. That part was done, now all they had to do was wait. Wait and see what happened with their Padrone, with Laurence Martel with Vito Bonnaro and with the D'Salvatores.

"So I hear Victor is one hell of a chess player," Sal said as he refilled his drink and passed the bottle on to the next man.

"The best," Joshua said and toasted his compari's, "the absolute best."

Next to him Leonardo nodded, a grim smile on his handsome features. "Absolutely the best," He agreed. "*Salute!*"

Alyssa and Victor had spent a wonderful dinner at an expensive but tropical island seafood place, Gio and Tony of course tagging along. Alyssa had to suppress a giggle it always amused her how much Gio Aprile could eat, he seemed a bottomless pit, but she was sure it had something to do with his overly, pumped up muscle mass.

That evening she had read, written some in her journals and turned in early, watching nature's light show: Lightning in the distance from a few far off storms on the ocean that never quite rolled in.

Victor had spent some time in the other room talking privately with Gio and Tony, going over plans for the morning and then made a call to someone. Since he spoke the whole call in Italian she had no idea to whom the call was, but it seemed to make him happy.

After that Victor came back in the room he shared with Alyssa and began to get ready for bed, as he was going to change for the night into his pajama's and prepare his insulin injection for himself, he briefly turned and regarded Alyssa for a moment. Now in just his slacks, and his undershirt, he looked even more grandfatherly, but she still had a healthy respect for the old man. She also had a sense of loyalty to him now that would never again waver.

The aging Don paused a moment in the doorway of the bathroom. "You know Alyssa," he spoke honestly, turning and facing her. "My late wife Isabella and I had always wanted a daughter. We had two beautiful sons, but Issy had always wanted a little girl to for her own, I guess in some way perhaps I did as well." His dark eyes searched hers for a moment just utter honesty between them, the sharing of two human souls. "After Michael, Issy couldn't have any more children. She tried and miscarried one early on. In many ways I see in you the daughter I never had. Good night, child." Victor spoke softly and then quietly turned and went into the bathroom.

As he injected his insulin into himself he replayed the day's events with Alyssa. He had meant what he said about accepting her and adopting her like a daughter/niece and was glad she had passed his test.

Had she refused his offer of loyalty or written that she wanted to leave, he would have had Gio drive her out somewhere on the Island and kill her. He knew his son was beginning to have deep feelings for the girl and there was no way he would have had his son do the unpleasant task of executing her. Not after Martel had invested so much in her. In many ways Alyssa was almost as good for his son as he had been in getting her integrated into the Family.

But Victor could feel the honesty in Alyssa now, the change in her. She truly was one of his family members, the same as if she really was his blood niece. He had no more reservations or doubts on her loyalty to either him or the Jerome Family.

Alyssa had snuggled under the covers and rolled over onto her side, a small smile of peace and contentment on her lips. Sleepily she closed her eyes and began to doze off, she had found her niche. This was without a doubt her family now and her life; the people she truly cared about now. She wouldn't want it any other way. That night she made peace with herself as well. All the lessons she had learned from Cesare, Victor, Rosette, Martel and the others gelling into a comfortable index in her head.

Like everyone else in the Family, she now had dedicated her heart and soul to the Jerome Family as an entity and to the men who ran it, Don Victor and Laurence Martel.
She was more than content to be exactly as Victor asked her, his niece, a daughter.

True she knew very well the darker side and what the men did behind closed doors and in their basements. They were not saints, but neither did they ask or demand of her to engage in that world, only to respect it and to understand that the Family and *La Cosa Nostra*, came first in their lives. It didn't change who the men were inside and as long as she followed the unspoken rules and codes that any other wife, mother, daughter, niece, etc followed then she knew her life here in the Jerome's was as safe and revered as could be.

Chapter 33- *October 15th 1987*

Martel had spotted his quarry by the next morning. He knew where his father was going to be staying and so discreetly he had circled the perimeter of the Sheridan Sands. Louie can easily blend in with this tourist/surfer crowd, he thought. And so he had staked out from a distance the beaches around the Sheridan Sands and sure enough, he finally spotted the man.

Louie was no inexperienced gunman though and he was clever enough and nearly always stayed as deep in the crowds of people as he could. Martel's instincts told him that Louie was going to wait until Victor was away from the people and the tourists, before trying his hit. Louie was a sniper at heart; he wasn't good at close contact kills and wouldn't risk even just two bodyguards taking him out. He was strictly 'contract for hire' and had no loyalties to any of this.

Martel marked him well in his mind and in his soul. The hunter was being stalked now, the game was on. Now came the long and tiring job of merely keeping Louie Gambini in his sites at all times until Martel felt he could take the man out quickly, quietly and efficiently.

With an iron will, Martel casually sat down near the line of foliage, a tourist off by himself reading. Every once in awhile the he would look up and mark Gambini, then return to his reading; but always he was aware that his target was there.

Martel had the same type of small long distance scope that Louie had and every once in awhile he would glance at the Sheridan Sands as well. When Louie suddenly perked up, Martel did also and scanned the elegant hotel. He saw his father and Alyssa flanked by Gio and Tony walking to the limo and being whisked away.

Louie Gambini casually rose up and stretched, put back on his gaudy Hawaiian surfing shirt and ambled off, looking exactly like some surfer dude who finally had enough sun and fun for the morning.

It was then that the slight chill coursed through Martel. He recognized that shirt Gambini wore! He had seen it in the dream/meditation he experienced the other day on the plane. Time seemed to slow and swirl briefly for him and then almost like some quantum hiccup speed back up. Martel swallowed dryly and briefly shook his head clearing his mind, his vigilance even more sharp and honed now.

As soon as Gambini moved off and left, Martel also casually waited until his target wouldn't spot him and then moved off and followed the hunter. Martel's body alive and focused as it always was when he locked onto his target.

Alyssa, Victor and the two guards took the hotel limo to a small but elegant restaurant on the east end of the island; this area was definitely less touristy and more for the high rollers and big spenders. Victor had told her to dress fairly nice that they would be going to some exclusive Country Club for brunch. She noticed Victor himself, usually always a nice, conservative dresser as well, was dressed extra dapper in a light grey suit and hat with a nice tie, handkerchief even a small white rose in his lapel.

The guards dressed in their usual dark suits but added ties on today, Gio carried one of the leather briefcases from the other day and she noticed it was handcuffed quite firmly around his thick wrist. Alyssa dressed in a nice light blue dress that came down slightly below her knees. Her only jewelry was the simple but elegant Kanji necklace that her teacher Martel had given her and the small key that unlocked Victor's insulin supply. In her small purse she carried 2 extra rolls of lifesavers for her uncle as well as one of the elegant hawk pens and a few small notepads.

"Ah Mr. Disarro," the elegant Maitre-d' greeted Victor and his group, "your party is already here." He led them down the steps to a couple of tables near a wonderful indoor fountain surrounded by small palms and flowers. At one table next to theirs, already sat two other guards and this is where Gio and Tony went to. At the table right next to the guard table, was another one that already had an elegant older couple sitting at it. They rose immediately as soon as Victor and company came in.

"*Buon giorno, Vittorio, mi amico!*" the older gentleman greeted Victor first. Both men hugged and embraced tightly and warmly, large smiles on both their faces. It was easy to see there was deep respect and friendship between them both.

"Vito, *benvenuto*," Victor held him at arms length and smiled. "My heart rejoices to see you again."

Alyssa noted that Vito Bonnaro was a small man, even smaller then Victor, more about her height, he like Victor also had a distinguished but neatly trimmed moustache, but he had a full head of thick salt and pepper hair. He like Victor, also wore an elegant diamond ring on his pinky and a wedding band and although he wore stately wire rimmed glasses Vito's eyes like Victor's conveyed strength, dignity and a charisma that seemed to be able to freeze men's blood or read into his opponents soul, it nearly took Alyssa's breath away. 'Two powerful dark suns!' Alyssa thought to herself, 'they could be brothers.'

There was no doubt in her mind that Vito Bonnaro was also a Man of Honor and a fellow Don, his mere presence and leadership like Victors conveyed a thousand unspoken words. Standing next to him was a very kind but strong looking woman. She was solid and slightly taller than her husband and very robust. Her eyes held grandmotherly warmth but also a matronly dignity that reminded Alyssa of Rosette but more so. Here was a woman who understood and respected her husbands' world but yet let no one push her around. Alyssa could see the way that the Bonnaro couple looked and smiled together, there was no doubt they were a team and had a lot of love and years between them.

"Ah, Lena…" Victor hugged her respectfully and spoke with her in Italian a few moments also.

Lena gave Victor a strong hug and a huge kiss on the cheek. It was very obvious to Alyssa that this couple were very dear and old friends to Victor.

Victor switched back to English and said, "I'd like to introduce my niece, Alyssa Disarro. Alyssa, these are special and close friends of ours, Vito Bonnaro and his wife Lena."

"Alyssa, nice to meet you," Don Vito spoke in heavily Italian-accented English to her, "My wife, she no speak English, but from both of us, is good to meet you, eh?"

He gave her a small polite hug and embrace and just like when Victor touched her; she could feel incredible strength and leadership in that simple embrace.

As she had seen others do to respected elders, she gave Mr. Bonnaro a warm hug and a gentle kiss on each cheek.

Lena gave Alyssa a huge hug that felt like a protective bear hugging a long lost cub. She grinned broadly and said something in Italian to both Vito and Victor and then smiled warmly at Alyssa.

"She, eh, says she glad to meet you, and glad you accompanied your Uncle here on vacation." Vito translated.

After the introductions, Vito reseated his wife and himself and Victor seated Alyssa and himself. Most of the talking was done in Sicilian and so Alyssa was totally lost on what was being said. In fact it was Vito who occasionally insisted on speaking in English for a while so Alyssa wouldn't feel "left out".

Alyssa noticed that at the guard table, Vito's guards seemed to look more dangerous and angry than the usual Jerome type guards: Leaner, hungrier and darker.

Since Tony Armanno was Sicilian he was able to converse quietly with the Bonnaro guards and act as a translator for Gio, but mostly the guards were silent, their eyes scanning quietly and alertly around.

"So Alyssa, you Uncle tell me that you and Laurence Martel have become how you say, very good friends, eh?" Vito chuckled at one point drawing back Alyssa's gaze to the powerful Don.

At the mere mention of his name, Alyssa had blushed which made Lena seem to smile even more broadly.

"Oh yes. She seems to be quite at ease with ol' Laurence." Victor chuckled and patted her hand gently and then repeated it in Italian for Lena's benefit.

Vito chuckled and his dark eyes pierced her soul, like Victor's she could feel him almost searching inside her soul. "Then that is a good thing." Vito smiled as their food was being served, "Lena and I have been together for many, many years. A true love and soulmate is worth more than anything else, and to, how you say, love someone you should truly be friends with them as well, eh?" he nodded sagely and then affectionately touched his wife's hand, a brief shared smile between them that spoke ages of love and companionship.

After that Victor and Vito seemed to switch to talking pretty much unto themselves in Italian only.

Breakfast being finished, Vito went to talk to his guards and to Lena privately in Italian while Victor pulled Alyssa aside a moment. "The Bonnaro's truly like you child, I hope you enjoy them as well. Now my dear," Victor spoke for her ears only, his dark eyes filling her with understanding and gentle instruction. "Vito and I have business to attend to, so today you and Lena will have the day to do sightseeing, shopping, whatever it is ladies like to do." Victor discreetly slipped a wad of cash into her purse. "One of Vito's men will be accompanying you both; I believe his name is Arrigo. Both Gio and Tony will be coming with Vito and me…"

Alyssa felt a brief moment of panic engulf her. How would she speak to Lena? Neither Arrigo nor Lena seemed to read, speak or understand

English nor did Alyssa understand Italian. Sure she had picked up a few words and phrases here and there from Rosette and the others in the Jerome Estates, but not enough to certainly be fluent in it or write it!! And what of her Uncle? What if something happened to him while he was separated from her? Who would give him his insulin shot or…

"Alyssa," Victor seemed to sense her brief rising fear. "You will be fine, trust me. Believe in me; do as I ask my dear. Everything will be all right." Her uncle assured her. "I have explained everything to Vito and Lena, they know about your inability to speak." He gently held her hand as his thumb stroked her fingers as though infusing her with his strength and faith.

It wasn't strictly herself that she was worried about, Alyssa glumly thought. But she had promised Victor, given him her oath. Obviously he needed to take care of some business with Vito. With a warm smile she nodded bravely acting like it was just fine.

"Good girl." Victor gave her a brief hug, "You'll do fine, why not go find a gift for Martel, eh?" he winked at her. He did so enjoy seeing her blush slightly whenever the big man's name was mentioned. "Besides," he whispered quickly, "Gio is with me, remember?" he briefly touched the key next to the kanji on her necklace.

Vito came back over to her after her and Victor had finished speaking, "It was good to meet you, *mia cara nipote*." He smiled and gave her another hug. "Arrigo Salvaggio will stay with you both and take good care of you, eh? You and Lena enjoy the sights, tonight we all meet back up again." she nodded and glanced briefly at the man named Arrigo who for a startling moment reminded her of a cross between Joshua and Leonardo but with even harder and darker eyes.

She smiled at him and watched Victor giving last minute instructions to Gio and Tony and even Arrigo as he pointed occasionally and discreetly to Alyssa. And then at once everyone seemed to move. Victor and Vito, flanked by Gio, Tony and Vito's other guard Luca.

Lena came up and gently put her hand on Alyssa's shoulder and gave it a reassuring squeeze as she and Alyssa watched the men all go. Only Arrigo remained with them and he was paying the bill. "I speak-a little *Inglese*." Lena confided to Alyssa, in a thick, heavy Sicilian accent. "Just-a no so *bene*, eh?" she winked. "*Noi donne*, we have-a *divertirsi*, eh?"

Alyssa smiled warmly at Lena and nodded, she knew the words so far Lena had used. *Donne* being 'women/ladies', and *divertirsi* meaning 'a fun time'… This may not be so bad after all!

Alyssa cast another quick glance at the dour Arrigo. Around 5'9, he was lean, olive skinned, classic Mediterranean looks but hard with darkly chiseled features and collar-length hair that he kept combed tightly back. He looked like the type of man who had no compulsions about killing anyone or anything and Alyssa was 100% certain, ol'

Arrigo probably had a garrote, a gun and maybe a stiletto stashed on him as well.

He spoke respectfully to Lena a moment and then like a protective guard dog just followed close by on the ladies heels.

Louie Gambini had been sitting outside the Sunset Palm Country Club, again acting the part of a tourist. He had cleaned up a bit and put on some expensive jewelry so as to at least look like he belonged there. He had stayed outside on a nearby bench though, reading the local newspaper, dark glasses covering his eyes as he occasionally glanced at the club waiting for Victor and Vito to emerge.

He had followed the hotel limo over when Victor and entourage had first arrived; so far everything was right on schedule. In a leather case by his feet was his most favorite sniper rifle, a Russian Dragunov SVD. In his hands the thing was absolutely flawless, and he wanted a perfect working gun on this hit.

When Louie Gambini first saw Victor and the group going in, it finally dawned on him after nearly 2 days of agonizing where he had seen that woman. She was one of his many captures done on the side for some of the various 'white slavery' gangs. This amused him to no end; did the great Don Victor Jerome have some white slave prostitute as his cover? He had always heard the Jerome's were not in that market.

Louie never liked anyone or anything to escape from him and he had half a mind after this hit, to take the woman out as well. After all, she may have remembered him from her initial capture. This continued to send bad vibes up and down his gut; he wanted no one alive who could possibly finger him on anything. Would she recognize him now, if she glanced at him? He decided to keep an even further distance from his target he didn't want to risk her pointing him out to Victor.

After awhile he spotted Victor, Vito and three guards get into a rental golf cart and head down towards the Country Club's private beach area.

Just as Louie was about to go follow the first group, he nearly collided with the exiting Lena, Alyssa and Arrigo.

"*Scusami!*" Lena nearly bowled him over, but made no other apologies or concessions to the man.

For the briefest of instances Alyssa and Louie Gambini locked eyes. Something icy cold and vile slid down her spine but she didn't know why, it was like that moment she would have those terrors... "Oh please not now, not while there is no Gio or Victor or Martel, don't let me have a terror now." Her mind grasped blindly. Why did this 'Hollywood-surfer type' fill her suddenly with so much dread and fear?

"*Affrettarsi passare*," Arrigo demanded Alyssa to hurry up and move along, "*Che accelera!*" The bodyguard didn't like his charges bunched up, it was not a good situation. "*Andiamo!*"

For a moment she could almost have sworn she heard Kageryu's voice in her head, "Hang on to Lena, Kanashii." The strong voice of her Teacher seemed to fill her both with soothing comfort and strength, "You'll be fine, just move along. Now move!" Instinctively she reached out and grabbed Lena's arm and the older woman pulled her along in a comforting and motherly fashion.

The hotel limo was already waiting and smoothly Arrigo got the two ladies and himself inside. "*Accelerare! Vai! Andiamo!*" he ordered the driver. The white limo with Lena Bonnaro, Alyssa and their bodyguard swiftly moved out.

For a brief moment Louie 'Kohana' Gambini tasted something so deliciously close; terrified and prey-like a part of him wanted to run after it, hunt it down and kill it. "Fly away now lil' bird, but ol' Louie will find you later." He chuckled darkly to himself, however right now he had a golf cart to rent and a powerful Crime Boss to kill.

Louie wasn't the only one who had been watching. The stealthy Laurence Martel had been watching the watcher, marking him from a distance and staying well hidden in the background. "Cat and mouse we play Louie..." Martel was getting anxious; he would be so happy to get his shot at Gambini and hopefully before Gambini took his shot at his father.

Martel had watched Victor, Vito and three of the guards get a large golf cart type beach vehicle and drive off down to the private area that was off limits to the public. With a resigned sigh he realized he would have to now double back and take the long way around, but in his mind he knew what he was looking for. A small single room beach cabin that was almost at the edge of the water. He was about to turn and go when he suddenly saw Alyssa, Lena and the other guard come out of the Country Club just as Gambini was heading to the cart rental area.

The Shadow Dragon tensed and it was again as if time stood still. He could almost see Gambini staring down at Alyssa. There was a look of smug satisfaction and predatory hunger on his face. Lena had moved on ahead ignoring the fellow and nearly plowing him down while the guard was beginning to get a bad feeling, probably his inner instinct that the jam-up was not a good situation all the way around.

'Move Kanashii, go!' Martel wondered why she was just standing there! Somehow even from way back here, without seeing her face, he could almost sense the waves of fear beginning to emanate from her. Martel's heart nearly sank in his chest. 'Not now Kanashii, not now...' He centered his mind and concentrated on the kanji around her neck, 'I am nearer than you think Kanashii, but go! Go! Hang on to Lena if you must, just get out of there.'

Thankfully she seemed to break out of her fear and do exactly as he envisioned. He saw her hand reach out and grab hold of Lena Bonnaro's arm as the matronly woman led her right into the awaiting limo with the darkly protective Arrigo on their heels. He too seemed to be aware of some intangible feeling and stayed extra alert and cautious as he quickly got the ladies and himself in the car and told the driver to go.

Martel noted with satisfaction that Arrigo was indeed a skilled bodyguard and had kept himself as a buffer between Gambini and the ladies at all times, one of his hands already half inside his dark sport coat probably resting on the handle of his gun.

Once they were away, Martel noted that Gambini stuck to his original plan and got a cart also. Somehow the D'Salvatores must have gotten him access to the Sunset Palms Country Club.

Martel disappeared back amongst the foliage and then loped up along some rugged hills; from here he had an excellent vantage point and could look for the cabin he had seen before. Far down below he saw the motorized golf cart with Victor, Vito and guards heading for a tiny point out to the west end near the strong surf.

He growled a few curses under his breath and then began to effortlessly jog his way off that direction as well. As he moved out he began assembling his own powerful sniper weapon on the fly. "Soon you will dance the dance of death with the Undertaker, Kohana." He centered his mind to the task ahead. He made sure to avoid the various nests of fire ants and other hungry ants that seemed to be built up here along the rugged hills, small fiddler crabs dancing away from him.

Alyssa and Lena trailed by the overly protective Arrigo had been shopping all morning, when they finally stopped at a small outdoor café for lunch. Already Lena had a bunch of shopping bags all stashed away in the limo. Since she spoke little to no English -she played dumb and spoke no English at all in the stores- and since none of the store keepers spoke any Italian, Lena made out like an Arab trader and often got the best bargains on things. To Alyssa it looked like Lena had bought presents for half the people on the island of Sicily and she would often wink to Alyssa and say things like "*Per mio figlio*, Gino" or "*Per mia abiatico*, Luccesia, *Mi* Grand baby."

So far Alyssa had found very little in the way of presents. She certainly had no want for anything for herself. She had gotten her Uncle Victor an elegant leather bound historical book on pirates knowing his penchant for collecting books and for Martel so far she had only found mostly cheap touristy 'oriental looking' things that she knew were not even worthy of giving to her beloved teacher but one thing did catch her eye for him. It was a coiled up dragon and half astride the coiled up dragon was an Oriental deity known as Kwan Ti. She knew this would have meaning to Martel because she had seen this oriental god Kwan Ti statue at his home.

Martel had told her the legend before; that Kwan Ti was the Asian god of War. He was a fearless strategist, powerful warrior and protector of his people.

What she liked best about the statue was that it reminded Alyssa for some very odd reason of Victor and Martel. Victor the noble elegant General, master strategist, protector and leader of the Jerome Family and Martel, the shadow dragon his ever-present supporter, enforcer and the protector of Victor.

Even Lena seemed to nod and smile, "For Martello, eh?" it always amused Alyssa that Lena seemed to get Laurence Martel's name wrong, and call him '*Martello*' but only later would Alyssa learn how very accurate Lena was. *Martello* was the Italian word for hammer and it was also a common Italian Mafia euphemism for underboss or someone's trusted "right hand man" or enforcer of the Family's wills and rules. Lena knew exactly who she meant, she knew very well the great Laurence Martel, son of Victor Jerome. She had raised him for many years as one of her own.

As the two ladies sat at the outdoor café sipping espresso and eating some antipasto, Lena would talk to Alyssa mostly in Sicilian with smatterings of English, as though Alyssa clearly understood every word.

Alyssa had not lived for so many months among Victor Jerome and his people without picking up at least some rudimentary Italian and at least 'key phrases', and even though she didn't understand a half of what Lena Bonnaro said, Alyssa found herself instinctually drawn to the maternal warmth and mentorship of the older woman.

Lena had been slightly briefed about Alyssa from both her husband and Victor Jerome. She was told Alyssa was a distant niece of Victors, related through a brother of Isabella and that the young girl had been in a terrible accident. But what the accident was, had never been told to her. She knew that Alyssa was trusted by Victor and that like Joshua, the Jerome family consigliere, Victor now had 'adopted' Alyssa Disarro as one of his own and had her under his wing.

Lena had spent many long loyal years with her beloved Vito and she often knew better than to ask too many questions, in fact she found if she often just waited and listened quietly she would usually figure things out on her own. While she and Vito were beloved childhood sweethearts and best friends, growing closer together with each passing year, she was still raised as *Mafioso* and that meant knowing the unwritten codes of omerta and how things worked in the Family. Like what was permitted to be asked and what wasn't.

She had known Victor and his family for many years as well; they were trusted allies and friends. She had watched Theodore Jerome grow up along side her own children and the Bonnaro Family and Lena along with her husband and their children were one of the very few people who knew 'Laurence Martel's' deepest secret of all, that he was in fact Victor's son.

Lena liked the younger woman Alyssa. She could tell whatever tragedy had befallen Alyssa had scarred her deeply both emotionally and physically, but yet the young woman had an inner strength and resilience that reminded Lena of herself in her youth.

During breakfast Victor had told her in Italian that Martel and Alyssa were quite close and Lena hoped in her heart that Theodore Jerome would indeed choose this girl as someone he may eventually marry.

Lena could tell by the way Alyssa would blush whenever the big man's name was mentioned, the Kanji she wore and the items she bought for him, that her heart was deeply in love with Victor's son. Lena had a feeling inside her that Alyssa would make a good wife to Theodore. She was strong, she dealt well with Family matters and she could tell Alyssa had an undying love and respect for her Uncle and the workings of *La Cosa Nostra*. She would be worthy.

And so Lena presided like a true Italian mother to the girl, protective, friendly and offering her strength and friendship. She knew now with *mannagge* in the air the young girl would need all the female mentorship in the ways of *La Cosa Nostra* she could get. After all, the wives of the Men of Honor needed their own fellowship and mentorship of other strong women as well.

Lena looked at Alyssa and smiled again as she continued telling the young woman of her travels and other things. She knew Alyssa didn't understand all of it, but in time she would, and Lena would happily keep telling her and tutoring her.

"*Padrona di casa, in futuro.*" Lena patted Alyssa's hand, 'future wife of the head of the Family' she would smile. I will teach you well.

After lunch they walked along some more, Alyssa was beginning to get tired and Arrigo was beginning to look more bored and grumpier by the minute. Always he was respectful and professional to Alyssa and Lena, but his occasional grumblings in Italian and dark dour looks at various fellow tourists were beginning to grate on everyone's nerves. However Lena seemed destined to look inside this one last store. "Arrigo, *calmati*," Lena said slightly exasperated. "*per un pelo emporio*, eh?"

All three went inside to look at this last store that seemed off the beaten path. Inside the store looked to have a bit of everything from candles to tourist gifts, jewelry, even local herbs and spices and remedies.

Alyssa was fascinated, the spicy scent of incense hung in the air, here and there were local herbs and remedies, hand crafted items and little discoveries of every description.

Tending the store was a venerable, dark skinned, island gentleman who must have been as ancient as the local folklore. "Ladies, gentleman, welcome to Elias's humble shop. You need any help you just ask ol' Elias, that's me." He smiled broadly and sincerely flashing a big smile. Alyssa liked him, he had character, color and she felt safe here. Even the dark, glowering Arrigo was calmed and pacified now, finding something on one of the shelves that seemed to interested him.

Lena was busy checking some fresh oregano and other herbs as well as some expensive but beautiful coral necklaces.

Alyssa was on the other side of the small store checking some coral men's rings, she was thinking of maybe getting a gift for Tommy DeLuca, or Gio Aprile or maybe some candy for Cesare.

"See anything you like, pretty lady?" Elias limped over towards Alyssa, "perhaps a pretty shell brooch or a coral ring?"

"She no-a *parlare!*" Lena began walking protectively towards Alyssa. "She have-a injury to she *voce.*" She continued pointing to her throat and miming an injury.

"Well that don't make any matter," Elias spoke gently to Alyssa, "I have a son who is deaf, we used to talk like this..." the man began 'speaking' with his fingers, his old dark wrinkled hands forming graceful signs and symbols in the code of International Sign language.

Unfortunately Alyssa understood none of what he was signing but she loved watching how graceful and fast the unspoken language was. "How could I have forgotten sign language?" Alyssa chastised herself, "I had always just thought it just for the deaf! But with this, I can talk as fast as he is..."

"Do you see how it flows?" He asked Alyssa, "Everything I am speaking to you I am saying with my hands as well." He smiled watching the spark of fire and interest suddenly in her eyes.

Alyssa nodded and smiled, she was mesmerized and a part of her ached with such longing to be able to talk like that, to have people understand her instead of painfully scratching out things.

"Here, watch." Elias slowly formed a simple gesture with his fingers that was easy and elegant. He repeated it twice more then spoke, "it means, '*Hello, good day.*' See like this..." he gently took Alyssa's smooth hand in his callous-hardened old one and showed her the sign. "You try it."

Even Arrigo had wandered over to watch; fascinated and enthralled, his head slightly tilted.

She signed out '*Hello, good day.*' A smile played across her lips and she could feel as though some inner part of her had just sprouted wings. It was as though the healing hawk was ready to try and fly again, her proud inner spirit calling to her to soar.

Both Lena the mother hen and Arrigo looked at one another and smiled.

"Come, child." Elias motioned with his head, "follow me." He limped back to behind the counter and began to dig around for a few minutes through some crates and boxes. After a few minutes and a triumphant, "Ah ha! Here it is!" he pulled out a very faded and well-worn book. It was titled 'Easy International Sign language ', "Here take it," He placed it in Alyssa's hands. "What's nice about sign language is that it is the same no matter what language. Italian, Spanish, English, the signs are all the same, you see?"

Almost reverently she opened the dusty cover and gently began skimming through the pages. Page after page had drawings or photos of hands signing numbers, the Alphabet, all kinds of words and phrases, all of it here in this thick book.

Her whole face lit up at the treasure and she felt even more free and happy inside, as if the hawk was finally ready to launch upon the wind, test her wings and fly.

"*Quanto costa per il libro?*" Lena walked over pointing to the book and fishing in her big purse.

"No, No..." the old man respectfully shook his head no, "Nothing, take it." Elias placed his hand briefly on Alyssa's shoulder, "It's to make your life a little easier, child." he smiled and looked at Lena and Arrigo, "My son is now passed on, but he and I had many deep and meaningful discussions in sign language." He again began to sign as he talked, "Maybe this will help you have meaningful communication with those you love."

Alyssa clutched the well-worn book to her chest, holding onto it for dear life. It was the most special book she would ever read and she couldn't wait to start! She held out her hand to Elias who warmly shook it.

"Here, *'thank-you'*, like this." The old man signed with his fingers.

Alyssa signed out *'thank you'* and her heart now soared among the clouds her soul taking flight on great elegant wings as her eyes alighted with inner happiness.

The rest of the afternoon Lena took Alyssa sightseeing with Arrigo in tow. Once again he seemed dour and sullen having to go look at a bunch of stuff that didn't interest him.
But Alyssa's face was buried deep in the book and when Lena wasn't looking Alyssa practiced and signed out the wondrous new language she had discovered. Only Arrigo seemed to notice out of the corner of his eye, with a slight amused and approving look.

At one point as they were listening to some tour-guide talking about some historical island place, Alyssa who had been sitting near one of the walls that overlooked the beautiful turquoise sea suddenly felt an icy cold chill slide down her neck and back. She gently closed the book and glanced up off towards the ocean, worry in her eyes.

Arrigo watched her intently a moment, but she quickly looked away.

"What was it?" It felt like something cruel, evil and calculating in the air. For a brief moment her heart lurched horribly and thought of her Uncle Victor, "Was he Ok? Had something happened?" The fear wanted to gel around her like a solid wall, "Oh please, no terrors!" she willed herself to clear her mind, to fight through the raw terror.

There were no old memories that haunted her this time, just cold tendrils of pure, raw icy fear that threatened to close around her. She glanced out towards the ocean, towards the beach but saw nothing, nothing solid she could grab onto.

"*Problema?*" Arrigo had sidled discreetly up to her looking a bit intense and concerned. "*Che cosa, inverso?*"

She had no idea what he was saying but she gathered he was trying to find out if there was some kind of problem or what was causing her fear. He seemed to be picking up her discomfort rather quickly. But what could she tell him? "I don't know? I just feel something?"' Besides, Arrigo couldn't read English anyway.

She simply shook her head for a moment and then as suddenly as it had come on the feeling of terror and dread left her, winked out as quickly as if someone had flicked off a light switch. Instead there was now just a dread feeling of tiredness, sadness and heaviness that seemed to smother her soul, but yet she had no idea why. Alyssa touched briefly the Kanji that Martel had given her; strangely it seemed so icy cold despite her body temperature and the warm tropical air. She smiled vaguely at Arrigo trying to convey that whatever feeling 'it' was had gone now. Slowly she and Arrigo went to rejoin Lena, her mind still wondering. Yet Arrigo still discreetly watched her with a concerned eye.

Victor Jerome and Vito Bonnaro sat inside the small beach side cabin. It was the last one on the row owned by the Country Club on their private beach, separated far from the others. Recent storms had shifted the beach and this cabin was dangerously close to the high tide line, even now they saw the waterline nearly up to the back steps. So the Country Club normally didn't rent it out anymore but for the right price and for just a few hours time, Victor Jerome was able to coax them into letting him use it.

It was a tiny place, little more than a living room, kitchenette, one bedroom and a bathroom. Gio and Luca had checked the inside out thoroughly first and then made some coffee for the two Dons while Tony stayed guard outside. Once Gio and Luca were convinced and satisfied that everything was safe for their bosses and they had their coffee, Gio unlocked the case that had been handcuffed to him and handed it to Victor. Then he and Luca went back outside to stand guard with Tony.

Outside, Tony had assembled two M-16 semi automatic rifles for mid to long-range work and all three guards checked and double checked their guns. Gio took one M-16 and gave the other to Luca to use, then the guards positioned themselves one on each side of the shack, alert and on duty. No one would be disturbing their two Dons.

Inside Vito and Victor sipped some coffee and spoke together in the traditional Sicilian dialect. "I have looked forward to this day for years, my dear friend." Victor raised a toast to Vito, "I have owed you so much in friendship, in favors and for all you have done for my *Famiglia* as well as for me personally as a friend."

"I feel the same way, my close friend." Vito said returning the toast, "There will be much in business for both of us. I am touched that you are turning over such generous ventures and businesses to the Bonnaro's" Vito was referring to the fact that Victor was turning more and more of the illegal aspects over to the Bonnaro's.

Victor nodded, "Things are more secure and safe right now in your country. This RICO shit," he shook his head almost sadly, "it has been slowly destroying 'our thing' that and the lack of omerta in this country have been eating away this thing of ours like a cancer. I predict it will get only worse in the U.S. Different gangs, different crime rings, different rackets, none of it is like before Vito."

"I understand." Vito nodded sagely, "And I think you will be very happy with some of the legitimate areas I will give to you in Italy. Banking, more export/import."

"I am already happy and pleased with everything you have given me, including some wonderful men like Leonardo, Martel..." Victor winked and let the sentence hang.

Even though the house had been checked for bugs, both men were old timers they were experienced enough to know even if an area seemed safe to still talk in code and in a round-about fashioned.

Vito smiled at the name of Martel. "He is one of the best; he turned out well my dear Vittorio." Vito sipped more coffee; "Your *Martello*, he will bring strength to the Family, make you proud."

"Yes, yes he will." Victor leaned back, glancing at the large picture window next to where the two men sat. It overlooked some high sand dunes and hills, once in awhile he would see one of the guards pass by but other than that, nothing moved out there except the ocean. "And again I thank you for his training as well as the men you have now offered to help the Jerome's settle this war with our old enemies."

Vito chuckled then, "D'Salvatore has bought one-way tickets to Palermo." He let the information sink into Victor for a moment. "Just for him and his wife, and I hear rumblings of him wanting to hook up with my old enemy the Graviano's."

"So he wants to flee does he?" Victor rejoiced in this news, "I will make sure he never makes that flight."

"The Bonnaro's will be at your side my friend, through all of it." Vito reached into the breast pocket of his suit coat and pulled out a small black velvet bag. "We solidify now, our alliance for all time, to you and to the next head of the Jerome family when it is his time." He untied the gold colored thread and poured out onto the table close to 600 thousand dollars worth of loose diamonds, they sparkled and glimmered with inner fire like a thousand light-filled rainbows.

"I am deeply honored, Vito." Victor silently and gently examined the exquisite diamonds then gently scooped them back into the bag. He then put the leather case on the table. "I now give to you as a gift to seal our alliance, something that has bought our Family a lot of profit in the past." He opened the case and inside was 6 sets of printing plates for $20, $50, and $100 bills. "Now since we are getting out of this particular aspect, I want them to have a home with you."

Vito was stunned for a moment. These were the famous Jerome printing plates he had heard vague rumors about, supposedly the best monetary printing plates ever devised, it was also rumored this was one of the main ways, in the early days of Victor's reign the Jerome's had made so much cash and assets, and now Victor was turning them over to him. Vito knew then his dear friend Victor truly was giving up more and more of the illegitimate aspects of the Family.

"Victor, I am…stunned." He said honestly looking into his friend and fellow Don's eyes. "A truly special gift indeed, thank you."

"You have provided so much to me Vito. And, you are providing even more in men for this war with my enemy. Were it not for your soldiers and assistance, I don't think the Jerome's would be successful in this vendetta against the D'Salvatores."

Vito just solemnly nodded at the compliment as each man secured his gifts of alliance from the other. "It's what brothers and family do for one another Victor. I know you would do no less for the Bonnaro's were the situations reversed. You, I respect. You are indeed like the Don's back in Sicily. Maybe you should consider moving back to your mother land, eh?" Vito gently teased. It did hurt him to know that La Cosa Nostra in the U.S.A was now down a path that would forever change it so radically from what it had started as back in Sicily and southern Italy. That his dear friend Vittorio was indeed one of the last of the great Don's in the States.

Gambini had parked far enough away and then walked on foot to the location he had chosen. The sand dunes provided a perfect shooters cover for a sniper like himself.

Stealthily, Louie had crawled the rest of the way, careful to avoid the angry fire-ant nests, until he was in position around 800 yards away from the small shack. Once there he hunkered down on his stomach and carefully put together his prized Russian Dragunov SVD, sniper rifle. After that he pulled out a fresh plug of chewing tobacco and placed it in his mouth, he always chewed on some when he was doing precise sniper gun work. It was like a meditative Zen thing with him; it calmed his body and allowed him to focus everything onto his work.

He knew he was quite a distance out, but thankfully he wouldn't have to use a silencer. The roar of the nearby ocean, as well as his distance from his targets would insure they wouldn't hear the sharp bark from the gun once he started, especially since the wind was gusting with a warm ferocity his way off the ocean.

All these factors were taken into account in the deadly hitman's mind with hardly any thought, after all, he was good at what he did and these things all came second nature to him now.

Gambini spit a brief wad of sticky tobacco juice around 5 feet to his left and then lay down on his stomach and became so still and immobile that after about 10 minutes a small sand spider and even a few fiddler crabs from a nearby sand dune began to crawl over him. He remained as still as a statue, one with the land and his gun as he focused intently down the scope.

Gio walked casually around the side of the house, his M-16 held comfortably but alertly in his hands. He watched as the ocean was still cresting towards its high tide mark, he figured maybe in another hour it would hit high water mark and then it would only be 5" from the steps of back door of the shack. He didn't mind though, it was a good location, they would be able to spot anyone coming from the ocean or from the long beach and he was sure he would have spotted anyone coming down the hills from in the distance.

He began thinking of his fiancée Clarissa back at home, she was so beautiful and she was so excited about the upcoming marriage in 4 months. He had been so happy when Patrizio had finally given him his blessing to marry his daughter, even if he did have to endure the older man's barbs. But he didn't care he had a lot of respect for Patrizio, just as he did for Martel. Both men were excellent mentors and had taught Gio so much of what it was to truly be a *Mafioso*. He felt the warm sun on his hard muscular body; this was a nice place down here. Maybe he and Clarissa would come here for their honeymoon…

"Hey Giovanni," Tony Armanno piped up interrupting the big man's thoughts. "I gotta go piss, eh?"

"Don't bother the bosses, just go off to the side there and go." Gio nodded his instructions. He moved closer to the corner of the front and side to cover Tony's post until he came back.

Louie controlled his breathing, remaining as still as the surrounding landscape. Down below in his sights the guards shifted around some at the house, talking to one another and then one moved off to go take a leak.

He re-sighted his first target through the scope, the muscle bound, bald one his mind marked the target. He flexed his finger and pulled the trigger. The first target fell instantly, never knowing what hit him, half his lower skull blown away.

Louie exhaled and smoothly re-sighted again; he aimed at the short thin fellow near the corner who was ready to walk up and find the dead bald guard. His finger flexed on the trigger again and the second target fell, the bullet entering right into his eye socket and exploding out the back of his skull.

With the slightest movement, he shifted the gun barely to the left and aimed at the guard taking a leak. The Dragunov recoiled slightly in Louie's tight grip as soldier number three dropped where he stood, still pissing; the bullet entering right through his heart.

A slight smile spread across Louie Gambini's face. Quietly he chewed at his tobacco plug, he was so close now. To be the one to kill Don Victor Jerome, it would be a worthy trophy indeed, his most famous hit yet. So many had tried but none had succeeded, and here he would be the one who finally got the hit on the powerful Crime Lord

So intent on his target now he didn't bother to spit the tobacco juice, he just swallowed it. He re-sighted again through the antireflective scope on his sniper rifle and aimed for the picture window where he saw the two dark forms of the great bosses talking. "Hell I may just take them both out." he thought, "Why not?" It would truly skyrocket his reputation through the roof and he hated leaving any witnesses who could come back and claim a vendetta on him. He truly did enjoy his work immensely.

A slight grin spread across his goateed face, either way, this would be his best piece of work yet. He carefully controlled his breathing, feeling every nerve alive in his body, feeling himself almost becoming one with his rifle. "And that fucking Martel thinks he's good..." Louie chuckled in his mind. "Not good enough to stop me from whacking his boss." Louie's finger flexed on the trigger as he prepared to take out Victor Jerome, so intent on his target that he didn't even notice the small fiddler crabs and sand spiders suddenly scurry off of him.

Inside the cottage, Victor had also pulled from the case, a bottle of expensive scotch to cement the bond of alliance and friendship between the two Families. He had gotten up grabbed a couple of glasses and then came and sat back down pouring him and Vito each a glass.

"To our alliances, to the tradition of *la cosa nostra*," Vito gave the traditional toast, raising his glass, "*Salute, mi compari* Vittorio."

"To our alliances and to the tradition of *our thing*," Victor echoed and raised his glass also "*Salute.*"

Suddenly there was the sound of exploding glass, like a rain of a thousand deadly glittering shards. The cup Victor had been holding exploded violently in his hand and a beam against the far wall seemed to burst from within as a high-powered bullet buried itself into it.

"Get down!" Vito sprang out of way surprisingly fast for an old man. Victor also instinctively moved quickly, both men now under the table and pressed down against the floor. Vito had drawn his Berretta pistol that he carried, "Are you hurt?" he whispered to his friend, looking concerned at Victor's hand.

"No, just cut from the glass." Victor glanced at his hand. Blood was flowing heavily and freely down his hand and arm, it was a fairly deep cut but not life threatening and it was better than the alternative, a bullet in his head. "I don't hear our men." Vito glanced at Victor a bit worried.

"They must have been hit." Victor listened intently for a moment. Almost at the same time, both men spotted the closet in the corner, away from any windows. "Let's go," they said nearly in unison.

"Are you carrying a weapon?" Vito whispered to Victor as they crawled down along the floor.

Victor just shook his head no, normally a man of his ranking had no need, it's why he had his bodyguards. "Well you got what you wanted old fool." he harshly chided himself, "Louie has made his move. But why isn't Martel here? You may have indeed bitten off more than you can chew old man, perhaps you should have bought more guards Perhaps you shouldn't have become so complacent and sure of yourself."

Vito slid a small 380 pistol across to him. "I figured you didn't, so I bought one along for you, eh?" He nodded briefly at Victor.

They crawled over to the closet opened it and dragged themselves inside. It was a tight fit even for two small old men. Both of them sat there pressed up against each other, "So now I hope us hens outfox the fox, eh?" Vito whispered. "This lone wolf triggerman, how did he take out all 3 of the guards?"

"I don't know." Victor began to get a bad sinking feeling. Had something delayed Martel, or worse, had this Gambini taken out his last living son? Was there more than just Gambini? Victor had never wanted to put Vito in danger, were his own plans now crumbling around him?

He fiddled around looking for one of his lifesavers; they must have fallen out of his
pocket while he was crawling into the closet. Victor could already feel the trembling in his muscles and nerves that was letting him know he had way too much insulin coursing through him. "*Vaffanculo.*" He mumbled softly. Would it even matter in a few minutes? Perhaps Gambini was walking down here right now to finish them off.

A small stifled chortle suddenly escaped Vito's lips, "*Merde*, Vittorio!" Vito cursed and chuckled softly, "I haven't been in gunfire like this since I was a young *cugine* back home!"

Victor couldn't see his friend and fellow Don in the closet next to him but he could feel him, feel Vito's confidence and trust in Victor. It boosted Victor's own confidence, acting like a soothing balm that allowed him to settle his mind and to center himself. "I know what you mean." He whispered quietly back.

And then instinctively both men fell deadly silent; both listening intently. Would Gambini torch the shack to drive them out? Would he come bursting in with a machine gun blazing?

A few minutes later they heard the front door open. "Mr. Jerome! Mr. Bonnaro!"

Victor felt sweet relief flood through him; it was the deep voice of his son and underboss Martel. "It's Martel!" Victor spoke.

"It's safe gentlemen." Martel said stalking inside looking for them, his own rising worry in his deep voice, as he saw all the blood stains on the floor. "Are you both Ok?"

The closet door opened and Vito and Victor emerged, "We're Ok." Vito said. "I think Victor got his hand injured though."

Almost immediately Martel was right there between the two men. He glanced with deep concern at his fathers bleeding and trembling hand.

"It's all right, Martel." Victor assured him, "It's just cut."

Martel saw his fathers roll of lifesavers on the floor and gently placed them in his father's hand as he began pulling some small hand towels out to wrap his fathers injured hand.

"It was Gambini all right," Martel spoke in Italian to both of them, "I'm afraid he was too far out ahead of me, the D'Salvatores must have bought him a temporary pass to the Country Club, he was able to rent a cart." He glanced darkly at his father a moment, wishing his father would have told him ahead of time where they would be.

His whole inner body was still shaking with anger at Gambini, his own slowness and the closeness at which he almost lost Victor and Vito. "Unfortunately they got all three of the outer guards."

"Shit." Victor's eyes blazed with anger and also sadness. "Vito, I'm so sorry."

"Easy my friend," Vito assured Victor, "we are in this together. We will mourn our soldiers. But the *Famiglias* live on; the Dons are safe, eh?" Vito then came over and hugged the giant Martel, "It is good to see you again, *Martello*, I have missed you *mio figlio!*"

Martel gently but warmly embraced the small form of Vito back, "And you as well Don Bonnaro, I'm just thankful you are safe and I am sorry about the loss of your men as well. Forgive my slowness." Martel's inner frustration shown through in the harshness of his icy eyes and the tenseness of his hard muscles.

"*Martello*," Don Bonnaro whispered sincerely to his ear, "It is not your fault. You are here now. We never lost confidence in you. I didn't. I know your father didn't."

"You took out Gambini?" Victor asked, his eyes still blazing in anger, it bothered him whenever he lost any of his Family members, but especially Gio Aprile. He knew Clarissa would now be without her future husband. He felt responsible for all his men and he had hoped no one would have been hurt on this gambit, except for Gambini. He had popped a few of the lifesavers in his mouth; so at least he didn't feel like he would pass out now at any moment.

A slow icy grin spread across the underbosses face, as he nodded his head and remembered. Remembered sneaking up on the prone figure of Gambini, already the man had taken out the 3 guards and was now aiming for the large picture window. Martel had no time to set up a formal shot; from nearly 200 yards away he had aimed his own gun on the fly, trusting his inner instinct and the deadly training from his masters.

The bullet from Martel's gun had entered the back of Gambini's head, killing him instantaneously but unfortunately causing the man to shoot his gun in reflex as he died. However, thankfully his aim was spoiled and he missed his intended target. Then, Gambini had simply dropped his head down on his arms as though sleeping, quite dead.

Martel had leapt down to the body but Louie was as dead as a doornail. He couldn't have shot him in a better location had he been concentrating. He pumped one more bullet into the now dead heart of his fallen enemy just for double-assurance of death and to sate his own anger and nerves and then had immediately run down the rest of the way to check on his father and Vito. "Yes, he is quite dead indeed." He assured both the men.

As the three men went out to check their fallen guards, Martel whispered to Victor's ear, "We need to get back ASAP. Joshua and I found out some useful information from that turncoat, Calendri. There will be a couple hit squads coming up into our territory any day now, only they really will be D'Salvatore hit-squads, men who won't be able to be turned."

"Understood Martel," Victor nodded. "We'll make arrangements to have Gio and Tony bought back to the states for their funerals and Luca sent back home to Sicily."

"I will do that." Martel spoke up. He was also taking their deaths personally, especially his right hand man, Gio Aprile. "It is my responsibility. You need to get back home to the Family. Please, *Padrino*."

"Very well," Victor sighed, "but hurry back to me my *Martello*, be safe."

Vito and Victor began heading off to the golf cart parked about 200 feet away. Vito carrying the leather case and Victor with the diamonds wrapped up and inside his pocket. Both men stopped a moment and glanced at the dour underboss easily carrying the bodies of the fallen bodyguards up away from the beach and into the shack.

"Go, please." Martel gently but firmly prodded his father; "I will meet up with you back home in 12 hours. This I promise you *padrone*."

Vito gently guided Victor to the golf cart and both of them rode back to the Country Club, Vito driving. "I am with you now, as well my brother." Vito looked at steadily at his friend. "Give me a day or two and I will meet you in New York City as well. I will have Arrigo see you safely off, tonight."

Victor nodded. "Thank you Vito." He turned around in the seat and glanced one last time back at the small shack that was now rapidly receding in the distance. He saw Martel striding back up the dunes, with a long knife/machete in his hand. The final closing play of the chess game would be rapidly coming now and he was determined to get the checkmate on Tito D'Salvatore.

After carrying the bodies of the three fallen guards inside, Martel had found a machete inside the shack and began to stride back up the dunes to deal with the body of Gambini. No funeral for this enemy of the Family.

He stripped whatever items he wanted off the dead body of Gambini, including the man's favorite Russian Dragunov sniper rifle and then with a hard swing of his arm, easily chopped off the head off his fallen enemy. He glanced around, finding what he was looking for, one of the huge Fire Ant mounds that was everywhere around here. He stirred up the nest a bit and then jammed the head right on top of the mound.

"You lost the final game, Louie. You were a worthy opponent, even my equal once. But no one and I mean no one, fucks with my father or my *Famiglia!*" the dark voice of the Shadow Dragon said. He spat on the decapitated head of his enemy watching it become engulfed in thousands of fire ants. By tonight he would have a nice clean trophy for his trophy room. He would come back later and collect his skull.

He quickly and efficiently buried the rest of Gambini's body deep within one of the sand dunes; the crabs and other ocean creatures in time would devour the rest of his body. He found Gambini's golf cart parked around a quarter mile over the last dune and then jumped in it and sped on towards the Country Club to take care of bribing the authorities and making sure the bodies of the fallen soldiers were on their way back home for burial. They would come back with him on the second VIJER private jet.

Alyssa had just gotten back about half an hour herself after Lena and Arrigo dropped her off at her elegant Sheridan Sands hotel. Finding no one else around like Gio or Tony, she just used the room key to let herself in and began to write in her journal. She was exhausted and tired from her day of sightseeing.

A half hour later the door opened and she saw Victor walk in, his hand wrapped in a towel and blood all over the arm and front of his suit. His eyes blazed with a fierce fire and determination in them and Alyssa knew instantly that something was very, very wrong.

She instantly leaped to her feet and ran over to see what had happened to her uncle, concern in her eyes. She wanted to tend to his injury, all tiredness suddenly gone from her. Where were Gio and Tony she wondered?

"Easy child, it's already been taken care of." He said firmly, holding her head gently in his hands. "Listen to me and listen to me carefully, Alyssa." He explained, his eyes seeming to convey a hundred emotions and orders at once into her. "We are going to have to leave early, as in right now. I don't have time to explain why or the details. There is much happening at home that I need to be there for."

Stunned, Alyssa simply nodded her understanding.

"Good girl." Victor released her face, giving her a quick hug and kiss on the forehead. "Go ahead and pack up, then help me pack up Gio and Tony's things."

She went and did as her uncle asked. She saw him use the other room key to go into the adjoining room that Gio and Tony had shared and he was in there for awhile, she even heard him talking on the phone in Italian to someone in there, but she had no idea who. Victor then stopped in the bathroom and carefully tended to his hand with a first aid kit, wrapping it carefully and then changing out of his bloodstained clothing into a fresh shirt and slacks.

Alyssa saw no sign of either Gio or Tony and indeed after hastily cramming her own stuff back into the suitcase she went to the other room to silently help her uncle. The guards had packed very lightly, only one small suitcase each. Victor threw their weapons in the case and then had Alyssa help him carry the suitcases downstairs to the waiting hotel limo. Alyssa herself personally carried her uncle's insulin supply and syringes in the metal lock box to transfer back to the airplanes refrigerator. This time she noticed that Arrigo was down there as well but no sign of the Bonnaro's or any other bodyguards.

Victor ushered her quickly into the car as Arrigo, Victor and the hotel doorman quickly loaded Victor, Alyssa's, Gio and Tony's stuff into the car. Victor spoke a bit in Italian to Arrigo, who now seemed totally alert and awake and not in the least bit dour.

She had tried a couple times to write to her Uncle to ask him what had happened to his hand or where Gio and Tony were or even to show him her new sign language book, but Victor seemed preoccupied, almost as wired up and anxious as Arrigo.

Finally she knew better than to press him to ask him anything. However she also knew whatever had happened, Victor was deeply shaken because she saw him chain eating the lifesavers he carried. She was quite certain whatever had him rattled had something to do with Family business and she knew better at that point to try and question or ask him anything else. She merely supported him and followed his every instruction from that point on, without any more questions.

"Thank you child," He finally spoke to her as they boarded his private plane.

Arrigo didn't follow with them but instead got back into the limo with the driver and departed.

"It means much to me your understanding and support." Victor continued and hugged her lightly. "Now, settle back and sleep child, we will be flying all night. Oh and…" Victor paused and looked deeply at her then, his eyes as emotionless and cold as black ice. He was deeply masking his feelings, being the total *Padrone* now. "I am afraid I have bad news I must tell you. Both Giovanni Aprile and Tony Armanno are dead we will be mourning them at home." And then her Uncle gave a deep sigh and simply said no more on that matter and abruptly turned away.

Numbly she did what her uncle requested, her soul in a total state of shock as she lay there on the small bed, her mind drifting off to the monotonous drone of the jet engines, Gio Aprile, dead?! What had happened? Her heart sunk, her mind remembered all the times she had been with the muscular man; he had been really a nice guy, a good friend to her. She felt a tear slip down her face and into the pillow, then another one. Poor Clarissa, she couldn't even imagine if someone told her so casually if Martel had died. Was Victor masking his emotions so hard because his own feelings were so hurt on this as well?

Alyssa swiped at a few of the tears as she let her heart and soul mourn for both Gio Aprile and Tony Armanno. Just what was going on in the Family? What had happened? Alyssa was certain that somewhere Lena Bonnaro was getting this same speech from her husband Vito. An almost slow dread and sorrow began to lay across her like a lead weight, it was though whatever was in the air now, was dangerous, hostile and somehow she knew it was far from over. Finally the sadness and tiredness overcame her and she fell into a fitful sleep, her dreams haunted by cruel, dark images.

Victor sat for the longest time staring out into the nothingness that was nighttime at 35,000 feet in the air as the private plane sped home. He mourned the loss of his two good men and what had happened but he also knew these things happened in this business. They were all in a war now and Gambini had to take his shot at Victor there in Jamaica and not at home in the states. His son had taken out Gambini and that was one less problem but now he knew that when he landed and returned the *mannagge* with the D'Salvatores would be on in full-gear.

"You missed me, Tito my old *nemico*," he thought to himself. "You want this old man? Then you come for me yourself you *stronzo bastardo!* However you and I Tito, we old men will finish this, we will finish what our fathers started."

With a sigh he popped a couple lifesavers in his mouth and then ambled over to the refrigerator to inject himself with his nightly insulin. With so much at stake now with the Family, the great 'Arbitrator' was going to have to call on all his reserve and cunning. He used a syringe

442

to draw out the insulin from the vial to the precise dose he needed and leaned up against the wall of the small plane. He pulled up his shirt and undershirt and then using an alcohol wipe swabbed the area of his stomach. With a well-practiced jab he drove the small needle into himself and injected the life saving insulin, once done he discarded the needle and tucked his shirts back in. His cut and bandaged hand throbbed in constant time with the droning jet engines.

Right now he felt so old in his bones and in his very soul. Pain often gnawed at him like a constant companion, he knew had Alyssa not donated a kidney to him, had the transplant not been successful he would have already been long dead. Now he still had so much to do in the short time he had left. He walked over to his medications and took his transplant anti-rejection drug and a couple of non-narcotic painkillers. He knew he was in for a very long next couple of days.

After finishing with his medicines and changing the bandage on his hand he ambled back to his seat, glancing once at the sleeping Alyssa. He saw that she had a book clutched to her as she slept and he glanced at the title, *International Sign Language Made Easy*. One of the old Don's hands gently pulled the blanket around her sleeping form as she shivered slightly and trembled in her dreams.

"Sleep well little one", he thought, "things are only going to get more hectic for you and for me; for all of us". Once again he suddenly felt some kind of strange connection between them, like he had that one day before his kidneys had failed and they had sensed each other outside the house. It was as though she was trying to once again tell him something from deep within her soul, like a silver thread was strung between them connecting them somehow.

"What are you trying to tell me, little one?" The old man softly whispered aloud. "This time I am trying to listen..."

She moaned deeply in her sleep and burrowed into the blanket he had placed on her but Victor could get no insight or answer. He gently touched her cheek and then returned to his own seat, where he sat and again brooded over the loss of his Family members. Victor never liked losing anyone in his Family, especially those who were so loyal. It had always been his secret weaknesses and one he kept well hidden, he cared for each and every one of his men and their families. Was it not the job of a true *padrone* and Don to care about even the lowest soldier or highest capo?

He forced himself to lay back and try to rest, he knew the next couple days were going to be long and fierce ones and he knew he would need all the rest he could get. He hoped his son, was also speeding on his way back to New York he would need him more than ever.

Joshua had Patrizio, Rocco, Cesare and Leonardo in the office at the Jerome Estates. He had immediately called the impromptu meeting together after he had gotten off the phone with Martel.

The consigliere glanced briefly at all his friends and capos, some were lighting up cigarettes, Cesare was chewing on a cannoli, Rocco anxiously cracking each of his knuckles and Leonardo sitting almost languidly on one of the overstuffed chairs, his blue-grey eyes like deadly lasers. "I heard from Martel. Victor is safe, Gambini missed." Joshua spoke the good news first.

"Taken out by Martel no doubt," Rocco smiled, "and hopefully, painfully."

"No doubt" Joshua stood and began to pace, chomping in agitation on his nicotine gum. "The important thing is Victor is safe and on his way home. Vito Bonnaro is safe and will be joining us also up here; he is in with us now fully."

An unspoken sigh of relief drifted around the room, only Leonardo seemed unsurprised at the news of the tight Bonnaro alliance. He simply nodded and continued watching Joshua like a hawk.

"The bad news is we have lost two good men. Giovanni Aprile and Tony Armanno were killed in action down there…" Joshua let the sentence hang a moment. While he did not know Tony well, he did have a lot of respect for Gio. All of the men knew of the upcoming marriage between Gio and Clarissa Fantenelli.

"What?" Patrizio suddenly looked up, "What was that?" the hand holding his cigarette began to tremble slightly and the old man's face looked as though it was he who had been shot.

"I'm sorry, Patrizio." Joshua came over to him, placed a hand on Patrizio's shoulder, "we all are." He could feel the silent grief and rage building inside the old man. He knew Patrizio would not vent it here, he was far too old-school for such displays.

"The D'Salvatores will pay for that too Patrizio, I personally promise you." Leonardo Tagretta spoke in his quiet voice. Only this time it was filled with such rage and restrained hatred that nearly all the men abruptly glanced at him. "Their deaths only fuel our vendetta against our enemies the D'Salvatores. *Buon' anima.*" Leonardo crossed himself. "*Riposa in pace*, Giovanni and Tony."

"*Buon' anima.*" The others grumbled softly, an old Sicilian form of "Rest his soul".

"Now," Joshua continued pacing, stopping briefly by Leonardo and glancing at him. Over the last few months Joshua and Leonardo had become fairly close friends and Joshua knew both Victor and Martel wanted to see Leonardo be given more responsibilities within the Family. "The boss will be here in the morning, he is in flying now as we speak, back from the islands. Martel is in route also but he is taking a later flight."

"I will pick up Martel." Leonardo quietly offered.

"Excellent, thank you Len." Joshua next moved on towards Caesar and Rocco, "We three will be picking up Victor, but all of us need to pack heavy and carry a lot of guards with us. We need to be alert because there will be some assassination squads courtesy of our *nemico's* running around out there with hard-on's for us."

"Great, wonderful." Patrizio glared and lit up another unfiltered Pall Mall. He was in his chain-smoking routine now, as he always did when stressed or troubled.

Joshua poured himself a fresh cup of coffee as he continued his briefing, "The D'Salvatores will be expecting us probably around the VIJER Corporation. I wouldn't be surprised if they have that covered closely. I've already called Danny Valsiglio and warned him but it means it's not safe to take the boss there. I would rather take the boss to your place Rocco, The Blue Parrot. Perhaps the D'Salvatores will not be expecting us to have a quickie meeting there, eh?"

"Sounds good to me my friend, I will have my men 'sweep and clean' the place well." He used the term that meant having a place checked out for bugs or any other spying devices.

"Pops," Joshua next stopped by Patrizio and gave the old man's shoulder a strong squeeze, "You are the most experienced man here. We need you," The consigliere paused, "I need you, to run the downtown area and groups. You're our wartime consigliere."

"Of course." Karloff's hardened face just nodded. "Gimme a few hours to get my older daughter up here to make arrangements for Gio and to stay with Clarissa, but I will set up at my main headquarters downtown and do what needs to be done."

Joshua just nodded in gratitude and moved back to go sit down at the desk. He could feel this thing in the air now, just as Leonardo had once told him and Joshua wanted this war finished and done with as quickly as possible with no more casualties for the Jerome's.

Cesare had stood up and begun pouring wine for all of them. "We will win this thing Josh." His eyes were as hard and cold as everyone else's. He began to hand out the glasses of wine to his fellow compari's, "If I have to go into D'Salvatore territory personally and bust his chops."

Joshua grabbed hold of Cesare's arm as the big man served up the drinks. "Your fire and strength encourage us all Cesare. I truly hope so as well, I trust in my bosses and I trust in all of you." He raised his glass in a toast. "To Gio and Tony; *buon' amina.* And to the longevity and strength of the Jerome Family, *Salute!*" he drank deeply.

"*Salute!*" the other men said nearly in unison and drank their wine as well. It would be a long night for them, each of them had work to do, things to organize within their crews and within their territories. Patrizio would have to break the awful news to his youngest daughter Clarissa, on the loss of her fiancé.

The small private plane bearing Victor and Alyssa finally touched down around 8:30 am. As they deplaned Victor spotted Cesare, Joshua and Rocco along with 3 other guards and another car of guards waiting for him. He was not surprised by the strong show of bodyguards, the war was revving up to its final conclusions now.

Joshua came over and embraced Victor tightly, whispering in Italian in his *padrone's* ear. "Everything is set up, but we will be taking you to the Blue Parrot and brief you there. It's not safe right now to go to the VIJER Corporation."

"I know." Victor hugged him back, "Thank you for handling everything Joshua. We need to get Alyssa out of here and back to the Estate immediately, eh?"

"Understood," He nodded, "but right now, you, are most important. We will take you to the Blue Parrot and then we will have the other car and two guards take Alyssa back to the Estate."

"Very well." Victor agreed. Already the luggage had been transferred over to the Jerome-2 limousine. He gave Rocco and Cesare a brief embrace as well and then all the men protectively surrounded their boss and Alyssa and ferried them into the awaiting car.

"Hey 'Lyss," Cesare gave her a quick hard embrace and slipped a Hershey's chocolate bar into her hand. "Welcome back, we missed you." He was the only one who even spoke to her as he helped her into the back next to Victor. "I'm so sorry about Gio," he quickly whispered into her ear, "I know he was a good friend to you." He gently patted her cheek a moment.

Alyssa clambered into the back and slipped the candy bar into her purse and clutched tightly onto her sign language book, she could tell the tension was astronomically high right now among all the men, so she simply quietly attempted to blend into the background as much as possible.

Still talking in Italian, Victor slid in the back with Alyssa, Joshua and Rocco and two guards while Cesare got in behind the wheel. The other guards piled into the second car and began following the large bulletproof limo as it began its journey on towards the Blue Parrot nightclub. "Martel will be here shortly as well. Take him directly to the Estate when he comes in, after my meeting at the Blue Parrot that is where I want to go too. The Bonnaro's are sending us a lot of muscle and soldiers to help in our war."

"I know, I know." Joshua said soothingly, he had heard all this from Victor last afternoon on the phone when Victor had called him from the Island. "I remember your instructions from last night, *padrone*." He smiled gently at his adopted father and boss.

"Forgive me Joshua; it has been a long night." Victor settled in, staring out the window at the passing buildings of the city as they sped downtown.

Joshua could tell his boss was stressed. Usually the famous 'Arbitrator' was as cool as a cucumber but something must have happened in the islands to rattle him. Joshua also noticed the bandaged hand of Victor; he would ask him later about it, not now.

He glanced over at Alyssa, she sat there with a look of concern and caring on her face, her eyes locked onto Victor as protectively as any of the guards. Briefly Joshua and Alyssa's eyes met; there was no hatred in either of their eyes this time. Alyssa looked wearily and with relief at the consigliere, almost as if she was happy to be back in his company as much as everyone else's. He could see deep sadness within her also; he knew she had befriended Gio Aprile as well. But for some reason her eyes held no more animosity towards him, just a tired resignation. He just nodded his head softly a moment, letting her know he recognized her feelings of mourning and then looked back out the window himself. Yes, he could tell a something had happened in her down there with Victor.

Occasionally Victor would speak here and there to Joshua or Rocco, briefing them on some small tidbits but he mainly kept his conversation censored, after all Alyssa was in the car with them and even if she couldn't understand fluent Italian it was considered taboo to talk 'business' in front of non-made members or associates.

The two cars pulled up in front of the Blue Parrot and Cesare, Rocco and the other men got out of the cars, ready to escort Victor into the nightclub and discuss business.

Victor just glanced at Alyssa and then said to Joshua in English, "You have Sal over there, take her back home, understand?" He then turned to Alyssa and leveled his gaze at her, "Alyssa, you will be going with Sal in that other car to the VIJER Corporation and then flying back home to the estates. You will be safe there."

Then everyone began to move at once and the men began walking up the sidewalk to the Blue Parrot as Alyssa was getting ready to get into the other car with the old capo Sal and one of the guards.

It was then Alyssa suddenly felt such an overriding fear and panic in her like she had never felt before. Not like the terrors from her amnesia, no this was vastly different. It was an all-engulfing fear for her Uncle, similar to what she had felt on the island yesterday when Victor had been with Vito, a vague permeating stench of utter terror that gripped her insides and twisted with a cruel hold. Dropping her book on the seat of the limo she suddenly bolted out of the car and up the sidewalk to him, she had no idea why, only that at that moment she had an overwhelming urge to at least give Victor a hug goodbye.

"Hey, come back!" Sal roared as she leaped past his grasp and raced towards her uncle.

Victor spun on heel, "Alyssa, what is it?" there was a distinct look of annoyance in his eyes, "You need to go back NOW!" he ordered firmly, angrily. "Go with Sal! Go home and wait for me there, I have no time for this!"

She could feel the hard and dark looks from Joshua, Rocco and even Cesare as well. This was Family business now, the middle of a blood war and she had no business being there, holding things up. Still every hair on the back of her neck was raised, as icy tendrils of fear gripped her heart and soul so strongly she nearly thought she would pass out. Time itself seemed to close in with a sluggish feeling around all of them, she saw her vision tunneling and she vividly remembered that day when Victor had been bought into the clinic with his failed kidneys. She hugged her Uncle tightly then and it was then he as well, seemed to pick up the same warning bells and unease as her. 'Oh child, why didn't you stay back in the car?' Victor's heart felt almost as hollow as that day Michael had been shot, a cruel premonition that surged through him like high voltage electricity.

Suddenly from nearby buildings men began to run out, there were staccato pops of gunfire, as chaos erupted around them all. Alyssa just instinctively gripped her Uncle harder and the both of them ended up somehow on the ground. She felt a sharp stab in the middle of her back and thought one of the men had knocked her and Victor down to get them of harms way.

A million thoughts seemed to go through the old man's eyes at once. He could have easily rolled her off but he lay there playing dead, remaining quiet and unmoving beneath Alyssa. After all he wasn't carrying a weapon himself; there was nothing he could do against this assassination squad. He hoped and prayed that if he and Alyssa didn't move, the assassins would think they had gotten their targets and leave.

Both of them heard the answering gunshots from their own men, curses in Italian, shouts and the stench of fear, death and bloodlust in the air. It was over as quickly as it started the squealing of tires in the distance as the surviving D'Salvatore hit squad leaped in cars and sped off from the scene of the ambush.

Time seemed to speed up again and Alyssa felt Victor roll her off of him as he got back up to his feet. She could hear Victor's angered voice barking in Italian and the angry voices of some of the other men.

'Get up girl!' Alyssa told herself, as she lay there on her stomach on the cold hard cement but it dawned on her then that she wasn't feeling to good. In fact, she couldn't even seem to feel anything from her mid back and below. Confused, she turned her head to her right and saw Rocco looming near her, his 357 Magnum in his hand. He was angrily talking to Joshua and there was a jagged cut on his head that was steadily dripping blood freely down his expensive sport coat. Joshua too was splattered with blood but Alyssa had no idea who's. "Oh damn, they've been hit!" she thought with a terrified fear. "What about my Uncle? What about Victor?"

She felt so numb and tired, with extreme effort she turned her head to the left and that is when she came face to face with Cesare "the Elf" Ciccerone. He was laying face down and unmoving on the cement next to her, only a few inches away from her face but half his face was blown away. His blood, brains and bone fragments were pooled around him and Alyssa as well. The one eye of his that remained stared lifelessly at her.

Alyssa felt the bile of terror rise in her throat and such a feeling of sorrow then that it tore her in half, "Oh God no!!! Not Cesare! Not the good-natured Cesare!" she felt hot tears streaming down her face, her anguish deep, "Oh shit! Cesare, get up please! Don't be dead!" she knew how dedicated he was to his Family and to his wife and children, he was the very first who had befriended her, been kind to her and now he lay there so violated and so brutally murdered. "Oh God!" her mind whimpered. She wrenched her head back to the right and began to feel a horrible, throbbing pain in her back, a descending cloud of pain and darkness threatening to close in around her like a cruel fist. She heard the talk switch back to English again but it sounded so far away, like it was in a tunnel.

"They got Cesare, Oh fuck!" Rocco's voice.

"Are you Ok?" Joshua's voice to someone, "…Boss what about you?"

"Yes! Yes! I'm fine Goddamn it!" Victor's angry voice, "Who else?"

A Mixture of various bodyguards' voices, "Sal's hit bad!" others confirming they were unharmed or un-hit.

"Alyssa!" Victor's voice again. His voice was intense and hard but not at her, "Oh dear child…" He kneeled down between his fallen capo and his niece and gently stroked her blood-splattered face. "Call an ambulance Rocco, get one now damn it! And call Weintraub!"

Alyssa could hear the rage in Victor's voice towards those who had attacked him and his crew. The tunnel zoomed deeper and it was the last words Alyssa remembered as darkness slipped over her, at least the pain was leaving her now. She was just so tired, felt so heavy. Why couldn't she move? Was someone lying on her back?

Tito D'Salvatore eyed his consigliere and his own war council. His world was falling apart, slowly but surely he began to realize now with a terrifying feeling of dread that the *mannagge* was not going his way. His underboss had gone missing and was feared dead, the hired gun, Gambini had missed his target in Jamaica and now his hit squad had missed again in taking out Victor Jerome or his consigliere at the Blue Parrot. "*Diavolo*, Vittorio!" Tito shouted. "He is the fucking devil himself, that Jerome *cazzone*! *Vaffanculo, diavolo!*" he downed a shot of scotch and poured himself another. He glared at consigliere Johnny

Baldovino and four of his trusted capos. "I thought you said you had him! You fuckin' promised we would have him!"

Baldovino lit up a cigarette, "I thought so too but he is slippery like a fucking eel!"

"So all we got out of our efforts were one of his capos, a couple of his bodyguards and some *mezza-morte* female? Not even anyone from his Top Administration?" Tito looked incredulous.

"Well I think the female was his niece?" Baldovino offered weakly.

"Fuck that!!!" Tito threw the empty shot glass near Johnny's feet where it shattered violently in a hundred shards. "It is not Victor! It was no one important! Don't you understand you stupid jamook!" Tito spun on him, "All it does is infuriate him more and fuels his vendetta further!"

"They are holed up good now, eh?" Said Sergio, he was one of the new capos who was really an undercover soldier of the Bonnaro's. But for now, Tito thought him a loyal capo from his association with his friends in Miami. "Maybe you need to step back yourself, let our squads go forth now and do their work. We can at least take out as many Jerome people as possible…" he was a dark dangerous man with a thick Sicilian accent and dark shifty eyes.

Johnny Baldovino didn't trust the man one iota but still spoke. "Maybe Sergio is right. Maybe it would be safest for you if you took Concetta and went down to Miami for a while, just in case…" he left the sentence hanging. He didn't dare say the unspoken words that the missing underboss Joey Calendri had tried to convey to him so many weeks ago, before he was killed. 'Before we lose this war, Tito, before we are all taken down by the Jerome's.'

Tito D'Salvatore had no intention of going to Miami; he had planned long ago to go somewhere even more distant. Back to Sicily, where he still had clan connections with the Graviano's, he knew even in Miami he wouldn't be truly safe. "Yeah sure," He said half-hearted, "I will consider it and let you all know."

He faced Baldovino, "See that the hit squads with the new muscle and soldiers from Sicily go out. They will be more successful, obviously our own men are fuckin' lousy shots." He thrust the cruel insult into his consigliere.

"Of course, Tito" Johnny walked away to make some calls, his own shoulders drooping. The other war council began to split up as well; going to make their remaining plans to send out the last ditch hit squads.

"Sergio, walk with me." D'Salvatore signaled to the capo. The small man fell into step with the grim faced Tito. "Sergio," he began once out of earshot of his own men, "Did you get me those first class tickets to Palermo? My wife and I will be leaving within in a few days."

"*Certamente*, Don D'Salvatore." Sergio nodded, "The arrangements have been made. You will be safe there, that is a good choice."

"Oh and Sergio," Tito stopped him a moment. "Say nothing to anyone, not even my own men. Let them think I am going to Miami if that is what they want to think."

A small dark smile played along the Sicilians face then. "Of course Don D'Salvatore. You know I will say nothing, your secret is safe with me, eh?" he lightly touched his boss's arm in affirmation and then strode off to make his own coded calls and secret arrangements.

Tito walked wearily to his wife's sewing room, where she sat sewing on a quilt. She looked so gaunt and hollow; the murder of Torenzo had sucked the life out of her. "Concetta, *cara mia*." he came in and sat next to her. "Would you like to get out of here now, to leave all this sorrow behind us?"

She looked up to her husband of nearly 35 years. "Oh yes, *marito mio*." Her tired old hands sought out his. "So much pain here, eh? Far too much pain now that our beloved Torenzo is gone. I have wanted to leave for a while now, please let us go."

"We will *mia cara*." He slid over and embraced his wife, kissed her gently on the forehead. "Definitely too much pain here. I will take you someplace nice, back to Sicily, our homeland. Would you like that?"

Her eyes which were clouded in illness and grief finally showed a hint of spark and life that Tito had not seen in her in years. "Oh yes, Tito. I would like that."

"Then I will make it so, my beloved." He stroked her cheek gently and wearily got to his feet.

"Let the fucking Jerome's have this city," he thought bitterly, "it isn't worth it anymore." So much this war had cost him and yet he had done so little to the powerful Jerome's. A smart man knew when to cut his losses and get out with his life. Besides, he figured he could hurt them more from the homeland of Sicily and like Victor he too felt the change in the air ever since RICO and the other anti-Organized Crime laws. The Golden Age of the true *Mafioso* was coming to an end in the United States. Too many new stakes and laws and ethics were out there now. No one had honor anymore, no one followed the old codes. Maybe that old dinosaur, Victor, his enemy of all these years was indeed smarter than he had given him credit for.

Thirteen hours after the ambush at the Blue Parrot, Victor and company sat in his downtown office at the VIJER Corporation. Surprisingly it had been being watched by a one of the undercover Bonnaro hit squads and not a D'Salvatore hit squad "You are either sharper than I thought my *nemico*," Victor thought bitterly, "Or damn lucky."

His beloved son and underboss, Martel was back here with him now. Also here in his war room was Joshua, Patrizio, Rocco and the other wartime capos; along with Vito Bonnaro, the Jerome's new arm in the alliance. With Martel and Vito here now, Victor knew things would go smoothly, or at least he desperately hoped.

Victor carefully listened to all the men talking to one another, their plans, their set ups, the reports coming in from their areas. "Whatever goes down, I only ask one thing." He suddenly interrupted the conversations his dark eyes boring into each of them and then looking at his friend Vito. "Tito D'Salvatore is mine. I want him and I want him alive if it is possible. He is my personal vendetta."

Vito nodded and threw Victor a compassionate glance. "He is yours my friend."

"Trust me Victor," Martel stopped by his father and refilled his glass of orange juice, "The D'Salvatore's are as closely watched as they are watching us. He can't take a shit without us or the Bonnaro's knowing about it."

"It is coming to a close for him now," Victor sipped his orange juice. "I feel it, he is a caged animal. I feel the tiredness and desperation of my old enemy."

Joshua felt the hair rise on the back of neck; it always spooked him when the boss spoke like that. Victor's uncanny insights and predictions were one of the things that made him the powerful boss that he was. Talk erupted around the table again, multiple conversations going on at once.

"How is your niece?" Vito gently touched Victor's arm, his eyes searching his friend.

Martel immediately straightened up at hearing Alyssa's name, his ears picking up the conversation between Victor and Vito. He had heard Alyssa had been shot in the ambush outside the Blue Parrot and taken to the hospital for emergency surgery but there had been no news since then, too much was going on all over the Family and they were in the middle of a war. He had just gotten in 10 hours ago himself and as underboss his duty was here now with his father, the Family always came first, no matter how much his heart worried for Kanashii.

"It was a deep wound to her back, thankfully it is not life threatening. It will be a slow recovery but Dr. Weintraub is certain she will walk again. It is only more fuel to fire my vengeance. She is strong, she will fully recover." This part Victor had said while looking discreetly at Martel. He could feel his son release the breath he had been holding.

"I am glad to hear." Vito nodded. "She is indeed a strong woman."

"She saved my life." Victor nodded wearily, he was bone tired and had not Alyssa ran up and hugged him when she did, the bullet that hit her would have hit him square in his heart. "That is twice I owe her." He barely whispered.

Only Joshua Demonico caught the faint declaration from his *padrone* and then once again the conversation drifted to more plans and other business.

Victor knew the next couple days were going to be long and stressful for all of them, with very little sleep for any of them.

Chapter 35- *October 17th 1987*

Alyssa began to wake up slowly, she felt someone petting and soothing her face and her head. "Where am I?" She wondered. Her eyes fought to open, to make sense of her surroundings. "Did I nod off in Martel's room? Was he finishing up a massage with me or am I in the peach-frilly room at the Jerome Estates, staying with Victor? Aren't we supposed to go on vacation soon?"

Random thoughts drifted in and out of her head, and then the pain began to bite at her back. She fought harder to regain her senses and her memory...

They had been on vacation; then they had to leave. Gio Aprile dead, then her Uncle injured, the shootout at the club as she ran to hug him, the fear and warning bells she had gotten moments before the attack...

She fought through the layers of sludge in her mind, like a drowning person struggling to swim to the surface of the water to breathe... "Oh God, Cesare! Rocco! Who else? Who else had been hit!!! Had her Uncle Victor been hit?"

She continued to feel the hand soothing her, almost gently trying to calm her, that voice that was talking to her, it was so familiar.

"Easy now, little one," The rough Brooklyn accent tried to gently soothe her, "You're Ok. Shhh, come on, easy now."

The hand was too smooth and young to be Victor's it was too small to be Martel's, it didn't feel or sound like Tommy DeLuca...Who the hell was touching her? With a rising panic she finally struggled to the surface, her eyes snapping open. She saw Joshua Demonico standing next to the bed, his hand resting on her brow.

"Easy, wake easy," he soothed softly again. His dark handsome features were showing concern and caring... "You're safe now. You're Ok, I'm here."

Joshua Demonico, showing kindness to her? Her mind tried to make sense of this. She was confused at first and then downright shocked, "*Joshua Demonico being nice to me?*"

She eyed him warily and he slowly withdrew his hand from her, seeing she was awake and coherent now. "You were hit, but Doc Weintraub says you will be Ok. Right now you are downtown in the hospital here, but I will arrange for you to leave today or tomorrow to go back to the estates where you can heal." He pulled a chair over and sat in it, straddling it backwards. "You just got out of surgery about five hours ago," Joshua continued. "It's been around 14 hours since you were shot."

Alyssa could tell he was not the type who was used to being a nursemaid and she could see his own nervousness at being around her, probably a part of him wanting to get back to the front lines of the Jerome-D'Salvatore war with the rest of his men.

Had Victor ordered him here to talk to her? Where was Martel? She wondered with a slow panic. "Oh please dear God, please, don't let Joshua be here to tell me that Martel is dead too! I could not handle that!" In desperation she reached for the kanji that should be around her neck, the one her teacher had given her, it was gone…

"Here, easy, I got it." Joshua saw the fear and pain creep into her eyes as her hand feebly felt at her throat. "I had to hold these things when you went in for surgery." He stood up and reached into his pocket pulling out the silver Kanji on the silken black cord. "He's fine Alyssa." Joshua said as though reading her mind. He reached over and began to gently put the necklace back on her. "Martel got back like12 hours ago, he stopped by to see you once, but you were in surgery then. The Boss, er, yer Uncle," he corrected himself, "He's fine too. He didn't even get hit…" He drifted off then, still sensing her confusion at his being here and feeling a bit awkward himself.

The pain was biting cruelly at her back and she realized she had one of those machines like she had last time, one that automatically injected morphine into her IV when she would push the button. She fumbled for the button and pushed it. She knew it would take a few minutes for it to take effect and so for now she had to endure the red hot fire of the pain that wanted to pound along every nerve in her back and legs.

"I'm sure this is a little awkward for both of us." Joshua stood up and reached into his pocket to pull out a nicotine gum square. "Look, when you first came here, I figured, it's just a woman, ya know? No big deal, but then…"

He paused and then rubbed his hand over his brow and down through his dark hair. This was not how he wanted this to come out. With a deep audible sigh, he sat back down backwards in the chair folding his arms across the back and then laid his chin on his arms, his dark piercing eyes watching her for a few moments. "Look, we've had our differences…" he finally began then, "We exactly have not been the best of friends, ya know?" the consigliere regarded her deeply for a moment longer as if debating with his own inner demons on telling her this intimate and personal part of his life.

But then he did; Joshua Demonico spoke freely and discreetly and honestly about how he had grown up on the streets, about Nico DeBasio and how Don Victor Jerome had literally adopted him as a son. He of course left out and censored any talk about illegal activities or 'Family business' but he told his story with his inner feelings and emotions, conveying to her his deep love and respect for Victor Jerome and the rest of the men.

"I love Victor Jerome more than my own mother, who basically left me on the streets." He finished his tale after about five minutes, "There is nothing I would not do for that man or this Family. And then here you come into his life and you end up giving him something I have never been able to give him; getting to save his life twice. First by donating a kidney to him and second by taking a bullet meant for him."

Joshua stood up and paced now as he frequently did, a graceful Panther with pent up energy, "When you first came here I had no trust for you, then there was a time I was even jealous of you, the way you had won over the trust of Martel, Cesare, Gio the rest of the Family..."

Alyssa watched him pacing like a great caged cat. Finally she was beginning to get insight into this passionate man, his emotions as liquid and volatile as molten lava, for good or bad.

"...Then to know that Victor had accepted you, adopted you as well. I changed my way of thinking, I mean. I got over my jealousy and was just thankful you were there to save Victor's life." He eyed her a moment, "Look, nobody made me come here I personally wanted to come see you. You know, to make my peace with you, understand?" his voice was sincere but gentle.

He walked back over to her and once again his elegantly manicured hand hesitantly came down and rested soothingly on her shoulder. "I know in my heart that for whatever reason, your being here has been important. It's helped Victor and if nothing else even seemed to bring luck to our Family. Victor and Martel and the others have accepted you and I do too. I felt kinda bad knowing I had judged you, the same way the men had first judged me, when they met me. They didn't know me or anything about me but Victor and Martel believed in me. So I will take a lesson from my mentors and believe in you too. You are my sister now Alyssa; I will revere and protect you as one would a younger sister."

She used the button on her bed to raise herself slightly as she wearily motioned for her writing tablet and a pen.

Joshua dug around in one of the desk drawers for some paper and then pulled out a pen from his own suit pocket. He handed the objects to her.

"*Fair enough Joshua, I will treat you the same, with respect and loyalty.*' She wrote, "*Thanks for sharing your story I am touched at your trusting me. How bad was I hit? Who else? When will I be able to see Martel or Victor? How's Rocco, I saw him hit too*..." she weakly handed the pad to Joshua.

"The bullet hit your mid-back but thankfully didn't go into the spinal cord. It just caused swelling in the area." The consigliere answered her questions, "Doc Weintraub said the paralysis you have is temporary, just from the swelling in your back, you should be able to get around and heal up fine in no time." Joshua assured her, "As to Martel, he is out an' about," he eluded shrugging his shoulders, "I dunno when he will be able to drop by; he's kinda busy, same with yer Uncle Victor."

Joshua averted his eyes for a moment gently laying the pad of paper back next to her, "Rocco is fine, it was just a grazing injury and he just needed a few stitches. We lost Cesare of course and Sal too, he died in surgery." he turned away.

'*I knew about Cesare*.' She scratched out on the pad, remembering that awful vision of her friend's head blown apart right next to her. '*I didn't know about Sal.*' She felt the tears hot and fresh on her cheeks from remembering the loss of Cesare, Gio, Tony and now Sal.

"Look," Joshua felt uncomfortable around a woman displaying emotions; it wasn't something he had any experience with. He had always just known a hard and cruel life.
He stroked her face again, softly, using some tissue to dab at her tears. But he did know right now her heart was hurting and in some odd way it was almost as if she was able to grieve on behalf of the men who had to remain stoic.

"I'll work on getting you moved by tonight back to the main house, Ok? I bet you'll feel more comfortable there. Lena Bonnaro is there and Rosette and all the other people as well, you will recover better in surroundings with people you trust and who care about, ya know?" he nodded.

"You remember Tommy, right?" Joshua tried to cheer her up some. "Well he's right outside, keeping watch on ya to keep ya safe. Along with that Bonnaro bodyguard you had, Arrigo Salvaggio. Mrs. Bonnaro told me you might like Arrigo here too…" Joshua paused then, realizing he was just rambling, that she was fighting consciousness as she was tired and hurting, besides he had things to do and a war to get back to, "We'll bring ya home. I promise ya 'Lyss." He unconsciously called her by the nickname Cesare used to.

She nodded tiredly and lay her head back heavily as the morphine began to affect her, it silenced the pain in her back and allowed her to once again begin drifting off into safe, mind-numbing sleep.

Her and the Panther no longer at war with one another, she mused as drugged sleep came upon her swiftly and comfortingly. While she knew she would never be as close to Joshua as she was to Cesare or Gio, the two of them had made their respected peace now as well.

This time the darkness that descended on her was warm and comforting, like an old friend. She was safe and right now she needed the darkness and sleep, needed to mentally escape the cruelty and all the death she had seen so vividly in the last couple of days. Vaguely at one point in time she was dimly aware of Tommy, Arrigo and Joshua wheeling her and a gurney onto a helicopter, while Dr. Weintraub groused, ranted and complained about his patient leaving too early, but then giving Tommy a bag of medications and their instructions for her.

"I will be over to see her soon!" Weintraub ordered. "You better keep her still, relaxed and healing! You understand me?" he threatened. "Or you will all deal with me!"

"We will doc, we will." Joshua assured him and slid the door shut on the helicopter as it sped off towards the Jerome Estates where Alyssa could be with her true family.

Chapter 36- *October 20th 1987*

Snow flurries were beginning to gracefully fall as the Sicilian bodyguards began to pack Tito and Concetta's luggage into his personal car. Tito's car was not as large and impressive as his enemy's Victor Jerome; however it was an elegant Lincoln Continental none-the-less. There were two other cars in the procession, another Lincoln in front of his that held 4 guards and a Cadillac in back that held another 3 bodyguards, and inside the middle car, riding with him would be two more.

Hindsight is a wonderful thing. And in hindsight, Tito D'Salvatore would have listened more to his own men, instead of giving so much trust and power to these new soldiers from Sicily but his own lack of planning, his grief at losing his only son and his own greed for power and impatience made him lose focus of his own foresight and planning.

Johnny Baldovino stood there with one other long time D'Salvatore capo Frankie Scalia and more of these damn Sicilian soldiers, that Tito had got from who knows where. The young Sicilian soldiers nodded silently to each other then turned and walked inside, leaving just Johnny and Frankie standing outside alone.

Every fiber of Johnny's soul told him that he was watching the Family and his life collapse before his very eyes, but what could he do? His boss seemed to be as crazy as a loon at this point. What was it Joey Calendri had once called him? Captain Ahab that was it, Tito was as obsessed and fanatical as the mythical Captain Ahab from Moby Dick and Johnny Baldovino didn't really want to see what fate would befall Tito; somehow, like ol' Capt. Ahab he didn't think it would be good.

"You gave away everything Tito," Johnny thought to himself sadly, "simply handed the Family away on a platter and for what?" Johnny watched as the procession of Tito, his wife and most of the young Sicilian bodyguards pulled away down the long driveway, towards the airport. He nudged his longtime friend and capo, "Come on let's go in and close up shop, I'll buy ya a beer, Frankie."

"Sounds good John," Frankie pulled his own trench-coat tighter around him and they both walked inside.

As they headed for the kitchen, it began to dawn on Johnny that it was awful quiet in here. Usually there was some guard or soldiers' wife in the kitchen making a snack or some men playing cards but now it was disturbingly empty only the large, elegant grandfather clock chimed ominously. He began to feel the hair on the back of his neck prickle a warning.

"Hey Frankie?" he asked quietly and abruptly stopped, wanting to simply back out of the house and run.

"What?" Frankie looked at him.

"It's awful quiet in here, huh?" Johnny felt his mouth go bone dry, his guts feel watery.

The chiming of the grandfather clock stopped then and suddenly four of the Sicilian soldiers burst through the kitchen with guns blazing. They were the undercover Bonnaro men.

Johnny felt the agonizing pain of hot lead as bullets tore into his flesh felt his very life force being shot out of him. "You so fucked up, Tito..." was Johnny's only last coherent thought as he was taken out along with Frankie and any other loyal D'Salvatore men.

Tito D'Salvatore sat in the back of the Lincoln holding onto his wife's hand as the cars sped onwards towards the airport. In his pocket he had the two first class tickets to Palermo Sicily that Sergio had picked up for him as ordered. He liked Sergio and the other Sicilian soldiers and thought, "Now these men, they know how to act in a Family. They know loyalty and omerta."

He glanced over at his wife and noticed she was finally beginning to look at peace after a long time. It warmed his heart to see his beloved happy about something again. He squeezed her hand and smiled briefly at her, "Fuck Victor and the Jerome's" he mused, "This 'thing of ours', is dead here now in the states. It is better to get out alive than go down with a sinking ship."

He suddenly noticed that the procession of cars sped right past the exit they should have taken to go to LaGuardia Airport. He glanced up uncertainly at Sergio who was sitting across from him in the front seat a gun suddenly in his hand and pointed discreetly at Tito; a dark, deadly look in the guard's eyes. Tito heard the locks ominously click shut on the Lincoln Continental as the driver locked them all in.

"Sergio?" Tito numbly asked, but he already knew the answer, knew it then with a frightening and deadly certainty in his very heart and soul. "You missed the airport exit."

The man just nodded solemnly, his eyes as cold and emotionless as a shark. "Just sit back and enjoy the ride, Don D'Salvatore."

Tito didn't dare want to frighten his wife, so he simply spoke no more and held her hand.

"What is it Tito?" she asked, confused. "What's going on?"

"Nothing *mia cara*," Tito kept his voice neutral, his eyes glued with fear and loathing on Sergio. "Nothing to worry about *mi amore*. We'll be there soon."

"Oh please, let them kill her quickly." Tito prayed silently. "Do what you want with me, but please let them kill her quickly."

Victor stood at the picture window in the VIJER building watching snow flurries falling over New York City. It was both beautiful and deceptive, concealing the hidden darkness of the war going on. He could feel it in the air, feel everything closing in now, as his own net tightened around the D'Salvatores' like a hangman's noose. The final play on his game plan coming into a checkmate.

Behind him he could hear the quiet hum of occasional voices as Joshua, Martel or some of the other men on the phones were talking; giving orders or receiving information from various Jerome and Bonnaro crews across the city.

"Fuck!" Joshua Demonico rudely slammed one of the phone receivers down hard.

Victor turned around looking at his consigliere. "What's the matter?" he asked.

"The Goddamn F.B.I is playing now as well." Joshua growled, "They just arrested Rocco and three of his soldiers as well as two of the Bonnaro's hit squads."

"That's why we have that defense attorney, Joshua." Martel's deep voice calmed all of them down, "The one we had Patrizio hire. Call him up and get him to work, we knew it was only a matter of time before the F.B.I got involved in our *mannagge* as well."

Joshua nodded and dialed up a number. Then spoke in his rapid fire pace to someone.

Martel walked over to where his father stood. "See anything out there?" he quietly asked.

"Victory, my *Martello*." Victor glanced at him a moment, "An end to this thing soon. I can feel it in the air. It is what I have been waiting for since 1957."

Martel placed his hand on his fathers shoulder and gave it a gentle reassuring squeeze. He could feel the weariness in his father's bones, the age that was so etched into the proud face of the Don. All of them were tired, but he could feel it as well, his father was right. The end was coming in sight rapidly.

"Alyssa is back at home." Victor spoke quietly in Italian to Martel, "Joshua bought her back the other day, he personally insisted on it."

The tall man raised one eyebrow and looked down at his father then cast a quick glance at the consigliere that was again on the phone with someone different now.

"You're a natural teacher and leader, Martel," Victor smiled warmly at him. "You can even get our hot-headed consigliere to make peace, eh?"

"Victor!" Joshua interrupted again, this time his voice held elation in it. "Bonnaro's men have got Tito! They wanna know where you want him!"

A sudden deafening silence seemed to fall over the entire boardroom as Victor turned and faced Joshua and the other men. "Tell them..." he paused suddenly feeling an almost otherworldly feeling about the whole situation, "Tell them to take him to warehouse #5 over on the docks."

Joshua excitedly relayed the information on the phone and hung up. "Yes!!" he crowed, a cruel smile playing on his handsome face, "Fuckin' Tito. Finally he will get what he deserves!"

Victor was strangely sedate and quiet. His heart was full of vendetta and revenge but yet an eerie calmness had seemed to fall over the room. "Martel, my coat and hat please. Carmine," Victor then spoke to the nearest bodyguard, "drive me over there."

Martel helped his father slip on his overcoat and hat, and Victor nodded discreetly to his underboss to come with. Martel deserved to be there, this was his vendetta too.

"You want me to go with?" Joshua asked his boss and adopted father excitedly.   Victor just quietly walked past Joshua with Martel protectively at his side, as though he had not even heard the question. Victor's mind was only on one thing now. "Does he want me to go with or what?" Joshua asked confused.

"No Joshua," Leonardo's voice spoke up then to him and the rest of the men. "He will be fine. This is private thing for Victor and Martel alone, eh?" the tombstone grey eyes of Len conveying complete understanding to Joshua.

"Oh, yeah. Of course." Joshua nodded understanding then, almost feeling stupid at his even asking. Of course if Victor had wanted him to come he would have asked him.

"Come," Leonardo leaned up against Joshua's shoulder, "we have work to do here, yes? Phones to man, we need to get the word out to pull back now."

"It's over now, isn't it?" one of the other guards asked.

"Yeah, I guess it is." Joshua smiled. "Let me call Pops and have him pull his war squad back." He dialed the number for where he knew Patrizio was hanging out.

Patrizio hung up the phone after finishing talking with Joshua and glanced at his crew. "Well fella's were outta here." He ground out his cigarette in the ashtray and reached for his own coat and hat.

One of his young soldiers helped him to put on his coat, knowing the old capo's arthritis was hurting him something awful in this cold weather.

"That's it? They got him then?" Patrizio's top soldier, Silvio asked.

"Yeah they did." Patrizio patted him on the shoulder, "Now it's for Victor to handle; now we get to go home and warm up and put this thing to bed." This cold weather always made the bullet in his back ache relentlessly. His souvenir from the great massacre in 1957, a chunk of lead still embedded in his upper back.

"I hear that Mr. P," the soldier who had been helping Patrizio put his coat on, patted him on the arm. "So you finally going to Florida now and retire or what?"

A round of laughter echoed among the four men as they began to walk out of the club, it was always a standing joke with Patrizio that he would retire and yet he never seemed to.

"Hey, stop busting my balls! Maybe this time I will, eh?" he laughed and paused to light up one of his cigarettes. The snow looked so beautiful as it fell across the city, had his heart not been aching for his dear Clarissa's loss of her fiancé Gio Aprile, he would have been full of nothing but happiness.

A beat up, black Ford suddenly screeched around a corner and came barreling at them, guns blazing at the group from the windows.

"Oh fuck!" Silvio shouted in fear and pulled out his revolver, "Duck, Pops!"

Time slowed agonizingly down for Patrizio Fantenelli, his old bones told him that his time had finally come. He saw the lighter he had been using to light his cigarette fall out of his hand in slow motion as numbness and shock began to overtake him. "Damn it! God damn it!" He felt himself falling to the pavement but surprisingly there was no pain, no pain at all in him.

He really had wanted to retire this time, now it would be permanent. He knew around him, his crew, his beloved friends and soldiers were going down as well. Whatever this rogue D'Salvatore hit squad was using was high caliber stuff, no small guns here, they had some powerful automatic weapons.

Five more cars suddenly converged on the scene as well, blocking the D'Salvatore hit squad from leaving. Gunshots from the other cars being shot at the black Ford, The F.B.I had arrived on the scene. "Federal Agents!!! Freeze! Drop your weapons!" the F.B.I ordered.

The D'Salvatore men immediately complied, tossing down high-powered automatic guns and putting their hands in the air, but their mission and carnage was complete. They had been the one hit squad sent out that had been the most successful.

As some of the F.B.I began handcuffing the D'Salvatore hitmen, other agents went and idly surveyed the sight of the grizzly massacre. *Caporegime* Patrizio Fantenelli and four of his top crew shot so full of holes by armor piercing bullets they looked like chopped up meat. Blood and gore from the carnage-filled scene began to trickle down the sidewalk and into the storm drain as other store owners and customers began to come out to view and gawk at the gruesome scene of the mob slaying.

Knowing that the F.B.I was out there and playing now, Martel and Victor did not use the Jerome 2 limo, instead Victor, Martel, Carmine and one other bodyguard piled into the junked up rental vehicle that Martel had been using to get about discreetly.

"I feel Tito's confusion." Victor spoke to Martel who was sitting next to him in the back seat. "I feel his fear, not at dying, but hoping he will die quickly and not hung up and tortured on a meat hook somewhere."

"Will he?" the deep baritone voice gently asked. "Will he die quickly?"

"I don't know my dear *Martello*," Victor answered honestly. They paused at a light as a squadron of police cars and ambulances raced down the opposite street. Victor felt a deep foreboding of dread for a moment and then it passed. He nodded and continued, "I do know, even I haven't decided yet. I know it will be very personal and the last set of bones this old man makes." Victor watched the snow drifting as it fell heavier and thicker now outside.

Victor sat back then quietly the rest of the trip, his mind a numbing blank. How long he had waited for this very day, how he had planned and plotted for it and yet now when it was finally here, he somehow never pictured it in this way. The two other men occasionally glanced at Victor or Martel but they also just rode quietly.

They pulled up to the long docks owned by the VIJER Import/Export Company and Carmine skillfully drove the car down behind the twisting paths to Warehouse #5, tires crunching and squeaking in the snow already covering the cement, no use coming in the front door and alerting everyone.

Three other cars were already parked out back behind here as well and a few guards stood in the cold hunched up but alert near the back door. They nodded in respect as soon as they saw Martel and Don Jerome exit the beat up car.

"He's inside, Boss." One of Martel's elite bodyguards, Dominick 'Nick' Pellegrio was standing there he gently stopped both the men for a moment. "The Bonnaro's men already killed his wife but Tito didn't witness it." He whispered to Victor.

"So be it," Victor idly nodded. "The Bonnaro's needed some blood to sate their capture of Tito. An enemy's family can be just as satisfying."

Martel nodded he knew how very true that was indeed, a small thin smile played briefly on his lips as he whispered to his father's ear, "At least Tito will have no idea whether she died fast or slow. The wondering will be agonizing enough." He informed his father, their minds once again thinking along the same path.

"So it will." Victor said quietly and then Don and underboss walked into the semi-darkened warehouse. The men's footsteps echoed ominously as they strode into the huge unheated, dimly lit building, the steam from their breath trailing behind them.

Normally the vast warehouse housed cargo either arriving or departing to overseas but today it was half empty, except for Tito D'Salvatore sitting on a lone chair surrounded by the Bonnaro men who had captured him. Their guns trained on him, he was going nowhere.

"So here we are my old enemy." Victor spoke to Tito in Italian. "So long have I waited for this it seems almost anticlimactic, eh?"

"Fuck you, Jerome!" Tito spit on the floor by Victor's feet, "Just whack me already you fucking old devil!"

Victor crossed his arms and glared daggers at his enemy. Would he have expected Tito to do anything less? Did he honestly think an old timer like Tito would beg for any mercy or quarter now? He half smiled and walked over to Martel a moment and spoke to him, the huge underboss handing something discreetly to his father.

Martel then stood back and motioned for the other men to do so as well. Out of deep respect for the aging Don, the men all stood way back giving Victor and his enemy plenty of room. They all knew this was to be Victor's set of bones, his vendetta. They would only interfere if something went wrong or Victor was in danger.

Victor walked back over to where Tito still sat, unmoving in the chair. "Tito, Tito." Victor shook his head. He could play the same cruel mind games Martel did; he had learned a thing or in this dark business as well. "Your wife is being tortured slowly even as we speak, her screams are most exquisite. She calls for you over and over and we just laugh at her."

"You fuckin' son of a bitch!" Tito roared to his feet actually daring to take a swing at his hated enemy.

Victor had nimbly moved out of the way, Tito was shocked just how nimbly. Something shiny flashed then in Victor's hand; a long wicked looking switchblade. "You expect any quarter now?" Victor roared just as darkly, electricity from the two old *padrones* in the air, "Did you give any to Michael? Did you give any to my family in 1957 you *fottuto bastardo!*"

"You got your Goddamn revenge when you killed my Torenzo!" Tito roared back in sorrow; anger and emotions flowing from both of the old men.

Again Tito lunged at Victor and again Victor was not where he was a moment ago, having once again nimbly ducked out of the way. Being a brown belt in judo definitely had its advantages.

"MY FUCKING VENDETTA, Tito!" Victor's voice roared with his own pain and anger like a wounded lion. "Torenzo's death can never compensate for that day in 1957, not ever!" Victor growled with such hatred and malice, it chilled the very air his eyes taking on the dreaded 'hard-light' look that could stop a freight train. Like two old lions fighting for territory the two old men danced the dance of death then.

Tito and Victor waded briefly in but it was over that fast, that quick. For a brief moment they were clasped together almost like an embrace and then Tito was knocked back, blood already blossoming on his suit.

Tito grabbed his shoulder in surprise where Victor had stabbed him and saw the blood flowing out from between his fingers, knowing in his heart he was going to die one way or the other. He realized then the other men were not going to get involved. If he was going to go down, he was going to go down trying to drag his enemy to hell with him. He had his own hatred and vendetta burning in his veins, knowing his *nemico* Victor Jerome had not only killed his son, his wife but also ruined anything he ever had. He was still the obsessed Captain Ahab; the injury from the knife only fueled his adrenaline further. "*Alla morte, tu figlio di puttana, Vittorio!*" he growled, "Go to hell!" and charged at Victor.

Again the two old Don's clashed briefly, this time Victor was able to use his foot to sweep his larger enemy's feet out from under him. Both of them went down in a bone crunching heap but Victor had the top superior position from the get go.

"No Tito, you go to hell!" Victor growled malevolently. He sat astride Tito's chest and with the skill of a butcher slaughtering a calf, expertly drew the razor sharp knife blade across his enemy's throat slashing his carotid veins and arteries. "My fucking vendetta, Tito!" Victor hissed at him cruelly as Tito's blood shot up in an arc over both of them.

Tito thrashed as a mad man in his death throes but Victor stayed atop him like a cowboy on a thrashing horse, the blood continuing to soak both of them.

In the warehouse the men could feel the waves of hatred and the scent of death as the two old Don's battled to the death. Martel briefly closed his eyes and drew in a deep breath, also sharing with his father the scent of feral and primal fear that was now coming off his enemy Tito. Tito's cruel death was sating Martel as much as Victor.

"It's going to take several long minutes for you to bleed to death, old *nemico!*" Victor taunted, "and I will feel every struggle, every dying heartbeat, every ounce of pain and shock and fear." Victor held on tighter, "For Michael, for my father Louis and my *Famiglia*, for ALL those in my family you have ever killed or harmed."

Tito made garbled wheezing noises from the gaping hole across his neck, his eyes wide in terror, he was weakening fast and Victor was feeling heavier and heavier on his chest; like the Grim Reaper riding him into death.

"Your bones have been the most important ones I've made, Tito." Victor spoke soothingly now almost gently. "My anger and vendetta of you drains like your blood flowing onto my floor. As your life fades so fades my anger and bitterness."

Tito, like a fish out of water, gave a final violent heave, trying to dislodge his hated enemy off of his chest but it was a vain gesture; he was already a dead man, dying slowly and painfully.

Victor clamped his thighs tight against Tito's ribs and stayed on, keeping him down. He could see the curtain of death finally coming over Tito's eyes.

"It's getting close to the end now Tito, I feel deaths gentle touch coming over you." Victor soothed. "But know this Tito Luciano D'Salvatore, you will not even escape me in death, for I most certainly see you in Hell someday and you will have to deal with me there as well." Victor's eyes glared intently down at his victim, willing him to die.

And Tito did exactly that, with a final convulsive groan that ran down the length of his body, he let loose his bladder and died beneath his enemy, Victor Jerome.

Weary Victor sat there on Tito's corpse a few moments longer, he was beyond exhausted, covered in his enemy's blood and he could feel his blood sugar dangerously low. He spat on Tito's face beneath him, and then said in Italian. "My vendetta with the D'Salvatores is now sated, *Finito!*"

Martel was at his side then, helping his exhausted father to his feet, discreetly feeding 3 of the lifesavers at once to his him. "Are you all right, Mr. Jerome?" he asked quietly.

"Yes Laurence, *Mio vindicare angelo della morte*, I am just fine." He allowed his son to half-support him as Martel draped a fresh blanket around him, covering the gore on his father.

A small smile played on Martel's lips. Yes, his father would be Ok; he was still teasing him with that damn nickname. "Giorgio, Nick," Martel quietly ordered to the two soldiers, "Please remain here and see that the warehouse is restored to its pristine condition. Take Mr. D'Salvatore and make him disappear forever in one of our safe places. Butcher the meat well."

"No problem boss." Nick nodded and then backed up with the other men, all of who were still looking in awe at the small, elderly Victor Jerome. It was not that these men had never seen a violent killing, or even a vendetta so thoroughly sated, but rarely did one ever see a Don of Victor's age personally extract such a thorough and physical vengeance on someone with so much agility and cruel finality.

Martel and two other guards bundled up their boss and carefully loaded him in the back of the car, "We are going home now, Victor." Martel spoke soothingly to his father, his hands finding the relaxing pressure points on his father's shoulders and neck as he relaxed the tension and pain out of him.

Victor smiled then at his son, a proud loving smile. He was safe and all was going to be Ok. He knew in his heart then that indeed the

Jerome's would live on and his son, Theodore Jerome, would be the perfect *Padrone* to lead them into the 21st century.

"The war will be ending rapidly now." Victor simply said as he sat back on the seat. His clothes uncomfortably sticky damp against his skin with the blood of the slain Tito. He couldn't wait to shower and clean up, he couldn't remember being this tired in a long time.

He was suddenly overcome by a powerful urge to sleep and so he dozed off on the trip back to the downtown penthouse apartment. Later he would clean up and relax before taking the helicopter back to his estates. Right now he knew everything was safe in the hands of Laurence Martel and his other Administration.

By the 3rd day in bed, back at the Jerome Estates, Alyssa could stand it no more, she had to get up and move around some. Tommy DeLuca, Lena Bonnaro and Arrigo Salvaggio, the bodyguard who had accompanied her and Lena around in Jamaica that day, had been the ones who had dutifully been taking care of her. She had been pretty much flat on her back in bed the whole time, unless she was going to the bathroom or moving around her room a bit. Even though Dr. Weintraub had encouraged her to move around a bit to keep any blood clots from forming in her, Lena and Arrigo had pretty much been quite strict about keeping her resting in bed, much to her dismay.

Meals, her pain medicines, books, whatever she wanted was bought up to her but now she wanted to go downstairs. She knew that there were lots of other wives and some families here at the Estate also seeking temporary shelter and companionship during the *mannagge*, as well as many Bonnaro soldiers and people staying as guests until they could get settled in town after the war was over or head back to Sicily. She often could hear their voices drifting up from downstairs.

She had hoped to see Martel, Victor, Joshua, *anyone* to get news but always news was kept censored from her and she figured from most of the wives and families staying here. She finally asked Tommy to help her get dressed and then began slowly using a cane to walk downstairs.

"Hey, Hey!" Tommy tried to stop her at first, "I don't think you're supposed to be wandering around, Alyssa." he had piped up, trying to stop her. But she had ignored him and simply limped slowly past him. He tried again, even going so far as to just try and firmly hold onto her arm and restrain her gently that way but she pulled free and he certainly was not going to get physical or forcibly restrain her. Instead he just threatened, "I'll call Weintraub! He'll tell you to rest!"

"Oh let him." Alyssa thought to herself, her mind was still in mourning and shock over the loss of her friends Cesare Ciccerone and Gio Aprile. She was going to go down stairs and listen for news, try and find Martel, Victor, someone and not Tommy or anyone else was going to stop her. With a grumbled curse under his breath he simply moved to her side to assist her, knowing he would not win this battle.

As Alyssa slowly made it downstairs into the main living room she saw it filled with many women and even children. It seemed like the families of many of the Jerome Family men were staying over here at the Estate to help out, keep each other company and stay safe.

Some of the women Alyssa noted looked shell-shocked and weary, some of them wept and grieved openly. She had met Cesare's wife, Lisa at Clarissa's bridal shower and she recognized Lisa Ciccerone in the living room, with 3 of Cesare's children. Lisa distraught was crying almost inconsolably as other women gently tended to her and helped her make funeral arrangements. She saw Clarissa Fantenelli, Patrizio's daughter half collapsed and crying in the arms of her older sister Olivia. Alyssa's heart ached for both of their families, especially as she remembered that vivid image of Cesare dead beside her on the sidewalk and remembered the way Gio seemed so different almost lighthearted when he was not on duty, the way he was always singing AC/DC's 'Dirty Deeds done Dirt Cheap' in his goofy off-key way.

Other women like Lena, Rosette, Emilia and several others, seemed to be all over the place running things in a smooth efficient manner feeding everyone, or getting coffee and food to incoming soldiers and guards. Many like Lena were sitting around in small intimate groups, talking sagely in English or Italian depending whether they were Jerome crew or Bonnaro crew ladies.

Alyssa dragged herself into the main living room and headed for the only empty chair she saw, Victor Jerome's recliner. It seemed no one was daring to sit there, in the *Padrone's* chair. She felt she needed to be here as well, to share in what the other women were going through, to show her support and to mourn those who were lost.

"Alyssa! *Ciò che stai facendo!*" she heard Lena's protective but strict voice as the woman chided her in Italian, probably saying the same things Tommy had to her about resting. However Alyssa kept moving until she got to Victor's chair and then just unceremoniously sank into it. She had wanted to go over and hug Lisa Ciccerone and Clarissa Fantenelli but she was too weary and felt light headed even from her short trip to the main living room.

A steaming cup of espresso was placed in her hands and a blanket protectively draped over her by Arrigo who had been down here with some other guards as well.

Briefly there was the murmur of many voices in Italian and English and she once again noted many women, especially the older matriarchs like Emilia crossed themselves again.

At first Alyssa had no idea why the other ladies had singled her out or seemed so intent on her, but then Rosette came over and kissed Alyssa on her cheeks, "Thank you for saving the life of our *Padrone* again. You are his *angelo custode*, his guardian angel. That is twice

467

now; you have protected the head of our Family." Lena nodded sagely at Rosette's words and said something in Italian, also kissing Alyssa on the cheek.

"She says; Victor is indeed blessed to have you as a niece." Rosette translated Lena's words for her. Then Rosette actually ordered Tommy and Arrigo to "let Alyssa be," that the ladies would now watch over her awhile. Reluctantly but obediently the two guards wandered back over with the rest of the men to drink coffee and talk amongst themselves.

Alyssa did exactly that. She sat in her Uncles chair, comforted in the soft blanket and warm espresso as she listened to all the conversations coming in. There was some occasional whispered talk of those who had been hit or killed in the war, like Cesare, Gio, Sal, and then as Alyssa found out Patrizio and 6 others. There was also talk of others who had been arrested by the Police and F.B.I. But the ladies overall seemed to talk of anything but the war that was raging between the Jerome's and D'Salvatores, as though it was either in bad taste or taboo she wasn't sure. At the news of Patrizio's death, her heart ached even more for Clarissa. Now, not only was her fiancé dead but so was her father. A small sigh of mourning for those who had been killed escaped her lips.

A warm, comforting fire blazed away in the massive fireplace and occasionally one of the ladies or either Arrigo or Tommy would come over with either her medications or to check that she was Ok. One thing she did notice is that Arrigo Salvaggio seemed to be very attentive to her ever since they had come back stateside. He always seemed to be looking at her with an intense concern or kindness in his dark eyes. The narcotic pain medicine she had been given earlier was rapidly taking effect and making her pleasantly drowsy and comfortably numb. Soon she just drifted off in a safe, content, nap.

She was suddenly aware of someone in her face even in her sleep and she lazily opened one eye and saw Dr. John Thomas Weintraub hovering over her scrutinizing her. "What's this I hear about you giving Tommy a hard time?" he grilled her lightly, "You're supposed to be resting, not running around all over the house."

This struck Alyssa as totally amusing since she was sitting in a reclining chair and had been napping. She stuck her tongue out at John Thomas. "Hey, hey…" he seemed to be revving up for one of his famous tirades, "You know that bullet came awfully close to burrowing in your spinal cord, missy! If you go running around all over the place you run the risk of ripping out the stitches or worse make your healing time substantially longer or crippling yourself…" he would have continued but Alyssa wearily reached up into his pocket pulled out his pen and prescription pad -since she had none of her pens or paper with her- and scrawled out, "*I'm just getting LIGHT walking to avoid blood clots and keep my muscles limber, don't gimme grief!*" that ought to keep the doc quiet she figured. "_Besides, I lost friends in this too, Doc._" She thrust the pad and pen back to him.

He read it and hemmed and hawed a moment, adjusted his perpetually off-kilter glasses then consented with an almost deep sigh of sorrow himself, "Yeah, well just don't over do it. Ok?" he ordered half heartedly, checked her over to make sure she was indeed Ok and then went over to see if the ladies would give him some of that coffee and blueberry muffins they were handing out to the guards. They did and Alyssa dozed back off.

Victor, Martel and two bodyguards went to the downtown penthouse apartment that was in the VIJER Corporation headquarters. The war was officially over and for now at least, the F.B.I was temporarily sated by their capture of the D'Salvatores hit squad and some Jerome/Bonnaro crews they had nabbed in the Blood war. Victor had showered and the guards took his bloodstained clothing to be taken away and burned. He had a fresh change of clothes here as well as his needed insulin, which his son had injected him with as soon as they got in.

After he was relaxing and finally eating some food with his son, he intently gazed over at Martel. "We will make the announcement soon." Victor said simply. "I am tired and want to retire now. You, my dear Theo, are now as ready as you will ever be to take the reins of the Family."

Martel looked up for a moment and looked to be opening his mouth to say something. Victor silenced any comments by wearily raising his hand. "Laurence... Theodore. I have watched you, now it is your time. You are a natural leader; the capos follow you and trust you. You got even our consigliere out of whatever slump he was in, you are a natural teacher. You got Alyssa, a broken outsider, to integrate seamlessly into our household and Family. You are a natural _padrone_." He paused and looked deeply at his son. "This is what we planned for, all those years ago. This..." Victor briefly waved his hand around, "I have worked hard to bring you much in legitimate businesses and to make hidden and profitable those illegitimate ones.

"We have the Bonnaro's as our backbone in Sicily and the Corella's and Del Giorno's fully support the Jerome's here." He continued, "We have rewarded those who will stand by us and destroyed those who have wanted to break us, like the D'Salvatores and the Romans. Now is your time, Theo. This is what the whole long play was for."

Martel didn't know what to say. Of course he knew his father was right, wasn't this what they had both worked nearly 15 years towards? Made so many sacrifices for?

"You are right of course, _padrone_." It wasn't that Martel thought he couldn't handle the Family, he knew these men and felt confidant in this life. It's just that time sped so rapidly forward to the underboss now, he had worked so hard during the last 15 years to be a 'shadow and ghost', to hide the ultimate secret and now soon everyone would know.

They would know he was Theodore Vittorio Jerome, Victor Jerome's son. A part of him had always liked the anonymity; being the supporting, underboss and protector of the Don. But now that was all to change. His life would become very busy and complicated for a while, especially as the Family adjusted to having a new leader at the helm. He knew his father would still be there to advise him and the Family. That Victor would act as a *consigliere de' facto* but it would now be Theodore who was thrust out into the limelight.

"Theo." His father whispered to him, as though sensing his son's inner conflicts. "You will do fine. I would not suggest transferring the reins of the Family over to you at this time if I didn't think you were ready, eh?" Victor's hand wearily reached over and cupped his son's neck pulling him forehead to forehead with him, their timeless gesture between father and son. "Your only fault is that you occasionally take things too hard and too personal, despite that massive wall you have up. I know, I feel it intensely around you on occasion, Theo." Victor sighed softly, "Learn to not be so hard on yourself sometimes. Even a good leader must know when to just move on gracefully, or to simply trust in those around you, otherwise you will become as consumed and obsessed as our *nemico*, Tito was." Victor gave his son's neck a gentle squeeze and released him. "Now, I really need to rest for awhile before we fly back to the Estate. I am so tired."

Martel nodded and helped escort his weary father to the bedroom to lie down and take a nap. After he had gotten his father settled in, he returned to the living room and flipped on the TV, watching bits of the Jerome-D'Salvatore war relived in all its media-hyped, bloody gore on the local news. It always amused him and others in the Family, just how 'off the mark' the media often was about them and the Family. The sensationalism they often used in hyping up "Mafia wars". His heart did ache though when they showed the massacre scene where Patrizio and his men had been shot or the body of Cesare being hauled off in a body bag.

With a sigh he went into the kitchen to brew himself some herbal tea, his mind wandering to Alyssa. He wondered how she was; he had been briefed on her medical condition earlier and knew she was thankfully going to be Ok. A part of him missed her and could see those playful emerald eyes of hers, the feisty hawk-like spirit that seemed to always cheer him up. In many ways she did remind him so much of Miyoko, a tough little fighter with an indomitable spirit but yet with a certain softness and reliance on him that drew him like a magnet to her. However he knew clearly she was her own unique soul, one that he had come to care for and crave dearly.

470

How would she deal with the news of him being Victor Jerome's son when that secret was revealed? How was she dealing with all this awful violence and cruelty of the war around her? She needed a teacher and someone who could be with her full time, and Laurence didn't know, especially now, if that was even possible. He knew his schedule would be hectic; his life turned temporarily upside down. He just didn't know if Kanashii could handle all that stress and even more importantly he didn't want to put her through that.

He knew she had been through so much already; the kidnapping, the amnesia, getting used to a whole new life, donating a kidney to Victor, seeing the horrors of *mannagge* up close and then being shot herself. She, like Victor deserved to rest, to be allowed to live stress free and not be thrust further into the craziness of his deepest secret being revealed and him taking over the reins of the Family. She had earned that right.

"But won't she be thrust into it anyway?" Martel could almost hear Sen's gravelly but sage voice in his head. "You read her note, know how she feels about you, don't you think she would rather face the craziness with someone she can trust?"

Martel sipped his tea and looked out the window over the grey, dull city. "Yes, but she needs someone who can be with her full time like I was before. The Family must come first!" his own voice echoed in his head.

"What are you really afraid of, Kageryu?" Sen's voice again, angry almost taunting.

Martel felt his anger rise, his hand that was tightly gripping his mug of tea, trembled with barely controlled inner conflict. He had done his role as teacher, as healer, it was time to cut the hawk loose and let her fly! He did not want to be the one to keep her tethered down. A part of him knew exactly what he was 'afraid of' as he vividly remembered what had happened to Miyoko. How she had been used as a pawn in a vendetta against him. Miyoko had loved him too and it had cost her, her life.

No, Kanashii-Taka must be set free from him. She had earned that much...

Later that day she was aware of a large hand lightly caressing her face, and the familiar deep baritone voice, "Hello Alyssa, wake up."

Martel! She snapped her eyes open and saw him kneeled in front of her on one knee. He looked tired and haggard, a thick five o'clock shadow on his angular face. His usually neatly fastidious clothing was wrinkled and she noticed some dark stains on his long trench coat. It looked eerily familiarly like dried blood. She didn't care though, she was just so happy to see her teacher alive and well.

"You left this in the limo on the day of the accident." His blue eyes pierced into her as he handed her the faded copy of 'Easy International Sign Language'.

Her book! Alyssa's heart soared as she snatched it up and clutched it in a death grip. Her book was back, she had thought it gone forever. She was going to reach out and hug her teacher but she felt that cold wall around him again. This time it was almost like an icy storm coming off a glacier, worse than she had ever felt it.

"Come, let's you and I go talk privately." Martel scooped up her body easily in his large arms and carried her to Victor's private Office, the one she had vague memories of being in that fateful day her and Cesare had gotten in trouble for talking about Family business. But she had no fear in her this time, she felt safe in her teacher's arms.

Martel put her gently down in the rich plush chair behind Victor's desk and then went to shut the door. "Nick," he quietly ordered one of the bodyguards, "See to it we're not disturbed." Nick, one of the elite bodyguards who worked directly for Martel, stood outside The Office door, and Martel gently closed the door behind him.

Martel walked back to Victor's desk over by Alyssa and sat one of his hips on the desk, regarding her. "I'm glad to see you up an about, glad that you were not hurt worse than you were. John Thomas says you're supposed to be taking it easy though, you don't want to throw out all those stitches…"

Alyssa quickly found a notepad and pen on Victors desk and feverishly wrote; "*Martel, you didn't come here just to tell me to take it easy did you? What's up? Is Victor Ok? Did something happen to someone else?*" she began to feel scared, had something happened to her Uncle? Why was Martel talking to her in here?

"Victor is fine, Alyssa." Martel assured her, "He sends his regards, in fact he just arrived here at the estate but he is exhausted and sleeping upstairs. I'm sure he'll talk to you in the morning as well, after he's rested for the night." He said folding his long arms over his chest. "I just wanted to make sure you were Ok and to let you know what was going on. As you know by now, we lost Gio and Tony as well as Cesare, Sal and Patrizio. We also lost…" Martel went on to name 10 other men, some Alyssa knew but most she didn't.

"I also wanted to let you know it's over for now. The war is finished. Some, like Rocco will be coming home in a bit, they got, detained." Martel alluded to those who had been picked up and arrested by the F.B.I. "I am sorry you were hurt little one, but I am also grateful that by fate or karma, you were there to save the life of Victor a second time." His eyes held honest warmth and compassion for her and also deep thankfulness.

Her heart began racing now, how she had longed to see Kageryu! To feel his familiar hands massaging her, his deep voice talking to her, the way he looked and talked and even the subtle manly scent of him.

But her inner instinct was telling her something was so very wrong, that he was way too distant and cold, almost shutting her out. What had happened? They had been getting along so well! Nervously she penned out, "*I'd give my life anytime for my Uncle Victor, or for you too Laurence! I had missed you so much while I was gone. Did you get my note I wrote before I left?*"

She had so much she wanted to say to her teacher. So many questions she wanted to ask him, to give him his gift she had picked out for him, to show him the book and the elegant sign language and how easy it could be to 'talk' with one's fingers instead of scratching all this out; hell even to do martial arts with him again, anything to be as content and happy as she was before when she was living with Laurence Martel in his house.

"Yes, Alyssa." He got off the desk and began walking around the elegant office he seemed unable to face her, which was so unlike her Shadow Dragon. "I got the note. That's what I wanted to talk to you about. I understand completely what you wrote and all, however..."

"Here it comes." Alyssa thought bitterly, like a sissy she could already feel her throat tightening up, her eyes beginning to feel salty with tears as she tried in vain to slam down her inner emotions.

"It's just that right now... Soon, things are going to get really crazy and hectic with me and the Family as well." He stopped and glanced at her, "It's not that I don't think you an attractive woman or anything but right now I just don't have time in my life for any kind of, relationship, like that." He tried to put conviction into his words.

It was the only time Alyssa had ever heard her teacher sound awkward. Usually he was so confidant, his speaking so certain and grounded. But it was Ok; she could at least sort of understand that reason. So maybe they wouldn't be dating but at least she would have her teacher and friend. "*So when can I move back into the house with you? Resume training and all, Kageryu?*" she handed the pad of paper to him with a shaking hand.

He read it and then quietly placed the pad face down on the desk without looking at her. "I don't think that is a good idea, Alyssa." Martel said quietly, his eyes almost seemed to pierce her like ice. "You're ready to live here with your Uncle Victor now. You have done exceedingly well in your lessons. You don't need me as a teacher anymore; you're ready to fly on your own... *Kanashii Taka.*" He barely whispered the name.

Alyssa felt her mouth go instantly dry and her stomach lurch into her throat. Not go back to Martel's house? He didn't want to be her teacher anymore? She felt her heart pounding in her ears and felt the tears come no matter how she tried to contain them. What had happened to him to make him so cold and distant all of a sudden? Had her note scared him away from her? Another tear ran unheeded down her cheek.

Martel turned away. He could not, would not, look into those penetratingly haunted eyes of hers. "Don't you see I'm doing this as a favor to you?" His mind screamed silently. It tore at his very heart and soul to say these things, to see her there looking as shocked and hurt as though he had suddenly reached out and stabbed her through the heart with his butterfly knife. "You don't want the kind of life I have to offer you, Kanashii. Damn It! I am trying to spare you, to protect you, because I do care so much for you." He growled in anguish within his mind.

Instead he silently buttoned up his overcoat then said without looking at her. "Look, I'm sorry Alyssa. I never meant to hurt you or give you the wrong impression."

He seemed at a total loss. A part of him wanted to yell, "No never mind, I was just mistaken, I really do want you near me forever." a part of him so loved her and yet was so tormented that he was simply at a loss right now for the first time in his life, unsure of himself and just as confused as she was. A part of him so wanted her close in every way and a part of him wanted her as far away from him as possible so she could never be used against him or harmed like Miyoko had been.

"Perhaps I'd better get going; I just seem to keep saying the wrong things. I will have your remaining things sent back up here to the house … I am sorry Alyssa." He said softly as he went to the door then quietly left and shut the door behind him without looking back, his own soul cracking in hurt and turmoil as well.

Alyssa just sat there dumbfounded and numb letting the tears come unheeded. What had just happened between her and Martel? Just what had suddenly slammed down between them? Her heartbreak and sadness would be in silence and it would be agonizingly deep.

Martel had gone to his own house to work out in his personal martial arts room, unleashing his fury and inner turmoil on his training dummy. He had not wanted to say the things he did to Kanashii and the look she had given him had torn such rents in the hardened wall he had worked so hard to build up around his emotions that it nearly drove him insane.

"What are you really afraid of Kageryu?" His own mind seemed to torment him over and over. He unleashed another flurry of roundhouse kicks and blows to the training dummy until it seemed like it would rip loose from the sturdy chains holding it to the ceiling and floor.

He knew damn well what he was worried about; worried that to allow his full love and emotions of Kanashii would be to jeopardize her. In Martel's mind, to love something was to doom it to die; it seemed his fate and karma for all the lives he had ever taken.

Cochran, Miyoko, Sen's family, his own mother Isabella, his brother Michael… His mind tortured him with visions of Kanashii being hideously killed by some other mob family with a vendetta against him.

Much like Tito D'Salvatores wife had been cruelly murdered in the vendetta with the Jerome's.

Martel knew so many ways to die, knew how to deliver them intimately. Knew from his own intimate experience that enemies, assassins and others would be just as happy with the death of a "loved one" as the enemy themselves. It's how he was raised by Vito Bonnaro, how the old school *Mafioso* operated, how even he had operated when he had taken out his vengeance on Tashima Katsuro's wife and children... "I won't put Kanashii in that kind of danger. I cannot!"

"But isn't she already in the center of things? Hasn't she been from the beginning?" this time he heard the gruff, arrogant voice of his first teacher Cochran in his soul... "She is not some 'unknowing' outsider! Has she not seen as much if not more than many seasoned soldiers in your Family? The girl was kidnapped against her will, she has learned to live and love in this Family, in the Jerome Family, she has passed every test you have thrown at her, that your father has thrown at her, she has endured it all!

"She knows what you are, what your Family is and has shown she accepts and loves you for <u>who</u> you are, accepts all the different sides of you; 'Kageryu', 'the Undertaker' and the 'Jerome Family underboss'. She wrote her honest feelings to you, including that even with most of her memories returned she chooses –this- life, with all of you.

"We all die, Kage. She has survived; the brutal kidnapping and beating by white slavers, donating a kidney to your father, coming face to face with Louie Gambini and even taking a bullet meant for your father. Through ALL this she endures, and why? Because of the loyalty she has for the members of this Family, because of her love and respect for you...

"Even Joshua has made peace with her but now you turn your back on her?" Martel could almost see Cochran sadly shaking his head at him, the way he did when he was disappointed in his student. "Even Sen tried to tell you as much... Think on it Kage and think on it well, you cannot truly control all things or people. No one can. Learn to live and to trust..." For a brief moment, Martel could have sworn he saw Cochran's reflection in the mirrored glass in front of him, the dark hazel eyes of the grizzled wolf, still his teacher, still one of the few men who could drive home a point with a cruel taunt of his voice.

With a sudden roar of rage and anguish, Martel thrust his hand at the reflection in the mirrored glass in the martial arts work out room and it cracked under the Dragon's onslaught of anger and confusion. He was oblivious to the flying glass and the blood that ran down his own fist. He saw his own reflection of fury, torment and exhaustion in the myriad of cracked mirror shards. With another savage scream he gracefully swung his foot in a roundhouse kick at the remaining cracked mirror and the whole entire section of it came loudly crashing down off the wall.

It was most satisfying to him as he saw the whole section of mirrored glass simply shatter and collapse with the violent explosion of his fury and slide down into one destroyed mess. Never had the underboss come undone like this, not ever. Not since he had worked so hard to put that wall up around his heart and emotions that day in Sen's yard when Sen branded him as a Ninjitsu. Like the ruined mirror he had just shattered, he then felt something deep inside his own soul come crashing down.

With a harsh grunt and a dark look and still ignoring the blood steadily dripping down his bare hands he simply walked off into his bedroom and collapsed onto his bed in utter physical, mental and spiritual exhaustion, where he would sleep a dreamless sleep for the next 10 hours.

Nearly two hours later after Martel's words to her, Alyssa emerged from the Office. No one had dared bothered her nor interrupted her in here. She had cried, raged inside and then drifted off into a brief exhausted nap. But now she blinked, woke up and then with sore cramped muscles and still red-rimmed eyes began to shuffle sorely out of the office.

She noticed Nick was now gone, instead Arrigo was standing there and talking to Leonardo Tagretta. The two obviously knew each other from before or were catching up on news from the homeland because Len leaned up casually against the wall near Arrigo and the two were chuckling and talking casually in rapid-fire Italian like two long-lost friends.

As soon as she opened the door Arrigo immediately glanced down at Alyssa with concern in his dark eyes and was instantly at her side saying something soothingly in Italian that she didn't understand.

Len sidled up to her other side, concern also on his face. "Ah, Miss Alyssa, maybe you should go back upstairs and rest now? Arrigo he been worried about you. He say you late for your medicines."

At first in her foul mood she tried to violently pull away from both of them but Len quickly and firmly grabbed her left arm. As weak as she was and as strongly muscular as Leonardo was, she was going nowhere.

"Shhh, easy now Alyssa..." His deceptively soft voice soothed with a hint of undeniable firmness, "Come on, take it easy, eh? The boss Victor is still sleeping, he really tired. Joshua is busy taking care of other things, so that leaves me to help out here right now."

Alyssa wondered where Rocco Benedarra or Carmine Marcallo was. Normally they were the ones who ran things at the Estates when the top Administration was busy. She was not used to seeing Leonardo here but she remembered Martel's words on all those who were lost.

All those who she had known so well: Gio, Cesare, Patrizio, Sal, Tony, and others, she still was deeply haunted by the image of her friend, Cesare, shot dead next to her on the pavement, his brains and blood mingling around her, his unblinking eye staring at her in death. She had a feeling there would be a lot of restructuring in the Family now, because of those killed or locked up in jail.

So now, apparently Mr. Leonardo Tagretta was the one temporarily running things, probably because he was so easily bi-lingual in Italian and could help the Bonnaro folks, like Arrigo and others feel more comfortable and because he was one of them as well.

She didn't really know Leonardo well except for briefly seeing him here and there since he normally worked downtown in the city with his crew. However his soothing voice and quiet, no-nonsense demeanor seemed to cut through her own inner turmoil. She also knew he was also an old world Man of Honor and obviously trying to keep everything running smoothly here now until his bosses took back over the reins, so she instinctively knew he would not be pushed or played with. He had things to do and a *Famiglia* to keep calm and running smoothly.

He loosened his grip some on her arm but his stormy grey eyes seemed to look deep into her heart conveying many thoughts at once, empathy, understanding but also unfaltering command. "I know you have had a tough time, Alyssa," his accented voice spoke gently, as though to a frightened animal. "Right now, even though this *mannagge* winding down, things they are still hectic. You no make my job any harder, Ok? Arrigo here, he likes you and was worried about you, insisted on keeping an eye on you himself..." The pony-tailed capo nodded towards Arrigo and made a gesture of his finger pointing to his eye and on the other side of her Arrigo nodded solemnly in agreement. Arrigo gently took her other arm again and also spoke in a low soothing voice, similar to Leonardo's.

"Arrigo say you really need to rest, that he and Lena have been deeply worried about you." Len continued, "Now, you help me out and listen to Arrigo and Lena, Ok? I know Tommy DeLuca should be back soon, I know you friends with him and trust him."

She wasn't going to argue or fight with Leonardo or Arrigo anymore. She had no beef with Len or the Bonnaro bodyguard, Arrigo and certainly didn't want to make their job any harder. She knew so many others in the Family were hurting a lot worse than her, she couldn't even imagine how Clarissa Fantenelli must be feeling right now, both her father and her fiancé dead, or Lisa Ciccerone, Cesare's wife and her now fatherless children. Alyssa just seemed to wilt in submission, nodded softly and sadly her eyes unable to look into the strong, intense eyes of Leonardo Tagretta.

"That's a girl." Len said gently, patted her hand in a kindly manner and then released her. He spoke briefly to Arrigo in Sicilian then walked off.

Arrigo continued to gently but firmly hold onto Alyssa and began to lead her back to her room, allowing her to use him as a crutch. He continued to converse with her in Italian but Alyssa just felt helpless, not knowing what he was saying. He just seemed to speak soothingly and quietly to her almost as if explaining something, as he helped lead her back upstairs.

Once back in her room, Alyssa just collapsed on her own bed in physical and mental anguish as she replayed Martel's words over and over in her head. "You're ready to live here with your Uncle Victor, now. You don't need me as a teacher anymore..." and then the man had simply walked out of her life without even a glance back. She felt her own inner grief fully renewed.

About 10 minutes later, Lena and Arrigo had come back into her room with her pain medications and some food. Alyssa could tell by the darkness that had fallen over the room it was probably well past dinnertime but her own inner grief and torment made her neither hungry or wanting any pain medication.

At first Lena and Arrigo had tried desperately to figure out what was wrong with Alyssa, why she was so sad and depressed. They talked to her, pleaded with her, even Lena in her broken English. "You inna pain? You wanna *dottore* Weintraub? Eh?" Lena seemed to be getting more and more worried at Alyssa's refusal of food, medication or any attention.

Finally Alyssa reached over and wearily pulled her pad of paper and pen from the nightstand. She hadn't lived among all these people of Victor's without learning some rudimentary words in Italian. She scrawled out... "*Col cuore spezzato, amore*." 'Broken-hearted love'. She knew it wasn't proper Italian, hell, she hoped she even spelled it right. But Lena seemed to understand her written communication immediately.

"Ah, *amore*," Lena nodded sagely. She gently stroked Alyssa's hair for a moment, the way a mother would soothe a daughter. She spoke briefly to Arrigo and Alyssa picked out the words '*amore*' and '*Martello*', in Lena's quick explanation to him.

Arrigo just solemnly nodded and then placed the tray of food and her dose of medicine on the nightstand, in case she wanted it later. "*Ci interessiamo tutti a te*," His dark eyes looked down at her a moment and one of his hands reached out and stroked her cheek gently almost lovingly. "*io ti ho particolarmente a cuore*." He said in an even more soft and intense voice.

"Arrigo!" Lena looked at him sternly a moment and slightly shook her head, almost like a warning. "*Lasciala stare, lei è di Laurence Martello!*"

Arrigo abruptly pulled his hand back, nodded once to Lena and his professional manner quickly slid back into place. "*Certamente Signora*

Bonnaro, *Ti prego, perdonami.*" He simply said and walked out of the room to resume standing guard by the door until Tommy came on duty.

A part of Alyssa was aching to know what had just been said between Lena and Arrigo! Whatever it was it seemed to have frustrated and shut down Arrigo Salvaggio almost instantly. "Shhh," Lena soothed for a moment. She spoke a few more calming sentences in Italian to her but like Lena and Arrigo's earlier exchange she had no idea what was actually said, only that she mentioned Martel (*Martello's*) name in it. Then with a quick kiss to her cheek the matronly Lena walked out giving Alyssa much needed privacy to sink into her own depression and sadness.

Later that evening she was dimly aware of Tommy DeLuca coming into her room to check on her bandage and surgery site on her back. "Hey, you Ok Alyssa? Lena and Arrigo tell me you're not taking your pain meds or eating." the baby-faced soldier asked her.

Alyssa did not want to go into this again, nor spread her private business with Martel all over the place. So she wrote nothing and chose to ignore his question, simply trying to burrow back into the covers.

"Suit yourself, Alyssa." Tommy merely said, "Your wound looks like it is healing well." He dropped another two codeine pills on the nightstand where her earlier untouched dose was. "If you need it, it's there." He patted her shoulder. "I can understand your sadness over the people we lost." He nodded. "Believe me, it bothers me as well." He gently replaced the covers over her. "Anything I can help you with?" he asked.

She just shook her head 'no' and turned away from him. He got to his feet with a small sigh. "I'll be outside if you need me for anything, Ok?" and then he too left.

Chapter 37- *October 21st 1987*

The next morning Alyssa woke up stiff and sore and decided she was going to go to the aviary. She was certain with all this war and *mannagge* going on that probably no one had taken care of Victor's little birds and more importantly she needed to get out and be by herself. She scooped the 4 codeine pills into a drawer in her nightstand and then slowly and in a great deal of pain got dressed.

She opened the door and saw some other Jerome guard there that she only vaguely recognized. The one Martel had called Nick the other day. Like Gio, Nick Pellegrio was another one of the elite bodyguards, another muscular man with hard, cold, unreadable eyes. She had seen him working out a lot at the Jerome gym before, often with Gio or the main head of the gym, Carmine Marcallo.

Nick glanced dourly at Alyssa. "You going down to breakfast, or what?" he gruffly asked in a thick Bronx accent. She just wearily nodded and began to limp sorely past him towards the stairs with her cane.

"Hey, wait. Chill out and slow down." He grumbled and offered his arm to help her. Apparently now that she had been adopted by Victor a lot of his bodyguards and men treated her much more carefully she noted.

Downstairs she was relieved to see Joshua Demonico but noted there was no Martel or Victor. Joshua was conversing away with Leonardo Tagretta and some other men, and she noted that most of the women and children were gone now. Only a few remained and many of them she could hear in the kitchens or cleaning up the Jerome manor trying to get things back to a routine. She saw no sign of Lena or Arrigo.

"Hey ya 'Lyss," Joshua came over and gave her shoulder a light squeeze. "Let me help ya here." He grabbed a plate and helped her load up some eggs, bacon and toast on it. She noted he filled it up with a lot more food than she would ever eat. "Tommy and some others tell me, you aren't eating so well. This concerns me." The Panther's dark eyes looked deeply at her a moment. "But, I'm glad to see you're eating now." He brought her plate to the table and helped her sit down. Then he whispered in her ear, "Everyone will be back over here later on. I know Victor has been repeatedly asking about you, he has just been really worn out by all this and also spending time with Vito Bonnaro. Trust me, he hasn't forgotten you, I promise. And I know Martel will undoubtedly be happy to see you again."

Alyssa sighed; she was not going to go into any detail or tell Joshua that she and Martel had already spoken and that Martel had basically abruptly and without true explanation had shut her out of his life. That grief was still too raw and an open wound on her very psyche. Joshua had effectively killed her appetite with that last comment, but she made a show of pushing her food around some and nibbling a few bites here and there, so they would all stop worrying about her and just leave her alone.

Victor sat in Martel's house here on the property along with Vito Bonnaro, just the three of them since Vito was one of the very few who knew Martel's true identity.

Martel had cleaned himself up and closed the door to his martial arts room; he would clean up the ruined mirror later after the meeting. Over his cut knuckles he wore some gauze covered in thin, ace-type bandages. Victor had glanced at his son's hands with a curious and concerned look but had said nothing.

Vito like many first time guests in Martel's house had been fascinated by the Asian décor and all the oriental statues and paintings. He threw a few friendly barbs at Theodore such as, "Not turning your back on your Italian heritage now, eh? The Asian Cosa Nostra, now that is something." He winked playfully at Laurence. Martel who was usually quick to either rise to the bait or else give withering looks that could silence even powerful men like Vito was strangely silent as if not hearing the comments at all, this Victor noticed as well.

The three men ate breakfast as they talked in Italian, "You know, Vito. You and Lena are welcome to stay at my place as long as you need." Victor assured his friend and fellow Don.

"Your generosity has been most kind, Vittorio." Vito nodded as he downed his orange juice, "I will however probably be getting a temporary place very soon in the nearby town. I have some of my men getting me a place to stay as we speak. Once you announce Theodore's taking over the Family and things are settled, however, we will all probably be going back to Sicily."

"I understand." Victor said, "I plan to make the announcement in about two weeks or less, of Theo's taking over. I want to give our allies on the Commission time to recover and calm down after this *mannagge* with the D'Salvatores, and I need to restructure people in my own Family."

"Of course, Victor." Don Vito agreed. "You know, I have around 5 of my men, including Arrigo Salvaggio who have expressed a desire to stay here in America and work directly for you, or rather Theodore, I should say." He winked at the large underboss soon to be the new Don of the Jerome Family.

"They are most welcome to stay Don Vito." Martel's weary sounding voice spoke. "I have seen Arrigo in action; he is an excellent soldier. His instincts are impeccable, I would even recommend him as my new Head of the elite bodyguards..." he glanced at his father and as though reading his mind added, "Len Tagretta, and several of the ladies like Rosette and others as well as myself are more than willing to work with all the new Sicilian immigrants and teach them English."

"Well that will be excellent then." Vito agreed, "Did you know Arrigo Salvaggio is a cousin to Leonardo Tagretta?" he smiled. "One of the few blood relatives Len has left from the old country. Even though Arrigo is from Napoli, a member of the *Camorrista*..." Vito referred to the Naples Organized Crime families commonly known as the Camorra, "...He has been one of mine for many years. A true *Mafiosi*, even if he isn't Sicilian." He chuckled good naturedly.

"Ah, that explains it. I thought those two got along quite well and seemed close." Victor finished off his coffee.

"Joshua is close with Len as well," Martel agreed, "In fact I am thinking of this for our Administration;" Martel looked at his father, "Joshua for our new underboss, and I am thinking of giving Leonardo a promotion to our new consigliere?" he quirked an eyebrow at his father, "Arrigo as our new head of the elite guards and Rocco as our new main capo for our downtown operations. I trust him implicitly and he is very in-tune with what is going on in the city. Patrizio had schooled him well."

"Don't ask me, Theo." Victor said sagely, kindly, "You will soon be the new leader; these are your decisions to make. However, are Rocco and the others freed from their stay with the Feds yet?"

"Their cases come up in 3 weeks." Martel said levelly, "that defense attorney Patrizio had got us assures us that he should be able to get their charges dropped."

"Have a backup plan, *mi angelo della morte*." Victor said casually. He knew that often what lawyers said didn't always come to pass. "Rocco and company may very well be 'guests of the state' for awhile, maybe up to several years or more."

Martel just nodded with a non-committal grunt. "Then how about Vincente Ardanno?"

"That's a good choice, especially since he works with Danny Valsiglio at the VIJER Corporation and he works our operations at the docks with the stevedores." Victor agreed. "Pull him up from the docks for now and have him come work up here at the Estates for awhile. We'll groom him up here."

Vito Bonnaro just idly listened to Martel and Victor making their plans for a while, as he finished his breakfast. Father and son smoothly re-aligning the Family structure for when Theodore would be announced as the new *Padrone*, it made him miss his own son Gino back at home.

"Vito, all of us are as usual indebted to you more than you can ever know." Victor turned back to his old friend. "Were it not for your extra soldiers and helping with the elaborate plan with DiMone and what not, we would not have won this thing as easily as we did."

Martel rose and began to gather the empty plates. "Very true," The deep voice echoed his father's sentiments. "I am also indebted to you not only for your support of the future of the Jerome's, but for all the training you gave me so long ago." He gently patted Vito on the shoulder. "You truly are like a second father to me, Vito."

"Nonsense Theodore," Vito smiled warmly at him, "You have always been like a son to me, to the Bonnaro Family. You will do just fine as the new *Padrone*, and the Jerome's and Bonnaro's will continue to be close allies. I am never farther away than a phone call or a visit." The two men's eyes conveyed deep respect, friendship and faith in one another.

It lightened Victor's heart immensely; he felt indeed things would go smoothly now. However he could sense some deep pain in his son, he knew better than to ask, although Victor had a very strong notion of what it was that bothered his son; and that it somehow involved the girl, Alyssa.

"Well gentlemen, if that is settled." Victor leaned back as Martel collected his empty breakfast dishes. "I suggest we make a quick trip down to the VIJER building and then come back here to the Estate later. I hear the ladies are whipping up a huge feast to celebrate our victory over the D'Salvatores and to mourn those who gave their lives for it."

"I will meet you all at the helipad, in an hour." Martel nodded to his father and Vito. "I have a few things to do here, first."

After the two men had left, Martel first quickly swept up the shattered glass from the huge mirrored wall he had broken in his anger, cleaned up the blood on the mat and then went to place a very special trophy down in his 'Trophy Room'.

As he flipped on the lights downstairs in his basement he walked over to the special tub filled with a variety of special chemical compounds, formalin, alcohol and a stabilized bleach compound. He used large rubber gloves to gently take out the now gleaming skull of his dead nemesis Louie Gambini and looked it over. It was perfect in every way, except for the 2" hole at the back of his skull, near the base where Martel's bullet had snuffed out the man's life. Carefully Martel dried it off and then walked over to the doorframe with his grisly trophy. He fished out his butterfly knife with one hand and carved a big notch on the door near the 219 other ones.

"Yours makes an even 220 Louie." He chuckled darkly, speaking aloud to the skull of his dead enemy. "Now you get to join Torenzo D'Salvatore, and Vito Roman as one of my truly special kills." He took the skull and placed it on a finished wooden stand that had "L.G" carved on it. He glanced at the skull as it sat in its final resting place deep in the heart of his basement, now destined to forever look at its killer whenever he worked on his guns down here.

As Martel glared at the skull, something seemed to tickle him at the base of his own skull, some nagging thought and dark karmic revelation. For whatever reason, the dead seemed to speak to him that day.

Theodore Jerome knew then without a doubt, that it was Louie Gambini who had been the one to first kidnap Alyssa for the Roman Families white slavery ring. The skull seemed to almost leer at him in its final insult to the man who had taken its life. Martel suddenly snatched the skull back up in his large hands and he briefly had half a mind to destroy the thing, to crush it under the power and weight of his foot, to stomp it into dust. He felt his own rage flare briefly in him again.

'Center yourself, Kageryu!' His mind warned him. 'Do not become like Joshua, white hot with anger and rage all the time. You have a *Famiglia* to run now, people whose lives will depend on you and your clear thinking.'

With a deep breath he mentally centered himself and replaced Louie's skull on its resting place. "You are so lucky you are already dead, Gambini." He muttered softly and then turning out the lights, left to join his father and Vito at the helipad.

After breakfast and pocketing two more of the pain pills that Rosette had plunked down in front of her, Alyssa walked off to the hall closet to find her coat. It was cold out now, in mid-October, only in the low 40's as the unusual cold spell continued to ride heavily over the New England area and more snow flurries were expected. Most of the guards who worked outside wore thick long overcoats or trench coats and leather gloves along with protection for their ears.

She noticed the house was much, more empty today of the wives, children and families of the capos, soldiers and associates who had been staying here. They had probably gone back to their own homes and lives to try and recover after the war.

Only a few of the Bonnaro folks seemed to be staying here as well as Clarissa Fantenelli who was still understandably inconsolable. Alyssa noticed that Joshua Demonico seemed to be spending a lot of time comforting her personally and giving her extra attention. Alyssa was certain Joshua had always liked her and now that Gio Aprile had been shot seemed to want to hopefully encourage Clarissa to be his girlfriend.

After dressing warmly in a coat and a scarf she flung open the door and began to limp out to the Aviary. She winced knowing it was going to be a very long and uncomfortable walk, but she was determined and she also knew if she asked any of the guards for a ride they would only tell her 'No' and try to force her to stay inside.

She heard a few shouts from the men inside but pulled shut the door before they could interfere with her. She hadn't gotten more than about 20 feet though when she heard the angry voices of Tommy DeLuca and Nick Pellegrio coming after her. "Whoa, hey, get back here!" they called in dark, exasperated voices.

Nick suddenly grabbed onto her shoulder rather roughly and this caused her back to rebel in agony. She involuntarily grunted in pain.

"Hey!" he glowered at her, "Where you goin' Missy? The bosses said everyone was supposed to stay *inside*!" he emphasized the word.

She glared back at him and tried to pull free of his strong grasp. She was no longer afraid of the guards and the men here. She would respect them but she held no fear of them. However she was determined to keep her oath to watch over Victor's birds, and more importantly her heart was still breaking deeply over the words Martel had said to her and his dumping her as his student. Depression made her angry and she cared less at this point the guards' orders.

"Yeah, come on, Alyssa." Tommy said trying to quickly defuse the situation. He did not want to see Nick get rough with Alyssa. "Where are you going, hun? Yer supposed to stay inside; you don't want Joshua getting all fired up now, do ya?"

This time she had remembered to bring her pad and pens with her. As she opened her purse to get the items her eyes fell on the Hershey bar Cesare had thrust in there on his last day alive, the day he had welcomed her back from Jamaica and then had been brutally shot. Her soul shattered anew once again as she remembered her friend Cesare and she quickly pulled out the pad and scrawled. "*I had promised Victor to take care of his birds, he entrusted it to me. Also, I am tired of staying inside I need some fresh air! Please! Nothing is going to happen, I promise!!!*"

Nick just narrowed his eyes at her, reminding her of some dark Rottweiler guard dog, and Tommy shook his head. He did not want a scene out here.

"Look 'Lyss, how about going down later? Huh? After Victor or Martel give their Ok?" Tommy tried again.

At the mention of Martel's name, Alyssa pulled forward again; the unexpected lurch actually freed her from Nick's grasp, as he had relaxed his hold on her. "Goddamn it!" he roared harshly at her and reached his well-muscled arm to snag her again.

Alyssa actually raised her cane against him, determined to actually fight him with it if he laid a hand on her again. Cesare had been the one who had first shown her the protective love of the Family and she would no longer be intimidated by the guards. She owed her uncle Victor the duty of taking care of his beloved finches. She had made him a promise and oath.

A dark-threatening look suddenly came over Nick Pellegrino and he truly looked like he might enjoy taking that cane away, beating her with it and then throwing her over his shoulder and forcibly taking her back in. As an elite bodyguard he was not used to people saying "No," to him or to his bosses direct orders, nor had he ever directly worked with Alyssa before.

"Nick, Nick!" Tommy quickly pushed his way between them. "Easy man, it's cool." He knew he was in a bad predicament here and things were quickly escalating. "Dominick," he used his friend's full name as glanced between the guard and Alyssa, "I got it; it's cool. I'll handle it Ok? Victor normally assigns me to work with her."

Tommy's words had the desired effect immediately placating the elite blackguard who backed off and growled, "Fine, whatever." He hunched his massive shoulders, "If the bosses get pissed, it's your shit to deal with Tommy." He shook his head and stalked angrily back into the house.

"Damn it, Alyssa!" Tommy half sighed in exasperation after Nick had moved off. "What the hell has gotten into you lately? Are you trying to get both of us in trouble?"

Alyssa felt the threat of tears in her eyes, but she was not going to cry in front of Tommy DeLuca. *"Tommy, please!"* She controlled her thoughts, focused every ounce of control on her writing. *"Please just take me to the aviary, I beg you. Please don't drag me back in the house. I need to check on the birds and have some time alone. I promise you nothing is going to happen. I owe the favor to Victor, I promised him I would take care of his birds."* One single tear managed to slipped out as she held the pad under Tommy DeLuca's nose, she knew in her weakened and pain-filled state he could easily overpower her and drag her back inside. But Tommy DeLuca was not only one of the few men who had been with Alyssa since the beginning of her stay with the Jerome's and her nursemaid, but he also liked her as a friend.

"Shit," he barely whispered under his breath, glancing around. "Damn it woman! Why do you do this to me, huh?" he relented. "Ok fine, but we make it quick and then get back to the house, Ok?"

She nodded then gently reached for his hand in trust. He gave her his arm to balance on, "But we are driving in my car there! You don't need to be walking or slipping on ice with your bad back," He gruffed.

He escorted her to the small, side parking lot where the guards normally parked and helped her into his mid-sized Ford Taurus. It reeked of cigarette smoke and coffee and was a cluttered mess, everything from music cassette cases to old empty boxes from Mario's Italian restaurant and McDonald's bags. A few cigarette butts spilled out of the overflowing ashtray and she noticed several empty and full cartons of Marlboro cigarettes here and there. Tommy DeLuca it seemed was a bit of a slob. He put his key into the ignition and turned the car over, immediately Sting and The Police blared out of his expensive stereo system singing '*Roxanne, you don't have to put on the Red light*'.

"Sorry" he muttered turning it down some. He casually grabbed a Colt 45 revolver that was sitting on the floor near Alyssa's feet and reaching over her he shoved it into the glove box. "Don't worry, it's not loaded." The baby-faced soldier half grumbled again as he put the car in gear and drove down the winding driveway towards the Aviary. They passed the giant, black JEROME-1 limo parked forlornly like some ghost ship near the corner of the lot and it only vividly reminded her of Cesare and the other men who had been killed.

"Do ya mind if I smoke?" he asked. She shook her head '*no*'; she didn't mind. Because of Victor's health, the house guards and soldiers were not allowed to smoke on duty unless they were in the back of the kitchen or one of the designated break rooms or outside. So those who did smoke often lit up as soon as they could get outside.

He lit up as they cruised down the driveway, it had been salted to keep it ice free but she could see the falling snowflakes getting heavier and fatter. Soon it would be covering the grounds again in fluffy, smothering whiteness. As they rounded the fork to where the Aviary was she caught a brief glance of her teachers house hidden in the pines and skeletal maple trees. Her heart lurched in her chest and part of her wanted to run down there and try talking to him, it only made her depression deeper and sharper.

They pulled up to the aviary and Tommy cut off the engine then got out to help her get out of the car. "Now remember," He reminded her gently, "we ain't got all day, right? I certainly don't want my ass busted by either Victor, Martel or Joshua for us running around outside, and neither do you." He sternly glanced at her a moment.

She just nodded wearily and then walked into the Aviary. The outer door was slightly stuck from the cold and with a tug she got it opened. Tommy was being nice and hanging out near his car smoking his cigarettes and letting her have peace and quiet and time alone.

Once in the inner aviary and after slipping on the protective dark smock she began to break the ice off the birds' water troughs and refill seed cups. She could tell it had been at least several days since anyone had been down here and so she had a lot to do. As she checked out a few of the nest boxes several of the finches landed on her chirping in her ears and chastising her lightly for being neglected. They became animated seeing they were getting fed and watered and they happily began singing and chirping and calling all at once.

As Victor had taught her she then began to check the nest boxes and the inhabitants detailing the information in a notebook that was kept down here just for that purpose. It had been awhile since she had been down here; first on vacation with Victor, then recovering from surgery in the hospital and then recovering here at the house, so it had been nearly 8 days since she had personally been in here. Obviously, someone (probably Joshua) had fed and watered the birds during that time but with the war that had just went on, it hadn't been done for the past 3-4 days.

She began to move down the rows of nest boxes checking inside each one. During the winter very rarely did any of the finches ever nest and lay eggs, Victor had explained to her, so she didn't expect to find any eggs or nestlings. In fact if she did find any eggs, Victor told her she was to toss them out and replace them with 'dummy eggs' small little plastic eggs, so it wouldn't drain the females and risk killing them. So far she didn't find any eggs, but at the 3rd nest box as she struggled to open the frozen lid she did find bird # 416, frozen dead inside. It was the bird Victor called Peppino or Peppi, the playful one that was Victor's personal favorite that always sought out his pockets and tried to escape in his little finch version of a jailbreak.

This time she had no control of the tears that ran down her face as her fingers scooped up the tiny little frozen body. Her vision blurred as she held the icy cold little body to her cheek and then cupped it tenderly.

So much death, so much of what she had loved gone... Why couldn't she just turn back time to 3 or 4 weeks ago, when all had been so well with Martel, when they were at that border of moving their relationship to something deeper, back 4 weeks ago when Gio Aprile, Cesare Ciccerone, chain-smoking Patrizio and all the rest were alive and happy and her life was good. Carrying the tiny, stiff, lifeless bird she walked to the inner chamber locked the outside door and sank down to the icy cold cement floor as her heart shattered in a million pieces.

She sat there rocking back and forth as the silent tears and anguish just kept coming upon her in waves. Her mind cruelly taunting her with memories both past and present; of her ex-fiancé betraying her with Mandy, her being kidnapped, falling in love with Laurence Martel, her close friendships with Gio, Cesare and the rest and then the terrible ways she had lost them always culminating with that horrible image of Cesare's face blown apart just inches from her own.

A few times she heard Tommy knocking on the outer door, even trying to pull it open, calling to her and begging her to come back out, but in her grief she was oblivious to it. All she could do was sit there on that cold floor, with no gloves or hat, cupping the tiny body of Peppi and letting her sorrow and anguish wash over her.

Tommy glanced at his watch again, he was getting frantic now, it had been nearly 3 hours she had been down here. He knew she had locked the outer door from the inside, there was no way he was getting into that aviary unless he went and got tools and took the door off the hinges. "Aw goddamn it, Lyss!" he growled, pissed off. "You promised me! Come on, I was nice to you! This is how you repay me? By giving me agita?" he was getting cold and agitated himself, he knew the bosses were going to be looking for them, he was half surprised that Nick or someone else hadn't already come down looking for them, he knew she was late on her noon-time meds.

A few times he had dug around the clutter of his car looking for a hammer or something to take the door off the hinges, but he had nothing to do the job with, not to mention he was half-afraid to mess up the Boss' aviary. They all knew the Aviary was Victor's special place and his alone. The fact Victor let Alyssa come down here and take care of his birds spoke volumes of his trust for her.

He had walked around trying to see into the screened areas and tried to plead with her but he could see nothing. A few times he thought he saw her sitting in a ball deep within the inner chamber but he wasn't sure. Since she was mute the constant peeping and chirping of the now fed finches drowned out her silent sobs and anguish. Tommy was seriously beginning to worry, had something happened to her? Had she slipped or fallen or worse collapsed?

"Fuck!!" he growled, "Ok, Alyssa that's it!" he yelled now at the end of his rope, "I'm going up to the house get a tool kit and Nick and we are both going to drag you back up to the house if we have to tie you up and sit on you!"

Still no answer from her from within…

"*Vaffanculo!!*" he angrily drove his gloved fist into the hood of his own car; he could already imagine the chewing out the bosses would give him over this screw up.

Suddenly the sweeping grill of the Jerome-1 limousine came over the rise and headed to the aviary, elite bodyguard Nick Pellegrio driving. It pulled up near Tommy's car and the thick muscled Nick got out and without even glancing at Tommy swept open the back door and held it open as Victor Jerome got out.

"Oh shit." Tommy thought, a cold fear closing in around his heart. "I am so dead."

Nick just stood like an imposing statue near the Limo as the small, powerful Victor walked slowly over towards Tommy DeLuca.

"Hey Mr. Jerome, I am so sorry…" Tommy began, "Really, I tried…" he began to explain.

"Mr. DeLuca," Victor interrupted him gently, one of his gloved hands on Tommy's arm. "It's Ok, really. Go back to the house and warm up, everything's fine, I assure you. You did nothing wrong, I promise." Victor smiled understandingly at him. "My niece is a determined and spirited woman, eh?" Victor chuckled lightly, "Now go, you look half frozen yourself. Everything is Ok." He assured his man.

Tommy nodded and then following the boss's orders, climbed into his Ford and quickly departed. He was not only cold, but hungry as well and had to pee like a racehorse.

Victor rapped hard on the outer door of his Aviary. "Child, open up, it's me." His calm but commanding voice gently called out.

She had pulled herself out of her dark daydreams surprised to see she had half fallen asleep. Her body ached relentlessly from sitting for nearly 4 hours outdoors in the icy cold, still injured and with no gloves or hat.

Alyssa knew better than to lock the *Padrone* of his own aviary or piss him off. So still carefully holding the tiny body of Peppino #416, she fought to unlock the door, then after unlocking it went and sank back down in the corner on the cold cement floor shivering and trembling in cold, not caring if she died in here like the little bird.

Victor calmly walked in and stood over where she sat in a heap on the floor. "Come here Child." He gently ordered, "Stand up. I am far too old and tired to get down there on the floor with you." Alyssa obediently stood up and gently edged over to him so that they stood side by side. She was sure she was a mess, her face and clothes soaked in her tears and anguish.

Victor gently removed his hat and smoothed back his distinguished remaining laurel of hair with a gloved hand, "It's cold out here Alyssa." He then pulled her close up against him, "You should be in the house where it's nice and warm, eh?" He removed his leather gloves and then let one of his arms drape across her shoulder, his old hand cupping her gently behind her neck and pulling her head forward until she was almost forehead to forehead with him, his gentle eyes locking on hers. "You are here to think, like I often come to do." The hand on her neck gently massaged her, his eyes conveying understanding and his own weariness. "To be out here in the cold for so long, it must be something very important you wrestle with, eh? Care to talk with a friend?" they briefly touched foreheads and then he released her.

She held up the tiny body of Peppino, now quite warm but still quite dead. Fresh tears tracked down her face as she held the bird out to Victor as if the great Mafia Don could somehow order the bird back alive again.

He gently took the dead bird from her hand. "Ah, little Peppi," Victor gently ran one thumb along the stiffened, feathered body. "He was with me for several long years, Alyssa. I knew his time was coming. This sudden cold snap must have been too much for the old fellow." Victor put the little body into his coat pocket, out of her sight. "He's flying free now and in a much better place, I'm sure."

Alyssa swiped at her nose, sniffed loudly and then dug out her notebook and pen. "*So much death Victor, so many dead, I wish I could turn back time and have Gio and Cesare and the others back...*" she enjoyed talking to Victor now, she wasn't about to clam up on her Uncle and in fact he was one of the very few she felt she could talk openly to. She had dearly missed seeing him since the day of the shooting.

"I know child." Victor nodded solemnly and she could see sadness in the great *Padrone's* eyes as well. "I know." He simply said recognizing her feelings of loss and mourning. "I miss them too, each and every one of them." He pulled her close again and gave her a warm hug and a kiss on the top of her head, slamming down his own emotions.

A good Don felt the loss of any of their men, they were all his responsibility and even though the Jerome's had been successful in their war, it didn't negate the fact that he was keenly aware of the ultimate sacrifice made by those who had died in the line of duty to the Family and the pain of those left behind. He had just gotten done talking with Lisa Ciccerone and Clarissa Fantenelli earlier. Patrizio was one of his best friends and oldest colleagues who had been with Victor since before he was the boss, and Cesare, the man had great potential and the ability to have made a wonderful consigliere, because he truly cared about his fellow compari's.

Alyssa hugged Victor tightly, savoring the familiar smell of his aftershave and peppermints on him, drawing warmth and strength from his body. She then gently released him and began writing again. Her body was now near numb from being out here so long was shivering and struggling to hold the pen, her body one mass of exquisite pain and stiffness. With a trembling hand she wrote out: "*Also I am hurt inside. I opened my heart and soul to someone who didn't share the same feelings. In fact he backed away rather fast, leaving me feeling totally stupid and embarrassed for opening up so much and worse, even thinking I could be loved by this person...*"

"Martel?" Victor eyed her levelly, his voice soft and understanding.

It only made the heartache that much worse. "*What?? He went and told you everything? Figures!*"

"Martel told me nothing." Victor's dark eyes looked deeply into hers with absolute frankness. "I or anyone else needs only to see your face whenever you are near him or hear his name mentioned, and now to feel your heartbreak and confusion over this."

"*So I guess your advice will be to 'get over it' and not make the same mistake twice.*" Alyssa scrawled out, mostly to quell the mind numbing pain in her half frozen hands.

Victor took the pad of paper from out of her hands and then cupped her frozen hands in his old ones, warming them with his own body heat, again those piercing eyes of his seemed to see within the darkest parts of her soul, to understand her like only he or Martel could. "Listen to me well, *cara mia*." He said, "You need to follow what is in your heart, in your soul. I happen to know something that you don't." he said, his eyes teasing lightly but speaking honestly "And that is, that the person you speak of, is also going through the same internal pain as you. His words to you were hollow and for the wrong reason. He didn't really mean what he said and said his words because he truly does care about you, not because he doesn't share your feelings. Listen with your heart and not just your ears and you will know this to be true."

Alyssa stood there dumbfounded again, her mind reeling, what was Victor saying? Could his words be true? She fought to replay the scene that day with Martel in the Office and desperately tried to see it from another perspective. Her heart was too fresh with pain and she was not the 'Arbitrator' and master that Victor was at reading people, so at the moment she just didn't see it. But she listened to what the Don was telling her, really listened.

"I am not going to give you the advice on the lovelorn, Alyssa." Victor gently explained, "But heed my words. You are not the only one hurting or confused right now. Do what you think you must, what your heart tells you to. If you don't, then the two of you might very well drift further and further away. If it is meant to be, it will be; but both of you need to be brutally honest with one another." He let go of her hands and took his leather gloves and gently placed them on her icy cold hands, as a father might to a beloved child.

"Now, I have said all I am going to say on that matter." He said ending the subject gently but succinctly, "I am freezing cold out here and I know you are as well. There is to be a nice dinner tonight, celebrating our ending of the *mannagge* with the D'Salvatores and to mourn the Family we lost." He quietly but firmly explained. "We are both going back to the house." He neatly replaced his own hat on his head and held his arm out to her.

There was no arguing with Victor, so Alyssa gently and lovingly held onto her uncle's arm as they both exited the Aviary and walked over to the Jerome-1 Limo where Nick was now opening the door for the two of them.

"Dominick," Victor called the guard by his given name, "Give him a burial somewhere appropriate, eh?" he winked privately at his elite guard as he placed the expired body of Peppi in the guards large gloved hand, then slid into the back seat with Alyssa.

Nick looked at the stiff body of the bird and wondered 'why me?' but of course what he said aloud was "Sure Mr. Jerome, no problem." He would dump the bird in the trash later after dropping off the boss and his niece.

Once she got inside she went to change and shower to warm up, placing her morning dose of pain meds with her 3 other doses. She took two of the codeine pills, or she knew she wouldn't be moving at all during dinner and because the pain of her injury was now near unbearable from sitting for hours on the cold cement floor of the aviary. She half debated returning the rest of the unused pain meds but a small plan was beginning to form in the back of her mind.

Lena and Vito had returned back to the Estates for the party so Lena had helped Alyssa brush out her hair, apply some make up and helped her dress for tonight's dinner. Alyssa had picked out a fairly nice dress since she could see Lena was dressed up and since she knew it was to be a semi-formal dinner.

Arrigo Salvaggio was back as well and he seemed to go between looking dour and forlorn whenever he saw Alyssa. It then dawned on her with a womans intuition that the Sicilian bodyguard was finding her attractive and she could feel as though Arrigo was trying to see what her feelings were about him, or to try and start a relationship her.

Whenever Lena was around he seemed silently dour and acted as a professional but whenever Lena was not there, he spoke to her like Len did, in that soft silky voice and was always trying to caress her arm or touch her. Not rudely, but honestly and sincerely, as though he was trying to convey what he truly felt about her. She saw it mostly with her eyes in the way Arrigo looked at her almost longingly and hopeful, his dark eyes filled with protective desire and want. It was perhaps the only time she was grateful that she didn't understand Italian, because her heart and soul was only for Laurence Martel and she had no idea how she would have even explained to Arrigo that she just wasn't interested in him as a potential lover.

Dinner was a large occasion with loads of food and the place jammed to the rafters with Jerome men and wives and the visiting

Bonnaro's people as well. Alyssa noted that Laurence Martel looked especially handsome in his dark suit and tie and as Victor had truthfully said, there indeed seemed to be some inner pain and torment in his icy blue eyes. Sadly, Martel seemed to be avoiding her at all costs and stayed constantly glued to Victor or Joshua and gave her no opportunity to try and get him alone to talk to him.

As with most of the mixed parties that had ladies and men present, the women stayed in groups by themselves off to one section and the men pretty much stayed off by themselves in another area, or wandered in and out of The Office when they wanted utter privacy or to talk 'business'. Only the bodyguards on duty seemed to mingle freely here and there.

Before the dinner Victor had made an eloquent toast to those who survived and to those who had been lost in the war, he also vaguely hinted that soon "Good news" would be announced within the next week or so that would benefit all of them, Jerome's and Bonnaro's alike. Alyssa noted he spoke his toast first in English and then Italian for the non-English speaking guests, and then finally ended with the solemn "*Buon' anima...*Rest their souls. *Salute!*"

"*Buon' anima, Salute!*" nearly everyone said at the same time, as they raised their glasses of sparkling wine or champagne to the two Don's, celebrating them.

Before the men and women had broken off in separate groups, Victor had come up to her during dessert, she was sitting between Tommy DeLuca and Lena Bonnaro, and standing behind her chair he hugged her tightly, kissed her head and said to everyone, "*Mia cara nipote*, I owe her my life twice, eh? She is truly *mi portafortuna* and *mia angelo custode*. My good luck charm and Guardian Angel." This statement bought smiles and nods from both Jerome and Bonnaro families. Then like the good host and diplomat that he was, Don Jerome drifted around to all his various guests offering happiness or condolences.

Alyssa had penned out a sincere letter of apology to Tommy when she first sat down next to him at dinner, for her earlier behavior at the Aviary towards him and her breaking her promise to him.

"Ah, don't worry about it." He brushed it off, "I can imagine these last weeks have been pretty rough on you. It's Ok, Alyssa." He lightly bumped her shoulder in the playful way Gio Aprile used to. "Just don't do it again, Ok?" he added with a wink.

Even Joshua had come over to her and spoke briefly to her ear, "It's good to see you 'Lyss. Hope you are feeling better." he gave her shoulder an almost too strong squeeze, "And stop giving my guards a hard time, Ok?" his dark eyes were both serious and playful at the same time. She nodded 'Yes' and gave his hand a quick squeeze of friendship back and he too moved on. Only Martel stayed notably absent and reserved from nearly everyone, keeping to himself. How she wished he would come over to her, talk to her.

As the men moved off by themselves to smoke cigars and talk, the ladies moved off to the other side and Arrigo followed along with Alyssa, his eyes seeming to bore into her as though hoping she could understand Italian and his heart. Whenever Lena was not right there by her he would sidle up to her and talk to her in a friendly way, his hand lightly brushing against her hand or arm. It was beginning to distinctly make Alyssa very uncomfortable and yet she was resolute not to go complaining to anyone. After all, she was single and he was being a gentleman if not a bit the overly flirty, Italian male.

During one time he had come over with a fresh glass of wine for her and again had begun to flirt lightly with her. While Arrigo was indeed handsome and a gentleman, Alyssa just simply was not interested in his advances, she went to gracefully move off from him; however his hand closed lightly around her wrist as he spoke low to her ear in Italian.

It was then she glanced up, perhaps hoping to find Lena, Clarissa, anyone she could go escape to but her eyes suddenly locked with the sapphire blue eyes of Laurence Martel around 10 feet away seeming to glare icy daggers right at her and Arrigo. She didn't know what to read in the eyes of the underboss, there seemed to be a mixture of jealousy, anger and also an almost eerie detachment all at the same time. Then with a slightly raised eyebrow he simply turned and harshly strode away back towards Victor.

Her heart ached in earnest; did Laurence think she was purposely inviting Arrigo's attentions? Couldn't he see that it was he, her Kageryu that she truly wanted? She wished she could have screamed at that point but her mute throat allowed her no voice.

With a sudden fury she yanked her hand away from Arrigo and glared at him, as she limped off to go find Lena or Rosette. She could feel the stunned and almost heartbroken surprise from Arrigo as she walked off.

"Arrigo," Leonardo calmly walked up to his cousin and stood with him shoulder to shoulder, speaking to his ear only in his home tongue. "We need to talk you and me, eh?" Leonardo watched Alyssa melt back with the other ladies almost hurriedly and with some fear in her eyes. "We need to have a long talk, before you get yourself seriously hurt my cousin." Len firmly guided Arrigo off to the side.

Martel had seen Arrigo talking to Alyssa, touching her; he had caught a few of the man's words to her in Italian, his simple declarations of his feelings to her... "Alyssa, why do you fight me so? Don't you know how much I care about you? If it is done with Martel then allow me to be the one to take care of you. My heart has fallen for you from the first time I met you..." A cold rage grew in the dragon's heart. A part of him wanted to go over and explain in cruel detail, exactly why Arrigo had no business taking care of her; because Kanashii was his!

'Is she?' His own mind taunted, 'didn't you discard her like yesterdays newspaper? Why shouldn't she be allowed to find happiness and someone to take care of her? Isn't that what you wanted you big *cafone*?'

He slammed his inner emotions down. 'What exactly do you want?' His mind bore into his heart and soul. 'For her to be happy and safe.' he tried to reason with himself.

He must have glared at her and Arrigo a bit longer, or harsher than he intended for he saw Leonardo Tagretta glance at him then, a touch of worry in the capo's eyes.

'Center yourself Kageryu; if you are going to set her free, then do so. You cannot have it both ways.' He pulled his gaze away and then abruptly walked off.

Chapter 38-

    Later that evening back in her room, Alyssa tossed and turned. There was no way she could get comfortable nor would sleep come to her. Her mind kept replaying the conversation of Martel's words in the office that day, and then the sadness of the loss of those she cared about and finally the hopeful words Victor had spoken to her in the Aviary earlier. "…You <u>are not</u> the only one hurting or confused right now. Do what you think you must, what your heart tells you to. If you don't, then the two of you might very well drift further and further away. If it is meant to be, it will be; But both of you need to be brutally honest with one another."

She sat up abruptly ignoring the sharp stab of pain in her back… No, enough was enough. She was going to talk to Martel damn it, make him listen, say what she had wanted to write in her heart that day in the office that she couldn't.

"…His words to you were hollow and for the wrong reason, he didn't really mean what he said, and said his words <u>because he truly does care about you,</u> not because he doesn't share your feelings…" Victor's words resounded with calm strength in her mind and she knew then that Martel did still indeed care about her. Had he not, he would never have glared at her the way he did when Arrigo was trying to flirt with her.

    Dragging herself out of bed and pulled open the draw on the nightstand, inside were 5 of the codeine tablets. She dug them out then swallowed all 5 of them at once with a large gulp of water. She was going to make her teacher listen to what was in her heart, and they were going to settle this.

She glanced at her bedside clock and saw it read nearly 2:20 am; well she knew he would be home. She hastily pulled on a warm fleecy pair of sweatpants and a cozy dark blue short-sleeved sweatshirt and then struggled to put on her socks and shoes. Her aching and healing back rebelled the whole time but she had anger coursing in her now, and she simply willed the pain to the background of her mind.

Cautiously she opened her door; surprised that there was no guard there. Either he was on break, or they simply stopped guarding her. She had a feeling it was the fact that since Victor Jerome had now formally adopted her, there was no need to guard her anymore. After all, she was one of them now, safe, an "insider" and a full-fledged family member of Victor Jerome's; his true niece.

She quietly trudged down to the kitchen area where she could hear the voices of a few guards and silky accented tones of one man she instantly recognized, Leonardo Tagretta. As soon as she walked into the kitchen a sudden deafening silence descended and several of the guards looked at her with stern if not concerned glances. They had been sitting around a small table playing cards, smoking and talking amongst themselves.

Leonardo was instantly on his feet and walked over to her. "What's the matter Miss Alyssa? You no can sleep?"

She dug into her purse and pulled out her notepad and pen. "*Leonardo, I need a huge favor, please.*" She held up the notepad for him, her eyes must have been alive with pleading and emotion.

"It depend." he pulled her over by the side where they could talk in private, "What do you need, eh?"

"*I need someone to drive me down to Martel's house. I must speak with him NOW, it's very important. Please Leonardo!!!*" her hands nearly trembling with emotion.

"I don't know Alyssa," Len frowned a moment, "it's kinda late eh? I don't think Mr. Martel want to be disturbed at two in the morning."

"PLEASE!!!" she underlined the word several times, then looked into Len's eyes, her heart pleading with him, conveying emotions and words that could not be said aloud or expressed on paper.

For several long seconds she and Tagretta looked deeply into one another's eyes. He knew that some emotional conflict was going on between her and Martel and he had told his cousin, Arrigo, earlier to knock it off with trying to put the moves on her. After all, Martel and Leonardo were close friends and Len had seen with his own eyes how close Alyssa and Martel were, even if his teacher Martel fought it.

Len knew how his own heart had felt about a dear girlfriend he had lost back In Sicily because he had not said the right things at the right time. They had been dating, but he was a rising soldier in the Bonnaro Family, putting off his relationship with her, she ended up in heartbreak marrying another man in the Bonnaro Family and Len still kicked himself for not marrying his soul mate. While he had many women and

496

comare, he had never found another who he loved as much as his first love, Sophia, who now belonged to another. It was one of the reasons he had agreed so willingly to come here to the states and stayed.

"Ok, Ok." His quiet voice soothed. "Let me get my coat and car keys, eh?"

He spoke briefly to his fellow crew and pointed briefly at Alyssa and then went to the closet near the kitchen to grab his leather jacket and gloves. It was only 25 degrees out there, bitterly cold for him.

Alyssa had limped over to the front room closet where she grabbed her own denim jacket. As she waited in the semi-dark foyer near the living room she caught sight of her book 'Easy International Sign Language' resting on one of the elegant marble topped tables. She quickly scooped it up and thrust it inside her jacket.

Leonardo now in his expensive jacket came back into the living room, his hair tightly retied in his ponytail and thin leather gloves on his hands. "Ok, let's go, eh? I notta have all night for this nonsense, you know." He tried to sound gruff, but with his understanding of the love between her and Martel it was hard for him to sound intimidating with her.

He offered her his strong hand to balance on and escorted her to his car, an elegant and sporty Porsche. The car was immaculately cared for and spotless. He helped her inside and then slid behind the wheel, the car started instantly with a deep growl of its sporty engine. "Ok, here we go." Len said gently and shifted the car into first gear.

Alyssa was quickly beginning to form a strong feeling of deep trust for Leonardo Tagretta the more she interacted with him. She could tell he was professional with his work and the *Famiglia*, but yet he was one of the few who knew how to also allow his heart to care for those who were in the Family with him. She glanced at him, thankfulness and gratitude for him in her eyes.

He mumbled something briefly in Italian under his breath and then said, "Let it be known that I not one to interfere in the ways of *amore'*, eh? I hope you know whatta you doing Alyssa. I truly hope it work out for you."

She just lightly touched his arm in gratitude and signed "*Thank you*" as she had learned from her book, then stared straight ahead again as his sporty car slowly drove down towards the darkened area where Laurence Martel's house was nestled in.

As they pulled into the driveway, only the small lights that illuminated the outer Japanese garden and walkway was softly lit up, every thing else was as dark as the grave at the underboss' house. Before Len's Porsche had even come to a complete stop she had flung the car door open and nearly leaped out.

"*Figlio di puttana!! Cazzo!*" Len yelped, "Are you nuts? Wait!" He was surprised she had not went under the wheels of his car or fallen down.

497

Alyssa dragged herself resolutely up the sidewalk, she could feel the codeine beginning to kick into her body now, her pain beginning to rapidly diminish and she had adrenaline and her own inner turmoil to fuel her on. She knew that Laurence Martel never locked his front door when he was home, after all, who was going to bother him here in the secure Jerome Estates with its deadly electric fence and patrolling guards?

Leonardo looked like he might have a heart attack right there on the spot as he saw her fling open the Martel's front door and simply walk in! Was she crazy? Didn't she know the deadly martial arts assassin and underboss could easily kill her before she got 10 feet in his house? One did not just bust into Laurence Martel's house like they owned it in the dead of night. In many ways Leonardo Tagretta knew Martel a lot better than she did and you didn't just surprise the man when he was sleeping unless you had a death wish.

Gut instinct kicked in then and Leonardo began sprinting towards the house, using the only way he knew to diffuse this potentially deadly situation, his voice. "Martel!" he screamed, "Martel *calmati, stai fermo*! It's Alyssa! It's Alyssa and Len!!!"

After flinging open the door she walked into the dark house, she could hear Len screaming something outside. After getting about 5 feet inside; she suddenly remembered to take her shoes off, as Martel always requested. She bent down to take off her shoes when she was dimly aware of something that had sailed right past her shoulder like a dark whispering breeze and buried itself into the wall with a soft '*Tink!*'

Every hair on her body stood on end and she suddenly felt as afraid as she did that day down in his basement. She stayed half crouched and didn't dare move a single muscle; somehow she knew if she did, she would be in grave danger.

"Martel, it's us! No shoot! *Essere facile!*" Len skidded into the living room and years of training as a bodyguard and a Man of Honor made him leap right in front of Alyssa, shielding her. "It's us, boss!" Len knew Alyssa had known no better. He felt his own hair prickling dangerously in the tense situation.

The lights instantly snapped on and Alyssa saw Laurence standing there in the hallway, with just his usual black pants on and no shirt. The giant's eyes were like two blue lasers of deadly anger. In one large hand his Berretta was pointed dead center at Leonardo's chest and in the other was some small metal object. It was then she saw the small oriental morning star embedded in the wall. Had she not bent down when she did it would have caught her in the neck or shoulder.

Martel quickly and angrily snapped the safety on the gun and thrust it into his waistband and she saw the dark look in his eyes leave as recognition of the two people in front of him sank in. She prayed she would never see that look in his eyes again, for she had a feeling it was the last look many of his victims saw before they died.

"Boss, *perdonare*, I sorry." Leonardo put his hands up in a placating gesture, "She just bolted in here! I tried to stop her, she is very determined..." Len seeing that Martel was awake now smoothly stepped away from Alyssa.

"So she is." Martel discreetly slipped the two other martial arts throwing stars into his pocket.

"She insisted on coming down," Len looked at his boss unspoken thoughts between them, "I couldn't let her walk all the way in the cold, eh? She wouldn't have taken no for an answer." He smiled lightly, trying to lighten the mood and then said something to Martel exclusively in Italian for a few moments.

Martel's eyes softened then and he nodded back to Leonardo. "It's all right Len, you did fine *mio tirocinante*. I have it from here. Go back to the house and have a good evening."

Leonardo Tagretta, his blood pressure and adrenaline now slowly cooling back to normal glared briefly down at Alyssa who just stood there, still looking between the two men and the wicked, oriental throwing star embedded deeply in the wall.

Now it was Leonardo's grey eyes that were like two dark angry storms. He muttered something under his breath in Italian at her that she knew was not nice or polite. "*Porco Dio!* You no ever do that to me again, you understand?" his voice while still quiet was filled with a very dark and dangerous edge to it. "You listen to my instructions next time or you get yourself killed! *Pazzo l'donna!*" he angrily shook his head and then strode off quietly closing the door behind him.

Martel casually walked over and easily pulled the razor-sharp throwing star out of the wall. "Bad mistake Kanashii." He said. "You would do well to listen to what Mr. Tagretta tells you next time."

Alyssa felt her heart sink, she had not wanted to come over here and piss off the man she loved, or worse get herself killed! This is not how this was supposed to be going, she had no idea that Martel would have waken up so violently but apparently his own men did. She felt her own shame and remorse at not listening more closely to them. Again she felt the tears of anger and hurt in her eyes, although this time she didn't even bother to try and hide them.

"It's late Alyssa." Martel said in a quiet almost subdued voice, "This couldn't have waited until the morning? I'll get my coat and take you back up to the house."

In her haste to come down here she had forgotten her pen and pad of paper. The codeine tablets she had taken were now fully kicked in, not only totally numbing her physical pain but making her mind more open and uncensored as well. Instinctively and in desperation she signed out to him: "*No! No! You listen now!*" Then she half ran to the kitchen where she knew he kept some paper and a pen.

She could hear him casually following behind her as she rummaged around the drawers got out the pen and paper and then scrawled out. *"We talk now, you and I..."*

Before she had written any more than that, Martel interrupted her and grabbed the pen, easily snatching it out of her hand. "I already told you the other day; I had no intention of hurting you. I apologized if there was a misunderstanding."

In blind rage and inner turmoil she physically swung at him. Why was he taking away her only means to talk to him? He easily deflected her blow, "Kanashii, Settle down." Her teacher instructed in a low, stern voice.

Couldn't he see the inner turmoil in her? Didn't he know how much she cared for him? As she went to grab for the pen in his hand, her sign language book, slid out from her coat and onto the floor.

"Besides," Martel said almost casually as he bent down to scoop up the book, "I think Arrigo Salvaggio is interested in you."

It was a cruel barb and with a grunt of rage she bought her fist down as hard as she could on her teachers shoulder as he was still bent down. However it was like striking a brick wall and had little effect on the giant who stood up with blinding speed.

She went to hit at him again, her body instinctively going into one of the basic martial arts stances he had taught her, she struck again and he just easily caught her hand and held it in a vice-like grip. "Stop!" he ordered in a semi-dangerous tone.

The two of them held that pose for several long seconds, the Dragon holding her small fist in his huge hand and she, the Hawk, glaring at him as unheeded tears streamed down her face.

"Kanashii, why do you do this to me?" His own heart ached in turmoil. Her pain touched him deeply and he was still upset that he had nearly harmed her with the throwing star. Why was she making this so hard? He knew the Arrigo comment had been a cold insult, in fact he couldn't believe that came out of his own mouth. "Because you still do care, you idiot!" Sen's voice seemed to taunt him. "You want her so bad it tears you in half."

Before he could ponder more, she suddenly took one of her legs and actually made a half decent side-kick at him. Of course he just easily twisted and deflected it with his large thigh. There was no way she could even make a dent in him, couldn't she see that? "Don't force me into conflict with you Kanashii-Taka, you cannot win." He tried to speak soothingly, but his eyes were still icy and business like. He lightly thrust her away from him, his hands loosely at his side in case she came at him again. He knew she was injured and recovering from getting shot and he had no want of harming her.

With a sudden dodge she actually spun away from him and ran around the side of the kitchen and drove both of her fists into the wall in utter frustration. "Why is he taking away my every means of communicating with him?" Her heart screamed in agony. In pure rage and frustration she had hit the wall and dodged out of the way of his grab, she knew now there was no way she was going to do any harm to Martel at this point, all she wanted was for him to hear her out, not drag her back up to the house. Victor's words rang in her soul like a mantra: "Do what you think you must, what your heart tells you to. If you don't, then the two of you might very well drift further and further away..."

She utterly trusted Victor, he knew his men like no one else and if he hinted that there was still a chance for her and Martel then she was not going to let it slip by. His 'Arrigo' comment had enraged her; somehow she knew Martel had said it because he too was indeed confused about their relationship, and didn't really want her to be with Arrigo Salvaggio at all. But couldn't the silly Dragon see that she had no want of Arrigo, she only wanted him.

The higher than normal dose of pain meds were flowing through her blood and nerves dulling all physical pain and giving her courage and bravado she would have never had while being sober. The crashing sleepiness of the codeine had not kicked in and all she had right now was the euphoria and the utter relief of her back pain. With a light twist she spun into the living room and began to purposely run right to the martial arts room. Her teacher wanted a conflict she would give him a conflict! He would listen to her. Her heart was aching as much as his and he would listen!

Martel watched Kanashii move with a speed and ease that with her recent injury she should have no business moving at. He began to seriously think she was on an overdose of something and this deeply worried him also. If she couldn't feel normal physical pain then she was in even graver danger of hurting herself. He had seen her ram her fists into his wall, leaving a small break/dent in the drywall. She was definitely feeling no physical pain. He spun also and nimbly followed her, before she did serious damage to his house, him or herself.

With an angered grunt she again drove her fists into the doorframe of his martial arts room, as though challenging him to face her and deal with her. As she sprinted inside and turned on the light, she noticed abruptly that the huge mirrored wall that normally was in here was gone. She saw a few dark splotches here and there and a few small shards of glass near the wall. She wondered what had happened to the mirrored wall, had something hit it? Had some fight between Martel and someone else occurred in here?

This time, she grabbed a quarterstaff from the wall, where the training weapons were. She knew she would have no chance against him in any hand-to-hand conflict and if he got hold of her it would be all over.

As Martel entered the room, he saw her in the center of the workout room with a Bo-staff in her hands, she swung it wildly at him and

501

gripped it in a way that told him she had no idea how to use it or what she was doing; just that she was one pissed off Kanashii.

"Alyssa," he tried one last time to reason with her, "Look, stop. You've already bruised and hurt your hands don't make things worse. Just put down the Bo staff, I'll take you back to the house and we can talk another day…"

But these were the wrong words to say, at the mention of going back to the main Estates she swung wildly at him again. But Martel was an expert and with one graceful move, his foot came up and the tall man swiftly kicked the quarterstaff out of her hands and into the air where he easily caught it one handed in mid-air in an elegant move that both shocked and stunned her.

She just stood there and blinked at him for a moment at the ease in which he was able to disarm her. "Kanashii, quit." He roughly threw the Bo staff into the corner his own eyes darkening now.

Had she been in her right mind, she would have felt the subtle dark-fire and warning tone in his voice. But her inner chaos and hurt at his words and the codeine tablets had her anywhere but her right mind.

A strangled grunt of pure agony and rage echoed in her lungs and throat, coming out no more than a soft inhuman growl of inner pain. 'Why won't you listen to me? Don't slam the door on me Kageryu! God Damn you, don't you see, don't you FEEL how much I care for you? I beg you do not shut the door on me, please!' Her mind and soul screamed. Her mind sank into a dark depression then and she knew in her heart and soul if he didn't want her, it would to be far too painful for her to exist in the same Family with him. She couldn't force him to like her but yet she knew her own heart could never love anyone else but him.

Her mind thought of the deadly electric fence, how Cesare's oldest daughter had accidentally fallen into it and fried to a crisp in a matter of seconds. The charred remains of the large bird of prey she had found one day there also…

No, if Kageryu was going to shut her out of his life forever, then so be it. She knew she could not force him to like or accept her and she would accept that, but her heart was filled with so much pain and emptiness that all she could think of was to join those friends of hers who had died in the *mannagge*. A soft resigned sigh seemed to rattle her very essence, she straightened up and gave him a deep bow of respect and then she turned to go past him and out of his house and life forever.

Martel having worked for many years as an assassin knew the intimate look of death as very few had. He knew when he saw a curtain fall behind her green eyes then that something had shattered deeply and with quiet resolve in her soul, the total lack of the will to live. The look she gave him so seized his heart and for whatever reasons made him think of what the last few moments of Miyoko's life must have been. A determined resolution to accept the utter fate of death, knowing there was no other way out.

"No!" the dragon roared then and snatched her up as she tried to dodge past him. He grabbed her easily and as he did that first night he grappled her down and tried to wrap his long arms and legs around her to restrain and calm her down. However this time there was no calming her, she fought with the strength of one who had so much adrenaline flowing through her and the utter pain and defeat of their soul that they had nothing to lose. She thrashed, struggled and tried to sink her teeth into him, the tears of pain and rage flowing down her cheeks.

Every instinct in him told him to 'choke her out', to use the moves he knew so well and had integrated into his very martial arts moves, the Judo *shime waza,* choke holds. But he also knew she was in total despair and her mind not very stable at this moment; also she obviously was feeling no pain. Never had the big man even debated before on such editing of his own instinctual martial arts moves. He wrapped one arm around her throat as he was behind her and leaned back, actually holding her backwards on top of him as he began to choke her out. His mind concentrated with every effort of his will to bring her to the lightest level of unconsciousness.

As he knew she would, she panicked nearly immediately as his huge arm cut off the blood to her brain, as easily as someone turned off a faucet. He could feel her thrash and struggle above him, could smell the panic coming off of her. Within a few seconds her struggling was already rapidly decreasing, her thrashing becoming more and more erratic and subdued. Her hands came up and almost seemed to plead with him, tapping his arm in a light gentle way, almost as if begging to release her. He knew this was normal as well; many victims who got choked-out did this same unusual move, almost as if before they dropped into unconsciousness (or death) they instinctively pleaded with their attacker. He felt her growing heavier atop him as her hands and legs began to become limp.

Immediately he released her and rolled her over, this time he atop her. Her eyes were partially rolled back into her skull, but because he had taken her only so lightly into the realm of unconsciousness she was already coming around.

The Wounded Hawk's emerald eyes seemed to stare at him balefully for a moment, and then again she began to fight him. "Kanashii, please, Stop! Don't make me do this to you." He said in a low sad tone himself. He swung his leg over her and attempted to hold her down as he had done that one day they had play fought hoping his sheer weight and size alone would be enough to hold her down.

She arched and struggled beneath him as he once again reached down and using his fingers pressed on the triangle of her throat where the carotid veins and arteries were, shutting down the blood to her brain. At one point she had nearly bridged up under him, but then her adrenaline left her, the injury in her back tore and her physical body pushed beyond its limits, simply shut down completely beneath him.

"Oh Kanashii, why do you do this to me, please stop fighting me. Please." he begged. The Undertaker, the man who had kill so many, who could maim in the most cruel and hideous of ways was touched beyond what he ever thought he could feel for this one feisty little hawk; his Kanashii. Again he felt a tear course down his own rough face, and drop onto Kanashii below him, another tear followed it.

This time, he still stayed atop her as he massaged the blood immediately back to her brain but as she came around this time he could see the physical pain and shock in her eyes, could see that the adrenaline-fueled rage and insanity had left her. His fingers instinctively began to sooth the median pressure points along her face and temple, and he immediately removed his full weight from her ribcage, which struggled to breath beneath him.

"Shhh, easy Kanashii. Settle now, settle. I see your pain; we will talk. Please stop fighting me, forgive me." He scooped her up in his arms and carried her to his bedroom. "*Gomennasai, Kanashii Taka.*" He barely whispered to her in Japanese.

She made no move to fight him at all. In fact she just lay surrendered, subdued and unmoving in his arms. Although she still had the codeine flowing through her, she felt the extreme pain in her back and the drug induced tiredness descending upon her. She had no urge to fight the Dragon anymore. The Hawk was completely and utterly grounded.

With the care and medical training he had learned from Cochran, he used his knife to cut away her shirt and examined her back. Thankfully from the outside she had only torn out four stitches, but he had no idea if she had torn anything internally. "Lay still, Kanashii." He quietly ordered as he used her now ruined shirt to lie atop her and loosely cover the wound in her back. He reached over and grabbed his phone, calling up to the main house. "Len, its Martel. Call Weintraub; get him down here for a house call. Thanks." He hung up the phone.

As they waited he made her comfortable and gently massaged her back, talking to her the whole time. "You are one of the most determined, bullheaded and feisty women I have ever known Kanashii. Are you sure you don't have Italian blood flowing somewhere in those veins? I guess it is true what they say about red heads, that you are indeed a spitfire. We will talk Kanashii; we will talk…" he soothed her. Nothing else was spoken by him though at that point while he merely massaged Alyssa into a light healing sleep.

Weintraub arrived at the Jerome estate about an hour later. Alyssa had fallen fast asleep on Martel's bed, unmoving from where he had laid her down. Weintraub and Martel woke her up and drove her down to the clinic here at the estate where they examined her wound and

504

were able to determine that for now, there was no internal tearing they could see beneath the flesh.

"We'll know more in the next few days, I don't think she tore any of the deep stitches though." Weintraub groused. "Just what the fuck was going on anyway? How did she injure herself?" he growled angrily at Martel.

Martel just met the doctor's hard eyes with his own cold stare. "Nothing doc," He calmly said, like his father, letting the doctor know he wasn't going to get the full tale. "A minor disagreement, but everything is fine now..." Martel's eyes seemed to bore into the doctor's soul, "everything will be just fine." He said as he grabbed one of the nearby suture kits.

"Well, it damn sure better..." Weintraub trailed off, "Jesus, Laurence." He looked up at the man, not really knowing what to say as together they finished cleaning up her wound and re-stitching it.

The whole time Alyssa had just lain there unmoving, uncomplaining, as though her inner soul was as numb as the rest of her. She had no more desire to run and fry herself on the electric fence, now she could only hope that when she and Martel talked he would truly see and understand what was in her heart and soul. Right now she was just so exhausted, in pain and tired.

"How many of those damn pain pills are you all feeding her?" John Thomas looked at her stoned eyes. "How many did you have darlin'?" he asked her. She wearily held up 5 fingers and waggled them at the doctor. "Well, since she's not on any other medication and she isn't showing any toxic side effects she should just sleep it off, I don't think there is any reason to give her a reversal drug. Just supervise her, make sure she sleeps on her side tonight and check her breathing in case it gets shallow, but she's looking pretty stable right now." Weintraub glared at both of them. "Keep her that way." He darkly ordered Martel. "I'll recheck her again tomorrow. I'll sleep here at the Estate for tonight just in case."

"Thanks doc." Laurence said softly, he was grateful for the old Family friend and physician. "I truly mean that."

"Yeah well..." Weintraub hemmed and harrumphed. He was always uncomfortable with receiving praise, he just did his job. "By the way, the game was a good one." He winked at Martel; in reference to the tickets Martel had gotten him a couple weeks ago and then yawned loudly. "I think we're all beat..." John Thomas announced. "Darlin'," he tapped Alyssa's shoulder, "How ya feeling?"

She gave him a thumbs-up sign. She was simply exhausted and now almost rather embarrassed at the rage that had come out of her own heart driving her to such madness, it made her understand how Joshua Demonico could lose his temper so easily. All she wanted to do now was shut down and sleep.

She was vaguely aware of Martel driving her to his home and then carrying her to the large king sized bed in his room, placing her in it. "Tonight you sleep it off, Kanashii. We will talk tomorrow when you are more awake and sober." He climbed into bed next to her determined to get a few more hours of rest himself. He noticed that as he lay there, she even in her half drowsed state this time turned towards him and pulled herself over, laying her head against his powerful chest.

He felt such warmth, desire and protection of her, as one of his long arms loosely wrapped around her shoulders. They would both lay this way unmoving and sleeping for the next 5 hours.

Chapter 39- *October 22nd 1987*

Victor sat downstairs with his men at breakfast the next morning. Talk was still drifting from everything to the Jerome's victory over the D'Salvatores, to which of the Bonnaro men wanted to stay on with the Jerome's full-time, after Vito and Lena returned back to Sicily.

It made Victor's heart feel good to see the house so full again of people and families. "Where is my niece this morning?" he had asked no one in particular.

"Leonardo said she went to talk to Martel late last night." Tommy DeLuca said to the boss.

"Ah, good," He mumbled under his breath, the fact that she must still be down there spoke well for the encounter.

"Yeah well, whatever happened down there, those two need to be a lot gentler with one another." Weintraub groused as he grabbed his own plate of breakfast, "G'morning, Vic." he mumbled.

"Why? What happened?" Victor asked casually.

"Hell, I dunno all the details. She had somehow ripped out a few of her stitches, but no information I could get out of either of them." The doctor sat down near his old friend, "emotionally they both seemed fine but offered no details."

"And this surprises you?" Victor chuckled and eyed his old friend.

"No, not really," Weintraub buttered his two English muffins, "I've never lived with so many people who can say so little about everything."

This bought a lot of chuckles from all the men; the code of omerta amongst the Jerome's was legendary. It was one of the vows they all took very seriously and it pleased Victor to know his niece was now taking it just as seriously. He had not made an error in accepting her; she truly was one of them in his heart and soul.

"I'll be checking her out later before I head back into the city, but I want to check you out this morning as well." The doctor eyed Victor the way a vampire eyes his victim.

"You have been looking a bit under the weather yourself you know..."

"In case you haven't noticed John Thomas, I've been busy! But, none-the-less, I will be generous and let you poke and prod, besides, I will be going into retirement soon, so you see, I will be living a lot more stress free." The old crime lord teased his friend good-naturedly.

Joshua Demonico who had entered the room and heard this last statement just stared at Victor. He knew there was to be restructuring in the Family, but Victor Jerome retiring? Who would be at the reins? He knew better to even ask Victor about it though and simply kept his mouth shut. All of the men would be finding out the biggest secret soon enough.

For once it was John Thomas who actually knew and had and inkling of what Victor spoke of, he simply raised an eyebrow and looked deeply at his friend. 'So you are finally turning it over to Theodore, are you?' His mind pondered. He smiled grimly to Victor, it had taken him so long and he had worked so hard to call the man 'Laurence Martel' and now he was going to have to learn to call him Theodore again.

"I think you just like making my life miserable, you persnickety-old-coot." John Thomas flung the barb at his lifelong friend.

"But of course I do, you broken-down sawbones." Victor smiled back at him. "It's my job." Around them all the men laughed, the grumpy old men were at it again.

Alyssa woke up as she felt her bedmate stir and gently unwrap his arm from around her. Her whole body was one mass of sore, aching muscles. The site where she had been shot and re-stitched up was throbbing as were as her knuckles, which were bruised and swollen; both injuries seemed to be throbbing in time with her heartbeat which was pounding in her head mercilessly. With a deep rattling sigh of discomfort she tried to roll over and out of bed.

"No more codeine for you." Martel said as he nimbly left the bed and walked into his master bathroom. He pulled out some Tylenol, some of his massage oil and some herbal capsules. He carried them all back into the bedroom, placed them on the bed, and then unwrapped the bandages on his own hand, so as not to get the massage oil on his bandages. He dropped a couple Tylenol and the herbal capsules on the table in front of Alyssa and got her some water to wash them down with.

Alyssa had immediately noticed the angry wounds on his left knuckles, wondering where he had gotten the injury from, and if it had anything to do with the broken mirrored wall in the martial arts workout room. She hungrily gulped down the pills when he returned with the water, hoping they would soon quell the soreness and pain. She noticed Martel seemed to move a little slow himself today. Not like he was in any physical pain, but almost as if he had some invisible weight on him, it was as though there seemed to be a million thoughts on the Shadow Dragon's mind.

"Lie on your stomach, Kanashii." Martel had simply said, as he began to rub the aromatic sweet oil on his hands. "I will talk some, we will eat breakfast and then I will listen to whatever you have to say to say to me."

She nodded as he helped her pull off her nightshirt and she rolled over onto her stomach. He sat next to her and began to massage her sore aching muscles. His healing touch was pure heaven. Somehow he always knew exactly the right combination of pressure and technique to heal, relax and bring relief to her body.

For several long minutes he said nothing, simply centered his mind and soul to the task at hand and finding the sore spots on Kanashii, went about relieving her pain and discomfort as he feel her body respond and relax to his healing touch.

"As promised, I will listen to whatever you have to say, shortly. But first I want you to hear what I have to say. Why I acted the way I did, why I said the things to you I said." His weary, baritone voice finally began. "There are going to be a lot of changes in the *Famiglia* as you can imagine from all this. With those close friends we lost like Gio and Cesare, and others out of the loop for awhile…" he eluded, "Like Carmine and Rocco and several others. New faces will be moving in permanently from the Bonnaro Family like Arrigo and a few others." Martel continued his healing work on her occasionally his hand caressing softly her neck or shoulder. "I'm sure it will be hectic with them settling in, learning English and other things. Other changes will be happening as well. Victor will be retiring soon from working…" he paused here for a several long moments as he watched Alyssa's rather surprised reaction. "There will be a new *padrone* to run our Family."

Alyssa turned her head and glanced behind her as though her mind seem to already know who this new *Padrone* would be.

"Yes, Kanashii, it will be me, and that is why at first I didn't want to continue our …" he paused, "our being together." He shifted positions and continued the massage of her, "But I realized that may have been a mistake." He said dryly, with a slight smirk on his face, "Obviously you are a very determined woman. But there is more to the tale, something that is going to be announced openly that I may have misjudged in how you will react to."

He sat back and she turned and looked at him full on, not at all ashamed of being topless in front of him. Alyssa noticed that he did glance at her body quite appreciatively.

"Alyssa." He said with honesty, his blue eyes peering deep into hers. "There is a very important truth you need to know. Number one, I am not who you think I am…"

She just stared at him for a moment. If he wasn't her 'Kageryu', her Martel, that she felt she knew, then who was he? But then again she had underestimated his reaction upon being woken up suddenly, so she just sat quietly and listened to him.

"…I think you deserve the truth, I trust you to keep the secret. After all, it will be announced soon enough." He sighed a moment and then settled next to her on the bed in a cross-legged position. Then the tall underboss spoke briefly and honestly about who he truly was. The son of Victor Jerome, how he had been raised in Europe, how he had spent many years in Vietnam and Japan. He obviously didn't go into detail about all he did and what his life had encompassed. Many of these things he had not even told his own father. Only Sen perhaps knew much of what had happened with Martel while he was in Asia, but even Sen did not know all the dark secrets that lurked in Martel's heart, what he had learned from Cochran. He spoke openly how he had been engaged to marry Miyoko, but how she had been used as a pawn in a vendetta against him. Again he did not go into the details of what had happened, only mentioned that she had been used against him and killed because of her connection to him.

"…I worried at first that if I opened up to you, took you into my life that I would be setting myself up for a repeat of what had happened with Miyoko. However, some more rational minds have convinced me that this could happen regardless and at any time whether you are with me or not.

"I was wrong in not giving you the benefit of the doubt in your own strong personality. You have proven you are indeed made of pretty stern stuff. That you have adapted to this thing of ours, to the Family and to our way of life is proof of this. My father has even called you his *portafortuna e angelo custode,* which translates as; a good luck charm and Guardian Angel. My father, our *Padrone* is a sage and wise man who I respect very much. If he calls you these things then it because he indeed means it."

Martel reached out and one of his hands caressed her soft cheek. "I do not really want you to go to Arrigo, and I do not want you to go away. I had only said that in order to protect you and myself as well, but I have decided it is only fair you deserve a say in this." He nimbly got off the bed and went and got a pen and pad of paper and returned and handed her the items.

"This life is not easy." Martel said again, this time he stood by the bed next to her, his hands loosely clasped in front of him. He looked both intimidating and yet weary at the same time. The sapphire eyes radiating honesty and yet a hundred emotions at once that Alyssa could not fully read. "You were not born into it so I don't expect you to fully understand, but you have shown us, shown me, that you are willing to accept and embrace it. If you want to be at my side, then you should know the downfalls, my beloved Kanashii." He spoke honestly but gently to her, "You or I could be killed, or jailed. We will frequently be spied on by the F.B.I, police and rival *Brugads*, or Families. There will be times I will keep very erratic hours, and times that like Lena; I will need you to be strong, wise and a true unquestioning partner.

"You will need to understand that no matter how close our hearts become, the *Famiglia* must always come first as an entity, it is just the way it is and has always been with all couples who are in this way of life. The Family will always be first in my life, especially if I am to now be its *padrone*, and it must be first in yours as well, so far as in understanding what I need to do.

"As before you will occasionally see and hear things and you must keep *omerta*, known as the 'code of silence' to all outsiders, at all times and around those you know are not a part of this life. People like Dr. Weintraub, DeLoccasio or our helicopter pilot Albert and others who are not a true part of us.

"You must understand that as before you will be treated with reverence and respect as long as you follow the rules and codes that have been handed down. You in turn must have respect for the Men of Honor in the Jerome Family, especially now as the wife of the *Padrone*." He looked strictly down at her then, blue eyes boring into her, "Which means if Len Tagretta tells you to 'wait' and not run in my house, you WILL listen to him. Which means if one of the guards gives you an order and tells you that you should remain inside for your protection, that you WILL listen to them..." he relaxed then and sat back down next to her.

"I have lived for nearly my entire life having to take care of no one but myself, watching out for no one but me, and so you must be patient with me if I occasionally make an error or don't seem as romantic or up-to-date on things as say Arrigo or Leonardo. I am just not used to having someone underfoot and constantly in my life in that way, however I am certainly willing to give it a go. I want to open that door to you Alyssa, my Kanashii, if you are willing to open that door to me."

She sat there stunned for a few moments, her heart slamming within her chest. He was inviting her into his life, far more deeply than she had even thought he would, or had dared hope. Before her he sat with just a quiet and calm expectation on his face, and yet her own body was nearly trembling with excitement and happiness. Of course she was willing to! Of course she would do whatever Martel, Theodore, Kageryu asked her!

She had been stunned at first when he had confessed that he was really Victor Jerome's son, but then a part of her was not really surprised at all. He and Victor were in so many ways alike, as much as they were different. Both had the uncanny ability to seem to read her deepest thoughts, to see into her heart. Both seemed truly born to this life and while they were both indeed different; Victor the great blinding sun, and Theodore the subtle but equally powerful force behind the sun, she knew in her heart that she could truly not love any man but him.

Tears of happiness came unheeded to her eyes, he had known how she felt, and more importantly he felt the same way! She bent down over the pad of paper and wrote feverishly; "*Oh Martel, Theodore, Kage, whomever… Your name is not important. What I wrote that day in the note is still how I feel. I LOVE YOU, you big ol' fool! I will do all of the above that you asked and spoke about, I am willing to make whatever sacrifices I must, I only ask to be in your life, no more no less.*" she handed him the notebook, and saw his eyes light up in that same way they always did when he had inner happiness in him.

With a totally straight face, he looked up at her and signed, "*OK*", with his large, elegant fingers.

Her heart soared even higher, he had read her book! Not only had he read it but also he was communicating to her in the wonderful unspoken language. She signed back, "*Ok,*" and "*I love you.*"

"Whoa, I'm not that far along." He pleaded gracefully. "I still have a lot to learn from the book, but we will learn it together."

"*It meant, 'I Love you'.*" she wrote out. "*And I do love you.*"

"I love you, Alyssa." He got back up and went to one of drawers and pulled out that small black lacquer box that she had given him from Sen.

It seemed like ages ago she had given that box to him, but yet it was less than a few months ago. He opened it up and showed her that it contained two elegant Kanji on silver chains. She recognized both the Kanji, one for Kageryu and one for Kanashii. His long fingers plucked out the one that said Kageryu and held it up. "Will you marry me, Kanashii?" he asked in a quiet tone, his deep voice filling her with the vibrations and resonance of its power.

He truly was a Man of Honor, as strong and powerful as his father and she knew he would make an excellent Don and husband. 'Yes', she nodded with a big grin on her face and then also signed out 'yes' with her hand.

"Then accept this as my token of our pledge to one another." He said as his long fingers fastened the Kanji around her neck that held his sign. "So as you wear my name, I shall be close to your heart." He said. After fastening it around her, he nodded at her to encourage her to do the same with the other Kanji.

With steady fingers, her small hands gently lifted the Kanji that said 'Kanashii', and he bent down so she could fasten it around his muscular neck. She then wrote out; "*So as you wear my name, I shall also be close to your heart*" and smiled at him.

"So you will, my Kanashii, so you will." He said and drew her close, doing what he had wanted to for a long time, embracing her fully in his arms. She was truly his now.

She felt the arousal of her own body, the need of him, and she kissed him full and deeply on the lips, as she felt his large hands caressing her body and her breasts.

The large dragon awoke with his full arousal and love and he lay her down beneath him, his hands running along the entire length of her petite body beneath him. Who's face do you see Kageryu? His mind asked in total serene peace...

The face of my beloved Kanashii, she who is to be my mate and my beloved wife.

The two of them made love then in his bed, he careful not to harm her back, but both of them were fiery and intense in their passions and she gave of herself to him fully and utterly. The Hawk and Dragon danced high above the earth in a dance that was theirs alone, one of love and total entwining.

As they both climaxed together he growled in her ear with a resonance that shook her very bones and sinew; "*Appartieni a me, anima e corpo!*" You are mine, body and soul.

She hung onto him and even though she had no idea what he had said to her in Italian, she released herself fully and utterly to him, giving all of herself in heart, mind and body to him; her soulmate, husband and her 'Dragon'. Whether he was the future *Padrone* of the Jerome Family, or an underboss, or a simple blue collar worker she would always love him and stand by him.

Afterwards they showered together, and Kageryu gently helped her bathe under the warm water; temporarily putting some plastic over her stitches to keep them dry.
Then quietly they worked side by side in the kitchen to whip up a late brunch just as they always had before; A comfortable silence and partnership flowing between them, two together working as one.

As they sat down to eat, he looked at her with a rather mischievous glance in his eyes, "Now, Kanashii." He barely was able to keep the smile off his face, "Was there something you wanted to talk to me about?"

Trying to keep her own grin off her face, she shook her head at him, then picked up a grape and flung with a deadly accuracy it at her teacher.

He of course neatly and easily caught it out of mid-air and casually ate it. "So I take that as a 'no' my feisty one." He chuckled softly.

Theodore had of course later that day told his father about his taking Alyssa as his fiancée. The old man had simply smiled and looked as though it was no surprise and he had known it to be all along. "She will do fine, my son." Victor said as he and Theodore sat alone in the Office, up at the main house. "I am glad you two were able to work it out. She will make a good partner for you." He said almost serenely.

"Are you always so damn sure of yourself Father?" Theo asked with a warm smile on his face as he poured him and his father some wine.

"Who me?" Victor chuckled ambiguously; "Maybe it just seems that way sometimes. I read people well eh? You have the same ability Theo, I've seen it in you time and time again, believe me. Trust your instinct and your gut feeling, especially now when you are to soon be the head of this family. Believe me when I confess to you there have been times I have taken my cue on someone or a situation by watching you and your slight reactions. You definitely have the gift of accurate insight and instinct."

The two men sat in silence a few moments drinking their wine and enjoying each other's company. "I have already begun to set things up for your taking over the Family with the other *Brugads*." Victor said matter-of-factly. "Of course the Corella's and Del Giorno's are fine with it and will welcome you with open arms as will the DiMones down in Miami. Calavicci not surprisingly is grousing about the whole thing, but then they were always obtuse D'Salvatore supporters, same with the Giancomo's. But they know better than to cause too many problems, especially with the strength of the Bonnaro's still as our allies and supplying additional muscle. We are still firmly on the Commission, for now, but your own force of will and strength will now have to hold the Family on it." Victor nodded honestly.

"I know," Theodore refilled their glasses, "That is not unexpected. Nor is Calavicci's open defiance with us, but I feel it is all empty words, no one wants any open warfare after what just happened with the D'Salvatores."

"No, no indeed." Victor smiled wanly, "The D'Salvatores will rebuild with a new Administration, and since there are no more bloodlines of D'Salvatores to the throne, we can approach them in a few months or years with a delegation of peace. Who knows who will run the Family now, probably whichever capos emerge that are the strongest."

Victor sat thoughtfully for a few moments. "And as I mentioned, there is so much legitimate avenues now for the Jerome's, thanks to my long planning and the Bonnaro's assistance. You have assets in Investments, overseas banking, Import/Export, waste management, and supply for local Italian restaurants." Theodore just silently nodded with his father's continuing plans and predictions. "Are you still wanting Joshua as underboss and Leonardo as your consigliere?" Victor eyed his son.

"Yes, I think they will both do well in their new positions." Theodore drank deeply of his wine.

"And you have some capos to promote, yes? After all some men are going to be a bit miffed because we are getting out of the more illegitimate aspects, so offer freely those who wish to join the Corella's or Del Giorno's, a chance to do so. Those who stay on with you, I humbly suggest you reward well."

"I will." Theodore nodded, absorbing his father's advice and long-term experience.

Victor looked long and hard at his son for a moment; a smile of amusement in his dark eyes, "So, any news you wish to tell me, *mio angelo della morte*?"

Theodore matched the subtle look at his father with his own hard blue eyes. The two knew each far too well, knew what the other was thinking before they even spoke it.

"You mean about Alyssa?" Theodore teased his father with a serious face. "Well, yes. I suppose there will be a wedding to announce after the announcement of your retirement." A smile lit up his angular face.

"Ah, excellent" Victor sat back a moment and then toasted his son with his wine glass, "*Salute*! I think you made a good choice, you have my blessings of course." he winked, then with a friendly barb of his own added, "But teach that girl some Italian eh? If she is going to be the wife of the *Padrone*, she had better at least understand the language."

"I plan to." Theodore toasted his father back. "In fact, I plan on getting the Bonnaro men to learn English, her to learn Italian and myself to learn more of that sign language book."

"Now all I need to be a happy man is grandchildren…" Victor teased unabashedly.

"Oh for chrissakes, Father!" Theodore raised an eyebrow at him with a deadpan look, "I am working on it."

This bought guffaws from the old man, which in turn made Theodore begin laughing until soon father and son were laughing so deeply, tears were nearly spilling down their faces.

After awhile Victor regained his composure, "This is excellent news though; the Family needs something positive to celebrate, considering what happened with Clarissa Fantenelli…"

Theodore nodded, "I see Joshua is quick to comfort her."

"Eh," Victor just said noncommittally. "He may be a bit to hot-headed and into himself for her taste, but if he can continue to tone himself down, she may very well fall for him, who knows."

"There is always Leonardo." Theodore refilled their glasses again.

"Len, ah yes Len," Victor leaned back in thought. "Now that would be a good match. But I sense in that flirtatious, old-world fellow, a man much like you were. A very deep and painful wall that he keeps up, he's not ready to commit fully to someone yet. Maybe in time, but not with Clarissa I don't think." Victor paused and glanced honestly at his son "However I am glad you asked finally asked Alyssa you stubborn man. Arrigo was definitely not her type, and I feared if he kept pushing her that some horrible accident might have befallen him."

"*Padre mio!*" Theodore actually almost but not quite looked shocked. "Me, interfere with Arrigo trying to flirt with Alyssa?"

A long silence sat between them, Victor's eyes twinkling with total humor and yet a truthful seriousness, "Do you really, want me to answer that, Theo?"

"Never mind," The tall man harrumphed. "Just never mind."

"Congratulations again, you and Alyssa will be perfect." Victor's idly waved his hand, "I know she will bring you much happiness, like your mother did to me. So tell me, do you still have that *comare*, Diana?"

Theodore turned a slight red at his temples, "Um, no. I think she left town..."

"I see." The Arbitrator said, seeming to understand the real answer behind his son's ambiguous answer. "I see."

"Well enough of that..." Theodore Jerome quickly changed the subject, "I know there are preparations to make for our announcement of your retirement, *Padrone*."
He came over and gently hugged his father and mentor. "I will catch up with you later, father."

Victor watched his tall son duck out under the doorway of the Office with a grace and a newfound lightness in his step. He could tell indeed his son was happy and in love, he could see it in his eyes, feel it in his heart. He was truly glad Theodore and Alyssa had worked things out, it would give the Family something pleasant to celebrate after all this death and the added stress of the announcement of Theodore as their new Padrone and head of the Family.

'You see there Issy,' Victor's mind thought to his beloved wife, 'Theo did drop that wall. Our true son has finally returned home to us'.

Chapter 40- *November 3rd 1987*

Alyssa felt so glad to be back with her beloved teacher and now fiancé in his oriental home. Each day she healed more in body, and each night she and Kageryu would explore the passions of one another's heart and soul in his bed. Even though Kage had asked her to keep quiet the announcement of their engagement until after all this business with funerals and his being announced as new head of the *famiglia*, it seemed as though the people in the Jerome family seemed to already sense that Alyssa and Martel were now exclusively an item. It was not uncommon for her or Martel to get discreet winks from some of the men, and even Victor had pulled her aside and whispered to her, "I am so happy for you *mia cara*. You are good for each other, eh?"

It would be Thanksgiving in a couple weeks and already Victor had ordered 150 turkeys, most that he gave away to those who worked with him that had families, others to local Catholic churches for their underprivileged and tons of other food to go with it.

Alyssa had gone with Laurence and Victor to Cesare's funeral, as well as Patrizio's a day later. There had also been separate funerals for Gio, Patrizio, Sal and all the other men lost. Even to those she did not know she had gone and quietly accompanied her Kageryu at each one; hugging gently the grieving widows, friends and family. These people were *her* people and Family too now.

Rocco and eight of the other men who had been arrested during the *mannagge* had their trials and while five had gotten off with light sentences, three others including Rocco were going to be in jail for longer, for at least 15 months to 8 years. Four of the Bonnaro men who had been picked up had been deported back immediately to Italy.

A week after Cesare's funeral, both Lena and Vito were headed back home with 10 of their soldiers, Victor flying them back to Sicily in his personal corporate jet. Alyssa was sorry to see Lena go, the two had begun to forge a deep friendship, and Lena, Arrigo and several other ladies from the kitchen had begun working with Alyssa in earnest to teach her the Italian language rich with Sicilian dialect.

And of course while Alyssa would never be able to speak it she would be able to understand and write it as well. Of course Victor and Theodore were completely fluent in it and she often found her Uncle and fiancé would speak to her only in Italian forcing her to learn the language that much faster.

Arrigo after finding out from Len, and of course hearing it proclaimed between the men themselves, of Alyssa's and Martel's getting back together, immediately stopped flirting with her. He had indeed truly found her attractive and would have continued to pursue her, had Martel not been interested. But one thing a Man of Honor learned quickly, beside the highly vaunted vow of omerta, was that one did not bother or mess with another made man's wife, girlfriend or fiancée. It was forbidden fruit to try and have a relationship with a nice woman who was dating, engaged or married to another Man of Honor. To do so could mean your death, and major Family *mannagges'* had been started by less.

And so Arrigo, like Leonardo being of the old school, nursed his heart over some wine and partying with his cousin and moved on. He would still be a faithful bodyguard to Alyssa, and be able to work efficiently around her, but he definitely would not be flirting with her. Alyssa was able to work just fine around Arrigo once he had backed off and stopped following her around like a love struck puppy and the two got along as well if not even better than before. After all, her heart only belonged to one man, her soul mate, Kageryu.

About eight of the Bonnaro soldiers would be remaining and living here permanently in the US, most of them in New York City and three at the nearby town, like Arrigo who would be working nearly exclusively at the Estate.

Before Bonnaro's had left, Lena and Alyssa had gone out to lunch in downtown NYC, with Arrigo, his cousin and capo Leonardo and a few other bodyguards along.

"Now Alyssa," Lena had spoken to her in Italian, with Len translating for her any parts she didn't understand. "I want to see you and *Martello...*" she winked at Alyssa.
(Not everyone knew yet about Laurence Martel being Victor's son. That had not been officially announced yet, but obviously Vito and Lena did.) "...In a few months or at least next year, eh? We have a nice palazzo near the shoreline that overlooks the ocean and Mt. Aetna, our volcano. It is beautiful with the olive and fig trees that over hang on the back patio and arbor. You, like *Martello* are like my own child; one of us, a true Bonnaro." She had kissed Alyssa then once on each cheek, her dark eyes full of understanding and quiet wisdom.

She whispered privately to Alyssa's ear only, "I am always available if you ever need to write or call, eh? You will do fine, just as I said, future wife to the *Padrone* of the Family." She smiled warmly and hugged the girl tightly. Alyssa would miss her mentor terribly but she would have her true love and husband Theodore, and the wisdom of Victor and the other members of the Jerome Family to help her now.

After Lena and Vito had left it seemed that for the next few days Victor, Theodore and half the Top Administration and capos were continually busy and running all over.

Alyssa spent her days either at the large Jerome Estates learning her Italian and studying and teaching sign language to both herself and others or else relaxing and writing in her journals at Kageryu's house.

Their house; she loved that phrase, and that feeling of knowing that she and Theodore were finally together, that she would support him in however he needed and he was there to continue being her soulmate, teacher and soon to be husband.

During the evenings when Theo came back from the City, she and Kageryu (Her sign language name for him was the sign for *'Dragon'* blending into the sign for *'shadow'*), would continue to work on her Italian lessons, martial arts, or he would read to her in his deep voice. Of course he continued her massages on her and in fact he began to teach her many of the same oriental philosophies and techniques he practiced since she had shown an interest in them; he even began to show her how to do the reiki/shiatsu massage on him.

Now it was Alyssa often doing the laundry or cleaning the house or tending his Zen garden, while he was often downtown with his father talking to capo's and helping to set in motion the restructuring for the Jerome Family, as well as making contacts and negotiations with the other Crime Families, like the Corella's and Del Giorno's.

They sat together one night, her and Kageryu in the living room, listening to some soft jazz on the stereo as he held her in his arms and they dined on Sushi together that he had bought back from the city. "*Kanashii*," he signed (her sign language name was the sign for '*Arrow*', followed by the sign for '*Hawk*'.) "I will be away for the next 3 days, staying downtown. I need you to stay here at our house. Do not leave unless you are accompanied by either Arrigo or Tommy. It will be during this time when I make my secret known about who I am. About me being Victor's son, Theodore Jerome..."

Alyssa was stunned how fast Theodore had picked up the unspoken, graceful sign language. The man seemed gifted with a higher than average intelligence and many things just seemed to come easy to him. Even though she was learning it quite fluently as well, but not as fast it seemed as he was.

He was also speaking in Italian as he was signing, and if she seemed confused by a word or a sign he would just quickly insert the English word for it.

"It will also be when my father Victor will announce his retirement," he continued, "and I will then be quite busy for the next few weeks, smoothing things over and taking care of business. I will announce our marriage formally as well, but I want to know two things. One, when would you like the wedding? And two, do you prefer to live here in this house or do you wish to move into the main house?" he finished signing and speaking in Italian and glanced down at her, his sapphire eyes filled with a tenderness and yet an almost hungry possessiveness for her.

She signed back, "*I know you will be busy love. I understand. As to a date for our wedding, I would marry you tomorrow, but I think Victor would be a bit miffed...*"

Kageryu chuckled at that, "Yes he would. Personally it wouldn't matter to me if we were the only two at the ceremony, just you and I, but I know my father. He will want to put on a real party."

Kanashii smiled at her fiancé, "*True. So let's say we make it a January wedding, after people have had the holidays with their families. That way it is still close, but gives Victor enough time to invite 'friends of his'.*" She smiled knowingly. It still amazed her just how easy it was to communicate in this non-spoken, non-written way of talking, how easy it flowed. She was so grateful to that mysterious old shop owner down in Jamaica for giving her the original book. Since then, Victor and Theodore had bought her a whole library and video collection of Sign Language instruction.

"So?" Theo prodded her playfully, "That answers one question, how about the other?"

"*Well...*" she thought long and hard. This house held so many memories for her, and she knew for Kageryu as well. "*Personally I like this house; you have gotten me addicted to the Asian style of* decorating my love." She teased, "*We can stay here, but of course use the main house for business or decorate parts of it in Asian décor. Overall, I like the privacy though of being down here with you, my love.*"

"*I do too, Kanashii.*" He signed and kissed her on the head, and then using his chopsticks gently fed her a piece of Sushi. "I do as well *mia amore*". He spoke to her.

"Last question," he spoke now and wrapped his arms around her, pulling her tight against him, breathing in the essence of her and simply enjoying the feel of her small body in his long arms. "Do you want to do only the standard wedding ceremony? I mean, I know my father, and he will be setting up the formal wedding to be at the Catholic cathedral St. Michael's downtown, but if you want, I can have Sen come by the next day, and you and I can also wed in a private and more intimate ceremony in my shinto" he motioned to the room where his shinto was.

"*Have Sen come and let's marry at your temple first.*" She smiled mischievously, "*He can come in 4 days for all I care and marry us and we can do your Father's 'official' ceremony in January. I just know I can't wait at least in my heart to be Mrs. Theodore 'Kageryu' Jerome.*"

He laughed at her use of Theodore Kageryu Jerome, "Ok, Ok. Fair enough, Kanashii. I will ask Sen to come over in 5 days from now, and we will be bonded together. But keep it secret my love."

"*Omerta and secrecy my beloved*" she signed at him and they kissed deeply. The best part of the evening time of course was being next to her Kageryu, in bed; making love to him and sleeping next to him. It always made her so safe and happy to awaken the next morning to her beloved and the way his eyes looked at her conveying deep emotions and love. She remembered she had never seen that possessive and hungry look in Jim's eyes when they had been together. No, she indeed knew her Kageryu loved her and she him unconditionally.

Theodore looked at the sleeping woman in his arms after they had made love that evening. Already he had begun to share more and more of himself with her, private things that he thought he would never tell another soul. While he would never tell her about any of his darker or illegal activities, even those in his past, he did open up more and tell her about his teachers Cochran, and Sen. Told her of his growing up in Giarre Sicily with the Bonnaro's and even his frustration at being on the 'outside' for so many years when he had returned. Through all of it Alyssa had not pushed him to tell her more than he felt comfortable with and through all of it she had always stood there at his side like a strong and comforting beacon to him. He had honestly never thought he would feel this way after what had happened with Miyoko, but he found in his heart a love for Alyssa that he knew no one could ever replace. He truly did need her as much as she needed him.

He was pleased at her honest love and curiosity at the Eastern philosophies and he was more than happy to now be her true 'teacher' as Sen was once to him, and begin teaching her the path of healing and of the eastern ways. Since Leonardo was now also his true student as well, he had merely told her that Len was studying with him too, but to keep it quiet. She had not asked for any other information, and indeed had kept quiet from everyone the fact that Leonardo also came and studied with Martel. Theodore Jerome had his own reasons he was now teaching Leonardo, but those were reasons he was not willing to discuss with anyone at this point, not even his father.

Arrigo Salvaggio had approached him shortly after Alyssa had moved back in with him and had apologized profusely at his trying to date her. Martel had assured the new bodyguard he had nothing to worry about, and that if anything Arrigo had been the final shove Martel needed to make up his mind and heart, so as not to lose his Kanashii forever. Laurence deeply trusted Arrigo, just as he did Len, and knew the bodyguard from Naples would be a very trusted ally in the future of the Jerome *famiglia*.

Theodore caressed the beautiful red hair of his beloved and his mind and heart drifted once again to how happy he truly was. In fact he could not remember such inner peace and contentment in all of his life.

Three days before Alyssa and Theodore Jerome were to be privately bonded in his Shinto at his house, by his best friend and martial arts Sensei, Sen Yamashita; Laurence Martel was in front of a giant meeting of his underworld peers.

The Top Administration of the Corella's and the Del Giorno's as well as around 15 of the Jerome Capo's and other allies to the Family, it was there that Victor Jerome made his formal announcement of retiring from being the head of the Family and turning it over to his son, his *true son*, who had indeed been alive all these years; Theodore Vittorio Jerome.

An almost palatable hush had fallen across the room in the Blue Parrot when the announcement had been made. Several of the old school *Mafioso's* crossed themselves when the secret of Laurence's identity was revealed, and others like, Joshua Demonico or Leonardo Tagretta, seemed to smile from within, it didn't shock them, somehow they knew just how uncannily alike father and son were.

Joshua like Alyssa, had always suspected, he too had noticed over the years that Victor never seemed to mourn or talk about his eldest son, Theodore the way he did Michael or Isabella. For many in the Jerome Family, it simply made no difference. After all, most had dealt with 'Laurence Martel' for years and both respected and trusted him as an underboss. Victor's son or not, many felt he was the logical choice to succeed Victor regardless.

However what seemed more shocking to everyone was Victor's going into semi-permanent retirement. Even though he assured everyone he would be acting as a *consigliere de' facto*, a counselor and advisor to Theodore, there were a few in the room who felt the old Jerome magic might be lost.

They would soon enough find out they were very wrong. That Theodore like his father had an instinctive grasp of how to truly run a *Brugad* and to take care of those who were friends, allies or enemies. He had been trained and groomed by the best, Vito Bonnaro and of course his father. His time in the orient had only further strengthened his inner ability to read friend or foe and deal with them in a totally efficient way. As well as instilled in him a sense of duty and honor to his Family and men, in some ways far more strict than the 'old school' men.

It was Leonardo who christened almost instinctively and uncannily, Theodore with the Italian name, "*il dragone*", or 'The Dragon'. It was now Theodore 'the Dragon' Jerome who was the *Padrone* and Leader of the Jerome Family, and Victor 'the Arbitrator', who would be enjoying the quiet peace of his retirement.

Later that afternoon at a much more private and formal sit down, in The Office at the Jerome Estates with only Jerome Family members, it would be Joshua Demonico promoted to underboss, and Leonardo Tagretta promoted to the Family's consigliere. Arrigo Salvaggio was also promoted and given the title of Head of the elite bodyguards. Tommy DeLuca was temporarily given Carmine Marcallo's position as head of the Jerome Estates and day-to-day operations. Dominick "Nick" Pellegrio was bumped up to Cesare's old job and made a capo as well. Marco Baldassare was also promoted to capo to take over running the Blue Parrot nightclub and Ricardo Orenda, manager and now owner, of The Harem was also promoted to capo.

The new captains and administration then shared wine and toasted to the new vitality and strength of the Family. "To our new leaders and to the new life and blood of the Jerome *Famiglia* and to those who will take 'this thing of ours' into the new century." Victor toasted.

"To my new Administration," Theo followed suit, "To those who I have vowed to care for as my own, to those who I rely to care for me, my *compari*, my brothers. And also to the great man who has brought the Family where it is today, my father and my *Padrone* always, Victor. *Salute!*"

"*Salute!*" all the Jerome men said nearly in unison.

Theodore then added, "I am also making the formal announcement of my upcoming marriage to Alyssa Disarro, the wedding will take place after the holidays at the end of January, and I request all of you to celebrate in my good fortune in this as well." Again the men of the Jerome Family toasted him with a hearty "*Salute!*" and drank with him.

The new Family was off to a good start; new strength flowed in her veins. Theodore glanced silently at his father, unspoken words between them. After all, his teacher was still at his side if he needed him, and Theodore would always respect and take to heart the old man's advice. In his mind, Victor would always be the last of the great Dons. A true Man of Honor with no equal.

Three days later Sen Yamashita was flown over on the helicopter to the Jerome Estates, and in private he helped conduct his former student and his best friend in a ceremony of bonding with his new wife, Kanashii. Although Alyssa didn't understand any of what was being said in Japanese, her fiancé either told her what to do in sign language or in English. In many ways this ceremony would be much more personal and loved by both Alyssa and Theodore, for it was just the two of them. Her and Kageryu, bonding in the way he felt most comfortable with, letting her into that world of his that he had worked so hard to keep hidden from everyone else.

Sen had bought some simple gifts and some elegant Asian treats and cakes, and he helped conduct the bonding ceremony between her and Kageryu. It mainly involved her doing an elaborate Tea Ceremony and serving it to her 'soon to be husband' and his ritualistic receiving of it. It was a complicated ceremony but yet so beautifully elegant, and the whole time Alyssa just felt the magnetic pull of the deep blue eyes and love of her beloved.

Kageryu was dressed in an elegant silk, black and beige, traditional Japanese male wedding Kimono that bore striking fiery red dragons around the border and Sen had bought her a traditional white Kimono called an *Uchikake*, to wear. Sen also wore an elegant black, men's Kimono without any embroidery on it. Both the men wore the traditional ceremonial *tanto* knife in their waistband and Sen had bought Alyssa an elegant fan that was required in the ceremony.

The Japanese ceremony seemed long and very involved, but to Kanashii she barely noticed, the whole time she just felt such happiness and love in her heart, knowing she was truly now where she was meant to be, at the side of her Kageryu.

The heady incense, that seemed to alter the senses and the red and white flickering candles in the elegant Shinto seemed to make the experience that much more mystical to her, especially since she didn't know all the intricacies of the ceremony. She did know that gifts were to be exchanged between her and her betrothed and also a gift to the Shinto, the shrine that Theodore had here in his house. Sen had already bought her some elegant bells and origami birds for her to give as her gift to the Shinto, but Alyssa already knew the perfect gift to give to her Kageryu. The General Kwan-Ti and dragon sculpture she had gotten him at the Island and had never given him yet, the one that eerily reminded her of Theodore and his father Victor.

When it was time to give the gifts, Martel presented her with a stunning oriental anklet bracelet made of platinum that bore an elegant kanji and small symbolic dragon on it. She gave him the statue, she could tell at once by reading his eyes and soul that he felt the same about it as she had. A smile crossed his face, and the blue eyes softened in deep appreciation as he looked at it. "*Mi padre, mio mentore.*" He barely whispered, 'My father; my mentor.' He too was reminded of the symbolism in it about him and Victor.

After the ceremony she changed out of the elegant wedding Kimono, and Martel and Sen changed into their more casual clothes as well, the three of them sat for a long time drinking *sake* and talking. Sen often taking her hand and telling her "You very good for this addle-brained Dragon, Kanashii, trust me!" and also letting her know he would always be a brother-in-law to her.

Sen had stayed over that night in the guest room, and Kageryu had made love to her that night with an even harder and more renewed vigor than before, almost as if he truly was a dragon. She gave into and lost herself in total ecstasy with him and fell asleep safe and sound in his tight embrace, for she was content and happy. No matter what now, no matter if the world stopped tomorrow, she was happy for at least to each other, her and Theodore Jerome were truly married.

Of course they carried on as though just engaged with the rest of the Family, after all they both knew Victor would be setting up a huge Italian style wedding for not only the Jerome Family, but probably to invite many other people, other Dons and made men from other families to celebrate the new Don of the Jerome Families marriage.

Thanksgiving was a truly a wonderful feast at the great Estates, and each day Alyssa became comfortable in a routine of getting to learn a bit about each of the people who worked at the Estate, the people and families of those who were in the Jerome Family and clan.

As November slipped into December, a truly picturesque winter descended on New York State that year, blanketing the Jerome Estates in at least a several inches of the powdery stuff, which gave it a cozy and almost magical feel. The temperatures dipped to icy daytime highs of only 30 and icy nights of only 20 degrees or so, prompting the great fireplaces to be lit up in the main house. Rosette, Emilia and the other women including Alyssa took great delight in having the house guards assist them in decorating the main house with wondrous Christmas decorations. Everything from candles in the windows to pine boughs around the banisters, and the centerpiece a great 15-foot tree that was set up and decorated in the main foyer near the double staircase that lead to the upstairs.

The Sicilian ladies went into overdrive preparing scores of Italian pastries, cookies and holiday treats for all, and it seemed the house always had the aroma of either hearty lasagnas, bruschettas, beef braciola, doughy Panettones, or the wafting scent of cinnamon and the sweet cheese of cannoli's and the enticing aromas of *pastaciotti*, rum *baba's*, biscotti's, tiramisu, decadent NY Cheese cakes and other Italian sweets. The wonderful smells alone could add on pounds to a person.

Since the *mannagge* was over, and people were celebrating all the good news including the new additional Bonnaro members, the joyous news of Victor's true heir alive and the upcoming marriage between Theodore's and Alyssa, the mood of the Family was truly in the holiday spirit.

Even the F.B.I and law enforcement seemed to be taking a break and leaving the Jerome's alone. Of course much of that had to do with Victor Jerome's clever foresight in putting much of his assets into more legitimate areas and passing off the more illegitimate ones to the Bonnaro's back in Sicily or rewarding old long time allies with them.

Alyssa's health had vastly improved and she had healed quickly indeed from her gunshot wound. As Dr. Weintraub had said thankfully the bullet had only torn up some muscle and nothing worse and she was almost totally back to normal now after donation of a kidney to her Uncle, and her whole ordeal at the hands of the Romans and the kidnappers.

Now that she was the true adopted niece of Victor, and had shown an interest in horseback riding, the snobby head of the stable, Ignasio DeLoccasio, had no choice but to let Alyssa go riding when she wanted. In fact his attitude towards her softened immensely when he found out that like Michael, she had a love of horses. And *Signore* DeLoccasio himself was more than happy to give her riding instruction. He was not a made member of the Family, but was like Dr. Weintraub an associate. However he came imported from northern Italy and was a master horseman. Often on cool winter days Alyssa would take one of the elegant Andalusian horses and go cantering across the great snow covered lawns or ride up near the now snow covered gardens. Her heart would soar as she would see Victor or Theodore watching her and she would happily wave to them as they would wave back.

Now, as he had forewarned her, it was Theodore who was often away for the day in downtown NYC, working hard with the other Commission Families and taking care of business at either the VIJER Corporation or handling Family Business either downtown or in the Office here at the Estate. As the new Don he was expected to be out much more frequently assuring associates and long time allies that all was still strong within the Jerome Family, that he being the new leader did not in any way weaken the power of the Family.

In fact during the first several weeks, it was not uncommon for those who outright disrespected or disavowed of the new Don to turn up missing, and word quickly spread among underworld associates, and those who dealt with the Jerome's that the 'Undertaker' did not take a break from avenging those who wronged the Jerome's just because he was now the head of the *Famiglia*.

Of course Alyssa did not know of any of these matters from Theodore. Family business was always censored from her just as it was from any other wife, mother or girlfriend. She overheard a lot more than she had before, especially now since she was becoming so proficient in the Sicilian tongue, but she had sworn an oath to her mate and husband of *omerta* and secrecy. She may indeed, accidentally overhear things, but they were not for her to discuss. Just like she overheard that Carmine Marcallo who was in prison was going to cut a deal with the feds and turn informant. She also overheard that he ended up dead two days later, on the orders of Theodore. Like his father, Victor, Theodore respected and demanded loyalty above all else.

It now meant Tommy and Nick's positions as majordomo's and head of the Gym and day-to-day operations, of the Jerome Estate would be permanent.

Also, Dominick 'Nick' Pellegrio now took over Cesare's job as official chauffeur and it was he who was the main driver of the massive Jerome-1 Limo. Nick was a hard-nosed man, and of course who would never be the jovial friendly man like Cesare was. Nick was always alert and on guard like some overzealous Guard Dog, or he was just menacingly silent and intimidating. To Alyssa, Nick reminded her of a cross between the bad points of Joshua and Gio Aprile. Intimidating, hard, arrogant and downright mean. However his bosses liked him and he was a silent and strict soldier for his Family.

Leonardo Tagretta thoroughly enjoyed his new promotion as family consigliere and he seemed born into the position. He was suave, elegant and indeed a great listener, advisor and assistant to both Joshua and Theodore. He often worked with the temerity and dedication of three men and he was seen nearly constantly at the Estate now. Alyssa and the others truly enjoyed having the silky voiced, experienced Len around.

His humor, dedication and calm voice made him a pleasure to work with, but always he was respected by everyone and took his job seriously.

Alyssa had apologized to him profusely for that night she had rushed into Martel's place nearly getting them both killed, and swore never to ignore his orders again. Len was a forgiving man of Family members and so of course had accepted her apology with a good natured, "You never do again, eh? Otherwise I show you some of those Aikido moves you Fiancé have been showing me." He said with a playful wink and the two had begun to form a friendship nearly as close as she had with the deceased Cesare Ciccerone. Of course since Leonardo was an excellent horseman and enjoyed riding, he and Alyssa often took long rides around the estate together, which only helped cement a deep respect and friendship between them. It was Leonardo who had the gentle patience to often work long hours with her teaching her to read and write in Italian, often as he told her about all the various sites and history of his homeland, and about his cousin Arrigo who had come originally from Napoli. But like everyone else around here, was an expert at speaking about many things, but keeping elegantly censored any conversation about 'Family business' or the *Mafioso* lifestyle.

Joshua was learning to fit well into the role of underboss, although he too spent a lot of time downtown working with many of the new capos and was not seen as often at the Estate as he was before.

Perhaps most enjoyable to Alyssa was that now she was able to spend much more time with her Uncle Victor as well. Even though Victor was always there to advise his son if he needed -and the two often talked a long time in the Office together after dinner- during the day, Victor thoroughly enjoyed helping set up the house with Christmas decorations or playing chess with Alyssa or practiced with her on her Italian as well.

Victor was much more open about his beloved wife Isabella, now that Alyssa and Theodore were to be husband and wife. Victor also told Alyssa the *true* story of what had happened to his younger son Michael and how the D'Salvatore animals had killed him in their vendetta against the Jerome's. He also mentioned how the long standing *mannagge* was started by the D'Salvatores cruel attack in the '57 Massacre that had cost Victor his blood family. Victor still censored all of his day-to-day talk on Family business, but now that she was to be a part of his son's life, he was more open about the past as though giving her a history of who the Jerome's were, and what had happened in the lives of those who were important to him and Theodore, would help her to understand the future of what her husband would now have to do.

She in turn was honest and told Victor what little she could remember from her past, and about her ex-fiancé, Jim who had run off with her supervisor Mandy.

"Pity for him, but good for us, eh child?" Victor always would tease her when she told the story. "Frankly I am glad the *stronzo cafone* did leave you, I think Theo is much better for you." He would wink. Often the two would simply read quietly in Victor's private library in front of the crackling fireplace, or they would bundle up together and Nick or Arrigo would drive them down to the Aviary to take care of the finches.

It was this time that would often live on in Alyssa's memories of being the most serene and content of her life. She still could not remember who her real parents were, or if she had any brothers or sisters, or even what the name of the town she had lived in was called. There were still glaring chunks in her memory like the holes in Swiss cheese especially regarding things before her being kidnapped. But her life now was full of nothing but love, contentment and a sense of belonging that made her so grateful for all that was in her life. In fact it sometimes scared her and she thought she would wake up, as though from a pleasant dream, and find that all this; her mate Theodore, her Uncle Victor, the love and belonging in the Jerome Family would simply vanish in a mist to have never taken place at all.

Victor seemed to be content and happy as well in his semi-retirement. He enjoyed planning the holidays for his men and their families and threw himself fully into planning along with Alyssa the upcoming wedding ceremony in January.

But while Alyssa was happy and content, and her heart and soul overflowing with love, there were times she would look over at her beloved Uncle Victor and feel sadness so profound it would shake her to her very core. She didn't know why, but it loomed there on occasion. Perhaps it was the way he seemed to be getting a bit paler, or his rapidly loosing weight despite Rosette and the ladies filling him with delicious Italian food. Maybe it was in the way Dr. Weintraub would often take Victor down to the clinic and the two would argue in hushed tones with one another. Or worse, the way Victor's hand would tremble a quite a bit more often when he would pick up a glass to drink and he would make a light joke of it. She didn't need to talk to Theodore about it, for she often saw the concerned look in his own blue eyes as he would occasionally look deeply at his father.

It was on December 22nd that Alyssa finally went and saw Dr. Weintraub, concerned because she was nearly a month overdue for her period. "Well dear heart." John Thomas shuffled the test result papers around then looked over his perpetually skewed glasses at her frankly, "It's because you're pregnant." He said trying to hide the grin on his face. "I'm assuming this is a good thing?" he asked.

She could only sit there and nod stupidly with a smile of her own on her face. Pregnant! She was now carrying her beloved Theodore's child. She ran over and hugged the doctor. "*Oh please don't tell Victor yet!*" she pleaded; "*He's got this elaborate wedding all set up and ...*" she scratched out on a piece of paper. Dr. Weintraub was the only one who had not learned any of the sign language.

"Darlin'," John Thomas said, "I won't tell Victor anything. You know there is such a thing as patient-doctor confidentiality, but between you and me, I don't think he would be offended." He winked at her in a conspiratorially manner, "You know, I think he realizes with you and Theo living in that small house together..." The doctor just left the sentence hanging. "Never-the-less, I won't say a peep. However, I think if you did tell him, he would be downright proud."

She blushed then, a deep blush. Then scratched out, "*Speaking of Victor…I have been worried about him, I mean, is there something I should know? He has been looking under the weather, is his diabetes under control? Has something else come up? Has…*"

John Thomas took the paper away from her before she wrote more. "Dear Alyssa." He looked at her sagely, "Now what did I just tell you about patient-doctor confidentiality?" he shook his head lightly, but Alyssa could see a hard and sad cloud come over the doctor's eyes as well, that he quickly hid. And unlike his usual self he didn't joke around about her question regarding Victor. It was this most of all that sent a cold chill down her heart, "You wanna discuss that you talk to Victor, Ok? You won't get anything from me. Now, enough on him, and lets talk about getting you on some prenatal vitamins and a prenatal check up, Ok?"

That evening as her and Kageryu were back in their Asian ranch style house she signed to him. "*Kage, I have something important to tell you. I hope it will please you… If not we need to discuss it now.*"

This got Theodore's full attention, and he looked at her with those piercing eyes of his. "What," He said levelly. "What is it Kanashii Taka?"

"*I, I'm pregnant. I found out today from Dr. Weintraub.*" She hoped that indeed this news would please him; she was so happy herself to find out that she was pregnant with her beloved's husband's child.

"What?" Theodore asked calmly again, as though he had not understood her the first time.

She began to slowly sign it again, but halfway through her signing, one of his large hands came up and quietly clasped hers, the other reaching down and gently touched her stomach. "You are pregnant with our child?" His voice was surprisingly low and quiet almost in a reverent awe. Alyssa nodded, her eyes filled with tears of happiness.

He pulled her close to him, enfolding her in his long arms, "Oh Kanashii," he whispered, "I am so pleased, so happy." He kissed her tenderly along her face. The two of them just sat for several long minutes as he held her tightly, so tightly she had to gently tap him and beg him to release her for fear of his great strength crushing her, he seemed so happy!

"Sorry, sorry." He mumbled, almost seeming awkward. "I'm just so happy, *mia tesoro.*"

"*Kage, Do you think we should tell Victor?*" she signed, "*I had wanted to wait until after our wedding he was planning in January, but… Well, Dr. Weintraub felt that it would be Ok to tell him now, I just didn't want Victor getting offended.*"

"Kanashii, my dear Kanashii," He crooned in a deep soothing voice, the voice that she could deny him nothing when he used. "My father may seem old fashioned, but he is a lot more progressive than you think, Hmm? Tell him, it will warm the old man's heart and soul trust me. It certainly warmed mine."

She nodded; she knew the perfect way and time to tell Victor. She would write it to him in a note for his Christmas present. She had went shopping in downtown NYC a few days ago with Arrigo, Tommy and Leonardo and picked out her presents (tons of them it seemed, she had so many people to give gifts too!) for her Uncle she had found two rare old books she knew he would love; one of them about Al Capone from the Chicago Outfit she knew he didn't have and one an old leather-bound Audubon book filled with various elegant bird pictures from nearly 50 years ago. Now she would tuck a card in there and a note with the news of her being pregnant with his grandchild.

Chapter 41-

Christmas was a huge festive occasion at the Jerome household, one that ran for two whole days of festivities, and large Italian Catholic holidays were even more impressive. On the 24th, Christmas Eve was the celebration for true Family, a time when she, Victor, Theodore and those single men without families, like Leonardo, Joshua and several other full time house guards celebrated. A wonderful dinner was served buffet style, and Victor and Theodore handed out several thick envelopes or gifts to the guards and the top Administration. Alyssa handed out her gifts to Leonardo, Arrigo, Tommy, Ignasio DeLoccasio and several others.

She would give Victor her present later, when the Men of Honor were done celebrating amongst themselves. As usual after dinner, the men had drifted off to talk some business and exchange gifts and Alyssa had joined the ladies in off to the side where she exchanged gifts, and conversation with Rosette, and many of the others while they drank wine or espresso as well.

After the men seemed to be done talking, Victor came to look her up and she steered him privately off to the side and handed him first the two elegantly wrapped books. Then after he was done admiring them she handed him the card, with her note inside.

She watched carefully the face of the great Arbitrator, and at first she could read no emotion on his face as he read and reread the note. But then she notice the tremble to his hand seem to get stronger and for the first time she could remember the great Don looked at her and she saw a single tear in the dark obsidian eye that rolled slowly down his cheek. "This is true?" he asked quietly indicating the note. "You are pregnant with Theodore's child?"

Hesitantly she nodded, hoping that he was not offended. She had never seen him act like this.

"*Bambina mia, che meravigliosa notizia,*" He whispered to her in Italian as he pulled her close, "My sweet precious child; *madre* who carries my grandchild. You now carry the next lineage of the Jerome line." And then another tear coursed down the old mans face. "My deepest hopes are not dead after all. You have indeed given me the greatest gift that an old man could want. A future for my family, eh?" He hugged her tightly and kissed her gently on the top of her head. "*Grazie,*" He whispered to her, "Thank you, dear Alyssa."

The next day the great Estate was then opened up to all those who had wives and children and they all came from all over New York for a true feast to behold. Alyssa saw Lisa Ciccerone and her children, and Clarissa Fantenelli accompanied by Joshua Demonico, and the whole house overflowed with laughter, food and love. A true Italian household. It was the greatest outpouring of family, food and fun Alyssa had ever seen or felt or experienced.

Victor had seen his son endure for many years, always a ghost behind the scenes, always having to remain on the outside. Now for the first time he was not only allowed to be in the forefront but allowed to experience all of it for himself as he truly was, Theodore Vittorio Jerome; Victor's son, the heir to the Family and the new Don.

He watched as Theodore integrated smoothly, he had seemingly adapted well to the change from being the quiet, intimidating, supporting underboss to now being the man whom everyone turned to for advice, arbitration and instruction. He was a natural and gracious leader and had an inborn calm and wisdom.

Victor knew his son fiercely upheld the same values in running a *Famiglia* as he himself did. He had seen Theodore's quiet anger and his decisive reaction when Carmine Marcallo had threatened to turn witness to the F.B.I. He had seen his son quietly and decisively order the execution of two associates who upon Victor's stepping down went to cause trouble between the Jerome's and the Corella's. He had even sent out a peace delegation to the new D'Salvatore family (now headed by one of the capos, Roberto "Bobby Rob" Corrado). The current broken regime of the D'Salvatores who still had a lot of DiMone and Bonnaro men, were more than happy to finally end the *mannagge* and make peace with the new Jerome leadership.

Theodore had a great trust and respect in those people he had picked to work with him and trusted them implicitly to carry out whatever orders he sent out. So far, all the orders he made were ones Victor would have made himself had he been in Theodore's shoes. Because of the reputation 'The Undertaker' had before, there was no questioning from any of the lower capo's or wondering if the new Don had what it took to control the *Famiglia*, they knew he did and they knew what would happen to those who broke omerta, or who disrespected the Family or the people in it.

As a result the transition between the Dons was flawless and smooth, and while Victor was always available to act as an advisor and *consigliere de'facto* the truth of the matter was, he was not really needed at all. However this didn't bother him whatsoever, he had only the utmost pride in the way his son was able to integrate so seamlessly into the role of the Jerome's new leader and now, today during the holidays, to be able to see Theodore finally be able to be himself, was the greatest gift of all.

'Perhaps it was all worth it my son' he thought to himself, 'perhaps it was indeed all worth it.' And then as if by some strange unspoken communication, father and son would often glance at one another, dark onyx eyes meeting the confident, piercing blue ones of his son. A small smile would be briefly shared between them.

Yet of course Victor and everyone in the Jerome Family from the highest Administration to the lowest associate or wife knew that Victor would always be the true *Padrone* of the whole Jerome Entity until the day he died. After all it was Victor's reputation and leadership that had made the Jerome Family what it was.

Victor had seen Theodore and Alyssa glow with the same inner contentment and happiness that Victor himself had felt when he had married his beloved Isabella so many decades ago. He knew the two complimented each other, and it was probably having Alyssa at home at night, beside him and at his side that tempered any stress that Theodore felt, during these hectic times. Victor could not remember his son ever being as strong and happy as he was now.

And his 'niece' Alyssa, she had positively flourished under the protective wing of the Family. How she had grown from a wounded, uncertain and frightened girl, to a lady who was confidant, calm almost serene. She worked hard to also integrate herself with everyone from the men's wives, to the kitchen ladies, to the bodyguards, capo's and Top Administration to make sure people were at ease, comfortable and taken care of.

She seemed to learn well and instinctively the lessons of being a true lady and wife to a Man of Honor. She knew the Family came first in her and her husbands' life, and she showed respect and omerta and an innate understanding of the codes and rules but without ever appearing kowtowed or weak. Never did she act the 'spoiled princess' or worse, always she was compassionate, respectful and even playful. Like a true hawk she was watchful and protective of those she loved and with an inner strength and resilience in her, Victor didn't wonder if maybe somewhere in her ancestry Italian blood truly did flow in her veins. She reminded Victor very much of the confidence and strength that Lena Bonnaro had.

Alyssa had worked hard to learn to understand the Italian language and was willing to teach whoever wanted to learn, her sign language. In fact her teaching others only helped her learn it better herself. And she worked to learn how to make some of the various Italian dishes and help out around the Estate with whatever needed to be done.

She was a gentle soul, but had a spirit as carefree as his birds, and she often looked like a vision of beauty when she would ride one of the great white Andalusian horses through the snow on the front lawn. It pleased Victor to see the elegant horses be enjoyed again. After his son Michael had died no one in the family except for some of the guards or occasionally Leonardo Tagretta would ever really ride them.

Now there seemed to be someone who appreciated them again, almost as much as Michael and Ignasio DeLoccasio was delighted to have an apt pupil to teach his riding and dressage skills to. It was a vision of beauty for Victor to see Alyssa and Leonardo ride side by side on the graceful and beautiful white horses as they galloped across the front lawn.

For the first time in many years since his beloved Issy and Michael had passed on, the great house was alive during various Holidays, filled with the sights, sounds and smells that made the old man's heart sing and remember the more pleasant times in his life. In many ways, Alyssa made him feel young again in mind, as he remembered his own pleasant memories with his brothers Max and Eddie, and then later with Isabella, Theodore and Michael. It seemed almost like the dreary funeral darkness that had sat over the Jerome Estates for nearly 14 years had lifted.

The mysterious girl he had rescued and then adopted as one of his own had indeed been a godsend. She had saved his life with her kidney giving him more precious time to put together his plans with his *mannagge* against the D'Salvatores and setting his plans in motion for Theodore's takeover. She had saved him from being shot that day in NYC giving him time to turn the Family over smoothly to his son, and she had been the one who had gotten his son to break down the iron wall that had encircled his heart and deadened his soul for so long.

And now she had given them both an even greater gift, she was now carrying Theodore's child. She had given Victor one final gift, something that neither; Max, Eddie or Michael had been able to give, a true blood heir to the Jerome line.

"I hope you are watching up there Issy." Victor thought as he watched Theodore and Alyssa dancing together a week later during the New Years Eve ball at the great house. "I hope you approve of her. She carries our grandbaby, I think she will give us a bunch of them, eh, mi amore?

"Remember when you once told me you didn't recognize your own son when he came home? Look at him now; he is beaming with happiness. I know how he feels. I never stopped feeling that way for you, my beloved." Victor felt another tear run down his worn face, "Ah the old get so sentimental, do they not, Issy?" he chuckled. He often still talked to his wife in private, in his mind. He knew she could hear him, he always knew she was there, just on the outside of him, he felt her intensely…

How Victor now longed to join her. To be with his beloved, to be with his brothers, his father and mother, "Is Mike there with you Issy? Does he see his brother so happy? Theo deserves it, eh? After all he has had to sacrifice. He deserves happiness now. Soon I will be with you Issy, do wait for me will you? I miss you more and more every day, and yet in many ways I feel you closer to me than ever. They are so happy together, those two. I'm putting on a big shindig for them at the same church we were married at …" Victor watched Theodore and Alyssa finish as the dance ended, the band started up again and Leonardo came over and gracefully asked permission to dance with Alyssa, she accepted and soon her and Len were elegantly dancing across the dance floor.

Theodore had walked over to him then and stood next to his father. "You feeling Ok, my *Padrone*?" He noted the soft tears in his father's eyes.

"Oh yes, Theo, just enjoying the party." Victor smiled at him, quickly wiping away any tears he had left from talking with Isabella, "Your girl she does look so pretty dancing out there doesn't she?"

"Yes she does." Theodore nodded in agreement. "Not jealous of Len dancing with her, are you?" Victor teased him lightly.

Theodore looked down at his father, their eyes meeting with total honesty and frankness. "No, not at all." He said. "Leonardo is a good man, I trust him deeply."

"Good." Victor patted his son's arm. "You shouldn't be, after all, I can feel it all the way over here. There is only one man Alyssa loves, and she is looking this way at him."

Indeed at that moment Alyssa had turned and smiled warmly at her husband, giving him a look that was reserved just for her Kageryu.

"I know." Theodore said softly. "I know indeed. The feeling is mutual, towards her."

As Theodore had rejoined the Family nearly 10 years ago he had come to learn that his father was one of the very few who had never taken on a *Comare*, or mistress. Victor and his mother, Isabella had been so in synch when she was alive, that Victor had just never needed or craved one. After Isabella had passed on, his Father had tried dating a few women, even taking a mistress for a while but his heart and soul was not in it. For Victor Jerome attraction to someone happened between his ears, he had to truly care about them, and while he often would go with his men to The Harem or other gentlemen's clubs, he just did so because it was expected of him as the Don.

Victor had no want of any female companionship, the Jerome Family was truly and utterly his 'mistress' that demanded all, and it was her alone that he fed and nurtured.

As Theodore watched Alyssa finish the dance with Leonardo, he could understand exactly what his father had felt. He had thought he would never feel that way again after Miyoko but he began to feel Sen might have been right. Perhaps karmic fate was indeed kinder to the enigmatic son of Victor. Perhaps he was either graced with another soul mate or Miyoko had never truly been destined to be his in the first place. Either way he didn't contemplate it to deeply, he was just thankful for what was.

The official wedding on January 15th 1988 at St. Michael's cathedral was one of the most talked about in Crime Family circles for many years. There were close to nearly 1500 people who had shown up, many from the Jerome Family of course, but also many guests from the Corella's, the Del Giorno's, even a few representatives from the Calavicci's and from a few crews in New Jersey. Even Antonio "Tony Coconuts" DiMone the boss of the Miami *brugad*, came down with his capo Joe Cinno. There were many non-made associates as well. Dr. Weintraub and his wife Melinda, Sen Yamashita, and an eclectic mix of people who worked closely with the Jerome's but were not necessarily in the Family Business.

Alyssa was indeed a bit unnerved by all the reporters and the not very well disguised F.B.I agents that cased the church and wedding, recording every detail and taking pictures of cars and license plates but they left them alone. However she steeled herself and ignored them, trusting utterly in her beloved Theodore. Discreet, imposing bodyguards like Nick Pellegrino, Arrigo and others kept nosey reporters and paparazzi away from bothering the guests at the wedding and away from the first reception at The Blue Parrot, where most of the guests went afterwards.

After the first reception, only those truly Family and close to the family were invited to spend the weekend at the elegant Jerome Estate for the 2nd reception that was far more intimate and informal.

Just like the formal Japanese wedding that she and Theodore had done in his private Shinto at his home, Alyssa was to learn that a huge traditional Italian wedding was just as intricate and formalized with its own rituals and codes.

She and Theo were given not "gifts" but tons of envelopes, all of them stuffed full of cold, hard cash. She noticed most of the *Brugad* members, spent more time talking to Theodore and Victor and showing face with them, than giving her a second glance, but yet it also seemed like she danced with nearly every male guest there -as was the custom-.

During the receptions, toasts were made and often the participants would signal their pleasure or agreement by clinking their champagne glasses with their spoons or forks, until at times the great hall sounded like a million tinkling bells. Tons of gifts were given out to the guests and Jordan Almonds, those delectable hard-shelled almond candies, were everywhere and much to her chagrin were gently tossed at her and Theodore instead of rice.

At the less formal reception back at the Estate was where things finally slowed down, and more of the men (Mainly the Jerome Family members) seemed to come up to her and welcome her fully and intimately into the fold of the *Brugad*. The true Jerome *Famiglia*, the one she always referred to with a capital "F", the Mafia Family.

It was there she often received more envelopes with cash, or sometimes, small trinkets and elegant gifts from those who knew her more closely. Men like Tommy DeLuca, Joshua Demonico, Leonardo Tagretta, and Arrigo Salvaggio, as well as several of the bodyguards she knew, as well as Danny Valsiglio from the VIJER Corporation and also associates like Master DeLoccasio, Albert Domenicci the current helicopter pilot and Dr. Weintraub. However Alyssa cared less about the gifts, she was just truly happy to have her Theo at her side and her friends and those she respected nearby and celebrating this happy moment in her life.

It was during this wedding that she indeed saw how busy her new husband was as the new Boss. It seemed he was constantly talking and interacting with everyone! Everyone wanted to bend the new Don's ear and pay their respects to him and assure him of their loyalty and continued business dealings with the Jerome Family. His own people in the Jerome's would monopolize him to congratulate him on his now leading the Family and to again confirm their continued loyalty to him, and congratulate those like Joshua and Leonardo who had been promoted. To Alyssa, her Kageryu always looked so handsome and professional as he literally towered over everyone around him.

Rosette, Lisa Ciccerone, Emilia and a few other seasoned Jerome Family ladies helped Alyssa through all the intricacies of the various ceremonies and receptions and stood faithfully by her as sisters and mentors and Matrons of honor. In fact she had chosen Cesare's Ciccerone's youngest daughter to be her flower girl and his middle son to be ring bearer.

By 11pm that night Alyssa was near complete and utter exhaustion. Thankfully her and Kageryu would have a 5 day honeymoon period together which to recuperate from all this.

Because Theodore was still needed close to home to help with Family matters, Alyssa and he spent their honeymoon locked away in his ranch house like old times. The two of them just sharing intimately together, cooking side by side or he filling her in on some of his tales of when he was in Vietnam and Japan, it always impressed Alyssa that the man was fluent in so many languages, English, Italian, Japanese, Korean, Vietnamese and now International sign language.

Of course he didn't tell her any of his more sordid or violent tales, or his stories of vendetta. Those were things that were to be taken to his own grave and things a Man of Honor just didn't discuss with a woman, no matter how much he loved her. And because Theodore so loved his Kanashii, tales of his dark side he would never tell her. She had seen his basement during his test and had been able to form her own opinions. There was nothing of his life as an assassin or *Mafioso* that ever would be discussed with her; in fact much of it was not even discussed with those men and *compari* in his own Family.

Only those who fellow men who had been there with him on various 'jobs' ever knew of that truly very dark and cruel side of him. Now that they were married, it seemed almost like Theodore worked even harder to keep that side even more removed from Alyssa's life than before. Instead he worked on being a good partner, husband and continued to be her teacher in martial arts and healing techniques since this was something that made both of them comfortable and bonded them in a deep common interest. Unlike Joshua who wanted to learn only the martial arts, Alyssa showed a true interest and level of commitment in being a true full-time student and so Kageryu took her in fully as once Sen and Cochran had taken him in. However, her true gift was not with 'destruction' but healing and so this is what he concentrated on with her, as well as defensive Karate. He began to teach her to understand the Japanese language as well, and the path of healing with herbs, massage and the Oriental philosophies. Because Theodore couldn't always work with Alyssa as much as he wanted to, he was able to get Sen Yamashita to work as a surrogate Sensei with Alyssa as well, or his other student Leonardo to work on her with some of her defensive karate sparring.

Victor came down for dinner one night with the newlyweds at their insistence to chat, play chess and socialize and the next night Joshua and Leonardo were invited down for an Italian feast as well.

Theodore was planning to take Alyssa to Sicily to visit Vito and Lena in 10 months, after the baby was born, since it would take some time to make and forge the necessary documents to get her a passport, visa, social security card and other things to make Sarah, truly 'Alyssa Disarro', now 'Alyssa Jerome', wife of Theodore Jerome.

Finally as the wintry weather slowly released its grip on the Northeast and slipped into late March and April, Theodore had gotten into a routine that worked well for him and his new wife. He was pleased to see that she had adapted so easily to going up to the house during the day and then back at his side at night. She was just now beginning to show her pregnancy, her body still well toned except for the bulge in her lower stomach that was their precious child.

Thankfully her pregnancy was so far a very easy one; she had no complications or morning sickness. While Victor worried over her still learning the martial arts, Theodore continued teaching her privately at their home the continued levels of the gentle Tai Chi and the smoother moves of Kenpo Karate, avoiding any rough contact or throws with her. He also taught her how to use the weapons so that she could practice solo, and already she was showing a good instinct on learning defensive moves with the Bo, the traditional Japanese quarterstaff.

Even though she had wanted to continue her riding lessons with Mr. DeLoccasio and Leonardo. Both Theodore and Victor had firmly put their foot down on that and said not until after her child was born.

Theodore knew he was being a bit over protective, but he indeed worried at times about his Kanashii and their child, she had already had so much happen in her short life with him. They had ridden together a few times she had gotten him to indulge her and go riding around the grounds together, even though she was far to good natured and kind to chuckle at his awkward appearance on a horse. And thankfully the horse was patient enough to put up with the giant man's ungainly attempts at being ridden by him.
Theodore was glad at least Leonardo was an avid horseman and could ride with Alyssa regularly when he was around.

Kageryu noticed Alyssa seemed to gravitate towards animals in general, whether his koi, his fathers Finches or the horses here on the Estates. In many ways she truly was his karmic opposite, a bringer of life and light to balance his darker nature. It was the thing that seemed to make him crave her even more; it was indeed as if she was his refuge on days when chaos was erupting all around him.

She had fully embraced his love of all things Oriental and he had continued to be her teacher and mentor, and concentrated much of his teachings on that which she seemed drawn too, the healing aspects. Whether teaching her the various herbs and supplements, or the intense reiki and shiatsu massage techniques, as well as some of the other healing and calming strategies, she proved to be a quick and eager learner, and it was not uncommon for her to mix up some herbal remedy or tea for Joshua's bout of flu, or when Nick came down with walking pneumonia. She had even learned to be able to relax and sooth her husband with some of the same basic massages and techniques he had used on her in the beginning.

Since she was such a dedicated student of the same Oriental lifestyle as him, he as her teacher had taken her down to Sen's shop and she had proudly gotten her first Kanji tattoo on her back, a small kanji symbol on her shoulder blade, for 'Healer'; A karmic opposite for his 'Bringer of Death' symbol.

While he had learned to live his life solo and as a self independent man, relying on no one, he would be the first to admit to his father, that he had come to very much enjoy and look forward to his Kanashii greeting him when he came home with a cup of his favorite green tea with chamomile or Mugwort, his favorite incense going and some Asian or Italian dinner cooking for the two of them. While they had only been together a short time as lovers and mates, for six months, he was already fully enjoying feeling her warm small body next to him at night, and on nights that he had to be away taking care of business, he grew to miss the heat of her body and soul next to him.

His first few months as the new Padrone had been filled with various small problems and re-establishing connections with the other Families, just as his father had warned him. And also just as his father had warned and taught him, he put his foot down firm and fast letting all be known whether it was those in the Jerome Family or in the other Families that he would tolerate no nonsense what-so-ever. Rapidly though, because of his former status and reputation he was quickly respected and taken indeed as a serious Don and Boss of his Family and the men in it.

He knew from the beginning that this would be something he would have to do personally, it was nothing his powerful father could do for him but all of his teachers from Vito Bonnaro, to Cochran, Sen and his own Father had groomed him for this and he took to it like a duck takes to water.

He was fortunate in that those he had chosen to work under him, both Joshua and Leonardo also were able to seamlessly and rapidly integrate into his Top Administration. And so the Jerome Family continued to flourish; if not a bit more subtly, under the new regime and leadership, with new ventures and new legitimate areas.

Theodore's biggest headache had been nothing at all to do with his being the new Boss, but that the normal winter flu epidemic had hit especially hard that year at his Family. Some like Nick and several of the newly immigrated Bonnaro men had gone on to developing Walking Pneumonia or severe bronchitis, and Dr. Weintraub, Tommy and Alyssa were kept constantly busy helping people out. Many of the soldiers and capos and their families though just needed lots of rest, and time to recuperate.

Hardest hit it seemed was his own father, Victor, who with his advancing age and his complications from his diabetes and the medicine he was on to avoid the rejection of his kidney transplant seemed especially hard hit and developed a severe case of pneumonia.

Victor staunchly and angrily refused to be hospitalized and so Dr. Weintraub, Tommy, himself and Alyssa had all worked around the clock to take care of the old man here at the Jerome Estates as they hoped the antibiotics and breathing treatments would kick in and work.

Alyssa and many of the other ladies like Rosette and Emilia would spend hours with the old *Padrone*, keeping him company, reading to him, bringing him his favorite Italian delicacies and basically working constantly to nurse him back to health. Finally it seemed by early April that he finally was beginning to rally and slowly recover.

A few times father and son had spoken privately, and Theodore already knew his fathers wishes, knew that Victor would not want to be kept alive when his time came.

As someone who was so familiar with death, it distressed Theodore that he could see his own father's life force slowly growing weaker over the months and ebbing away. He could tell his father was readying himself for his final transition into death, since all that he had worked hard to accomplish was nearing an end.

As a Buddhist practitioner, Kageryu understood the logical necessity of Victor's coming time to pass, but as a human being who was now in touch with emotions he had not felt in years, it was as though a black cloak sat around his shoulders, weighing him down. He loved his father dearly and could not even imagine the man's wisdom and guidance not there for him.

But it seemed for now at least, that Theodore would have his beloved father around just as the first signs of spring were thawing the North-Eastern US. A more morbid part of him felt that his father was fighting to hang on for one event, and one event only, and that was to see his grandchild born. Deep in Theodore's heart almost like some precognition he truly felt that once Alyssa had her child that Victor would be moving on to the afterlife.

Chapter 42- *April 25th 1988*

Springs warm air flowed over New York and the Jerome Estates, bathing it in warming sunshine and life renewed. Now during late April, the crocus' and daffodils were in full bloom; the grass was springing back to its emerald green and the hint of warmer summer days soon to be washed over the land.

Alyssa had just finished breakfast in the main house, as Theodore had been downtown all last night taking care of business at the VIJER Corporation. He was due back later this afternoon or evening.

"Morning, everyone." Joshua said as he grabbed some coffee and some Danishes. He seemed to be a much better 'morning person' now that he and Clarissa had begun to steadily date.

She signed to him. *"You hanging around the house today or going downtown as well?"*

"Always going downtown," He winked briefly. Next to Theodore, Joshua had surprisingly learned the sign language the fastest and easiest. "Gotta take care of business and take Clarissa, out to lunch." She smiled and signed: *"Have fun, be good."*

"Me, good? Never!" Josh chuckled and after giving her a quick light squeeze on the shoulder moved off to talk to Tommy DeLuca.

"Ah, *Signora* Alyssa," Leonardo spoke to her in Italian as he nudged in next to her, also wrestling up some breakfast. He preferred strong espresso and biscotti along with some fresh fruit. He could be rather a health nut at times. During the winter he had been working out at the gym and had added quite a bit of tone and muscle to him. "How is Victor, eh? I don't see him much anymore? He is recuperating Ok?"

Alyssa also carried her ever present pen and paper, as not everyone understood the sign language as fluently as Theodore, Joshua and herself. Leonardo was learning it fairly well, but still had some difficulty in it. "*Improving more every day,*" She signed, "*I was just getting ready to go down to the aviary to take care of the birds soon.*"
She had to write out '*Aviary*', '*Go down to*' and '*birds*' for him, as those signs eluded him.

"Aren't they all nesting now or something?" Len asked. He used to keep homing pigeons when he was younger in Sicily and so did have some understanding of the care of birds.

"*Yep,*" She nodded, "*Should be a bunch of new nestlings within the next 28 days.*"

"Ah," Leonardo nodded as he gulped down some Sicilian blood orange slices, "That should make Victor happy, eh? Maybe he come down and visit them soon. I bet it would cheer him up."

"*So are you still riding my favorite horse, Andario for me? Keeping him in shape?*" she asked him. Since Kageryu had pretty much put the brakes on her riding until after she had her child, she had asked Leonardo to exercise the great elegant Andalusian stallion for her. She knew Len enjoyed riding and as a young lad in Sicily had grown up around horses. He rode with the grace and mastery of one who was truly at one with the horse.

"Eh, here and there, when I can." Len answered truthfully. "I know DeLoccasio has been riding him regularly and I rode him a few times last week, I take him out tomorrow and give him a good workout, Ok?"

She nodded her thanks to Len and they talked briefly about horses for a little while until he too moved off to finish his breakfast and then turn his attention to Family business. Like Joshua, he would also be departing for downtown today to meet up with Theodore, apparently there was some big meeting going on, and most of the Top Administration, capos and many of the soldiers were to be meeting downtown at the Blue Parrot.

In fact by the time Alyssa was ready to depart down to the aviary the house seemed relatively empty. Normally this didn't bother her, but today for some reason it gave her an unexpected and dark chill and she didn't know why.

She began to walk the long walk down to the Aviary, when she bumped into the captain of the guard Arrigo. "Where go, you?" he asked in badly broken English, in that silky but dark voice eerily reminiscent of his cousin Len's.

"*Down to the aviary*" she repeated. Thankfully Arrigo had also picked up the sign language fairly well, and his English was coming along good also. He enjoyed practicing it with her as he didn't feel so self conscious if he messed up.

"I get car, drive you, eh?" he said.

"*Come on, Arrigo!*" she pleaded, her fingers flying through the signs, "*It's a nice day, let me walk. I'm pregnant, not crippled!*"

"Yeah but..." he paused. "Oh, Ok!" he relented in a gentle manner. "But I drive by soon an' a check you out. See you up, Ok?"

Alyssa smiled gently, "*Check ON you, Arrigo.*" She explained the correct terms in English, "*I will drive by and check ON you and see TO you; otherwise it sounds like you are trying to get a hot date with me and look down my shirt.*" She smiled softly.

The two had become friends and he still enjoyed working as her personal bodyguard, so he was never offended by her gentle teachings and lighthearted corrections. But he did blush a bit as she explained what he had said. "No, I no do that!" He hastily corrected himself, "But I will how you say, check ON you then, and see TO you."

She smiled and nodded and gave him a gentle squeeze on his arm. "*Very good,*" She signed. The wonderful thing about International Sign Language was that it was the same no matter what language, so it was truly 'multi-linguistic'.

As she walked down the paved drive enjoying the warm air on her skin, she meandered slowly taking time to wave here and there to some of the distantly patrolling guards who waved back. She stopped to pick some daffodils and a few tulips to carry with her.

She could hear the small finches peeping and chirping long before she even got to them, and it was a sound that always warmed her heart. As she went inside she placed the flowers she had picked into the wires of the outer gate, where they seemed to brighten the surroundings and announce the rebirth of the land and the Jerome Family itself. As Alyssa slipped on the dark smock to cover her clothes and turned on the radio to the classical music PBS station, she could have sworn she felt a twitching in her stomach.

She placed her hand on her belly and felt for it again. There it was again! Her child was moving within her. Somehow she already knew in her heart and soul that it was going to be a boy, and although she and Kage had already picked out both male and female names. The boys' name they had picked out would be Victor Theodore Jerome, it was tradition in the Jerome Family for first born male children to have the middle name of their father, and both her and Theodore agreed to name him Victor in honor of his grandfather, an old Italian tradition. She also knew in her heart, that he would be a large child, and would inherit his fathers' unusually tall size when he was full-grown. She smiled and caressed her own belly as she felt Victor Theodore doing some flip flops in her stomach and then settle down as she began to work at feeding the birds and tending to them. The baby seemed to like the Aviary as well.

She had been in the aviary for nearly two hours; everything seemed unusually quiet today as so many were away in the city. Suddenly she saw the long, black Jerome-1 limo crest over the driveway and come to a stop beside the Aviary. Nick Pellegrio got out and opened the door for Victor, who wearily got out, spoke quietly to Nick's ear for a few moments and then to Alyssa's complete and utter surprise the long limo actually left.

Alyssa hastily walked to the outer door and had already opened it for her Uncle. He still looked so thin and pale; he had lost a lot of weight during his illness and now relied on a cane full time to help steady him. Slowly and with great effort he made it inside the aviary. For the first time, she saw him as the one thing she had never seen Victor as and that was frail and weak.

She held out the door for him, and he paused as he saw the flowers and pulled one off the aviary and handed it to her, a smile on his face, his dark eyes still full of wisdom and power that had made him the *Padrone* for many decades.

"Ah, hello my dear Alyssa," He said as he ambled into the aviary, and handed her the flower he had pulled out from the doorframe. She accepted it and placed it in her long red hair, behind her ear. He smiled and held out his hand to her, "Come help me sit down, will you."

She led him over to one of the two plastic chairs that were kept in the outer section of the aviary.

"Much better," he lowered himself slowly almost painfully with a small grunt into the chair then relaxed. "I was looking for you earlier; Nick said you were down here."

It had been a long couple months since Victor himself had been down in the aviary and at the sound of his voice all the little finches began to chirp and sing excitedly, many landing and frantically swarming on the other side of the screen. In fact Alyssa couldn't ever remember them being so fired up and vocal, almost as if they were intensely trying to reach the man. It sent an involuntary shudder down her back.

"How is that grandchild of mine doing today," Victor eyed her sweetly, he gently reached out, "May I?"

She nodded *'yes'*; as the old Don placed his hand gently on her belly.

"Oh he will be a strong one, I just know." He winked at her.

Did Victor feel like her, that her child was going to be a son as well? She beamed at him when he said that and scrawled out, "*I, we, are going to name him Victor Theodore Jerome*." Her Uncle never had gotten the hang of the Sign Language, but Alyssa was beginning to think it was because his eyesight had been failing him recently from his diabetes.

"That's wonderful, Child." He said and then had a round of coughing, even though he was supposedly healing he still sounded so bad, so frail. He pulled out a handkerchief and coughed hard into it, Alyssa noted when he put it back in his pocket it was red with blood. "How are you doing, Mother?" he wheezed as he regained himself.

"Fine, good! But Victor, I am worried about you." She held the pad out for him to read.

Somehow she knew his eyes were not focusing on the words, behind her the tiny finches seemed to be getting more frantic in their peeping and chirping, almost clamoring in a frenzied swarm along the screen. Her body was beginning to get tremors at the birds' strange actions.

Alyssa was beginning to get nervous and concerned now, Nick had driven the huge car back up to the house, there were no guards anywhere in site and her Uncle seemed to be getting even paler by the moment. She got to her feet, small little sounds of whispered alarm in her unspeaking throat.

"Ah, ah. No," Victor reached out and his hand grabbed her wrist gently but with a hard determined strength that totally surprised her. "Alyssa, no. I never did like hospitals, do you understand? I love you though child, so sit and keep me company, eh?" the eyes bore into her with the strength, leadership and power that she had always known in him, and his grip on her wrist was quite tight.

Obediently she sat back down and he immediately released her wrist. She pulled her chair right next to him so they were practically touching, leg-to-leg and shoulder-to-shoulder.

"Good, excellent child," He said soothingly. "Now, I just want to talk. So let this old man talk, Ok dear lady?" he put his hand on her shoulder and pulled her even closer to him.

She could feel the shaking in his muscles and could smell an almost faint odor of fruit or almonds about him. She was wracking her brain trying to remember what it meant! She knew she had read somewhere that when a diabetic had an odor of fruit or almonds around them it meant something important and very bad!

"You know, there were days I cursed my decision to save you, and cursed your decision to want to stay here..." he began.

His frank statement had so surprised Alyssa that she could do nothing at that moment but sit there and listen with an almost morbid fascination.

"...That day in Vito Roman's hideous kennel I kept asking myself, why am I really doing this?" he continued, "But then, each day it seemed that there was some unseen reason you were sent here to be with the Jerome's." his hand gripped around her wrist again with that surprising strength, "You and I have had our ups and downs, there was a time I saw you as helpless, saw you as a threat, wondered if you were a *nemico*, but no... No." he said, his voice softening, "You are as

I had said before, a true guardian angel..." he turned away from her and his body was seized again in a fit of coughing.

He released her wrist again and coughed into his handkerchief but this time when he was done, it just dropped to the floor, Alyssa could clearly see fresh blood in it now.

Alarm and panic shown in her eyes, 'Oh God! She had to get someone, this wasn't right! Her Uncle needed someone!' she nearly abruptly stood up.

"Sit, Alyssa." Victor said, it was still a command and even though the eyes were clouding it was almost as if the wily old *Padrone* knew exactly what he was doing. "Please. Do not leave me alone child." He said in such a tender voice that it nearly shook her to her core.

This time there were tears in the old man's eyes and when he spoke now it was in Italian, "I have made many decisions in my life, Alyssa. Ones that at least I always felt were for the best, for my *brugad* Family and my blood family, but I have come to realize that saving you that day from the Roman's was indeed one of the best I ever made."

He turned and faced her head on, his hand cupped behind her neck and he pulled her until she was forehead to forehead with him. Victor began to talk then to her of his younger days, about his friends, his enemies, about his sadness and his happiness and Alyssa sat there and listened as tears began to roll down her eyes, matching the tears that rolled down Victor's great wise eyes.

"The estate is so beautiful, so full of life. It is coming to life again, and coming full circle. I am tired child and I am ready to be with Issy and Michael and my brothers and my parents..." Victor looked then into a corner and his face smiled in such a tender smile it nearly broke Alyssa's heart. "*Mia Amore...*" Victor seemed to speak to nothing, to the empty corner, "Soon, I will be with you, I feel you so close my beloved, my only beloved, and it makes me so happy to see you here with me..."

He turned his attention back to Alyssa and she could see his eyes were beginning to cloud with a grey haze now, he was dying. "You have seen so much death, young one. Yes, but you will also see so much life now. I have never regretted any of my decisions Alyssa, not a single one. Even my beloved son Theo has taught me the wonderment of destiny and fate.

"You and Theodore are strong, you will stand by him as he runs this Family, and the Jerome Family will endure, and continue to prosper. You were meant for him, like Issy was to me..." Victor's voice was beginning to fade and waver; he would speak occasionally in English and switch back to Italian in mid-sentence. He released her neck and leaned up heavily against her, his shoulder against her shoulder.

Behind them both an almost palatable hush had suddenly descended upon the finches who sat half clustered up against the screen, and then without warning they began to keen as one in an almost eerie wail.

Alyssa had never heard the birds make that sound before, and it caused her hair to stand on end, her blood to chill in her veins.

Victor seemed to flinch in pain as if he had heard that eerie noise before, long ago in his past. His full weight was leaning against Alyssa and for an old, frail man he was growing surprisingly heavy. "Help me lie on the floor child; it's hard to sit up." He gently asked, his voice a low wheeze as though gasping for air.

Every shred of common sense was telling her to run and get help, but she somehow knew the awful truth that her beloved Uncle and benefactor was rapidly dying. That he indeed knew exactly what he had done when he had sent Nick and the car away, to come down here and to talk to her. She knew in her heart and soul if she ran to get someone her Uncle would already be dead long before she got back with help.

Victor sensed her indecision as only a man caught between two worlds can. "Sit with me, Child. You have seen harsh death, now sit with me and face it on a gentle nature."

She nodded numbly as her tears streamed silently down her face unheeded as she remembered Gio, Cesare.... Dear Cesare his brains blown out all around her.

"Alyssa..." Victor was whispering now, "It is not bad, do you understand child? It is not scary. This Aviary has always been a place of safety and solitude for me, always. I am honored you name the little one after me, deeply honored. Theodore is a good man, a very good man. He will protect and take good care of you; he is a true Man of Honor... You have always bought me happiness dear child, and I meant what I said that day. If I could have had a daughter she would have been you, but I think fate made it otherwise so you could be with Theo..."

Victor lay there for awhile, his chest struggling in wheezing gasps as Alyssa cradled his head in her lap. Oh how she prayed that some guards would come patrolling along! *Where were they? Usually she always saw some guards around, where was everyone?*

Finally, his eyes opened up once more and looked at her, "I'm tired now child..." he barely muttered. "I need to sleep. Watch over me, will you? I know you..." his voice faltered and he abruptly glanced over to his left, to the corner again. "Issy..." A small peaceful smile came on his lips then and his eyes closed and his muscles suddenly tensed up like a thousand iron bands, and then he was completely and utterly still.

The great Don, the powerful Father and *Padrone* of the Jerome Family legacy, the one whom the F.B.I had labeled as one of the most powerful, feared and dangerous of the Mafia 'Godfathers' died peacefully in his aviary.

Alyssa let the tears fall on her Uncles face as she bent down and kissed his forehead.

'Oh god no…" her mind reeled, 'Oh please Victor, please, not you too, Uncle…' Alyssa railed silently, letting her tears fall and drop onto the unmoving and dead body of her beloved Uncle. Her soul cried out then that day and though she had no voice to give it, her sorrow echoed in the strange keening wail that the finches in the aviary had begun to sing. It was the same cry they had echoed that day during the awful storm of the great 1957 Jerome-Felani Massacre.

After a few moments, she gently laid her Uncles head on the floor, and covered him with the daffodils she had entwined in the Aviary wire. She then with a sudden cold conviction opened the main outer door and propped it open with one of the chairs, then calmly walking to the inner door, she opened that one as well, propping it open with the other plastic chair.

She walked back into the main aviary where the finches were now beginning to fly around almost frantically, she threw up her hands and began to herd them out the around the small aviary until every finch in that place was circling wildly.

They flew as a single unit, circling faster and faster, until seeing the open doors they flew straight through them in a neat swarm out and into the open sky. Up and towards the clouds taking wing to freedom through the warm spring air, higher and higher the flight of birds flew as though bearing Victor's soul along with them. Higher over the elegant Jerome Estate they soared, disappearing far off into the distance.

It was only then the guards began running down in a panic to the aviary.

The funeral for Victor Jerome was what the newspapers and media called one of the last great 'Mafia Don funerals'. It was attended by close to 3000 people from every walk of life and not all of them that would be considered 'mobbed up'. Italian storeowners in downtown NYC mourned, as did clergy, politicians, little old ladies, even the media as well as many people who had never even met the enigmatic Victor Jerome. He was indeed the last of the great ones, the 'Old dinosaurs' the true 'Godfathers'. None however mourned him as much as those who truly knew him, his *Famiglia* and his family.

The F.B.I and the newspapers made much ado and predictions about the Jerome Family collapsing now without the powerful leadership of its most famous *Padrone*, and this made Theodore quite happy. He much preferred the Jerome's be ghosts' and out of the media spotlight. Victor had indeed done well by his Family before he died and played his final gambit with a chilling certainty and accuracy that had indeed insured continued strength for his son's Top Administration.

For many months John Thomas seemed the most inconsolable of all; for he had lost his best friend who had been with him from his school days. Inside the Jerome Family the mood was grim and heavy, and it was during this time when Theodore's true measure of leadership was put to the ultimate test.

Without Victor around, a few in the *Famiglia* and those who had claimed to be allies tried to weasel out of former deals or jump ship. Like his father before him, Theodore was just as powerful a leader and tactician. He rewarded well those who remained loyal and aided him and with his devoted Top Administration, and capos discreetly and decisively took out those who opposed him or caused any problems. Vito Bonnaro and his family of course stood just as solidly behind the Jerome's as they always had.

On September 24th 1988 Alyssa gave birth to a healthy 8 lb 2 oz boy, who was indeed christened Vittorio Theodore Jerome.

Epilogue:

It was during the late fall, as Alyssa sat outside the porch with her pen in hand and journal open on her lap. She watched some of the guards bringing in decorations for Thanksgiving; giant bundled corn stalk husks, hay bales and pumpkins.

She was aware of the familiar light footfalls next to her and she looked up and saw her beloved husband next to her. "*Hi you two,*" She signed. Kageryu was holding a bundled up young Victor Theodore Jerome. His hair was dark like his grandfather, but he had the blue/grey eyes that looked like they may become green someday like his mothers.

"Hello yourself, my beautiful little Hawk." Theodore said as he adjusted young Victor gently in his huge hands. The child looked so tiny clutched gently in the arms of his giant father. "What are you up to?" He asked, his eyes looking at his Kanashii with love.

"*Trying to write, my husband,*" she signed. "*But I don't know; I'm stuck here. I don't know even how to begin!*"

"Well, why not start from the beginning Kanashii? After all, just write what is in your heart and soul, eh?" He leaned down and kissed the top of her fiery red hair.

She nodded and felt a blush come across her neck. He still made her blush with love and desire, and she knew he always would, her Kageryu.

"I am going to take little one inside for awhile. I think Rosette and the others want to start him young in raising him in the Italian way." He winked playfully at her, "Later, you and I have martial arts, and you have still yet to throw your teacher off you."
He teased her.

She playfully stuck her tongue out at him her green eyes teasing him back.

"Hmm, so that is challenge accepted then, I take it my Kanashii?" He grinned deeply. "Come along Victor, let's go see what Rosette and the ladies have going in the kitchens, we will come harass your Mother in a bit." He gave her another kiss and then walked inside the large estate.

Alyssa watched as Leonardo Tagretta came cantering elegantly down the lane on the great white Andalusian stallion, Andario. He was riding bareback today and rode elegantly around as the horse pranced gracefully beneath him, Leonardo was indeed a natural rider. He spoke softly in Italian to the horse a moment, settling it beneath him then looking up he smiled and waved briefly to Alyssa, then with a playful gleam in his grey eyes he dug his heels into Andario's flanks and gave the stallion his head allowing the horse to gallop wildly down the lawn, both of them riding as one on the wings of the wind.

She looked the other way and saw Joshua Demonico and Tommy DeLuca leaning up against one of the cars talking together. Tommy had recently given up smoking and now he too was chewing incessantly the nicotine gum, Joshua was just as addicted to the gum as ever. Her Uncle Victor had been right the Family would indeed endure.

Finally it dawned on her then. With a sudden smile of inspiration she leaned back in the Adirondack chair, and began to write feverishly...

'*I, then known as Sarah was jogging briskly down the forest trail; this was something I often did. Hiking through the local forest preserve was my favorite way to exercise and also to meditate. It was not unusual for me to cover 5-6 miles in a single day, especially if something was troubling me...*"

* * * * *